HIS WISH WAS

Alexandria had never experienced such a restless sensation while wide awake before, and gave a strangled gasp. What was he doing? How dare he touch her so intimately! Oh, Lord, she could scarcely breathe! She squirmed away from his relentless touch.

"Be still, my dove," Sharif commanded lazily, his deep voice gentling against the harsh wailing of the sandstorm without. "It will soon pass, this cursed *simoon*, and we shall go on to my kingdom."

"No! I'd sooner die in this sandstorm than be your—your woman, or go anywhere with you!" she choked out, summoning the remnants of her pride and defiance.

"Ah, beloved little liar," he breathed. "You were born for the joys of life—not to squander that Allah-given gift on the desert sands. Accept what is written in the stars, *habibah!* Let me be your master!"

"No, I just can't—you mustn't. Stop it! Never, never, never . . ."

Alexandria moaned denials, but the vows sighed into oblivion as his mouth again captured hers, drawing a response against her will. His touch filled her with a euphoria and giddiness she could neither control nor comprehend—and now she wasn't in any position to force him to stop!

Desert Captive

PENELOPE NERI

ZEBRA BOOKS
KENSINGTON PUBLISHING CORP.

ZEBRA BOOKS

are published by

Kensington Publishing Corp.
475 Park Avenue South
New York, NY 10016

First printing: September, 1988

Printed in the United States of America

To
Patricia Bascon.
With love and thanks
for your friendship and encouragement.

From afar, his heart called to her,
From across the sands and the sea.
Like one entranced, she answered
The call of destiny.

"I come to you, my desert lord!
But—are you what you seem?
Are you flesh and blood, and heart and soul?
Or only a desert dream?"

Prologue

"Oh, look, just look! You broke my dolly, you beast! She's all hurted, an' it's your fault. I hate you, Sha-Sha!"

Tears streamed down the little girl's face as she picked up her beloved baby and cradled it to her pinafored bosom. Her lower lip trembled, for there was an ugly crack in the painted porcelain face that she was certain even clever Fatima could not mend. Oh, poor, poor Lucy! She'd been her favorite baby, for she'd come by ship to Alexandria, Egypt, from far across the sea. Her Grandmother Harding, whom she'd never once met, had sent it just for her a month ago, on her fourth birthday, cozy in a box lined with straw which Mama said had been posted all the way from somewhere called Ingland. And now poor little Lucy's cheek was broked. . . .

The boy, eight years her senior, eyed her scornfully, his fists planted arrogantly on his hips.

"Pah!" He dismissed her grief with all the airy superiority of a twelve-year-old. "You are but an infant, and a girl at that! What did you expect? There can be no war without casualties, foolish one! Your stupid Lucy-doll is a hero, wounded by the rebellious Murid ben-Azad while defending the life of the great *amir*, Sharif! She will receive honor and rewards for her courage. Perhaps I will give her fifty—no, a hundred!—white racing camels, and a score of the finest Arabian horses in all the desert!" he boasted. "Here, give that stupid doll to me!"

"No! You hurt her, Sha-Sha!" Alexandria accused, using the name she'd given the boy when they'd first met. She hadn't

9

been able to pronounce his name properly then, 'cos she'd still been just a baby, and so it had been "Sha-Sha" ever since. "Lucy doesn't like you no more. An' she don't want no horr'ble camels. She just wants a new—a new—f-face, so's she'll be-be p-pretty 'gain!"

Great hiccupping sobs sounded from behind the doll pressed close to her damp face, and the boy felt, for the first time, an uncomfortable pang of guilt to see his little friend so upset. It had been an accident, true, but the doll's sorry state had been his fault nonetheless. While acting out the part of his treacherous uncle, Murid ben-Azad, he had dealt his porcelain "attacker" a mighty blow with his jeweled "dagger"—albeit that dagger was really just a lowly camel-stick, and the jeweled hilt entirely of his imagination. . . .

"When my father is once again *amir* of al-Azadel, he will send you a thousand such toys," he promised stiffly, hoping she'd dry her eyes. "And each one will be far grander than your ugly old Lucy."

"Don't want t'ousand dollies," the little girl sniffed, rubbing her teary eyes on her dolly's petticoats. "Want Lucy's f-face pretty 'gain."

The boy looked cross. He was the son of *Amir* Malik ben-Azad, and as heir to his father's province in the mountains of northwestern Algeria, accustomed to getting his own way. He scowled at her, his handsome black eyes sulky beneath their fringing of inky-black lashes. His head was capped with short, curly black hair. His fair skin, the heritage of his Caucasian Berber people, now tanned a pale gold, was just beginning to show the suggestion of a beard in the faint bluish shadows at the chin and jaws. Very soon, he would become a striking young man, but for now he was but a boy, with one foot on the threshold of adulthood. He impatiently tapped the sandy ground of the courtyard with his camel-stick and tried to appear aloof.

"By Allah, I do not know why I bother with you, unless it is to learn English! It cannot be that I find your company pleasing, for you are such a crybaby!" he said scornfully, and added a string of insults in his native Tamahaq for good measure.

"And you're just a b-big b-bully, Sha-Sha!" she retorted.

"Bully? Guard your tongue! You will not speak to me in that way, girl!" he said arrogantly, for he was often his most arrogant when feeling his most guilty! Besides, although the women of his tribe were allowed certain freedoms rare to other desert peoples, retaliating hotly with a show of temper and the calling of names when a man had spoken was unthinkable! "I had thought to take you for a ride on Aswad, but now I won't," he said punishingly. "You can stay here with the other women and wait for your mother to give birth. I pray to Allah that she gives Harding-Pasha a son this time, instead of a worthless girl!" He rolled his dark eyes in a look that spoke volumes.

"Don't care!" Alexandria Harding defied him, pouting. It was a lie, for she loved horses with a passion and a ride on Sha-Sha's glossy, spirited black colt was a rare treat indeed. "Don't want to ride your stupid ole horse anyway! It's ugly n' nasty— just like you! Go away, you mean boy. I hate you!"

Tight-lipped at her cutting remarks about his beloved blooded black colt, Sharif nodded. "Yes. It is only fitting you should stay home! My beautiful Aswad would not wish to have such a baby as you ride him with me, for then we would have to go slowly—as befits a horse who carries a little *bint*, a small girl. Alone, Aswad and I will fly like the desert wind!"

He spun on his heel and began to stride quickly away across the courtyard, past the splashing fountains and the shady date palms towards the stables of the great white house that basked in the scorching Egyptian sun.

Little Alexa, as she was known, trotted after him, half-tempted to beg his forgiveness, for she would have liked to ride the colt with him and it was worth telling a fib to do so. Aswad liked her. He always nuzzled her cheek and then her pinny pockets with his velvety nose and mouth, in search of the sugar cubes she gave him! Still, her fierce little temper had not abated, nor her pride, which had been wounded by Sha-Sha's name-calling, and glancing down at the doll's caved-in porcelain cheek was a powerful reminder that the horrid boy was everything she'd said he was. Poor Lucy was ugly now. She'd never, never *ever* be pretty again, an' it was all his fault. As she looked at the ruined dolly cradled in her little arms,

11

tears filled her green eyes anew. With a burst of renewed fury, she picked up a small, withered coconut that had fallen prematurely from the towering fronded palms way above the house, and hurled it after Sha-Sha, pleased when it struck him squarely between the shoulder-blades just as he was about to enter the stables.

"Oww!" he cried, and spun to face her. "That hurt!"

"Good for you! You're not my fr'end no more!" she crowed, and crossed her eyes and stuck out her small pink tongue as far as she could in a horrible grimace. "You—you Gatherer-of-Camel-Dung!" It was an epithet he'd taught her himself.

"Pah! Go back to your nurse, Apricot-Hair!" he taunted back, knowing how she loathed him teasing her about her hair-coloring, which was a rare pale-reddish brown color that secretly he found fascinating and almost beautiful, though he'd never admit that to *her*. With his parting shot, he left.

Alexa sighed. Her anger had vanished, replaced by the keen awareness that she'd have to spend the entire day—and possibly tomorrow too—alone, until Sha-Sha's temper cooled. And there was nothing much to do without Sha-Sha to play with. Mama was in her bedroom with the blinds down. She seemed awful sick, and Fatima had said not to 'sturb her. It had to be something to do with her tummy growing so fat, the little girl had decided, for her Mama's tummy had gotten bigger and bigger every day for weeks now. Was it like her own tummy aches, which Fatima said were caused by eating too many figs and dates, she wondered, though her mother hadn't seemed to like dates or figs much at all? Or worse, perhaps Mama had a terrible sickness? Perhaps her tummy would burst, and she might even go to heaven and become an angel, like Sha-Sha told her his mother had done when he was born.

Of a sudden, Alexa was afraid. All of Uncle Malik's serving women were with her mother. The English doctor had been called that morning too, and Fatima, her nurse, who always laughed and smiled and sang to her, had not smiled once that morning. She'd looked worried and had prayed to her god Allah for Harding-Pasha's wife. Alexa had sensed that something was very wrong by the way they'd all behaved. . . .

Still, she thought, brightening at the recollection, Papa had

12

said at breakfast that very soon she would have a new baby brother or sister to play with, and that was something to look forward to, she supposed. She sighed again. She did hope the baby arrived soon, so she could play with it while Mama was sick and Sha-Sha still cross with her. Would it come up from the harbor in a big box with a thick brown wrapper that had stamps pasted on it with pictures of the Oueen of Ingland? Would it arrive all wrapped up in straw like Lucy had done? she wondered. Where *did* baby sisters or brothers come from, anyway? She hadn't seen any in the native bazaar, though she'd certainly seen everything else for sale there.

"Well, however the baby comes, I do hope it's a girl-baby an' not a horr'd boy like that Sha-Sha, don't you, Lucy, my dear?" she whispered to the doll, and skipped off to find her nurse, Fatima.

"You have been a true friend to me, Harding-Pasha. I will not forget all you have done for me and my son these past two years." The *amir*'s voice was thick with emotion.

"It was my pleasure, Malik. You and those of your household have been gracious guests. We'll miss you, old chap." The other man's voice cracked, and he turned where he sat cross-legged upon a pile of cushions to busy himself in pouring another tiny cupful of strong, thick black coffee for them both, a tactic designed to hide the emotion in his face. Jonathan Harding was British to the core, and unlike the natives of this volatile country, the British did not display their feelings readily in public.

Nonetheless, his words were sincere, his dismay at the imminent departure of a dear friend genuine. He sighed. It was damned funny how life went! When the Consul had asked him to share his home with the *amir* and his household, Jonathan had been outraged, seeing the prolonged visit of the overthrown Imochagh chieftain as an imposition and a very possible hindrance to his archaeological excavations in the Valley of the Pharaohs.

But, the British Consul to Egypt had explained delicately, the Crown could not afford to implicate itself in native trivial

13

wars by taking sides, nor by giving sanctuary to Malik ben-Azad—or at least, not officially, it couldn't! It was a matter of diplomacy. Surely Jonathan could see that, and appreciate the sensitive position they were in? The feeling was that the peaceful, intelligent, and well-educated Malik ben-Azad was by far the better man for the job of governing the mountain province of al-Azadel in northwest Africa, and of controlling the warlike tribes of that area, who bitterly resented French and British government intrusion into their affairs. Oh, yes, a far better choice than his younger brother, Murid, who was a hotheaded throwback to the bandit "Tuaregs" of an earlier century. Since it was but a matter of time before the *amir* regained his former power and overthrew his rebellious brother, allowing him to pass his time of forced exile in the comfortable, officially neutral home of a "personal friend"— an archaeologist who was a visitor to Egypt, and who just happened to be a British citizen—would go a long way as a gesture of goodwill. . . .

Jonathan had talked it over with his wife, Elizabeth, and she'd agreed. And what had been begun reluctantly would now also end reluctantly, he acknowledged, for over the past two years since Malik's brother had forced him into exile and slain many of his followers in a bloody revolt, the two diverse men had, to the surprise of both, become fast friends: almost as inseparable as their children, Malik's only son, Sharif, and Jonathan Harding's little daughter, Alexandria, who'd been born in and named for this very city. But now, regrettably, that friendship was ended. It was doubtful they'd ever see each other again.

"And I will miss you and your most gracious lady, my friend," Malik said warmly in answer to Jonathan Harding's comment. "But word came for me by messenger this morning. By the Grace of Allah, it is over! My brother, Murid, is dead. My people have retaken our mountain fortress of al-Azadel, and Murid's followers have deserted his cause and sworn new allegiance to me, their *amir*. It is time. I will return to al-Azadel to lead my people into a new way of life. A prosperous, peaceful way of life, without the old customs of robbing the caravans for horses and camels and slaves."

"I have every confidence that you'll succeed," Jonathan agreed sincerely. "And it goes without saying that I wish you all the very best of luck, Malik, my friend."

"Your good wishes are accepted, Harding-Pasha," Malik rejoined gratefully.

He glanced up as a servant entered the long, white room, which was scattered comfortably with beautiful rugs and silk cushions strewn about the mosaic-patterned tile floor after the Eastern fashion, rather than with the hot and uncomfortable overstuffed furniture of the West. "Yes? What is it, Hamal?"

"May it please you, my lord, the doctor-*hakim* wishes to speak with Harding-Pasha at once!"

"I'll be right there," Jonathan said hurriedly, springing to his feet. "You'll excuse me, won't you, Malik? My wife, you know—"

"But of course! Go at once, my friend, and may Allah attend you both in this difficult hour, and bless you with a strong son!" He touched his fingertips to his brow, and then to his heart. "Peace be with you. We will say our farewells at another time."

It was an hour later that Jonathan found Alexa seated in a corner of the sun-washed courtyard, her precious doll held firmly between her little knees. She seemed intent on mending a rather gruesome-looking crack that had caved in one side of the pretty, painted face by packing it with an oozy lump of gray clay. She looked up as he approached, and gave him a sweet, sunny smile that made her eyes shine ever greener, in vivid contrast to her chestnut-colored ringlets and the smears of clay daubing her rosy cheeks.

"Hello, there, poppet," he greeted her, forcing himself to smile despite his anxiety for his wife and the frail infant child she had delivered. "How's Papa's favorite girl this afternoon?"

"I'm very well, thank you, Papa," she said demurely, accepting the kiss he planted upon her brow. "But my dear Lucy is ind'sposed. I'm making her all better, just like Doctor Tom is making Mama better. Look!"

"Hmm. Poor old Lucy," Jonathan commiserated, taking

15

Alexa and her doll into his arms. He settled her comfortably on his knee as he sat upon the rim of one of the fountains, and carefully inspected her repairs. "Mmm. Jolly good! I'd say you're doing a fine job of patching her up, poppet."

"It was Fatima's idea. Sha-Sha says Lucy's a hero now, 'cos he hurted her when we were playing battle, see? But he just said that to make me feel better," she said softly with a wisdom beyond her years. "He was sorry he hurted Lucy, see?"

"I do believe you're right, Miss Alexandria! Sha-Sha's your friend, and I'm sure he felt very badly that Lucy was—er—injured by him in battle," Jonathan agreed solemnly, wondering how best to break the news to his little daughter. "But Alexa, enough of Lucy's injury for now, mmm? I have some news for you—two pieces of news, actually. Can you guess what?" She shook her head, wide-eyed. "Well, the first news is that you have a brand-new baby brother! Isn't that wonderful?"

"A brother?" She wrinkled her little snub nose in disappointment. "Oh! I s'pose so, Papa." She eyed him intently, as if perhaps the baby might be hidden in his pocket. "Where is it? How did it get here? Did it come up from the harbor in a box filled with straw, like my dear Lucy?"

Jonathan hid a smile. "No, no, not this time. The stork brought *him,* just a short while ago. He's with your mama, and in a moment you can come with me to see them both, if you promise to tiptoe and be very quiet. Can you?"

"I pr'mise, Papa. What's the other s'prise?"

"Well, your mama and I have decided that we've been here in Egypt quite long enough! We're all going home to England to live, Alexa—won't that be fun? You'll be able to meet your Grandmother Harding at last, and your Grandmother Turner, and Uncle David too. Uncle David and Aunt Julie have a little boy called Dan, you know, who's just a bit older than you. Dan is your cousin, and I expect you'll have fine old times playing together. You'll see, Alexa. It'll be marvelous!"

"Can Sha-Sha come too?" she asked hopefully, voicing the question he'd dreaded.

"Well, no, I'm afraid not. You see, Sha-Sha and his father will be leaving Egypt for their own home very soon."

A sudden squeezing sensation gripped Alexa's little chest. Her lower lip trembled. "You mean, we must go 'way and leave Sha-Sha and Uncle Malik and Fatima and Rida an'—an' everyone?" It was a thought too horrible to contemplate, for she had loved them all for half her lifetime.

"Well, yes, I'm afraid so. But Sha-Sha and his father would have been leaving us very soon anyway, poppet," he explained gently, trying to soften the blow. "They're planning to go back to al-Azadel, just as we're planning to go home to England. Come on, poppet, where's that sunny smile! You'll make lots of new friends there, I just know it."

"But I don't *want* to go to Ingland!" Alexa cried, her eyes filling with tears. "I don't want to leave Sha-Sha an' Aswad an' everyone! Why do we have to go, Papa, why, why?" she pleaded.

"Because your new baby brother is very, very tiny, Alexa, and not terribly strong," her father explained gently. "Come, dry your eyes, poppet, and try very hard to be grown up, and not pout and make your poor mama worry about you being unhappy, won't you? You see, my pet, that old sun up there is far too hot for a tiny baby, and whether we want to leave here or not, the doctor says we must. Your new little brother's very weak as it is. The weather here might make him sicker. He has to go home to England, where it's cool and where there are good doctors who can see that he grows stronger every day."

She jumped down from his lap, her tear-streaked little face suddenly shining with a solution. "I know, Papa! We'll send that ole baby to Gran'mother Harding! Fatima can put him in a box with straw 'round him, an' stick stamps on it, and then we can all stay here instead!"

"I'm sorry, poppet, but we simply can't do that," her father said with regret. "A new baby needs his mama and his papa and his big sister to go with him. He's far too little to go all that way alone without some help. Do you know whose help he needs most of all? More than anyone's?"

"Uh-huh?" She shook her head, making her reddish-brown curls jiggle engagingly.

"Yours! He needs his big, grown-up sister, Alexandria Victoria Elizabeth Harding! You must help Mama to take care

17

of him, Alexa, for you are older and very clever, and you know so much more than he knows. Will you promise me that you'll always help Mama take care of your baby brother?"

"Is a pr'mise like when Sha-Sha says I must swear by the Beard of the Prophet?" she demanded gravely.

"Why, something like that, yes!" her father agreed, hiding a smile.

"Then I swear by the Beard of the Prophet that I'll always take care of him, for always an' always an' always—but only when Lucy don't need me. I love my dear Lucy. She'll always be my very fav'rite baby, you know, Papa."

"Good enough!" Jonathan Harding declared, standing up and taking her sticky little hand in his. "Now! Let's go and see Mama and Master Keene Harding."

"Keene? But I want to see that old boy-baby the stork brought Mama!" Alexa pouted in disappointment.

"And so you will, my dear. You see, that's your new brother's name, Keene Michael David, after your grandfathers on both sides of the family."

"Oh! His name's almost big as mine!" She giggled. "Now, come along, Lucy, my dear. Don't dawdle so!" the little girl told her dolly, now tucked in the crook of her arm.

Hand in hand, she and her father left the sunlit courtyard, oblivious of the burning dark eyes—bright with unmanly tears—that watched their departure through a latticed window.

"You will come back, my little friend!" Sha-Sha muttered fiercely under his breath. "I, Sharif al-Azim, heir to al-Mamlaka al-Azadel, swear that you will!"

Sharif had returned to the courtyard out of guilt, intending to offer his crushed little friend the treat he'd promised before their quarrel, a ride on Aswad, his colt, only to overhear the disturbing conversation between Alexa and her father, Jonathan-Pasha. His anger at her was spent now, replaced by a sense of imminent loss.

"If it is the will of Allah and of *kismet* that we should be parted, then so be it," he muttered. "But someday, when you are grown, you *will* return to me, my little friend. Our destiny is written in the stars!"

18

Chapter One

Harding House, Riverside, London, 1860

"Come to me, little one! O Zerdali, jewel amongst women, fairer than all the women of the sands, come to me!"

That deep hypnotic voice, that commanding voice, its timbre the rough-smoothness of raw silk—oh, how that voice drew her! She dearly wanted to answer its summons, but dare not!

"My lord, I cannot!" she implored the voice. *"I dare not. . . . Please don't ask it of me!"*

Alexa stirred restlessly, mumbling in her fitful sleep as the dream took over once again: the same deliciously disturbing dream she'd had so many times since she was a little girl. Her lips moved. Her long lashes fluttered against her cheek. She flung out one pale, slender arm and sighed deeply, thrusting the crisp bedsheet and a forgotten novel aside as the now-familiar images unraveled through her mind in a slow-moving caravan.

Pale desert sands—a gleaming ocean frozen into endless gray eddies and waves—billowed beyond and about her oasis bower in the silvery moonlight. Upon the crest of a nearby dune waited an Arabian steed. The proud stallion seemed sculpted from the night itself, while his rider cut an equally commanding figure, cloaked in silhouette-black against an indigo sky spangled with blazing stars.

"My lord!" she whispered, and her heartbeat quickened.

The rider was as still and silent as the desert all about him. Only the dark-blue cloth that turbaned his head and masked his lower face like a brigand's fluttered gently in the night wind. The same chill breeze rippled the flowing hems of his indigo *jelabia* to reveal the sudden shimmer of a blade: the long, curved *takoba* dagger of the Tuaregs, which he wore thrust into the sash at his hip. His hair was hidden now by the dark wrappings of his headdress, but Alexa knew—oh, how well she knew!—the midnight blackness of that hidden hair; the silky, glossy texture of those inky curls beneath her fingertips; the smoldering ardor of ebony eyes aflame with desire as he came slowly riding across the shifting sands toward her. . . .

Somewhere within the house, a door slammed.

She jerked awake, and her heart skipped a beat. Her eyes flew open. She stared upward, not at fronded date palms dancing like feathery black plumes against a starry sky, but at the whiteness of her bedroom ceiling in the moonlight that streamed through the window.

The sound had been as loud and angry as a gunshot in the hushed house, and its violence and her subconscious straining for it all night long, even in the depths of sleep, had wakened her, she realized drowsily. Keene had a bad habit of slamming doors that she'd been unable to break him of.

She drew a shaky breath and tried to control the frenetic galloping of her heart, breathing deeply and calmly until its throbbing grew more even and controlled. The remnants of the dream receded as reality intruded. She let it go without fighting to recall each vivid detail. The dream would return, as it always did, if not this night, then the next. It had done so since her childhood. But the door—well, that was another matter! She'd heard it slam! That could mean only one thing, at this ungodly hour: Keene had come home at last, and she could finally confront him with the terrible accusations Charles Marchant had made against him. . . .

She tossed aside the tangled sheets and padded across the room in search of her dressing gown, outwardly composed, inwardly seething with mixed emotions. Hurriedly knotting the sash about her waist, she smoothed her waist-length, sleep-tousled chestnut hair away from her shoulders and started downstairs, moving blindly through the darkened house with the ease of one who knew it intimately.

A single gas lamp had remained lit in the study against her younger brother's return. Pausing by the opened door, Alexa saw him standing here, rocking a little on his heels. In one hand he held a glass and in the other a decanter filled with whiskey, which he was sloshing into it. His fair hair was disheveled. His collar and tie were untidily loosened. He tossed off a greedy gulp or two before he noticed Alexa standing in the doorway, and reeled unsteadily to face her. Judging by his appearance, he'd been drinking heavily long before he arrived home, she realized with a deepening sense of forboding. *Not again, please God, not again!* she prayed silently, and wished fervently that she were less cowardly, more like the stalwart heroines of the novels she devoured. They'd never yearn to bury their heads like silly ostriches and escape from the harsh realities and responsibilities of life. They'd meet them head-on, and with an aplomb she could only dream of. . . .

"Well, well, sister dear! Having trouble sleeping, were you?" he jeered, his handsome face twisted into an unpleasant sneer as he saw her standing there.

"Never mind me. Where were you, Keene?" Alexa stated baldly, taking a hesitant step or two into the room. "You haven't been home for three days! I was afraid you'd—"

"What? Done a mischief to myself?" He snorted, his upper lip curling in contempt. "Don't make me laugh! The only thing you're ever afraid of is the prospect of my being in trouble, and thereby tarnishing the fine old Harding name. Isn't that right, Alex?!"

In the pool of amber light that spilled from the glass chimney of the lamp, Keene saw the color drain from about his sister's lush coral mouth. Simultaneously, two spots of hectic crimson rose in her cheeks. Ha! Good for her, that beautiful, harping bitch! If she hadn't been riled before, she was thoroughly so now. He experienced a glow of malicious satisfaction at seeing the Ice Maiden so shaken from her customary cool and calm demeanor. Who did she think she was, anyway? His conscience, Devil take her?

"I suppose you're right, after a fashion," Alexa admitted very softly at length, and he knew by the slight tremor in her

21

voice the enormous self-control it took to refrain from screaming at him like a fishwife. She had a temper, had Alexa, which she controlled with varying degrees of success on such occasions. "I *was* worried that you might be in trouble. And with good reason, don't you think? After all, I'm still your legal guardian until next year, and it wouldn't be the first time you've disgraced us, would it?"

She paused to make her point and let it sink home, but Keene's expression remained unmoved.

"Oh, get on with it!" he urged, irritated. "Let's have your little sermon and be done with it! I don't have all night to listen to your blasted preaching!"

"Very well. Charles Marchant was here yesterday! He made some very serious accusations against you, Keene. In fact, he said—he said he'd taken the matter to the authorities and sworn out a warrant for your arrest!"

"Good God! On what charge?"

"That you a-attacked his wife!" she whispered. "I—I was so afraid the police had already apprehended you when you didn't come home. . . ."

With her shocking announcement, the evil grin Keene wore disappeared, as if the grin were chalk wiped from a slate by a damp rag. Oh, Christ, here it was again, he could tell! She'd rake it all back up, all that messy business with the little slut of a parlor maid. In her mind, Alexa had obviously believed Marchant's accusations because of Keene's lurid past exploits, and had had him tried, found guilty, and hanged, he could tell it by her expression. That blasted old fool Marchant and his trumped-up charges—!

Nausea filled him despite his scorn. With her shocking disclosure, his bloody skull had started to ache abominably again, and he felt the beginning of another of his migraines that had pained him since he was a child. The headaches were becoming more frequent now, and even the bloody liquor couldn't dull the pain anymore. Neither could opiates, though God knows, he'd tried them all. Unfortunately, he'd grown immune to the effects of laudanum long since.

The pain increased, as if hammers were pounding in his skull. Bright lights flashed behind his eyes and cold sweat beaded his brow. Oh Christ, he'd had enough, more than enough! Just because Alex controlled the Harding purse strings didn't mean she could run his life forever, damn her. . . .

"And so you believed him, of course, hook, line, and sinker?" he responded at length. "Damn you, Alexa! Must I go on paying for my mistake for the rest of my life?" he gritted through clenched teeth. "Having you doubt me at every turn, listening to you accuse me, hearing you take others' words against mine, because of that one mistake? Have you never heard of the old admonition to 'forgive and forget,' sister mine?"

"Forgive, perhaps, but forget—?" A sigh escaped Alexa. "I only wish I could! I've tried, but I can't forget it, Keene! When one's own brother does something so—so despicable as what you did to that poor girl two years ago, it can never be completely forgotten like just a little 'mistake,' as you call it!" Alex reminded him bitterly, memory twisting her lovely face into harsh lines as she added firmly, "And nor should it ever be forgotten! Now, what about Marchant's wife—and please, don't try to ignore the issue this time," she warned him, trying to sound in control and calmer than she felt. "He told me he caught you red-handed with his wife. That you hurt her, and— and—that you—!" She couldn't bring herself to say it. It was too distasteful a word for a young woman such as herself to say aloud.

Keene scowled moodily at her, looking for all the world like a truculent schoolboy. "Raped her? What? Can't you say it, my dear? Oh, damn Marchant to hell! If the old goat can't please his young bride, then that's his problem. Whatever he told you, it certainly wasn't rape!" he growled. "So forget all about his pathetic, empty little threats and go on back to bed. They're just the whinings of an impotent old idiot who's discovered he's been cuckolded by a younger man, nothing more. And Alexa—when I want your interference in my affairs in the future, I'll ask for it."

He turned back to the whiskey decanter and poured himself another hefty drink. As he did so, the lamplight illumined his face. Two livid scratches scored his cheek from eye to jaw, she saw, and there were tiny beads of dried blood clinging like rubies to the scratches. A narrow, angry ring encircled his throat like a red cord below the St. Christopher medallion she'd bought him for his sixteenth birthday, which he always wore on a thin silver chain. It looked as if someone had wound their hand through its length and twisted it tight—desperately tight. A sick feeling stirred deep in her belly. A throbbing began in her temple.

"Your face!" she blurted out, feeling suddenly short of breath, for it was like a nightmare relived to see those marks upon him again. "If Marchant's lying, what—what on earth happened to you?"

On reflex, Keene reached up to finger the scratches. "These?" He laughed. "Ah, yes, I'd almost forgotten! Well, let's see. How can I word it for your delicate ears, sister dear?" He paused. "Shall we just say that I tangled with a moody cat? A fickle, amoral little she-cat named Cynthia Marchant! She started off by purring in my arms, and then decided to scratch me to ribbons instead when her husband appeared on the scene, trumpeting like a cuckolded bull-elephant!" He cocked a rakish eyebrow at Alexa's shocked expression. "Oh, my! Does such plain talk offend your prim sensibilities, my dear? Do forgive me! But in all honesty, that's exactly what happened. Dear old Charles surprised me royally 'tupping' his lovely little wife in his own bed, and the impotent old bastard was—"

"Stop it!" she cried, covering her ears with her hands. "I won't be put off by your—your coarseness, not this time, Keene. I insist that you tell me what happened to your face! The truth."

"I told you, and that's that. If you don't like my explanations, then mind your own bloody business, Alex! My damned head aches like the devil and I'm going to bed. If you want to stand here and rant and rave all night, that's up to you. Good night, sister dear!"

He snatched up the decanter and wove his way past her to the door.

"I'm warning you, Keene," Alex threatened unsteadily as he drew level with her, though she was half-afraid of the evil glitter in her brother's blue eyes. "You won't be able to wriggle out of this scrape. Marchant was deadly serious. The police are out there now, combing London for you! When they find you, you'll be arrested, jailed, and forced to stand trial. I smoothed things over for you the last time, but I can't this time, don't you see? I can't bribe Scotland Yard! Marchant's an influential, wealthy man, and he means business, Keene. He's out for your blood. I think if he could, he'd see you hanged!''

Her dramatic outburst crackled on what seemed an endless silence before either of them spoke again.

''My God, you're serious aren't you?'' he said softly at length, meeting her frightened green eyes with his own blue ones.

''Very, I'm afraid.'' She gave a soft sigh of despair.

''And Marchant's really been to the police? You weren't just trying to frighten me?'' There was incredulity in his tone, and the dawnings of fear.

''Yes—or so he said. He told me he'd sworn out a warrant against you first thing yesterday morning.''

''Good God!'' Keene exclaimed with feeling. ''The man's a bloody fool! He can't truly believe I raped his wife, for crying out loud?''

''On the contrary, it seems he does.''

''But—it's a filthy lie! Cynthia and I—well, we'd been having an affair for some time, I admit it. She invited me to a dinner party at their home last night. All of the other guests were playing billiards or gossiping after dinner, and she was bored silly. She's so much younger than her husband and his friends' wives, you see?'' Stiffly, Alexa nodded. ''Cyn invited me upstairs, and, well, what with one thing leading to another, we ended up in her bed.'' He shrugged. ''To make a long story short, her husband came into the room soon after and surprised us *in flagrante delicto,* I believe the legal term is.''

''I'm sorry, but that pat little explanation won't do, Keene, not this time! Marchant said—he said his wife had bruises— that her clothing was torn! Does that sound like the results of a—a passionate, romantic tryst?''

''Oh, I don't for a minute doubt she had a bruise or two,'' he said levelly and with no apparent surprise. ''The lovely Cyn Marchant's a tigress—a beautiful, man-eating tigress! Oh,

Lord, don't look at me that way, Alex! The real world is far, far more sordid than your simpering romantic novels. Your paper heroes and heroines have no relationship whatsoever to real flesh and blood men and women with needs and lusts and greeds that are far from pretty. Christ! For all that you're four years older than me, you're so bloody innocent about such matters, Alex! However, let me try to explain to you.

"There *are* some women in this world—though admittedly they're quite few and far between—who, believe it or not, perversely *enjoy* being handled roughly by their lovers. They're called masochists, I believe, and Cynthia is one of them. She enjoys a man whose attentions are somewhat less than—er—gentle, shall we say? It's all just a wonderful, bawdy game with Cyn, you see, the old 'ravish and conquer.' But I never dreamed that deceitful little bitch wouldn't tearfully 'fess up and tell the truth to her old man after he thrashed me and threw me out!"

He looked up, saw the doubt in his sister's eyes, and nervously wet his lips with his tongue. The hammers were still beating a tattoo in his head. "Come now, Alexa, I've explained how it was, and how I came by these scratches—surely you believe me?" he demanded hoarsely. "For God's sake, woman, you have to! You're my sister!"

"Keene, I—I want to, truly I do, but I—" Her voice broke off lamely. Her eyes slid away from his.

"But you can't?" he snarled, finishing for her.

"Marchant was very convincing, Keene, very!" she cried, half-pleading, half-defiant. "You have no idea how frightening he was. And besides, that other time with Polly—those scratches on your cheek then! Keene, I'm only human! What am I supposed to believe? Your denials, or my own eyes and ears?"

"'That other time,' 'that other time'—that's all I've heard since it happened! I was little more than a boy myself then, and that chit was a cheap little East End trollop who was more than eager—despite what her coarse lout of a father might have said to the contrary—to squeeze more money out of you! Christ! She'd probably had more men in her time than I've had collar studs! But this—this time is different. Alexa, if what you say is

26

true, I'm a wanted man! I could spend years in prison for something I didn't do! I swear to you, on our mother's grave, I'm innocent! Tell me *you* believe in me, at least. Tell me you don't believe me guilty of raping another man's wife—of forcing myself on a woman."

Her eyes came to rest on the livid purplish welt encircling his neck, then were drawn back to the deep, bloody scratches on his cheek. Her gaze met his fleetingly, then again slid uncomfortably away. She swallowed, trembling all over, her mouth working soundlessly like a gasping fish. She wanted to reassure him—to say *something*—but couldn't bring herself to speak at all.

Keene gave a short, harsh bark of a laugh. "Well, I suppose your silence says it all, doesn't it? Thanks for the vote of confidence, sister mine! That's all I needed to know." He started through the door.

"Keene, wait! If it was really as you've told me, we have to talk, decide what to do. You can't just walk out like this!" she cried after him, suddenly finding her tongue.

No. He couldn't simply turn his back on this matter and pretend it hadn't happened; couldn't duck his responsibilities as he had so many times in the past and leave everything to her. They had to talk, to decide on some plan of action! And besides, before she'd died their mama had asked her to take care of poor, troubled Keene, her incorrigible, violent-tempered younger brother, had she not? It was a habit too long ingrained in Alexa to break now, whatever he'd done. Furthermore, despite his unpleasantness towards her, he was still her younger brother. She loved him, though he was often a difficult person to love, and harder still to like. It was her duty as his guardian to try to sort this mess out and stand beside him, to the bitter end, if need be, whatever scandal or shame it brought upon their family name.

"You can't run!" she whispered again. "It'll only make matters worse."

At the foot of the stairs in the paneled entryway, he turned and looked back at her over his shoulder, his fingers already closing over the front doorknob. His expression was pained.

"Can't I?" he asked mockingly, rubbing his temples. "Just

watch me! And if the police should come sniffing around, do me one last favor: tell them I've left Harding House for good, and won't be coming back. Tell them you have no idea where I can be found. And don't worry about lying to them, my holier-than-thou sister! Once I walk out of here, it'll be the truth!"

The anger that had been building inside her burst free at last.

"Go then, confound you, Keene! Go, if you're too bloody cowardly to stay and face the consequences of your actions like a man! Perhaps it'll be for the best. I'm tired of making excuses for your wild behavior, for your drinking and gambling, and having to bail you out of one scrape after the other! Go if you must—and don't come back!"

He slammed the door for a second time as he stormed out into the night, leaving her with tears of frustration and anguish at her outburst shining in her green eyes.

When, after a fitful, exhausted sleep, she awakened the next morning to a perfect English spring day of warbling birds and budding boughs, she found his bed had not been slept in. As he'd threatened—and as she'd screamed at him to do—Keene was gone.

Over eighteen months would pass without word from him. Almost two years would come and go before she learned the terrible error in judgment she'd made that night. Everything Keene had told her had been the truth. . . .

Chapter Two

Algiers, Northwest Africa, 1862

Algiers, the teeming capital of Algeria that overlooked the vivid waters of the bay, promised to be exotic beyond even her wildest imaginings, Alexa thought as she tentatively made her way down the precarious wooden gangplank of the *L'Aventure*, the grubby little French vessel that had brought her safely through the Straits of Gibraltar and across the sparkling Mediterranean on the first leg of her search for her missing brother.

Dan, her lawyer cousin, had discovered a clue to her brother's disappearance from some of the more unsavory members of his clientele: the gaming-house proprietors to whom Keene had been indebted for several thousand pounds. Keene Harding's gambling debts had been left unpaid when he fled the authorities and the country. His dunners' considerable interest in finding him had resulted in their uncovering his trail as far as Paris. There, Alexa had been astounded to learn, they'd discovered that Keene had enlisted in the French Foreign Legion to put himself beyond the long arm of the law— and themselves!

No sooner had Dan told her this than Alexa had pensioned off old Sally, the cook, given notice to the maid, closed up Harding Hall, left the keys and her business affairs in Dan's capable hands, and sold the double rope of matched pearls her mother had bequeathed her to a reputable jeweler in the City. She'd decided to use the proceeds from their sale to finance her search for Keene's whereabouts, for she was determined to

29

find him and somehow right the enormous wrong she'd done him.

France being the obvious starting point for her quest, she'd traveled by ferry and then by train to the city of Paris, where—by means of flirtatious glances, tearful cajolings, and several hefty bribes—she'd at last uncovered the knowledge she sought.

Keene, a recruiting officer had reluctantly informed her, had indeed joined the *Legion Etrangere* the year previous. From there he had been dispatched to the Foreign Legion headquarters of Sidi-bel-Abbes, Northwest Africa, from which he had doubtless been assigned to some desert outpost by now.

Was he certain the young man he remembered had been her brother? she'd asked the recruiting officer anxiously. Surely with so many young men enlisting each week, he could have been mistaken. The recruiting officer had bristled at such an idea. He, a soldier of thirty-five years' honorable service to France, forget such an insolent, abrasive young man? Forget one with such an unusual first name who had also been British, and who had worn about his neck a medallion of St. Christopher, an unusual trinket for an Englishman to wear? *Mon Dieu*, was it likely he would have forgotten? Alexa had agreed that it was not. The man's description of the silver rope-chain and the medal she herself had bought as a gift for Keene was the final proof she needed that she was headed in the right direction.

At last, she'd thought optimistically, she had a place to begin her search! And there was an excellent chance she'd be able to find her brother. Once she'd done so, she'd try her utmost to make amends to him, though it wouldn't be easy. Keene—well, unlike her, Keene had always been of an unforgiving nature, and jealous of Alexa's position as the oldest and her closeness to their father. She secretly doubted he'd meet her halfway, or even with any pretense at civility! But even so, since she'd discovered just a few week ago that she'd misjudged him, and that he'd been telling her the truth about his affair with Charles Marchant's wife, she *had* to try! After all, she'd let him leave Harding Hall that night with harsh and hate-filled words between them. She'd stubbornly allowed his past behavior to color her judgment of the incident, and in the process had badly let her brother down when he'd needed her support most. She knew she couldn't live with her guilt if she didn't find him and ask his forgiveness!

The moment she disembarked, there were white-robed natives everywhere about her, clamoring in strident tones for the *ma'mselle* to hire their services as porters or guides, or to buy their fruits and other exotic wares.

Choosing a smiling moustached fellow who seemed less persistent than his countrymen, she paid a native porter to see her and her luggage safely transported aboard the man's weathered *gharry*, an Indian-style canopied open carriage drawn by a scrawny mule. She opened her lacy parasol with a practiced twirl and leaned comfortably back against the brown leather seat to enjoy her first views of Algiers' New Quarter as they drove to what Muhammed, her driver, described as a predominantly British hotel, the Grand Empress, which was just a few streets distant from the government buildings of the French, of whose North African Republic Algiers was a part.

The drive through the dusty, sun-drenched streets of the city gave Alexa a leisurely opportunity to see the sights she'd hitherto only read about in a battered guidebook another passenger of the *L'Aventure* had graciously loaned her, and to put her memory to work to recall the tidbits of Algiers' history she'd read in its pages.

Along with Morocco, Libya, and Tunisia, Algeria had formerly been one of the rich and powerful Barbary States whose unscrupulous rulers had, until as recently as the last century, offered protection from fierce pirates to those foreign vessels which sailed the vivid turquoise waters of the Mediterranean—in return for a rich tribute paid to themselves! Those who were unwilling or unable to pay these hefty tributes had found their cargoes taken, and their crews and passengers sold into slavery. This cruel practice had flourished until effective military intervention from both the British and French governments had—at least, officially—ended such goings-on. After suffering enormous losses from naval attacks upon Tripoli and Algiers by the American and British forces as recently as 1815 and 1816, the lands of the Barbary States had been divided amongst several European powers, with Algeria in North Africa becoming first a colony, then a republic of France.

As would be expected from her position between Tunisia and Morocco, Algeria reflected centuries of Arab, Berber, and Moslem influence, the guidebook had promised. Alexa was not disappointed. The blinding white of Algiers' graceful Islamic architecture, with its mosques and slender minarets, its grilled archways and tiled courtyards and white, flat-roofed buildings, was everything she had anticipated in the way of things foreign and mysterious, she saw as she gazed eagerly about her—as were the hundreds of *dhows* with their lateen sails furled that bobbed about on the vivid blue waters of the harbor.

The exotic dress of the various peoples to be found in the teeming markets, tenements, bazaars, and sidewalk cafes of the city they drove through was also fascinating. What a stunning contrast to the grimy, drab costermongers of the London markets were the rug sellers and brass merchants of Algiers! There were fierce-looking Turks with their red *fez* or "flower-pot" hats and curly-toed, yellow felt slippers, rubbing shoulders with the peddlers of pottery and exotic fruits, bearded sidewalk astrologers and fortune-tellers, money-lenders, and the dapperly uniformed soldiers of the famed French *Legion Etrangere*. There were, too, many stuffy British civil servants attired in colonial white garb, which was considered *de rigueur* for proper English gentlemen in such tropic climes.

She glimpsed amongst the kaleidoscopic variety of faces the hawk-featured faces of fair-skinned Berbers, fierce nomadic tribesmen whose home was the forbidding and little-known Sahara to the south, and also the swarthy Bedouins, who herded their flocks of sheep and goats from desert oasis to desert oasis the winter long, and who returned to their palatial homes in the white-walled oasis cities only for the blistering months of summer.

The more modern portion of the city, Alexa's native driver Muhammed told her in answer to her barrage of questions concerning the offices of the French Foreign Legion, was situated here on this low hillside overlooking the vivid waters of the Bay of Algiers. She would find the officials she sought in these buildings, Muhammed promised, within the cool, colonial-style offices from which the French conducted the governing of the Republic.

The adventurous traveler seeking exotic sights and a vastly unfamiliar culture must climb the narrow maze of streets to the higher slopes of Algiers, Muhammed disclosed, flashing her a broad grin that revealed twin rows of sparkling white teeth against olive skin. He must visit the fabled Casbah, or citadel, which had once presided over the ancient Moorish quarter but was now the name for the area where the majority of Algiers' natives lived and worked amongst narrow, mazelike streets. Each street had an exotic name that was reminiscent of the tales of *The Thousand and One Nights*, Alexa heard, smiling with delight: names such as the Street of the Tent-Makers, the Street of the Rug-Sellers, or the Street of the Workers in Brass.

It was here—not in the New Quarter, but in the teeming bazaars of the mysterious, fabled Casbah—that Alexa found herself two days after her arrival, to both her secret delight and her dismay.

Remembering the successful use of both her feminine wiles and a hefty bribe or two at the Legion offices in Paris, she'd confidently determined to use the same speedy and effective methods upon the officials here at the British Consulate. She'd hoped she could persuade them to provide her further information concerning her brother's whereabouts and later, all going well, an escort to wherever he might be. Men were a gullible lot, she'd soon decided in Paris. The majority of them could easily be coerced into doing anything a woman desired by the judicious use of her enigmatic smiles, tears, or cold, hard cash. Why should the officials of Algiers prove any different?

But alas, her efforts had all come to naught! The officials at the Algiers British Consulate and also at the Legion offices had proven incorruptible! They'd curtly told her she was wasting her time, and pointed out that her brother had severed all former ties with England and his citizenship by joining the Legion's numbers. They insisted that she return to England immediately, where she belonged, washing their hands of all responsibility for her safety should she remain. Algiers, they had sternly cautioned her to a man, was a dangerous place, a totally unsuitable place for a well-bred and unescorted, naive young white woman such as herself. It was advice she was to hear over and over in the next few days until she was sick of hearing it!

But while she was leaving the Legion for the last time, angry and dispirited by the stony-faced reception she had received there, a young military clerk had beckoned to her to follow him. Curious despite her disappointment and indignation, she had followed him outside, and thence to a sidewalk cafe in the cool, dark shadows of a nearby building.

"*Mademoiselle,* I do believe I can 'elp you to find your brother," the clerk had divulged as he drew out a chair for her to sit at a small round table, and took the seat opposite for himself.

"I see," Alexa had responded warily to his announcement. "And what, may I ask, will this information cost me, sir?" Her shabby treatment at the hands of both French and British officials over the past two days had left her decidedly wary of offers of help from any quarter!

"Cost you? Ah, *mademoiselle,* it will cost you nothing, I promise! I merely wish to be of help to a charming young lady." The clerk had grinned disarmingly, his boyish face wreathed with smiles. "You see, I remember your brother very well, *Mademoiselle* Harding, because his name, Keene, is an unusual one, *n'est ce pas,* and because *M'sieu* Harding's papers were one of the first I processed on my arrival here almost two years ago. I also remember distinctly the very fine Saint Christopher medallion which he wore on a chain about his neck, for you see, *mademoiselle,* I have one just like it, although mine is made of gold! Is this young man not the Keene Harding you are searching for, *mademoiselle?*"

"Why yes, that's him!" Alexa exclaimed, her eyes shining. "I gave the Saint Christopher medal to him myself, on his sixteenth birthday! Oh, *M'sieu* Etoile, where is he? Tell me,

34

where has the Legion sent my brother?"

"While you were speaking with my commandant, I took the liberty of looking up his name in the records. After arriving at Sidi-bel-Abbes, your brother was assigned to a remote outpost in the desert, *mademoiselle.*" He frowned. "Fort Valeureux, it is called. Alas, Valeureux lies in very dangerous, very inhospitable terrain! I do not wish to disappoint you, *Mademoiselle* Harding, but the Legion will not help you to go there, however charmingly you might plead. It is a grueling journey for the brave men posted there. For a young white woman—impossible! Why, even for a native familiar with the desert, it would prove a most difficult journey to undertake, *mademoiselle!* For you to even contemplate making such a hazardous journey would be quite out of the question!"

Like all the others, the young military clerk had openly dismissed the idea of a mere woman undertaking such an outlandish quest.

But after thanking the young man for his assistance, Alexa had returned to her hotel to consider what to do next, having no intention whatsoever of taking his advice and leaving Algeria. Indeed, no! She had many admirable traits, but the ability to blindly, docilely follow orders was not one of them. Tenacity—if not courage—was. "A native who is familiar with the desert," young Etoile had unwittingly suggested, and his disparaging words had stuck in Alexa's mind. Mmmm. But where on earth was she to find such a person? The answer had been ridiculously simple, so simple she could have kicked herself for not seeing it immediately! Since "natives" tended to be found most readily in the "native" quarters of a city, she would go straight to the horse's mouth, so to speak; she would scour the mysterious Casbah for her guide, and the British Consulate and French Foreign Legion officials could all go to blazes, those stuffy old stick-in-the-muds—!

And so, here she was.

The *muezzin*'s wailing cry from the lofty minaret of a nearby mosque had just called the faithful to noon prayer when Alexa left the cool, dark shadows of the Grand Empress Hotel yet again, two days later. She made her way across a sun-washed courtyard where fountains splashed and doves strutted and cooed, to the waiting *gharry* she'd instructed the hotel porter to hire for her use. There being no one nearby to hand her inside the vehicle, she gave a shrug, hoisted her skirts, and clambered unaided into her seat.

In thoughtful silence, she sat beneath the carriage's shady fringed canopy and waited for the time of prayer to end. The date-palm-lined streets about her were now miraculously deserted save for the few Europeans still strolling about. All the followers of Islam, her driver among them, had disappeared inside the nearby buildings to perform their devotions. Five times each and every day they removed their sandals, unrolled their small prayer rugs, and knelt down upon them, prostrating themselves in the direction of the Holy City of Mecca. The *muezzin*'s call to prayer and the response of the Muslim population of Algiers to his cries had by now become a common occurrence to Alexa since her arrival in Algiers, for the Muslims prayed in the same fashion at dawn, at noon, at four in the afternoon, at sunset, and at nightfall. Though a Christian herself, she could not help but admire their devotion, and the way their religion seemed to play an integral part in their lives.

Her thoughts drifting while she patiently awaited her driver's return, she considered again how incredible it was that she was really here, in Algeria, despite her cousin Dan's heated protests. Her train of thought inevitably returned to that sunny Sunday afternoon some weeks before when her life had been turned upside down a second time by Charles Marchant's explosive reentry into her life.

The months since Keene stormed out into the night had been pure torment for Alexa. Alone, she'd had to stare down the contemptuous glances that were cast in her direction when she was forced to go into the City to shop. Shopkeepers had been barely civil to her. Doors had been none too politely slammed in her face. Invitations to teas and suppers and even charitable functions had dwindled and finally ceased. With her head held high, she'd had to turn a deaf ear to the cruelly loud whispers of the gossips who'd pointed her out as "the only sister of that disgraceful young man! You know, the one who—" Then, just when she was beginning to hope she'd finally lived the scandal down by her own impeccable behavior, and had come to accept that Keene had fled England under a cloud of disgrace and threat of imprisonment, and that there was every chance she might never see him again, Marchant had appeared on her doorstep at Harding Hall, disheveled and distraught, and her world had been turned upside down again.

In embarrassed and sometimes scarcely coherent tones, Marchant had confessed that he had been terribly wrong about Keene. He had, he'd said, falsely accused her younger brother of ravishing his wife upon his last fateful visit to their home. He'd returned to Harding Hall in an attempt to right the wrong he'd done him!

Marchant, it transpired, had just that afternoon arrived home from a shooting expedition up in Scotland far earlier than expected. By so doing he'd surprised his beautiful, bored young wife in bed with her latest lover, one of his own young bank clerks! It had been patently obvious even to stuffy old Marchant that his faithless Cynthia had been no reluctant participant in the passionate wrestling match he'd interrupted! In the face of his terrible anger and under the pressure of threats that he would divorce her for adultery and toss her out of his home, penniless and naked, Cynthia had tearfully confessed to having indulged in several torrid affairs, among them her earlier trysts with young Keene Harding. In the process, she'd also admitted to her outraged husband that she'd lied about Keene's "brutal" attack upon her, and that she'd been not an innocent victim of his unbridled animal lust, but a willing participant in their very torrid lovemaking.

Alexa had been almost as shattered by this revelation as poor cuckolded Charles. She'd realized immediately the grave injustice she'd done Keene, and had been overwhelmed by guilt. Her father had asked her to watch out for her wild young brother, and to try to keep him to the straight-and-narrow path. Her poor mama, who'd gone into a steady decline after receiving the news of Jonathan Harding's death in distant Egypt and never recovered fully from her grief, had implored Alexa to do likewise. Oh yes, she'd let both of her parents down, and Keene too! She should have supported him, believed in him, whatever he'd been guilty of in the past. Surely, she thought, tears filling her eyes, as his sister who

37

loved him, she'd owed him the benefit of the doubt.

"*Excusez-moi! Excusez-moi!* Shall we soon depart, *mam'selle?*" Muhammed was asking, grinning expectantly up at her. His inquiry broke into her thoughts.

She blinked back her tears, and saw that her driver was none other than the same Moroccan fellow who'd driven her to her hotel upon her arrival in Algiers. His broad, sunny smile was like that of an old friend.

"Why, hello again, Muhammed! How are you?" she inquired, smiling warmly in response.

"Very well, *merci, mademoiselle!*" Muhammed returned with a bashful grin. "May I ask where is it you wish me to take you today, *mademoiselle?*"

"I wish to go into the Casbah," she declared firmly, ignoring his immediate look of astonishment and disapproval. "Please, drive on when you're ready."

Muhammed opened his mouth to protest but thought better of it. He shrugged, then clambered up to his seat on the *gharry* without another word, much to Alexa's secret amusement.

When they were finally under way, the driver quickly left the newer part of the city for the old, his mule straining up the lower streets to the ancient Moorish quarter that sprawled across the upper hillsides like a frowsy old bawd decked out in shabby finery.

Alexa saw to her relief that the streets were far less crowded at this time of day, for most if not all of the population preferred to sleep away the hottest hours following the noon prayers. Still, the Casbah's rabbit warren of narrow, cobbled streets was thronged with bargain-hunters and haggling sellers nonetheless, and alive with all the noisy confusion and exotic color, sights and pungent smells that Alexa had anticipated she would find at the native bazaar. True, she thought with a smile of delight as she looked about her, she had embarked on this journey primarily to make amends with Keene. But in all honesty, she had also embraced with wide-open arms the prospect of new sights, excitement, and possible adventures to rival those she read about so avidly! Her life in staid and proper England as a twenty-four-year-old spinster living alone with little to occupy her days had grown immeasurably dull. She hungered for some sort of diversion as a fish craved water!

Alighting from her carriage, she opened her parasol and bade her driver wait for her return.

"Meet me back here, would you, Muhammed? I should be gone for—oh, about an hour, with any luck. But if my—business—here should take longer, I'll pay you extra for your trouble if you'll wait for me." She flashed him a hopeful smile that would have melted the heart of a moneylender.

"What is this you say? You would go into the Casbah alone, *mademoiselle?*" Muhammed gasped, his eyes growing round and wide with disbelief, the bluish whites stark against his olive complexion. "Ah, *mais, non, non,* this I cannot possibly permit! Why, it is most unsafe—and most unwise. There are thieves and cutthroats everywhere in these parts—wicked men who might seek to harm you, *mademoiselle!* Perhaps—yes, Muhammed had best escort you, *non?*"

Alexa had accepted his offer with relief and gratitude, and Muhammed had given a small, ragged beggar boy a coin to watch his vehicle before they set off on foot.

The labyrinth of narrow, twisting streets, each one lined with blank white walls or ornate grilled windows, were pooled for the greater part in inky shadow, but the gloom was pierced here and there by dazzling shafts of sunlight. The uneasy feeling that hundreds of eyes watched her from behind those shadowed grills scared her a little, if the truth were known, and Alexa welcomed the Moroccan's company more than she cared to admit. She stepped out briskly, looking cool and composed in her sprigged white muslin dress, a shady leghorn straw hat perched fetchingly atop her coppery ringlets and festooned with saucy green ribbons. Muhammed meanwhile dogged her heels like a faithful shadow.

Weaving her way amongst the crowds of white-robed men and black-robed women, rendered formless and faceless and peculiarly sexless beneath the concealing veils of *purdah,* she was still keenly aware of the sensation of unseen hostile eyes watching her, following her every little movement from behind those somber veils or from the concealment of those narrow, arabesqued black grills. Since she had no guilty conscience and certainly no dark secrets to hide, she didn't know why it should

39

bother her so to know that she was being watched, but it did so regardless. It was a disquieting sensation that raised the fine hairs at her nape in tingling awareness: one she would ever after associate with her visit to the Casbah, the City of a Thousand Watching Eyes, she thought, giving it her own appropriate title. . . .

Realizing belatedly that she was acting like an overimaginative, naive little twit, she forced her thoughts away from such silliness and turned her attention outward to her surroundings instead.

Hand-loomed rugs were heaped everywhere against the towering walls of the dusty street. Each rug was unique, although their patterns included no woven animals or human figures, Muhammed explained to her, for the Muslim religion forbade the depiction of living creatures. Still, they were beautifully crafted, with ornate borders of flowers and vines in a seemingly endless variety of patterns, woven in blue and gold, black and crimson, or natural, creamy white. Each one felt soft to her touch.

Further on, metal workers were busily hammering floral designs onto oval trays or platters of brass. Nearby, a vendor of caged birds and parrots in wicker prisons nudged his captives out of their slumber and into full-throated, warbling song or deafening squawks for the *mademoiselle*'s benefit. There were camels and donkeys everywhere too, each poor beast heavily laden, all resolutely picking their plodding way through the jostling crowds while their masters ran behind, heaping insults upon the animals' heads. The exotic aromas of sizzling skewered meats, baking wheels of flat breads, and steaming mounds of yellow rice and the reek of clarified butter and hot oils wafted from the food vendors' stalls and mingled with the sweet or musky scents of vast arrays of spices and flagons of perfumes and scented oils.

They passed a wide stairway that led down into some murky cafe or other, and although Muhammed attempted to chivy her quickly past it, Alexa paused. She was doubly curious to see what was inside, since Muhammed seemed determined she should not!

Peering curiously down through the gloomy opening, she

was shocked to glimpse a half-naked female dancer, clothed in swirling, gauzy veils decorated with slivers of bright mirror, writhing and twirling before a circle of hawk-faced men! Smiling a seductive smile, her heavy-lidded eyes darkened and ringed exotically with kohl and antimony, the dancer undulated her torso and moved her breasts, hips, and belly in time to the rhythmic music of wailing flutes and the insistent heartbeat of several small drums. The dancer provided a counterpoint to the exciting music by chinking her *zals*, the tiny bells she wore fastened to her fingers. The air that billowed out from the place was thick with the heavy aromas of Turkish coffee and pungent cigar smoke, the steam of water-pipes, and the subtle scent of something else Alexa could not define—some dark and primitive, pungent odor that was more an atmosphere than a true scent, she realized, sniffing and straining her eyes to see more of the intriguing—scandalous—goings-on within the shadowed cafe.

"*Non, non, ma'm'selle,* this very wicked place! Certainly not for English young lady's eyes, *ewellah,* indeed *non!* Come, come, let us move on!" Muhammed insisted, stepping before her and effectively blocking her curious gaze. With a resigned shrug, Alexa obediently did as he asked.

"Perhaps," her escort suggested as they stepped aside to avoid a heavily veiled woman passing by with a wooden tray of flat bread loaves balanced effortlessly upon her head, "if the *mademoiselle* would but tell Muhammed what it is she is looking for in the bazaar, he would know where it might be found, and she could purchase it and return safely to her hotel very soon, yes?" He was obviously ill at ease with the responsibility of being her escort that she'd unwittingly thrust upon him.

"Oh, very well!" she agreed, resigned to accepting his offer. Over the past hour, seeing the sometimes openly disapproving, often lecherous, and frequently hostile or speculative way some of the men of the Casbah regarded her, with her unveiled face, uncovered hair, and—in their eyes—shockingly immodest European attire, she'd come to realize she would need Muhammed's help if she were to do what she'd come here to do, like it or not.

41

"I came to the Casbah hoping to find a guide, Muhammed—someone honest who knows the desert well and would be willing, for a fee, to escort me safely to Fort Valeureux. It's a French fort that lies deep in the Sahara, far to the south of Sidi-bel-Abbes."

Her cool announcement obviously horrified Muhammed. He gaped at her, slack-jawed and sputtering incoherently. "Fort Valeureux! I know of it, yes, yes, of course, everyone does. But such a journey—why, it is impossible! Surely you are making the leetle joke with Muhammed, *oui, mademoiselle?*" He eyed her hopefully.

"On the contrary, I'm very serious!" Alexa said firmly. "My brother is a legionnaire at Valeureux, and I must see him, to talk with him. It is—it is a matter of our family honor, you see?"

Her mention of family honor had obviously touched a familiar chord in the Moroccan, for now Muhammed nodded solemnly in understanding, though appearing no less troubled. "Ah, yes, I understand, dear lady, indeed yes. And I only wish there was some way I could help you, but you cannot attempt this! The desert is—"

"I know, I know!" Alexa cut in irritably. "The desert is 'no place for an unescorted white woman'! I've been told exactly that so many times since I arrived in Algiers, I know it by heart! But I don't care what everyone says, don't you see?" she continued, her jaw obstinately set. "I've made up my mind to do this, and somehow, somewhere, I shall find a guide and do it!"

"Guide, missy? *Englesy* missie want guide?" piped up a young voice at her elbow.

Alexa spun around to see a native youth hovering at her side. He wore a white turban and a belted, long-sleeved cotton tunic that reached his knees, with baggy white cotton breeches beneath. His feet were brown, dirty, and bare, yet his eyes were bright and dark in his golden-bronzed face, and his smile irrepressibly young and eager—and greedy.

"Why, yes!" she agreed, smiling down at the youth. "Do you know of someone who might be willing to—"

"*Wellah!* Don't listen to his nonsense! Be off with you, you

42

young monkey!" Muhammed growled, scowling fiercely at the boy as he interrupted. "Stop your pestering, boy, and leave the *mam'selle* be! *Allez! Allez!*"

"Cemal, my honored father—he plans a holy pilgrimage to Mecca across the Red Sea!" the boy managed to gasp out, sidestepping Muhammed's tall, bony frame as he tried to shove the lad away from Alexa. The youth's head bobbed about like a nestling owl's in an effort to meet her eyes over or around Muhammed's arms or broad frame. "It is a pilgrimage every good Muslim must make at least once in his lifetime, according to our faith, you understand? Some while ago, he worked for the *Englesy* at the consulate, and speaks very good English, missie. He knows the desert better than any other too! Perhaps he would be willing to escort the missie, if the price was right." He grinned craftily. "The road the pilgrims' camel caravan will take is very long, but it is the same as the road to the fort for many, many miles, and—"

"By Allah, art thou deaf, O Donkey Ears? Be off with you, I said!" Muhammed thundered, trying to cuff the lad now, although the boy nimbly avoided his blows by ducking to left and to right and running around behind Alexa for protection, the dust of the street riding in eddies in his wake.

"Muhammed, leave him be, please!" Alexa insisted crossly, their antics making her dizzy. "I want to hear what he has to say!"

The boy shot her a smug grin as Muhammed shrugged, scowled, and stepped aside, his arms crossed over his chest. He made a horrible, vulgar gesture and a grimace in the Moroccan's direction, which Muhammed, with great fortitude, managed to refrain from answering with a hefty kick.

"As I was saying, missie, before this interfering fellow interrupted, my father Cemal ben-Hussein plans a pilgrimage to Mecca. The caravan will depart two days from now. I believe the fort of the *Franziwas* is but two—perhaps three?—days off the pilgrims' road. Perhaps my father would be willing to take the missie with us, yes?"

"Do you think he might? Oh, I hope so. Tell me, where is your father? Could you take me to him, so we can discuss it and agree upon a price?"

"Ah, yes, we will go at once, missie, never fear! You will follow me." The boy jerked his head, then remembered the Moroccan and added aloofly over his shoulder, "And you may follow also—but only if the missie wishes you should do so— and if you will stay silent, O Thou Interfering One!"

Completely ignoring the venomous glare the furious Moroccan sizzled at him, the youth plunged into the thick of the crowds. Without hesitation, Alexa dove between the jostling bodies in his wake, trying breathlessly to keep up.

Hours before the *muezzin* called the faithful to prayer that sunset, Alexa—flushed with triumph and glowing with anticipation of the great adventure about to unfold before her—had hired herself a guide!

Her rendezvous with destiny was about to begin, she sensed. Whatever lay ahead from here on would be solely the results of her own actions, combined with the *kismet*, or fate, that ruled all men. A tingle of excitement rippled through her as she tumbled wearily into her bed at the hotel that night. Tomorrow, she would make the train journey south to Sidi-bel-Abbes, and there meet up with Cemal, her guide, and his son, Nabal, once more, and join the pilgrims' caravan.

The sands of the Sahara awaited her—and the magical promise of a desert dream.

Chapter Three

Lord! If only Cousin Dan and Pauline could see me now! Alexa thought, smothering a giggle.

The snorting sound that resulted caused her guide, the very proper Cemal, to glance at her with a curious frown, perhaps wondering if the heat had already affected her mind, as it did so many Europeans.

It was peculiar, but having shed her hot Victorian clothing this morning in favor of the flowing robes of a Bedouin native woman, it seemed as if she had shed her prim and stuffy inhibitions right along with her stays! In the silky red-and-black-patterned *caftan* which Cemal had acquired for her to wear under a flowing overrobe, she felt gloriously free! She could move as her body was intended by nature to move with a lithe, natural grace unhampered by whalebone corsets, numerous petticoats, and tightly buttoned, high-heeled boots that always pinched. Free to wear her long, golden-chestnut hair loose and flowing beneath her veils, instead of tightly parted and scraped back into the severe braided knots or loops dictated by current fashion, both of which pained her scalp and sometimes left her with a throbbing headache. And, as if she were a butterfly emerging from a chrysalis, she suddenly realized she was completely free to *think* for herself too! She could relish the great adventure unfolding before her, for out here, the pressures of running a household, instructing servants, and trying to make ends meet on a too-tight budget were blissfully gone! Having found such freedom and excitement, could she ever consider relinquishing it and returning to the stuffy Victorian life she'd once known? Mmm.

45

Probably not. She doubted if she'd ever be the same again. . . .

"The moon has risen. Shall we depart, mistress?" Cemal inquired, looking up at her curiously.

Only her strange, faintly slanted green eyes—eyes that Cemal fancied belonged more properly in the face of an Eastern *jinn* rather than a proper British missie—showed amidst the girl's concealing veils, which were prettily edged with tinkling silver coins like those of the other *hareem*, the women of the waiting caravan. Those eyes were brimful with sparkling merriment, dancing and flashing like a sultan's treasure trove of rare emeralds with sheer enjoyment, he saw, and he wondered at the cause of her high spirits. Cemal shrugged. It was not for him, a mere guide, to wonder about such things. Besides, was it not said that the British were a people of great honor, but alas, all mad, to the very last one of them? Why then should their women be any different, sadly pampered and indulged as were the wives and daughters of the *Englesy?*

"Yes! We shall depart, Cemal!" she sang out, laughter burbling in her voice as she parroted her answer to his solemn question.

With a grunt that said everything and nothing, Cemal muttered the words that would make her camel rise to its feet, then gave it a gentle thwack across the rump with a stout camel-stick when it stubbornly refused to do so.

"Offspring of a cross-eyed she-goat!" Cemal cursed, and thwacked the animal a second time to prove his mastery.

He hurriedly stepped back as the beast heaved itself off its lumpy knees to stand, favoring him with a sulky hiss and a contemptuous curl of its split upper lip. The hiss revealed large teeth stained deep yellow, as if from the camel's smoking of many Turkish cigarettes.

"Oh my stars!" Alexa exclaimed, hanging on for dear life and rising skyward rapidly. She gasped as she looked down from the three-pronged saddle atop her mount's lofty single hump, some seven feet above the ground.

In response to the unfamiliar sound, the animal's gooselike neck skewed around. The female camel chewed thoughtfully on its massive cud and fluttered a curly eyelash or two in her direction, obviously disdaining her riding skills.

46

"Something is wrong, mistress?" Cemal cried anxiously.

"No—no, nothing's wrong, Cemal. It's just that—well, the saddle's a lot farther from the ground than I'd expected!"

"Ah! *Ewellah*, it is indeed! But don't be afraid. Missie will soon grow used to riding this most unworthy beast," Nabal, Cemal's roguish young son, reassured her. "Before many miles of desert lie behind us, the missie will ride as easily as do the Bedouin women, who weave and churn the she-camel's milk into butter and cheese with one foot upon their camel's neck as they ride! Come! Let's make haste, my father. The caravan leaves, and I have no wish to taste its dust and dung upon my tongue from dusk till dawn, as we must if we fall behind the others."

His father muttered agreement.

The pilgrim caravan began to move out, unwinding like a ragged, darker ribbon unfurling across the endless dark-gold of the desert sands in the amethyst light of evening. There were many, many camels in their caravan, over a thousand in all, Alexa guessed, some bearing riders, others loaded down with enormous burdens, some with their young trotting along beside them. From time to time, the camel-calves tried to duck their heads to suckle at their mothers' swollen teats, bleating and snorting piteously when they discovered that they could not. Each teat had been tied with twine close to the end of the duct in the Bedouin fashion, to prevent the milk from being drained at will by the nursing camels. The reason for this, Cemal had explained to Alexa earlier that day when she'd noticed this peculiar practice, was that the she-camels' milk provided life-giving nourishment for both man and horse alike if an oasis should prove dried up or the goatskin waterbags were emptied. Consequently, the camel-calves were permitted to nurse only twice a day, in the early morning and at evening.

There were donkeys too, and a few hardy Arabian horses, caparisoned with flowing silken coverings hung all about with red and gold tassels and bells. There were also a few sheep and goats bleating and scampering about, chivied along by young native boys brandishing sticks. Camels hissed and spat and plodded sedately along. Donkeys brayed. Lambs baaed for their missing mothers, chickens carried in wicker coops cackled and

47

fussed and lost their feathers in snowy flurries; bells tinkled, women and girls chattered noisily, various *sheiks* bragged and boasted and shouted commands, and amidst it all the children laughed and shrieked and played in and out of the serpentine column as children must, wherever they might be. Following them all came the servants, who outnumbered them all, on foot.

Cemal's camel began stepping out with an easy, rolling gait and fell neatly into line behind the beasts before it. Accordingly, Alexa's seasoned beast followed suit. The unexpected movement almost unseated her from the perilously high wooden saddle arrangement in which she sat, for it was neither a forward-and-backward rocking motion, nor a side-to-side swaying motion, but a peculiar combination of both! She concentrated all her attention on maintaining both her seat and her tasseled camel-hair reins, and before she knew it, the sun-dried mud-brick walls of the city of Sidi-bel-Abbes, about which they'd congregated as dusk began to fall, had shrunk to the size of low, dark smudges against the indigo horizon. They were on their way at last!

As Cemal had warned her, the desert evening was cold by comparison with the scorching heat of day. The air grew steadily cooler as they continued on and true night fell in dark amethyst drifts across the rubbled sand. A full, round moon rose and floated way above the vast sandy wastes below, far larger and more silvery than it had ever seemed in the night sky above Harding House. Even the stars seemed larger, brighter, out here, shards of celestial crystal reflecting the moon's ethereal shimmer. They seemed close enough to reach out and pluck like flowers. The breeze lifted, stirring her robes and the robes of all those who were a part of the caravan. It was blessedly cool, blessedly sweet, that night breeze, after the heat and noxious smells of crowded Sidi-bel-Abbes, and Alexa sighed with relief.

"The missie is more comfortable now, yes?" Cemal asked from the back of his camel after what seemed at least a hundred miles of desert lay behind them. His bright, dark eyes seemed to take on a liquid sheen in the moonlight, shining like lumps of coal above his generously hooked nose and gray-streaked beard.

"The missie is—adjusting, shall we say?" Alexa replied diplomatically, wincing and wondering if she'd be able to walk at all once the camel halted—if they ever halted, which she was beginning to doubt! Her bottom and back and thighs felt completely numb. She was certain she was dead from the waist down.

"Ah. Very good!" Cemal declared with enormous satisfaction, taking her comment at face value. "Tell me, missie, is not Cemal the very best of escorts, the most perfect of all guides, as he promised the missie in the bazaar of the Casbah?" he asked slyly, obviously fishing for a compliment.

"A guide above all guides, and an escort above all escorts!" Alexa agreed solemnly. Cemal positively beamed, basking in her flowery praises. Nabal shot her a cheeky, knowing grin before lashing his camel into a lope and riding on ahead, his actions scorning the snail-like pace of his father and the prim *Englesy* missie.

The sky was lightening, turning gray and violet in the east, when the noisy caravan halted to rest during the coming heat of day. They had ridden throughout the night without stopping, and had covered a good many miles by Alexa's reckoning.

A tiny oasis, hardly more than a pothole in the sand to Alexa's untrained eye, appeared. But the oasis, on closer inspection, boasted a very small spring, its source shielded from grit by a tiny man-made wall of mud that curved about it like a protective arm. A pair of disgruntled-looking date palms tossed ragged heads in the dawn breeze, and spiny thorn bushes and a few acacias struggled for life amongst scattered white rocks.

As had the other camel-drivers, Cemal reined in his mount and harshly commanded it to couch with a guttural *"Ikh-kh-kh!"*

The beast—to his obvious surprise—obediently knelt with a single command. He came over to Alexa's mount and bade it do likewise, offering his arm to steady her as she staggered from

49

her perch. She was grateful beyond words for that arm and tottered like a drunkard to where Nabal was grudgingly erecting her tent—a woman's labor, by his people's reckoning—without once feeling her feet.

In the twinkling of an eye, there were low tents raised everywhere about the tiny spring, Bedouin tents with roofs of tightly stretched black goatskins, with separate walls, or skirts, of gaily striped cloth hanging down from each side for shade or shelter, held firmly in place by wooden pegs. Numerous carpets and small rugs and plump cushions were unloaded from the camels' packs and strewn within the tents to soften the hard ground.

Their tents erected, the women patiently went to fill their goatskins from the spring's modest trickle of water, their movements making the many little silver disks that adorned their headdresses jingle muscically. Still other women congregated about small fires and were already busily preparing a meal, patting balls of dough into flat little bread loaves, which they roasted buried in the embers of the fires. Meanwhile, their menfolk honed their knives and slaughtered a goat or a lamb for roasting on sharp skewers, before gathering at the tent of a hospitable *sheik* to partake of little cups of black coffee while the evening meal was being readied—a custom that she would witness countless times on their journey, Cemal divulged. Some of the *sheiks* even permitted their prized Arabian mares to nose their dainty heads under the tents' awnings. The men gently petted the horses and crooned to them while they conversed with their guests, and this seemed, to a fascinated Alexa, evidence of a fondness for their beasts she had not seen exhibited toward their womenfolk!

"Nabal will fetch the missie her supper as soon as the men have eaten," Cemal promised a little apologetically, mistakenly thinking she was eyeing the roasting lambs and kids on skewers over nearby fires with a hungry eye. "Meanwhile, we must discuss the dangers we might encounter on the morrow, so that we are prepared."

"Tomorrow?" Alexa echoed stupidly, sinking down with a sigh of gratitude onto the small fringed rug Nabal had at last unrolled before the opening to her tent, and yawning hugely.

She was far too exhausted to think about tomorrow just yet! Were her derriere and feet still there? They were, and painfully so, now that feeling was returning to them. She wanted nothing more than to be permitted to sleep, but it seemed Cemal had other ideas.

"Tomorrow," Cemal repeated with enormous patience while she chafed her numbed feet, as if addressing one of those whom Allah had chosen to afflict with enormous stupidity. "The caravan will follow the accustomed route of the pilgrims on the long road to Mecca, while we must journey on alone in the opposite direction, alas, to the fortress of the *Franziwa* Legionnaires, which lies in the very heart of the desert provinces of the Tuareg peoples. Allah protect us from their thievery, but there is a very fine chance those devil-robbers will be watching us, missie, though we will not see them, for the Tuaregs are demons who can vanish into thin air, if it is their will! It is for this reason that I suggested we dress most humbly, and carry nothing of obvious wealth, yes?"

"I remember," Alexa acknowledged, wide-awake now, her tingling, prickling limbs forgotten. Her heart had begun to beat very fast in response to his comment about the robber Tuaregs, and flutters of apprehension stirred in her belly. "Go on," she urged him.

"If, by some great and unhappy fortune, those desert-demons should approach us, you must say nothing that will give your identity away, missie. You must not raise your eyes to any of their number, for if you do so, we will be discovered!"

He said the latter in such a doom-filled voice, Alexa all but choked on the knot of fear that rose up her throat.

"What—what would happen then?" she asked in a quavery voice, and could have kicked herself seconds later for voicing a question she really didn't want an answer to.

"The Tuaregs are robbers, missie—bloodthirsty pirates who plunder the wealth of the caravans that must cross the desert sands. The very name by which others know them, given them by their enemy, the Bedouin, means the 'Lost Souls,' for it is said they have forsaken many of the laws of Allah, and pay little heed to the sacred writings of His Blessed Prophet. They rob others as a way of life, for riches, for camels, for horses.

And they take captives, both men and women, to sell as slaves in the secret slave bazaars of the cities. One such as you, one with your rare coloring and—alas, yes, gentle missie!—your great beauty, would be a rare prize for a Tuareg chieftain. You would become the brightest jewel of his mountain *hareem!*"

She gulped. "Oh! I see. Then if we should encounter these 'Lost Souls,' I'll certainly do my best to remain silent, I promise," Alexa agreed hurriedly. "And I'll keep my eyes down, as do your women, if these—brigands—should surprise us."

"It would be well if the missie also watched the ways of the women of my people, and wiser still if she were to behave in much the same manner," Cemal hinted.

"I'll try!" Alexa promised, although she was trembling inside. She had come so far—too far to cowardly back out now at the first scent of possible danger! There would be no turning back for her, she told herself firmly, not until she had done what she set out to do and made things right between herself and poor Keene. "I promise, Cemal. I'll do nothing that would endanger our lives."

Her guide nodded and bowed his head. "Cemal is grateful. The missie is a woman possessed of rare wisdom. Wisdom almost befitting that of a man. Ah! Here is my son now, with food for you. May Allah protect you as you sleep, Missie Harding," the Arab declared, touching his fingertips to his brow and then his breast by way of salutation. Without further words, he made his way to one of the campfires, no doubt to eat with the other men as was the custom of the Arab peoples, leaving her alone with Nabal.

"I bring very fine roasted kid for missie's supper. *Englesy* missie like goat meat, yes? I can find camel meat, maybe, if not." The lad smiled innocently, his teeth very white against the pale bronze of his complexion.

"Goat will be sufficient," Alexa insisted hurriedly. "Er—what is this on the side here?"

"What would it be but *couscous*, missie? And there is some camel cheese also, and here dates with *samn*, or camel butter, and flat bread. I bring you very fine supper, yes?" he suggested with a sly grin, obviously well aware that everything he had described within her flattish wooden bowl was totally unfamiliar to her. His eyes, bright and intelligent and as dark as his father's, sparkled with deviltry.

Well, two could play at his rascal's game, Alex decided, hiding a smile. The Arab boy, for all his unusual manner of dress and different customs, was not so very different to that beguiling scamp of a "nephew" she'd left back in England, Dan and Pauline's son known to one and all as Sweet William.

"Camel cheese!" she exclaimed in apparent delight. "And dates too! Oh, how wonderful, Nabal—you've brought my favorite foods! Mmmm, delicious!" And with every evidence of enjoyment, she munched a mouthful of pungent cheese as if it were manna from heaven—and with a prayer that she would not gag.

"Your—your favorite, missie?" Nabal echoed, obviously crestfallen that what had promised to be a fine joke had misfired.

Swallowing with difficulty, Alexa nodded and beamed her enjoyment of the repast. Nabal scowled.

"Pah! I must go now and eat with the other men," the lad decided, disgust etched on his face. Apparently, he'd come to the conclusion that the English missie promised to be less fun than he had anticipated. "It is not fitting that a man should eat in the company of a woman," he scoffed, and took off at a jaunty stride, leaving a relieved Alex alone.

To her surprise, the *couscous*, a sort of floury dumpling boiled in a savory, spicy sauce, proved tasty; the plump dates chewy, sticky and gritty but good, after the fashion of dates; the roasted goat meat not unpleasant at all after the first few bites, when one's palate had grown accustomed to its flavor. Only that tough, curdy cheese seemed totally beyond her swallowing powers, no matter how she steeled herself to eat it with the stern reminder that food was in scarce supply in these parts and that it was a sin to waste even the smallest portion! But in the end, she couldn't eat it. She buried the small wedge deep in the sand, scoured out her platter with still more gritty sand, washed her sticky fingers also in the sand as she saw others doing, left her dish by the tent opening, and crawled inside.

Dawn was breaking in lemon and mauve streaks on the eastern horizon when her weary head touched the softness of heaped rugs and cushions spread over the sand for her comfort. With an unladylike grunt of sheer bliss, Alexa plunged deeply into sleep, and into the seductive arms of her shadowy dream-lover.

Late afternoon of the following day, the leader of a little *escouade* of Legionnaires, reconnoitering the native villages in the vicinity of the oasis of Yasmeen, three days' journey from Fort Valeureux, raised his arm to signal the men riding behind him to halt as they crested a large dune. To a man, they did so.

Below, in the bloody rays of the dying desert sun that turned the waters of the green oasis pool to rust and gold, were a number of Bedouin tents. Their striped silken skirts fluttered in the lifting twilight breezes. There were several servants moving about, a number of kneeling camels, and a few horses grazing on wisps of bleached vegetation .

"Corporal O'Day!"

"Surr?"

"Take a look through here. Tell me, what do you see?"

The corporal, Timothy O'Day, took the field glasses from his leader, raised them to his eyes, and adjusted the focus. After a few moments he said, "I see a small native caravan, surr. My estimate is twenty camels, four horses. As for civilians, there's two older men, neither of whom appear t' be carrying stolen carbines, a small *hareem* of perhaps three women, an' their servants. I'd say 'tis a peaceful Bedouin camp we're after seein', surr. A *sheik* and his family party an' servants broken off from their main caravan for some reason."

"Would you indeed, Corporal?" his leader said with a derisive smile. "How fortunate I am to have your expert opinion! However, I believe you're in grave error, soldier. What *I*, the leader of this *escouade*, see through those glasses is a hostile encampment of filthy natives, obviously planning an attack on our fort, whose camels meanwhile are fouling the watering hole of this strategically vital oasis!"

"Surr?" O'Day queried, his eyes registering astonishment.

"If you'll pardon me sayin', 'tis my opinion you're wrong, surr!"

"Ah, but I didn't ask your opinion, O'Day. I asked what you saw, and you told me. But obviously, your eyes deceived you. Right?"

Corporal O'Day licked his lips. "Well, no, surr, I—"

"A simple yes or no will be sufficient, soldier!" the sergeant rasped.

"Er—yes, surr!"

"Very good, Corporal. We are in accord. Men!" he began, turning in his saddle to face the remainder of his squad. "Corporal O'Day and I are in complete agreement that it's probable the native encampment up ahead contains hostiles. I intend to find out exactly what these sly bastards are doing way out here, as is my duty. You three—LeBraun, Gianetti, and St. Pierre—will remain here, to act as our backup while the rest of us go in. Corporal Gianetti, I'm leaving you in charge. Have the men pitch the tents. At first sign of trouble from our direction, you know what to do. We'll be depending on you to cover our retreat, should we find ourselves in deep water."

"Oui, m'sieu le sergeant!" the Italian responded promptly, though in badly accented French. His leader nodded approval.

"Good man. O'Day, you and the rest follow me!" He rode off ahead of them on his horse, while the remaining three men followed at a slower pace on their sturdy military mules.

"They do not look 'ostile to me, Timothy, *mon brave!*" Henri Toussant murmured to his friend the Irishman. "What is our beloved Sergeant Le Fou up to now, eh?"

At another moment, O'Day would have grinned at the nickname the men of the barracks had bestowed upon the sergeant—*Le Fou*, The Crazy One. But right now, the uneasy sensation of forboding in his belly wouldn't permit a grin. Call it Gaelic precognition, or intuition, or just a pure and simple gut-feeling he had, he felt something was about to go wrong— aye, and badly wrong.

"Up to no good, I'm after bettin'! Only the Blessed Saints know for sure, Henri, but I don't like the feel o' these here doin's a wee bit!" He crossed himself as they rode on, his actions drawing a mocking chuckle of laughter from the third man riding with them after the sergeant, a man known simply as Flechette.

"Afraid, *mon ami?*" mocked Flechette. "Pah! I, for one, would enjoy a little target practice before supper, and what better targets than a handful of stinking Arabs fermenting an attack on our beloved fort, *hein?*"

"Then ye're as mad as t' sergeant, to be sure, Flechette!" O'Day growled, but the third man merely laughed again in response.

Several yards from the oasis, the sergeant reined in his mount. The others halted their mules, and saw how the Bedouins, obviously peacefully about the business of preparing their evening meal, had also halted their preparations and were now silently watching the soldiers' approach.

"You, there, O'Day," the sergeant called to the corporal.

"Surr?" O'Day kneed his mount alongside the other man's horse.

"Since your Arabic's a damned sight better than mine, I'll let you do the talking. Tell them we want to speak with their *sheik*, and ask them what the devil they're doing here."

O'Day did so, and an imposing, dignified Bedouin man wearing a burnoose held in place with black *agals* stepped forward as spokesman. He had a fine black beard streaked lightly with gray, and dark intelligent eyes that dominated his long, lean face.

"He says his name is *Sheik* Hussein ben-Fadil. He and his brother and their two wives were accompanying his daughter to meet her betrothed when they encountered a sandstorm and lost their bearings, surr. He says he welcomes you, and offers you the hospitality of his camp, as is the Bedouin custom. He says as his honored guests, we need have no fear of him, but will be treated with every courtesy."

His superior snorted. "Does he indeed? Well, you tell him that I say he's a bloody old liar whose mangy camels are fouling the watering hole, O'Day," the sergeant said calmly. "Tell him I believe he and this miserable camp of his are hostile to those of the Legion, and very probably the flank for a Tuareg attack on our fort. Tell him I spit on his false offers of hospitality!"

"What? But—I can't tell him that, surr!" O'Day protested,

56

aghast. "Honor's everything t' these Bedouins! He'll lose face."

"You can tell him, and you will—unless you wish to be court-martialed, that is, Corporal. Refusing an order is a very serious offense, you know."

O'Day licked his dry lips. Being court-martialed was the greatest fear of every man in the Legion, for the French military penal institutions were harsh indeed. Few men survived their rigors with both health and sanity intact. And besides, hadn't he left his beloved Ireland to escape a British prison cell and the long arm of the law? Sweat beading his brow, he swallowed, heartsick, and translated word for word what his sergeant had said.

The Arab chieftain was astounded. His bronzed face grew harsh. His black eyes ignited. His expression grew doubly hawklike in his fury. He raised his arm and shouted something, and at once another man came running. They conferred in heated tones, and then the *sheik* turned back to the Legion sergeant and said something in cold, measured tones laced with contempt.

"What's that he's jabbering, O'Day?"

"He says—he says for all that ye are *Englesy*—English—ye are a man wi' out honor, surr. He says t' speak wi' the likes of ye defiles his very lips. He says for ye and your men t' leave his camp, before ye force him t' defend his honorable name."

"Oh, he does, does he now? Bloody nerve of the fellow! Flechette! Show this Arab upstart how we deal with his sort!"

"My pleasure, *mon sergeant!*" Flechette agreed eagerly, and before O'Day could utter any protest, he had drawn his service revolver from its unsnapped holster and fired it point blank at the *sheik's* chest!

The Bedouin jerked backward, blood blossoming in crimson gouts across his white *jelabia*. He staggered and fell. As he did so, the second Bedouin tore a curved dagger from his sash and with a bloodcurdling, howling cry to his God, charged Flechette's mount. Flechette's second bullet slammed into his belly, and the Arab twitched and fell to his side, screaming in agony.

At once, all hell broke loose about the oasis. The three women huddled beneath the date palms began clawing at their veils and tearing at their hair, weeping and wailing in sorrow and terror for the deaths of their menfolk and in fear of their own lives. The camel-herders and other servants screamed and fled into the desert. There was chaos as tents were overturned by frightened livestock stampeded by the gunshots, but in the midst of it, the unperturbed sergeant merely smiled.

"O'Day, Toussant—see their precious horses and camels soundly run off, on the double, men!" he ordered, his blue eyes glittering with some unholy inner light. "do the same with their beggarly servants too. A few days of stumbling around out here without water or mounts will teach them a stern lesson, I do believe. Meanwhile, I must interrogate the remaining—er—prisoners. Flechette? You'll assist me."

As Flechette dismounted, Toussant looked furtively across at O'Day, and saw that his friend's face had grown as white as his own.

"*Mon Dieu!* He is a fiend!" Toussant breathed. "I want no part of this mess!"

Timothy, feeling close to vomiting, nodded shaken agreement as Toussant wheeled his mule and rode out after the fast-disappearing camels.

His heart pounding, O'Day watched the two men dismount and begin to make their way slowly toward the screaming women. He found, despite the sergeant's commands, he was unable to move to follow Henri. He could only sit his mule and watch. Oh Blessed Sweet Mary, what had he done! What had his very compliance, his silence, made him a part of this time? Cold-blooded murder, that was what! There was no other word fer it. And now—? He swallowed. Jaysus! He had a fair idea of what the sergeant intended now, and he liked it even less than the shootings. . . .

Hating himself for his cowardice, but finding to his enormous guilt and shame that he lacked the courage to do anything about it, he forced himself to move and followed Toussant's mule. Some distance from the oasis, he set about running off camels and horses, now quietly milling about, as his sergeant had commanded, and tried desperately to pretend he didn't know what was going on under the date palms. . . .

"Well, well, Flechette, what have we here?" the sergeant

mused aloud meanwhile.

He stood less than fifteen feet from the three Bedouin women, his fists on his hips, his legs braced apart. There was a broad grin upon his handsome, bronzed face beneath his *kepi*.

"They certainly appear to be women, but—who can say for sure with all those robes and such? It's very possible they're men in disguise! Ah, yes, Flechette, filthy cutthroat spies, merely biding their time until we turn our back before they attack us, wouldn't you say?" His sun-bleached blond brows rose in mocking speculation.

Flechette eagerly licked his lips, a hot glitter in his own eyes that boded ill. "Oui, very possibly. We must take no chances, eh, *m'sieu le sergeant?*"

"Quite, Corporal. We think alike, you and I. You, girl! Come here!"

He beckoned to the smallest of the women, the only one of the three whose face was veiled, indicating she was a *bint*, a virgin maid, for the nomadic Bedouin women rarely covered their faces out in the desert, veiling only when they returned to the cities.

The girl obviously understood his gestures, if not his words, for she shrank from his pointing finger, babbling incoherently as she clung to the older woman's arm, beseeching them to help her.

"It would appear she's reluctant and needs persuading, Flechette—a sure sign that she has something to hide, wouldn't you say? Get her to her feet and bring her to me, at once."

Apparently oblivious to the shrieks and the flailing fists the two older women rained down upon him in a futile attempt to force him to let her be, Flechette grabbed the girl about the waist and hauled her upright. She was clawing and spitting and kicking out like a cornered animal.

"What luck! She's a little wildcat!" Flechette crowed, gripping her wrists and dragging her across the sand to stand before his superior officer.

At once the sergeant hooked his finger in the light cloth of her face-covering and tore the concealing veil from the girl's face, the silver coins that adorned her brow chinking noisily as he did so. Like his companion, he seemed deaf to the cries of the other women, who were clinging to each other and sobbing now.

"Well, well, who'd have thought it? A dusky pearl is what we have here, Flechette. I wonder, does her body match this charming, innocent little face?"

His expression eager, his eyes aglitter now with lust, the sergeant tore off the girl's overrobe and tossed it to the sand.

Clad only in her richly embroidered *caftan* of yellow and white, beneath it baggy trousers that were cuffed tight at the ankles, the girl stood mutely before him, trying neither to flee him nor fight him off. It was as if she had already accepted the outcome as inevitable, and was resigned to her fate. She simply stood there, her head bowed beneath a curtain of raven-black hair, her hands by her sides. She was trembling violently, but other than this only her pallor and her dark eyes showed her true terror, for they were enormous in her oval face. Great, shiny tears slipped down her cheeks.

The sergeant was breathing thickly now, his fists clenching and unclenching by his sides as if he fought for control of himself. Suddenly, he muttered a foul oath and clamped the fingers of both hands over the neck of the girl's *caftan*. He yanked hard, brutally rending the thin cloth in two. The sudden, violent action bared her budding young breasts and torso clear to the waist.

"Sweet Christ!" the sergeant groaned. Impatient now, he hauled her roughly to him, knotting his fingers in her long, thick hair, winding them tightly in its inky length so that she moaned with the fiery agony in her scalp. His brutal, greedy mouth ground down over hers, tearing her lip, while he covered the soft mound of a breast with his hard hand and kneaded it roughly—so roughly she cried out in pain.

"*Prenez-garde!* Ze little bitch 'as a knife!" Flechette warned him in the nick of time.

The cry brought the lust-crazed sergeant to his senses. Like lightning, he trapped the slenderly boned wrist that had withdrawn the small, sharp dagger the girl had hidden in her palm. He gripped tighter and tighter until her fingers grew numb, and she was forced to release the weapon or suffer a broken bone. She uttered a pitiful whimper of pain, but with a harsh, triumphant laugh, the man drew back his hand and slapped her viciously across the face, first to the left, then to the right, then to the left once more, before he flung her down to her knees on the sand at his feet. Following her down, he straddled her body, pinioning it securely beneath the weight of his own.

Still fighting desperately, she managed to worm her arms free, clawing for his eyes. Her fingers tangled instead in the length of a slim silver chain about his neck, breaking it. But, breathing heavily, the sergeant overpowered her with ease, trapping both slender wrists in one of his large and powerful hands and yanking them securely up, above her head. With the other hand he unbuttoned the fastenings of his uniform trousers and ripped her pantaloons down to her knees.

"Fight me, would you, eh, you little Bedouin *bint?*" he rasped, prodding his knee between her thighs to pry them apart. "We'll see if there's any fight left when I'm done with you, by God!"

"Ah, *mon ami,* do not be greedy! Save some for me, eh?" Flechette urged, unfastening his own belt buckle and fly buttons as he went to help the sergeant hold the girl down.

O'Day heard the high screams that followed then, for sounds carried great distances out there in the open desert. He heard them, and he sank down onto his knees in the sand and covered his ears with his hands to drown out the sound—but could not. The cries still ringing in his mind, he wished to God, the Virgin Mary, and all the Blessed Saints that he were man enough to return to the oasis and see them silenced. But he didn't dare.

Alexa's little party broke away from the main caravan late the next day, for all had slept as the burning sun climbed to her zenith during the hellish heat of morning and early afternoon.

Atop her trusty camel—which she'd privately decided to call Mary, after the Mary of nursery-rhyme fame, on account of her contrariness—they set off at a tangent to the main caravan, leaving behind the noisy throng and with it, the safety of its vast numbers.

Contrary Mary plodded sedately along behind Cemal's camel, chewing thoughtfully on a wad of thornbush she had snatched as a farewell snack upon leaving the oasis, while Nabal trailed behind, leading the three pack-beasts loaded down with their goatskin tents and her clothing.

Nothing but endless dunes and valleys of golden sand, broken occasionally by a ruined *kella*, or ancient watchtower, stretched ahead of them, behind them, to either side of them. Nothing but the painfully bright azure vault of the sky and the brilliant medallion of the sun arched above them, casting their shadows in inky silhouettes upon the burning sands as they moved steadily onward.

And yet the Sahara had a savage, pitiless beauty that was uniquely its own, Alexa decided. It was the beauty of seemingly endless space and boundless skies, of clear, clear light and pure, sweet air. There were no smoking chimney pots belching their black flags skyward here, no buildings smutty with soot and grime, as there had been in London. If the lack of Britain's lush greenery were a fault, it was in part compensated for by that sensation of limitless space.

The journey was grueling for Alexa that third afternoon, for her muscles had not yet recovered from their punishment of the days before. About two hours after the moon had risen, Cemal, obviously sensing her extreme discomfort, called a halt. He and Nabal busily set about pitching their tents, lighting their cooking fire, and preparing supper; black coffee for themselves and a simple meal of flat bread dipped in a small pot of honey, more roasted goat meat, heavily salted, and sour-tasting milk swigged from a hairy skin, its very tartness prized by the desert peoples for its refreshing qualities.

"Alas, missie, we have not your favorite camel-cheese this evening!" Nabal apologized, his cheeky grin bordering on the malicious.

Alexa, her veil unfastened to allow her to eat comfortably, returned his comment with a sugary-sweet smile. "Pray, do not concern yourself on a lowly woman's account, O Very Small and Spiteful Child," she said silkily, paying him back in kind. "Those of us who are *grown* have learned to do without such treats, unlike a mere child, whose needs must ever be satisfied at once lest he kick his heels and cry."

She was rewarded by seeing Nabal's face flush in anger at being so demeaningly termed a child—which, by Arab reckoning, was almost as demeaning as being termed a woman, or worse, a Christian. He muttered something under his breath in Arabic which needed little translation, causing Cemal's dark eyes to snap toward his son like black magnets and his generously lipped mouth to tighten amidst his luxuriant pepper-and-salt beard.

"My most unworthy son forgets the great honor the missie does us by hiring our most humble selves to escort her to the fort of the *Franziwas!*" Cemal said sharply. A dark, expressive brow raised above his penetrating black eyes. "He forgets also that the missie has laid claim to our hospitality, and that according to our Arab customs, as hosts we are bound to behave with respect and graciousness toward a guest. Perhaps a beating would remind him, yes, my son?"

Nabal scowled, but added hurriedly in Alexa's direction, "A thousand pardons, missie!"

"Accepted," Alexa agreed readily, and gave the chastened boy a warm and friendly smile, which obviously took Nabal aback somewhat. He returned it with an uncertain grin of his own, a grin that implied a truce was in order, much to Alexa's relief.

They finished their evening meal companionably. Cemal had just begun drawing with a stick in the sand, outlining for Alexa's benefit the miles they had yet to travel, when Nabal suddenly jolted upright, his head cocked to one side, every muscle in his lean body tensed and alert.

"Be silent and listen well, my father!" he hissed. "Someone comes!"

Cemal listened, hearing nothing. "Pah! There is no one there. I would have heard them too were it so, my son. You are like a woman or a little child that hears the desert *ghrôl* calling their name in the darkness, and is afraid of shadows!" his father accused.

"Nay, my father, this is no one-eyed monster!" Nabal

63

insisted. "The sound was that of men—many men, and horses and camels too!"

Scarcely had the lad uttered these words than Alexa saw the dark and ominous silhouettes that encircled their little camp: the frightening figures of several robed men mounted upon horses and camels, silently waiting, watching, scant feet away!

Her heart began to skip and jump erratically, threatening to leap from her very breast. The hair at her nape rose. Dear God, were they real, or desert phantoms? And if they were flesh-and-blood men, how had they been able to move so silently, to come so close to their little camp without so much as a sight or sound to announce their coming? More terrifyingly, who were these men, and what was their purpose?

Cemal's hoarse whisper explained everything. "Allah protect us, they are the Blue Men!" he hissed. "Beware, Tuaregs!"

And with a broad and beaming crocodile-smile of greeting, he rose from his cross-legged position before the fire and went to meet their unwelcome guests.

Chapter Four

"Greetings, my lords! Greetings!" Cemal cried, bowing deeply to the shadowy riders. "May I offer you and your men the hospitality of my humble camp? I am Cemal ben-Yussef, a poor man indeed, a man of few camels and not a single horse, yet all that I have is yours for the—for the asking." Despite Cemal's best efforts, his expression denied the truth of his latter statement.

"Count yourself among the fortunate of Allah that we are indeed asking this night, Old One, rather than taking!" declared a tall, heavyset man in an Arabic dialect, and the robed band of men all about him laughed. "I am *Sheik* Kadar ben-Selim and I would have you welcome my master. Perhaps you have heard of al-Azim, the Defender? My lord chieftain and I would share your fire for the night, my friend. We have ridden long and hard."

"Then you are welcome, sirs," Cemal declared, none too eagerly, gesturing to the flickering circle of ruddy firelight. "Eat and rest for—er—for as long as it pleases you to do so."

"Ah, Father, we will indeed!" Kadar grinned, for it was obvious the fawning fellow greatly feared him and his companions. Despite his generous invitation, Kadar was certain the man was silently beseeching Allah to make him and his companions ride on before too much time had passed, or too many of his precious provisions been consumed! "And fear not, O Trembling One," he continued. "We are not minded to rob you of your scrawny camels, nor to linger long by your fire. Nor—for that matter—to drink you dry of coffee! Our business lies elsewhere. By the grace of Allah, we ride to meet the caravan of my betrothed, a little Bedouin pearl whose beauty outshines the very moon, and whose dowry will swell my camel herds to bursting!" Kadar reassured Cemal with the roguish grin of a prospective bridegroom. "Alas, it would seem her honored father's caravan must have lost its way, for it was not at our appointed meeting place. You passed it, perhaps, on your travels?"

"Alas, sir, since we departed the caravan bound for Mecca two days ago, we have met with no one," Cemal said.

"Hmm. They have no doubt gone on, then, in search of another oasis to the west of here. Surely we will find that they await us there. Ah, al-Azim comes!"

A man swung lithely down from the back of his black Arabian stallion, and strode forward from the shadows and into the light of the fire. He was taller than Kadar, his second-in-command, and leaner, yet for all his height he moved with the boneless grace of a desert lion. He strode slowly toward the little camp, and the others of his band stepped back in deference to allow him to pass. When he came alongside Alexa's nervous guide, he halted and murmured his thanks to Cemal for his offer of hospitality, much to the little man's ill-concealed surprise, and then turned and said something to his second-in-command.

Kadar barked an order to the other riders to follow suit and dismount.

At once, Cemal made a surreptitious gesture to Nabal, and immediately the boy started scurrying about like a desert scorpion, dusting off a small fringed rug and spreading it before the fire for the Tuareg chieftain; bringing pillows to cushion him where he sat; tossing a handful of precious coffee grounds into the brass pot of doubly precious water heating over the fire.

Nabal eyed the towering stranger uncertainly, bowing as he backed away, and the chieftain took his seat. He swallowed, for once in his young life decidedly nervous. It was difficult to determine if his humble efforts had pleased or displeased al-Azim, for he wore a dark-blue *tagilmust*—a turban headdress with the loose end drawn across the face after the manner of the Tuareg tribes. It effectively concealed his lower features from the lad, and allowed only his brooding dark eyes to show. They were, Nabal observed with a shiver, as piercing as a hawk's, and potentially as ruthless.

With a budding merchant's shrewd eye, Nabal also noted the fine quality of the man's flowing dark-blue robe as he took his seat cross-legged upon the brightly woven rug, thrusting the indigo-dyed folds casually aside as he did so. His actions exposed the magnificent embroidery of silver and gold threads that bordered the short white *caftan* he wore beneath it; the fine, generously cut silk of his baggy white *sirwal*, trousers that were tucked into soft knee-length boots of the finest dark suede. With the merest flicker of an eyelid, Nabal also took in the shining splendor of a curved dagger, its hilt of gold and precious jewels thrust carelessly into the crimson *hezaam*, or sash, at his lean waist.

Alexa, still frozen in her huddled position by the fire, noted that wicked dagger too, watching it with the horrified fascination of a rabbit watching a snake as the robber-chieftain withdrew it from his sash and set it carefully beside him on the rug. She began to tremble uncontrollably, imagining the blade's cold steel curved against the pulse at her throat in a deadly caress, and she swallowed only with enormous effort and quickly looked down at her hands, clenched in her lap, as if the answers to all the mysteries of the universe lay there. . . .

"Wellah! You, boy! O thou worthless only son of a lazy mother, bring food for our lords, al-Azim and Kadar!" Cemal snapped, giving a transfixed Nabal a hefty kick in his bony rump to get him moving. The kick served its purpose, much to Cemal's relief. Nabal fairly flew to the platter of roasted goat and unleavened bread, and began assembling a vast communal platter for their uninvited guests to dip into in the nomad fashion.

"And you, foolish girl! What are you gaping at? Can it be you have never seen such great and noble lords before? Be off to your tent, where one of the *hareem* rightly belongs!" Cemal ranted at Alexa. Knowing she could not understand his words, he grasped her by the elbow and jolted her to her feet, thrusting her roughly in the direction of the tent to make his meaning transparently clear, and praying she would not protest.

Alexa, rudely jolted from her terror into violent movement by the impetus of Cemal's hefty palm planted in the middle of her back, lost her balance and sprawled forward, missing the crackling camel-dung fire by only an inch or so.

Aghast, Cemal rolled his eyes heavenward and muttered a silent but fervent prayer for Blessed Allah to intervene and deliver them, for of a certainty they were now doomed to discovery. . . .

For a second, Alexa lay there on her belly, winded, before she recovered her wits and remembered what she and Cemal had discussed the day before, and the folly of drawing attention to herself in any way if they were met by Tuaregs. She hastily scrambled to her knees, her heart thumping wildly. As she did so, she made her second grave mistake.

Fearing her clumsiness had drawn the Tuareg chieftain's notice, she raised her eyes to check—and to her horror found herself gazing into the robber-chieftain's smoldering eyes. The blood drained from her face, for it was as if she had touched a live coal with her fingertips! His ebony eyes glittered like twin chips of jet flecked with tiny golden flames as they mirrored the dancing light of the campfire in their inky depths!

A thrill ran through her, dancing and shivering up and down her spine and spreading through her body to curl her very toes. Her heart lurched violently in her breast. The fine little hairs rose in tingling waves at the nape of her neck. Her body grew warm and pulsing in an immediate, compelling, and totally feminine reaction to the man's very glance upon her; a glance that was at once so sensual, so primitive, so unexpected, and so very strangely *familiar* that she felt close to swooning as she stared openly at him, transfixed. In that moment, she forgot every vow she had made Cemal, every vow she had ever made herself. Dear God, she couldn't tear her gaze from his even had her very life depended on it, for they were the *same ebony eyes that had haunted her dreams!*

She swayed as she knelt there, and would, she was certain, have fainted clear away had not the chieftain's deep voice forced her sharply back to reality.

"By the Beard of the Prophet, who are you, *marra?*" al-Azim demanded harshly. "Who is your father, girl, and from what

68

province do you come?"

Had she imagined the recognition that flared up in his eyes, mirroring her own? Oh, surely she must have! And what was it he was asking—demanding her—in that imperious tone? Helpless to understand the language he spoke, much less answer him, she beseechingly glanced back over her shoulder at Cemal, who was wringing his hands in anguish across the fire from them.

"Alas, my worthless slave girl is of the afflicted of Allah, my lord. Forgive her clumsiness and her ill manners, but she cannot answer. She is mute, sir, and has been so from her birth—or so that cur of a slave merchant swore to me in the market!"

"Ah." Sharif nodded in understanding, and Alexa fancied— trembling like a reed in the wind upon her knees before him— she thought she saw the light that had flared in his midnight eyes gutter and dim in disappointment. She remembered her pose again then, and swiftly looked down at the darkened sand beneath her knees, a picture of abject humility.

"To your woman's quarters, girl! What can you be thinking of, to stare at our noble guests so rudely, eh?" Cemal barked. "A virtuous maiden does not seek to catch the eye of strange men, unless she is a common dancing girl from the Street of the Courtesans! Shameless *bint* of an unwed mother, be off with you!"

"A moment more, little one," al-Azim murmured, his tone as deep and silken as a caress now.

He reached out and crooked his finger beneath her chin, raising her veiled face to his and thus forcing her startled, anguished green eyes to meet his own once more. He stared into them for so long and with such intensity, it seemed to Alexa that his gaze must surely be able to strip away her veil and see the face, so pale with fear, so ivory-complexioned, beneath it.

"By Allah, surely she has the green eyes of Zerdali!" the Tuareg chieftain said softly.

"Her eyes? Why—er—yes, my lord, her eyes are rare jewels, indeed they are! Her master told me she was the—er— the daughter of a Circassian woman, stolen from her lands and ravished by her captors. This clumsy girl was the babe they planted in the woman's belly."

"Ah, I see, Old One," he murmured, yet he was unable to keep the irritation and regret from his tone. "Then be gone with you, girl! Be gone, and swiftly, before I forget you have a master and steal you away to replace the lovely *houri* who has haunted my dreams!"

Alexa did not understand the words he spoke, but their tone was clear, as was his abrupt gesture of dismissal. She had annoyed him, and he wished her to be gone. Needing no further bidding, she scurried to her own side of the tent, scuttled beneath the curtain, and drew the cloth partition down behind her. It was a flimsy barrier, that cloth, but better than nothing, offering at least a sense of security, even if it was a false one.

Like an animal run to ground, her breathing rapid and unsteady, her heart pounding, she huddled on her pile of rugs and cushions and lay there, waiting for that awful moment when the partition would be rudely torn aside. She would see the Tuareg chieftain towering there in the moonlight, lust raging in his eyes, his arms cruel and imprisoning as he forced her to her back upon the hot sand beneath him and slaked his evil thirsts upon her helpless body. . . .

But then—oh, then she remembered that his eyes were the eyes of her dream-lover's, and that the arms that had imprisoned her in her dreams had never once been cruel, but had encircled her with tenderness, passion, and love. That the lean, golden body that had claimed hers, mastered her feminine softness with its muscled male hardness in those shameless, delicious dreams, had not been brutal with animal lust, but tenderly enflaming as it brushed hers, molded to hers, imparting the delightful warmth and ardor of desire.

Could this man be he, the lover of her dreams whose compelling voice had commanded her to come to him from across a distant continent even as she slept? No! Of course not! Such things couldn't happen, and she was a fool to imagine for one instant that they could. A woman's fantasies, her dream-lovers, did not materialize as flesh-and-blood, virile males; did not become real except, perhaps, in fairy tales, suitable only for gullible children who knew no better.

Well, she was a woman, not a child. A mature, rational, informed woman, not a feather-brained, flighty nitwit with a lurid imagination fed upon scandalous romantic novels. Rape, torture, captivity, slavery—*they* were the harsh realities out here in this savage, beautiful land. Her romantic dreams were only beautiful images of her deepest, darkest, dearest desires, nothing more. Pretty, empty pictures of her childhood's secret longings to return to Egypt and the land of her birth, longings that must be left behind upon waking. She really must pull herself together and think, even prepare to defend herself, if need be. . . .

Scrabbling about and fumbling beneath the rugs and cushions in the tent's pitch-black interior, she encountered the stout camel-stick she'd seen Nabal leave behind when strewing her floor-coverings about. She grasped it firmly, determined to use it to advantage and defend her honor and her life to the last breath, should the occasion arise.

It did not. And against all Alexa's vows to the contrary, she drifted into sleep at long, long last, still clutching the stick tightly—and uncomfortably—to her breast.

When she awoke to Nabal's shaking the next morning, the sun was already high in the sky. The Tuareg Blue Men had vanished as if they'd never been.

"What does *zerdali* mean, Cemal?" Alexa asked. That single word had lodged in her memory since the Tuareg chieftain had spoken it the evening before. It had continued to nag at her memory throughout the hurried breaking of their fast, the striking of their camp, and their swift ride on through the cool, sweet hours of dawn, when she had murmured it a time or two aloud.

"*Zerdali,* missie?" Cemal chuckled. "Why, it is a name—a most foolish, fond name, such as a man might call his woman when they are alone together—or the pet name a man might give his favorite little daughter."

71

"Does it have a meaning?"

"It does, it does. The *zerdali* is the sweet, wild apricot that grows in the walled courtyards of the oasis cities."

"Wild apricot!" Alexa repeated, tawny brows arching in astonishment. The funny little endearment plucked a long-forgotten chord in her memory that came, then quickly vanished. "How strange!"

"Why do you ask me this, Missie Hard-ing?"

"That robber—the chieftain of the band—it was one of the words he said to me. Or at least, that was how it sounded. For some reason, I remembered it when I woke up."

Cemal shrugged. "Pah! Put it from your mind! Who knows why the Tuaregs do or say anything! They are a lawless people, an uncivilized tribe of thieving murderers, as their name implies! They steal down from their hidden strongholds in the mountains to rob the caravans as they pass, and then return with their stolen booty. We were lucky indeed that it was the band of Malik ben-Azad's son who surprised us, missie, and not some other band of lawless dogs. I have heard that Sharif al-Azim is much like his father, and strives to lead his people out of the darkness of blind custom and into the light of progress. He wants to teach his people that the old Tuareg ways of robbing the caravans, of plundering and killing, are no longer the road to prosperity, as they were in the past. Thanks be to Allah it was al-Azim the Defender who found us, and no other!"

"But if that is so, what was he doing out here in the desert by night, with that band of cutthroats armed to the teeth with daggers and carbines?" Alexa reasoned.

"The other one, the Bedouin *sheik* Kadar, told me they were riding to meet the caravan of his betrothed's father. The men with him were to be their escort and bodyguard against attack from other hostile tribes. When they return to their hidden stronghold in the mountains, Kadar and the maiden, Muriel, will be wed."

"I see! Then that explains it. I suppose we should be thankful they were about peaceful business and left us unharmed!"

"Very thankful, missie. A caravan which has been attacked by the Blue Men is not a pretty sight, not even for the eyes of one who has seen many, many terrible things in his long lifetime as has Cemal."

"Why do they call them the Blue Men?" she asked curiously.

"The name comes from the robes they wear, missie. The cloth from which they are made is dyed by steeping it in expensive indigo dyes—a color greatly prized by the Tuareg nobles. A fine, costly new robe will leave a blue coloring upon the fair skin of the wearer, and it is this symbol of their wealth that gives them their name. Now, let us be on our way!"

For two more nights and many more miles, they rode in either easy conversation or amicable silence, broken only by the playing of Nábal upon a reed flute. It appeared he could play only one tune, and he played it over and over, a shrilling, eerie piping on the dark coolness that unsettled Alexa's already unsettled stomach. Still, it was preferable to traveling during daylight hours, when heat and thirst became unbearable.

When they traveled in the hours of daylight, shortly after dawn and in the late afternoon, sweat streamed from her brow hour in and hour out, stinging her eyes with its saltiness. More sweat soaked her hair beneath her robe, for all that she'd taken to braiding it for coolness. Deluges of sweat streamed down her back, poured down the valley between her breasts, stinging her chafed buttocks and thighs and soaking her *caftan*.

She tried to concentrate on the scenery all about her rather than upon her discomforts, but it was a pastime that soon palled. There was little more to see except gravelly sand and sky, and still more sand and sky, though occasionally a lone desert hawk wheeled in the blazing blue overhead, or a littering of brilliantly white rocks and a twisted thornbush broke the endless gold of the hills and valleys. Once, shortly before dusk, she even spied a small leaping mouselike creature that disappeared from view so swiftly, she wondered afterward if her eyes were not playing tricks on her. Hot—oh, God, it was so hellishly hot! Her head began to ache, its throbbing matching the throbbing of her aching body. Oh, what she would give to tear off her clothes and plunge headfirst into a pool of cool water! She groaned, wiping the perspiration from her brow with her palm, and drawing it away dripping wet. She may as well pine for the moon, out here, as to yearn for a gleaming pool. . . .

Heaving a sigh, she gazed up ahead as their camels crested a large dune, and her mouth dropped open in disbelief.

There, not far ahead of them, was what appeared to be a large oasis, and at its heart was the gleaming pool she had wished for! Low date palms with scaled, spiny trunks lined its banks, their fronds offering dark pools of shade on the burning sands beneath them. She licked her cracked lips and rubbed her gritty, smarting eyes. Was what she was seeing real—or but a cruel mirage?

"Cemal—?" she began uncertainly.

"Ah, yes, it is real, missie! Your eyes do not deceive you! Yonder lies the oasis of Yasmeen. We will water our camels and fill our goatskins to bursting, and rest there in the shade of the palms until night falls once again, and the missie is refreshed and able to continue."

But the anticipation that soared through Alexa—and indeed seemed to give new life to Cemal and his son, who kicked their camels into a rapid lope—was to be short-lived.

When they were still some distance from the oasis, it became apparent that others had arrived there before them. The bodies of two Arab men lay sprawled upon the sand, dried blood congealed in pools beneath them, glossy-armored swarms of small flies clouding their eyes, their noses, their mouths, their wounds. And under the palms, huddled so closely together they were like a single-bodied, three-headed figure, were the surviving women.

As they rode nearer, she realized that the women were weeping and clinging to each other. They hid their faces beneath their torn veils and implored Cemal and Nabal, who were still advancing on their loping camels, not to harm them, for pity's sake and for the love of Allah the Merciful!

Alexa yanked hard on the reins of Contrary Mary, but it was too late. She had seen the bodies—the bloody wounds—the buzzing flies—and felt her stomach heave.

"Oh, my God, Cemal, what have we here?" she cried. Her green eyes were dark with horror.

Cemal appeared grim, Nabal unusually silent. The older man heaved an enormous sigh, and said sorrowfully as he turned his dark eyes to hers, "I am very much afraid, my poor missie, that we have found the lost caravan of Kadar ben-Selim's betrothed!"

Chapter Five

The youngest of the women, a beautiful child of perhaps fifteen or sixteen, shrank from Alexa as she approached with a goatskin of water and some cloths she had torn from one of the voluminous petticoats hidden beneath the rugs upon a baggage camel with the remainder of her clothing. When Alexa knelt beside her, the Bedouin girl cried out and cringed from her, hiding her face in her hands and beseeching her God in Arabic to protect her. She was trembling violently.

"Please, Cemal, won't you tell her I don't mean to frighten or hurt her, but only to bathe her wounds and give her some comfort?"

Cemal spoke softly to the girl, "Do not be afraid, my daughter. The green-eyed one is gentle and good, for all that she is a stranger to our lands. I swear by the Prophet that she wants only to help you. Let her, Daughter, for you are hurt and have need of her help!"

His words had the desired effect, though the terror never quite left the girl's huge, tormented dark eyes. Her hands dropped to her side, and she eyed Alexa with open suspicion, muttering something under her breath.

"There. You may tend to her now, missie, if that is your wish. But she still fears you for the color of your eyes. She is certain you are a wicked *jinn*, a spirit who might try to harm her further!"

"Oh, please, tell her that's nonsense! Tell her I might very well be a hated white woman, but I'm certainly no *jinn!*" Alexa said sharply, and to prove it, she unfastened the veil that hid her face and smiled at the girl, who gasped in surprise to see

76

that a white woman hid beneath the veils.

Poor little thing! Alexa's heart went out to Muriel in pity, for her lovely, innocent face was darkened by ugly bruises, livid against the golden hue of her complexion. Her upper lip had torn and bled profusely, swelling to three times its normal size, though the blood was dried and crusty now. The fine robes she'd worn were little better than tatters, torn from her body by her attackers and now hastily gathered about her. Beneath them, Alexa could see still more bruises mottling her upper arms, her thighs, her small breasts.

Alexa fought back the tears that smarted in her eyes as her heart went out to the poor battered native girl. It was obvious that she'd been brutally beaten and in all probability raped by one or more of the men who'd killed the two Bedouins. The other women—one of whom seemed to be the girl's mother, the other perhaps an aunt or other relative—seemed grieving and frightened, but otherwise unharmed. Cemal managed to persuade them that their charge would be quite safe with the white woman, and drew them aside to talk while Nabal drew water, built a small fire, and brewed fragrant tea for them all in a brass pot.

Alexa soaked one of her cloths in water from the oasis and reached out to the girl's face, dabbing gently at the caked blood that disfigured her mouth.

"There, there, sweetheart," she crooned as she did so. "It's all over now, you poor little thing. Whoever those brutes were, they're gone now, and won't be coming back." Her gentle, soothing voice, the light yet sure touch of her hands, seemed to have the desired effect. As she bathed each bruise, as she wiped away the rusty smears of blood that stained the girl's mottled inner thighs, she felt the tension begin to drain from Muriel's trembling body; saw the lustrous dark lashes begin to droop over liquid dark eyes as exhaustion and tears replaced the horrified wakefulness of moments before. Her body soon grew limp with fatigue save for her little fists, which she kept tightly clenched despite Alexa's efforts to open them and bathe her scratched hands.

When the girl had been bathed, her hurts tended to as efficiently as she was able, Alexa ducked inside one of the low

Bedouin tents, found a clean, untorn robe belonging to one of the women, and brought it back to cover the girl, pressing her down on the shaded sand beneath a date palm and spreading the garment over her. Despite the heat, the girl's skin seemed overly cool to the touch—a result of the shock she'd undergone, Alexa guessed. The two other native women darted her uncertain smiles as she brought them dishes of the steaming tea Nabal had brewed, and bade them by gestures to offer another dish to the girl to warm her.

"Well, I've done all I can do for her or the others!" Alexa announced with obvious regret, rejoining Cemal and his son by the fire and pouring a dish of reviving tea for herself. "I suppose time will heal the rest. Is she who you feared, Cemal—is that poor battered little creature *Sheik* Kadar's bride?" Her slim hope that Cemal had been wrong died as her guide slowly nodded.

"Alas, she was the one whose caravan the Tuaregs sought, missie, yes! Her name is Muriel bat-Hussein. Her father's caravan was caught in a sandstorm—a small one lasting but an hour or so, but sufficient for her honored father—who was unfamiliar with these parts—to lose his way. In the confusion, they missed the place where they were to meet with their Tuareg escort, and instead found their way here, to the oasis of Yasmeen. Muriel's father decided they must wait here, in the hope that Kadar would find them. Instead, a patrol of *Franziwa* surprised them! There were four men in all, clad in the uniform of Legionnaires. They were rude and angry, and claimed Muriel's father's camels had fouled the oasis and that they planned to spy upon the French fort with an eye to attacking. When the girl's father insisted they were wrong, and that his caravan was a peaceful one, boasting only the few horses and camels which were his daughter's dowry, and their numbers far too few to attack anyone, their officer accused them of being liars, filthy heathen savages. When Muriel's father threatened to call the anger of the Tuaregs down upon the heads of the hated *Rhoumi* in retaliation for their insults, they shot first him and then his brother in cold blood, then they fired their revolvers to drive off the animals, even to the very last one of them, although to be without a horse or a camel out here in the desert means certain death! And then, ah, then one of them noticed the girl. . . ." Cemal shook his head sorrowfully. "Muriel bat-Hussein's mother, Noura, said that two of the soldiers seemed ashamed of the killing, seeing the bodies in the sand, hearing the women wailing and shrieking and tearing their hair in grief, as is the custom of our people. The two soldiers implored the other two to ride away with them and leave the girl untouched, but they laughed in their faces!" Cemal bowed his head sorrowfully. "Alas, the rest you can imagine, missie. . . ."

She nodded mutely and closed her eyes, feeling sickened to her stomach. Oh, yes, she could imagine it very well—too well, in fact. She'd imagined something very similar overtaking her the night the Tuaregs had come to their camp, but she had been fortunate, thanks to Cemal's disguise, and the men had ridden on without harming her, thank God. She shivered and when she opened her eyes, she found Cemal and Nabal regarding her curiously. "Well?" she said at length, "What now? Do we take those poor women along with us, or remain with them until Kadar's band arrives—if it arrives?"

Cemal's expression was aghast. "By the Beard of the Prophet, missie, you would have us wait here for the Tuaregs, knowing what they will find?"

"What else can we do?" Alexa asked.

"We must ride on to the fortress of the *Franziwa,*" her guide insisted, "and with all possible haste! Heed me, I implore you, mistress, for Cemal would live long enough to see the sons of his Nabal born into this world—*ewellah,* perhaps even the sons of his *grandsons!* If we stay here, we tempt the terrible thirst for revenge that will fill Kadar ben-Selim when he learns what has befallen his betrothed. It will spill over like a brimming dish of poison upon all who are near, whether they be innocent or guilty. Have I not told you, missie, that the Tuareg lords are pitiless? Ha! They are doubly ruthless when angered! And did I not tell you that they are masters in the arts of torture? Aiee! We must ride on—ride like the very winds! Linger, and we will surely be slain!"

Reluctant as she was to leave the women, Alexa could see the wisdom in Cemal's reasoning—and she had no more wish to face the terrible anger of Kadar than did Cemal.

After Cemal and Nabal had buried the dead men in the sand, they left dates, meats, and bread with the three women by the oasis pool, as well as one of the baggage camels. The women thanked them in such a piteous manner it brought tears to Alexa's eyes, especially when the girl, Muriel, clasped her hands between her own and kissed them in gratitude.

They rode swiftly away soon afterward, with many backward glances over their shoulders to see if, by some awful chance, they were already being pursued.

As welcome as the oasis had seemed, rising cool and green amidst the hot desert sands, Alexa did not in the least regret leaving it behind them. Rather than a place of refreshment and refuge, the oasis of Yasmeen had become a place of death and despair.

They reached the perimeters of the French Legion fort late the following afternoon, and Alexa heaved a sigh of relief mingled with twinges of apprehension.

Well, the first part of her task was almost over. Despite Dan's and Pauline's warnings, and against the heated advice of the stuffy diplomats at the British Residency in Algiers, she had crossed the Sahara with only a native guide, and survived intact! Yes, she'd arrived. Now, she fancied, came the hardest part of all: seeing Keene again, and trying to make amends between them. It would not be easy, for she knew him to be a proud and unforgiving young man who could be viciously cruel when his will was crossed, but she would try her hardest. She would tell him she'd been wrong, and beg his forgiveness. She'd implore him to return with her to England and Harding House the moment his five-year enlistment was ended, if it should transpire that he could not somehow be released earlier. The rest would be up to him. Forgiveness was not something you could force someone to feel. It was a gift, its giving dependent on the generosity of the giver and, perhaps, on the worthiness of the receiver.

Since Keene had left England, he had reached his majority. Now that he was twenty-one, her guardianship of him had officially ended. She had no lawful means to persuade him to do her bidding. She could only hope that his soldier's life and the deprivations and rigors of the life he'd lived for almost two years now had matured him, without hardening him further. He was his own man, true, but surely, in his heart of hearts, he would want to come home, now that the threat of trial and imprisonment for a crime he did not commit had been removed, and the blemish upon his name washed away. And surely—surely he still felt *some* little affection for her, his only sister, however angry he might have been when he stormed from Harding House that night and swore he'd never return. After all, she was the only family he had left! Well, she'd find out soon enough, one way or the other, she realized grimly, and her belly turned over and growled in apprehension.

The white walls of Fort Valeureux, tinged a rosy pink by the bloody rays of the dying sun, rose from a relatively flat, sandy plain. From the flagpole that towered above the massive fort, the tricolored flag of France, white, blue, and red, fluttered halfheartedly in the sultry breeze. The massive double gates were closed, yet she saw the white neckcloths of the sentries' regulation *kepis* fluttering in that same breeze as they stood watch in the deep embrasures directly above and to either side of them. There was no sense in putting it off any longer. She was here, and the sooner she got her unpleasant task over and done with, the better she'd feel. . . .

She cleared her throat. "Well, I'm ready. I suppose the time has come to say goodbye, to both of you. Cemal, you and Nabal have been the—the very best of guides, and the most—the most perfect escorts." She swallowed. "You have protected me, advised me, and shown me how best to get along in your foreign lands, and no amount of money can repay you for your care. I thank you both, from the very bottom of my heart, dear Cemal and Nabal!" She smiled, and Cemal shuffled his feet and averted his dark and sorrowful eyes.

"The missie made herself ready very quickly, yes? And very charming missie looks! Most proper English lady now, yes?" Cemal coughed, embarrassed. "Behold! I found this for you in the packs," he added, jabbing a parasol in her direction. "Umbrella very proper, very British. You must carry it always."

"'Umbrella' very proper indeed, good Cemal," Alexa agreed grave-faced. "Thank you for finding it for me."

"It is the custom of my people to give one who is departing a gift, missie," Nabal piped in, and there was a wicked gleam in his sloe-black eyes that might have warned her of his deviltry had her own eyes not strangely filled with tears at that very moment. "And so, I have a gift for you!"

"You have?"

With great solemnity, he handed her a small something, wrapped tidily in a square of her own petticoat cloth. "The missie will open it when she reaches the fort, yes? When she sees what great gift Nabal has given her, she will remember him with a warm heart, and hope he walks in the path Allah has chosen for him all the days of his unworthy life, yes?"

"Yes. The missie will," Alexa promised.

She accepted the arm Cemal held out to her, and let him help her up into Mary's saddle, whereupon he removed his foot from the camel's folded knees.

The camel, obviously in a rare biddable frame of mind, unfolded, first backlegs, then forelegs.

"Good girl, Mary!" Alexa praised, and gave the surly beast an affectionate slap on the hump. This valiant if somewhat moth-eaten ship-of-the-desert had carried her safely—though with a modicum of comfort—over many hazardous miles. Despite her somewhat sullen and disagreeable personality and her disgusting habit of spitting and hissing, Alexa'd grown rather fond of the unfragrant creature. With a last glance at the two men, she urged the camel forward.

"Goodbye!"

So saying, she kicked Contrary Mary into the perilous lope that was the camel's approximation of a gallop, and headed her toward the fort.

"Farewell, and Allah be with you!" Cemal called, staring misty-eyed after the strange British missie as she rode slowly away. She had, he realized, with her bravery and her willingness to try his customs, and her gentleness in all things, touched his mercenary old heart in some mysterious fashion during their journey.

He had turned and started back to the tent, planning to take the well-deserved nap he'd been promising himself for many

82

miles, when he heard a peal of merry laughter float across the sands toward him. It came from Missie Har-ding, who had already ridden halfway to the massive gates of the fort. What was it she was saying? He could not make out the words, for they sounded very much like the garbled speech of the *Franziwa*.

"*Touché, Nabal! Touché*, you young rascal!" Alexa called over her shoulder.

"Well? What did the missie say, O my son?" he asked the lad, who was grinning broadly and returning the missie's energetic wave.

"Only that she was most grateful for the gift I gave her," Nabal said with a mysterious, gloating smile.

"Gift? Ah, yes, that gift! And what was inside the cloth, you rogue? What trinket did you steal from me now, worthless offspring of an unhappy father?"

"Only a small piece of camel-cheese that the missie misplaced at the oasis, my father. You see, I found it buried in the sand when I took down the tent and knew she would want to have it back. She said it was her favorite food, after all!" He grinned slyly.

Cemal, his brow creased with a frown, shook his head. *Camel-cheese* the favorite food of a proper British missie? By the Blessed Beard of the Prophet, now he had heard everything! Still, it was said that the British were all mad— every last one of them! Why should Missie Harding be any different?

Chapter Six

"I would very much like to tell you, *chère mademoiselle*, that as Commanding Officer here at Fort Valeureux, I am 'appy to welcome you here. Alas, I cannot in good conscience say it is so!" the commandant, one Major André Laroussse, said with regret and every evidence of considerable irritation. "After all, it is a military outpost we're running, *Mademoiselle* Harding, not a hostel for young ladies wishing to make ze little visit with a younger brother!"

He tapped his pencil upon his desk and regarded her thoughtfully, his stern gaze softening by the minute until his blue eyes reflected somewhat less than his former military detachment. *Sacré Bleu!* How *could* he regard such a vision as Alexandria Harding dispassionately? He'd been André Larousse the man long before he'd become a soldier of *La Belle France*, a true Frenchman who adored all women, and especially those of such stunning beauty as the *mademoiselle anglaise!*

It was little wonder the two sentries who had been manning the gates upon her arrival had believed they were suffering from *cafard*—the desert madness that afflicted so many good men posted to these parts—on seeing her advance over a nearby dune as if materializing from nowhere. What a woman! She had coolly ridden across the sandy plain and up to the fort upon her moth-eaten camel like a desert princess, one incongruously arrayed in a ruffled white gown and an enormous pink hat sporting silk cabbage-roses and festoons of netting, as if arriving simply to take afternoon tea!

When the guards had challenged her at the gates, she had

sweetly asked the stunned men if they might please be so kind as to permit her to see her brother, one of the Legionnaires by the name of Keene Harding, all the while pertly twirling her parasol! If the vivid beauty of her flowing chestnut-colored hair and stunning green eyes, coupled with a flawless rose-tinged complexion and a slender rounded figure that was sheer perfection, had not been enough to render them speechless, then her casual inquiry from atop her camel surely had!

Larousse realized belatedly that he had been staring across the desktop at her for several moments without speaking. Embarrassed, he cleared his throat as he tore his eyes from her. "Ahh-hhem. I repeat, *mademoiselle*, that it was a grave mistake for you to come here!" he said curtly in an attempt to cover his earlier bedazzlement.

"And I repeat, *m'sieu le commandant*, that I really had no choice! You see, before my brother left England to enlist in your country's Foreign Legion, we quarreled bitterly. I accused him of terrible things, Major. Things I later learned he was completely innocent of. At the time, he asked me if I believed him capable of those crimes, and I, his own flesh and blood, couldn't answer him, nor offer the support and trust he needed. I know that I wronged him terribly, *m'sieu*, and that this is why he left our home and ran off to join the Legion, swearing never to return. Later, when I discovered he'd told me the truth, I couldn't live with my guilt. I can't leave here without knowing I've *tried* to make amends to him."

Her voice was husky as she finished, choked with unshed tears. There was a sheen in her faintly slanted, fascinating green eyes that indicated tears were about to spill down her rosy cheeks as she toyed distractedly with the wide pink sash of her gown. She sighed, then raised her distraught face to his and boldly looked him full in the eye, before quickly lowering her lashes with a flutter. Although flirtation and her feminine wiles had not moved the British and Legion officials in Algiers one iota, she instinctively knew that they would work beautifully upon André Larousse. Why, it was there, in his eyes! She had as good as won him over!

Sure enough, in that moment André Larousse felt the full, glorious impact of her stunning beauty, her potent femininity, coupled with a strength of will and steely spirit hitherto unseen as she added huskily, "You simply *must* let me see him, Major Larousee! I have come so far and at such great risk to be here today. Believe me, I shall not leave this fort until I have spoken with my brother, and I defy you or your men to force me to do so!"

Her stubborn little chin jutted now with determination, and he saw that, yes, there was steely obstinacy in the depths of those green eyes that her glistening tears and her damp lashes could not quite hide. He looked away to conceal a smile of amused admiration, busying himself by withdrawing an official form from a drawer in his desk and scratching his signature across the bottom. Beauty and determination, and fire and spirit too! What a prize for some fortunate man the lovely *mademoiselle* would prove some day. . . .

He tossed the pencil aside and smiled, conceding her victory. "Very well! I confess, you have convinced me of your determination, my dear young lady. I've decided to permit you to see this rascal brother of yours. But, when you have spoken with him and mended this matter between you, I must regretfully insist that you return to Sidi-bel-Abbes *immediately*. You see, Fort Valeureux is under constant threat of attack from the Arabs. The natives of these parts resent my country's attempts to control their people and bring them under our government's protection and rule. At any moment, we could find ourselves surrounded and under heavy fire, pinned down by the overwhelming numbers of an Arab *harka*, as we have so many times before! Such a situation would hardly be pleasant for you, *mademoiselle*, as you must appreciate. During an attack, my men would have more than enough to occupy themselves, without the additional burden of defending your so lovely self against being killed or captured by those bloodthirsty savages. The Arabs would not deal at all gently with you should you fall into their hands, *mademoiselle*."

"You said you'd permit me to speak with Keene, Major, and that is all I ask. Do so, and I promise I'll leave here without troubling you further."

Larousse nodded and stood, coming around his desk to stand

beside her.

It occurred to Alexa as he did so that the major was a rather handsome man of perhaps thirty-five or so years, though it was hard to determine his age. His dark-brown, close-clipped hair was distinguished with threadings of silver at the temples, his hussar's moustache neatly trimmed. His eyes were honest and direct and a most engaging cornflower-blue against the leathery bronze of his complexion, which was nearly as dark as any Arab's. In his crisply pressed uniform of black jacket and white breeches, he was every inch a professional soldier: competent, farsighted, resourceful. The major was the sort of cool, brave fighting man for which the French Foreign Legion had become famous throughout the world. Her silly heart fluttered as he smiled down at her.

"Very well, *chère mademoiselle,* you shall see him immediately. And I think you will be pleasantly surprised by what you find! Our young Sergeant Harding has shaped up into an excellent soldier, despite my initial doubts concerning his character when he was first attached to this unit. He seemed a trifle—'ow you say?—ah yes, impetuous, hotheaded, somewhat surly when given an order by one of his superior officers. Fortunately, that behavior is now of the past. He has proven himself worthy, *mademoiselle,* a man of courage and bravery under fire, and has already been promoted to the rank of sergeant—a rank not won lightly by the men of the Legion, you understand?"

He touched her elbow, and she rose gracefully to stand beside him, her lovely head tilted like a bronze blossom to one side as she regarded him expectantly. "While we talked," Larousse continued, "my Adjutant, Captain Boch, has been seeing that my own quarters were made ready for your use while you are with us, Miss Harding. I trust you will feel comfortable there for your brief visit? If there is anything I can do personally, you have only to ask. Your brother will join you after he has made himself presentable. The sergeant and his *escouade*—that is, the squad under his command—returned just a while ago from a patrol in the desert. According to his report, while reconnoitering, they were set upon by a party of Tuaregs, the brigands of the desert, *mademoiselle.* They barely escaped with their lives after skirmishing with those blood-thirsty devils. *Corporal Bouton!"*

A heavyset man appeared at once in the opened doorway of the office, stood rigidly at attention, and snapped a smart salute. *"Oui, m'sieu mon commandant?"*

"Escort Mademoiselle Harding to my quarters, Corporal. See that she is given anything she might require for her comfort, if it is within our limited means to provide it."

"At once, Major Larousse! *Mademoiselle?"* The corporal stepped back, offering Alexa his elbow. She responded with a gracious inclination of her head and placed her slender little hand upon his beefy arm, murmuring to the commandant, "Thank you for your kindness and understanding, Major."

"My pleasure, *mademoiselle,"* the major answered, bringing his heels together and offering her a gallant bow. The pair turned to go. "One more thing, *mademoiselle,"* the major called after her.

"Yes?"

"I would respectfully suggest that you confine yourself to my quarters as much as it is possible, *mademoiselle.* My men have been stationed here at Valeureux for many, many months. Some have fallen victim to *cafard,* others to—shall we say—differing forms of madness? You are a beautiful, charming woman and, *mademoiselle,* the only white woman for thousands of miles—!" He coughed, appearing somewhat embarrassed. "Need I go on?"

Alexa shook her head. A blush deepened the rose in her cheeks. "No, sir, you need not. I understand quite well. I'll try to see that my presence here causes as little inconvenience to your men and your routine as possible, Major."

She left his office on the arm of the lucky corporal, who was agog at his good fortune.

André Larousse, commandant of Fort Valeureux and a confirmed bachelor, sighed and stared after her like a lovesick puppy, wishing he had been able to think of some further point to discuss, some further hazard to caution her about, any ruse to delay her banishment to his quarters.

As she walked away from him, her slender yet womanly hips swung provocatively beneath the delightful gown she wore, rustling and stirring the full skirts so that with a whispering of silk, a glimpse of her trim little ankles was revealed along with, he realized belatedly, the surprising fact that the *mademoiselle* was, of all things, *barefooted* as she tripped along beside the portly corporal! *Mon Dieu!* Those delicious little bare feet, the toes so pink, so innocent, so vulnerable—!

Larousse tried to speak, but found to his dismay his lips were dry, his tongue tied, and speech impossible. Neither shoes nor boots, *hein?* And what else, he wondered, had the delightful *anglaise* opted to dispense with by way of clothing in the hellish North African heat? Sheer wisps of silk stocking on her dainty feet, obviously. Perhaps a lacy under-chemise too, layers of frothy petticoats, a satin corset?

Mon Dieu, Larousse! he upbraided himself sternly. *Enough of this self-inflicted torture!* Was he not an officer and a respectable gentleman of France? Then what was wrong with him, to be thinking such licentious thoughts about such an obviously respectable young lady? Of a certainty, on his next leave in Algiers he would have to seek out one of those reeking, smoky hashish dens in the heart of the Casbah. In their dark and undoubtedly evil cellars, bewitching, half-clad native dancing girls from the Street of the Courtesans undulated their hips and bellies and derrieres and tinkled their little bells. Their erotic gyrations drove a man to madness, it was rumored—or to explosions of unimaginable pleasure!

But despite his self-reproach, Alexandria Harding had crossed the enclosed sandy parade ground and moved on into the heavy shadows of the covered walkways that fronted *la caserne,* the barracks, headed for the officers' quarters beyond, before André was finally able to tear himself away and return to his official duties. And even then, her face smiled seductively up at him from each tedious form he was supposed to complete!

The major's quarters were spartan in the extreme, as befitted a professional soldier, Alexa found.

A simple flagstone floor, faultlessly swept, bore a narrow wooden cot. On it was unrolled a thin tick mattress of straw, supported by taut ropes. The cot was the room's only concession to comfort. A lone, crudely fashioned wooden chair, a small table, and a narrow cupboard of singular plainness positioned solidly against one wall were the only furnishings.

After the exotic grace and charm and perfect serviceability of her goatskin Bedouin tent, this little cell and its sticks of furniture seemed ugly beyond belief! Was this barrenness and utter lack of beauty necessary? Was it simply a matter of the Legion's straightened finances, or a calculated facet of the Legionnaires' lives? Alexa wondered. Perhaps this austerity was part and parcel of the strict discipline and denial they practiced? If that were so, did the renunciation of all that was graceful and pleasing to the eye add to their invincibility as fighting men?

She frowned as she unpinned her hat and set it upon the solitary table. How had Keene, used to the somewhat shabby yet comfortable and eye-pleasing decor of Harding House and a life of relative ease, fare here? What kind of man had such an environment carved him into? The major had seemed proud of the changes that had taken place in the young man, but they were improvements a soldier would naturally applaud. Would she?

Too nervous to take advantage of the major's horrible cot despite her fatigue and the corporal's kind urgings before he left her alone that she have a "leetle nap" before supper was served, she paced restlessly up and down the room's narrow confines, going over and over in her mind what she would say to Keene when she came face to face with him again, and discarding each approach as swiftly as it occurred to her. She was ridiculously grateful for the sharp rap upon the door that interrupted her agonized tangle of thoughts.

"Café, mademoiselle!"

The young soldier goggled at her as she accepted the steaming mug of coffee he offered for her refreshment, and turned beet-red when she thanked him. He tried to snap a dashing salute, forgot the tray in his hand, and dropped it with a resounding clang. He went through an agony of embarrassed fumbling before he was able to salute, regain the tray, and depart. Alexa saved her giggle until he had safely disappeared. Poor boy! Would her presence have a similar effect on all the men stationed here? She hoped not!

The coffee was surprisingly good, hot and strong and somehow soothing to her nerves. She was not half-finished sipping it when there came another knock at the door. Supper—already?

But before she could rise from the edge of the cot to answer it, Keene strode in and slammed the door behind him—a bad habit that the Legion had apparently been unable to drum out of him.

For a moment, the sight of him left her openmouthed and speechless, for he had changed almost beyond her recognition and become a stranger. Oh, he was still handsome, very handsome indeed, but it was the chiseled, muscular hardness of a grown man he had about him now, rather than the transient, softer male beauty of youth. The desert sun, despite the white *kepi* he slapped impatiently against his thigh, had bleached his hair and brows almost to white-gold, while burnishing his face the color of dark honey. There were lighter lines winging outward from about his eyes where he had squinted against that burning sun, and more bracketing his hard, uncompromising mouth. It was a mouth that held no hint of softness, no promise of mercy or compassion whatsoever in its harsh lines. His blue eyes were equally ruthless. She doubted, from the looks of him alone, that there was much that could still move him to pity, never mind tears, and a knot of agony tightened in her breast. She'd come too late. . . .

"Keene?" she whispered, rising slowly to her feet, an uncertain smile of welcome starting to form upon her lips.

"Who did you expect, sister dear? Genghis Khan?"

She flinched under his sneering words as if struck, the smile dying. So. At least he hadn't changed completely; he was still unpleasant, still only too eager to mock and hurt her, without giving an inch to meet her halfway.

"How—how have you been, Keene?" she stammered.

"'How have you been, Keene?'" he mimicked. He gave a harsh laugh that was chilling. "Good God, you haven't changed a bit, have you, Alex? We might be at a bloody tea party, instead of a fort in the blasted Sahara, swarming with cutthroat savages out for white blood! How the devil do you think I've been, you little idiot—it's been eighteen months of pure hell out here! As a matter of fact, I'd just returned from patrol when I heard you were here. I'm tired and hungry and in need of a good, stiff drink, so if it's all the same to you, I suggest we get straight to the point, sister dear, and get this charade over with. Tell me what the blazes you're doing here, Alex. Why did you come? God knows, it wasn't my doing—or my wish—that you should!"

"I know that! But oh, Keene, I had to! I had to find you so I could apologize, and ask you to please come home!" she cried hoarsely, the words escaping her in a torrent. She reached out to touch his cheek, to turn his face to hers in the hope of reaching him, of finding some residue of softness buried deep within him. But he flung off her affectionate gesture with an oath so foul, the blood drained from her face.

"To apologize? Damn it, *why?*" he demanded. "Give me one reason, Alexa. Has that drafty old house grown too empty for you to live in all alone? Does Papa's precious pet weary of the sound of her own heart beating, her own footsteps echoing, her own harping companionship?"

So. He wanted her to grovel, did he, to spell out her shame, her mistake, her guilt and loneliness? Well, so be it. If that was what it took, she'd do it. She owed him that much.

"I've missed you, yes, of course I have," she began. "But—more than that—I know now that I wronged you terribly, Keene, didn't I? I believed the angry words of a stranger over your word as my brother! Cynthia Marchant lied to hide her affairs from her husband and to protect herself, I know that now. You see, her husband came to see me again. He told me he'd—he'd surprised her with another man, and that when he'd threatened to divorce her, she'd told him everything—oh, about you, about how she'd lied and told him you'd attacked her—about her other lovers too. I didn't know the truth until after it was too late to beg your forgiveness, don't you see? And so, I'm begging you now, Keene. Please, please forgive me for ever doubting you!" There were tears streaming down her lovely pale face, and her hands, clasped tightly together, were trembling violently while she awaited his answer, hardly daring to draw a breath.

"Forgive you? The hell I will! You're too bloody late," he rasped. "Your apologies, your little entreaties—they've come too damned late, don't you see? I was immature, foolish, a frightened, confused boy desperately in need of your support and trust—ah yes, and your love—back then. The drinking and the gambling I drowned myself in night after night weren't sins; they were desperate cries for help, sister dear, that you ignored utterly!" They'd been cries of pain too, he remembered bitterly, from the pounding agony in his skull that still returned time and time again to torture him. But she didn't need to know about that. He didn't want—or need—her pity, damn her.

"When you told me that Marchant had been to the police, I knew I was in deep water, and I panicked. I was afraid—more afraid than I've ever been in my life. Our mama appointed you my guardian before she died, Alex. She trusted you to give me the guidance and support I needed. You let me down in my hour of needing you most. And in doing so, you let our mother down too! But that's all in the past now. I don't need your help anymore," he rasped, striding closer and closer to her.

Instinctively, she shrank from him until she felt a whitewashed wall hard at her back. His eyes were blazing with anger as he towered over her.

"I've found what I need here, in the Legion. They protect their own here, Alex, they stand by their own kind to the bitter end, if need be—they don't toss you to the wolves at the first whiff of trouble, as you would have tossed me to the authorities. Listen to me, and listen well, Alex. I don't want your belated, tearful apologies, nor do I need them, d' you hear me? Now go home, damn you—go back to where you belong! Get out of my life and for God's sake, stay out or so help me I'll make you wish you'd never been born!"

Hurt her! the sly little voices whispered in his brain. *Go on, hurt her! That's what she wants—what all women want! Strike her down, hurt her the way she hurt you with her mistrust! She deserves it. She's earned it, hasn't she, eh, sonny . . . hasn't she? She. Me. He. We. See! You see what a woman can do, old son? How they can make you love them and want to please them with their soft, false smiles and their sly, lying ways. And then, when they've got you, they betray you!*

"You betrayed me!" he spat, egged on by the snickering voices, trembling with fury. "You've never once trusted me, not once! Now you come here, asking for my forgiveness? Never, Alex, I'll never forgive you! You were always Papa's favorite, always the one he—!"

Keene was shouting now, ranting on and on like a madman, his fists clenched at his sides as if he might strike her as he loomed threateningly over her, Alexa realized fearfully, instinctively shrinking into herself to offer a smaller target for his rage. She saw that his eyes were glittering strangely; with anger, yes, but also something more, something frightening. His bronze complexion was mottled an ugly, violent red in his fury. His awful, thickened breathing broke heavy and wheezing from his slitted lips as if from some deranged animal—

All at once, the door flew open, crashing back against the wall. Major Larousse stood upon the threshold with arms akimbo and polished booted feet planted apart. Despite the thundering shouts, alternated with a woman's tear-filled pleading that he'd heard from his Adjutant's quarters close by, he was unprepared for the scene that met his eyes as he flung open the door.

He saw *Mademoiselle* Harding pressed flat against the wall as if trying to shrink into it, her eyes wide with horror, while her brother towered menacingly over her but a hairbreadth from losing his temper and brutally striking her! His chivalrous nature recoiled to think that the young soldier would treat his lovely sister—indeed any woman—in such an outrageous, cowardly fashion.

"Harding!" he demanded sternly. "Back away! What the

94

devil is the meaning of this?" he roared.

"Major Larousse, sir!"

At once Keene took a smart step away from Alexa and whirled to face his commanding officer, coming immediately to attention and saluting. "By your leave sir, I—I don't know what came over me, sir!"

He blinked like one awakening from a dream, and flicked his head as if to clear it. His shoulders, belligerently braced seconds before, slumped now. His fists uncurled like giant bronze flowers unfurling against his lean thighs. "I'm deeply sorry, sir. My—my behavior was unforgivable."

Larousse's cornflower-blue eyes were hard. *"C'est vrai, mon sergeant!* In that, you are quite correct! Your conduct is a disgrace to the Legion, and to all gentlemen worthy of ze name! But I believe it is your sister who deserves your apology, not I. Little *mademoiselle*, you are unharmed?" Larousse asked gently, turning to Alexa.

Alexa could not find the words to answer him. She was still too stunned to do so. She simply nodded mutely.

"Well, Sergeant? I am waiting. What have you to say to the *mademoiselle?"*

Keene wet his lips and turned to his sister. "I'm sorry, Alexa, truly sorry! I lost my temper, and my behavior was unforgivable. But seeing you here, of all places, after hoping and praying for so damned long that somehow, someday, you'd learn the truth, and remembering the way we parted company, with hard words and accusations, I, well, I suppose my feelings got the best of me and took a bad turn! As I said, I'd come in from a patrol just before you arrived. I'm completely exhausted. The desert—the blasted heat and never knowing when you'll be attacked next, or from where—it plays on a man's nerves, it wears him down, Alexa, believe me, it does. That's no excuse for my rotten treatment of you, I know, love, but it's the plain truth. I'll be myself again after a good night's sleep, I swear it. We'll talk out our problems in the morning. I'll be a good boy then, Sis, cross my heart!"

He gave her a sheepish, boyish grin, looking like a naughty schoolboy caught in the act of some minor misdeed. The grin confused her completely, because at heart she wanted so badly to believe he was telling her the truth, and that his hateful behavior had truly been caused by stress and fatigue. *Was* he sincere, or merely a more mature, more dangerously clever version of the old, sly Keene?

Major Larousse glanced at Alexa. "Well, *mademoiselle?* Do you accept the sergeant's apology, or do I place him on report for his disgraceful behavior?"

"Oh, please, there's no need for that, Major, really there isn't. I'm sure Keene must have reacted as he did out of—of fatigue. As he said, a good night's sleep for both of us will do wonders." She tried to smile brightly, but failed. Her lower lip still quivered uncontrollably.

The brave little gesture intended to convince her brother's commanding officer and spare him disciplinary action was noticed by Larousse, and touched the major deeply. Harding, in his opinion, did not deserve such a sister, but the girl's devotion to him was plain. For her sake, if not her brother's, he intended to see to it that she received the hearing she deserved after coming so far to make amends with her brother for some nonsensical, probably imaginary, wrong she had done him.

"That may be so, *mademoiselle.* However, since the sergeant has a few days' leave coming to him, and since he is quite obviously in need of rest and recuperation of some kind, I believe I have a solution which will benefit you both. Sergeant Harding, I've already informed your sister that she cannot stay here at the fort for any longer than is absolutely necessary. Accordingly, I am appointing you her escort back to Sidi-bel-Abbes, where you will see her safely aboard a train bound for Algiers with a suitable traveling companion. You will pick six men to accompany you, and prepare to leave first thing in the morning. Do I make myself clear?"

"*Oui, m'sieu mon commandant!* Quite clear. Thank you, sir!"

"Furthermore, I will permit no more outbursts of this shocking nature, Sergeant. You will raise neither your voice nor your fists to your sister ever again. Do so, and you will answer to me. You understand?"

"Yes, sir!" Keene responded smartly. A muscle worked in

his jaw as he swallowed his rage. Damn Alexa's soul! Damn that conniving bitch! She'd done it again, twisted things around to make him look bad, just as she'd always done with their father. Larousse was eyeing her as if she were a goddess on a pedestal, faultless and perfect, he thought jealously. *You'll pay, sister dear!* he vowed silently. *You'll pay for turning him against me! He choked back a sob of rage and remained stiffly at attention, his handsome face impassive.*

"Very well, Sergeant. You may now make your way to the mess hall for supper. Dismissed!"

Keene saluted Larousse, who stepped aside to allow him to exit. He did so, striding smartly.

"So! Do my orders meet with your approval, *chère mademoiselle?*" Larousse asked when they were alone again. His heart was pounding madly, and he found himself quite giddy at the idea that they were alone. The faint fragrance of roses that clung to her person made him dizzy, as if he'd drunk several glasses of potent wine.

"Very much so, Major," Alexa murmured gratefully. "I'm sure Keene and I will be able to come to some sort of understanding during the journey back to the city."

"That was my hope entirely!" the major admitted with a charming smile. "Now, let's forget this moment's unpleasantness, shall we? Er, forgive me if I'm being too forward, but I was wondering if I might invite you to join me for supper this evening, *M'selle* Harding? It is selfish of me to ask, I know, when you are undoubtedly exhausted from your journey, but you have no idea how long it's been since I've enjoyed the company of a lovely and charming young woman such as yourself! I can promise you only miserable food, alas—but food accompanied by the most excellent wines between here and Paris! Please, *mademoiselle,* won't you bring a little beauty into a soldier's lonely existence, and accept my invitation?"

His gentleness, his charm, his chivalrous manner were like a balm to her wounded spirit after Keene's cold and violent welcome. A little smile curved her lips. True, Larousse had said he was asking her out of selfishness, but she had a shrewd idea that intuitively he'd known she should not be left alone to lick the wounds Keene had so cruelly dealt her in private. He was asking her as much for her own sake as for his.

"I would be honored, Major Larousse," she said with a wider smile, bobbing him a charming curtsy.

"André. If we are to be dinner companions, I insist that you call me André, *chère mademoiselle*."

"Of course! And you must call me Alexandra, André."

Chapter Seven

"My lord Sharif, I protest your orders! I would ride after those murdering *Franziwa* dogs at once!" Kadar demanded. His black eyes were crackling with fury. His fingers curled lovingly about the hilt of his curved dagger as if he fondled a favorite woman.

Sharif al-Azim, his chieftain, knew that with this lust for vengeance burning in his veins, the Bedouin's blade would not go unblooded for long.

"Kadar, my brother, you know I would not stop you from going after these men," he began. "The rage and grief you are feeling are my own rage and grief! Your thirst for vengeance is my thirst. Were the two of us not raised as brothers when our mothers died giving us life? Did we two not suckle at the breasts of the same nurse? And it is because I value your life"—a ghost of a smile curved Sharif's hard mouth, yet never reached his troubled black eyes—"that I urge you to postpone your quest for vengeance until the furnace of your temper cools. Better a brief delay until dawn, Brother-of-My-Childhood, than your death in a hasty attack in which you and your men are outnumbered. The severing of our friendship under such conditions would weigh heavy on my heart, be it the will of Allah or nay."

Kadar scowled, his hooked nose dominating his angular, handsome face. "By the Beard of the Prophet, you ask much of me, Sharif! You know if it is your command that I wait until dawn, I have no choice but to obey you, for I have sworn you my allegiance. But mark me well, Brother, it is the throats of the *Franziwa* dogs that will be severed, not our friendship! I will hunt them down and slay them, to the last cowardly Christian dog! It is their blood that will water the desert sands! Before Allah, I swear it!"

He strode off, leaving Sharif seated alone beside the fire.

The flames writhed, orange-and-golden fire-demons who cast their fleeting images upon the darkened amber of the sands of Yasmeen, and danced upon the surface of the still pool beneath the date palms in ripples of rust and gold. They also cast the chieftain's face first in revealing ruddy light, and then in mysterious shadow. Sharif rested his chin upon his balled fist as he gazed into their depths, deep in troubled thought.

They had found the missing caravan of Muriel's father that same afternoon, here at the oasis of Yasmeen. Three shocked and weeping women were all that had remained of its people. From a tearful Noura, the girl's mother, they had learned of the cowardly and unprovoked attack upon the peaceful caravan by French soldiers; an attack which had left Noura's husband and his brother dead, Muriel beaten and raped, and their servants, camel herds, and horses driven off. The three women had been left defenseless by their attackers, at the mercy of the sun and the desert predators—both four- and two-legged—which in this harsh land was a sentence as severe as any execution.

So too had Noura told of the coming of those others; a humble pilgrim bound for Mecca with his young son, accompanied by a beautiful white woman with the slanted green eyes of a *jinn*, dressed as a Bedouin. Before they'd left, the man and his son had buried the dead deep in the sand, where the bodies would be hidden from the carrion birds and the jackals, while the green-eyed woman had comforted them in their sorrow and tended their wounds. She'd even made certain that they received food and were sheltered before continuing on her way. Yes, she was certain the one who had saved their lives had been a beautiful, green-eyed white woman, Noura had confirmed when pressed by Sharif. Pale-skinned, and with flowing hair little less wondrous than the color of her eyes, for it was the warm hue of apricots, only darker . . .

Her vivid description had stolen the breath from Sharif's

lips. It would appear that old rogue, Cemal, was a teller-of-tales to rival even the best on the Street of Storytellers! "I am but a petty merchant, my lord," he had humbly told Sharif. "I am a simple pilgrim, bound for the Holy City of Mecca," he had told Noura. He had also lied when Sharif's Tuareg band had claimed the hospitality of his little camp that night, after the custom of the nomadic tribes of their people, for he'd implied the green-eyed maiden was but a lowly slave girl, and a mute one at that! The crafty rascal had protected his young mistress well, Sharif mused, for at the time he'd not for an instant thought to doubt the truth of the man's story.

"Zerdali!" he breathed on the coolness of the night wind. "Was it in truth your beloved eyes into which I gazed that night? Were you so very close that I could hear the frantic beating of your little heart, like a frightened dove's, and yet I knew you not? Have you come to me at last from across the seas and across the desert sands, that I might claim you as my bride, beloved *houri*?"

There was no answer on the breeze. But that night, she came to him again in his dreams. That fleeting night, he dwelt again in Paradise. . . .

"Oh, hang them all!" Alexa grumbled, mopping her streaming face with an already sodden scrap of a handkerchief, and wishing dearly she had not listened to her brother and Major Larousse.

As the major—or André, as she thought of him now—had planned, she and her escort of six Legionnaires, led by her brother, had left Fort Valeureux in the cool gray hours that preceded the dawn here in the desert, when only the paling beams of moonlight and fading starlight stretched ghostly fingers across the hushed white dunes. Alexa had not needed to look back over her shoulder to know that André's blue eyes—and perhaps the eyes of several score other men—watched her with longing as she rode away.

Against her wishes and innate good sense, she'd given in to André's and Keene's insistence that she wear European clothing for the journey, rather than the red-and-black native *caftan* that had proven so cool and comfortable before. She regretted it bitterly now. The divided riding skirt and matching jacket with a lacy *jabot* spilling over at the collar had proved an instrument of torture today, for it had chafed her tender skin and proven stifling to boot. Tomorrow, she would wear what she chose, and Keene's protests could go hang!

Keene had been curtly polite to her during that evening at Valeureux, and then again today, the first full day of their journey. But to Alexa's regret, they'd not discussed their problems any further since their argument. Keene had claimed he had far too much to do to see her escort suitably equipped to take the time to discuss what was obviously past discussing. She'd tried, he'd told her, but failed. As far as he was concerned, that was an end to the matter. He'd made no secret of the fact either that he resented having been elected to serve as her escort, though he never let his pose of the perfect, chastened brother slip in the major's presence—no, not for a second! He was far too clever for that. She had a shrewd suspicion he intended to keep up his delaying tactics, and avoid any further confrontations.

During the heat of that first morning, he'd ridden ahead of the rest of them, scouting the terrain they had yet to travel, and she'd scarcely seen him. Now, it was shortly before dusk. They'd halted and erected the white campaign tents of the Legion about a scrubby water hole. Corporal O'Day, one of the other men who spoke more than a smattering of English, had been elected to serve as cook. Alexa had volunteered to help him, but had been curtly—and rudely—rebuffed. With a shrug, she consigned him and Keene to the devil and decided to let him get on with his chores alone, offended by his hostility. Mopping her streaming face, she retreated to the canvas prison of her tent, with white walls that reflected the dazzling afternoon sunlight but seemed to trap its scorching heat within them.

She loosened her clothing and stretched out upon the canvas ground cover, falling at once into a deep yet fitful sleep. Immediately, it seemed, her recurring dream began to unfold for the first time since she'd left home, the strangely disturbing

102

yet delightful images flickering through her mind with all the wondrous colors and pageantry of a magic-lantern show.

"Zerdali!"

"My lord!"

"I have waited for thee so long, habibah!"

"The waiting is past, my lord. I'm here now. I have come to you!"

She lay upon a low, silk-draped couch, the caress of the night wind stroking her body, which was clothed only in jewels and bangles of precious metals. A slim circlet of silver bound her brow, and from it suspended the cool weight of a priceless teardrop emerald. Silver bangles encircled her upper arms, and matching anklets with tiny, tinkling bells adorned her feet. Her heavy mane of golden-chestnut hair flowed over the edge of the couch and swept the mosaic-tiled floor below in glorious, rippling waves. Its color captured the blazing glow of brass dish-lamps set in alcoves, and held strands of it prisoner in chains of copper and gold. Gauzy hangings fluttered against the walls, dancing in the breeze from the arched windows, each one of which boasted a lattice of intricate arabesques. Through them she could see the indigo sky, sequined by a million-million frosty stars, and a silvery moon that hung in the darkened heavens like a soothsayer's crystal ball.

A man's broad-shouldered silhouette blotted the starry night from her view as he loomed over where she lay. His scent was of aromatic sandalwood, clean and pleasant to her flaring nostrils as he lowered his ebony head to hers.

"Aaah, Zerdali, my Zerdali!" he murmured huskily, and she heard herself gasp as his large hands tenderly framed her face. Then his warm mouth covered hers, demanding and yet curiously gentle all at once. His tongue-tip danced along the meeting of her lips, outlining their yielding softness.

"You will learn how a woman kisses a man, Zerdali. It is an art that will bring us both pleasure. But first, you must open your mouth to mine, little one," he whispered, and shyly her lips parted beneath his.

103

His tongue slid between them, and she shivered at the erotic sensations his moist, intimate caresses unleashed in her body. The very bones seemed to melt within her, leaving only trembling, burning flesh in their wake. Her senses reeled. Her thoughts whirled, like tiny snowflakes shaken in a glass sphere. Was this rapture but a kiss—? Oh, Lord! She was drowning in a warm sea of exquisite pleasure that flowed from his lips to hers, and filled her veins with molten honey. She clung to him, to his powerfully muscled arms, his broad, smooth back, uttering little birdlike cries against his lips as his tongue delicately stroked her teeth, then slipped deeper into the moist, hidden recesses of her mouth to play teasingly with her own. As he kissed her, she gazed into his sensual eyes, heavy-lidded with desire, and saw tiny flecks of gold flaring in their inky depths; a reflection of the fire within his soul—or a reflection of her own desire?

When he broke away, it was only to rain still more kisses over her throat, or trace the delicate shells of her ears with his lips and tongue. His warm breath tickled, made ripples of pleasure shiver up and down her spine and center deep in her loins as a throbbing pulse. She felt the graze of his hand upon her bared shoulder as he nuzzled her ears, and shivered and arched like a purring kitten to follow its path as his palm moved slowly, oh, so slowly, downward, to encompass the soft curve of her breast. His fingertips trapped the rising coral peak there in a tender trap, and she moaned with delight as he fondled the sensitive nipple, silently—shamelessly—begging for more . . . and more . . . and still more.

"Soon I come to claim thee as my woman, Zerdali!" came his husky voice. *"The sands of time are running out; the hour draws ever nearer. Do not fear me, Zerdali. Do not fight against the fate which is yours. It was written in the stars that you would be mine, from the moment of your birth. . . ."*

With his whispered words, the images and sensations began to dissolve, spreading out before vanishing like reflections mirrored in a still pool, disturbed by a falling leaf.

"No! Please, don't go! Wait! Come back!" she cried, reaching out to recapture those fading dreams. But it was no use. The warmth and substance of the dream-lover she'd embraced

began to vanish like smoke upon the wind. The gauzy-curtained bower, the silken couch, receded . . .

She awoke with a start, and stifled a groan of disappointment at finding herself in the suffocating Legion tent, her body bathed in perspiration, and Corporal O'Day impatiently calling her name from the tent flap, bidding her come to the fire for supper.

"There ye are, ma'am," the Irishman muttered moments later, passing her a tin plate of unappetizing, greasy beef stew, which had obviously been warmed straight from the ration cans it came in, the latter now half-buried in the sand. He also handed her a chunk of dry bread and an enamel mug of steaming coffee.

Seeing her unenthusiastic expression, O'Day scowled and shrugged. "Aye, ma'am, it's not much, t' be true. But I'm after thinkin' it'll be the best ye'll be tasting until you're safe an' snug in yer fine hotel in Sidi-bel-Abbes, m' lady."

Was she mistaken, or was there a definite bite of sarcasm to his tone? And if so, why? As far as she knew, she'd done or said nothing to irritate the man, unless—? Could he have taken her expression for criticism of his skills as cook?

"Thank you, Corporal. I'm sure I've eaten worse in my lifetime." She sat down and sampled a spoonful of the stew, hastily washing it down with a swig of scalding coffee. "Mmm. At least the coffee's good. That's something to be grateful for."

The corporal was a homely fellow at first glance, with the oft-broken, badly-mended nose of a pugilist. Yet when he smiled, as he suddenly did now, his battered features took on a roguish charm. Then, before her very eyes, the reluctant smile vanished as suddenly as it had appeared! He scowled blackly at her as if she'd somehow tricked him into smiling, muttered a curse under his breath, and abruptly left her. He went across to the baggage animals and rummaged in one of the packs, busying himself—she was almost certain—in pretending to look for some missing item!

Well, Alexa thought, wasn't he the moody, mercurial one! She'd never seen such a marked change of mood in a man! Still, it seemed that more than one of the men Keene had chosen to form the *escouade* of six that made up her escort was a little

105

strange. Another of their number—a Corporal Flechette—
gave her the creeps each time he looked her way, which to
Alexa's mind was far too often. *That* one, with his sly glances
from puffy, drooping eyelids that gave him a decidedly sinister
aspect, and fleshy lips that he frequently wet with lizardlike
swipes of his tongue, reminded her of a predatory snake eyeing
his next meal! She'd liked Corporal O'Day initially, but now
decided that perhaps only the young Italian, Gianetti, and
another gentle Frenchman with protruding ears named Henri
Toussant or Soucant or something similar were in any way
likeable. Keene, however, seemed on friendly terms with all of
them, and had obviously led them on several prior patrols.
Henceforth, she decided, she'd definitely give both O'Day and
Flechette wide berth during their journey, or know the reason
why! Their quixotic moods disturbed her.

"Ma'am?"

For a second or two, she was so deep in speculation about the
horrible Flechette—wondering what particularly awful crime
he'd committed to make him flee justice and seek the sanctuary
of the Legion—that she didn't notice the sheepish Irish
corporal standing before her with the coffeepot held in his
shaking hand.

"Ma'am? Beggin' yer pardon, ma'am, but 'tis sorry I am fer
speakin' t' ye so rudely a while ago, ma'am."

Well, well! It seems she'd underestimated the man!
"Apology accepted, Corporal," she responded. Her cool tone
dismissed him, yet the Irishman was either slow to take the
hint, or obstinately refused to. He still stood before her. She
sighed. He obviously intended to remain standing there until
she relented and said something more to ease the animosity
between them. "I said your apology is accepted, Corporal.
Think nothing more of it, unless—is there something else you
wished to ask me?"

"Ask, ma'am, no. But t' be sure, ma'am, there's somethin' I
believe I have to be tellin' ye. 'Tis about ye're brother, ma'am,
it is!"

"My brother? What about him?" she asked, puzzled. O'Day
wore a deeply worried expression on his battered features.
Even his dark-blue eyes seemed furtive and reluctant to meet

her own. *Guilt,* she decided intuitively, the man was riddled with it! Now what on earth had he to be guilty about?

"Well, ye see, ma'am, it's like this," O'Day began. "I was part o' this same patrol five days ago. Our *escouade* was led by yer brother then, just like now. A little before nightfall, we came upon a—*Jaysus!*"

He broke off as something shiny flashed past, inches from his shoulder. A small knife thudded into the hard sandy ground of the oasis between them, and remained upright with its hilt aquiver from the impact.

Alexa and Corporal O'Day looked up sharply in horror to see the soldier named Flechette lounging on one elbow against his bedroll only a few feet away. How long had he been there, listening as she and O'Day talked? Alexa wondered.

"Ah! *Sacré bleu!* What a careless fool I am! Please, forgive me, *mademoiselle,* and you too, my old friend? I was but practicing my knife-throwing, and foolishly sent the blade astray. It was fortunate it landed harmlessly where it did, *n'est-ce pas?* Another inch or two to the left, and—pouf!—our poor O'Day would be missing his ear!" Flechette's sly grin belied his apologies.

O'Day licked his lips, seemingly hypnotized and unable to look away from the Frenchman even when a rider trotted into the camp and sprang down from his camel.

"Ah, Timothy, *mon ami, regardez!* Our brave sergeant has returned! No doubt he will be anxious for 'is supper, *non?*" Flechette said softly. "To work with you, Corporal! Ze chef should nevaire be idle!"

"Aye," O'Day agreed, swallowing. "I'd best see t' Sergeant Harding's supper right away. Ye'll have t' excuse me, ma'am?" With obvious difficulty, he drew his eyes from Flechette and back to her.

"Of course, Corporal. Perhaps we can finish our chat later?"

"Perhaps," the corporal agreed doubtfully, and bolted like a frightened rabbit to the fire and the stew kettle. There he began ladling the greasy mess onto a platter for the sergeant as if his very life depended upon it. As, perhaps, it did.

Flechette rose lazily to his feet and strolled across to where

Alexa sat. He crouched down before her, brushing her long skirts with the toe of his boot, and plucked the dagger from the dirt, wiping the shining steel blade on the thigh of his trousers as he squatted back on his haunches.

"You must not make too much of my friend's ramblings, *mademoiselle*," he advised her. "Poor O'Day—he suffers badly from ze *cafard*, you know? It is a madness that afflicts many of us out here in the desert, but those of us who are overly fond of liquor seem to be stricken worst of all. So it is with my friend the Irishman. He has a great fondness for whiskey."

He smiled, catlike, his heavy-lidded eyes flickering over her face, lingering greedily on her lips for a moment before dropping to stare at the swell of her breasts outlined by the cloth of her jacket. "Other men have a passion for other things. Perhaps beautiful women such as yourself, eh?"

Alexa stiffened. The innuendo in his tone was unmistakable! She felt heat fill her cheeks, and knew they were stained a furious crimson with her indignation.

"I accept your apology, and also your explanation regarding the corporal, Corporal Flechette. Please, feel free to find your own supper now," she prompted, wishing he'd leave her alone.

"But of course, if that is what you wish. It was just that I did not want you to think badly of my good friend, O'Day, or to take his crazy mutterings too seriously, poor fellow. Friends should stick together, should they not? It is *trés dangereux* out here, you know, a very hostile land. One never knows when one will be attacked—perhaps as we sleep all alone in our tents one night? Friends can make ze difference in such a situation, eh? And it is my fondest wish that I and the so-lovely *mademoiselle* will also become quite intimate friends!"

He reached for her hand, obviously intending to kiss it, Gallic fashion, but Alexa tore her hand free of his sweaty grasp as if he were a snake about to strike.

"Don't touch me, you disgusting excuse for a man!" she snapped, her nostrils flared in outrage. "Do you think me a total innocent, too naive to understand what you're implying? On the contrary, *m'sieu*, I've met your kind before! They're sixpence a dozen back in England!" she scoffed, green eyes blazing. "Now, if you would be so kind, I would prefer that you return to your side of the fire and leave me alone—at once! And take your nasty little knife and your innuendos with you!"

"You wrong me with your harsh accusations, *mademoiselle!*" Flechette denied silkily, though his eyes were hard and angry now, "I certainly intended no insult to the lovely sister of our so-beloved sergeant. I simply hoped to offer you my friendship, for one never knows when one might need a friend out here."

"Is that so, Corporal? But I assure you, you'd be the very last person I would choose for that honor!" Alexa gritted, her green eyes still crackling.

With a gallant yet somehow mocking incline of his head, Flechette moved away, taking his dagger with him. Despite her words, he resumed his comfortable sprawl only a few feet from her.

The nerve of the man! She was trembling inside, but she'd be damned if she let that horrible toad see he'd succeeded in upsetting her! She gazed steadfastly at the crimson beauty of the sunset falling over the desert sands instead, and ignored him, although she knew he glanced speculatively in her direction from time to time. Let him! she thought, irritated. A word to Keene would put a stop to his nonsense in short order!

Some of the other men came to the fire then, offering her polite greetings. She returned their courteous words warmly, welcoming the brief distraction they offered. Her thoughts returned once again to O'Day, and whatever it was he'd been on the brink of disclosing to her. The poor, troubled man had seemed so distraught—guilty, almost—and in need of unburdening himself to someone. Had it merely been the *cafard* talking, as the odious Flechette had implied, or had he been about to tell her what crime he'd committed that had sent him fleeing from the arms of the law to this remote and inhospitable outpost? It was probable. Her cousin Dan, in his efforts to deter her from making this journey alone, had warned her that although the majority of the men of the French Foreign Legion were simply career soldiers serving France, many others who were not of French origin were fugitives from the laws of other countries. Their enlistment guaranteed them immunity from prosecution for the duration of their service, and the cloak of

French citizenship afterward, should they desire it. Was O'Day a wanted man in his native Ireland, she wondered?

She looked up as Keene took a seat on the rocks beside her, a steaming tin mug of coffee in his hand. He looked bronzed, fit, and relaxed.

"So. How have my men been treating you?" her brother inquired, regarding her speculatively. Poor devils, he mused. His men's tongues must be fairly hanging out with lusting after his sister, the beautiful bitch, who—despite a rigorous day's journey in blistering heat—still somehow contrived to look cool and regal! Ah, yes, reluctant as he was to admit it, although still a spinster at the advanced age of twenty-four, by which time most girls were married and already mothers back home, his domineering bitch of a sister was nonetheless a beauty, even by exacting British standards. Her unmarried condition was one of choice, not one dictated by lack of proposals. She'd turned down at least a dozen offers for her hand that he knew of, claiming her guardianship of himself her reason for so doing. Keene smirked. How his men, too long without seeing a white woman, let alone bedding one, must secretly be panting after her!

He averted his face and grinned broadly, the grin deepening as he caught Flechette's lewd wink and returned it. What had that sly bastard of a Frenchman said to rile her? he wondered casually, relishing his sister's obvious discomfort. Right now, she looked angry enough to explode, if the telltale hectic spots of crimson in her cheeks were anything to go by!

"For the most part, your men have been very kind," she murmured in answer to his question, casting a pointed glance at Flechette, which Keene ignored.

"Good! So very glad to hear it, old girl! Hate to think one of my men had been acting in too familiar a fashion toward my big sister. Why, I might be forced to clap the awful chap in irons, eh, Flechette, my friend?"

"Alas, yes, *mon ami!*" Flechette agreed, enjoying the look of undisguised dismay upon Alexa Harding's face as it dawned on her that the two of them were fast friends, and that Keene was actually poking fun at her distress.

So! That was the way the wind blew, was it? she thought,

distaste stamped on her strong, beautiful features. The two of them were in cahoots, and Keene had clearly implied in which direction his loyalties lay. She might as well forgo any attempt to explain Flechette's insulting behavior toward her. In this matter, she was clearly on her own. . . .

"We should make good time tomorrow, I believe, if we break camp about three hours after moonrise tonight. I thought we'd plan the next halt at the oasis of Yasmeen, during the noonday heat," Keene was observing. "It's a damned good spot, as far as oases go. Lots of water, some grass, a few date palms—the best oasis between here and Sidi-bel-Abbes, as a matter of fact. All the little comforts of home, right, Flechette?"

"Indeed, *mon sergeant.* It is said that a man can find every comfort he might wish for at ze lovely oasis of Yasmeen!"

The pair exchanged secretive glances and chuckled at some private joke.

Alexa bristled. They were like ill-mannered children, crowing over some scrape they'd got away with scot-free.

"Keene, if you have a moment, I'd been hoping to discuss our—personal matters—with you?" Alexa ventured, trying to change the direction of the conversation. "In private."

"Later, Alex," he promised airily. "Right now, I really must see about posting some sentries for the night. I suggest you turn in soon. I plan an early start in the morning. Good night." With a faint, triumphant smirk, he drained his coffee mug, nodded, and left her by the fire.

Well aware that the slimy Flechette was still watching her, she decided to take Keene's advice and retire early. She rose and headed for her baggage, still loaded onto Contrary Mary, and rummaged inside the bulky roll for some items of clothing before going to her tent. As she went, she heard Flechette call after her: "Sleep well, my lovely *mademoiselle!* May all your dreams be of me, *cherie!*"

Alexa snorted. "Impossible, *m'sieu,*" she retorted softly, "for if that were so, they would not be dreams, but nightmares!" So saying, she stormed into her tent.

Chapter Eight

Despite the coolness of the nights out in the desert, when temperatures dropped several degrees, her tent seemed almost as suffocating after moonrise as before. Alex rummaged amongst the bundle of belongings she'd unloaded from her camel and at last found what she'd been looking for—a long, white nightgown of sheer silk with ribbon-ties at the shoulders. It was the coolest item of clothing she possessed.

She undressed and slipped the nightgown on, loving the feel of its cool silk slipping like water over her bare skin as she smoothed it down about her hips. Her hair she untangled with a few brisk, efficient brush strokes, then twisted into a heavy knot at the nape of her neck which she fastened with a tortoiseshell comb. Her sketchy toilet completed, she was about to lie down when she recalled Flechette's insolent manner and the bold leer he'd given her as she left the campfire. On reflection, it wasn't too farfetched to wonder if he might indulge in some nocturnal wandering in the direction of her tent after the others fell asleep.

"Well! I'll certainly lock my door on you, lecherous *M'sieu* Toad!" she muttered grimly. She quickly knelt to the tent flap, fastening the cords that closed it from the inside with a series of complex knots she dearly hoped would serve to keep him out.

Feeling far cooler than she had all day, she lay down and dropped into a deep and dreamless sleep.

"Aux armes! Aux armes!"

Keene's roared commands wakened her what seemed only seconds later. The edge of alarm in his voice acted like ice water dashed in her face. She sat up, blinking in the pitch-blackness of the tent. Her heart was thumping wildly in fear for she heard muffled oaths and yells now, frightening sounds carried from the camp outside, as well as the rattling of rifles being readied for firing. Dear God! There was trouble, by the sound of it! What on earth was going on out there?

She scrambled to the tent flap, cursing the clever knots she'd tied so smugly the evening before. In the dark, and with fingers made clumsy by panic, she couldn't unfasten them! The blood seemed to congeal in her veins as she heard more cries from outside. They sounded—oh, God!—they sounded like battle cries, though not in any language she understood! The ululating whoops of challenge sent frissons of terror sweeping through her:

"Ul-ul-ul-ul-ul-ullah Akbar!"

The last knot gave! With a frightened whimper, Alexa tugged aside the tent flap. She was about to scramble through the opening when, in the same moment, she saw dozens of native riders pour over the crest of a nearby dune, sweeping down the hillside toward their camp and the scattered soldiers of the Legion! Their robes streamed behind them with the swiftness of their ride as they careened downhill to the little camp, galloping across the moonlit sands and uttering bloodcurdling cries as they came.

Each one of her escorts was already awake and alert, she saw with wide, horrified eyes. They'd hastily prepared to meet the oncoming tide and now lay upon their bellies in the sand, their rifles shouldered and cocked. The camels, still heavily laden, formed living barricades for their masters.

"Fire!" she heard Keene roar, and the guns cracked, the bullets whined, simultaneously as one thundering report.

An approaching Arab rider—then two—three—toppled with up-flung arms beneath the bodies of falling camels or horses, yet the rest came on: an unstoppable, surging, death-bearing flood that was awful to behold!

"Fire!" came the order again, and there was a note of fierce exultation in his cry.

The voice drew and held her. Alexa saw Keene off to one side, his saber drawn and brandished aloft, his fair hair disheveled, his handsome face radiant with savage joy as he commanded his brave men, giving the order to fire and fire again.

Off to her right, Corporal O'Day's rifle clicked hollowly. With an oath, he wriggled backward on his belly, using his camel as a barricade to cover his retreat. He gathered fresh ammunition and began to rapidly reload. As he did so, the flash of Alexa's white nightgown in the nearby tent opening caught his eye for a fleeting instant.

How small and vulnerable she was, crouched there, her face ashen with terror in the moonlight, her eyes overly bright. *Jaysus!* As a seasoned soldier, he knew there was no use fighting. Hopelessly outnumbered, they didn't have the chance of a snowball in hell against the fierce Tuaregs, an enemy who believed that death in battle against a Christian foe assured them of Paradise, no less. No hope at all, but the hope of a quick and merciful death, while a white woman like her wouldn't even have that to look forward to—! *Jaysus!* Even Harding's sister didn't deserve to end up at the mercy o' these howling, savage heathens.

"Run fer it, colleen!" O'Day screamed at her. "'Tis yer only hope! Take yer camel and ride back t' the fort!"

"*My brother!*" She mouthed the agonized words silently.

"Damn the murthering scum!" O'Day growled, "Look at him! Did he think o' you? Nay, colleen, that madman's enjoyin' this, all the blood an' glory o' it! Damn ye, woman, run, I tell ye!"

Grim and pale in the graying moonlight, O'Day cracked his rifle barrel, fixed his bayonet, and swung to meet a bearded, white-robed devil wielding a shimmering curved dagger. Despite his wild Irish whoop, his answering challenge was somehow sadly hollow.

The rush of mounted tribesmen was soon over. To a man, they now leaped from their galloping horses or racing camels to battle the hated *Franziwas* on foot, hand to hand upon the pale oasis sands. They wielded heavy battle lances or curved daggers, describing sweeping arcs that caught the moonlight in

114

rainbows of silver-fire as they fought.

In answer, the seven men of the Legion battled courageously, as befitted their valiant reputation, fixing their bayonets against their attackers when their ammunition ran out, and using the hefty butts of their rifles as clubs when sabers or bayonets were lost or shattered.

And to a man, of a sudden it dawned on them that they were all still standing or knocked senseless: that *not one* of them had been killed or mortally wounded. In the same breath they asked themselves why that should be. The awful truth slammed home. They wouldn't be killed, not even if they courted death. *The Tuaregs meant to take them alive!*

Alexa stared mutely at the chaos of the moonlit oasis before her, paralyzed with fear. Camels lay dead or dying in the sand, innocent victims of bullets from either side. Tents had been overturned. The stew kettle had fallen into the fire, adding the stench of burning meat to the nightmarish scene. She saw her brother fiercely struggling with one heavyset Arab, then suddenly utter a groaning cry and go limp beneath his bludgeoning rifle butt. She saw O'Day likewise silenced, then jug-eared Toussant fold to the sand on his knees and pitch forward on his belly. He lay still.

They were all dead. She was the only one left alive!

She swallowed, trembling all over as a burnoosed Arab gave guttural orders to left and right. With an angry gesture, he pointed to one of the sprawled bodies—Flechette's, she thought—and two of the Arabs dragged the man upright. A third pounded four sharp stakes into the hard dirt about the oasis. A moment more, and Flechette, groaning now as he came to, had been spread-eagled. His arms and legs were stretched taut between the stakes. His wrists and ankles were tightly lashed to them by ropes of camel hair. Meanwhile, the other bodies were dragged unceremoniously to one side, and another tribesman set to guarding them with a curved dagger cradled in his arms.

A guard—for dead men? But surely dead men posed no threat to anyone! And then Alexa saw Keene stir, his arm raised to his head, and she knew with a blinding flash of intuition that not one of them was actually dead. They'd all

115

been scrupulously kept alive, but for what purpose? The answer was obvious, for hadn't Cemal told her that the Tuaregs were masters in the art of torture? Obviously that was what these savages intended, to torture their captives one after the other—!

The realization broke down the woolly walls of befuddlement her mind had erected for her defense. Her belly heaved. Her pulse thundered sickeningly in her ears. Oh, God, she couldn't let Keene go through that! She'd promised Mama. She couldn't let her down, or Keene either, not again. He wouldn't be lying there, facing a drawn-out, agonizing death, had he and his men not been escorting her to safety! It was all her fault, and she had to do something before those bloodthirsty savages killed them all. . . .

O'Day'd screamed something at her, she distantly remembered—something about riding back to the fort? That was it. He'd meant for her to bring them help. She had to try. If they were slaughtered, it would be her fault; their blood would be on her hands. . . .

A curious calm and detachment settled over her as she ducked back inside the tent and crawled across the canvas to the rear side, the one farthest from the Arabs but closest to where Contrary Mary had been tethered. Adrenaline flowed through her veins, giving her courage and a strength of purpose she'd never guessed she possessed before. She scooped out a hollow in the sand, then tugged at the tent's tautly pegged walls until they slackened, leaving an opening big enough for her to crawl under.

A moment later, she was out in the night, the pale sands of the Sahara undulating like bolts of grayed silk before and all about her, tiny stars bright as glimpses of candlelight spied through a tattered curtain in the heavens yawning above.

Thank God, Contrary Mary was still saddled, couched quietly in the shadows of a thornbush chewing her cud, with apparent disregard for the chaotic sounds of battle beyond.

Alexa hoisted her nightgown and scrambled up into the lofty saddle, risking a glance over her shoulder as she dropped safely into it. So far, so good.

"Up, Mary! Come on, up with you, girl!" Alexa whispered.

To her undying gratitude, the cantankerous beast rose up off her knees without preamble, and heaved herself to standing. She yanked on the reins and headed Mary toward the nearest dune, knowing once she was up and over it, she would be completely hidden from the camp by a mountain of sand. The Arabs seemed too busy with their first captive to notice a rider escaping in the other direction! Since there was every chance their attackers had been unaware of her presence with the Legionnaires, the odds of her getting away undetected were better than even. Once out of sight of their camp, she'd throw caution to the winds and ride like the devil back to Fort Valeureux.

"Come on, old girl, you can do it!" she urged the camel. "Just a few more yards, and we're home free—!"

While standing in the bright moonlight, watching Kadar order the prisoners bound hand and foot, Sharif felt a tingling sensation raise the fine hairs at the nape of his neck. A compelling force—something quite beyond his control—made him straighten up and look beyond the ruined camp of the *Franziwas* to the sugary sand hills that encircled it on three sides.

A thrill ran through him as his searching gaze found the woman; a tingling sensation of destiny at last fulfilled.

With strands of her long hair streaming out behind her like a veil upon the night wind, her bare limbs pearlescent beneath the moon and starlight, the woman who had haunted his dreams for half a lifetime rode her camel to the crest of a dune. For a fleeting moment, she remained poised there, a vision spun of milky moonbeams and magic, before she disappeared from his view.

Sharif's ebony eyes blazed with sudden fire.

"Zerdali!" he breathed softly, his voice husky with longing. "At last you have come to me. . . ."

Alexa turned and risked a glance behind her, seeing nothing but the rolling swells of the desert sands at her back, like the

117

enormous troughs of a frozen sea. With a low, triumphant whoop, she gave voice to the giddy surge of relief welling up from deep within her. Thank God, she'd escaped without notice—!

But as she was about to turn back to the moonlit terrain unfolding ahead of her, the wild bubble of exhilaration that had filled her abruptly burst. *Please oh God no no!* An Arab rider had crested the dune at her back!

For a moment, horse and rider were both motionless, a silhouette carved in ebony from the lighter amethyst of the sky and the enormous round lantern of the moon beyond. And then, the dark horse reared up on its haunches, its forelegs pawing air as its rider hauled hard on the reins and looked about him, scanning the desert sands with the piercing eyes of a hawk that sees and understands everything, and to whom nothing of the desert can be hidden.

She felt rather than saw the moment when he spotted her, for it was as if an arrow had sung home to bury itself deep in her breast. Another moment, and the flash of his dark robes and darker horse blurred in her vision as he kicked his steed into a gallop and started after her!

Swallowing a frightened sob, she furiously drummed her heels into her camel's sides, trying to milk still more speed from the gamely loping beast while knowing, deep in her heart, that although prized for its endurance, a camel was not bred for speed, as was the flying Arabian horse of her pursuer. Sand flew in drifts from beneath Mary's broad round hooves, yet it flew with agonizing lack of haste.

"Try, Mary, for God's sake, try!" she panted, flinging her wind-whipped hair away from her face to once again glance over her shoulder. *No!* The Arab was gaining on her! Its passage soundless on the desert sands, the racing hooves of the black horse carried him closer and closer with every second, like a silent ebony shadow swiftly racing the scudding moon across the pale face of the earth. And Mary was tiring. She uttered protesting little grunts and wheezing snorts with every labored stride she took now. Her sides heaved with exhaustion. Her mouth hung open. A few moments more, Alexa sensed, and she would drop. . . .

Her heart lurched in terror as, true to her expectations, Mary faltered, losing her footing as she strained to crest a towering dune. She went down in a flurry of hooves and sand that flung Alexa forcibly from the saddle and into the air. She landed heavily, but the impetus sent her rolling over and over, head over heels, spinning like a hoop until she came to an abrupt halt at the bottom, the breath jolted from her.

For a second, she was too winded to react. But then, opening eyes lidded with sand, she saw to her horror that she'd rolled to a stop but inches away from the prancing hooves of her pursuer's horse!

Sucking in a terrified, shaky breath, she looked up into the face of the rider who towered above her. She glimpsed the wicked gleam of a pair of burning dark eyes from above his concealing veil before, hurriedly scrambling to her feet, her heart pounding as if it would burst from her chest, she took off at a run.

The soft, sun-warmed sand dragged at her bare feet as she tried vainly to outrun him on foot. Her nightgown tangled and flapped about her legs and hampered her progress as if in league with her enemy. Still, she ran blindly on. Nothing could save her now. Her two feet could never outdistance such a magnificent horse! Logically, she knew she couldn't hope to escape him, but she had to try! Her very life depended upon it.

I won't make it easy for that murdering savage! she sobbed silently as she fled, hearing the breath rasping from her lungs like a pair of wheezing bellows upon the cool night air. *Maybe he'll kill me anyway—but I'll be damned if I'll make it easy for the brute! I'll fight him! I'll fight him as long as I draw breath—*

Her sobs were no longer silent but agonizingly loud as the horse drew alongside her. Its hooves worked like dark pistons. Its mane and tail streamed like midnight banners in the wind. Flecks of foam lathered its mouth. She could feel the beast, smell the hot reek of its sweat, sense the brooding, ruthless presence of the man astride him as together, one inseparable, deadly force, they bore down upon her. The man's flowing dark robe whipped about him in the wind, flailing her back like a lash as he leaned low from the saddle to sweep her up before him.

119

She shrieked as she felt a powerful arm coil about her waist and wrest her from the ground. Although airborne for a second or two, she still struggled with blind fury to free herself from that viselike grip, her legs windmilling on air.

"You savage!" she screamed. "You murdering savage! Let me go, damn you!"

She struck out blindly, hammering at any part of either him or his horse that she could strike. She tore at the strong fingers that were clamped about her waist in an effort to break his grip, writhing from side to side in a desperate effort to squirm free of her precarious perch upon the saddle before him and regain the sand and at least a chance of escape. It was no use. Those arms, those steely hands, refused to free her! Her captor simply held her firmly about the waist and let her struggle and struggle and go on struggling until she was no longer screaming curses or wriggling to escape him, but exhausted and weeping bitterly with defeat, huge dry sobs shuddering through her body. Damn him! He had used her very resistance to his advantage, letting her tire herself out!

Sharif al-Azim reined in his lathered horse. His heart was pounding—not from his exertions, but from that peculiar sensation of destiny about to be fulfilled that had prickled through him back at the oasis. He swung a leg over his saddle and lithely dismounted, dragging the woman after him to stand upon the sand at his side. Holding her firmly by one wrist, he swung her about to face him, eager to see her face and learn, once and for all, if she was truly the woman of his dreams. His ebony eyes were aflame with the desire to *know*, once and for all, as he brushed the tangled mane of hair from her face.

A woman grown now.

Beautiful beyond compare.

His beloved, the *houri* who had filled his dreams!

Zerdali—!

Ah, could he in truth have ever doubted it? The woman was none other than she, he saw, and his heartbeat quickened. No other could possess those matchless eyes, twin emerald jewels aglitter now with hatred of him and frustration at her capture. No one but Zerdali could possess such lips as she, a mouth as lush and ripe as the sweetest pomegranate, a mouth destined to

120

know his kisses. The temptation to sample her lips, to drink at last from the sweet wellspring of her mouth, was strong, but Sharif denied himself. She would not welcome his kisses nor embraces, not now, for she eyed him like a tigress, passionate in her hatred of him! So be it. The time would come for them, as it had been destined to come since the moment of their births. . . .

Aware that she was eyeing him with equal, if reluctant, curiosity, he reached up and drew aside the indigo veil that masked his lower face: the *tagilmust* worn by all the men of his tribe to protect the soul. His piercing black eyes were intent on her expression as he showed himself to her. Would she recognize him from *her* dreams, perhaps? he wondered. Would she find his looks as pleasing to her eyes as he found her lovely face and form? For a moment, the proud Tuareg chieftain suffered an agony of doubt.

Alexa sucked in a gasp of disbelief as he drew aside his indigo veil. Dear God, how could that be? It was him again! Her captor was the Tuareg chieftain al-Azim, who'd demanded hospitality at Cemal's oasis camp that night! Even more incredulously, his face was that of the mysterious lover of her dreams! Those hooded, ebony eyes, the lashes impossibly sooty and long under stormy black brows, were *his* eyes, obsidian jewels in a setting of bronze flesh, blue-shadowed at the cheeks. That nose, long and aquiline, that mouth, so hard and unsmiling now, was *his* nose, *his* lips! That handsome, ruthless lean face with its clefted chin and jaw of sculpted granite—yes, they were *his* chin and jaw! She was almost—but not quite—tempted to tear his turban headdress away, and ascertain for herself if his hair was also as dark as the heavens wheeling above them, the unruly halo of glossy, inky curls she remembered from her dreams. . . .

"So, little one," Sharif murmured in his native Tamahaq, a smile curving his hard mouth now, "it is as I thought. We have met and loved a thousand times—in the realms of sleep!"

Alexa gulped as she looked up at him, wondering what it was he had said. Was he threatening her with rape? Threatening to kill her? Torture her? She licked her dry lips, discovering there was gritty sand still clinging to them from her fall.

121

"What is it you want from me?" she began nervously, her throat seeming parched with fear. "I—I have nothing—no camels except that poor beast back there—no horses—no money—nothing! You've chosen the wrong victim this time!"

Sharif, despite having understood every brave word she'd said, made no comment, though secretly this proof of her undaunted spirit gladdened his heart. Giving no sign that he'd understood either her words or their tone, he drew the swirling cloak from his back and draped it around her shoulders, both to conceal the loveliness of her body—only partially hidden from his view by her revealing garment—from others' eyes, and to keep the cold night wind from chilling her.

At once, she flung the cloak angrily aside, scorning his gentle actions which were so at odds with her expectations. Her defiance goaded him to punish her in some way, but to her surprise, her savage captor merely chuckled.

"O, what a woman art thou, Zerdali!" he murmured. "A bride fit to carry the sons of Sharif al-Azim in her womb! Our children will be lions of the desert, my jewel-amongst-women. Hawks of the winds! Princes amongst men!"

Alexa had caught only the familiar term "Zerdali" amidst his soft-spoken comments, and she latched onto it like a dog tossed a juicy bone.

"And I'm not your Zerdali, damn you!" she protested, and before he guessed her intent, she'd sidestepped him and was off and running again.

With the lithe grace of a desert lion himself, Sharif pursued her on foot, bringing her down in a flying leap with his arms fastened about her slender hips. He would have landed heavily upon her, had he not reached out and broken the impact with his palms in the nick of time.

Alexa's darkest fears seemed about to come true as his weight slammed her heavily beneath him onto the sand. Bright moonlight bathed the desert wastes as if it were not night but day. With his face so very close to hers now she could see little golden flecks in the lambent depths of his eyes, like tiny flames! Her breasts were crushed beneath the broadness of his chest, her wrists firmly pinioned above her head by his fingers. Her hips were imprisoned by his lean flanks, his thighs and knees cruelly holding down her legs. She was helpless, at his mercy, as powerless as if bound by thongs of steel.

Beneath his chest, Sharif could feel the softness of her breasts pressed close to his; could discern the wild, frightened tempo of her heart as it throbbed against his ribs. Ah, how her soft lips tempted him! How the lush curves of her female body quickened his desire! Was he wise to deny her body's alluring promise—or but proving himself a fool? By Allah, had he not waited a lifetime for this woman? Should he now postpone the moment he had longed for—or take her here, upon the warm desert sands, claiming her savagely as his woman? he wondered, desire rising fiercely through him. Kadar, Abdul, Akli—they were of the old ways of the Tuareg bands who had roamed the deserts since time began, plundering the caravans, stealing spices, camels, and the fairest of the women to carry away to their secret mountain fortresses, to serve their pleasure in the hidden *hareems*. Should he, Sharif al-Azim, only son of the chieftain Malik ben-Azad, follow blindly the customs of his people—or his heart, which bade him wait?

Alexa scarcely dared to breathe as she lay crushed beneath him, watching the conflicting emotions flicker across that harsh, handsome face like moths flitting about a dark flame. She saw the lust in his smoldering ebony eyes, the indecision in his swarthy, striking face, and then, after what seemed an eternity, the new resolve that gleamed in their obsidian depths.

"Allah has smiled upon you, my beauty!" Sharif declared, grinning wickedly now. He stood, reached down, took her wrists, and yanked her to her feet. "Your 'murdering savage' has spared you—for now!"

That black-eyed demon was laughing at her! How dare he, Alexa thought. What right had he to smile and eye her so scornfully? But then, she quickly realized, as her captor, with the power of life or death over her, he had all the rights he needed!

"You won't get away with this, you animal—you brute!" she said softly, all the vehemence in her heart loaded in her tone. "Major Larousse will find out what happened here tonight. He'll send a patrol out looking for us—and when he does, you'll be sorry!"

But to her disappointment, the man's face was bland and expressionless. He didn't understand her threats, obviously. Perhaps if she shouted?

"Do you hear me, you black-hearted savage? I said the *Franziwas* will be here any minute, looking for us!" She screamed the lie at the top of her lungs, emphasizing the Arab word she'd learned from Cemal.

"*Franziwas?*" Sharif echoed innocently, quirking a dark brow in her direction.

Good. The brute had finally understood her!

"That's right—*Franziwas!*" she agreed with relish, mustering a determined expression she was far from feeling. "The French will be here very soon, with hundreds of reinforcements, you'll see!"

"Pah! *Franziwas*—zzuut!" he said again, and drew his finger across his throat in a violent gesture that needed no translation whatsoever. Not when coupled with his bloodthirsty, pitiless smile.

"Oh, my God!" Alexa whispered, her face blanching in the moonlight.

And then, high and ululating on the desert wind, she heard an inhuman scream of agony.

It was too much, that tortured cry ripping the silence of the hushed sands asunder on a night already fraught with terror. Alexa's mind could withstand no more. With a sigh, her knees gave way. Everything turned black as she crumpled to the sand at Sharif's feet.

Chapter Nine

"*Alexa!*" rasped the voice. "*For God's sake, Alexa, wake up!*"

The urgent whisper penetrated the black depths into which Alexa had plummeted. She opened her eyes, and saw the sky before her. Its ashes-and-charcoal hues were just beginning to lighten with streaks of sulphur and mauve in the east. Sighing, she turned her head and saw walls to the other three sides. Peculiarly, they were of striped cloth, like those of a pavilion or Bedouin tent.

"Cemal?" she mumbled, stretching hugely as she dragged her ragged thoughts together. "Is that you? Are you ready to go on?"

She was disoriented, and for a moment believed herself still en route to Fort Valeureux with the guide, Cemal.

Rubbing her eyes, she sat up, her hands encountering the fuzzy-velvet feel of fringed rugs strewn beneath her, the plump give of silken pillows scattered about her in the gloomy half-light. She shook her head in an effort to clear it. Where was she? Everything seemed foggy, as if she'd been drugged. . . .

"*Sweet Christ, Alexa, wake up! You've got to help me!*"

Keene's voice! But what on earth was he doing here? Wasn't he supposed to be at the fort?

A gurgling shriek shattered the preternatural hush of dawn, sending chills sweeping through Alexa. The shriek was abruptly cut off, and the silence in its wake was somehow even more terrifying.

She was wide awake now, acutely aware of all that had happened moments before she fainted—what was it, an hour, maybe more, ago? She remembered everything only too well now! The Tuaregs had attacked her escort . . . one of their tribesmen had taken her prisoner . . . and that awful cry she'd heard had been her last conscious memory! She swallowed, feeling sick to her stomach! Her knees were trembling as if she had a raging fever, yet she was clammy with dread. Obviously, she was the Arabs' prisoner. What would they do with her?

Remembering suddenly that she'd thought she heard Keene's voice from somewhere close by, she tried moving her arms and legs, and found to her relief that she had not been bound, as she'd seen the other prisoners bound before she'd attempted to ride for help. That devilish brute on the black horse must have believed her too deeply unconscious to bother about tying her.

"Keene?" she whispered softly, then again, louder this time, "Keene! Are you there? Where are you? I can't see you!"

"Thank God! I'm over here, by the side of the tent!"

She crawled in the direction of his voice and raised the striped cloth skirt. Keene lay in the sand just a few feet away, his wrists bound behind his back with camel-hair ropes, his ankles similarly bound. Sweat streamed from his face, slick and shiny in the fading moonlight. His eyes—in that same grayed, ethereal light—were dark with pain and fear.

Wetting her lips, she glanced nervously to left and right. There were many camels and horses tethered off to one side; a number of Tuaregs were some distance away, yelling and arguing excitedly over something in their midst. Flechette, she realized, sickened anew. The Legionnaires—O'Day and the Italian corporal Gianetti, the Frenchman Toussant and another man whose name she couldn't remember—were also bound, but huddled together several yards from where Keene lay. They were being guarded by a Tuareg whose back was to both her and the men. He was straining to watch the torture of the prisoner, judging by the angle of his head.

"Oh, my God!" she whispered hoarsely, tears filling her eyes. "Why, Keene? Why did they attack us? We did nothing to harm them! And that man, Flechette, what did . . . what have they . . . what are they doing to him?" She closed her eyes, unable to voice her fears. "Are they—?"

"Torturing him? Oh, Christ, yes!" Keene confirmed bitterly, his voice breaking. "Didn't you hear those god-awful screams? Good for him, damn his soul! He'd betray his own mother, that one! He told them everything, every damned, lying thing they wanted to hear! He lied, Alex, about the Arab girl and about those two old men that were shot. He told the Tuaregs—oh, sweet Christ—he told them *I* was a partner to it all!"

His excited babbling ceased as he drew a shuddering breath, obviously trying to get a grip on himself. "They said—they said I'm to be kept alive, until they reach their mountain hideout. Then they'll torture and kill me too! Alexa, for the love of God, Alexa, you have to untie me, help me to escape!"

"What do you mean? What was it Flechette told them?"

"My Arabic's not good, but I figured it out from what they were screaming at Flechette. A native girl and her caravan were attacked at an oasis north of here a few days ago. She was raped and beaten, her father and another man killed. She claims their attackers were part of a French Legion patrol! The man she was on her way to marry—Kadar ben-something-or-other his name is—is one of those bastards out there, and he's after blood! They attacked our escort intending to force us to tell them the names of the patrol responsible for what happened that day. Christ, Alexa, Flechette and I were a part of that patrol! I sent him and some of the others to reconnoiter, and when they came back, Flechette seemed—edgy. He had blood on his clothes, scratches. He told me they'd run into a band of Tuaregs and skirmished them, barely escaping with their lives. And like a fool, I believed him! When he—when he couldn't take any more of their torture—when they kept on demanding and insisting that he give them the names of the other men with him—oh, lord, Alexa, he gave them *my name* to shut them up! He lied so they'd let him die!"

He closed his eyes, runnels of sweat glistening in the meager light as they trickled down his face. Beneath his deep tan, he was ashen, she saw, biting her lip.

"I saw what was left of that caravan. Flechette was responsible for that?" She shuddered with revulsion as he nodded, then suddenly remembered a scrap of the peculiar

127

conversation she'd heard between Keene and Flechette concerning the "comforts" to be found at the oasis of Yasmeen, and her distaste for the sly, somehow suspicious manner in which they'd spoken then. What had their crafty smiles, their veiled hints, implied? A sudden, chilling twinge of doubt swept through her, and with it a strong sensation of *déja vu*, as if a single, terrible moment of her life were happening all over again.

"Keene, you didn't—*swear* to me that you didn't!—know anything about what happened to that girl?" God forgive her for asking, she thought with a frisson of self-disgust, but she had to!

Keene's eyes flew open. For a moment, the abject fear in his eyes was gone. A withering contempt took its place. "You'd ask me that, at a time like this?" He moaned. "Oh, Dear God, *you'd* doubt me? Then what hope do I have that *they'll* believe me! None!" he ground out between clenched jaws. "Sweet Christ, you doubted me once, but discovered you were wrong," he moaned hoarsely. "Did you learn nothing from that lesson? Flechette's desperate, can't you see? He's trying to save his own skin by implicating me, I swear it! I'm innocent, but they'll torture me anyway! They won't give a damn whether I tell them the truth or not, those Tuareg bastards. Sweet Jesus, Sis, I'm so afraid! *Help me!*"

His shoulders were heaving. Muffled sobs escaped him despite his clenched jaws. Alexa was aghast, for never in her life before this had she seen her brother cry, not even as a little boy; tears were alien to him. How could she think of refusing to help him? And how could she have doubted him, even for an instant? She couldn't let those—those savages torture and kill him if there was a chance she could help him to escape, however slim that chance was.

She scrambled beneath the folds of the tent, darting a hurried glance to left and right. The Arab guard was still watching the others, his attention diverted. To her right were tethered the camels and horses, and beyond them, nothing but desert and sky.

She sucked in a shaky breath and crawled on her hands and knees to Keene. Her heart was beating so painfully, she feared it would burst from her breast at any minute.

Keene stiffened in terror at the brush of her clammy fingers, then relaxed as she began to work at loosening the knots, tugging and working frantically for what seemed an eternity before the first knot came free. The others, despite her clumsiness, seemed easier, and moments later he was groaning and flexing his numbed arms and hands in partial freedom.

Cautiously, she glanced up, relieved to see the native guard had not turned or altered his position.

"I'll get the other knots—your fingers will be too stiff for a while," she whispered, and at once she began yanking at the ropes lashing his ankles together, her fingers feverish with urgency. "What do we do about the others?" she murmured as she worked. "We can't escape and leave them behind to be tortured!"

"Do we have a choice?" Keene rasped back, surreptitiously moving his legs to restore feeling to them. "Make a move in their direction, and our friend the sentry over there will be down on us like a ton of bricks!"

"And if we don't try, they'll be killed inch by inch! Could you live with yourself, knowing you'd left them behind to die so horribly? You know we can't do that, Keene! There's two of us. Surely we could do *something*. Maybe I could create a scene—to draw their attention—while you released them." In all honesty, she'd rather have run for her life than attempt any such thing, but managed to quell such cowardly urges. She'd have to live with herself afterward.

"All right," Keene agreed with obvious reluctance. "But I think you should be the one to untie the others. My bloody hands are still half-numb! I'll run off their camels. That should keep them busy for a while. Agreed?"

She managed a tremulous smile, though her belly heaved at the thought of braving the Arab guard to untie the Legionnaires. He still lovingly cradled his curved dagger while he egged on the torturer!

"Agreed!" she whispered, her voice almost inaudible.

He smiled, and for a second he was the old Keene, her bronzed and arrogant, incredibly handsome younger brother. "That's my Alex! Go to it, then, old girl, and good luck! Stand by for some Harding 'fireworks'!"

With a nod, she glanced about her, mentally gauging the distance between herself and the other captive Legionnaires while Keene crouched low to the ground and dodged between the tents, headed for the camels. Thirty feet? she wondered. Less? Surely it couldn't be as far as it seemed? And the guard—! What if he should turn and see her before she reached O'Day and the others? She swallowed, aware of the thunder of her pulse in her ears, acutely aware of the risk she was running. What she and Keene intended would surely be punished by swift and merciless death at the hands of the Tuaregs, should they be caught.

Far above, the paling moon took refuge behind a cloud, dimming the last silvery shimmer of her revealing light. The sun was rising, a golden fireball staining the sky sulphur-yellow far in the east. Dawn was nearly breaking. It was now or never, she knew. Her last chance.

She took one step, two—and the guard suddenly yawned and shifted. She froze, exposed in her vulnerable position. If he turned, he couldn't help but see her silhouetted against the pale sands! But the Tuareg only said something scornful or threatening over his shoulder to his captives, and laughed. In the next moment, Flechette started screaming again, screaming horribly over and over, and the guard's head jerked around, his attention at once ghoulishly riveted on the tortured man.

It was awful, that endless screaming, but awful or nay, it served Alexa's purpose. She grasped the folds of her nightgown and dashed barefooted the remainder of the way, dropping down behind where O'Day and Toussant were huddled, and breathlessly squirming the last two or three feet on her belly in the sand until she was directly behind them.

"Don't make a sound," she cautioned the men softly. "I'll untie you, if I can. Confound it! If only we had a knife!"

"My boot! There's a knife inside it!" O'Day rasped. He edged his body around in an attempt to give her access to the weapon.

Moving like a snail, scarcely daring to draw breath, she slipped her hand down inside his boot and drew forth the cold length of steel. O'Day muttered a prayer of thanks as she sawed through the bonds at his wrists, then did likewise for Toussant, but both men wisely kept their arms behind their backs to maintain the illusion that they were still bound.

"'Tis grand ye are, colleen!" praised O'Day from the corner of his mouth.

"Ah, *oui*, what a woman of courage the little *mademoiselle* is! Give me the knife now, and I will free Gianetti and St. Pierre, and take care of our watchful friend, yes?" jug-eared Henri Toussant hissed, giving her an encouraging smile.

She nodded. "Here, take it. My brother's seeing to a diversion. When it comes, we've got to be ready!" She didn't need to explain what it was they had to be ready to do. They already knew, for their only options were to fight for escape and a chance at life, or certain, lingering death.

But then, paling with horror, Alexa saw the Tuareg chieftain who'd captured her break away from the others and stride off alone, headed for the tent she'd left to free Keene! In another second or two, he'd find her gone and sound an alarm, then the game would be up for all of them! Unless—?

An agony of indecision made burning heat and freezing cold sweep alternately through her body. But in her heart, she knew from the first she had no choice. It was one life versus five lives, and the scales tipped heavily in favor of the five. . . .

She began to scrabble backward on her hands and knees, away from the men, and in the final second before she acted, an incredulous O'Day saw the danger, realized her plan, and hissed frantically, "No, ye blessed little fool!"

But it was too late; too late even as he said the words, for Alexa had straightened up and was running, making no attempt to conceal herself as she tore through the very heart of the ruined camp, heading away from the Legionnaires, away from the camels, and away from Keene. She was screaming at the top of her lungs, her flowing hair and sheerly clad body drawing the eye of every Tuareg in sight as she did so—exactly as she'd planned.

At once, the chieftain spotted her. His black eyes narrowed first in disbelief, then in fury.

"You, Selim!" he barked to one of his men, gripping him by the shoulder, "After her! I'll have your cursed head if another has harmed her before you catch her!"

The youth grinned and hared after the slim girl, easily outdistancing the others who'd thought to catch the fair-skinned beauty for themselves. He left them behind one by one as his booted feet gobbled up the sandy expanse in great leaping strides.

"By Allah, woman, you're a gazelle, and swift indeed! But 'tis no use to flee, pretty one!" he panted. "For Selim is fond of his head, and will bring you safe to his lord, untouched by other hands!"

The tone of his voice, if not his meaning, registered on Alexa, but served as a goad rather than a means of slowing her down! Surely any minute Keene's diversion would be underway, and the youth would then be forced to return to camp to help his fellows regain their mounts! If only she could keep running for a little while longer!

Hurry! Hurry! Hurry! The words, screamed a litany in her brain, were the impetus that kept her going even when a cramp knifed through her side and squeezed fiery agony into her lungs. Her bare feet flew over rocks and thorns, yet she felt no pain. It was as if they were no longer a living part of her flesh, but relentless, pumping machines, running, running, running until they could run no more.

"Uggah!" Her arms flew up as she turned her ankle on a small rock and fell heavily forward.

Selim—pounding doggedly along close behind her—growled an oath as he, in turn, tripped over her legs as she fell! Together in a tangle of limbs, they scuffled, but Alexa rolled free first and sprang to her feet. She began raining punches down over Selim's head and shoulders as if they were hailstones, gasping with pain at the new agony she discovered shooting through her ankle when her foot touched the ground, partially crippled yet still frantic to escape him. One fist connected solidly with his eye; the other smacked full into his mouth. A lifetime spent trying to control her temper and refrain from physical violence was forgotten in a single breath as her instincts for survival surfaced. She couldn't run anymore, not on her injured ankle, but damn it, she was far from cowed yet! *For God's sake, Keene, hurry, hurry!* she sobbed silently, battering the Arab's head with all the strength she could summon.

"By Allah, thou she-devil!" Selim rasped, his bruised eye watering. He tasted blood on his tongue from where his teeth had snapped together on it. He grabbed for slender wrists that would not be still; for a slimly curved ivory body that would not be held fast, but instead squirmed like a scorpion pinned by a rock! The laughter of his companions suddenly reached the mortified Selim, reddening his ears, adding to his determination to overpower her. So the others would mock him, eh? Then by the Prophet, their laughter would be brief and hollow! he vowed, and knotted his fingers in the girl's flying hair, jerking her backward to her knees. But she wriggled sideways and swung at him despite his grip, clawing for his eyes, yanking the cloth of his turban headdress forward over them so that, for all practical purposes, he was now blinded! More laughter ran in his ears.

"Daughter of an obstinate she-camel!" Selim ranted, unable to see and trying to tear the cloth away without losing his grip on her hair. "I shall yet turn you over to my lord Sharif, and bid him welcome his spitting tigress!"

"Ah, she is too spirited for thee, my young friend!" jeered one of the Tuareg band.

"Tame her, Selim, my brother—lest she tear out thy liver and eat it alive!"

"For the honor of all men, lad, catch the green-eyed witch, and swiftly!"

"And when you have, hand her over to me!" roared another boastfully. "For I have mastered the thousand-and-one caresses to make this tigress purr! I will teach her her woman's place—beneath a man!"

"Indeed, my friend? And how will that be, since it's said you've yet to teach that place to your own wives?" sneered another.

The men all roared with bawdy laughter at the boaster's crestfallen expression.

"Enough!" commanded a stern voice at their backs, and to a man they turned to see their chieftain, al-Azim, standing behind them.

He cut a commanding figure with his flowing dark cloak

swinging from broad shoulders, his massive fists planted on lean hips. His long, muscular legs, clothed in baggy silken breeches tucked into kid boots at the knees, were braced apart on the stony ground. His magnificent ebony eyes were crackling with anger above the *tagilmust*.

"You, Selim—bring the woman to me. The rest of you, there is yet much work to be done, if we would break camp and turn our faces to al-Azadel before the sun climbs high in the sky!"

Sheepish now, the men nodded and began moving back to the camp under the forbidding eyes of their leader. Selim gave Alexa a triumphant smile and a shove in the small of the back to get her moving in his chieftain's direction.

She responded with a muttered curse and an icy glare that would have made a lesser man quail, and began gamely limping toward Sharif, with Selim prodding her from time to time to keep her moving. Any second now, surely, she thought, Keene would begin stirring things up, and then the sparks would fly! This hateful boy—and his doubly hateful chieftain—would find out very soon the foolishness of trying to capture the brave men of the Legion—and Alexandria Harding!

When she was standing before the Tuareg lord, she tossed her wild, tangled mane of chestnut-colored hair over her shoulders, planted her fists on her hips exactly as he was doing, and met his glittering black eyes with her own crackling green ones without flinching.

A reluctant smile twitched at the corners of Sharif's mouth, but was swiftly hidden. "Brave little fool!" he growled in disgusted admiration. "You are fortunate my men did not kill you!"

She gave no sign that she'd understood a word of his language, of course, but continued to meet his eyes glare for glare. By Allah, her green eyes were challenging his to be the first to weaken and look away, he suddenly realized, amazed that she was recklessly testing his authority over her, and in so doing threatening his authority over his men. His long-awaited Zerdali or nay, he could not permit that!

Without further words, he impatiently stepped closer and grasped her wrist, hauling her after him as he strode back toward the tent, dragging her along behind him so swiftly, her feet scarcely touched the sand. She hoped and limped after him, gasping at the pain repeatedly shooting through her ankle when it touched the hard ground, but her captor was pitiless. He neither looked back in her direction nor slowed his pace until they had returned to the oasis. The *sheik*, Kadar, at once strode forward to meet them.

"The *Franziwa* cur is dead, Allah curse him," Kadar announced with relish, "and the sun not yet fully risen! Pah! A Tuareg or a Bedouin would not have died so easily nor so swiftly as that pariah dog!" he observed with contempt.

Sharif nodded soberly, but with none of the gloating satisfaction of his friend in his eyes. "So be it! Death was a fitting punishment for what the *Franziwa* did. No true man would slay two helpless travelers unprovoked, nor rape and beat a helpless girl-child. That is not the way of the warriors of the desert, for all that the white men call us savages! Our young maidens wander alone and unafraid, herding their flocks in the desert unprotected, fearing no man of Islam will violate their innocence, do they not? *Ewellah*, let the jackals and the vultures fight over his worthless corpse!" he said finally. "And the other—what of the *Englesy* dog?"

"Ah, that one yet lives, my lord. He has not been harmed, by my orders. His men will be released to survive as best they can in the desert, but the yellow-haired sergeant will be our 'guest' until we return to al-Azadel. There, before our people, I intend to bring Muriel forward so that she may accuse her attacker to his face. She will show the people proof of his sins, and all eyes will see and all hearts will know that this man and no other is the guilty one. Then shall I slay the *Englesy*, inch by inch. His ears and his eyes will fall victim to my sword. He will suffer a thousand small deaths before he draws his last breath. His death will prove to all who are a witness to it that Kadar ben-Selim is a man of honor. A man who will avenge the wrongs done to him and to all his followers, without pity or mercy." His eyes shifted coldly to the captive girl still held in Sharif's grip, who glowered defiantly back at him. "I claim this captive *bint* also, my lord!" he added, eyeing Alexa with unconcealed contempt.

"By what right?" demanded Sharif, taken aback by Kadar's

135

announcement. "Was it not I who rode her down when she fled across the desert? I who took the woman captive? Nay, Kadar! By the laws of the desert, she is my prize!"

"Not so, my lord Sharif. She is the sister of the *Englesy* dog—the Frenchman swore it!—and as such her life belongs to me. Before he dies, her brother will be forced to watch his sister dishonored, as my bride was dishonored by him! He will watch, he will hear her screams—and yet be helpless to save her!"

"No. I forbid it!" Sharif countered softly, yet with a grating edge of steel to his voice. "The Frenchman's death and the death of the other English cur will avenge your betrothed's kinsmen. But the girl is mine, and mine she will remain!"

"She is of his blood. Her fate is mine to decide, according to the ancient laws of our people. Two have been slain, and two will die in their place. But the lost innocence of the maid who was promised me by her father from birth remains unavenged! For this reason, I have greater claim to the girl! Through her shall I avenge the loss of my honor. I'll remove this blemish from the name of Kadar ben-Selim, and from the daughter of Hussein! 'An eye for an eye,' it is written, O my chieftain. Would you go against the sacred writings of the Prophet?"

"I go against nothing! The girl is innocent of wrongdoing, my brother. She's the white woman that Noura told us of—the green-eyed one who offered our women help and kindness at the oasis of Yasmeen. Would you harm one who has sought only to help our people in your thirst for vengeance?"

Kadar laughed harshly. "By Allah, you speak eloquently in her defense, my lord Sharif! But is it truly her innocent, kind heart that compels you—or the fair, fresh curves of her body? She is a woman of rare beauty, my lord, beauty and fire! I say her beauty has blinded your eyes to what is right, and deafened your ears to my cries for justice and vengeance!"

"Never fear, justice will be served, Kadar," Sharif assured him sternly. "Yet its hand will be tempered by mercy, where mercy is warranted, as will the hand of vengeance. As for the girl, she is mine! Argue with me no more, for I have spoken," he warned.

"Pah, Brother, I fear for you! Mercy makes a fool of justice,

136

and of the man who, in his misguided wisdom, offers it! We will speak more of rights and justice later, when we return to al-Azadel. Meanwhile, keep the woman safe in your care, my friend, if it pleases you to do so. Your lord father will decide her fate fairly and wisely when we return to the mountains, and unlike you he will do so without the hot fire of lust heating his loins and marring his judgment! I will abide by his decision, Brother. Will you?"

"He is my chieftain too, Kadar ben-Selim, as well as my father. Do I have a choice? I cannot . . ."

Meanwhile, Alexa had given up her useless struggles. She now stood quietly, making good use of the brief respite to take the weight off her throbbing, swollen ankle while the two men spoke together heatedly. She didn't understand a word of what they were saying, but guessed they were arguing about her, squabbling over her fate. Swallowing, she decided she wouldn't even think about that! There were too many uncomfortable possibilities, and she was far too frightened to consider any one of them without giving way to tears and panic. Instead, she bit her lip, gnawing at it anxiously. What on earth had happened to Keene's diversion? Had he been apprehended before he could bring it off? Or—Lord, no!—perhaps been killed while trying to escape? And what of O'Day and Toussant and the rest of the prisoners? Where were they? The Legionnaires and their guard had disappeared.

She was suddenly aware that there was great activity all about her on the part of the tribesmen who'd attacked them. In the golden light of dawn, spilling like melted honey across the oasis sands, she saw that the Tuaregs were burying their dead in the sand, breaking their hastily erected camp, bundling up tents and rugs and loading them onto camels, covering cooking fires with sand, filling goatskins from the watering hole. Obviously, the band of desert brigands intended to move out, and very soon, by the look of things. What would happen to her, to all of them, before they left?

A shout broke through her uneasy thoughts, and she saw one of the camel-tenders running toward them. He began talking rapidly and gesticulating wildly, pointing from the camels and then to the distant dunes. Whatever he was saying made the other man—Kadar, was it?—furiously angry. With what sounded like an oath, he began running for his white racing camel, shouting orders to some of the other men to follow suit as he went. Several of them swiftly mounted up and rode out after him, brandishing daggers or stolen carbines above their heads. Thank God! Keene must have escaped, she realized with a fierce surge of hope and elation rising through her. He was free! Obviously they'd only just discovered his disappearance! But, if that were so, why hadn't he—

A soft, wet animal nose nuzzled and blew against her bare shoulder, nudging her off-balance and interrupting her turbulent train of thought. Glancing over her shoulder, she saw that the chieftain's black stallion had been brought forward by a servant, saddled and bridled. Despite everything, she was mildly surprised at the gentleness of the magnificent animal's gesture toward her, for a lifetime's love of horses had taught her that stallions were rarely affectionate creatures.

"Zerdali!" commanded the chieftain. "We ride!"

She raised puzzled eyes to his; green eyes muddied with confusion, pain and fear commingled. But in the next moment, Sharif had grasped her about the waist and tossed her up onto the stallion's ornate, crimson-leather saddle, before springing lithely up behind her, and his meaning was clear.

As he mounted, his tanned hands brushed against her breasts as he leaned forward to gather the tasseled reins in his fists. On reflex, she recoiled and shrank from his touch and from the hard warmth of his broad chest pressed against her shoulder and arm where she sat sideways before him. But his arm curled around her, tightening its grip possessively, asserting his mastery over her. He'd never let her go, never, she realized, fighting back tears. She could tell by the possessive hold he had on her that he considered her his property, to do with as he wished.

With a whoop, her captor kicked the stallion into a gallop, and like a dark arrow it shot forward. She gave a startled cry and, despite her aversion to him, gripped the Tuareg's corded arm to steady herself. The feel of rippling muscles and warm, hard male flesh braided tautly over bone beneath the cloth of his full sleeves made her hurriedly release him again the very moment she'd regained her balance. She heard him chuckle wickedly, his breath rising, warm and intimate, against her tumbling hair as they galloped swiftly across the desert sands. Other riders on laden camels or horses joined them as they rode, and soon their swift-moving caravan drew level with and quickly overtook the sorry men of her escort, who were doggedly trudging along on foot.

The Legionnaires were a pitiful lot now. They no longer wore the Legion *képis* that would have served to shield their heads and throats from the scorching desert sun. They'd also been stripped of their precious canteens, their food and water, their tents for shade, and their weapons. Even their sturdy leather boots had been taken. Without these necessities, they were doomed men, as Kadar had fully intended. They'd not taken part in the tragedy at the oasis of Yasmeen, but neither had they lifted a finger to prevent it, he had reasoned, and for this omission, they would die a slow death beneath the broiling sun. Only the mercy of Allah could spare them now!

The Arabs jeered and reviled the men of the Legion as they passed them by, brazenly leading the abandoned Legionnaires' stolen camels and mules behind their own.

"O'Day!" Alexa screamed desperately as she spotted the Irishman among the others. "O'Day, help me!"

"There's nothing I can do, colleen!" O'Day yelled sadly as the black stallion thundered past them, the sand churned up by its flying hooves spraying over the sorry handful of men. "Yer brother left us to them, girl! Sweet Jaysus! The black-hearted bastard betrayed his own flesh 'n' blood, t' the savages!"

With a sickening sense of betrayal, Alexa realized O'Day's screamed words were true: she had waited for her brother's diversion, but even as she'd risked her own life to save him and the others, he'd coldheartedly ridden away to save his own skin.

Now only the harsh Sahara and an unknown, terrifying future at her captor's hands lay ahead of her, growing ever closer beneath the stallion's flying black hooves.

Chapter Ten

The hours blurred and ran together. Alexa lost all sense of time and direction, for each hour that passed, each mile they traveled, was like the last. Endless azure skies canopying endless wastes of stone and sand followed still more stone and sand.

The sun beat down like a fiery, blind white eye. Waves of heat distorted distance and shapes, shimmering over the baking land like curving columns of watery glass. Occasionally, the black silhouette of a ruined *kella* or ancient watchtower broke the monotony of the flat plains or rolling dunes, or the remains of a crumbling, abandoned village, half buried in sand, lay beneath the sun like the bleached bones of some long-dead animal. But other than that, the terrain remained monotonously unchanged mile after mile and mile.

The faint hope Alexa had harbored that Major Larousse would learn of the Tuaregs' attack on her escort and that he and his Legionnaires would come riding to her rescue dwindled miserably in those first hours of her captivity, and finally died. It could be days, perhaps weeks, before André learned that his men had disappeared, and she with them. Perhaps the only clues to what had happened to them all would be the bodies of O'Day and the others, found in the sand, for it was doubtful if any of the Legionnaires would survive the desert to carry the tale back to Fort Valeureux. And even if—by some miracle—one should, the news would arrive too late to help her. André would never find her now. They'd gone too far.

The pace of the band slowed after a while, when they caught up with another, smaller caravan. This one included in its

140

number the Bedouin girl Muriel and the other women Alexa had met with her at the oasis of Yasmeen. The two caravans combined to form one larger one, but of the *sheik* Kadar and his followers who had ridden in pursuit of her brother, there was no sign. Alexa was glad. She feared the Arab chieftain with the angry black eyes and the hawklike nose out of all proportion to the little she'd seen of him, for she suspected from his expression when he'd looked at her so intently that he hated her and meant her nothing but harm. The young Tuareg chieftain upon whose horse she rode, though feared almost as much, seemed the more even-tempered of the two. She decided she'd prefer to stay with him, if forced to make a choice, although it was unlikely she'd be granted any say in her fate. She suspected al-Azim had even argued with the one called Kadar to keep her for himself, though the suspicion gave her cold comfort, since his purpose in doing so was obviously not to admire her from afar! Her stomach turned over with dread. She was alone, and at the mercy of these veiled and frightening desert pirates. What would they do with her—what?

The Arab girl Muriel, her bruises still apparent but faded now, gave her a shy yet reassuring smile of greeting as Alexa slithered wearily down from the back of the horse at Sharif's command to dismount. But there was no opportunity for communication between the two of them then, for her captor wasted no time in dismounting himself and chivying her into one side of a hastily erected goatskin tent, posting guards before it, and indicating harshly that she was to rest before he left her alone.

To her surprise, she fell into exhausted sleep the moment her head touched the soft rugs beneath it, waking only when the blazing disk of the desert sun had already faded from the sky and, in place of its brilliance, dark panther-shadows again stalked the sands on inky paws.

She saw through the tent opening that the moon had risen while she slept, attended by a sprinkling of stars. She also glimpsed the bulky silhouettes of the two men, seated cross-legged before the tent, whom Sharif had earlier set there to prevent her escaping. Fragrant camel-dung cooking fires had been lit, and the aroma of roasting bread and pungent *samn*, clarified butter, mingled with the smoky, herbal scents of burning dung that wafted on the cooling night air.

Soon after, Muriel ducked beneath the cloth partition that divided the tent into two areas—one for the *hareem*, or womenfolk, the other for the men—bearing a shallow bowl of food. Within it there was rice with pieces of savory lamb, honeyed dates, and flat bread. She also brought a goatskin of *léban*, foaming fresh milk, still warm from the camel.

With a smile of thanks to the girl, Alexa forced herself to eat well, despite having little appetite. Her fears for her future at the hands of the Tuaregs had effectively quelled any true hunger pangs she might have possessed, but if she proved brave enough—or desperate enough—to attempt an escape in the future, given the opportunity, she would need all her strength and wits about her. She forced herself to chew and swallow, chew and swallow, with this hope in mind.

While she ate, Muriel gestured to her foot, obviously aware that she had wrenched it trying to escape. How did the girl know? Had the chieftain told her of it? Alexa wondered. She drew up the hem of her nightgown, revealing a badly swollen ankle. It had turned a puffy black and blue in places during her travels.

Clucking her sympathy, Muriel left the tent, returning moments later with a paper lantern in one hand, which she hung from the tent's skin roof. She carried a bundled garment and a vermilion wooden chest containing her mirror, her combs, her bangles, her simples, and other precious items.

Kneeling at Alexa's feet, she gently massaged her injured foot with a sweet-smelling ointment drawn from the potions in her precious chest, warming it in her palms by the lamp's tiny flicker of light and heat. Afterward, she bound a slim length of soft goatskin firmly about the ankle and fastened it in place with narrow hemp cords, which she cut into serviceable lengths using a small, sharp dagger taken from the leather braid at her waist. When she was finished, she placed the knife down upon a pillow, rocked back on her heels, and smiled shyly.

Alexa saw the dagger lying there, and her heartbeat quickened. Her mouth grew dry with anxiety. Could she? Dare she? Oh, Lord, she had to do *something!* To meekly accept her

142

captivity and its consequences was unthinkable, but she was terrified of what her abductors might do should she offer any resistance! Flechette's horrible, prolonged death, the threat of being skinned alive inch by agonizing inch as he had been, was still sharp and fresh in her memory. Fear, she'd learned, was far more persuasive than the ephemeral promises and possible rewards of courage. Yet, if the end result was to be the same, her death—regardless of whether she accepted her capture meekly or fought against it to her last breath—surely it would be better to fight?

Muriel's gentleness proved too much for Alexa to bear, following so close on the heels of the attack on their camp and her harrowing capture. To her dismay, she suddenly burst into tears. Great, heaving sobs tore from her, out of control. Once started, she couldn't stop. Scalding tears rolled down her cheeks as she rocked back and forth, choking with misery.

She felt Muriel's slim arms go about her as the younger Arab girl pressed her head to her small bosom, crooning softly all the while as if she were cradling a babe, and combing her hair through with her slim fingers in an effort to reassure her.

"Hush, now, hush, my sister. No one is going to harm you, I swear it upon the Beard of the Prophet, Zerdali!"

But Alexa could not understand her comforting words. She clung to the Bedouin girl and wept uncontrollably until she felt numb and empty inside: emptied of the entire gamut of her emotions, so that only a brittle shell remained encasing a single, compelling desire that now overrode her former fear. The fierce determination to escape her captor . . .

Muriel brushed her tear-dampened hair away from her wet cheeks at length, murmuring shushing sounds. She slipped a full hooded cloak of some dark cloth over Alexa's head, smoothing its folds down about her. As she did so, Alexa seized the opportunity she'd been waiting for and quickly palmed the girl's small dagger, her actions concealed by the flowing folds of the hooded robe. She hated to take advantage of the Bedouin girl's gentleness and trust, but what choice did she have? Survival must be her only consideration now. She had no intention of using the wicked little weapon she'd stolen against Muriel, but anyone else who attempted to lay hands upon her would discover she was far from helpless! She had no intention of becoming the victim of the Tuareg chieftain's lust.

"Come, you have wept long enough, Zerdali, my sister," Muriel urged. "Now you must dry your eyes and look to what the future holds for you, instead of yearning for the past. It is Allah's will that you are here, and no mortal man or woman may change His will, nor the whims of Kismet. Soon we will turn our faces to the mountains of al-Azadel. We will ride the night long, and it will grow very cold. You will need this covering to keep you warm, yes, my sister?" She indicated the garment, and made a shivering motion, pointing to the darkened night sky beyond the tent as she did so.

Alexa caught her meaning and nodded, clasping Muriel's hand warmly between her own to show her thanks, smothering a stirring of guilt. The small dagger felt heavy where she'd hidden it, slipped into the wide hems of the robe, but the girl smiled in delight that she'd understood her actions and obviously suspected nothing.

"Good, very good! We are able to understand each other a little without need for words! Soon we will both be newcomers to al-Azadel, but it will not seem so strange there if we two are already friends, think you not? From the moment you were kind to me at the oasis of Yasmeen, I knew you were not like those *Franziwas*, who hate the God of Islam and my people. You are good and gentle, Zerdali, as are many *Englesy*, who have often proven friends to my people in the past. Your heart is filled only with sweetness and caring. That terrible day at the oasis of Yasmeen, I was ashamed and hurting. You showed me kindness and hospitality worthy of a Bedouin woman, who shares whatever little she might have, and gladly, with those less fortunate. That is why I do not believe what my cousin Selim has told my mother—that you are the sister of the *Englesy* dog who harmed me! But if, Allah forbid it, it is truly so, then I forgive you. Although you may be of one seed, you are not one in heart."

"I'm sorry, I don't understand you!" Alexa cried softly, shrugging in frustration. She held out her hands, palms upward, and shook her head.

Muriel smiled, patting her cheek. She was fascinated by her

new friend's milky complexion, her golden-chestnut hair, and her slanted eyes which, though strangely green like a *jinn*'s, were nonetheless very gentle and sad.

"Ah, in truth, I know you do not speak my tongue, Zerdali! But the language of friendship and love is not of the tongue, but of the heart. For now, we understand each other well enough. The other will follow in time. Come," she said, rising to her feet and gesturing to Alexa to follow her. "I have much work to do. I must take down this tent and see it securely loaded upon my camel, and do the same with the rugs and pots before we ride on. Meanwhile, you will ride ahead with the chieftain, Sharif al-Azim. Do you know, he has forbidden any other to have the care of you, and forbidden even to leave you in the hands of the *hareem!* It is obvious he looks upon you with favor, Zerdali, as a woman to be prized, for all that you are an unbeliever! Is that not an honor?"

So saying, Muriel led an uncomprehending Alexa by the hand outside in the moonlight to where Sharif was already mounted on his prancing stallion. He looked down at her, robed now in the concealing folds of the hooded Bedouin *jelabia* from head to toe, then nodded his approval. He said something teasing to the Arab girl before leaning low in the saddle and sweeping Alexa up into his arms, and Muriel giggled and covered her mouth with her hands.

Sharif lifted her and brought her close against the warmth and broadness of his torso. His arms went about her once again to gather up the reins, so close their bodies were pressed tightly together in an intimate fashion that made Alexa tremble with apprehension. This time, when his fingertips again grazed the peaks of her breasts above her cloak, she knew it was no accident on his part! That lecherous rogue! His fingertips had lingered far too long against her bosom for it to be accidental, and to her dismay, her sensitive nipples stirred, swelling into hard, tight buds against her clothing. She heard him chuckle wickedly, deep in his throat, at her body's involuntary—treacherous!—response.

"Have you no shame, no decency in you at all? Stop it, you savage devil!" she hissed. "Don't you dare touch me so intimately again!" Furious, she slapped his hand away. But he

145

only laughed deeply once again and drew her still closer to him, so close she could feel the throb of his heartbeat against her arm; feel the rising heat of his hard body seeping even through the folds of their clothing; smell the warm, rugged, overtly male scent of him sharp in her flaring nostrils. His scent was strangely disturbing to her senses, and somehow familiar, she fancied, though why it should be, she had no idea.

"Ah, you scorn me now, *habibah,* but soon you will sigh for my touch!" Sharif threatened huskily against her hair, knowing full well the effect his warm, moist breath would have upon her as he murmured in her ear. "Soon Zerdali will beg for the honey of my lips on hers, and for much more that I will teach her!"

She glanced up at him, scowling, infuriated by his taunting tone—and even more so by her body's strange reaction to his moist breath in her ear. Prickly gooseflesh had risen in tingling waves up and down her arms and trickled down her spine, making her arch against him for one brief, reckless moment, before hurriedly shrinking away.

Starlight glinted in her green eyes as she hissed back at him, "I don't understand your heathen tongue, but for all that I've a fair idea of what you're threatening me with, given the chance! I swear you won't get away with it, you—you lawless savage! Major Larousse will come looking for me, and when he does, you'll wish to your heathen god that you'd nev—"

She was destined never to finish her outburst, for Sharif could withstand his impulses no longer. He caught her chin between his thumb and forefinger, jerked her head roughly backward beneath his, and silenced her lips with his hungry mouth, draining the breath and the words from her with his kisses and making her eyes widen into round, green pools of astonishment at the same time.

Hungrily, he kissed her, parting her lips with his hard, demanding mouth and greedily exploring deep between them with his insistent tongue. He'd planned only to shock her into silence with a gentle touch of his lips to hers, yet once he started, all restraint fled him. He kissed her passionately, as a man starved too long for his beloved's honeyed lips kisses, his mouth hot and ardent and savagely sweet.

Alexa's stunned senses reeled under this fresh assault. She

screamed against his hateful mouth and tried to shove him away, her palms thrusting with all her strength at his broad chest. But his hold only tightened about her, arching her pliant and helpless across his horse and across his corded thighs until he had drunk his fill of her sweetness, and swallowed her furious protests on his own warm breath.

When he at last released her, she was breathless and for once struck dumb, the curses and threats she had wanted to scream at him when freed temporarily forgotten in her shock. Her breasts heaved. A pulse throbbed in the pit of her belly. Her mouth worked soundlessly as she stared at him, and she furiously rubbed her knuckles across it to rid it of the taste of him.

He smiled, his expression wicked. His midnight eyes glinted roguishly in the silvery starlight, the tiny golden flecks in their inky depths flared up like embers fanned into flame. The flash of his teeth was startlingly white against his swarthy complexion as he grinned down at her, and she frowned, suddenly breathless. His smile had pricked a dormant memory in her mind, as if he had grinned down at her in just that rascal's way a lifetime ago. For a fleeting second she tried to hold on to the image, to identify it with someone she had known who resembled him in some way, but then in the twinkling of an eye, it was lost, and he was again a hated stranger and her captor.

"So, I have found a way to silence you, eh, Zerdali?" he exclaimed aloud, obviously pleased with himself. "By Allah, it is a most pleasant way to silence you too, for there is honey on your lips although there are aloes on your tongue—and I, alas, am cursed with a sweet tooth!"

Still chuckling, he rose in the saddle and signaled to his band with a flourish of his upraised arm. "Al-Azadel awaits! Turn your faces to home, my people! We ride!" he commanded, and then they were off once again, traveling on over the moonwashed, ghostly pallor of the sands to an unknown destination, while the lingering sensation of his stolen kisses branded her lips like fire.

They rode throughout the cool of that night. Despite Alexa's determined efforts to stay wide awake and defend herself against that brute's advances—or against any other attack he might launch against her—the steady, monotonous rhythm of the stallion's smooth gait rocked her to sleep as if she were in a baby's down-lined cradle. Her eyelids drooped, the lashes trembling upon her pale-rose cheeks like tawny butterflies at rest upon the petals of a velvet rose. Her head bowed like a lovely, weighty blossom upon a weary stem. She sighed heavily and sank back upon her captor's chest, her body loose and relaxed against him in slumber.

An overwhelming tenderness swept through Sharif as she leaned against him, her fear of him forgotten in sleep. Carefully, so as not to waken her, he shifted his position somewhat in the saddle to better support her weight upon his chest. Her hair, dark as copper in the moonlight, was uncovered against the cool zephyrs, and so he pulled up the hood of her cloak and settled it warmly about her, brushing her pale brow with his lips before covering her.

"Sleep, my little apricot," he murmured, smiling fondly down at her as she slept exhausted in his arms. "Our journey is yet a long one, and sleep will heal and strengthen thee. The past hours have been hard for you to bear, I know, little one, but soon your painful memories will fade, Zerdali, I swear it. Newer, happier memories will replace them." He regarded her silently for several moments before speaking again. "One day, you will come to love me, as it was foretold long ago by the astrologer."

Those predictions, made so long ago, came back to him in the cool starry night, as clearly as if the voice of bearded old Maimun murmured them in his ears even now.

If he closed his eyes, he was a lad of twelve again, puffed up with all the arrogance of youth and imminent manhood, but trembling like a babe for all that as he waited in the house of the Turkish astrologer Maimun. The walls of his house, Sharif recalled, had been made beautiful with tile murals of the twelve signs of the zodiac, and with gold-veined marble maps of the heavens and the stars, dazzling and mysterious.

Maimun had greeted the lad's return to his household gravely and with great respect, gesturing him to be seated upon cushions and partake of coffee as if he warranted the respect of a grown man, rather than a stripling boy. Sharif had politely accepted. Not until the Eastern formalities of host and hospitality had been dispensed with, and the required three cupfuls of coffee drained at last, had Maimun unrolled the carefully inked star charts he'd prepared, and spread them across the low brass table between them.

"It was a most interesting challenge to cast the horoscopes of yourself and the little *Englesy* maiden, young master," he'd said at length, scanning the circles described on the heavy parchment and the scribblings of sidereal calculations, conjunctions, and trines clustered all about them on the parchment before him. "Pisces, the maid's sign, and yourself, the sign of Scorpio—ah, both interesting, complex sun-signs indeed! You are certain the times and places of birth were correct for both of you, hmm?"

"*Ewellah*, learned Master Maimun!" Sharif had replied, a little impatiently. "The girl's nurse had no doubt of the time and place of her birth, and my honored father no doubt of my own. Please, sir, tell me what you've learned!"

Maimun had apparently taken pity on the anxious young fellow and without further ado had ceased his teasing delaying tactics and solemnly begun:

"It is written in the stars that the desert hawk and his young will once again rule the mountains of al-Azadel!" he had begun his prophecy, and shivers of anticipation had danced up and down Sharif's spine. "I see great success in your houses, a success that will last for two decades. Twenty years will pass in which you and your lord father, the *amir*, will rule in peace and prosperity, guiding the Imochagh to progress through new ways of life in which bloodshed will have no part. Your daggers will be sheathed. The old ways of robbing the desert caravans for their riches will come to an end for the al-Malik. New ways of livelihood will be embraced. Peaceful trade with others not of your tribe will be undertaken to south, east , and west. The cultivation of crops and their irrigation will be studied, and the knowledge gainfully employed. The breeding and building of strong, healthy herds to provide meat and milk for your people and to sell to others will flourish and bring great prosperity to

149

your kingdom. Do you understand?"

"*Ewellah!* It will be so, for it is my father's dearest wish that the al-Malik should profit from such ventures!" Sharif had exclaimed, his dark eyes shining.

Maimun had smiled indulgently, long accustomed to the awe of others at his skills of prophecy, which had often been proven uncannily accurate.

"Peace will prevail," the astrologer had continued more soberly, "but will last only until the sons of your enemies are grown to manhood. These enemies are ones who are tied to thee by the bonds of blood.

"Then, in the month following Ramadan, shortly after the Night of Power in the twentieth year, there will come a period of deep unrest; a time of both light and darkness, sorrow and joy, for both you and your people, young master. Times are always unsettled when the planets Mars and Venus together rule the heavens, bringing discord on one hand, and moments of great harmony on the other, you understand? But it is also then that the promise of love will be fulfilled for you and the maid, young master, for it is in this time of strife that the paths of your two destinies will cross once more! Your beloved will return to thee from the West, grown in beauty and grace—yet in this time of your greatest joy will also come the threat of war and death, and a loss of all you hold dear. Brothers suckled at the same breast will in a single breath become deadly enemies, and this woman will be the cause. Deceit and deception will flourish like wild roses in the garden of trust, and jealousy will poison their sharpest thorns and wither their brightest blossoms. It will be a time when a gift of beauty might harbor death in its perfumed bosom, so beware, young master, beware, for love and hatred will ride the same horse!"

Maimun had appeared grave indeed, and the boy Sharif had swallowed nervously.

"But our love *will* triumph over this—this hatred, will it not?" Sharif had demanded doubtfully, his voice cracking. "By Allah, you speak in riddles, Old One, and I would have your meaning clear! Explain!"

"Ah, if only I could! But the future is entirely clear to no mortal man, my little lord. We who have been given the power

150

to divine the influence of the stars upon those below can only interpret what the signs suggest, and use our skills to guess at their true meaning. The ultimate course of any man's life is governed by himself, his strengths and his weaknesses and the choices he is moved to make. Not in a diviner's arts."

"And you can tell me no more?"

Maimun had smiled. "Alas, no! I see great promise in your charts, certainly, and a woman's love returned to you in full measure. But whether that love will triumph over adversity, I cannot tell. However, I can offer you a few words of advice that might stand you in good stead in matters of the heart, and which seem from my calculations to have a bearing on your future. Would you hear them, or nay?"

"*Ewellah*, teacher, I would!"

"Then remember this, my young friend: that a caged songbird cannot love her keeper. In order for her to love him, she must be offered the chance of freedom, not be kept a prisoner. A heart imprisoned feeds on resentment, and love becomes lost amidst the desire to be free. The keeper must be willing to take the risk of losing the songbird, and loosen the latch and permit her to fly free—or to choose to return to him and remain by his side always. It must be as she chooses, if he is ever to gain her love."

"What?" he'd cried, disappointed by this enigmatic advice. "But that's foolish! The little bird would certainly fly away, master, and her keeper would lose the pleasure of her company and enjoy her sweet song no more! Such a keeper would be a fool, I say," Sharif had declared, "when he could keep a close watch on the door and keep her always for himself."

Maimun had shrugged. A snowy eyebrow had lifted. "Perhaps. And then again, perhaps such a keeper would possess a wisdom granted few men? Do you not see, my son, that a heart, like a songbird, cannot be caged? It cannot be coerced and forced into loving someone any more than that bird can be forced to sing in captivity, Sharif. A heart too, my son, must be given a choice. Remember my words in the future, and in time you will understand, and will act upon them with the wisdom that will come when you are grown."

He'd scowled, not understanding at all. "In truth, I do not

see how this advice will affect me, but I thank you for it anyway, Master Maimun," he'd said haughtily, insufferable, arrogant little rogue that he'd been. Paying the astrologer, he'd left, certain he'd squandered his money.

But as the years passed, he'd forgotten none of Maimun's predictions, each one of which had come true with chilling accuracy. He'd begun to realize then that Maimun had been gifted far beyond his youthful expectations. This year was the twentieth year since then. It was the month following Ramadan, the Muslim month of fasting and prayer. The Night of Power had come and gone, and his beloved *had* come to him from the West, exactly as Maimun had long ago foretold, grown in beauty and grace. . . .

"And so you see," Sharif continued aloud to the sleeping woman cradled in his arms, "I feared never to see thee again, Zerdali, when we were parted as children that first time. My spirit was as heavy as the stones of the desert, my heart torn with the grief of our leave-taking! But the astrologer gave me hope. He charted the heavens for us both and plotted the paths of our stars from the very moments of our births. Maimun showed me how, in time, the paths of our destinies would cross once more. The future I have dreamed for us will come to be, *ya habibah*, my beloved one. It will come to be!"

It was sultry mid-morning of the following day when Selim spied a hazy reddish glow in the sky ahead of them. He turned his camel and kicked it into a lope, urging the beast back to his chieftain's side with all possible haste.

"*Simoom*, my lord!" he cried, pointing back the way he had come. "It rises from the west!"

Alexa, seated before Sharif on his horse, caught his meaning and looked in the direction the lad was pointing. She saw a vast, smoky cloud directly in their path, growing closer by the second. She frowned, the jittery, headachy feeling she'd had since earlier that morning intensifying with alarm. What could it be? Surely not fire, way out here in the desert. After all, what was there to burn? Yet, if not fire, what else could explain the strange lack of air which made it difficult to breathe?

She had little time to wonder, for at once, everywhere was action all about her! The servants caught the reins of their masters' or mistresses' camels and bade them couch on their knees. Their riders swiftly dismounted and lay down alongside the beasts, faces pressed to the sand, robes pulled tightly over them. The servants hastily untied the animals' burdens and followed suit. The camels too stretched out their swanlike necks flat atop the ground, closed their long-lashed eyes, and stoppered their clever nostrils, their massive humps now egg-shaped boulders rising from the desert floor.

Seeing his people prepared, Sharif quickly swung down from his own horse, pulling Alexa after him. He sternly commanded Aswad to drop to its knees. When it had done so, he removed its saddle blanket and securely fastened the cloth over the beast's head and eyes, before dropping to the sand and hauling Alexa down beside him. When his fingers coiled around her wrist, she yelped in surprise, for a small charge of electricity had leaped from his flesh to hers, like a tiny arrow of lightning: a result of the electricity in the air. But ignoring her noisy protests, he stretched out, forcing her to lay beside him, and covered them both completely with the full folds of his cloak.

For but a few moments, all the caravan lay eerily still and waiting, hardly breathing. Not a camel stirred, though the stolen Legion mules brayed in fear and tried to break their tethers and run.

The *simoom,* the hot, dry wind of the desert, laden with fine sand, was not long in reaching them. It swept onward, howling, drawing closer and closer to where they were like a cloud of hungry locusts darkening the sky, violently whirling and swirling. Within seconds, the smothering, blinding powder-storm was everywhere, heavy and choking on the air, drowning the lungs of those who had not taken proper concealment as if it were water.

Pressed to the length of Sharif's hard and aggressively male body, Alexa hardly dared to breathe. He, like the moaning *simoom,* seemed everywhere, confound him! His strong arms were about her, holding her pressed to his length beneath the wind-tugged folds of the flapping cloak. His rough cheeks were molded against her softer cheeks. His broad chest crushed the

153

softly swelling curves of her breasts. His lean, hard flanks and thighs were tight against her belly and hips and—oh, Lord!—she was almost certain she could feel the rising hardness of his maleness pressing against her, like a burning rod between them despite their clothing!

Embarrassment flamed in her cheeks, yet through her belly stole curling warmth: a shameful, licking heat in response to his overt maleness that horrified her by its sheer primitiveness, and more so by its betrayal! Was she a wanton Jezebel that this—this desert pirate could stir such feelings of confusion in her body? Lord, she simply had to get free of him! She was suffocating. He was too close, too warm, too male, too everything! Besides, she couldn't breathe under the cloak.

"Let me out of here!" she cried in panic, her voice muffled by the fold. "Please! I—I can't breathe—please—!" she implored him, squirming away from the prodding pressure of what was, she was certain now, his arrogant manhood pricking at her belly.

To her amazement, the chieftain answered her in equally muffled *English*—and English that held more than a hint of laughter in its tone, to boot!

"Fear not, O Innocent One, for it is not the mighty *wezand* of Sharif that prods your little belly so painfully, but the hilt of his *taboka,* his dagger, which is—Allah the Fruitful be praised!—by far the smaller weapon!"

"You speak English!" she exclaimed, angered by this discovery of his deceit and even more so by the mortification of knowing he'd correctly guessed the cause of her discomfort. "You lied to me!"

"Not so, my angry dove. Rather, I was silent, and how can silence be a lie?" Sharif confessed. She knew by his muffled, teasing tone that he was still laughing at her and not really apologetic at all, although in the stuffy darkness beneath the cloak they shared she could not see his hateful handsome face.

"But you let me scream at you, thinking you didn't understand me, you deceitful brute!" she hissed, wanting to slap him soundly for making such a fool of her.

"*Ewellah,* in truth, I did," Sharif confessed amicably, "for it suited my purpose to seem naught but an uncomprehending

154

'savage brute' in your eyes, beloved! After all, being ignorant of your tongue, how could you expect me to heed your demands to free you, eh? It is written that sometimes it is wiser to seem the fool than to reveal one's secret talents!"

His grip tightened when, still unaware of the approaching danger and ignorant of why the entire caravan was behaving so strangely, Alexa struggled and tried to rise from the safety of their cover, pressed close to the shielding bulk of his horse.

"*Wellah,* be still now, woman! The *simoom* will soon pass," he growled, holding her furiously wriggling body still. "It is but a small sandstorm, this one. If you are to be al-Azim's woman, you must learn the patience of the desert peoples and wait. To leave shelter before the sandstorm has passed would mean certain death for thee, with sand filling your nose and choking that lovely mouth. Ah, *habibah,* lie still in my arms. Al-Azim will make you forget the *sheytàn,* the devil-wind!"

Her furious retort died on her lips as a firm male hand swept down the length of her body. His palm limned her full, womanly curves with heat and a tingling, warm sensation that was alarmingly pleasant. His touch confused her utterly! It had been so long since anyone had shown her affection with a gentle embrace, a touch—not since her mama had died, in fact, had anyone hugged her or reached out to hold and comfort her, and Keene had never been demonstrative in any way. Since she was affectionate by nature herself, she'd secretly yearned to be held in someone's protective arms—but not here, and not by his arms, thank you very much!

She strove to trap his marauding hand, wanting desperately to halt its path, afraid of what other liberties she might permit if she allowed him to continue. But with a low chuckle of laughter, he snared her fingers between his own and held them trapped, continuing to caress her body gently above the folds of her garment with his free hand, and to whisper wicked endearments in her ears.

"The two of us here beneath my cloak reminds me of the summer tents of my people, the Imochagh, Zerdali, when we follow our herds to grazing," he murmured in a soothing, lazy drawl. "When the moon's light is hidden and only the stars may mark his path, a young man will slip into the tent of his

155

beloved, and seek her out in the shadows amongst the other sleeping women of her father's *hareem*. He will take her in his arms . . . like so . . . and drink deeply of her scent. Then they secretly embrace and caress each other until dawn paints the heavens, like so . . . and like so, although the girl's mother sleeps but an arm's length away to guard her daughter's virtue! Ah, do not tremble so, *habibah!* Do not be afraid, my little dove, for my caresses and kisses will only delight, not harm you!"

Despite his words, she trembled uncontrollably, for everywhere he touched her, everywhere he caressed her, it seemed heat trailed in the wake of his fingers. To her shame, when he had stroked down the delicately ridged line of her spine with an agonizing lack of haste, his caresses continued even lower. His smooth palm glided over and then cupped each rounded mound of her buttocks, molding her firmly against his hard loins. He touched her in a way no man had ever dared to touch her before, a way that made her shiver with wicked pleasure and grow weak and shivery as if she'd taken a fever. And then his hand curled about her waist and reached lower to rub the very pit of her belly above her robe, moving in lazy, lingering circular motions about her navel, before skimming up over her midriff and cupping the soft mound of each breast in turn in his palm.

She flinched as he fondled her gently, shrinking away from his hand and muttering halfhearted protests, but he didn't stop. Instead, he nibbled at her earlobes, while his fingers captured her sensitive, virginal nipples, lazily teasing the tiny nubbins of flesh with the ball of his thumb until they swelled to double their original size, and became unbearably swollen and sensitive. To her horror, his bold hand slid lower, moving downward over her shrinking belly until it lodged possessively over the fleecy mound between her thighs. There it remained, very still and firmly pressing, his body heat spreading like fire from his palm, through her clothing to the most secret core of her body, while his lips dragged lightly over her throat and his tongue darted at the feathery hairs at her nape.

A throbbing began deep inside her, pulsing in time to the racing beat of her heart. She'd never experienced such a

156

restless sensation while wide awake before, and gave a strangled gasp. What was he doing? How dare he touch her so intimately! Oh, Lord, she could scarce breathe! Oh, Lord, she had to make him stop somehow. She couldn't let him do anything he wanted to her, but how could she stop him? To leave the confines of the billowing cloak meant certain death, he'd implied. But to stay and permit him this languorous freedom of her body—what greater disaster did *that* imply? she wondered in anguish. His touch was so shockingly bold, so provocative, so knowing and sensual. He stirred strange, frightening feelings within her that proper young ladies, she was certain, were not supposed to feel, and certainly not under these circumstances, the Tuareg chieftain having stolen her away from her escort and obviously being intent on rape rather than romance! She couldn't let him continue to touch her so. She told herself she hated him! He was her enemy, her captor. She loathed him, feared him . . . didn't she? Her erotic dreams of half a lifetime—dreams of this man and her together, lost in each other's arms, slaves to the delights of love and desire that so dangerously approximated her feelings at this very moment—had clearly not been spinsterish fantasies at all. They'd been premonitions of disaster! Warnings she should have heeded with heart and soul, instead of blindly rushing headlong into the arms of her dark destiny! She shivered away from his touch, squirming to free herself, searching for the hard ridge of the little dagger she'd concealed to defend herself, and which he'd surely discover at any moment. Yet his fingers locked fast about her wrist like a manacle. He would not let her go, confound him!

"Be still, Zerdali, my dove," he commanded lazily, his deep voice peculiarly hypnotic and gentling against the harsh wailing of the sandstorm without. Like a drug, its timbre weakened her, robbed her of the will to resist him. "It will be soon past, this cursed *simoom*, and we shall go on to Al-Azadel."

"No! I'd sooner die here in this sandstorm than be your— your woman, or go anywhere with you!" she choked out, summoning the remnants of her pride and defiance and resistance.

"Liar!" he countered huskily, brushing his lips against hers

157

in a feathery way that sent tingles through her and made their warm breaths commingle.

The womanly fragrance of her hair, her woman's musk, her flesh were an aphrodisiac to Sharif in the close confines beneath the cloak. He inhaled, taking her scent and her essence deeply into him, as was the way of his people between a man and a woman. The mating of two mouths in the Western fashion of kisses was a foreign delight, one only recently practiced amongst the Tuaregs, a pleasing new love-art he'd eagerly—and expertly—acquired and practiced in anticipation of her coming. "Ah, beloved little liar! You were born for the joys of life, Zerdali, for the delights of desire and a great and lasting love—not to squander that Allah-given life on the desert sands, your blood poured out beneath a Bedouin dagger! Accept what is written in the stars, *habibah!* Let me be your master! Let me make you sing like the strings of the *anzad!*"

"No. I just can't—you mustn't. Please, let me go! No. Stop it! Never, never, never!"

She moaned denials, but the vows sighed into oblivion as his mouth again captured hers, sweetly demanding, drawing a response from her against her will. Little by little, her clamped lips softened beneath his insistent mouth, yielding, opening to him, until the tip of his tongue could penetrate their silken petals, and taste the moist sweetness that lay beyond. Her cries of protests became muffled sighs of pleasure, and she shuddered, shaken to the core by the sensations unfolding inside her. His lips ignited tiny, exquisite little explosions deep within her belly, and aftershocks that spiraled from it even to her breasts, her fingertips, her toes, filling her with a euphoria and expectant giddiness she could neither control nor comprehend.

His firm lips, warm and moist, expertly nuzzled the corners of her mouth, teasing the slight indentations there. His tongue trailed sensually across her lips, then his mouth grazed the flaming curves of her cheeks and—very slowly—found the soft shells of her ears, tracing their sensitive whorls with all the delicacy of an artist's brush.

She shivered, her fingers curling involuntarily about his upper arms. Her nails dug deep into their corded curves.

"Stop—oh, yes, you must! Please, I beg you, no more!" she cried against him. Yet, perversely, there was a wild and wicked, reckless part of her that wantonly hoped he would refuse; that hoped he would go on and take command, that he would wrest the onus of decision from her conscience and make love to her.

Well-versed from an early age in the ways of women in passion, Sharif guessed the thoughts and fears that whirled in Alexa's mind; knew the confusion and conflict within her in that moment. She was innocent, he knew it; a lovely virgin maiden who had known no man's touch before his. His heart sang with joy. By Allah, her body was as creamy as *léban* to his touch, as firm and ripe as a pomegranate for his loving! She responded to his caresses like a Persian nightingale, long imprisoned in a cage, now offered the freedom of an open door, coming alive under his touch! But he would not take advantage of her innocent, eager responses, not now, not here. Her maidenhead was her woman's precious gift to him, her virginity a jewel too priceless to be lightly taken. He would woo her gift from her as a lover should, with tenderness.

For now, the little intimacies that had passed between them were enough, although they left his need unquenched. The kisses he had given her, the delights yet to come at which his caresses had hinted at, would serve as embers to keep her desire for him smoldering! So had the secretive fondlings of lovers in the summer tents of the Imochagh served time and time again, Sharif remembered, and he marveled anew at the ancient wisdom that had designed such a pattern of courtship for his people. Stolen caresses, secret fondlings, combined with the element of danger inherent in discovery and a strict denial of the ultimate act of coupling itself, only served to heighten and sweeten the joys of passion that would be theirs when a man took his bride and claimed her innocence. Zerdali's lingering memories of his kisses and caresses, her own imagination of what *might* have been between them would build her fires. When he came to her again, she would burst into glorious, passionate conflagration, like a desert wildflower blooming under the rare spring rains, and he would teach her the joys of passion!

"*Ya habibah,* I hear thee—and obey. It shall be as you wish, little virgin," Sharif promised craftily but with every evidence of solemnity. "I will caress your loveliness no more, although your lips are sweeter than the sweetest honeycomb, your breasts more firm than ripened peaches, your eyes more lovely than the brightest stars!"

"Thank you," she whispered primly, taken aback—and wondered why his words did not bring the relief or reassurance she craved, why she felt rejected and somehow disappointed when he withdrew his hands from her body and lay decorously still beside her.

Sharif heard the wondering edge of disappointment in her tone, and silently chuckled. Already it was beginning. . . .

The *simoom* lasted a full half hour more. When it had passed over, the people of the caravan arose, shaking the clogging dust from their garments and bodies, and bidding their camels rise.

The desert had altered with the advent of the *simoom*. Great drifts of sand had been shifted by its whirling-dervish dance until there was little that was recognizable in the land about them. Sharif ordered a halt until the caravan had righted itself, and the camel-herders could rid the beasts' heavy burdens of the driven sand collected within their loads.

Swollen goatskins of lukewarm water or tangy, fermenting *léban* were passed about, and everyone swigged his or her mouth free of powdery sand—though none spat out the precious liquid, but instead swallowed it down, grit and all. Water and milk were too hard to come by in the desert to waste even a single drop.

Chapter Eleven

Alexa was silent as they rode on throughout that late afternoon, unable to believe the way she had responded to Sharif's disgusting advances, or to reconcile her behavior with her deeply ingrained principles.

Her mother had brought her up to be a lady, both in thought and manner, hadn't she? What little she knew of what went on between a man and his wife in the privacy of their bedroom had implied that it was a wife's responsibility to submit to her husband's baser male instincts and to bear the children in which they sooner or later resulted. There had been no indication whatsoever that a normal, decent woman would find any pleasure in the act, or in the furtive fondlings that led up to it, she thought, deeply ashamed of herself.

Remembering how excited the devilishly handsome Tuareg's touch had made her sent heat to her cheeks. Oh, lord, what on earth was wrong with her? She'd been kissed twice in her life before today; pleasant enough experiences to be sure, but certainly nothing to compare with the earth-shattering, bone-melting delight of *his* kisses! And she'd never, in her entire life, suspected for a minute that she was capable of such intense or shameful reactions to a man. Surely feeling such— such wicked pleasure in a stranger's intimate exploration of her body was a terrible sin, a secret she must carry with her to her grave, and let no one suspect she was guilty of. She'd have to be strong, and try desperately to withstand such weakness on her part in the future, she decided.

Riding before Sharif after the *simoom* had passed was sheer torture. Every graze, every bump of his hard, lean body against

161

hers, however accidental, now held a threat—not only that her closeness might enflame him, but that his closeness might rekindle those shocking responses in herself! She held her body rigid before him, her back ramrod straight, determined to subdue her sordid animal instincts by willpower as she flinched against every jarring motion of the stallion, instead of adjusting her body to fit its gait. By the time they halted to make camp that night below the crumbling walls of an ancient watchtower, she was aching in every part of her, bad-tempered at herself and at him for bringing it forcefully home that she was flawed; a wanton, a wicked Jezebel masquerading in the trappings of a lady while within them beat the heart and body of a born harlot.

Muriel erected their tent as usual, and wearing a secretive little smile, returned from the well bearing a brass basin which held a cup or two of murky water scented with what smelled like oil of roses.

"You are not used to the ways of the desert, my poor sister," she said, smiling despite Alexa's irritable scowl, "and I am certain the sand with which we cleanse ourselves would not be gentle to your soft skin. And so, here, I've brought you well water to wash yourself, perfumed with oil of roses. I steeped it myself last summer, from the roses that grew in my father's city gardens. Does it not smell wonderful?" She made signs, pretending to cup the water and splash her face.

Alexa grasped her meaning immediately. Muriel was offering her a chance to wash herself! Only the promise of her release could have pleased her more! That, or the news that Sharif had been trampled to death by a thirst-crazed camel, confound him!

"Oh, bless you, Muriel! What a dear, thoughtful person you are!" she exclaimed, her bad temper miraculously vanishing beneath a delighted smile.

Muriel laughed with pleasure, happy to see her friend's spirits lifted by her simple treat as she set down the carved comb and clean garments that she'd brought for Alexa to wear after her bath. She pressed her finger across her lips and pointed to the basin, then to the far side of the tent where Sharif and his men congregated noisily over the ubiquitous

162

evening rounds of black coffee or green tea, to which they had invited the keeper of the *kella* and his sons. "You must promise to say nothing of this extravagance to anyone, Zerdali, for it is considered a grave sin to waste water in this way, out here in the desert. But—"she winked—"it will be our little secret! It is my hope that you'll enjoy your wash!"

With a conspiratorial grin, Muriel left Alexa alone, returning to the tent she shared with her mother, Noura, and her aunt. Quickly, Alexa unrolled the skirt of the goatskin tent and drew it down for privacy, eager to get started and wash the sweat and dust from her body. In heavy gloom now, she stripped off the flowing cloak and tossed it aside, then peeled off the silk nightgown beneath, which had become plastered to her body with the heat. Mmm! Heaven! The water was tepid, its scent glorious. Naked now, she eagerly tore a strip from the hem of her discarded gown to serve as a crude washcloth, and dipped it into the precious water.

Oh, how cool it felt, how soothing! She slowly bathed her face, her throat, her breasts, reveling in the heady fragrance of roses that enveloped her and in the delicious sensations of cool water on her skin and of being clean again at last. She'd always taken access to water for drinking or bathing for granted, until she came here. She'd never do so again, she vowed, vigorously swishing the wet cloth over her belly, rinsing it out, raising one leg to wash it thoroughly, then the other.

But when she washed between her legs, the friction of the slippery cloth reminded her of Sharif's caresses upon that part of her body earlier that day, although the cloth of her robe had prevented him from actually touching her skin then. Her movements slowed. Her eyes grew dreamy, heavy-lidded, and a peculiar languor flowed through her. What if the washcloth were his hands? she mused, a little breathless at the wicked thought. How would it feel if he touched her there? Would she find it pleasant—as pleasant as his kisses and the fondling way in which he'd cupped her breasts, teasing the crests until they'd hardened and waves of pleasure had swamped through her? Would that pulsing, ticklish feeling make her squirm with frustration yet again, and long to press her body hard against his to ease its yearnings? Or had it been but a one-time reaction to him, never to be repeated—?

She caught herself in mid-fantasy and uttered an unladylike curse. For goodness' sake, what was she thinking of! With an exasperated sigh at her train of thought, she abruptly flung the washcloth into the basin and set it aside, near the opening to the tent. The warm air soon dried her body without need of a towel. Feeling refreshed for the first time in days, she took up the comb Muriel'd brought and began combing the tangles from her hair, perching amongst the plump pillows and woven rugs, which felt as soft as velvet to her bare body. She wielded the comb with lazy, unconsciously seductive strokes, working the teeth from the crown of her head and all the way through her long, chestnut hair to the curling ends that fell loosely about her waist, to free it of snarls and knots. She hummed as she did so, completely unaware that she was being watched, of the ebony eyes that smoldered in the gloom by the tent's opening.

For the first time, Sharif—who had come to the tent bearing a bowl of figs and dates, intending only to talk with her—gazed upon her naked beauty. By Blessed Fatima's Thighs, what a woman the little girl he remembered had become! Her flesh was pale as the finest pink Italian marble in the shadows, and more lushly curved than he had expected. Her hair gleamed softly, a mantle of dark fire shot through with gold without the light to lift its color. Her breasts were two snowy doves, nestled sweetly together. The tiny, virginal nipples were exquisite little rubies in a coral setting, sweetmeats he hungered to devour. From her creamy breasts, her figure dipped into a slender little waist the span of his two hands, then flared into full, womanly hips fashioned to cradle a man's hips as he loved her, or to carry the sons they'd make together. She nestled amongst the pillows like a small, pale-feathered bird in a cozy bower, her long, shapely legs curled to one side, permitting him a tiny glimpse of the soft thatch of curls that mounded at the junction of her thighs. His manhood rose in response to her delectable charms. The clamor of desire that had settled into a gnawing ache deep in his belly flared up, demanding release. He knotted his fists, and felt the breath in his throat become a husky rasp of passion. He needed her. He wanted her. He'd wanted her for far too long to look upon her naked this way and again deny himself the rapture of her body! And yet, he still hesitated to take her against her will. To do so went against a lifetime's protective instincts, and he possessed many such instincts where she was concerned. It went against the caution of the astrologer Maimun's ancient prophecy too . . . but, by Allah, how she stirred him—!

"Get out!" she screamed, suddenly glancing up to see him there, watching her. She sprang to her feet, looking desperately about her for something to cover herself with, but her discarded clothes lay across the tent, heaped at his feet. She snatched up two pillows instead, and held them before her like plump shields. "You—you Peeping Tom! Get out of here!"

Sharif grinned and took a step inside the tent, letting the skirt fall behind him as he did so. In the gloom with her, he bent down and set the bowl of dates he'd brought at his feet, his dark, hungry eyes flickering over her, noting the creamy curves the little pillows could not conceal.

"You are beautiful," he said huskily, as if she'd never screamed at him.

His calm compliment, huskily voiced, obviously sincere, silenced her, caught her off guard for a moment. It was virtually impossible to remain angry at someone who called you beautiful! She clamped her jaws shut, nonplussed, only too well aware of the kindling in his eyes. Oh, Lord, what could she do? she wondered, swallowing nervously. His lust was obvious, and she was so very naked and vulnerable.

"Please. I—I won't scream anymore, I promise, not if you'll just—go. We'll pretend this never happened. Oh, please, won't you just go?" she whispered hopefully.

"You are even lovelier than in my dreams," he said softly again, ignoring her protests, and her hopes sank. "I desire thee more than I've desired any other woman. Will you not come to me, Zerdali, of your own free will? Will you not let me teach you the meaning of desire?" He held out his hand to her, inviting her to clasp it. His dark eyes were aflame as he looked down at her, his handsome, lean face stark with passion in the shadows.

Some primitive part of her ached to reach out, to place her

trembling hand within his far larger one and accept his sensual invitation. Somehow, it was as if she'd known him always, as if it would be quite proper and right and pleasant to do so. However, the prim Victorian miss that kept sentinel within her was outraged by his offer! The nerve of him, to expect her to meekly fall victim to his animal lust for the price of a few flowery compliments! Did he think she was some common tart, accustomed to selling her favors to any Tom, Dick, or Achmed? Well! She would show him once and for all the lofty price she placed upon her virtue, yes, indeed. But—how to do it? *The dagger!* she remembered. Muriel's little knife! She'd hidden it by slipping it into the wide hems of her cloak. If only she could recover it, she could defend herself against his assault! But her clothes were heaped several feet away, at his feet.

Fighting to appear outwardly calm despite the turbulent thoughts whirling in her mind, she glowered at him.

"I am not a harlot, Tuareg, to give myself to you simply for the asking!" she said coldly, crisply, tossing her head. "For your information, my name is Miss Alexandria Elizabeth Harding. Of course, that means nothing to you, but I'm a—a woman of considerable—er—influence in my country," she lied. "I swear, if you'd just notify the British Consulate in Algiers that you've kidnapped me, they'd pay you a hefty ransom for my safe return, unmolested."

He chuckled admiringly at her hauteur, for naked as she was and with only two plump pillows to conceal her breasts and sex and ward him off, she nevertheless managed to appear haughty, and to sound as aloof as a queen. He wondered how she'd look when she finally writhed in total abandon beneath him, her lips and breasts swollen from his kisses, her magnificent hair tangled, her slanted green eyes glazed with passion?

"Ah, but you underestimate your charms, lovely *Mademoiselle* Harding! Even a sultan's treasure could not repay me for your loss! Besides, Alex-an-dria Hard-ing, you want me, I can tell," he accused, waggling a finger at her playfully. "So, why do you deny the passion you feel?" he asked, his voice a lazy, purring caress. "You are no harlot, we both know that, but—

you are still a woman, with a woman's body. And were not women, like us men, created by Allah, fashioned to receive pleasure, as well as to give it? Tell me the truth now? Did your blood not race just a little when I kissed you during the *simoom*? Did your heart not pound a beat or two faster? Did you not feel the flutter of wings in your belly when I touched you? *Ewellah*, it was so! I know it was, for your lovely eyes betray your thoughts! Neither can your body tell lies to mine, Zerdali, though your lips might try to do so! Look at your breasts—see how hard they have grown! You desire me, as I desire you."

When had he stepped so close? she wondered, aghast at how near he'd grown while his silky words mesmerized her. She wet her lips, trembling all over.

"Step back, you devil! Get away from me!"

"Ah, but how then can I hold you, kiss you?"

"You can't. I—I won't let you! That's quite enough, you rogue! Step back—you're far too close!"

"Does my closeness frighten you so, then?"

"Yes! No—oh, God, yes! Please, please, no closer!"

"But I will be gentle, little one. So very gentle. See? Ah, your cheek feels soft as the breast of a dove to my hand. Smooth as the petal of a rose . . ."

"I—said—don't—touch—me!" she hissed, jerking her head away.

"And look, how your lips quiver, like the moist stamens of an opened flower, trembling before a hummingbird. Let me taste your nectar, beloved. Let me sip it. . . ."

His poetic words, his deep, cajoling voice, almost lulled her into obeying, so hypnotic were they. With a start, she realized suddenly that she was straining ever so slightly toward him where she stood; that involuntarily she had started to raise her lips ever so slightly to meet his and succumb to his trap! The knowledge horrified her. Oh, but he was dangerous, far more dangerous than she'd ever estimated!

"No, *damn* you!" she screeched.

Suddenly, she thrust him forcibly away, the surprise of her attack knocking him off balance, sending him sprawling on his back to the scattered rugs and upsetting her basin of bathing water. She sprang across the tent and dove for the hidden dagger. An agonizing, endless instant of fumbling, and she'd torn it loose, held it ready on a level with her waist as she whirled to face him.

"If you try to touch me, I swear I'll cut you!" she threatened shakily, and wondered if he could possibly hear the agonized pounding of her heart. "Please, don't make me do it!" she warned, half-pleading, half-threatening. "I'm quite dangerous when roused, believe me. I have a terrible temper, everyone tells me so, and I'll—I-ll make mincemeat of you!"

In answer to her brave boast—which in all honesty amused rather than intimidated him—he inclined his head as if accepting that she had gained the upper hand. To her surprise, he sat down, cross-legged, on the rugs, and began munching the dates he'd brought, popping them into his mouth one after the other and noisily spitting out the pits in a manner calculated to hold her disgusted attention.

"If you think you can outlast me, you're wrong," she declared stonily. "I am a woman of considerable determination and enormous patience."

He shrugged and spat another date pit, remarking casually with Eastern fatalism, "All things are in the hands of Allah, are they not?"

He was laughing as he said the words; she could hear it in his tone! She gritted her jaw and took up a belligerent stance, determined to stand there, the little knife held in readiness, for as long as it took, even should it take all night. Minutes passed. More followed. Her considerable determination wavered. Her endless patience frayed. Her hand trembled with the strain of holding the knife in midair. Her knees felt weak and ready to buckle. Oh, Lord, she almost wished he'd try something— anything!—to break the unnerving immobility!

Suddenly, she heard a dull thud to one side of the tent. She whirled to face the sound, but there was nothing there; no turbaned henchman come to aid his chieftain, nothing but unthreatening, deep shadow, and the skirts of the tent rippling in the night wind. Another dull thud sounded, this time in the opposite direction. Again, she spun to face it, and in the same moment that she realized that he—and the dates he had lobbed to distract her—was the cause of the sound, he sprang out of the gloom like an attacking panther, grasped her by the hips, and in the same lithe move used the impetus of his spring to fling her backward beneath him. She landed across the heaped rugs with a startled "Ooof!"

He lay half across her, smothering her. His steely fingers were clamped about her wrist. His broad chest pinned her, immobile, to the rugs beneath them, like a pinned butterfly in a collector's glass display case.

"Drop it, little one," he menaced silkily. "I have no wish to snap your pretty wrist!"

His ruthless tone was one she had not heard him use before. It was chilling in its mercilessness, and showed a side of him she had hoped never to see. Swallowing, she let the dagger fall, riveted on the looming silhouette of his head and shoulders above her, painfully conscious of his hard flanks angled across her hips and with the disquieting knowledge that he was very much aroused, and she was very much naked.

If only she could faint away in a swoon, like other women would at such a threatening moment! A sudden fainting on her part might detract him from his purpose, or at the very least, render her insensible to its outcome! But she had never been much of a one for swooning at even the most propitious of times, and she doubted she'd be able to start now. She could only endure, and pray she came out of this with her life and sanity intact, if not her innocence. . . .

Her rash actions had forced a proximity between them that Sharif, in all honesty, had not anticipated, but one which, once forced, he could not help but turn to his advantage, desiring her as he did.

His manhood surged in response to the rounded, wriggling length of her pinned so deliciously naked beneath him. His senses reeled at the fragrance of roses and the delicate feminine musk which rose from her body to tease his nostrils, a scent as potent and euphoric as the dream-smoke of the poppy flower. He could feel the thud of her heart against his ribs. He could hear the shaky rasp of her breathing, like a gazelle run to ground by a hunter. He could feel the trembling of her body beneath him. All this, but nothing—neither her fear of him nor his own long-standing, hard-won restraint, nor her very

169

innocence—could halt him now. The moment of reason had come, and gone. He desired her, and he would take her.

His warm breath fanned her cheek as he dipped his dark head to hers. His mouth covered her soft mouth in the gloom, slanting across her lips, fitting them to his own. He kissed her gently at first, playing his tongue along her clamped lips, darting the very tip between them until, as she made to open her mouth in a protest, his tongue seized the advantage and surged between them.

His kisses deepened, becoming ardent and so sensual they left her breathless with rising sensations too wild and wicked to contemplate. As he kissed her, he released her wrist and instead sought out the fullness of her breasts, fitting the firm little mound to the cup of his large hand, squeezing, fondling, teasing the sensitive flesh.

Her hands, loosened now, came up in a last attempt to force him from her. But instead, she found her fingertips grazing over his shoulders and arms, and with fascination she discovered where braided tendons and muscles made curving ridges over bone beneath the cloth of his robe, then gave way to the smooth, broad expanse of his back.

Meanwhile, his fingers captured a tender nipple, working it gently between thumb and finger until it blossomed in his hand like some ripened berry he ached to taste. The breath caught huskily in her throat as he circled the throbbing little nub of flesh with his fingertips, then moistened it delicately with lips and tongue. She felt her flesh ruche beneath his teasing lips, felt a tingling, electrical sensation gather and build and snake through her from nipples to loins with a sizzle that arched her upward, clear off the rugs, as if struck by a tiny bolt of lightning.

"Damn you, you devil!" she cried.

She fell back, sighing helplessly as his mouth nuzzled the little valley between her breasts, moving lower to flicker like summer lightning across her flat belly. He teased the rim of her navel and dipped his tongue into its miniature well until she giggled at the ticklish sensation. In a haze of mindless, sensual pleasure in which fear and protest were forgotten, she felt the trace of his fingertips and the graze of his palm against the

170

silken inner surfaces of her thighs as he parted them. She knew what he intended, and yet was powerless to prevent him, though her conscience clamored that she must . . . she . . . really . . . must . . . do . . . something.

Somehow, he was now as naked as she, his burning, virile body pressed hard over hers, his lips on hers, his fingers playing teasingly over and within her most secret folds as he kissed her. His intimate caresses yielded a moist response from her body that made her cheeks burn with shame, and yet she had little time to dwell upon it. His chest rubbing sensually against her tender, swollen breasts, he lifted himself up and loomed between her parted thighs. He pressed forward, bringing his lips fully against hers, his rigid, silken warmth parting her nether lips, nudging deeper between them. He hesitated but a moment and then, before terror could erode her languor and render her tense and resistant beneath him, he'd gathered her up into his arms and kissed her ardently, even as he eased himself into her tight sheath.

He took her maidenhead with such gentleness, with such care not to hurt her any more than was absolutely necessary, that it was done before she realized the moment she dreaded had come and gone. Where was the agonized rending in two she'd feared? She'd felt no true pain; only a moment's burning discomfort followed by a pressing fullness, a delicious expectancy now, as he eased forward again and thrust deeply into her. He lodged his entire length in the tight, hot sheath of her body with a groan of delight that tore from his lips with a fervor that stunned her.

When he had given her body a moment to grow used to his presence, he withdrew and began his thrusts, plunging deep and then almost withdrawing again and again until she could no longer withstand his sensual torture. Her arms curled about his chest, drawing him down upon her, holding him fast within her body. Together, they began to move as one, her body imitating and answering the movements of his in the instinctive, ageless dance of passion as she arched upward to meet his plungings.

Time and again, she sobbed with the agony of delight with which he filled her. Her breaths became little strangled gasps as

171

the mysterious pressure building deep in her loins grew and grew. It mounted in urgency until she suddenly felt as if she'd exploded in a myriad of colored petals! Oh, Lord! she wondered, dazed and spinning—spinning, like a whirling top of blurred colors—was this how it was meant to be? This glorious explosion of sensation? This voluptuous delight washing over her? She'd never even imagined that such pleasure could exist for a woman! She lay still while colored starbursts filled her vision, though her eyes were tightly closed. Warm pulses that shook her to the core rippled through her body like warm tides. They left her weeping with the profound release and beauty of her rapture, drained so utterly that in their wake she quickly fell asleep. Sharif's triumphant groan of fulfillment was the last sound she heard.

She awoke much later to see that the skirt of the tent had been raised. Through it, a rectangle of paling charcoal and a single morning star alerted her that night was fast fading to dawn. She must have fallen asleep, she realized fuzzily, and then, in the same moment, she remembered Sharif, remembered what had happened between them! Horrified, she remembered too how her protests had become whimpered pleas for his kisses and caresses, her struggles fierce embraces that *she*, not he, had initiated. Shame filled her. Oh, Lord, how could she have surrendered to him so easily? How could she have given in with so little protest? Unsuccessfully fighting back tears of self-reproach, she struggled to sit up.

It was then that she saw him, still sprawled half-naked beside her. He appeared lazy and sleek, content as a well-fed cat after a particularly toothsome feast of canary, and had obviously been watching her as she slept. The knowledge angered her. Bad enough he had used his wiles to gain her surrender, but did he have to sit there and—and gloat over his innocent victim, that scoundrel?

"Peace unto you this morning, *habibah*," he greeted her, his tone a caress. His dark eyes adored her. "The beauty of *zohra*, the dawn star, pales beside the loveliness of you, beloved."

She scowled at him in reply, her eyes almost crossing in her endeavor to put on a furious face. If he expected to find her meek and biddable after what had happened, he'd be disappointed! Perhaps she had surrendered to him—more out of curiosity than anything else, of course—but that moment of unenlightened weakness had passed, never to return.

"You animal!" she answered him softly, her green eyes glittering with hatred and contempt. "You savage, unspeakable animal! It wasn't enough that you tortured one of my escort to death, and turned the rest loose to die a slow death in the desert! It wasn't enough that you falsely accused my brother and forced him to flee too! Did you have to add my—my rape to your list of unspeakable crimes?" she accused him, her own guilt adding an acidic sharpness to her tone.

He flinched in shock, and his ebony eyes hardened. The adoration in their depths became irritation. Twenty years, and she was yet as obstinate as a she-donkey, as single-minded as ever, still able to move him to anger in the blink of an eye, still unable to admit her part in what had happened, or that she'd found pleasure as well as he!

"You are wrong, *habibah*. Your brother was guilty, damned by his companion's word. And let us not speak of rape either, little fool, while we are speaking of guilt and innocence, for if I had in truth raped you, you would not have begged me for more, believe me. Rape is an act of hate and violence, of brutality and pain. Do not confuse it with what passed between us, innocent one. That was passion, desire, and pleasure, and on my part, an act of love."

"Huh! How prettily you dress up your guilt with words, my Tuareg lord! But words change nothing. You forced your attentions on me, admit it! You stole the innocence which rightly belonged to the decent, respectable man I would have chosen for my husband. What you experienced last night was nothing more than lust, crude animal lust. Love? Ha! An—an ignorant, barbaric savage like you isn't capable of anything *remotely* approaching something so fine and noble as love!"

Her face flamed. Her scornful tongue had run away with her caution and reason in her guilt, she realized as her last words shuddered in the silence that followed them. She glanced across at him and saw a momentary flash of pain, naked and raw, flit across his stern, dark features in the gray light. In that moment, she wished with all her heart that she had the power

173

to take her words back, to recant. She knew that what she'd said was a terrible accusation to make, and that in all honesty she'd wronged him by it. This man had taken her innocence, true, but he'd been gentle with her when another might have been unspeakably cruel. And yet, to admit that he had not—in all honesty—used force, had used caresses rather than blows to override her initial protests, would be to admit her own guilt! If she admitted that, she would have to admit to him and to herself that she was attracted to him in some way; that she'd secretly welcomed his advances, and that her sensual nature had actively enjoyed every delicious minute of them. And that she could never do!

A muscle twitched in his swarthy jaw. Anger filled his eyes, making the tiny yellow flecks in their midnight depths flare in a shower of gold. He clenched his fists, and for a moment she wondered if he would strike her, but he did not. He only twisted the copper amulet that encircled his upper arm, as if he would dearly have loved to twist her pretty throat instead, and glowered at her.

Sharif had known a pain more wounding than a physical blow as she spat out her tirade, and he'd flinched as if struck. Hot on its heels came that spurt of anger. That little innocent! She'd accused him of rape, had said he was "incapable of love." Had she not seen Muriel with her own eyes, witnessed for herself the aftermath of her own brother's brutal, insane "love" for a woman? That she could still defend him, that she could, in the same breath, compare his own tender lovemaking to *that* unspeakable act, stunned him and filled him with fury! By Allah, she did not, could not, know what she was saying! Heat filled him, white-hot and virulent. The urge to shake her until her teeth rattled and she saw reason was strong upon him, but the upbringing of his proud people forbade that an Imochagh warrior of his rank should ever show his anger or emotion before others. He tightened his jaw, and mastered the momentary weakness. Without a word in his defense, nor even a flicker of an eye to demonstrate how deeply her accusations had wounded him, he pulled his robe over his head, shucked on his *sirwal* and boots, ducked under the tent, and left her alone.

His departure was, somehow, more chastening to Alexa than if he'd argued the point or turned on her in anger. The yawning silence in the wake of his leaving made her feel hollow and not very admirable, as if somehow she were the one in the wrong. She remembered his whispered endearments. The velvet caress of his midnight eyes. The gentle way he'd kissed her, caressed her, held her in his arms and made her come alive with passion, and she squirmed with guilt as she mentally compared them to Muriel's purpling bruises, degraded pride, and battered spirit. Perhaps it hadn't been an act of love for her, true, but—something about the expression in his eyes last night, and the depth of sorrow in their dark pools just a while ago, said that for him, it had been exactly that: an act of love, which she'd desecrated with her words.

They camped where they were for the following day—both to rest the animals and to enjoy the hospitality of the *kella* keeper and his family, Muriel confided—then rose three hours after midnight of the next morning and continued on through the cool dark hours before dawn. They kept moving well into the saffron-and-mauve skies of early morning which followed.

She found herself again mounted before Sharif, but his teasing smiles and wicked grins were a thing of the past. He spoke to her now in harsh, stilted phrases, and then only when forced to do so. That peculiar feeling of familiarity that had been between them from the first was quite gone now. They were hostile strangers, and for some reason, Alexa found it saddened her. She missed the exciting, delicious spark of attraction that had flared between them, the wicked banter and flowery compliments he'd casually tossed her way, and wished she could bring all that back again. What had she to look forward to now, or to occupy her restless thoughts? Nothing but endless deserts of golden sand, endless skies of brilliant blue, and her endless fears for what fate held in store for her at the end of their journey, churning over and over in her mind.

Would he hand her over to Kadar without a second thought, now that she had displeased him? she wondered apprehensively.

Soon, still small and in the distance, Alexa saw low-lying

masses of land upon the hazy horizon: masses which, from here, appeared capped in white. Snow-peaked mountains? she asked herself silently, and decided it could not possibly be, not out here! Yet as they drew closer and closer, she saw that her first impression had been correct. There were indeed mountains ahead, but the "snow" she had imagined was not snow, but masses of fluffy white cloud.

The terrain altered noticeably as they approached the mountains. Rugged rock formations rose in unbelievable fashion seemingly from nowhere, as if a giant hand had set down a huge, golden loaf of crusty bread in the midst of the desert, making a wall between the sands and whatever kingdom lay beyond the soaring, craggy ranges.

The land their caravan now crossed was called the *sahel*, the shore of the desert. It was littered with rocks and an occasional straggling thorn or date palm, tamarisk trees or twisted olive bushes, fighting for life amidst the arid soil. Spiny cacti were as numerous as stones here in the foothills, yet sere grasses grew in abundance. Alexa spied a pair of tiny gazelles that bounded away as they neared them, and several lizards scuttled out of the path of their mounts' hooves. She started to voice her pleasure at these signs of wildlife to Sharif, then remembered their quarrel and fell moodily silent. There were Sodom apple trees with bitter-tasting yellow fruits and gum-arabic-yielding acacia trees with fuzzy yellow spires of blossom, long thorns, and narrow, pointed leaves much in evidence. Such plant life offered rare and welcome sights of greenery and flowers after days of barren desert.

To her eyes, the caravan seemed intent on riding straight through the solid mountain range. But at the last moment, it turned, and Alexa saw an opening chasm amongst the rocks of foothills, little wider than a goat path.

The lead animals started up a narrow, almost hidden defile, concealed partially by enormous camel-colored boulders. The defile was only a few feet wide and stony as it twisted back and forth, hairpin fashion, leading them deeper and deeper and ever higher into the mountains.

Soon, she discovered when she dared to glance over her shoulder, the *sahel* lay far below, the gnarled acacias little bigger than pale yellow mushrooms from this vantage point. She twined her fingers through the stallion's rough-silk mane. She had never been overly fond of heights, and her stomach contracted, causing her to hurriedly focus her attention on the track ahead, which suddenly took yet another sharp turn and opened up into a deep, sloping ravine, carpeted with sturdy grasses and sandy soil and even a few hardy wildflowers.

To her amazement, there were trees growing out of the rocky soil here; wild plum, apricot, and even pomegranate trees, fashioned into crooked, witchy shapes by sun and wind and, yes, perhaps even rain, if the gauzy clouds huddled sheeplike against the mountains' topmost ridges were any indication. They passed a youth herding a vast number of goats, which leaped up to watch their passage from the craggy lookout points of huge rocks and outcroppings, their golden-slitted eyes curiously demonic. Their herder touched his fingertips to his forehead and then his breast in courteous salute, and then waved to the chieftain a less formal, friendlier greeting, his toothy grin wide and sparkling white against his swarthy, clean-shaven complexion.

"La Bes, master, *La Bes! Ilham'dilla!"*

To Alexa's surprise, her captor laughed and waved back, *"Ilham'dilla!* How goes it, goatherd?" To which the boy replied, "By the Grace of Allah, all is well, my prince!"

Alexa could feel the stallion straining to gallop beneath her now as they neared the end of the ravine, yet it was some time before she saw the reason for the old stallion's eagerness; he scented home, and there, up ahead, was the entrance to it in the form of a lovely stone gateway. The gateway was cleverly constructed across a mountain pass, so that the arms of the pass formed walls of natural rock formations to both east and west. It was arched at its center and flanked by imitation towers on either side, each one adorned with pretty, intricate tile mosaics and surmounted by delicate fretwork.

As they approached, two armed sentries wearing the turban *tagilmust* headdresses and flowing cloaks and baggy *sirwal* of her captors appeared and challenged them from atop the walls. They grinned and saluted as Sharif rose in the saddle and gave the obligatory password in a loud, resonant cry that echoed like a peal of thunder throughout the tiny valleys and mountain passes. With a salute, brandishing their long wooden staffs or the wickedly curved *takoba* daggers above their heads, the sentries beckoned them on. With Sharif now at its head, the caravan of camels and horses swept under the gateway and traveled still deeper into the very heart of the mountain-walled al-Mamlaka al-Azadel, the Prosperous Kingdom.

Small, flat-roofed houses built of whitewashed mud bricks perched upon the winding slopes, like limpets clinging to a stony breakwater. Each had a tiny courtyard at its center where sparkling fountains played and carefully tended and watered fruit trees of every kind flourished. Upon the rooftops, chickens scratched and goats bleated.

In lofty contrast, the cupolas and minarets of an ornate little mosque rose above the flat-roofed houses, gently reminding Alexa with its sweeping Moslem religious symbols atop them that she was still a prisoner of the followers of Islam, albeit those followers were the Tuareg "Lost Ones," and far less devout than most of their faith.

The central bazaar through which they passed was a miniature of the bazaar she had visited in Algiers, with vendors hawking their wares and singing the praises of their goods at the top of their lungs. There were the sellers of richly woven Persian rugs and carpets she so admired for their colorful floral artistry, sitting cross-legged in the dust; the sellers of leather goods and embroidered cloth, lengths of exquisite silk in rainbow hues, bolts of fine, sheer "muslin" from the Iraqi city of Mosul; of brassware lamps and bowls and figures; of all manner of baskets and wood carvings, flat wheels of bread and thick, black Turkish coffee or green tea by the thimble-sized cupful.

The people of al-Azadel were as diverse as their goods, from the *marabouts*, the priests, in their somber, traditional robes, to half-naked, fair-skinned children; from a ragged, one-eyed beggar to the greedy moneylenders, and barechested grinning fellow riding on the back of a wide-horned ox. The young women of al-Azadel were enchanting, dark-eyed beauties most of whom, like the other nomadic tribes of the desert, left their fair faces uncovered. Instead of the dark, concealing robes of city women in *purdah*, the young women of al-Azadel wore sheer, flower-embroidered veils thrown over their heads and flowing exotically about their shoulders as they went about their shopping, with embroidered tunics and swirling skirts of bright colors beneath them. Necklaces of coins and bells and silver bangles about their wrists and ankles chinked musically as they walked.

To Alexa, the sights, the sounds—a heady cacophony of street cries, drums, flutes and bells, braying donkeys, neighing horses, bellowing oxen, bleating goats, and the numerous scents—of tea and coffee, of exotic cinnamon and cloves and other spices, of camel dung and perfumes commingling with the sun-ripened fragrance of fruits piled high in woven baskets—was just as she imagined a scene from the *Arabian Nights* would appear if the descriptions could come alive!

And then, glancing up, she saw above the city the towers, walls, cupolas, and minarets of a little white palace befitting a fairy-tale prince, the Palace of the Clouds, where lived the *amir* Azid Malik ben-Azad, ruler of al-Mamlaka al-Azadel, the Prosperous Kingdom, and his son and heir, Sharif al-Azim, the Defender.

She wet her lips nervously and dared a glance over her shoulder at the face of her captor. He appeared stern and aloof still, and her belly turned over in apprehension. What would happen to her now? She sighed. For better or worse, for good or evil, she was here at last, a prisoner in the mountain stronghold of the Tuareg brigands.

Chapter Twelve

Well, well, who'd have thought it, eh? You've outrun them this far, Keene, old boy! You thought they'd carve you into little pieces of meat back there at the oasis, and those bloody Arabs thought so too, didn't they? But they were wrong, all wrong! He! He! He! No, sonny, they were too damned stupid to keep you prisoner, so to Hell and be damned with the lot of them, miserable tadpoles. Mmm. They got Flech, though. Got him, all right. Sliver by sliver and piece by piece. Yes, sir, it's too late for ole Flech. Serves him right tho', that sly bastard. He got what was coming to him. Got it good! He should never have told them your name, Keene, old son. There's honor in silence, eh, sonny? Absolute silence equals absolute honor. Absolute silence equals absolute hush, totally mum. Mum's the word! That's what Flech should have kept, mum. Numb. Hum. Tight as a drum. Not a single crumb. That's the sum. Bum. Bum. Tiddley-tum.

The soft cadence of the murmuring voices gradually drowned out the fiery agony in his skull. Keene, reeling in the saddle of his stolen camel, almost sobbed with relief as the pain ebbed. It became a dull, constant aching that he had—over the years since the headaches had first begun—long since learned to cope with, if not welcome with open arms.

He flung back his throbbing head and stared above him with horribly bloodshot eyes. The lids were almost swollen shut by the two enormous blisters that covered them. His face was burned black. His lips had grown bloody and cracked from the merciless sun that blazed down on him from the empty sky above; a sky without clouds, empty of blessed rain, empty of all things save for that single blistering, blind eye, burning everything in sight as it stared sightlessly down upon the world below.

Oh, please God, he needed water! Oh, Jesus Christ, he needed water so damned badly! Twice since dawn he'd cupped his hands and drunk his own piss, but now he was too dried out to piss any more. Try as he might, it wouldn't come, not a bloody drop nor a trickle! Who'd have thought it would ever come to this, that he'd be praying for the sight of his own piss! He lowered his head upon his chest and began to laugh, hoarsely first, then hysterically. Soon the maniacal laughter turned to harsh sobs, although it was dry sobs that wracked him, for God knew, there wasn't enough moisture left anywhere within him to squeeze out enough for a single tear. Not a single tear nor a drop of piss . . .

Piss. Hiss. Pretty pretty miss. Give me a kiss. What bliss!

The voices were back again. They whispered in his ear, filling his mind like moldy, rustling leaves in a damp wind, or evil little elves snickering and sniggering dirty things to him. He strained with every ounce of his remaining strength to listen to them, to obey their commands as he always had, afraid if he ignored them even once they would go away and never return. That they'd leave him in agonized silence, alone with the stabbing, clawing pain in his skull, not knowing what to do nor where to turn. He needed the voices! Without their anesthetic mutterings, without their constant stream of advice, he was doomed. . . .

Ah, yes, that's it, all right! You're doomed without us, Keene, old boy. Need our help, don't you? Die of thirst if we don't tell you what to do, won't you? they crowed. *He! He! He! That's easy, sonny. Arabs got you into this mess, well, let 'em get you out of it, blasted tadpole bastards, always running around with dishrags on their heads! Wheezy. Sleazy. Easy—easy as peasy, let them get you out! They're honor-bound t' give you the hospitality of their tents—why, that's their jolly old code, don't ye know? Ask it, and they can't refuse to help, no, no, they can't! Turn around, Keene, old son. Backtrack and demand their bloody hospitality! That should knock 'em for a loop, troop, coop, stoop, hoop—keep 'em guessing, eh, old son? Turn back and ask 'em!*

"I hear you!" he screamed, his hands clamped over his ears.

"I'll do it! For God's sake, leave me alooone!"

Somehow, he managed to obey. Somehow, he found the strength to turn his camel's head around, to face it in the direction he had come, in the direction from which he knew the Bedouin *sheik* Kadar ben-Selim and his men were riding in pursuit of him, as thirsty for his life's blood as he was for water.

For two days now—ever since Alexa had helped him to escape—he'd managed to stay one step ahead of them, but his luck was fast running out. Without protective clothing to shield his body from the sun's burning rays, without water, without rest for the camel, he'd be a dead man within hours. *He didn't care about dying, but he didn't want to die slowly!*

It was the fault of the voices, he thought bitterly as his camel plodded back across the burning pale sands. For all that they eased his pain, his problems were all their fault, their doing. They wouldn't leave him alone, they wouldn't let him be! They were the ones who'd told him to hurt the Arab girl at the oasis of Yasmeen, and urged him to do those awful things to her; they, and the evil, wicked Frenchman Flechette, who'd been the Devil, of course, and their ally. They were the ones who'd always told him to do bad things, to hurt people—just like that parlormaid years ago. Poor little Polly. Alexa had cried that time and said he was evil and wicked, but none of it was his doing, not really. Couldn't she see that? Couldn't she understand? He was Keene Michael David Harding, and he was a good boy, his mama'd always said so. Good boys didn't hurt people. They didn't do hateful things to them, so why was Alexa always so mean to him? Why'd she always blame him and say he was bad, bad, bad, and look at him that way with her witch's green eyes all filled up with tears? He wasn't bad—he wasn't! Why couldn't she love him instead of condemning him? It served her right she'd had to stay with the Arabs. It would serve her right if they carved her up into little pieces just like ole Flechette. . . .

The sudden dusk of the desert was falling, swallowing up form and light like a great, greedy dark mouth when Keene's camel crested yet another dune. He dragged himself upright in the saddle and saw through eyes almost swollen shut the little Bedouin camp below: two black goatskin tents and a number of camels pitched alongside a tiny oasis he'd missed completely himself earlier that morning, for it was no bigger than a muddy pothole in the ground.

They're damned clever, these Arabs! Clever, ever, never, lever! Be careful, sonny! the voices cautioned, and he nodded solemn agreement as he started his stolen camel down the rise.

"*Sheik* Kadar! Look! Aiee, can it be? The *Englesy* returns to us!" a guard cried, snatching up his rifle and slinging it over his shoulder as he hurried forward to halt the intruder.

"What!" Kadar exclaimed, springing from his seat about the campfire where he had been serving coffee for his men, as was the duty of a *sheik*. He drew the curved dagger from the sash at his belt. His black eyes flamed with hatred. "Are you certain, Yussef?"

"*Ewellah*, my lord, I am! See for yourself! He comes!"

Kadar looked, and saw that young Yussef's keen eyesight had not failed him, for through the deepening twilight shadows rode a man in the uniform of the hated *Franziwa* Legionnaires, mounted upon one of Kadar's own racing camels—a white female stolen from their herd three days before, when they'd attacked the Legion patrol and taken this same man prisoner. The *Englesy's* hair was bleached pure white, his flesh black from repeated burnings under the hot desert sun. He'd tied himself into the saddle and was slumped to one side. If there was life yet left in him, there was not much of it, Kadar realized. He clamped a steadying hand over Yussef's shoulder.

"Hold your fire, my friend," he said softly, "for I am of a mind to make him pay for what he did to my woman, and an easy death by bullet for that jackal does not sit well with the plans I've made for him. Let him approach! Let us see what it is he wants of us, what he will tell us. Then we will take action."

"As you will, my lord," Yussef agreed as the others of their party filed out of the tent at their backs. Some had their fists clasped over the hilts of their daggers in readiness, or cradled their rifles in their arms like babes. All muttered curses against the Englishman.

"Hey, you bloody Arabs!" Keene yelled, reining in his camel

a few dozen yards from their camp and hauling himself upright like a drunkard. "You've a visitor out here!" He raggedly waved his arm over his head, the effort to do so draining the remainder of his strength and almost lurching him from the high, three-pronged saddle to the sand. He swayed and seemed about to topple, but then with superhuman strength managed to right himself and cling grimly to his reins.

"We are here, *Englesy!*" Kadar, his eyes narrowed and catching the firelight like chips of obsidian, rejoined. "Do you return to surrender yourself to our justice?"

"Not bloody likely!" Keene rasped, grinning crookedly as if he were drunk. He could barely sit he was so weakened, if the truth were known, but he put on a good front nonetheless. "Never! I'm innocent, you damned monkeys, you hear me? Truth is, I came back to claim your famous hospitality and protection, my friends! Three days and three nights as your honored guest—isn't that how it goes out here?" There was a taunting edge to his croaking voice that grated upon Kadar's already shredded patience.

The *sheik* blanched. "*Ewellah.* It is so, *Englesy.*"

"Then I ask your hospitality, *sheik*, old chum."

"No, sir, he cannot!" Yussef cut in before his *sheik* could answer, his eyes wide with alarm. "Such a jackal as this one—after what he did to your bride—after he killed her father and uncle in cold blood—by Allah, surely our honor need not extend to such offal as him, my lord?"

"If only that were so, Yussef," Kadar gritted through clenched jaws. "But alas, the *Englesy* is right. It is written that any man, even be he guilty of the foulest crimes and even should he be a man's mortal enemy, can lay claim to the hospitality of a Bedouin tent. For three nights and three days, we are honor-bound to treat him as our guest, to offer him the comforts of our tents, and our protection. Only afterward may we lay hands upon him and take revenge for the hurt and deaths of our loved ones!"

"Honor, my lord? Pah! What does such offal know of honor! He deserves no such consideration, I say!"

"Nevertheless, I will not sacrifice my own honor because

this dog has none. Take his camel, Yussef, and fetch him a bowl of fresh *léban* to drink. You, Akbar, see that he receives clean garments and food, if he is able to eat. I command you, all of you, to treat him as you would care for any welcome traveler, my friends!"

"If it is your command, we will, sir," Yussef agreed, though with ill-concealed resentment and through teeth gritted with anger. He went forward to lead the hated *Englesy*'s mount to the herd, while others carried the rider down from its back to the tent.

For two nights and two days, Keene Harding languished in the midst of his enemies like a Turkish sultan. He drank the fresh, foaming camel milk they served him, and devoured a little of the sheep they'd slaughtered and roasted in his honor, according to their ancient customs of hospitality. Still, it seemed to Yussef's eyes that he would not recover, for he lay weak and moaning, raving in delirium on a soft bed of sheep's wool framed with tamarisk wood, well into the second day.

"He is yet weak, my lord," Yussef said with a cruel grin of anticipation. "And tomorrow is the third day he has shared our tents. He is not strong enough to go anywhere. Our hunt for him is over!"

"Not so hasty! Be on your guard, my young friend," his *sheik* cautioned. "It is my thought that he is mad, and the mad are often far cleverer and far stronger than we give them credit. Don't relax your vigil simply because he *seems* weak, for he is as cunning as the desert fox!"

"Never fear. He will not escape Yussef, my lord Kadar," the young lad reassured his *sheik* confidently.

They found Yussef the next morning, lying naked in a pool of his own blood. His clothes, his prized rifle, and his dagger were gone, along with his brace of fine riding camels, stolen from the herd under the very eyes of a guard. Several goatskins of milk and oasis water were missing. So too was the *Englesy*, Keene Harding, gone, vanished into the night like a desert ghost while all in the camp slumbered.

"That jackal will pay for what he has done!" Kadar cried after he had wept over the body of the fallen youth. He raised his clenched fist to the sky, and his men saw that his eyes were terrible, black and emptied of all but rage and vengeance. "By Allah, I swear it!" he vowed. "I shall not rest until I have taken my revenge upon him, and upon the woman who shares his blood. The vengeance of Kadar ben-Selim will be written in blood upon the desert sands!"

al-Azadel

The Prosperous Kingdom

Chapter Thirteen

Alexa sighed as she gazed from the arch-shaped window.

Her view extended down the rocky mountain valley to the little kingdom of al-Azadel below. From here, the whitewashed, flat-roofed buildings seemed no larger than those of a toy village, the people as small as marionettes, but they were real nonetheless. Real and, in comparison to herself, free, and for that, she envied them, be they beggar or prince!

The wrought-iron grill that filled in the archway before her was lovely, an attractive design of sweeping arabesques and ornate scrolls, yet like the servants and the opulent quarters she had been given, lovely or not, it too only served to keep her prisoner. Her fingers clenched around the ornate metal curls so tightly, the knuckles showed white as tears welled in her eyes, blinding her to the beautiful view. She gulped, bravely fighting the torrent of weeping that threatened. Was this, she wondered bleakly, to form the pattern of her life from now on: endless days spent in idleness in a lavish prison cell, denied freedom, denied companionship, yet fed and watered and cared for as if she were a pampered pet in a golden cage?

The memory of those scorching days and starlit nights when she had crossed the deserts to reach al-Azadel filled her mind. How preferable even that had been to this monotony, albeit she had been taken captive and lost her innocence to the Tuareg chieftain! At least the journey had offered variety to her days, and she had had the Bedouin girl Muriel for company, even if fear of what awaited her at her final destination had served to sharpen even the simplest pleasures. Here, she had no one.

"Oh, Keene, why?" she whispered, blinking rapidly. "How

could you have ridden off to save your own skin? How could you have condemned me to this life—you, my own flesh and blood? I did what you asked—I freed you, didn't I? I proved that I trusted you, didn't I—didn't I? Oh, God, help me!"

She shuddered, tightening her fists to quell the hot flood of bitter resentment and anger that rose through her and replaced her self-pity and despair of moments before. With enormous effort, she mastered her temper yet again, more out of habit than from any true need to exercise control over her emotions here. After two long weeks in this lavish prison cell of tiled floors, colorful mosaic walls, and gauzy wall-hangings, she'd discovered that even if she hurled the brass bowl of fruits set out for her pleasure clear across her apartments, or dashed to smithereens the elegant glass pitcher of cool mountain-spring water provided to quench her thirst, or tear the hangings to shreds, no punishment would be forthcoming! A serving woman would simply appear, as if conjured from thin air by some Eastern magic, her bare feet pattering over the tiled floor. She would remove the debris, offering a respectful bow as she exited again. Alexa sighed. All the servants' expressions were uniformly bland. Their dark eyes shifted uncomfortably from the questions in Alexa's eyes, and that was that. None of them volunteered information, or heeded her insistent demands to speak with their chieftain when they served her meals or brought her basins of water to bathe. Nor did they explain the frequent sounds of gunfire she'd heard off in the distance. They merely smiled and shrugged an apology at their inability to comprehend her, which further frustrated Alexa to the point of making her want to scream—not that that would have had any results either!

The nights had been just as difficult to bear, for when she lay upon her silken-draped divan, she discovered she was rarely tired, having had little to occupy her thoughts or drain her physically during the day. It was then, when the moon shone full and silvery-round as a soothsayer's crystal ball through the latticed arched windows, that her thoughts turned insidiously to Sharif. Despite her determined efforts to force her thoughts elsewhere, she could not forget how damnably handsome he was: how disturbing as a man, with his wicked, inky-black eyes fringed with ebony lashes that would have been the envy of any woman, and with those glossy, blue-black commas of curly hair clinging to his noble head. Inevitably, memories of his stolen kisses, his bold caresses, and his ardent lovemaking would follow. Her willful thoughts strayed again and again to those moments when their bodies had been pressed intimately together; to that night in the camp by the ruined *kella* when he'd swept her off her prim feet, taken her innocence, and made her his woman.

Oh, what was wrong with her? she wondered irritably for the hundredth time. Why did she continually think about that awful brute, and relive every shameful detail of what he'd done to her? And why hadn't he bothered her since they'd reached his mountain stronghold? she wondered, frightened by the almost petulant direction of her thoughts. Out in the desert, it'd been quite obvious that he lusted after her, so why hadn't he come to her apartments since reaching al-Azadel? She couldn't help wondering if perhaps he'd found her undesirable, or lacking in some way that she was too innocent to define.

She glanced up disinterestedly as a woman entered, anticipating yet another serving girl. She was surprised to see that her visitor was older than most of the women she had seen to date, and definitely not of the servant class. Tall and slender and fair-skinned, the woman possessed the graceful yet self-assured carriage of a Berber queen. Her striking features were more Western than Eastern, a long yet narrow, elegant nose and high cheekbones cast in the same aristocratic fair-skinned complexion as the other Tuareg noblewomen she'd glimpsed upon her arrival in the *hareem*, yet given character by the fine lines at the corner of her eyes and across her broad brow, and by expressive dark brows and a well-defined chin that hinted at an obstinate, determined nature. Her mouth was wide, but the lips too elegantly molded to be considered lush or full. Large, intelligent dark eyes swept over Alexa with a thick, sooty fanning of the lashes. Alexa had a strong feeling that in that single glance, she had been expertly assessed.

"*La Bes!* Welcome to al-Azadel, Zerdali!" the woman said softly, inclining her head and spreading her arms gracefully.

The many silver bangles that encircled her slender wrists chinked musically as she did so. Smiling, she crossed the room and stood before Alexa, looking composed and elegant in a *caftan* of indigo-blue cloth, a color that seemed highly favored among both women and men here, Alexa had observed. The flowing garment's sleeves were wide at the wrists and the skirts reached almost to her ankles, where the curling toes of her Turkish slippers showed beneath. A belt of linked silver disks encircled her slim waist, each one engraved with flowers, and from them were suspended several little keys and a small, sharp dagger. She looked, Alexa thought, like the *chatelaine* of some medieval castle.

"You must forgive our long delay in making you welcome," the woman continued, "but many things have happened in the past fourteen days since you arrived. The rival tribe of my husband's nephew, Tabor ben-Murid, has long coveted our kingdom and its fortress. Unfortunately, the al-Tabor chose to wage a surprise attack upon our little city shortly after your arrival! In the confusion that followed, I was unable to welcome you as I would have wished to do. Please, Daughter, accept my apologies! Thanks be to Allah, and to the warrior skills with which He blessed my lord husband and his son, Sharif, our enemies were put to flight. Those difficult times are now past, and I'm here to greet you at last! Tell me, Zerdali, have you been treated well? Have my servants made you comfortable here?"

Alexa, once she'd recovered from her initial surprise at learning the woman spoke well-modulated, lilting English, nodded. "Why, yes, thank you, they have, quite comfortable." She drew a deep breath and steeled herself to add, "But comfort is the least of my concerns, ma'am! Instead, I'd very much like to know why I'm being held pris—"

"Ah, I am glad to hear it," the woman cut in with a warm smile, ignoring whatever it was Alexa had been about to add. "I'd instructed my servants to see that you lacked for nothing, and I'm relieved to discover that my wishes were carried out in my absence. But perhaps there is something else you wish for?" she asked, dark brows arched in inquiry. "If so, you have only to ask and, if it is within our power here at al-Azadel, it will be given you. Your apartments are to your liking?"

"Well, yes, they're quite beautiful, but—"

"They are lovely, aren't they?" the woman agreed with a smile. "These rooms once belonged to Bikkelu, my lord husband Malik's first wife. He loved Sharif's mother very dearly, and wanted always to please her, and so he commanded these apartments be added to the original *hareem*, the women's quarters, for her pleasure. We call this tower wing of the palace the Mist *serai*, or palace, for it seems to reach into the very clouds. The view of the valley and the gentle rain mists that drift about this tower is one the lady Bikkelu especially prized after long winter months spent traveling the hot desert sands with the herds. Come, let me show you!"

She crossed the room and, gently taking Alexa's elbow, led her back to the grilled archway she had left before the woman's arrival.

"You see, from here—if you look over there just . . . so . . . you may watch the sun as it rises," she promised, pointing. "It is truly a miracle of beauty to watch it coming up from behind the dark ridges of the mountains, bringing light to the new day, and to see the golden rays of its warmth burning off the mists of night."

"I'm sure it is," Alexa agreed, a little ungraciously, "but—I would much prefer to admire the mists and sunrises as a *free* woman!" she said pointedly, meeting the woman's dark eyes with her own determined green ones. Like it or not, the woman would hear what she had to say, she vowed. "These apartments, however lovely, are nothing more than an elegant prison, as I'm sure you're very well aware!"

If her directness upset or irritated the woman in some way, neither her eyes nor her expression betrayed her, Alexa observed. This close to her—less than a foot away—Alexa could smell the faint, elusive fragrance of rose water that enveloped her, and was poignantly reminded of her own mother in that moment, for the perfume of roses had been her mama's favorite too, as it was her own. She could also admire close up the magnificent artistry of the silver necklaces looped about her throat and resting upon her full breasts, and the bracelets, chased with curling flower designs, that encircled

193

her slender wrists.

"Ah, yes," the woman said thoughtfully. "Your freedom. You poor child, you must forgive my thoughtlessness, but you see, it is so difficult for me to remember that you did not come here of your own free will! After all, your arrival had been awaited for so very long!"

"Awaited?" Alexa exclaimed. "But that's impossible! My coming here couldn't have been expected! Until two months ago, I'd never even thought of leaving England, let alone imagined being abducted and made the captive of—of some desert robber!" she said scornfully.

"Ah, but the dreams foretold your coming, Zerdali—the *dreams! Wellah!* Did that rascal Sharif not tell you that he has dreamed of your coming for many, many years? And did he not ask you if you had perhaps ever dreamed of him?" She could tell from Alexa's shocked expression that he had not, though perhaps the girl had indeed dreamed of him. In a gesture that was both motherly and affectionate, the woman reached out and brushed a long, curling tendril of chestnut hair from Alexa's cheek, gazing at her fondly. "Often he described you to me, Zerdali—your unusual hair, your rare green eyes, that fair complexion. And seeing you at last, I no longer wonder that his dreams of you bewitched him, made him swear a vow before Allah that he would take no other as his bride but you. You are indeed as lovely as any *houri* sent from Paradise!"

Too startled by this surprising revelation to react to the caress, Alexa shook her head emphatically. "Your lord Sharif told me nothing, but I suppose that's hardly surprising, since our few conversations to date have proven somewhat strained," she explained wryly. Fuming, she turned away, hugging herself about the arms. "Besides, I had no wish to talk to him about anything! He abducted me, carried me off by force," she added hotly. "He and his band of cutthroats left my escort to die a slow and agonizing death in the desert, after they killed one of the men! Surely you can appreciate that I was in little mood for conversations about his dreams!"

Her cheeks bloomed scarlet and her eyes crackled, seeming even more emerald and electric as they flashed with anger in the lacy patterns of sunlight that streamed through the grilled

194

window and played over her lovely, indignant face.

Husky laughter escaped the woman as she chuckled with delight. "Ah, I see that you still have spirit, Zerdali, as well as that uncommon beauty! That is good, for a spirited woman is much prized by our menfolk. The Imochagh—the Free Ones, as we call ourselves—are not like the other tribes who roam the deserts. Those others regard their womenfolk as little better than chattel, and treat their sisters, wives, and daughters as shamefully as they would treat the lowliest camp dog! Amongst the Imochagh, Zerdali, women have position and honor, and are respected. Their opinions are valued. They're entitled to own property of their own, but are not considered property themselves! In this, I think perhaps they are even more fortunate than the women of the *Englesy*, although it is a great sultana, a queen rather than a king, who rules your lands. In your country, it is true that women have very few rights, yes?"

Seeing Alexa's expression unmoved by either her reassurances or her attempts at casual conversation, the older woman sighed. Her expression grew solemn as she slowly continued, "Alas, on the matter of your escort, I can give you no word of consolation, except to say that I have no doubt that Sharif did what he felt was right. He is a fair man, most of the time."

"Oh, come now!" Alexa cried, whirling to face her. "Was it fair to torture a man to death without benefit of a trial to prove his guilt, or a jury of his peers to convict him? Was it fair to leave other innocent men to die horribly of heat and thirst?"

"And was it 'fair' for those same men to watch in silence as two innocent men were murdered in cold blood, and a virgin maid brutally defiled by two of their number?" The woman shook her head sorrowfully. "Can you not see, Zerdali, that those who watched but did nothing were as guilty as the *Franziwa* who fired the gun or the *Englesy* who ravished the girl? Those others could so easily have prevented what happened at the oasis of Yasmeen, and yet not one of them lifted a finger to do so because the victims were of another race! Our lord Sharif is known by his people as a just man, one not given to cruelty. In that he is much like his father, my lord husband. You knew of Muriel bat-Hussein, and the tragedy that befell her and her family at the oasis of Yasmeen?"

"Yes, of course! And I agree that it was awful, just awful. But Flechette, the man responsible for that, *died* for his crimes," Alexa said earnestly. "Wasn't his torture and death enough to see justice served? Neither I nor the remainder of my escort had anything to do with that. I'm certain they knew nothing about it. They were good men, and I just know they didn't! Oh please, isn't there something you could do to help me get back to Algiers? I must return to England, don't you see? I can't stay here for the rest of my life, I just can't!"

The woman looked at her with a pitying expression. "I am afraid that is impossible, Zerdali," she said gently.

"Impossible? But why?"

"Because your fate yet hangs in the balance, little one!" the woman explained. "Muriel's betrothed, Kadar ben-Selim, made his position very clear to Sharif before he rode in pursuit of your brother. He has demanded that you be handed over to him to do with as he sees fit, once he returns to al-Azadel. According to the laws of my people, that is his right."

Alexa paled. "To—to do with as he sees fit?" she echoed. She remembered all too clearly the fierce argument that had taken place between the hawk-faced man and the chieftain, Sharif, when she was first captured. She recalled the naked hatred and contempt for her that had burned like hot coals in Kadar's black eyes, and her mouth tasted suddenly foul with apprehension. Her stomach did uneasy flip-flops. "W-what does that imply?"

"It implies exactly what it says, Zerdali," the woman said with a sigh. "If my lord husband, the prince, rules that you are to be handed over to Kadar—as he must—then Sharif will have no choice but to comply. Kadar will then have the power of life and death over you! It will be for Kadar alone to decide if you are to live or die, and if he allows you to live, in what manner you will pass the remainder of your days. *The rest of your life,* Zerdali, for of a certainty, there'll be no chance given you to escape him once you belong to him."

"But—that's barbaric! You can't hold people against their will, nor make slaves of them! This is the nineteenth century, not the Dark Ages! Besides, I'm innocent of any wrongdoing!" Alexa cried desperately. "I've done nothing wrong, do you hear me, nothing! Surely that must count for something, if there is any justice amongst your people at all?"

"Ah, I hear you, little one. And I know that you are innocent. But your brother—*he* was not innocent!" she insisted with gentle reproof in her tone. "And the old laws are still the ones we live by here. Is it not true that you helped your brother to escape Kadar's vengeance? That you untied him so that he might flee?"

"I helped him, yes, of course I did. He's my brother—I couldn't let him suffer torture for something he didn't do! He told me—he swore to me—that he had no part in what happened to Muriel and the others." Her chin raised defiantly, challenging the older woman to contradict her. "He swore his innocence to me—and *I believed him*. I still believe him," she insisted.

"You believed in him, and yet he left you to the mercy of his enemies?"

The woman's quiet words cut like razors.

"You make it sound so cowardly of him, but it wasn't like that! He left to bring help, I'm sure of it, not because he was guilty or afraid for himself, but because we were outnumbered. He had no choice, don't you see?" she tried to convince the woman, and in so doing, attempted to convince herself.

A veil seemed to drop over the woman's eyes. She made no attempt to argue Keene's guilt with the girl, or make any further comment on the matter other than to cluck soothingly in an effort to calm her. She looked, the woman thought, like a frightened kitten bravely about to spit and claw in defense of its life, despite its escalating fear.

"There, there, calm yourself, little one! Try to forget about your brother for the time being, and think instead of your own predicament. There is no need for you to become upset, nor to be afraid for the future—if you'll be sensible. You see, it is to avoid just such an unpleasant future for you at Kadar's hands that Lord Sharif and I have—conspired—together!"

"You and—and Sharif?"

"But of course Sharif!" Her expression softened at mention of the young man's name. "Did you not know that he loves you, Zerdali? He has waited many, many years for you to come

197

to him as his dreams foretold, only to be forced to accept the possibility that he might lose you to Kadar now that you are finally here. And because he loves you—and because I love him as the son that Allah chose to deny me—you must trust us to help you! You must promise that you will do all that we ask of you! Will you swear, Daughter, upon the name of your Christian God, to say nothing to any other of what we have planned for you, when the time comes for me to tell it to you?"

"You ask too much! You speak of Sharif's love, but how can he possibly love me? He doesn't even know me! What he feels for me is lust, nothing more nor less. And how do I know that I can trust either of you?" Alexa demanded, wrestling with her tortured emotions in an effort to subdue the fear that was uppermost and which grappled to control her. "Nothing that has happened to me so far has inspired my trust in anyone here!" Her thoughts careened crazily while she fought to regain her composure following her outburst. *Oh, Dear Lord, they intended to hand her over to Kadar when he returned from his hunt for Keene!* Then why was she stalling? Why didn't she simply tell the woman yes, yes, that she'd do anything to avoid falling into the Bedouin *sheik*'s hands? Surely any fate was better than that, she thought bleakly, remembering Flechette's agonized screams for mercy and death that had gone unanswered. Nevertheless, she wet her lips nervously and demanded in a calmer voice, "You ask for my promise, ma'am, but what about yours? How can I trust any of you?"

"Because you have no choice," the woman pointed out. "Because everyone must trust someone in this life. Because you want desperately to live, to be free!"

There was a crackling silence for several moments in the wake of her words.

"Then I suppose my answer must be yes," Alexa said at length, though with obvious reluctance. As the woman had said, what choice did she really have?

The woman nodded. "Good. Now, let me introduce myself. I'm the lady Kairee, the *Amir* Malik ben-Azad's second and only living wife, and the mother of his three daughters. Come, we will join the rest of the *hareem* and you shall meet the others. It is my thought that you have been left all alone for far too long. Some companionship will lighten your heart and give strength to your spirit. Perhaps, when you get to know us and learn our customs, you will even find you could come to like living here. Later we will speak more of those—other—matters, yes?" she added in a conspiratorial whisper.

Feeling more confused than ever, Alexa followed the lady Kairee from her apartments.

The quarters of the *hareem* opened off a long, wide corridor that led from her own tower apartments in the Mist *serai* to the main buildings of the palace. They were almost as opulent as those she had just left, yet the views from the arched and grilled windows could not compete with the lovely vista of green and gold and white from her own, as the lady Kairee had implied, Alexa noticed at once. Her eyes sought and found the grilled casements like that of a captured animal who jealously watches its cage doors with a view to escape. The scenes through the lattices were of bleak and forbidding, rugged mountain ranges or lonely, craggy red peaks, framed by small glimpses of dazzling blue sky and fleecy clouds. They had none of the color and panorama of "her" view of the little valley and the tiny city below.

The vast high-ceilinged, white-walled room they entered was scattered with comfortable low divans hung with silken hangings in a rainbow of hues, from the deep violet-blue of dusk to the hazy powder-blue dusted with gold that followed the dawn. Upon the walls, colorful mosaics of tiny tiles arranged in pleasing patterns delighted the eyes, and the blue-tiled floors were softened with thickly woven, fringed carpets in shades of blue and gold and crimson. The Persian carpets added a luxurious quality to the already lavish decor.

Gleaming brass dish-lamps hung from the ceiling by chains, but were unlit as yet for it was still early in the day, and glorious golden sunlight flooded the room, bringing the colors of mosaic and carpet alike to vivid life. Low brass tables held wooden platters of fruits and sweetmeats, and elegant, long-necked glass pitchers containing water were also close at hand. From one end of the room, a wide arched portal supported by slender white columns led out to a shady courtyard lined with still more columns. There reed cages of pretty songbirds hung in leafy fruit trees, warbling and trilling joyously, and peacocks stalked aloofly by with a sweep of their trailing jeweled tails, uttering harsh calls. From the other end of the room, a few shallow steps led down to an unseen area, hidden from Alexa's view by a wall and by fronded palms potted in great earthenware bowls, and further screened by light- and dark-blue hangings, from beyond which carried the splashing song of water fountains, and muted feminine laughter.

It was here, Alexa realized, in this vast communal chamber and in the many small, heavily guarded private apartments leading off it, that the women of the *hareem* of *Amir* Malik ben-Azad—wife, daughters, sister, cousins, nieces—reclined or gossiped or otherwise whiled away their afternoons, attended by their Inandan serving women, who were distinguishable from the Tuareg—or Imochagh—noblewomen by their darker complexions and their humble manner.

In one corner, a regal young woman who resembled the lady Kairee was seated cross-legged upon a huge pillow, playing an instrument that looked like a skin-covered mandolin. Both her singing and playing were haunting and sweet, and reminded Alexa fleetingly of the rascally Nabal, Cemal's young son, who had piped his flute so mournfully in the desert. Another young woman was humming to the melody as she labored busily at her embroidery, lovely geometric designs in colorful yarn flowing out from her nimble fingers to edge the fringed camel saddlebag of pure white wool upon which she was working.

Chatter and music ceased abruptly, and every one of the women looked up as they entered, the serving girls offering the lady Kairee a respectful bobbing of their heads, the others giving her warm smiles of greeting. To the last woman, their dark eyes at once shifted from Kairee to Alexa, and regarded her with frank curiosity they made no attempt to conceal. All but one of them seemed friendly, however, and offered her a shy smile of welcome.

As Alexa's eyes met the hostile, cinnamon brown eyes of the last girl—a sulky-lipped little creature with thick, raven-black hair that tumbled clear to her waist and a dusky complexion several shades darker than all the others—she recoiled at the naked hatred in their depths before quickly looking away. When, involuntarily, she found herself drawn to look back at the girl seconds later, she wondered if she'd been mistaken, for those hostile eyes were hostile no more! They were serene and bright with warmth and welcome now, as was the generous smile that curved her small red mouth.

"My daughters," the lady Kairee said, smiling fondly at the gathering. "I bring you the lady Zerdali. I bid you greet her as our honored guest at last, and welcome her to the *hareem*."

Like a flock of pretty, chattering birds, they jumped to their feet and jostled each other to get closest to Alexa. A wave of pretty perfumes surrounded her as they admired her hair, her eyes, her creamy complexion. Alexa glimpsed pretty Muriel's oval face and shyly welcoming smile amongst the sea of strange female faces, and mouthed a relieved greeting. At last—a familiar face!

The women introduced themselves one by one then. There were Drisana and Hestia, two of Kairee's three daughters; and an older woman named Zada, who was the *amir*'s widowed sister apparently; and her two middle-aged daughters, Jamila and Cynara; and her four granddaughters; and several others whose names she forgot almost as soon as she had learned them, there were so many! Soon, only one remained to introduce herself, and there was an uncomfortable silence as the other women waited for this last young woman to do so. With a contemptuous tossing of her head, she stepped forward and made a graceful bow.

"*Salam un'alaykum!* Peace be with you, and welcome, Lady Zerdali! My name is Raisha," purred the sulky-lipped girl in throaty, heavily accented English, clasping Alexa's hand between her own as she did so. "We are going to be the dearest of friends, you and I, I just know it, for we are both outsiders here, in our own fashion, and however hard we try, we will never be anything more."

The other women exchanged shocked glances, then turned to Alexa to see how she would respond to the woman's calculatedly disturbing comment.

But in answer to the other girl's silky greeting, Alexa only smiled and nodded politely, murmuring, "I'm sure, after such warm greetings as I have been given today, we will all be friends," and the tension was broken.

Still, as the women returned to their embroidery and music, Alexa silently wondered about the girl's hostile manner, and the coolness of the other women toward her.

Are you and I to be friends, Raisha? she pondered. *I truly wonder about that! Indeed, dare I trust anyone to be my friend here—a true friend—or must I constantly be on my guard against my "jailers," like any captive?*

Remembering the fleeting, unveiled glimpse of pure hostility she'd recognized for a moment in Raisha's eyes, she feared the latter would prove the case.

Chapter Fourteen

Sharif pulled aside the grilled aperture and gestured the turbaned man beside him to peer through it.

"There she is, Kahlil!" he murmured. "Did I lie when I told you she had grown to great beauty?"

For a few moments, the man watched yet said nothing. He simply stared through the small opening to where Alexa, robed in a *caftan* of iridescent blue and green like the shimmering "eyes" of a peacock's tail, sat beside a shallow marble bathing pool that was colored a delicate rose. Tears filled the man's blue-gray eyes above the indigo veiling he wore with the loose end pulled across his lower face in the manner of the Tuaregs. Although shadows hid the expression in Alexa's eyes, the sunlight burnished her glorious hair, worn caught up at the temples with pearl-studded combs and then tumbling loosely down her back to her waist. One toe she trailed in the still waters of the bathing pool while she gazed thoughtfully at her reflection, a lovely study in pensive feminine beauty, the man thought, a knot constricting his throat. Then, to his disappointment, another young woman who was relaxing in the bathing pool, submerged to her shoulders, cupped a handful of water and dashed it in Alexa's face, splashing the girl and banishing the lovely picture she had created.

"Too much thinking will of a certainty cause you many wrinkles, Zerdali!" he heard the girl cry teasingly in broken Tamahaq—the Imochagh tongue. "You will look like the lady Kairee before too long—as wrinkled as a date!"

He saw how Alexa tossed her damp hair and laughed, answering uncertainly in the same difficult tongue, "Better

203

wrinkles from too much thought than an empty head from too little! And shame on you, Raisha! The lady Kairee isn't wrinkled at all, she's a very handsome woman. Why, I do believe you're jealous of the attention she pays me, aren't you?" Alexa teased.

"Not at all, my friend! Since it seems the lady's attention only brings one hard work, I prefer to let you remain her favorite!" Grinning, the girl stuck out her tongue and clambered lithely from the pool.

At once, a darker-skinned serving girl hurried forward and wound a fresh white towel about her streaming body. Leading her across to a low divan, the servant gestured to the girl to lie down there and began gently patting her dry with another fluffy towel. This task completed to her satisfaction, she began massaging fragrant oils into the supple dusky-gold of her smooth skin, while another servant appeared with more cloths to briskly towel her long, thick black hair dry, and to brush and perfume it.

"You seem troubled today, Zerdali," the girl, who was lying on her stomach now while the servant smoothed oil into her calves, observed, glancing across at Alexa. Her cheek resting upon her arms, she regarded Alexa with slitted cinnamon-brown eyes. "Perhaps a massage would relax you. It always soothes me."

"No, thank you. I've had enough of baths and massages and perfumes and oils to last me a lifetime, Raisha," Alexa answered her frankly. "But no amount of pampering can make up for what I want most of all!"

"Ah yes, your freedom. Poor little Zerdali! It is so hard for me to understand what you're feeling, for my own people have never been truly free. We Inandan are neither slaves nor yet servants, you see, but ancient *custom* binds us as surely as chains to serve our patrons, the Imochagh lords." She sighed wistfully. "I wonder how it feels to be free, to owe allegiance to no one but yourself?"

Alexa grimaced, then appeared wistful. "Ah, Raisha, it's something you can't fully appreciate until it's taken away from you, I'm afraid. Have your people always served the Tuaregs— I mean, the Imochagh, then?"

"For as long as time," Raisha confirmed.

She wriggled to get comfortable. "Mmm, lower, Leila—yes, that's it, to the left a little," she instructed her masseuse, and the serving girl's supple fingers moved down over her back, gently kneading the knobs of her spine. Raisha continued, "We Inandan serve the nobles in many ways—oh, as blacksmiths and silversmiths, like Ahoudan, my father, and also as saddle-makers and marriage-brokers between the Imochagh families. The men of my family are artisans, you see, gifted by Allah with the talents to perform such diverse skills. In return for the services they perform and the things my people are commissioned to make for the *imaheren*, the nobles, they are rewarded with 'gifts'—a share in the harvests, perhaps, or animals from the herds for meat, or a bolt of fine cloth. In this way, we make our living. So you see, although we are not slaves, we are still dependent upon the generosity of our lords for our livelihood, having no crops or herds of our own."

"Mm," Alexa observed, fascinated by this unusual yet symbiotic relationship. "And are the Imochagh permitted to marry with the Inandan?" she wondered aloud. Raisha's accounting of the relationship between the Imochagh nobles and the Inandan serving classes had started her puzzling about Raisha's elevated position amongst the *hareem* of the *amir*, Malik ben-Azad. Raisha was Inandan, was she not? What, then, was her position here at the palace? Why did the lady Kairee and her daughters maintain an aloof distance from the girl which, although they never once treated her harshly or spoke to her unkindly, was nevertheless obvious to even a casual observer?

"There have been no marriages between our people as yet, my sister," Raisha said evasively, turning her head away from Alexa's curious gaze. "The Imochagh pride themselves on their fair Berber skins, and look down upon us Inandan because of our darker complexions. But, as with all things, there will come a first time, will there not?"

"Pah! Not in your lifetime I fear, Raisha! You know very well that an Imochagh lord will never marry a dark-skinned Inandan witch!" interrupted a scornful voice. "Though it is

205

possible he enjoys using one in his bed!"

Furious, Raisha leaned up on her elbows to glower at the intruder. Her cinnamon-brown eyes snapped with fury. "Fatima! I should have known it was you, spiteful one!" she hissed, swinging her legs over the side of the divan and gathering the towel about her as she stood up. "And who are you to mock me, old woman? Since your paps dried up in your youth, you are worse than useless—little more than a Bedouin slave here!"

The Bedouin woman, plump and well-advanced in years, smiled sweetly. "*Ewellah,* it is so. But better a Bedouin slave than an Inandan whore with ambitions that exceed her position!"

"Whore? How dare you call me a whore! You lie, Fatima! By Allah-Who-Knows-All-Things, I was never his whore! Our lord took me to his bed because he loves me—!"

"Loves you? Ha! Ha! That's a good one! What fanciful dreams you have, Raisha! Everyone knows you seduced our lord with your wicked dancing at the wedding of his sister, the lady Drisana. He lay with you to ease his body, stupid girl, and that is all," Fatima crowed. "A man's lusts are ruled by his swollen *weezan,* not his heart, as you would realize if you were not so blinded by conceit!"

Fatima turned to Alexa and smiled fondly, her lined, plump face softening noticeably as she looked upon the confused girl, who was attempting to follow their sharp exchange of words with little success.

"Come now, my lady Zerdali, to your apartments with you, at once! The *marabout* is here to give you your daily lesson, and he is an impatient fellow, as you should know by now. Hurry, girl, if you would not anger him! Quickly, quickly, now! And as for you," she cautioned Raisha, "hold your tongue!"

Alexa rose and obediently followed the woman who had been assigned to her as her personal maid away from the baths. She winked at Raisha over her shoulder as she went, for Raisha, despite her initial misgivings about her, had become the closest thing she had to a friend, though she felt closer to Fatima. For some reason, she had felt completely at ease with the old woman from the moment they had met, and it seemed Fatima had felt the same, for from the first moment of their introduction by Lady Kairee a month ago, Fatima had embraced her with tears in her eyes and called her "daughter" as if they had been companions for many years, rather than moments. Alexa had found the sharp-tongued old woman an amusing and soothing companion, and enjoyed the fuss she made over her and her merry habit of singing and humming as she tended her every need.

"Well? What is it to be today, dear Fatima?" she asked as they made their way down the long, wide corridor that led to her tower quarters in the Mist *serai*. "More of Master Hakim's blessed teachings of the Holy Koran, or will we study Tamahaq yet again?"

Tamahaq was the language spoken by the Imochagh nobles, a Berber dialect that she had found relatively easy to learn since she'd always prided herself on having an ear for languages, a talent her governess had nurtured when drilling her in French, which she'd spoken fluently for as long as she could remember. Tamahaq, with its alphabet of twenty-three simple and thirteen compound letters, had proved a challenge, and at times the pronunciation of its sounds had all but defied her Western tongue. But it was a challenge she was mastering little by little, and she was improving by means of daily conversations with the women of the *hareem*, who were always ready to help her, she'd discovered. Drisana, Jamila, and Hestia, the lady Kairee's three married daughters, had been particularly eager to help her, and had each taken the time to correct her mistakes and to gently advise her in the proper way of speaking their language. On the other hand, poor little Muriel, her mother Noura, and her aunt could speak neither Tamahaq nor English, and over the past few weeks it seemed to Alexa that their budding friendship, founded on mutual kindness, had dwindled. Besides, between her daily language lessons and the teachings in the Islamic faith that she was receiving every day from the old *marabout*, or priest, Master Hakim—instruction she received at the lady Kairee's insistence—she had seen little of the Bedouin girl. On the rare occasions when they'd met, Raisha always seemed to appear from nowhere and drag her away to see some new marvel or other, leaving poor Muriel alone again. Alexa frowned. She'd come to the conclusion that her first impressions of Raisha had been false, but now she was at times beginning to feel stifled by the girl's overly possessive manner and her jealousy.

As if reading her thoughts, Fatima observed as a servant opened the double doors leading to the Mist *serai*, "Ah, that Raisha! She's a sly, conniving dark-skinned witch! Did I not warn you to keep your distance where she's concerned, but no, you persist in ignoring Fatima's advice! What am I to do with you, eh, stubborn little one?"

"Oh, come, Fatima, don't be so spiteful. Raisha's quite harmless. She's just jealous of you and the others, and wants to keep me for her friend alone. When my novelty has worn off, she'll find something else to amuse her. After all, she doesn't seem to have any friends within the *hareem*. I feel sorry for her at times."

"Pah! Friendships are earned, they are not a birthright, Zerdali. Feel sorry for her if you wish, but do not let pity lull you into trusting her. After all, she has no cause to be fond of you, of all people, especially since you'll soon be—"

Fatima broke off suddenly, blushed and hurriedly added, "—Especially since you'll soon be—er—" Her voice trailed away.

"Especially since I'll soon be what?" Alexa demanded, her tawny brows raised in suspicion. Fatima seemed to be a party to whatever it was the lady Kairee had planned for her, and so she jumped at any chance to quiz Fatima for more information.

"Why, especially since you will soon be—er—speaking Tamahaq far better than she, and will be way, way above her in station," Fatima said, covering clumsily. "The Imochagh consider the Inandan crafty, sly folk, little better than dark-skinned Gypsies! And they do so with reason, *habibah*, make no mistake. It is said"—she wet her lips nervously—"it is said they possess powers!"

Alexa halted and turned to face the shorter woman, laughter dancing in her green eyes. "Powers? You mean, magical powers?"

"So it is said—and I, Fatima, have seen some of their magic for myself, *ewellah*, indeed, so you need not laugh! Believe me, it is a brave man who denies the Inandan anything, for if he does, he will find his wives barren and sickening, his daughters languishing with fever, his milk camels' udders dried up, his breeding camels sterile! Such is the power of their *tezma,* their evil eye!"

"Oh, rubbish!" Alexa laughed. "I'm sure it's nothing but a coincidence when such things happen. Shame on you for believing in such things, Fatima. I can understand a Tuareg who has never once left the desert clinging to such superstitious nonsense, but not you, a woman of the world! Didn't you tell me you'd traveled to Damascus and to Egypt? That you'd crossed the Red Sea and visited the holy shrines at Mecca and Medina and other places? Surely you're above such beliefs, dear Fatima!" she teased.

"I know what I know, and I've seen what I've seen!" the woman insisted obstinately. "Allah protect us from that witch, Raisha. . . ."

The turbaned man turned away from the grilled aperture and shook his head with a sigh.

"Has she gone then, my friend?" Sharif asked, disappointed, for he had hoped to gaze upon Zerdali's beauty himself.

"*Ewellah,* she's gone to her apartments with her serving woman," Kahlil confirmed.

Sharif clapped his hands, and a servant appeared and bowed deeply.

"Bring us tea, Akli," his master commanded, "and some refreshment for my guest."

The servant bowed and quickly exited as Sharif gestured Kahlil to take a seat upon a low divan. He took a seat opposite himself.

"Be seated, my friend, and compose yourself. The years since you saw Zerdali last have been many. I think the shock was too great for you, after so long?"

"You're right, my lord Sharif," the man replied wearily. "Yet I'm more encouraged than I can say to see her grown so—perfectly—to womanhood. Tell me, do her studies go well?"

"Better than I had dared to hope! Hakim, the *marabout,* tells me they are proceeding very quickly, and that she is eager to learn and remembers everything he teaches her. In a few days, she will be ready."

The blue-gray eyes above the man's indigo veiling darkened. "Already? Ah, I wonder. If she is as determined and obstinate as the lady Kairee says, she will not accept what you have planned readily, my lord. I implore you, do as I asked! Give her the choice to say yes or no to your plan. Let her decide for herself if she'll go along with it, or would rather bide her time and trust to whatever decision your lord father makes in this matter."

Sharif's black eyes smoldered. "Ah, Kahlil, if only I had the luxury of time to allow Zerdali a choice. But Kadar could return any day now, and I dare not delay until she's had time to consider her options. She's still furious with me for abducting her, Kairee says, and would not willingly go along with our plans. For her sake, it must be done my way."

"Has Kadar not yet found the one he seeks?"

"The messenger from him said not. Zerdali's brother fled into Tanezrouft, that desert-within-a-desert that we call the Land of Fear and Thirst, after killing one of Kadar's men. Alas, Kahlil, even should he survive the wastelands of Tanezrouft, Kadar is sworn to find him and slay him, and the girl with him. Kadar would suffer death himself before he'd let him flee a second time unpunished!"

He noticed suddenly that the older man's pale hands shook upon hearing his words, and that what little could be seen of his weathered, deeply tanned complexion had grown ashen beneath the bronze. Reaching over, he poured them each a small cupful of the steaming sweet tea so favored by his people which the servant had silently set before them, pressing the small cup into the older man's chill hand and wrapping his fingers about it.

"Come, drink, Kahlil, and draw strength. By Allah, I would never have spoken so bluntly had I known my words still had the power to grieve you. Forgive me, sir."

The man drained the cup, and seemed to gain a little color from the benefits of the scalding, syrupy beverage. His hands no longer trembled.

210

"Ah, now, do not blame yourself, Sharif. The fault lies in me, not in you. Knowing all that I know, I should be able to harden my heart against him. *Ewellah*, my head tells me to cast him out of my heart—but my heart refuses to forsake him!"

Sharif nodded in understanding and pity. "I understand. A strong tree may bear both good and poor fruit, it is written, but does that same tree not give life and sustenance to both? Why, then, should a man be different from a tree?"

"It is so," Kahlil agreed. "But a skillful gardener would prune out the branches that are spoiled, Sharif, to permit the good to flourish and grow unhampered. So must I cut this twisted love from my heart! That branch has grown evil fruit, and is no longer worthy of the tree. It must be destroyed, before it destroys others." He paused. "But on the matter of Zerdali, again, I ask you one last time, Sharif—can the girl not be told, and given a choice?"

"No. This way is the only way! I will not risk her life to grant her the freedom of choice!"

"You love her still?"

"More than ever! I've loved her for a lifetime," he said simply.

"And does she return your love?"

The chieftain scowled. "How can she, my friend? During the journey here, she hated me for abducting her, and had only harsh words for me. She called me 'savage' and 'heathen' in response to my words of love! And since then, the lady Kairee has kept her closely guarded, as she once watched over my sisters! But she will learn to love me, Kahlil. By Allah, she will learn if it takes me the rest of my days to teach her!"

Kahlil's fears ebbed. He found he was able to chuckle at Sharif's determined optimism. " 'Heathen savage,' eh? Ha! She is little changed, I believe! I wish you great good fortune then, my lord, for I remember her most clearly as an obstinate little creature—more obstinate than many donkeys! She will not easily forget your trickery in this matter!"

Sharif grimaced. "My thanks for your reassurances, Kahlil! They comfort me not at all!" he observed with a rueful grin, which soon faded. "Besides, there is little trickery about it. After all, is it not written that a woman's silence in such matters signifies her consent?"

"Ah, it is so written, yes. But I very much doubt she would be silent *if* she knew what it was you plan to do!"

Sharif's handsome, clean-shaven face grew dark and stern once more. "Perhaps you're right, but as I said before, I dare not take that risk. Is it agreed between us then? You will not stand in my way, despite Zerdali's ignorance?"

"It is agreed. I think perhaps you're right, after all. I see no other way out of it. She will need your protection when Kadar returns, I know, for there is a chance he will refuse a blood-payment in return for his losses."

"Then thanks be to Allah, it is settled between us! I will send the Inandan matchmaker to your household with the gifts I've chosen without delay. You can expect my man Ahoudan there before sunset, to discuss the details. And you will not be disappointed nor shamed by the gifts I have chosen, Kahlil, for they are many and precious, and will show you the honor and esteem in which I hold you, although they are but a small symbol of the great love I carry in my soul and heart for Zerdali. In truth, she is the breath of my life! Fifty of my finest white racing camels will be yours, each one a female, each one chosen for its beauty and swiftness, each one heavy with young. Upon their backs will rest only the finest three-pronged saddles of leather and tamarisk wood, the best my Inandan saddle makers can produce. There will be embroidered saddlebags, heavy with bolts of indigo cloth for your honored wife, the lady Yasmeen, stitched by the women of my father's *hareem*, and ornaments of silver and armbands of beaten copper for yourself. There will be spices and perfumes and rare herbs, and rose and fruit trees from the famed gardens of Damascus to plant in your own terrace gardens."

"You are too generous, my young lord," Kahlil said softly, inclining his head. "But such riches are not necessary. I humbly ask only for your gentleness and patience with her, nothing more."

"They are already hers, I swear it," Sharif responded. "And my generosity is nothing in comparison with yours, for you have given me the greatest gift any man could give another!"

Their eyes met in mutual admiration and respect.

"Go in peace, Kahlil!" Sharif said huskily. "May Allah guide you safely, always and in all things. My only regret in this matter is that from this moment forth, custom decrees that we may no longer address each other directly, face to face, man to man. I have enjoyed our games of chess in the past, and will miss them after this day. You were always a cunning opponent, Kahlil."

"Your regret is my own, Sharif," the man replied with obvious emotion. "Guard her carefully, my son."

"With my life, Father," Sharif answered, and he embraced the older man fiercely, repeating, "With my very life and soul!"

Chapter Fifteen

Ahoudan, the Inandan silversmith, pumped energetically at the skin bellows in his workshop. His burly dark-brown arms bulged with effort as air was forced out of the bellows, wheezing as if it came from a pair of faulty lungs. The charcoal fire roared and leaped up to twice its former size, its heat licking lovingly at Ahoudan's already ruddy, streaming face, and sending giant tongues of light skittering across the shadowed whitewashed walls.

The hour was late—long past the time of the *muezzin*'s call to sunset prayers, when Ahoudan usually ceased his day's labors, closed up his forge, and sent his apprentices home for the night, before leaving himself for the little whitewashed, flat-roofed house he shared with his wife, Boucha. But the pieces he had been commissioned to design and cast in silver for his master, Sharif al-Azim, had yet to be completed, and he had only a few hours left in which to do so.

"Ah, these young lords!" he muttered to himself. "Everything is rush, rush, rush! Do they never plan ahead? Do they never consider that such things take time, if the workmanship is to be of the finest? No, of course not! All at once, they want something done, and tomorrow is not good enough, oh, no, my friend Ahoudan—it must be ready *yesterday!*" He shook his head ruefully. "Ah, well, never mind, Ahoudan, never mind the lateness of the hour," he consoled himself. "You are a master of your craft, and the young lord will reward your long hours of work and your talents generously! The hard part is already done, and the finished piece exquisite, if I do say so myself, *ewellah!* Only the simple one is left, and that too only a

214

moment from being cast! Patience is all it takes, Ahoudan, you old jackal, and a steady hand and eye. . . ."

Still muttering and humming to himself, the finest silversmith of al-Azadel—or indeed, the finest Inandan artisan anywhere, by Allah!—wiped his brow on the trailing end of his grimy white turban, and repeated his labor, pumping again at the goatskin bellows, not satisfied until the furnace fire was a shimmering cavern of heat, orange and crimson and a pure, pale topaz that was almost white. When it was hot enough for his needs, he turned from the furnace and back to his worktable. There he carefully inspected the two halves of the intricate mold he had designed and prepared, using the lost-wax process, over the past three days since Sharif had summoned him. From this mold, a solid silver object could be cast.

Using a camel-hair brush to ascertain that his mold was free of all traces of wax and dust, Ahoudan next took up a long-handled crucible and heated the silver he would use to cast his creation to the melting point, plunging it deep into the heart of his fiery furnace. When it had reached the point which years of experience, his artist's skill, and an acquired sixth sense told him was the proper one, he removed the molten silver from the fire and poured it quickly into the bronze mold, locking the two halves together. This done, he picked up the mold again with long-handled pincers and, while it was yet red-hot, he plunged the bronze mold into a vat of cool water, reeling as clouds of steam billowed out to fill his workshop and turn his face a deep, dark red.

"*Wellah!* It is done!" he crowed softly, nodding in satisfaction as he drew the cooled mold from the water some time later.

The moon had risen by the time Ahoudan parted the cooled mold and removed the small object within. It was an Egyptian *ankh* cast in fine silver, a span-sized, T-shaped cross with a loop at the top: the ancient symbol of life and of the soul, and an ornament highly favored by the Imochagh nobles. The edges were a little ragged as yet, but soon, under Ahoudan's skilled hands, the roughness would be ground away with fine sand until the talisman was as flawless and softly gleaming as

215

moonlight. Ah, *wellah*, only when it was as smooth and silken as the flesh of a virgin's inner thigh would he take up hammer and fine chisel and etch the delicate tracery of designs his master had described upon it: tiny damask roses, each one set inside a lozenge-shaped border and connected by a curling vine. The rose, his master had told him with a sheepish smile, was an Eastern flower highly favored by the women of the *Englesy*, and Ahoudan had guessed that the gifts were intended for the captured beauty named Zerdali, who had been whisked away to the women's quarters of the palace *hareem* upon her arrival at al-Azadel, where she'd been strictly hidden from view ever since.

It had proven no surprise to Ahoudan, therefore, when he had been summoned to the Palace of the Clouds and his young lord's chambers, and learned that his Inandan matchmaker's talents were to be called upon as well as his silversmith's arts. The only part of it that puzzled him was the secrecy involved, and the foreign one named Kahlil's part in all of this? Why, Ahoudan wondered, had the *amir*'s Christian friend been presented with Lord Sharif's generous, costly gifts as if he were the father of the bride? By the Prophet's Beard, it was an intriguing question, and one Ahoudan had pondered long and hard. . . .

Pausing a moment to stretch the kinks from his aching back, Ahoudan crossed the untidy workshop to a corner where something was protected from curious eyes and from smoke and dust by a covering of fine cloth. Drawing it aside, Ahoudan appraised the object beneath with a pride that rivaled that of a mother admiring her newborn child, for like a mother, he had created this wondrous beauty, had brought it forth in a labor of love and agony, had breathed life into it with the breath of his body and the caress of his hands and, he sometimes fancied, at the cost of a small part of his soul.

A delicate, spherical cage of silver wires hung on a dainty chain. The globe enclosed a little bird with spread wings that appeared about to soar into flight from a slender branch at any moment, or to warble an exquisite song. Except for its silver coloring, the bird and the branch were extraordinarily lifelike, each tiny feather, each bright and lively eye, each grain and knot and tissue-fine leaf in the branch delicately, painstakingly detailed. Curiously, Lord Sharif had commanded that the cage be fashioned without a door. "Songbirds," he had told Ahoudan in a mysterious voice, "should be granted their freedom, if they are ever to love their master and stay with him by choice." The enigmatic remark had seemed to Ahoudan like a piece of some complex riddle, and he had shrugged and agreed without bothering to puzzle it out. Such complicated thinking was better left to educated men such as his lord, he decided, nobles who had time to waste in frivolous intellectual pursuits that profited them nothing.

"Ah, Ahoudan, you are a wonder!" he praised himself, his calloused fingertips tracing the delicate creation he'd fashioned. "A Persian nightingale to delight the little dove whose beauty has bewitched our young lord's senses!" He chuckled. "*Ewellah*, truly, it is fitting!"

"What is fitting, O my father?" demanded an irritable voice.

"Raisha, my daughter!" Ahoudan cried, startled to hear her voice so suddenly from the ruddy shadows. How long had she been there, watching him? he wondered, annoyed by her stealth. How many of his mutterings had she overheard? *Wellah*, she was more cat than woman, this one, always slinking about and surprising people! For all that she was his daughter, and for all that he had a great liking for cats, he had no liking for his youngest daughter, headstrong, selfish Raisha. She had a way of ferreting out secrets however carefully one guarded them, and he had an uneasy forboding that the secret he was in possession of was one she'd give a great deal to discover.

He slipped the cover over the silver songbird in its cage, his body concealing his actions from her, before turning to face her and asking, "Well, what do you here at this late hour, Raisha? Why are you not among the women of our lords' *hareem*, as is your place? Or else visiting our poor mother, who has missed you these past months, instead of coming here?"

By the light of the glowing fire, he watched warily as Raisha drew away the veil that covered her face and head. He had wondered why she had donned her veil, but the answer was obvious when he saw that her eyes were swollen from crying,

217

her small red mouth twisted into a sulky pout.

"I am here because I do not know what to do, where to go, or to whom to turn, my father!" she wailed hoarsely as if she had cried for many, many hours. "Tonight, my lord Sharif refused me his bed yet again!" Her slim, dusky fingers twined together in her anguish as she continued bitterly, pacing back and forth. "I humbled myself, Father—I threw myself at his feet like the lowliest Negro *aklan* and begged him to favor me tonight! With tears in my eyes, I reminded him that he has not summoned me to his apartments for many, many weeks, that he has ignored me since he returned from the desert. But he would not be persuaded. Instead, he was *kind!*" she hissed. "He took my hand and raised me to stand before him. He said that although he found me beautiful, and although I had pleased him greatly in the past, I must now return to my father's household. He said that he'd given the lady Kairee orders to see that I left the *hareem*, and—and that my possessions had already been taken to my father's house." Her mouth twisted with bitterness. Her cinnamon-brown eyes were hard and cold, muddy pools of fury as she hissed, "He offered gifts to placate me, O my father, as if I were not his favored one amongst women but a dancing girl from the Street of the Courtesans! He treated me like a common harlot who could be bought and used and—and discarded without thought! O my clever father, I beg you, help me!" she pleaded with the old man, her arms outstretched in entreaty. "You are wise in the ways of our Imochagh lords. Tell me—what have I done to displease him! How have I failed! How can I regain his favor and his love—how, *how?*"

Ahoudan eyed his daughter sternly and with obvious disapproval, not a whit moved by either her upset or her hurt.

"Pah! Now you cry, eh? Good for you, girl! Perhaps now you will listen to your father, who has the wisdom of his years to guide you! Did I not warn you at the lady Drisana's wedding that nothing but ill would befall you if you cast your eyes in Sharif's direction, foolish daughter? And yet, you disobeyed me and flaunted yourself! Ah, don't deny it, Raisha, don't—I am not yet blind! I saw how you danced that night, with your painted eyes and your painted lips. Your dance was for his pleasure alone! You heated his blood with lust for you, but now the fire has burned out and you find you are cast aside. *Wellah*, what did you expect? That our lord would marry you? Why? Why should he marry one who throws herself at his feet and offers her body with her dancing? Does a herder buy the camel that gives him her milk freely? And you are a bigger fool to hope that one of the *imajeghan* would take the likes of you as his bride when he has already tasted the delights of your body! Wake up, O my daughter! Do not let your pride and ambition blind you to the truth. You are *Inandan*, and you are barren. One would be enough, but both facts make marriage to Sharif al-Azim impossible for you. Accept it now, and instead cast about for another husband before you are too old for marriage. Perhaps an older man who has lost a wife and needs someone to pleasure his loins occasionally and to care for his little ones. Such a one would not care that his seed could find no root in your belly, as would a younger man."

"No!" Raisha cried with a shudder. "I won't take an ugly old man for a mate, and nor will I care for his children. It is my beautiful Sharif I love, only Sharif I will take as my own! If I cannot have him for my husband, I will have no man!"

"Pah! You are a romantic and a fool! Does love put rice and lamb in your belly, and bangles of silver around your wrists? I ask you. Does love clothe you and protect you, eh, Daughter?" Ahoudan sputtered, waving his hammer in her direction.

"Can a man I have no love for make me feel as if I am the most beautiful woman in the world when he lies with me? Can his caresses make my heart sing like the strings of the *anzad*? No, no, no!" She stamped her little foot petulantly. "There must be something I can do to make Sharif smile upon me again. Some potion I may drink? If you will not help me, then I shall ask Mother Boucha," Raisha threatened ominously, her eyes flashing angrily. "She won't scold me and tell me to forget Sharif. She'll understand how I feel. She'll know of a way. . . ."

"What way?" Ahoudan jeered. "With her potions of herbs and spells, her arts of *tezma*, her evil eye? Ha, Daughter, try if you must, but this time your mother's skills will be useless, I promise you!" he declared, growing increasingly annoyed by his daughter's stubborn persistence. "It will take far more than that to draw Sharif's eyes from his beloved's, for tomorrow they will be joined as—"

Too late, Ahoudan caught himself. He clamped his mouth shut, hoping his daughter had been too upset to notice his slip or had not realized the implication of his words, but Raisha was certainly no fool. She pounced like a cat pouncing upon a mouse, claws unsheathed!

"Beloved?" she echoed sharply, her stance alert now. "Who, pray, is Sharif's 'beloved,' and how are they to be joined?" She took two steps toward her father, her ornaments chinking noisily. Involuntarily, the man shrank back against the wall. "Tell me, Father!" she threatened, changing to *tenet*, the secret language used among the Inandan blacksmiths, to voice her demands. "You know something you do not wish to tell me, yes? What are you hiding? What is it you know?"

"I know nothing!" Ahoudan insisted lamely, lapsing into *tenet* himself. He nervously wet his lips. When Raisha was angry, as she was now, she scared him a little, if truth were known, for he was a gentle, even-tempered fellow who rarely raised his voice except to indulge in mild scoldings, while his daughter possessed a violent temper that caused her to throw things, more often than not, and to simmer for days in a broth of revenge that was terrible to behold. "Nothing!" he repeated.

"You lie, Father!" she accused. "You mentioned Sharif's beloved, I heard you! Who is she? Is it Radwane's daughter, that goat-eyed Raishatu?" She watched his eyes carefully. "Or Hamzetta's scrawny offspring?" Not a flicker, she saw, her eyes intent upon her father's. Who could it be then? she wondered, racking her memory. Which one amongst the Imochagh noblemen's daughters might have caught Sharif's eye in the past few weeks since he'd returned from the desert with that green-eyed Zerdali as his captive—

Her heart skipped a beat in her breast and fluttered painfully as her chest constricted in sudden agony. *No, no, anyone but she!* The glimmer of a truth she did not want to even consider had struck her like lightning from the heavens. Surely not— Zerdali? Surely Sharif had not lost his heart to the green-eyed, foreign beauty? Why, she could never hope to compete with one such as she! A lump formed in Raisha's throat, too huge

220

and hurtful to swallow. It choked, how it burned! Had her lord in truth cast her aside for Zerdali, with her fiery mane and her pale, pale skin, and her lovely face and form? Did that explain the *marabout*'s long hours closeted with Zerdali in her apartments, teaching her the Tamahaq tongue, the Writings of the Prophet? Aiee, surely it did—it all made sense to her now!

"Ah-ha! His beloved is Zerdali, is she not?" Raisha exclaimed, the words ground out from between her clenched teeth. She watched her father's eyes, and sure enough, something flared there, although his expression remained impassive, and her last, fragile hope died.

"No!" Ahoudan insisted, blustering in his guilt and confusion. "You're wrong, quite wrong!"

"If I am wrong," Raisha hissed, her eyes glowing, "then you are not my father! It *is* Zerdali Sharif loves, and it is she he means to join with—as his wife, *ewellah!*"

"Nonsense, girl! Utter nonsense."

"Not nonsense but truth, my father! If I am wrong, swear it to me by the Beard of the Prophet, and I will believe thee!"

"Go away!" Ahoudan suggested crossly, backed into a corner, for deeply religious in his beliefs as were all of the Inandan, unlike their far-less-devout lords, he could not bring himself to swear falsely, and his daughter knew it.

Raisha crowed with triumph. "Ah, so it *is* Zerdali! I knew it! When are they to be wed?" There was silence. "Did my lord ask you to fashion gifts for his bride?" Silence again. "He must have," Raisha reasoned aloud, "for you are the finest silversmith in al-Azadel, and he would want nothing but the best for his beloved bride!" Her voice trembled with hurt and outrage. "So. Is that why you're still here this evening, Father!" she accused. "Do you work late into the night to fashion the lady Zerdali's wedding gifts from her lord?" She almost spat the words, her fingers clamped over the edges of her robes to keep from striking out blindly in an explosion of temper. "If so, I fancy the happy day is to be soon, else why would you keep such late hours? When, Father? Tomorrow? The day after? Two days? Tell me!"

Ahoudan's shoulders slumped. He was defeated, and he knew it. Softly he admitted in *tenet,* "Tomorrow. They are to be wed

221

tomorrow, Daughter. Zerdali is the one of whom Sharif has dreamed these many years. He will take her as his bride, and your part in his life will then be over. Accept it, and do as I ask," he implored her. "Find a good man, an honest, loving man for a husband, and be happy with what you have, instead of pining for the impossible."

Yet even as he beseeched her, he knew his words fell upon deaf ears. She turned from him and crossed the room, casting about until she spied the objects hidden under the cloth that he had tried to keep from her view. She drew off the cover and a low, jealous sigh hissed from her lips.

"Truly, they are beautiful—the finest you have ever made, my father," she said softly, grudgingly. "My lord's love for the woman must be great indeed for him to commission such lovely, costly gifts for her."

Ahoudan nodded and began to relax. Raisha seemed to be growing resigned to the idea, little by little, much to his relief. "Ah, indeed, yes, very great!"

"And yet, he wishes his wedding to her to be a secret?" She frowned in puzzlement, her nose wrinkling. "He must, for I have heard no talk of it in the palace. Now, I wonder, why is that?"

Her father squirmed in discomfort, for Sharif had indeed sworn him to secrecy. It would not do to admit as much to Raisha, however. "Secret? No, not a secret exactly! After all, a wedding is a public ceremony, and the *amir*'s attendance, the feasting and the dancing which is to follow, can hardly be concealed!"

"That is true. But—if there is no need for secrecy, then why had I not heard of our lord's decision to take a wife until now?" She thought for a moment, then said thoughtfully, "Perhaps the secrecy was not meant to hide the truth, as you say, but to *postpone* it from being made public until the last possible moment for some reason. Now I wonder, what could that reason be?" She eyed her father, yet his shrug was genuine. Whatever that reason might be, Raisha was convinced her father knew nothing more than he had told her. . . .

"And you will be the one to slaughter the sacred sheep for the feast? You will play the sacred *tendi* for the dancing and preside over the entertainment?" she asked slyly.

"But of course!" Ahoudan acknowledged, beaming with pride. "Did our lord not choose his favorite among the Inandan, his trustworthy, talented Ahoudan, to handle everything for him as it should be handled?" He puffed up like a rooster, for he was as proud of his talents as marriage-broker and master-of-ceremonies for the Imochagh as he was of his silversmithing talents. "The wedding feast will be all that is expected for *Amir* Malik's son, and more."

"Good! Then it will be a simple matter for you to select your daughter Raisha as one of the dancing girls, will it not?"

"My daughter Raisha?" he exclaimed, suddenly realizing what she had said. "No! I forbid it! It would not be fitting!" protested the old man.

"Fitting or not, I want to dance for him one last time, Father—to show our fine lord what a prize he has thrown away so carelessly for the sake of his fair-skinned bride, who has no hint of passion for a man in her body, nor fire in her blood to bring him pleasure!"

Raisha made her expression humbly imploring, and allowed a tear to slip down her dusky cheek in the firelight. "Please, beloved Father, please grant me this one small request? Let me have my little revenge on Sharif, so I can cast him out of my heart forever. Perhaps then I'll be able to do as you ask, and find myself a fitting Inandan husband," she wheedled.

"You will say nothing to anyone before the wedding takes place if I agree?" Ahoudan said hopefully. After all, what harm could Raisha's dancing do this time, except perhaps to whet the bridegroom's appetite for his wedding night?

"My lips will be sealed, and as silent as a *marabout*'s tomb, my father!" Raisha promised demurely, with just the right note of melancholy eagerness.

"Oh, very well, then," Ahoudan agreed with a relieved sigh. Perhaps after this, she'd take herself a husband and settle down as he'd asked, he thought hopefully. "You may dance at the wedding, Daughter."

Chapter Sixteen

"Hurry, hurry, I say!"

"I *am* hurrying, Fatima—though I honestly don't see why there's such a blessed need to! After all, I've been a Christian for the past twenty-odd years, so I don't see why a few minutes more will do me any harm. Why not simply ask the *marabout* to wait?" Alexa reasoned as she struggled into the garments Fatima had brought her to wear that morning.

Fatima rolled her eyes and shook her head. "Pah! It is not the *marabout* I am worried about, little one, but the *amir!* Allah forbid we should attract our lord Malik's displeasure today, of all days!"

"Why? Is there something else special about today—other than my becoming a Muslim, I mean?"

"Why—no, of course not!" Fatima retorted hastily, brushing out Alexa's long, chestnut-colored hair until it gleamed a rich, reddish-golden-brown hue in the morning light, while the girl struggled to tie the sash about her waist. "It's just that—what with the celebrations and everything going on for your conversion to the True Faith today—it would be better for everyone concerned if our prince's temper were also good, *ewellah?* And, since he's impatient by nature and just can't abide being kept waiting, hurry, Daughter, hurry!" Fatima scolded.

"There! I'm ready! I don't know why you insisted I wear this garish crimson, but I will, just to please you. Well? How do I look?"

Alexa twirled about for Fatima's approval. As she did so, the flared, slitted skirts of her crimson silk costume, the hems sewn with silver coins, flew up and outward, revealing the matching crimson pantaloons beneath. These, though baggy at the calf, were tight at the ankles, where several heavy silver bangles chinked together noisily. The sleeves and bodice of the exotic costume were form-fitting and embroidered, as were the silver-embroidered Turkish slippers with the curling toes she wore on her feet.

Fatima beamed. Despite the girl's concern about the costume's uncomplimentary crimson color, Fatima decided it suited her, for it cast a rosy glow upon her creamy skin, and made her rare chestnut hair appear even redder by comparison. With her eyelids darkened subtly by Fatima's skillful application of kohl earlier, and her cheeks and her soft coral lips tinted slightly with rouge to heighten their natural hue, she was very feminine, very innocently seductive this morning. The crimson costume only added to her vivid beauty. Besides, Fatima mused guiltily, remembering the tiny lie she had told Zerdali moments before, what other color but crimson would she wear for the *very* special occasion the lady Kairee had planned for her today?

"Hush now, enough of your grumbling! Despite your misgivings, the color well becomes you, Daughter," Fatima reassured her. "Now, just the headdress, and you are ready!"

Moments later, the tall headdress settled securely atop her loose and flowing hair, its tinkling silver ornaments catching the light and sparkling as they dangled about her face, Fatima declared Alexa dressed to her satisfaction. She clapped her hands and, as if they had been waiting for just such a summons, lady Kairee and the women of the *hareem* appeared from nowhere, exclaiming over her appearance and offering her compliments like a flock of pretty, noisy parakeets. They were followed by four burly, turbaned Inandan males bearing what looked like a huge brass tray draped with a red fringed cloth between them. This they set down upon the tiled floor close to where Alexa—mollified by all the attention she'd been receiving—stood waiting, feeling embarrassed by the *hareem*'s lavish compliments. She'd been taken to the baths at dawn, and had been scrubbed, oiled, perfumed, manicured, pedicured, groomed, and dressed with the care befitting a queen! All this simply for her day of conversion from the Christian to the Islamic faith? Ah well, who was she to question the customs here? And, she thought sadly, since it was highly unlikely she would ever see England again—if the lady Kairee and Fatima were to be believed—the sooner she accepted her new life and its customs and made the best of it in all its unusual facets, the easier it would be for her.

"You have done well, Fatima!" Kairee praised, taking Alexa by the hand. "She is even lovelier today!" So saying, she kissed Alexa fondly upon the cheek and led her to the huge oval tray set upon the floor, handing her onto it as if she were handing her into a grand carriage. "Be seated here, my dear," she urged, and with raised brows, Alexa did as she asked, taking a seat cross-legged in the center of the peculiar tray.

"Now remember, Zerdali, that everything I have asked you to do these past weeks has been for your own good, for your continued safety, and, ah yes, your happiness. The same is true for everything that will take place today, however confusing or unusual things may seem." There was a hint of anxiety in her dark eyes, Alexa fancied, and a sensation of foreboding fluttered in her belly. "Now, trust me, Daughter, and do all that you are bidden without question."

Alexa nodded and gave her a hesitant smile. "I'll try."

The lady Kairee nodded in satisfaction. "That is all I can ask. You are an intelligent woman, as well as a very lovely one, and I know you will do your best. Now. Do you remember what you must say when the priest asks if you will accept the Muslim faith?"

"I answer him, '*La ilaha illa Allah: wa-Mohammed rasul Allah!*' There is no god but God, and Mohammed is His Prophet."

"Good, very good. Well, you are ready! I have done all I can. Go in peace now, Daughter. May Allah grant you great happiness—and very good fortune!"

To Alexa's surprise, each of the four husky Inandans grasped a corner of the flat tray. She gasped as she was hoisted easily aloft on their burly shoulders, riding high above the heads of the cheering *hareem*, and carried in this fashion from her chambers. The women, calling her name and waving, hurried after her as she was carried over tiled floors strewn with flower petals, through the long corridors of the *hareem*, and out of the palace proper.

Alexa had to fight down the urge to giggle, for she felt ridiculous sitting cross-legged, balanced precariously on a tray borne way up in the air, as if she were part of a mad magician's music-hall act. Still, in some ways it was rather pleasant, being carried along like a queen, and her former apprehension vanished and became a sense of keen anticipation—and fun!

The Inandans carried her from the palace and through a small portion of the city, running down narrow, twisting streets with many steps that were lined with towering buildings with little balconies that almost met far above her. The people of al-Azadel cheered and waved as she was borne past them, and to her surprise her bearers scattered coins in their wake, which they eagerly scrambled after. They carried her to the little white-walled mosque where Hakim, the *marabout* who had instructed her in the Koran's teachings and the tenets of the Muslim faith for the past weeks, awaited her, along with other *marabouts*.

At Hakim's bidding, she dismounted from her peculiar litter and followed them inside the mosque to a vast open room with a lofty domed ceiling. Intricate, endlessly repeating friezes of carved wood or tile ornamented the walls of the inner mosque, their patterns framing graceful, Arabic inscriptions taken from the Koran. The floor beneath her feet was of white marble, veined with pink. The vivid mosaics, the complex friezes, the wood and mother-of-pearl-inlaid pulpits and prayer-niches were of such dazzling beauty, they left her wide-eyed and breathless, and Hakim had to speak her name twice before she realized he was addressing her, and that her conversion was about to begin.

She obediently answered the many questions the *marabouts* put to her. Did she accept the Muslim faith as her own? Did she accept Allah as the only God, and Muhammed as His Prophet? Since privately she had always believed that there was only one God, be His name God, or Allah, or Buddha or Jehovah or what-have-you, and that other than the differing styles of worship, most religions were founded on the same basic beliefs as her

227

own Christian religion, she answered that she did, giving the replies Hakim had coached her in these past weeks. All that remained was to scrawl her signature on the papers stern Hakim unrolled and spread out before her, and then what seemed only minutes later, the *marabout* was smiling and bidding her, "Go in peace, Zerdali, Daughter of Islam!" and she was being handed back up onto her litter.

Her Inandan servants carried her back to the Palace of the Clouds and to a vast open central courtyard where many people were gathered, most lolling comfortably on their elbows upon small rugs, others seated cross-legged, still others astride the magnificent, milling white racing camels which the Tuaregs were renowned for breeding, or upon prancing caparisoned Arabian mares. Their silks and tassels and fringed coverings made brilliant splashes of rippling color in the sunshine and the cool mountain breeze that stirred them. Despite the throngs of people, from her vantage point above the crowds Alexa unerringly recognized Sharif, for all that he wore his *tagilmust*—the indigo-blue covering that, Fatima had told her, the Tuareg males believed protected their souls—wound about his lower face.

He was seated cross-legged upon heaped rugs and cushions beneath an ornate canopy at the far end of the courtyard. Her heart leaped in her breast and a stabbing heat filled the pit of her belly when she felt his ebony eyes meet and lock with hers across the heads thronging the vast courtyard. It was as if the two of them were quite alone, tinglingly aware of each other's presence, despite the noisy throng to all sides. His gaze made her weak, peculiarly breathless, and excited for some reason she could not fathom.

Oh, Lord, these past weeks I'd almost forgotten how very handsome he is! she thought, unnerved by the smoldering midnight eyes that consumed her above the mysterious veiling he wore, and which only added to his virile enigma and allure. With great effort, feeling heat sweep through her body as she did so, she tore her gaze from Sharif to the man seated cross-legged beside him. He was strikingly handsome too, yet far older than Sharif. His face was unveiled, revealing a pair of intelligent dark eyes under brooding black brows, a strong

228

nose, and a neatly trimmed, pointed beard threaded with silver. For some reason, he also appeared familiar to her, though Alexa could not recall having ever seen him before today.

Her porters carried her slowly across the courtyard, between the waves of cheering people that parted respectfully. They set the huge brass litter down very carefully before Sharif and the other man, who was obviously his father, the *amir* Malik, and a third man who was also heavily robed and veiled, though in white. This third man rose as she was gently set down upon the sandy ground and came toward her, extending his hand to assist her in rising to her feet.

Offering him a shy smile of gratitude, she glanced up at the eyes revealed above the *tagilmust*'s concealing folds and saw a pair of the saddest eyes she had ever seen looking back at her—*blue* eyes! Why, the heavily robed man was no Tuareg surely, not with those troubled, light eyes? But then, she recalled that Fatima had once mentioned that some of the Tuareg were blue-eyed, and the mystery seemed solved. Before she had time to ponder this intriguing question any further, the man had taken her gently by the hand and led her to stand before Sharif and his father. While she offered the prince a respectful bow as the lady Kairee had instructed earlier that morning, the two older men exchanged a few rapid words in Tamahaq that she didn't understand, and then the blue-eyed one gravely placed her hand in Sharif's large brown one, kissed her lightly upon the brow, and bowed to the *amir* and his son.

"The woman Zerdali, my lord Sharif!" he said softly. "I give her into your keeping. Guard her wisely and well."

"Wisely and well, and with tenderness, friend Kahlil, fear not!" Sharif replied softly.

"So! Here at last is that jewel-amongst-women my son has coveted these many years!" *Amir* Malik declared with amusement, slapping his son heartily across the back. "Truly, Kahlil, the little blossom I remember from distant Egypt has flowered to great beauty! I cannot blame my worthless son for refusing to accept any other as his bride. She is a prize worthy of the wait."

"My humble thanks, Prince Malik," Kahlil murmured, bowing. "You do me great honor." He cast Sharif a pointed

229

glance, and the younger man gave a barely perceptible nod in reply. "And now, by your leave, I shall rejoin my lady wife."

"The contracts have all been completed?"

"They have, my prince. At the mosque, just a short while ago. Both were completed and signed by Zerdali, before *marabout* witnesses."

"Ah, then all is well! Go to your woman now, Kahlil, my friend, and enjoy the celebrations Ahoudan has prepared for this happy day. May the costly gifts my son has given you in some small way repay you for the priceless gift you have given him and our family this day. May the fruits of their union be many, and the joy and pride of both our houses great!"

"You are both too generous. Thank you, my lord and friend Malik."

The man named Kahlil touched his brow and his breast and bowed again before leaving.

After he had left them, Malik turned his attention to the girl before him, whose hand was still clasped tightly in that of his son. That she seemed less than eager for it to remain so was obvious, and Malik hid a smile at her maidenly shyness and reserve, which were attributes he admired and heartily approved in a bride.

"Welcome, at last, Daughter," the prince said softly, his appreciative eyes taking in the lovely picture she made in her crimson bridal robes. "My heart is filled with joy that you have come to al-Azadel at last. Allah knows, I had begun to fear this young rogue would never see me supplied with grand-children—"

"Patience, Father, patience!" Sharif cautioned, hurriedly cutting in with a low-voiced aside to his father. "My Zerdali is a little shy and your teasing will alarm her, I fear. Give her time to adjust to our customs first. Then—why, I am certain your wish will be granted very soon—perhaps before the next spring rains, eh?" Sharif winked.

Malik nodded, his eyes twinkling. "I doubt it not, if you are in truth your father's son! But tell me, Daughter," he continued, turning to Zerdali, "did you freely agree to all that has taken place today?" Her shyness, to his eyes, seemed marked. In fact, she appeared to be trying to twist her hand free of

230

his son's.

Puzzled, Alexa glanced toward Sharif, who seemed suddenly to be holding his breath, and then back to the prince. "Why, yes of course!" she answered, wondering why the *amir* should ever have thought otherwise about her conversion.

"You see, Father, she is as eager as I!" Sharif said hurriedly in Tamahaq. Grinning, he glanced up at Zerdali's confused face, relieved to see by her expression that she had understood little of their latter exchange. "So! We meet again, eh, little one?" Sharif murmured, his ebony eyes dancing wickedly as he looked up into her eyes. "And not before time! Come, sit beside your 'savage brute,' beloved!"

Thoroughly unsettled by his searching, teasing expression and by his scornful endearments, she tried to pull her hand free of his tight grasp again, but he would not release her. Instead, he tugged her sharply down to sit at his side, and held her there with fingers of steel clamped about her wrist—though his restraining hand was concealed by the folds of their robes from the watching eyes of his father. "Ahoudan! We are ready to begin!" he announced, hoping for a diversion.

Ahoudan, silversmith and master-of-ceremonies, robed today in his finest garments, stepped forward, drawing himself up to his full height. His chest was swelled with pride. He raised his hand and snapped his fingers. "Musicians!" he commanded. "Play on!"

At once, the Inandan musicians began to play, the sweet strumming of the *anzads* and the tapping of the goatskin *tendis* and flutes rising above the heads of the gathering. Simultaneously, servants began moving about the courtyard, bearing huge platters piled high with food: fluffy saffron rice with morsels of lamb and herbs scattered over it; *nashuuf*, the savory dish of lentils, buttermilk, onions and barley; *kabobs*, those tender morsels of marinated goat or lamb and vegetables speared upon skewers and roasted over hot coals. There were baskets of flat bread too, to be torn into strips and dipped into the delicious, frothy gruel made of yoghurt and butterfat and green onions called *madiid;* bowls of sweet onions and radishes, plump apricots and plums, sticky dates, black olives, pomegranates, and other fruits, and for the sweet-toothed, little crêpes soaked in honey that were known by the amusing name of *bint-sahn,* girl-on-a-plate, owing to their delectable sweetness. The aroma of the syrupy green tea the Tuaregs prized, as well as the spicy, dark fragrance of Turkish coffee, mingled with the aromas of the rich foods as the servants moved amongst the gathering, pouring the steaming beverages from elegant, spouted brass pots into thimble-sized cups.

Sharif, his veil unfastened now in order to partake of the meal, wadded a tasty morsel of the yellow rice and lamb heaped before him in his fingers, after the Tuareg custom, and offered it to Alexa. Somewhat surprised—for she had never seen the men eating with the women as they were doing today— she obligingly opened her mouth and Sharif popped the food inside, much to the amusement of everyone about them. Several bawdy roars of approval rose from Sharif's men, among whom Alexa recognized young Selim, who'd tried to catch her that first day. The lady Kairee, seated now alongside her husband with her daughters and their families arrayed behind her, caught Alexa's eye and nodded her approval. Caught up in the relaxed, festive mood, with the delicious foods and the lively, boisterous music, she blushed with pleasure, basking under her praise, and even granted Sharif a fleeting smile as he offered her another mouthful, this of *bint-sahn,* dripping honey. It tasted delicious, and she shyly said so, hoping against hope he would not respond with sarcasm. She was doubtful, for after all, the last time she had spoken with him had been the night he had taken her, and she had afterwards accused him of being little better than a rutting beast incapable of love. She was relieved when she heard him answer her in a teasing way.

"Sweet, *ewellah,* sweet indeed! But not half so sweet as thou, my flower!" he whispered in reply, and though she did not understand his flowery Tamahaq compliment, its meaning was plain in his burning dark eyes.

She looked quickly away, disconcerted by her treacherous body's unexpected reaction to his nearness, his husky voice, his unsettlingly handsome face, for he made her bones melt within her, her knees tremble, made the breath catch in her throat and her respiration shallow and rapid. . . .

Dish after dish disappeared as the afternoon wore on. The bright blue of the sky was darkening to the lavender hues of dusk when bowls of warmed water scented with lemon or roses and fresh cloths were finally brought so that the replete guests might wash and dry their fingers.

This completed, torches were lit about the perimeters of the courtyard and a sumptuous presentation of gifts followed, each item being set before Sharif and Alexa momentarily before being whisked away to their apartments to make room for the next. The finest Persian rugs were unrolled before her eyes; bolts of prized indigo cloth and silks of every hue, some embroidered, some plain, were unfurled for her inspection; there was a fancily carved rosewood coffer too that reminded Alexa of the one in which Muriel had stored her jewels and medicines—this one lined with vials of perfume and lotions; bowls and platters of the fine brasswork and other, somewhat more curious gifts presented by the blue-eyed Kahlil and his shy wife, lovely, sad-eyed Yasmeen, the most unusual being a nomad tent of black goatskins with a bed frame of tamarisk wood.

"A tent? Isn't that a strange gift to give someone?" Alexa voiced her puzzlement aloud.

"Strange? No, not at all. It is our custom on—er—such an occasion," Sharif replied casually and shrugged, inclining his head in gratitude to the couple. "Just offer them your thanks, Zerdali. That is all that is required of you."

Alexa did so, still privately thinking a tent was a strange gift to give someone on the occasion of their conversion to a different faith! A copy of the works of the Koran would have been more appropriate, but then, the tent was hardly less fitting than the other lavish gifts that had been heaped before her! *Don't be so ungrateful, you wretch!* she told herself silently, and flashed Kahlil and his demure wife a warm smile of thanks.

Next, Ahoudan led forth a beautiful Arabian mare that drew murmurs of approval from the crowd. Her shining coat was the color of smoke, with darker charcoal dapplings upon her hindquarters, her legs, and her dainty muzzle. Her streaming mane and tail were of silvery-gray silk, her saddle and bridle of the finest scarlet leather, adorned with plump tassels at the bit and breast.

Malik waved his hand toward the animal and declared, "The mare is for you, my newest daughter, a gift from the lady Kairee and myself. She was sired by Aswad, Sharif's black stallion, and is named 'Rabi,' the Breeze, for like the gentle wind she is both swift and light-footed. May she carry you swiftly and safely always."

"For me?" Alexa asked breathlessly, starry-eyed as Ahoudan led the animal forward to stand in front of her. She was scarcely able to believe the generosity of the prince and his wife as she reached out and petted the little mare's velvety nose. Rabi tossed her smoky gray head and nickered in pleasure. "Oh Prince Malik, thank you!" Alexa told the prince, her eyes dancing with pleasure, much to Malik and Kairee's satisfaction. Uncertainly, she turned and asked Sharif, "Oh, but I—I will be allowed to leave the palace to ride her sometimes, won't I?"

Sharif nodded. "Of course, whenever you wish—providing it is safe to do so, and on condition that you are accompanied. After all, my love, you are not a prisoner here! There are many pleasant little valleys in these mountains that you would enjoy exploring by horseback, as I do, but since al-Azadel's recent skirmishes with my cousin Tabor and his people, such outings cannot safely be undertaken without an armed escort. I had planned to go hawking in a day or two. Perhaps you would like to ride with me and try Rabi for the first time?"

Would she! Overcome with anticipation, she could say nothing. She merely nodded happily, foolishly, in reply, feeling far more warmly welcomed to al-Azadel than she had ever felt before this day. Perhaps, as the lady Kairee had once suggested, she would come to enjoy her life here, in time.

After the pretty mare had been led away to the stables, Ahoudan brought forward the last gifts himself, each one set upon a plump pillow of indigo-colored velvet, which he handed to Sharif.

"And lastly, my own gifts to you, little one," Sharif murmured, and from one of the pillows he lifted an exquisite silver *ankh*, over three inches long, its softly gleaming surface chased all over with a delicate trellis of roses and vines. The *ankh* hung upon a dainty silver chain which Sharif lifted over Alexa's head. He sat back and admired the way the pendant gleamed where it nestled against the crimson cloth, lodged snugly in the narrow valley between her firm, ripe little breasts. If only it were his hands or his head resting there, rather than the cool metal, he thought in wicked anticipation. . . .

"Well? Is my first gift to your liking?" Sharif asked, for her expression was perturbed rather than delighted. "The *ankh* is the symbol of eternity, you know."

"Why—yes—it's beautiful, but of course I couldn't possibly accept it!" Alexa answered primly, lifting the chain over her head and returning the pendant to him. "I'm sorry, but it wouldn't be—proper—for me to accept anything as—as personal as jewelry from you, my lord—nor from any other man, come to that, unless he were my fiancé, of course, or my husband."

Sharif's dark eyes widened in frank disbelief at her explanation, then flashed with merriment. "What is this you say?" he queried, and when she repeated her prim explanation of her refusal, he threw back his head and roared with laughter. "Ah, Zerdali, you have much yet to learn about being a woman, I believe!" he declared. "Most of your sex would have taken my gift greedily, and without second thought, whereas you— But, if that is your decision, then so be it! Take my gifts away, good Ahoudan," he told the astonished craftsman. "They have been admired but rejected, alas. I will give them to the lady Zerdali when she has come to know me better!" He gave the artisan a conspiratorial wink.

Ahoudan, somewhat disgruntled that his painstaking efforts had been so summarily rebuffed, muttered under his breath as he carried away the fine silver pieces he had labored over so long and hard. He carried them to a small room of the palace that opened out onto the courtyard, where his daughter and the other dancing girls craned their heads to watch the goings-on in the courtyard beyond while they awaited his summons to entertain the gathering.

"You there, all of you, go! Hurry now! Delight the guests with your dancing!" Ahoudan shouted irritably, snapping his

235

fingers at the girls, and they bustled out into the courtyard, leaving Raisha and her father alone.

"Surely she has not refused my lord Sharif's gifts?" Raisha demanded, incredulous that the fair-skinned foreign woman would dare to insult her lord before everyone by refusing his wedding presents.

Her cinnamon-brown eyes, ringed heavily with kohl and lidded with blue antimony tonight, flashed jealously. Her cheeks and lips were rouged, and she wore a gauzy lavender veil pinned over her waist-length black hair with jeweled combs. Her small breasts were barely concealed by a sleeveless violet bolero, trimmed with amethyst-colored teardrop beads that jiggled with her indignant breathing. The brief garment ended where her ribs began, and the two halves of it were held in place between her breasts by only a single, fragile clip. Her smooth abdomen, hips, and belly had been perfumed and oiled and were quite bare, undulating sinuously with her movements. An amethyst bauble winked slyly from her navel, below which the jeweled band of her gauzy skirts—merely floating panels of diaphanous cloth—rode low upon her hips. She wore nothing beneath her filmy attire save for a narrow strip of silky cloth between her legs that hardly satisfied the demands of modesty. The slightest movement on Raisha's part revealed long, tantalizing glimpses of supple bare legs with tinkling bells dangling from a chain at her ankles, and a glimpse of her rounded derriere. It was a costume calculated to tease, to torment, to drive a man to lust and madness, and Raisha knew it. She knew it, and she intended to use that knowledge and her dancer's arts to the fullest limits.

Her father, suddenly jolted from his disappointment by the sight of his wayward daughter so scantily clad, hurriedly set the gifts aside.

"And what is this?" he demanded, shaking a fist at her. "Are you a harlot, that you display yourself in this fashion? A Turkish courtesan? Cover your nakedness, minx!"

"No, Father!" Raisha crowed, smiling gleefully. "You promised that I should dance for my lord one last time, and dance I shall!" She pouted. "Sharif will not forget this night, I swear it! Nor will he—or Zerdali—ever forget Raisha! He

236

will regret casting me aside a thousand times before the sun rises again over al-Azadel!"

Before Ahoudan could protest further, Raisha ducked under his outstretched arm and through the doorway, tiny bells tinkling as she ran lightly across the sandy courtyard to the crowds assembled about the troupe of dancers, respectable Inandan daughters performing the traditional women's fertility and rejoicing dances suitable for such celebrations. Raisha waited until they were done, and then signaled the musicians to play her music.

With the first beats of the *tendi*, the center of the courtyard remained empty, save for the dancing light of the flickering torches as they guttered and writhed in the wind. Then Raisha ran between the watchers and into the center of the circle, taking up a pose with her head demurely downcast. The tempo of the music altered, became slow and dreamy as the lutelike strains of the *anzad* picked out the melody, and as the music flowed like lazy water over the ears of the listeners, so too did Raisha's body begin to flow, hips and belly rotating slowly, so slowly, her graceful arms weaving oiled patterns above her, snakelike, in the air. The muscles of her stomach undulated like a flowing bolt of cloth rippled by the wind, barely shifting the veils of her gauzy skirts to tease the senses of the watching men with a fleeting vision of slim, bared thigh, or a delicately turned calf or ankle.

The tempo quickened, the tapping of the *tendi* a rapid heartbeat now that was matched by the gyrations and spasms of Raisha's twitching hips, describing slow revolutions in the air around her. She leaned backward, her arms and her long hair and veil sweeping the ground behind her, her only movement the uncanny, undulating play of her stomach muscles as they shivered and danced and rippled beneath the smooth brown flesh of her belly in time to her music. The men in her audience gave a collective sigh and arched closer, wetting their lips as Raisha began to arch even further backward, her head almost resting upon the ground behind her. Behind her half-closed, sensual brown eyes, she saw how the men watched her, lusted with gleaming eyes and moistened lips just for her, and a swift thrill of pleasure coursed through her, firing her movements to

237

even greater sensuality. Sharif could not fail to want her again after tonight, she knew it. Not now, when she danced only for him. . . .

Alexa looked on curiously, fascinated by the blatantly erotic quality of her former friend's dancing. She'd had no idea that Raisha could dance this way! The manner in which she moved her body had stirred something dark and primitive in the crowd that was tangible to her senses, yet as elusive as the electric tang of a coming storm as it rode the wind. Shocked, she found her palms were moist, and that she was half holding her breath as Raisha danced. Young Selim, across the circle from her, was watching openmouthed, his dark eyes heavy-lidded and riveted on Raisha, the expression on his face naked with lust.

Involuntarily, Alexa turned to look at Sharif, wondering what effect the Inandan girl's dancing might be having on him, and curious to see if his expression in any way matched Selim's. But to her surprise, she saw that at some point Sharif had left her side. As she glanced about her, the lady Kairee rose and came to her side, beckoning to some of the servants as she did so.

"It is time, my dear," she murmured to Zerdali as the servants set the tray-litter down before her again. "Go now, and remember what I told you: that everything that has taken place today—or that will take place tonight—is for your safety, your happiness."

"But Kairee—I don't understand! Where is it that I'm to go?" Alexa asked, puzzled, for it seemed the celebrations were not yet ended, and she was reluctant to leave them. A sudden hope filled her. Was it possible they were releasing her at last? she wondered. It was unlikely. But nonetheless, she took her place upon the litter and allowed the four bearers to hoist her aloft.

"You will be taken to your lord's apartments, my child!" Kairee told her, looking up at her, hating the look of betrayal that sprang instantly into the girl's green eyes. "Tonight, you will take your rightful place in al-Azadel and share his bed." Kairee's glance slid away from the look of accusation that filled Alexa's horrified expression.

238

"You tricked me!" she accused, panic-stricken. "Both of you—you and Fatima too, you tricked me!" she cried, terrified and desperate to escape from her high perch. "How could you? I trusted you!"

"No, Daughter!" Kairee denied. "This is no betrayal. It will be for the best, you'll see. In time you will understand and thank me!" To the bearers she ordered, "Take the lady Zerdali to her lord's apartments, quickly now!"

And like a sacrificial offering on a brazen platter, Alexa was carried swiftly away from the torchlit courtyard, through the winding corridors to Sharif's private chambers, where he awaited her coming.

Meanwhile, Raisha danced, calculating her steps and her movements so that each one brought her closer and still closer to where Sharif and his father, the *amir*, were seated upon their rugs and satin pillows.

Her gyrations were growing wilder and more sensual, more primitive, more savage and frenzied with each step she took. At last, as the drums, the wailing flutes, and the bells at her fingers reached an exciting, towering crescendo, she flung herself face down on the sand before the *amir* and his party, her veils and her long, dark hair sweeping over her as she did so.

"Magnificent, Raisha!" the prince declared, tossing her a handful of silver coins. "You have fired my blood with your dancing tonight—and, I have no doubt, the blood of every man here who has watched you!"

Raisha, her teeth bared in a broad, triumphant smile, slowly raised her head to bask in her prince's praises—and to gaze into Sharif's ebony eyes and see for herself the desire that glittered for her in their depths.

Gone!

To her dismay, the space beside the prince where Sharif had sat and the one next to him where Zerdali had curled beside him were quite empty now. Sharif had left—he had not even seen the dance she had created just for him, the dance that she had danced to win him away from his fair-skinned beauty and back into her arms! As she took her bows and accepted the coins showered upon her—and numerous invitations to sell her favors to the men of al-Azadel—she tasted the bile of jealousy and hurt as sour as acid on her tongue. Sharif had insulted her! He had used her body and cast her aside as if she were of little account. A dagger of hatred twisted deep in her vitals. *Ewellah,* he would know the depths of her hurt! He too would know the pain of losing one beloved to him. She, Raisha, would make certain that he did!

Choking back a sob, she scanned the crowd and found the one she sought amongst the eager men there: young Selim, Muriel's cousin and a favorite of Sharif. He had been in the desert with Sharif when Zerdali had been abducted, and she knew that he had wanted her for many, many months. Tonight, she would grant him his wish, and after, when he lay drained and indulgent beside her, she would ask questions, and he would give answers. By morning, she would know all that there was to know of Zerdali—and also any other secrets worthy of knowing that she could use against her rival. . . .

Chapter Seventeen

The moon rose like a Turkish scimitar. She cast the teardrop white towers of the Palace of the Clouds as graceful black shadows against the sleeping face of the mountain, and showered ethereal light through the arched windows of Sharif's apartments and onto Alexa's face, illuminating her pallor.

She stood very still exactly where her litter had deposited her, at the arched doorway to Sharif's apartments. Outwardly, she seemed calm as she stared across the bedchamber through the far casements to the moon-drenched terraced gardens that lay beyond. Yet inside she seethed with the hurt of Fatima and Kairee's betrayal, and with apprehension. The last time she'd been alone with Sharif, she'd angered him terribly, though he'd tried to conceal it from her. What would he do? Would he be cruel in revenge?

Sharif, lying upon one elbow on his divan and watching her silently by the glow of a single dish-lamp, was certain she saw nothing through the window but a wider boundary to her prison, heard only the beating of her small, frightened heart in her ears, for her creamy complexion was deathly pale, her green eyes dilated and luminous, like drowned emeralds shimmering under the gleaming waters of an oasis pool.

Despite what has already taken place between us, she still fears me, Sharif realized. *To her, I am still just a savage heathen brute. She wants me as a woman wants a man, and yet she despises me, believes me capable of lust, yet incapable of love!* The knowledge that she had learned to hate and fear him before she'd learned to love him as he loved her saddened him, and tainted the joy of

241

his love and desire with a bittersweet pain. If only they'd had more time! But alas, there was none.

"Come here to me, beloved," he commanded.

His tone was warm but compelling, yet for all the effect his words had upon her, it might have been only in his mind that he spoke.

She ignored him utterly and instead scampered away from him, across the tiled floors of his apartments, to the windows. Her crimson robes made a silky, rustling whisper as she went, and the ornaments of her headdress tinkled musically, like wind chimes. She took up a new, tense stance before the grilled, arched windows, staring out as if she would have liked to hurl herself through them to the rocks far below—or wriggle through the lattices to gain her freedom.

But as he watched her, her chin came up with new resolve, and her expression changed from one of terror to one of readiness to fight or flee, despite a suspicious sheen in her eyes that caught the light and the quivering of her full lower lip as she hooked her slender fingers over the wrought-iron arabesques that barred her escape. She curled her fingers in tight arches, as if they were claws that could bend the metal and free her.

"No!" she whispered, answering him at last, and her voice broke as she spoke. "I will not!"

"You will come to me," he repeated sternly. "I command it!"

"Command all you wish! You may think you own me, but you don't. To everyone else here you may be a prince, but to me you're just a murdering savage!"

Her tone was flatter now, yet somehow she managed to sound even more determined. A muscle worked in her jaw as she swallowed, as if despite her determination to resist him, she inwardly feared the consequences of defiance.

He rose from the divan, uncoiling with the lazy grace of a dark leopard to stand.

Her eyes flickered sideways to watch him, returning smartly to her view of the valley below and the rooftops of the little houses of the city drenched in silver-gray moonlight. Yet that single, fleeting glimpse of him had been enough to set her heart hammering in her breast all over again. Gone were the sumptuously embroidered garments he had worn for the feast. In their place he now wore only a pair of baggy white silken breeches, and his wicked dagger, much in evidence, shining like a crescent of moonlight against his lean thigh as he strode slowly across the floor toward her. Ten feet. Six feet. Three. There he halted, towering over her. A fist of terror clenched in the pit of her belly. Her breath was suddenly labored, painful, trapped somewhere beneath her ribs. Oh, God, he was so tall, so powerful, far more powerful than she, and she had no one in this entire city to cry out to for help, no one to turn to! She trembled inside. She wanted to run. She thought she might swoon. But she did none of these things. She only stood there. Tense. Waiting.

"I might well be a 'murdering savage' in your opinion," he said softly, "but I am also your husband."

Her head snapped up so sharply, he could hear the click of the bones in her delicate neck as she turned to look at him.

"What? *What* did you say?" she breathed, incredulous, the blood draining from her cheeks.

"I said, my beauty, that like it or not, I am also your husband."

She stared at him openmouthed, shocked into silence. Was he drunk? He seemed quite sober, to her eyes, and besides, alcohol was forbidden those of the Muslim faith. Nor did he appear to be mad. But—surely he couldn't be serious? She gave a nervous, mirthless little laugh. "Oh, come now, prince! You can't believe I'm naive enough to fall for that transparent ploy to bring me to your bed again. Don't you think I would know if we'd been married or not?" she demanded in her most stinging tones.

"Perhaps in your country. In mine, knowing little of our customs, it is possible you would not."

He suddenly moved, closing the distance between them, trapping her with a weighty hand placed on each of her shoulders before she could evade him. He could feel her trembling beneath his touch, knew the vulnerability of the small-boned frame in his strong grip. He knew that she must be only too aware of his greater strength too, yet her defiant spirit

243

would not permit her to back down, to quake or quail before him, and warmth and pride filled his heart.

"The documents you signed at the mosque, and the feast with its dancing and gifts—in the eyes of the priests of this land, and by our laws, you are my bride, like it or nay, beloved."

She seemed to shrink beneath his touch in horror, her flesh drawing back beneath his palms. "No! That can't be true! The papers—they were only to acknowledge my change of faith!"

"Were they?" he taunted, and he saw the dawning of suspicion, then truth fill her eyes, widening them first with disbelief and then with anger and rejection of the knowledge. "Are you quite certain?"

"But I gave no consent to any marriage between us!"

"It was not required. Your silence alone was sufficient to signify your willingness, according to the Writings of the Prophet."

"But I was ignorant of your intentions! How *could* I protest?" she screamed at him, outraged by his calm admission of trickery.

"That," he said with regret, "was what I counted upon most, your ignorance of many of our customs. Forgive me my deceit in this, little one, but it was necessary, alas."

"Necessary? *Necessary?* By whose reckoning? Yours? And for what reason? To give you license to force yourself on me again?"

"No, Zerdali. To insure you the protection of my name against Kadar."

"Kadar again? But he's miles from here! Don't blame him for your—for your little maneuver!"

He sensed her intent the moment it was born. She sprang at him, but he moved with the speed of lightning to trap both her wrists tight in his huge grip in the second before she would have clawed at his eyes, her temper boiling over.

"No, little tigress! You'll not sink your claws in me, not on our wedding night!" he vowed. "And not when fighting can do us both so little good."

He gripped her by the upper arms and dragged her against him, holding her tightly so that her feet were swept clear off the tiled floor and her soft breasts crushed hard against him. He would silence her protests with passion, not force, and in the process her anger would be forgotten, he hoped.

"*Ewellah*, let me taste your sweetness, desert flower," Sharif whispered ardently against her mouth, "rather than feel the sharpness of your talons. Let me savor again the nectar that lies hidden within thee, for whether you protest or nay, I will have you," he murmured, his tone firm, brooking no refusal despite the husky quality that betrayed his desire for her. "You are my bride. It is my right, as your lord and husband. It is your duty, as my bride. Surrender to me, little one! Surrender to yourself, and to the passion that waits within you, and forget all else in my arms . . . !"

How many nights had she imagined stroking his hard-muscled shoulders, learning the texture of his smooth, golden body, so lean and male in comparison to her own soft curves? How many nights had she burned to feel his touch again? Too many . . . far too many. It would be so easy to surrender, as he demanded.

How could you! her conscience railed. *How could you want him? This man would kill your brother without a second thought, even as he commanded that awful Flechette to be tortured and killed, even as he permitted your escort to die in the desert. What sort of monster are you, that you could desire such a man? What decent, moral woman would willingly give herself to a cold-blooded murderer?*

Me, her wanton, shameless self answered. *"There's something about him that draws me. I would! I will!*

Oh, Lord, had she sunk so low?

"Perhaps what you said is true," she countered. "Perhaps according to your laws, you are my husband. But as far as I'm concerned, you're still a murderer and my brother's accuser, nothing more! For that, and for what you'll do to him if you should find him, I hate you, husband or no! Whether we are married or not changes nothing. You may wait and hope a hundred years for me to love you, but that day will never come, Sharif. I'll never truly be your bride except in name. My body might crave yours, but my heart will never belong to you, never!"

But Sharif had seen the answering sparks that ignited in her green eyes whenever he looked at her, had sensed the heated response of her body to his closeness. He was certain that despite her vows to the contrary, it was not hatred she felt for him. There was something else too, the first fragile kindling of some other emotion. Perhaps, if he could force her to admit that she did not hate him, he could make her realize what it was she truly felt: recognition of him as a man she could love and one to whom the passionate, mature woman dormant within her girl's body could respond with equal passion. There was, he fancied, a ring of uncertainty in her voice when she spoke of her brother that betrayed her doubts of his innocence, though she'd never admit her fears to anyone, least of all to him.

"Then here, little tigress," he gritted softly, drawing his long, curved dagger with its jeweled hilt from the belt at his waist. "If it is truly only hatred you feel for Sharif, my death and freedom that you crave above all things, I give you the means to accomplish your heart's desire: my *takoba*, with a blade forged of the finest Toledo steel. Take it! Slay me, Zerdali! Sever my hated head from my body, and you will be free, your brother safe!"

Surprising even herself, she at once sprang forward and tore the jeweled dagger from his hands. Trembling, she gripped the weighty weapon in her two fists and clumsily swung it aloft.

Lamplight flashed off the heavy crescent blade in shimmers and bursts of gold. The razor edge was a deadly silver thread that drew her eyes like a magnet, honed and sharpened to part an enemy's head from his body in a single clean stroke. She gazed at his beautiful, bare throat, mesmerized by the steady pulse of life she saw beating strongly amidst the shadows at its base. A shudder ran through her. She was suddenly overwhelmed by the urge to run her fingers down his tan throat to the hollows below, and press her lips to the heartbeat there. . . .

Sharif stood motionless and waiting, the golden puddle of light shed from the lighted brass dish-lamps limning his tall, lean body with a fuzzy halo of topaz light against the shadows, and striking a bluish gleam in the midnight-black commas of his curling hair. He angled his dark head a little to one side, baring the vulnerable, smooth tanned column of his throat, offering it in sacrifice to the dagger's curved embrace.

"So? Do you not hate me? Do you not hate yourself for wanting me? Then kill me, Zerdali! Do it now, and be free!"

She wet her lips as doubt overwhelmed her, as unbidden and unwanted memories stormed her defenses. Her slitted gaze traveling upwards to his chiseled lips, she remembered vividly how he'd kissed her amidst the powder-storm of the *simoom*, and then again under the blazing stars of the desert sky that last, unforgettable time by the ruined *kella*. She recalled how she had responded to his kisses and the nearness and warmth of his male body with a sexual intensity that had shaken her to the core; how she'd wanted him ever since that night with a hunger that confused and terrified her more than anything in her twenty-four years of life had ever done. The blade trembled madly in her fists. Oh, God, what was wrong with her, *what*? She did hate him, didn't she? There was no rhyme or reason to the way he made her feel! Love him as a husband, she never, never could, but desire him, want him as a woman wants a man? Oh, yes, oh yes yes yes . . . !

"Why are you waiting?" he demanded.

With a sob, she hurled the dagger far from her, and it fell to one corner of the chamber with a noisy clatter.

"Damn you! Damn you, I can't kill you!" she sobbed. "I can't."

"Because you desire me more than you desire revenge, is that not so?" he demanded. "Because you desire me more than you desire your freedom? More than you hate me?"

"Yes. Oh, yes, damn you!" she confessed brokenly, her green eyes swimming with tears.

"Then, come!" He held out his arms to her. An invitation, which she could accept or refuse.

With a cry, she stepped into his embrace and arched her body against his, lifting her mouth hungrily to meet his. By offering her the chance to take his life, he had forced her to acknowledge her true feelings toward him. By making her his bride without her consent, he'd released her from the torment of guilt and misplaced loyalty to Keene her willingness would have created. She could not quite determine what it was she wanted from this man, her thoughts were so confused, nor exactly when her feelings had altered, softened toward him, yet

247

she wanted him anyway, with a fervor that drove all other considerations from her mind.

Her feet left the floor as his arms enfolded her. Her breasts were crushed against his broad torso. Her belly and hips were plastered against the hardness of his flanks like a second skin as he cradled her weight against his body. His desire for her was palpable, the swollen ridge of his manhood fiery against her belly, its warmth sending heat pulsing through her loins. She gasped as his lips slashed over hers, hot, eager, demanding, his tongue-tip prying them apart, her mouth yielding, parting, as he kissed her in a way that made her bones melt in her trembling flesh.

A cry that could have been a final whimper of protest or acceptance of defeat faded in her throat as his tongue surged into the soft, wet recesses of her mouth. She was breathing shallowly as the very tip of his tongue met her own tongue and warred gently with it, and to her shame she heard herself sob, "At last! At last!" the moment his lips left hers to draw breath.

A shudder of wild longing wracked her body, longing only he could assuage. How could she have pretended—lied—to herself? That sweetness—the drugging languor and warmth lapping through her, eroding her will—sapping her resistence—oh, Lord, she wanted it, wanted him, wanted it all!

Darting and playing, snakelike, his tongue stroked her own hesitant tongue in a swirling, twining dance that thrilled her with its sensuality. Tentatively, she answered with her own tongue, and felt the chest beneath her palms heave as a shudder of need moved through him. His teeth dragged hungrily on her lower lip, gnawing the soft flesh as if he would devour her. His breathing was thickened and unsteady as his hands danced over her curves, moving to cup the taut mounds of her buttocks. He stroked and caressed them, tugging her hard against his hips as he did so, so that she could feel his readiness, learn for herself how compelling was his need of her, as he ground his hips against her.

"Sharif, oh, Sharif . . . !" she whispered throatily. Don't . . . don't stop!"

He saw the confusion that lingered still in her eyes, and knew how desperately she fought the conflicting feelings inside her, of right versus wrong. The rewards of pleasure weighed against all that she had been taught from childhood was wicked. In that moment, he saw that taking her as his bride without her consent had been the only way for her to ever acknowledge her desire for him without guilt accompanying the admission. And too, by making her his bride, he had absolved her of the responsiblity of fighting him off, as her sense of duty and her upbringing decreed she must to defend her honor, although her passionate female instincts might urge her to surrender.

Whispering endearments, he mouthed the tiny hollows that lay in shadow along the base of her throat, moistening them with his tongue while his eager fingers drew the tinkling headdress from her hair and cast it aside. He outlined the shells of her ears, his tongue-tip wetly teasing each little ridge and fold while he deftly unfastened the sash at her waist. She moaned deep in her throat, pressing back against his hands. Seized by desire, he impatiently tore the silken robe down from her shoulders, baring her to the waist. His ebony eyes devoured her. His hands explored her creamy flesh, sliding up and over her warm skin to capture her firm little breasts, and play with their full curves. As his palms cupped her in heat and sensation, she shuddered and arched her head back in sheer pleasure, so that its glorious length swung free like a curtain down her back to brush her waist.

Touch me, she implored silently. *Oh, touch me just that way!*

"You are fair and white as *léban,* beloved," he said huskily. "Your skin is silken-smooth, soft and fragrant as the petals of rose. Tonight, I shall taste all of you, beloved. There will be no part of your flesh that is a stranger to my lips, my touch—!"

His sensual promises thrilled her. Still uttering endearments, his lips traced the pulse at the hollow of her throat, then moved down over the delicate ridge of her collarbone to the start of the shadowed little valley between her breasts. He dipped his ebony head lower until his lips brushed her right breast, teasing the little nub of flesh at its peak with a curling tongue-tip. His sweet breath fanned the coral crest with damp warmth.

"By Allah, Zerdali, you are even lovelier than my dreams!

249

Your little breasts are ripe for my loving. See how your nipples beg to be drawn deep into my mouth, their sweetness savored!" His dark head moved lower still, his jet-black curls tickling erotically as they brushed her sensitive, exposed flesh. With exquisite slowness, he covered a tiny coral bud and the pink flush that encircled it and drew it deep into his mouth as he had promised, licking delicately, swirling his tongue-tip around and around it and suckling gently until the ruched bud grew slippery, blossomed, hardened.

Gasping, she threaded her fingers through his inky curls, kneading the glossy softness beneath her hands. Her breathing grew shallow and unsteady, as if she'd run a mile or more, and her knees threatened to buckle.

A low sound uttered in his throat—a growl or a moan, she could not say—then he was kneeling at her feet, his rough hair tickling her belly as his tongue danced about the tiny well of her navel, or nuzzled the smooth flesh that stretched taut across her hipbones.

"No part left unsampled, *habibah,* jewel-amongst-women . . . !" She felt the butterfly caress of his hands as he stroked down her thighs, drawing the silken pantaloons away with his caresses until they fell about her ankles. She stepped free of them and drew a deep, shaky breath as his devilish lips traveled over her thighs, lingering to tousle the crown of curls at their joining. With a will of their own, her trembling thighs parted slightly, permitting him access to the secret, hidden folds that were moist with longing for his caresses, his kisses, his lips. She made little incoherent sounds as his fingers slipped inside her, as his tongue flicked delicately over the very bud of her womanhood, readying her, making her as moist and trembling as a fragile leaf, wet with the dews of dawn, trembles in a current of warm air. With a sob of pleasure and sweet pain commingled her knees gave way.

Without a word, he swept her up into his arms and bore her to the divan, raining little kisses over her hair as he set her down amidst its soft, silken pillows, like a delicate bird brought to a rainbow-colored nest. She was a vision beyond even his wildest imaginings as she lay there, quite still, waiting, watching him, her eyes curtained by her long, tawny lashes, her perfect breasts rising and falling visibly with anticipation.

Sharif's love and desire for Alexa was, as he looked down at her, heightened by his sense of the danger threatening her—danger in the form of Kadar, and the threat his return posed to their happiness. It quickened the already racing tempo of his heart and tightened the full hardness at his loins almost unbearably. Who knew when Kadar might return and demand that Zerdali be handed over to him, forcing a confrontation between them that could only end in death for himself, or death by his hand for the man who'd been as close to him as any brother for nearly thirty years? In this way, he realized sadly, would the prophecy made many years ago by the Egyptian astrologer, Maimun, be fulfilled. *Brothers suckled at the same breast will, in a single breath, become enemies, and this woman will be the cause,* he had foretold, and it was all happening as he had predicted. And who knew when his father, the *amir,* might somehow learn of Kadar's greater claim to the girl by reason of their ancient laws of vengeance, and discover that the son in whom he trusted had confided only half-truths of Zerdali's coming to al-Azadel?

His tanned face burned as if a fever raged in him. His ebony eyes were as turbulent as the dark clouds that gathered before a storm. Long before that time came, he must bind Zerdali to him by more than the bonds of passion. They must be united in love and trust, joined in spirit as well as body, or be destroyed!

"This day I have taken a bride, Zerdali," he told her softly, looking down at her as she lay watching him, "but you have also taken a husband. Be patient, for just a moment more, little one, while I light another lamp. There will be no secrets between us henceforth. As I have enjoyed the beauty of your nakedness, so shall you have the knowledge of mine."

He strode across the chamber away from her, his movements lithe and masculinely graceful as a desert lion's, his stride proud and self-assured. A true warrior of the Imochagh noble caste such as he never merely walked any more than he openly expressed anger: he strode the world with an air of manly arrogance, as one accustomed to obedience from those of lesser birth. That fierce pride was confirmed by every step he took, each word he spoke. In the desert provinces over which he held

251

domain, he was truly a desert prince, Alexa thought, and a curious sense of pride that such a man as he had chosen her, not as his courtesan or plaything but as his bride, filled her as she watched him.

Moments later, the gentle radiance of a second brass dish-lamp spilled across the divan, throwing the remainder of the vast room into shadows so dark that the two of them seemed to float on a golden island within a midnight sea. It seemed to Alexa that she and Sharif were all alone in the world. No one else, nothing else, existed save for the two of them, with the pounding of her heart and the sweetfire aching in her body.

As he returned to the divan, she averted her eyes and looked away, but he leaned down, tilted her face up to his, and brushed her reddened lips with his own, declaring in a teasing voice, "Do not be modest and turn your head, little one, but behold your husband, my lady Zerdali, as Allah sent him forth into this world!"

Shyly, she looked, and saw that, as she had feared, he was now quite naked. His ebony-capped head sat proudly upon broad shoulders that curved with braids of muscle and sinew, and gleamed as if burnished in the amber light shed by the dish-lamps. His bronze torso was bare, unmarked save for a narrow T of dark hair. His fists were planted arrogantly upon his lean hips, and upon his muscular left upper arm, he wore a broad armlet of soapstone, honed and polished and fired to smooth, obsidian blackness, that she had not noticed until now.

Noting her eyes upon his curious ornament, he smiled. "This is a talisman, one worn only by the warriors of my people. Such armlets are crafted by our Inandan artisans from stone mined in the farthest, desolate reaches of our mountains. It is said that its wearing will ward off the blows of a man's enemy—and grant him great virility!"

He chuckled as he saw, despite the meager light, how she blushed at his words, adding, "But fear not, little virgin, armlet or nay, my virility has yet to fail me!"

The crimson deepened in her cheeks, yet Alexa was curious despite her embarrassment and could not draw her eyes away from him! She had never seen a grown man naked before, and her eyes traveled slowly over his striking male form as if she

252

intended to commit it to memory.

He was a strong, ruggedly beautiful man, perfect and whole and more than a little appealing to her with his chiseled, handsome face and fine, athletic physique. She swallowed the taste of fear that rose, suddenly, in her mouth, for this powerful, wickedly handsome desert prince was now her husband, or so he had sworn, and by the laws of this land, she belonged to him, and as he had reassured her, he was certainly virile. The dark furring of wiry black curls that lay like a slim shadow across his chest tapered to a thin, dark line that arrowed downward on reaching the hard plateau of his belly, only to reassert itself as a luxuriant ebony thatch at his groin. From there, his circumcised root rose proudly, erect and ready as a battle staff, unquestionably male, undeniably potent and threatening. The lean span of his hips, his hard, flat buttocks, the corded power of his muscular horseman's thighs—he was lacking in no part of him, she saw, and she quivered and wet her lips as sudden apprehension filled her, stealing her breath away.

"Speak, *habibah!*" he urged hoarsely, seeing the sudden apprehension in her eyes. "Do you find your husband pleasing?" He forced his tone to sound casual, for he was half afraid of her answer.

Slowly, she nodded and whispered, "Yes. Oh, God, yes!"

With a smile, he went to her and took her in his arms, drawing her close in an embrace that she returned without restraint.

"I will love you now, Zerdali," he murmured fiercely. "Tonight, we will truly become man and wife, yes? Do you desire me, *habibah?*"

His words, deliciously accented, had a peculiarly medieval flavor in their translation from the flowery, poetic Tamahaq of his thoughts to the less familiar English. As always, his voice sent heat licking through her body in spiraling waves.

"Yes," she whispered. "Love me, Sharif!"

She lay curved against him naked, her shimmering green eyes languid with passion, her breasts rising and falling with mounting ardor, the nipples ripened into tiny, ruby jewels at their crests. He leaned over her, dipped his dark head to hers.

253

Her lips parted to yield to his kisses, to allow them to deepen and reach burning depths that seemed to touch and sear her soul. Her tongue-tip touched and played with his. Their quickened breaths commingled and exchanged, her heart's measured beat now leaping and thundering out of control with her mounting excitement. She felt a great shudder run through his hard, virile body, pressed along the length of her own. Felt his staff pressing eagerly to meet her flesh with, what seemed, a will of its own.

"Sharif . . . Sharif!" she whispered against his mouth, his name a blessing, an invitation, a caress.

"Soon, *habibah,* very soon . . ."

A low moan escaped her as he cupped her breast and suckled her, swirling the fiery lash of his tongue around and around the sensitive, ruched flesh of each ripened nipple until she moaned and gasped and implored him to take her, and he knew that she was truly ready for him. Her body writhed upon the silken coverlet with the escalating torment that rose through her. His touch and his kisses were no longer enough. . . . And then, wondrously, he lifted her astride him, guiding her hips downwards until she straddled the burning length of him. In a second, he'd slipped deep inside her, burying himself to the hilt.

With a low, astonished cry of delight, she instinctively began to move her hips, undulating them beneath his steadying hands, setting the pace of their lovemaking and the depth she would take him into herself as she desired, and using her newfound sensual talents to drive him to madness. She arched her head backward so that her breasts rose impudently to meet his caresses, moving upon him to the pulsing rhythm that sang in her blood. Her cloak of lamplit hair swept her buttocks and his strong tan thighs behind her, then swirled over them, across his chest, wrapping about his throat as she rode him to the heights, moving quickly, then slowly, so slowly, then quickly again, almost rising from him only to plunge downward at the very moment of withdrawal.

The sweat sprang from Sharif's brow and beaded his chest and palms with the effort it cost him to delay his own release. By Allah, she was a tigress, a goddess of passion, a she-devil to

254

torment him so. . . .

The fierce, aching monster of need in her loins craved the relief that only he could bring. She came in an explosion of colored lights that were blinding in their vivid magic, wave after wave of ecstasy bursting through her as warm ripples of sensation. Her nipples grew rigid. Her body grew still and taut as a bowstring outwardly, while deep within her, a secret maelstrom of sensation pooled and eddied and tore itself free. Her fingers clawed on air, and then somehow twined themselves in the thick black curls of his hair, which felt soft and rough all at once, like raw silk to the touch, and deliciously alive in her euphoric state.

While she was still lost in the velvet languor of rapture, Sharif rolled her beneath him, spreading her thighs high and wide and driving deep into her honeyed well, possessing her utterly.

Green eyes wide with wonder at the glorious ecstasy he'd shown her, Alexa gazed dreamily up into his lean, rugged face in the moonlight, as if seeing him for the first time.

His eyes were closed. The dark smudge of his lashes rested upon the golden bronze of his cheeks. His chiseled lips were barely parted, his handsome, swarthy features transported as he rode between her thighs again and again. He alternated his powerful thrusts with slow and sensuous, snakelike gyrations of his flanks as she had done; undulations that made her gasp and grit her teeth, and groan and moan aloud with the sheer, animal pleasure rising through her all over again; unbearable, breathless pleasure that clawed and clamored for release. With a cry, she twined her arms about his neck, wrapped her slender legs about his hips to hold him fast within her, and matched her movements to the rhythm of his dance.

"Zerdali, Zerdali . . ." he whispered huskily. "You are mine now, forever, and for always! I have waited a lifetime for thee—for this moment between us! Love me, *habibah!* Sing for me, my desert songbird : . . !"

A surge of emotion swept through her with his impassioned command. She clung to him fiercely and together this time, moving as one, they climbed the stairway to heaven's gates, lips and bodies joined in the age-old dance of love until, with cries and kisses, Alexa sang the love-song Sharif had bade her sing, finding her release a second time with fluting notes of ecstasy. Together, their souls took flight and soared to the blazing stars.

Later, when the wild throbbing of their hearts had slowed to a more measured tempo, Sharif rolled from her to lie by her side. Tenderly, he brushed a strand of dampened hair from her flushed cheek and kissed her brow, her nose, her soft lips. She smiled sleepily and sighed, snuggling into his body warmth like a small kitten exhausted from its rompings, fitting her slender feminine curves snugly to his leaner male form.

"And so? Do you still fear me now, beloved?" he asked softly, an amused smile glinting in his dark eyes and curving his lips, for in the moonlight she was the picture of a woman who had been well loved by her man, and her answer he already knew at heart. "Do you still fear the savage Tuareg bandit who has made you his woman?" he teased.

Her eyelids fluttered open. She cast dreamy green eyes up to look at him. The lashes, thick and tawny, fluttered momentarily. "No," she murmured drowsily at length, struggling to keep her eyes open. "No, I'm not afraid of you, not anymore."

"Then let me hear you say it, Zerdali! Say that you are the beloved wife of Sharif al-Azim, and his woman alone."

"I am the bride of Sharif al-Azim," she echoed obediently, her voice like one in a deep trance. "I am his, and no other's." She sighed heavily and her eyelids fluttered closed again, the lashes resting upon her cheeks like dark crescent-moons.

"Good enough, little one," he whispered, brushing his lips across her soft mouth. "Good enough, for the time being. Tonight, you have learned the power of desire. Soon, you will learn also how to love me. It is a good new beginning, little Apricot-Hair."

He curled his arms about her and drew the loose, warm weight of her body against his chest. Stroking her hair, he gazed through the arabesqued windows at the starlit skies beyond their bower, lost in thought.

From a spirited, lovely child, his Zerdali had grown into a

Affix
stamp
here

ZEBRA HOME SUBSCRIPTION SERVICES, INC.

P.O. BOX 5214

120 BRIGHTON ROAD

CLIFTON, NEW JERSEY 07015-5214

FREE

ZEBRA BOOK CERTIFICATE

ZEBRA HOME BOOK SUBSCRIPTION SERVICE, INC.

YES! Please start my subscription to Zebra Historical Romances and send me my free Zebra Novel along with my first month's Romances. I understand that I may preview these four new Zebra Historical Romances Free for 10 days. If I'm not satisfied with them I may return the four books within 10 days and owe nothing. Otherwise I will pay just $3.50 each; a total of $14.00 (a $15.80 value—I save $1.80). Then each month I will receive the 4 newest titles as soon as they come off the press for the same 10 day Free preview and low price. I may return any shipment and I may cancel this arrangement at any time. There is no minimum number of books to buy and there are no shipping, handling or postage charges. Regardless of what I do, the FREE book is mine to keep.

Name _____
            (Please Print)

Address _____ Apt. # _____

City _____ State _____ Zip _____

Telephone ( ) _____

Signature _____
            (if under 18, parent or guardian must sign)

Terms and offer subject to change without notice.

MAIL IN THE COUPON BELOW TODAY

To get your Free **ZEBRA HISTORICAL ROMANCE** fill out the coupon below and send it in today. As soon as we receive the coupon, we'll send your first month's books to preview Free for 10 days along with your **FREE NOVEL**.

GET FREE GIFT

ACCEPT YOUR FREE GIFT
AND EXPERIENCE MORE OF
THE PASSION AND ADVENTURE
YOU LIKE IN A
HISTORICAL ROMANCE

Zebra Romances are the finest novels of their kind and are written with the adult woman in mind. All of our books are written by authors who really know how to weave tales of romantic adventure in the historical settings you love.

Because our readers tell us these books sell out very fast in the stores, Zebra has made arrangements for you to receive at home the four newest titles published each month. You'll never miss a title and home delivery is so convenient. With your first shipment we'll even send you a FREE Zebra Historical Romance as our gift just for trying our home subscription service. No obligation.

BIG SAVINGS
AND **FREE** HOME DELIVERY

Each month, the Zebra Home Subscription Service will send you the four newest titles as soon as they are published. (We ship these books to our subscribers even before we send them to the stores.) You may preview them *Free for 10 days.* If you like them as much as we think you will, you'll pay just $3.50 each and *save $1.80 each month off the cover price.* AND *you'll also get FREE HOME DELIVERY.* There is never a charge for shipping, handling or postage and there is no minimum you must buy. If you decide not to keep any shipment, simply return it within 10 days, no questions asked, and owe nothing.

breathtaking, passionate woman, he mused. *Ewellah*, every moment, every second of those long and empty years of waiting had been worthwhile. . . .

A cool mountain zephyr drifted into the chamber, chilling their heated bodies. Sharif pulled a silken coverlet over them and as he did so, Alexa stirred, burrowing more snugly against him. She fitted her hand into his larger one.

"Mmm. I feel so safe, so warm and sleepy, Sha-Sha," she murmured drowsily.

Sharif's smile broadened. Awake, she had not recognized him. But, in her deepest dreams, she remembered their childhood. He was certain that, in the deepest reaches of her mind, she also remembered him!

The *houri* of his dreams was a fantasy no more. Tonight, she had stepped from Paradise into his arms, and become reality.

Chapter Eighteen

Alexa awoke first the next morning to beams of sunlight streaming through the arched windows and playing over her face. Still in that euphoric state halfway between waking and sleeping, she stretched languorously and opened her eyes, lazily watching the minute dust motes that swirled and danced like gold dust spun by a dust-devil in the shafts.

A delicious sensation of well-being pervaded every inch of her, from head to her toes, which she wiggled in sheer pleasure. She felt sleek and content as never before, and she stretched once again before snuggling back into the divan's downy comfort.

A disgruntled, sleepy male, muttering a protest close at hand, shattered her complacency, for as she wriggled to get comfortable, her elbow had cracked against Sharif's skull! In a rush, the events of the night before flooded through her, along with an acute awareness of where she was, and with whom, and why, and vivid flashes of memory that only served to make her cheeks burn.

Moving stealthily, she slid back under the silken coverlet, careful to keep a prudent distance between her own body and that of the aggressively male brute sprawled only inches away from her. He lay on his belly this morning, cradling his ebony head on his bent arms. His torso was bare to the waist, where the coverlet had twisted about him in sleep. She could see the rippling delineations of his muscles across his back and shoulders; the somehow vulnerable little ridges of his spine; the dark shadows of hair at his armpits. Fortunately, the sheeting concealed his buttocks, outlining their hard, spare curves but revealing nothing.

She felt quite affectionate toward him as she drank in this secret picture of him in repose, for he revealed a side of him she'd never seen before: a man far different from the controlled, arrogant Tuareg lord he had seemed in his desert domain. With his swarthy cheek cradled on his elbow, his long dark lashes resting like smudges of charcoal against the taut flesh of his cheekbones, he seemed as young and innocent as a little boy. Yet—she remembered only too well the havoc those dangerous lips could wreak upon her resolve, the perilously sweet pleasure of his caresses, and the drugging, sapping warmth of his lovemaking!

Dear Lord, had she really given herself to this dark and handsome stranger last night, and had she truly responded like the wanton, eager tigress her memory suggested, returning kiss for kiss, caress for eager caress? It seemed she had, for her lips still tingled with remembrances of his kisses. Her breasts surged anew with sudden sensation, the nipples ripening to hard little nubbins of flesh with a will all of their own. Oh, Lord, she had indeed responded in that shameless way, and having done so once, her treacherous body seemed bent on doing so again and again!

She was about to edge herself off the divan, dress, and flee for the comparative safety—and distance—of her own apartments in the Mist *serai*, when Sharif rolled over, onto his back. One out-flung arm landed across her hips, lodging there and trapping her. Swallowing, she saw that with his movement the concealing coverlet had slipped from him to the floor, and that his lower body was now quite bared to her eyes.

She could feel the rush of heat fill her cheeks again, for as she gazed at him, her eyes were drawn inexorably downward over the dark furring that clung jealously to his chest and was flanked on either side by a flat brown nipple, to the hard belly below, and thence to his powerful loins. Surprised, she saw that his maleness, curled innocently against his thigh, was far smaller, far less intimidating and threatening this morning than it had been the night before. . . .

"Continue to look upon him so, *habibah*, and he will grow proud and eager once more!" a lazy voice drawled.

259

Alexa jumped in guilty surprise. Her cheeks were bright pink with embarrassment as she realized Sharif was not only wide awake, but watching her with sleepy dark eyes that held a twinkle in their depths. Like a hot desert wind as it caressed her body, his gaze dropped from her face to her breasts, for she was every bit as naked as he. He wet his lips and winked wickedly at her, and as if by magic, at the mere sight of her his root stirred against her thigh. She glanced down, saw that it was again as she remembered, and quickly looked away, staring at the mosaics on the far wall, the fluttering gauzy draperies—anything rather than look at It—or at him.

"There, little one! Did I not tell you the truth?" Sharif murmured with a chuckle, enjoying her confused modesty. Leaning over to face her, he boldly cupped her left breast in his hand, fondling it as he pressed his lips to hers. He darted his tongue across her lips as he kneaded the little mound gently and rubbed the ball of his thumb over the sensitive crest.

She tried to move away, but found herself pulled abruptly back down across his chest. He framed her face between his palms so that he could plant a long and thorough kiss full upon her mouth, one that stole her breath away with its sweet-fire hunger. As he kissed her, he stroked her hair, and then his fingertips skimmed down the delicate knobs of her spine to caress her buttocks. He kneaded and squeezed them gently, pressing her against the ridge of his manhood as he did so until she was breathless with kisses and quivering from his caresses.

"A very good morning to you, Zerdali," he greeted huskily, looking up at her with a roguish smile as he traced the angle of her cheek and jaw and gently tweaked her nose. "Did my little bride sleep well?"

The wicked grin he wore betrayed his question as a teasing one, for her face still bore the blurred and rosy contours of a woman sated by a night of pleasure in the arms of her man. "Tell me," he continued hopefully, "would you start this day as we ended the last—or in some other pleasing fashion?"

"In any other fashion but the one you're thinking of!" she insisted hotly, pulling free of his arms. He let her go, chuckling as she sprang from the divan with her chestnut hair flying behind her, for she'd obviously quite forgotten for the moment

260

that she was nude and that her charms were exposed to his view in the dawn light!

Belatedly, she snatched up the coverlet from the floor and wound it tight about her. "If I may," she said in a controlled, tight little voice, "I should like to bathe."

"*Ewellah!* But of course!" Sharif agreed, his grin deepening. "As would I! We will enjoy a refreshing, cleansing bath together, *habibah*—and then your husband will teach you more of the delights that can be ours to share. Come, little one!"

He sprang from the bed and held out his hand invitingly.

Aghast, she shook her head, ignoring his hand. Bathe with him! What could he be thinking of!

"Very well," Sharif said with mock severity. "If my little wife will not be obedient, I must persuade her to obey me!"

With that, he strode purposefully across the chamber toward her. Before she could escape him—with the coverlet's folds hampering her feet—he'd scooped her up into his arms and was laughing as he swept her, protesting loudly, across his chamber and through a curtained entrance to another vast room.

"My private baths," he declared as he set her on her feet.

Alexa saw several steps beyond her, leading down to a sunken pool lined with mosaic tiles in varying shades of blue that gave the water a sparkling turquoise color. More tiled areas and low, gold-veined marble divans flanked the bathing area, and huge flagons of crystal with water-lily crystal stoppers—no doubt containing oils and perfumed soaps or lotions of some sort—were set in readiness upon them.

One side of the baths was opened to the air and views of the terraced palace gardens beyond, made bright with blooming sprays of purple and magenta bougainvillea, and rambling pink- and flame-colored roses. A panoramic view of the dawn sky and the rose-washed mountain passes colliding with one another filled one side of the walls, as if a lovely mural had been painted there. The scent of dewy jasmine and roses wafted into the room to tease her nose, and the wakening chorus of hidden birds filled the air with their glad song.

"I gave orders last night that no one was to disturb us this

261

morning," Sharif revealed, his tone husky with desire. "Our privacy will not be intruded upon by servants, you have my word. We shall spend many hours in pleasure here together, so that you may come to know me better."

"No! Last night was a mistake, surely you see that? It changed nothing," she insisted, looking up at him with an earnest expression upon her lovely face. "I don't want to know you better, nor be your wife! It's barbaric, the way you brought me here, held me prisoner all these weeks, tricked me into this farce of a marriage that I knew nothing of! I demand that you end this charade and set me free!"

She made to turn her back on him and walk away, but with a speed that belied his still-lazy expression, he caught her wrist and drew her back, spinning her against his chest.

"In the light of morning, you sing a different song, little nightingale," he murmured, his tone half-threatening, half-teasing. "Do you forget so soon how by moonlight you begged me to love you, *habibah?*" His eyelids drooped sensually. "Then let me remind you once more, eh?"

As he spoke, she felt the coverlet slipping from her grip, the cool air of dawn racing over her body. Of a sudden, she again stood naked in his embrace, pressed mounded breasts to flat chest and pelvis to pelvis against the man who last night she'd called her husband but who, in the saffron light of dawn, had become a stranger yet again.

He idly stroked her thigh, and then his fingertips grazed like fire across her belly and downward to the silky curls of her mound. He teased the tawny thatch with his palm, then gently explored her most secret places, his skilled fingers parting her hidden petals and moving delicately within her, leaving her weak with rising pleasure and the languor that accompanied desire. The sweet sensations he aroused with his touch made her lean limply into his embrace, the will to resist him weakening with every passing moment. Another second, and she would be lost all over again! With enormous effort, she wrenched free.

"Stop it, Sharif! This is all wrong, so wrong!" she cried softly, filled with confusion. "I hardly know you, although

262

we've been lovers—and—and although you insist that we're married!"

"Come, come, Zerdali! From my understanding, such matters are little different in your England. Many young women marry men they scarcely know, and yet they grow to love them as husbands, and to find happiness in their marriages and in the children they make together. Love will come to us in time, I know it will. One day, you will discover that from feeling only passion, you have grown to love me, as I love thee! Try to forget your English ways of thinking. They belong to your past, to a woman named Alex-and-ria Harding and another world where everything was far different from the ways of my land, and the land of Zerdali, princess of al-Azadel. What I have to offer you is a future here, which one day, Allah permitting, will be *our* world, and that of our children."

"You arrogant, unfeeling animal!" she hissed at him, unable to believe his self-serving logic. "What about what I want? Does that count for nothing? You tell me to forget my past, and offer me a future here with you instead, as if it were a great gift I cannot resist. But it's a world and a future that holds nothing for me! Can't you understand that it's a life and a world I hate, and want no part of? No, my lord Sharif, not even the promise of your lovemaking, pleasant as it is, could begin to make up for the loss of my freedom! I'm not some mindless, docile creature, suited to spend years of my life quietly embroidering myself insane in your palace *hareem,* or meekly awaiting your summons to share your bed like some—some—favorite concubine! I want more than that from my life, don't you see?" She drew a deep, shaky breath. "I want a man I can love and respect for my husband, one who can share my interests, and be my friend as well as my lover. Someone I can laugh with, share hopes and dreams and fears with, share my life with. Damn you for your arrogance in thinking I could ever willingly settle for less!"

She'd wanted to anger him by telling him her true feelings, all of them, hoping in anger he'd be diverted from his original purpose of seducing her again, and would realize how futile his hopes that she'd come to love him truly were. But as always,

263

his lean tanned face was implacable, the only indication she had succeeded in her goal the twitch of a muscle in his jaw.

"By the Spleen of the Prophet, you are unreasonable, woman!" he gritted. "I offer you a life that other women only dream of, with every comfort at your fingertips! I give you my name, your position here as my wife, my love, and my heart. I lay at your feet the chance for our marriage to be all you could ever wish it to be, if you were only willing to try, and yet you toss these things back in my face, rejected as if they were worthless stones instead of opportunities for new beginnings! You are stubborn, my lady Zerdali, as stubborn and obstinate as a donkey. By Allah, I know not why I desire thee above all others, nor why my heart has chosen thee, for you are of a certainly lacking in every one of the qualities I had hop—"

"*My lord Sharif!*"

The male voice, raised in alarm, carried clearly from the bedchamber beyond to the adjoining baths, cutting off whatever Sharif had been about to say.

"I gave orders I was not to be disturbed, curse you!" he growled. "Go, before I have your head!"

"Forgive me, but your father summons you, sir! The al-Tabor have taken the southern gate!"

"I come at once!" Sharif called back over his shoulder, scowling blackly now. To Alexa, he only nodded curtly, without smiling.

"My cousin's tribe, the al-Tabor, has attacked our city. I must go at once. Return to your apartments. We will continue this little—discussion—when I return."

With palpable reluctance, he bent down and pressed his lips to her brow in farewell. "May Allah watch over you until we are together again, O Obstinate One!"

Then he turned on his heels and left her alone. She heard him moving quickly about in the chamber adjoining as he dressed, and then afterward there was only silence, interspersed with distant cracking sounds that were like the muted popping of champagne corks.

"O Obstinate One," he'd called her in parting! Not beloved, not little one, nor his favorite endearment, *habibah*, but Obstinate One! She shrugged. Well, in that regard, she supposed she couldn't really blame him. He'd tried so hard to convince her that their love was destined to be, without success. And she *was* stubborn, as obstinate as any donkey— her papa'd said so many a time—though she felt she had every right to be stubborn, under the trying circumstances! With the thought, something stirred in her memory, as if the argument that had flared between them moments ago had been played out many times before in similar fashion. Frowning, she tried to clutch at the memory, to hold it fast and examine it more closely, but it slipped through her fingers like fine sand and was gone. When she glanced up again, the room was still empty, except for herself and the disquieting, unexpressed anger Sharif had left behind him as an invisible, crackling presence in the room.

In a fit of pique that he'd left before she could wring some promise from him to release her, or at the very least, the hope of some worthwhile means to fill her hours and days to look forward to, she picked up the coverlet and hurled it in his wake, feeling again the tug of a half-buried memory as she did so, but shrugging it aside as nonsense. . . .

Her outburst—which had in all honesty stemmed more from her own guilt and shame than true anger at him or chafing over her captivity—now thoroughly vented, she sighed and turned resolutely from the doorway, contemplating the glinting oval of turquoise water before her. It looked inviting, cool and refreshing in the sunlight with the reflections of the shrubbery shifting over its sparkling surface, and so she waded down the marble steps and into the water, shivering as it rushed around her, taking every part of her into its cool embrace.

As she closed her eyes and drifted in the sun-washed pool, she found to her disgust that she was disappointed that Sharif had left, and secretly resented the urgent summons that had resulted in his having to leaving her to her own devices. If he were here with her in the sunlit turquoise pool, as he'd intended, the arms that cradled her would not have been cool, watery ones, but strong masculine ones, warm with desire. . . . Oh, confound him, despite her protests to the contrary, his lovemaking had stirred feelings within her that she'd been convinced, as an old maid of twenty-four with no marriage prospects ahead of her, she'd never experience! Now thoroughly awakened, she had a sinking feeling those secret, hungry yearnings would never again lie dormant for very long. *Oh, Alexa, you wicked, weak creature, for shame on you, for shame....*

So immersed was she in trying to sort out her conflicting emotions regarding Sharif, it didn't occur to her for some while that he was in danger from the attack of Tabor's tribe upon the city; that he might be wounded, or captured by the enemy in battle, or even slain, if the battle went against them. When such thoughts did occur much later, she was stunned by the depth of her anxiety for his safety. Was it simply that she feared for herself and her own safety if al-Azadel were taken, and Sharif his cousin's prisoner, or even dead? Or was it some other, deeper reason that filled her with gnawing apprehension, an anxiety that would not be laid to rest until he returned safely to her?

Chapter Nineteen

The attack was far worse than Sharif had expected. The al-Tabor had chosen the hours before dawn, when a man's wakefulness was at its lowest ebb, to launch a surprise attack on the guards who manned the little stone gateway across the mountain pass leading to al-Azadel, slitting the sleeping sentries' throats and opening the gate wide for their tribesmen to enter the mountain kingdom.

The citizens of al-Azadel had awakened to the sounds of gunfire, shouts, and screams as a bloody dawn broke, making the sky pink above the ragged mountain tops, to see enemy tribesmen, armed to the teeth and screaming to Allah to favor their cause, running through the streets of their city. Rising from their sleeping rugs, the menfolk of the al-Malik had hastily taken up daggers, lances, knives, or antiquated firearms and stumbled out to meet their attackers, to add their resistance to the *amir*'s small yet courageous palace guardsmen, many of whom had still been celebrating their lord's wedding when first word of the al-Tabor attack reached them, since Imochagh wedding festivities rarely lasted less than three days.

"Is it possible they knew we would be unprepared for an attack?" Sharif wondered shrewdly, slipping a belt of cartridges over his shoulder and loading his rifle.

"I wondered the same thing, my son," his father, Malik, scowling darkly, agreed. "Their attack seems too perfectly timed to have been chosen by chance, to my mind. I believe they somehow learned of your wedding, and took the opportunity to strike this dawn knowing the festivities would have our greater attention, and our men would be unprepared. Were it not for Selim, who raised the alarm when he spotted two of the al-Tabor clambering up the cliffs to the palace proper, we would have been dead in our beds with our throats slit before the guard could be called out to repel them! As it was, our warriors were able to press them back down into the city, where they now hide like rats in the houses of our people, as I told you."

"Selim sounded the alarm?"

"*Ewellah*. The lad was awake—"

"At such an hour? How so?"

Malik grinned, despite the severity of the situation. "It seems your lovely dancing girl, Raisha, had looked upon him with more than favor after the feast, and took him to her bed! When he untangled himself from her arms a while ago to go outside and make water, he saw something metallic catch the light in the valley below. He watched, and as it grew closer, he realized it was a *takoba,* carried by someone climbing stealthily up the hillside toward the palace. The lad used his wits and wasted no time. He sounded the alarm, took up his own dagger, and went to meet them."

"A promising fellow, to all accounts," Sharif acknowledged with grim approval. "I must commend him later. For now, we have other things to worry about." He flashed his father a smile, then wound the *tagilmust* about his lower face. "By the grace of Allah, we will secure our city very quickly, my lord father."

"So be it!" Malik replied, gripping his son's shoulder, then hurriedly embracing him. "Be off with you!"

With that gruffly affectionate farewell, Sharif the Defender was gone to lead his men, and to rid his city of the al-Tabor "rats" who'd infested its walls.

"Surely the fighting must be over with by now," Alexa muttered, craning her head from the window of her apartments in the Mist *serai* to the city far below. The sun was setting, staining the white rooftops red with its rays.

Over twelve hours had passed since Sharif had bid her a curt

268

farewell, and left her alone, hours in which her anxiety had grown with every passing minute. "The gunfire stopped hours ago. I've seen little movement down there since. Surely it's all over with?" There was a note of hopefulness in her tone.

Her companion grunted. "The way I heard it, the al-Tabor took refuge in the houses of our people at knife- or gunpoint when they realized their bid to take our city had failed," Fatima explained, her plump face frowning. "Those sly jackals thought to take many innocents hostage to insure their own safe exit from our city, but their plan failed. Sharif has refused to bargain with them, you see; he's sworn he will not be blackmailed! He'll wait, he has told their spokesmen, for as long as he must, until either their prisoners are released and they surrender to his men, or until they grow rash and determine to fight their way free, and fall beneath his waiting blade. Al-Azadel is enclosed by twisting mountain passes," Fatima observed with the air of a seasoned battle commander, "like a maze that is all but impenetrable to outsiders. The al-Tabor are reckless, dreaming fools to think they ever stood a chance of taking our city and escaping with their worthless lives!"

She said the latter with such relish, Alexa darted a surprised glance at her, for the woman, although cursed with an acid tongue at times, was at heart a gentle soul, who hated bloodshed of any kind.

"Well! You do sound fierce!"

"*Ewellah*, I am! The al-Tabor killed my husband and my baby daughter in one of their attacks many, many years ago. I would be a liar, would I not, little one, if I pretended any fondness for them?"

Poor Fatima, Alexa thought, looking at the woman with sympathy and increased understanding now. "Oh, yes. I should think you would."

She turned from the window and instead paced up and down, needing to do something to drain off the nervous energy filling her. The silence now was somehow worse than the screams and sharp reports that had carried faintly to them earlier, for it seemed, in the light of the setting sun, a brooding, ominous silence. She whirled about as someone entered her chambers, and saw the lady Kairee hovering there. In her anxiety, her irritation over Kairee's betrayal of her trust was forgotten and forgiven, as swiftly as Fatima's deviousness had been earlier, when she'd returned to her apartments in the Mist *serai* from Sharif's bedchamber to find the older woman nervously awaiting her return, her eyes red-rimmed from crying, begging her to understand why they had tricked her into marriage with Sharif.

"Oh, Kairee, what's going on? Do you know anything? Have the al-Tabor been driven off?"

"Most of them, yes," Kairee divulged, taking Alexa's hand and leading the anxious girl to one of the divans. "Sharif and his men were able to round up most of them. The rest either fled back to their camp in the *sahel,* or took refuge in some of the houses, hoping to bargain their freedom for the lives of their hostages."

"So Fatima said. And what happened? Did they succeed?"

Kairee shook her head, her dark, expressive eyes grave. "Fortunately no, my dear. When they heard that Sharif would not be blackmailed, they were desperate and decided to fight their way to freedom. In the process, many were slain."

"Then it's over!" Alexa cried with relief.

"Almost," Kairee acknowledged. "One of Sharif's men is certain he saw one, perhaps two others, evade his men and take refuge in the Street of the Silversmiths. They are searching for these others now. By nightfall, Allah willing, our city will be safe once more."

"Then Sharif is unhurt? He wasn't wounded in the fighting?"

Kairee smiled, touched by the girl's obvious concern for her bridegroom. She'd feared Alexa might be angry and resentful toward her for the part she'd played in arranging her clandestine wedding, and had spent a sleepless night in worrying that she'd feel nothing but hatred toward Sharif. Furthermore, when she'd heard of the al-Tabor attack, she'd wondered if Zerdali would secretly welcome his convenient death in battle, and be hoping that just such a terrible thing would happen. Obviously, she'd underestimated the girl's attraction to her husband's handsome son—or Sharif's ability to charm! Either way, she was delighted that she had done so.

"Don't worry, my dear, your husband was well and unwounded when I glimpsed him in the streets below but a moment ago! My husband told me he fought like a lion in the battle, and that the al-Tabor fled before his *takoba* like locusts before the fire!" She squeezed Alexa's cold hand. "I'm certain when those last few men have been found, he will come to you at once."

Alexa nodded, peculiarly relieved to hear Kairee's reassurances that Sharif was safe.

But despite what the woman had said, Sharif didn't come to her that night, nor the following day.

Raisha was smiling as she watched the pink rays of the sun creep across the flat white rooftop of her mother's little house. The plan she'd conceived as she finished her dancing at the wedding of Sharif and the lady Zerdali had succeeded beyond her wildest dreams! She'd passed the night in pleasant enough dalliance with the youth Selim, who—if he'd lacked the expertise of Sharif as a lover—had nonetheless proved energetic and lusty and eager to learn. Three times he had mounted her during the night, and ridden her to noisy climax. Each time, she'd dutifully applauded his masculinity and performance with gasps and sighs and breathless little moans, and called him a "man amongst men." By the time he was hard and ready for his fourth sampling of her delights, she'd known she owned him, body, heart, and soul!

Afterward, as they lay together upon the rooftop, his head pillowed upon her breasts, she'd stroked his curly hair and idly asked him questions: casual-seeming, unimportant questions. Selim, in complete innocence and eager to please her in the flush of first love he was feeling for the beautiful, experienced woman who had taught him the arts of love, had answered readily.

"Ah, it was a beautiful wedding today, was it not, my love?" she'd said dreamily, tickling his earlobe. "And the lady Zerdali, my dearest friend, the loveliest bride!" She allowed a wistful sigh to escape her lips.

"Lovely, yes. But you were by far the lovelier, Raisha! Why, when you danced tonight, half the men of al-Azadel wanted you for themselves."

"Only half?" She'd pouted.

"Nay, my sweetmeat, in truth *all* of them wanted you—but only half of them were bold enough to say so, with their wives beside them!"

She'd laughed softly, her husky voice like the slow, lazy trickle of honey sliding over a spoon. "And whom did I choose to please me?"

"You chose me, my beloved, the unworthy Selim, who found Paradise in your arms tonight, and still cannot believe that Allah has blessed him so!"

"Dear boy!" She'd sighed. "I only hope the lady Zerdali is as content in her wedding bed tonight as I am in your arms."

"Truly?"

"Truly. You are magnificent, Selim, like a young stallion, virile and lusty! No woman could ask for more."

Flattered by her lavish praises, Selim had grinned broadly.

For a few moments, silence had rested between them while Raisha gazed up at the stars twinkling far above in the indigo sky, and at the moon, curved like the slim crescent blade of a Turkish scimitar directly above the rooftop of her father's house, where she often slept to enjoy the coolness, and considered how best to part Selim from what he knew about the foreign woman's coming to al-Azadel.

"I suppose the lady Zerdali must have been accompanied by a rich caravan when our lord met her in the desert," she'd said casually. "She must be a very great lady where she came from for our prince's son to take her as his bride?"

Selim had shrugged. "I don't know about that. She had no large caravan when we first found her!"

"Found her?"

"*Ewellah,* found. I remember *Sheik* Kadar was filled with fury that day, you see, for the evening before we had found the caravan of my cousin Muriel, and had learned that her father and uncle had been slain by *Franziwas,* and she herself— violated. He'd sworn to find the men who had done these things, and to satisfy his vengeance upon them. Late that

272

afternoon, we spotted a handful of the *Franziwa* Legionnaires camped by an oasis for the night, and against Sharif's wishes, Kadar attacked them. He told us to be careful to take them alive, for he wished to learn from them who it was had done these terrible things to his betrothed and her family.

"Fate smiled upon Kadar. He had one of the Frenchmen tortured to make him talk, and before he died, the man confessed that he was one of the guilty ones, and that another man, an *Englesy*, had been his partner. Kadar ordered the English sergeant bound, intending to bring him to al-Azadel and see justice served by having him executed before all. Meanwhile, Sharif suddenly sprang astride his horse and rode away. At first, we all thought he'd ridden off to be alone, to regain control of his temper, for as you know, that is his habit when he is angered, and he was very angry that Kadar had disobeyed his commands. But when he returned, he was no longer alone, nor angry. He brought with him the white woman, Zerdali. It seemed she'd been hiding in one of the tents when we attacked, but had slipped away to try and bring help for her escort. Sharif claimed the captive woman as his prize, after the customs of the Imochagh, but by then Kadar had learned from the dying Frenchman that the girl was the *Englesy*'s sister, and he was determined he would keep her for himself. He swore she would suffer the same fate as my poor little cousin."

"They quarreled?"

"*Ewellah,* bitterly, for both insisted they had the greater right to the girl. And then—"

"Yes? What then?" Raisha had demanded eagerly, all ears.

"Someone discovered that the *Englesy* had been freed by his sister, and had escaped with one of our finest mounts. Kadar took his closest followers and rode after him."

"And in so doing, relinquished his claim to the woman?"

"Kadar?" Selim had snorted. "You know that Kadar relinquishes nothing that he considers his, and that he has ever been envious of Sharif! No, he told Sharif to keep the girl safe in his care, and that our prince would decide who had the greater claim to her upon his return to the mountains."

"And so Sharif married her, in order to give his claim the

273

greater weight!" Raisha had exclaimed.

"And because he loves her. Everyone could see that she fascinated him as we rode home to al-Azadel. He would not let her out of his sight! It was as if she had bewitched him with her beauty."

Raisha had chosen to ignore that last remark, for it was not news she wanted to hear—though the rest had been unexpectedly juicy. Little Zerdali, wanted by two men, one for love, the other for revenge, perhaps even death! Raisha had smirked. What a delicious entanglement—and she'd wager every silver bangle she possessed that the *amir* knew nothing of Kadar's legal claims upon the woman he called daughter-in-law. Perhaps she'd tell him, though it was unlikely he'd believe the word of an Inandan serving girl who'd happened to enjoy his son's favors for a few brief months before being cast aside, and who could be considered malicious rather than honest! No, perhaps it would be better to wait a little while, and see what other opportunities to oust Zerdali from favor presented themselves.

"Where are you going, my love?" she'd asked Selim sweetly as he rose from her side. "Do you leave poor little Raisha's arms already?"

Selim had seemed shamefaced. "In truth, my sweetmeat, my bladder is as a goatskin ready to burst! I go to make water, and then I'll return."

"A moment apart from you will be a lifetime!" Raisha had sighed, raising her slender hand to her forehead to give him an unimpeded view of her pert breasts in the gray light of predawn. "Hurry back to me, young master-of-love!"

Gulping, Selim had hurried off to do exactly as she'd commanded, and there, as he relieved himself over a convenient bush, gazing into the little valley below the craggy hillside he had chosen, he'd seen the glint of metal in the puny light, winking far below. Suddenly alert, he'd ducked down and watched the place, and moments later had realized what it was he'd seen: men, armed men in turbans and robes, scaling the steep, undefended side of the mountain pass upon which the Palace of the Clouds was built. One of their daggers had caught the light and thence his keen eye as it glinted.

By Allah, surely they must be men of the al-Tabor, and enemies of the al-Malik! he'd reasoned. Raisha had been forgotten as he'd backed away, then turned and raced for the palace, yelling an alarm and a call to arms as he went.

Raisha, mollified at first by Selim's churlishness, had understood his hasty departure when the fighting broke out. She'd hurried down the outer stairs and into the little house proper, shaking awake her mother and father.

Ahoudan had decided to go at once to see if there was any way in which his smith's talents could serve the *amir*, though reluctant to leave his *hareem* unprotected in his absence. Plump Boucha, his wife, might be a nag and a shrew, but he was used to her and her ways. And Raisha, however sorely she might try him with her loose morals, her intrigue, and her disobedience, was still his daughter, Allah pity him his misfortune!

"Barricade the doorway with your looms, Boucha, my dove! Raisha—help your mother with those sacks of rice, foolish girl, don't just stand there! Dangerous men are about, killing our friends and neighbors! Quickly, quickly!"

The sound of shots and cries and running feet had been growing louder, and the shrill, terrified screams of horses had carried on the dawn breeze. Certain his women were secure from harm, Ahoudan had left his house and hurried to the palace. From there, he would go directly to his forge, if there were weapons that needed sharpening or daggers needing repair. By Allah, how his blood sang! Not since he was a young man and had battled the al-Murid had he felt so alive . . . !

For the greater part of that day, Boucha and her daughter cowered in the darkened confines of their little house, behind a barricade of weaving looms, rice sacks, goatskins, huge earthenware oil jars, and whatever household goods seemed to offer the best barrier to an al-Tabor tribesman bent on entering their humble abode. But as the hours passed uneventfully, Raisha's irritation grew, and her initial fear lessened in proportion to it.

"Enough of this nonsense," she told her mother. "The danger must already be past. Why, I haven't heard any shots since the time of the noon prayers, over three hours ago!"

"Then why has your father not returned?" Boucha snapped, her plump face oily with sweat.

"You know him, Mother!" Raisha said scornfully. "He is probably sipping coffee in the palace at this very moment, listening to some storyteller exaggerate the attack today, his wife and daughter forgotten. Come, let's move all this away from the door, and see to cooking supper. My belly is as empty as a chicken's head!"

They'd all but completed their task of unbarring the door when two men came racing down the Street of the Silversmiths, robes flying behind them, turbans lost. Before Raisha or Boucha could duck back inside, the men were upon them, jostling them roughly back inside their dwelling with harsh commands.

"Who are you, Rude Ones?" Boucha snapped. "Get out of my house!"

"Shut up, old woman!" one of the men growled, revealing the dagger in his fist. "A silent tongue will serve me best today. Another word from you, and I cut yours from your mouth."

Boucha agreed, nodding furiously, her lips now tightly pursed, her eyes round saucers of terror. She backed into a corner and slid down until she was sitting mutely in it, watching the two men with the scared fascination of a cornered animal watching a snake.

Not so Raisha. She moved to replace the barriers she and her mother had removed moments before.

"What are you doing, girl?" the second man, who wore a beard, demanded. "Sit over there with your mother, or it'll be the worse for you!"

"Fools!" Raisha retorted to the astounded fugitives, who could not believe her foolhardiness. "If you would hide from the men of the al-Malik, is it not better for this house to appear secured from the outside?"

"You're right, girl, it is," the bearded one agreed at once. "Quickly, Yasah, help her!"

When the barricades had been replaced, Raisha fetched a goatskin from where it hung upon a peg in the corner and offered it to the pair. "Running must be thirsty work," she observed slyly. "Here, have some. It's goat's milk, fresh

276

this morning."

They accepted in turn, swigging gratefully.

"You seem very friendly," the one named Ali said, eyeing her speculatively. "By Allah, if only others of your city had behaved as you, we would be lords here by now, and strutting about the Palace of the Clouds with Tabor as the new *amir* of al-Azadel!"

The other one, Yasah, nodded and grinned nastily. "*Ewellah*, Ali—and Malik's head decorating a spike at the city gates, as a warning to all that the al-Tabor are a tribe to be reckoned with!"

"As I said before, you are both fools—indeed, all of the al-Tabor are fools, if they think to take Malik by force in his own mountain stronghold!" Raisha said with scorn. "These mountains are his territory, known by him as well as the back of his hand! He requires only a small force to defend his kingdom, for its rocky walls are a defense in themselves."

"By Allah!" Ali declared mockingly. "We have wandered into the dwelling of a female *sheik*, wise in the arts of warfare and strategy. Tell me, pretty one, how would you take al-Azadel, then?"

"That's obvious," Raisha said with a look of patent disgust. "A lioness cannot be easily taken when she hunts alone. When cornered, she will fight to the death, and not care how many lives she takes with her. But—if she has a cub—well, that is a completely different matter, is it not? Then she must use caution, or risk the life of her young. Such a lioness can be captured, for in her concern for her cub, she grows anxious—and careless."

She raised her brows inquiringly, wondering if these woolly-headed louts would catch her meaning, or if she would be forced to explain in plain talk. She need not have worried. Ali, the brighter of the two, she suspected, understood at once.

"Sharif al-Azim, you mean? You'd take him by stealth, and through him the *amir* and al-Azadel?"

"I would."

"Raisha! Be silent!" her mother pleaded, finding her tongue in her outrage at her daughter's treachery.

"I warned you, woman!" Yasah snarled, raising his dagger

and jabbing it threateningly in the woman's direction. Boucha backed down again with a muffled whimper.

"It could be done that way, yes," Raisha allowed, speaking quickly to draw their attention away from her mother and back to herself, for Yasah seemed quite capable of slitting the woman's throat. "However, Malik is no fool, nor is his son. Take Sharif captive, and there is no doubt in my mind that the noble fool and his father would refuse to meet any demands you might make. They'd prefer Sharif's death at your lord Tabor's hands rather than relinquish one inch of al-Azadel to his control by surrendering."

She smiled, catlike, the tension easing from her body as she realized she held them spellbound, that her ideas had them transfixed. Her smile deepened. "No, my friends, Sharif would not prove Malik's weakness, they would not let it prove so. But—there is one who might well prove Sharif's undoing, and through him, his father's."

"A son? Is that it?"

"No, my friend Ali. Sharif's bride!"

"Bride? Pah, you lie, girl! Everyone knows that Sharif has never taken a wife! Our lord Tabor has four, as the Prophet allows, and twice as many women to serve his pleasures, and he often scorns his lord cousin for the lack of women in his life! They wonder, in the tents and villages of the al-Tabor, if he is enamored of young boys instead."

Raisha laughed scornfully on hearing this. "Young boys? Sharif al-Azim? By Allah, never was any man so wrongly judged! Sharif is a man of lusty appetites, and all of them manly ones. A woman that has shared his bed and known his lovemaking can never find pleasure with another. Beside his skills in the arts of love and delight, all men are but pale shadows of Sharif!" She sighed.

"And how do you know this?"

"You are impertinent to ask, Master Ali!" Raisha retorted too quickly, and the men nudged each other and grinned wolfishly, licking their lips as they appraised the young woman anew.

"It would appear our little Inandan traitress has been pricked by her lord's dagger a time or two, eh, girl?"

"He loved me, before *she* came here!" Raisha insisted, tossing her head. "I shared his bed, his confidence, his concerns—I was everything to him! I would have been his bride, I know it, had she not come to al-Azadel. I hate her! I would do anything to rid Sharif of her, and regain my place in his heart! Anything."

"That's well enough, but what about us? We can't do a cursed thing about Sharif and this woman of his, not while we're trapped here!" Yasah pointed out. "I hear the al-Malik guards coming nearer by the second, Ali! If we wait much longer here, we'll be done for! Let's go!"

"Wait! That's exactly what they'll expect you to do—to stupidly make a run for it!" Raisha argued. "Try it, and they'll cut you down. Now, did anyone see you come in here?"

The two men exchanged glances and shook their heads. "I think not," Ali answered.

"Then there is every chance that no one knows that the two of you even exist, in the confusion of the fighting. Stay here until the guards return to the palace. I know a way down the mountain, one that is impossible mounted, but quite passable on foot. I'll take you after moonrise—if you give me your word you'll tell your lord Tabor what I have said?"

The fugitives were about to agree when they heard tramping feet in the street outside, and the shouts of Sharif's guards as they searched the houses nearby. As Yasah had said, they were getting closer by the second.

"Quickly! Get in here!" Raisha urged, gesturing to the empty earthenware oil jars, each one of which was quite large enough to hold a man.

"Are we Ali Baba of Omar the Tentmaker's Tales, that we are to hide in jars?" Ali sneered, fear giving him a decidedly evil cast.

"And am I Scheherazade, to spin stories to prevent you from losing your stupid heads?" Raisha hissed. "Get inside, quickly now, quickly!"

The two men had no choice, for already Raisha could hear Sharif's voice, very close to the doorway of their little house. They clambered inside the jars, and ducked down in the nick of time.

279

"Ahoudan! Are you inside?" Sharif roared.

"Oh, Sharif!" Raisha cried, quickly throwing aside the looms and sacks that blocked the opening. She flung herself down at his feet and pressed her lips to his dusty boots. "O my lord Sharif, Praise Allah, you have come to save us at last! I was so very frightened—what with all the gunshots, and the cries! My father is not here, you see. He left my mother and me here alone, to see if your lord father required his services at the palace."

"Get up, girl," Sharif said curtly, glancing over her shoulder into the gloomy little dwelling. "One of your neighbors says he spotted someone running this way—that he thought they'd come in here. Are you alone?"

"Why yes, my lord—but we were so frightened! That is why we barricaded the door, don't you see? Come, look inside, if you wish. There is no one here but us poor, helpless women. Is that not so, Mother?" Raisha scowled, for her mother refused to answer, her lips still tightly pursed. "Mother?" the girl repeated.

"J-j-just the two of us," Boucha agreed, but her eyes rolled frantically in her plump face, like one of the Afflicted of Allah, and her plump, silver-ringed fingers twitched toward the earthenware oil jars in the corner, as if taken by a spasm.

Sharif jerked his head, gesturing to two of his men to look about the room. Satisfied it was empty save for the two women, they exited and shook their heads. "There's no one there, my lord—not unless you count a fat spider or two! They must have escaped down the mountainside."

"Go up on the roof. If you find nothing there either, we'll ride down the mountain and see if we can find any trace of them."

One of his men climbed the outside stairway of whitewashed mud bricks to the roof. There was a rumpled sleeping mat of gaily striped wool to one side, a few chickens, and a wicker dovecote, from which pigeons rose in a flutter of white wings as the guard strode about the roof. A devil-eyed black she-goat, her udders swollen, was tethered to one side. She eyed him calmly, gave an irritable bleat, and chewed some more at her fraying tether.

"Nothing here, sir, not unless you count goats, pigeons, and a few scrawny chickens amongst the fugitives!" he called cheerfully down to his chieftain.

Sharif grinned, his smile belying the fatigue that haunted his ebony eyes and the white rings of dried sweat that circled his garments, evidence of the many hard-won skirmishes he had entered into to secure his city and her people that day.

"So be it, then. Mount up, men! We will turn our faces toward the desert and overtake these jackals before they reach their master. And when we find them, we will send their heads to Tabor in a wicker basket. We will make of them an example that will cause Tabor to think twice before he attacks my kingdom again . . . !"

With that ominous threat, he strode to his horse and sprang lithely astride it, wheeling the stallion about and kneeing it into a swift canter through the winding flagstoned little streets of al-Azadel. His men followed him quickly away from the Street of the Silversmiths.

Raisha watched him go, finally releasing the anxious breath she had been holding and licking her dry lips nervously. She had come so close to discovery, so very close! Perhaps, if Sharif had not spent a sleepless wedding night with his precious Zerdali in his bed, he would have been alert enough to notice her unusual nervousness. As it was, his fatigue had served her well. . . .

"You may come out now, my friends," she said softly, and rapped once upon the earthenware jars. "They are gone."

It was well after moonrise before Raisha was able to escort the pair down the perilous mountain path she had told them of, and later still before she judged them far enough along on their road to find the remainder of the way with ease.

"My part is done for now," she whispered, her cinnamon eyes bright and malicious in the starlight. "What happens next is up to you."

"Will you aid us from within?" Ali asked.

She nodded.

"But how? They will be on the alert after this, and it will be difficult, if not impossible, to slip away from the city unseen."

"I've already thought of that. Here, take these," she said,

and handed Ali a woven basket with a lid.

"Food?" he asked, grinning, for his belly was growling loudly to remind him he had not eaten since the evening before, over twenty-four hours ago.

"No, stupid one, not food!" she snapped. "Do you think of nothing but your empty bellies? Just take the basket and go! When you reach your camp, give it at once to your chieftain and tell him what I have suggested. By all accounts, Tabor is no fool. He will know what to do. And remember, the *woman* is the key in this, not Sharif. Take her, and Sharif will bend like a reed in the *simoom*, and do anything you ask."

They nodded and began scurrying away from her. In seconds, the darkness of the mountains had swallowed them whole.

Chapter Twenty

She knew it. She knew she was dreaming again—the first time she'd dreamed since coming to al-Azadel—yet it was not the same erotic dream of a shadowy lover she'd had so many times before in her life. No, this one was very different!

In this dream, she was somewhere dark and frightening, floating like a phantom above the ground, aware that she was dreaming yet alert to her surroundings. She was in a place of shadows and looming boulders shaped like menacing creatures. A place where danger and evil rode the wind that moaned in the caves and chasms, bringing the threat of death on its cool current . . .

On she floated, looking down. She was able to discern a lighter, twisting path between the shadows and the rocks below, perhaps a winding goat path or something similar. Down this path came a handful of men, dark as shades themselves in their indigo robes. Snatches of their conversation carried to her where she floated:

". . . *are you certain you heard something . . . ?*"

". . . *leave the horses . . . go up here on foot were I not . . . ?*"

". . . *but my lord Sharif . . . surely they would never have risked . . .*"

And then, below her, just ahead of the men she'd heard and recognized as her husband and his men, she saw a shadow move, detach itself from the denser shadows about it, and crouch forward, arm raised aloft. A second shadow mirrored its threatening actions from across the snaking path!

An ambush! she realized. She opened her mouth to scream an alarm, to warn the unsuspecting men who were coming up the path to meet their deaths. But to her horror, in her dream she could not cry a warning. It was as if her throat was paralyzed, her tongue cut out! She could only utter incoherent, useless babbling sounds as the shadows erupted from their hiding places and fell upon the unsuspecting men, bludgeoning their heads with weighty rocks, thrusting their daggers into yielding flesh, arms raising and falling again and again until their dark blood splattered the boulders and glistened in ruby splashes over the sandy earth in the cold light of the moon. . . ."

"*Shaaa-Shaaa!*"

Alexa suddenly sat bolt upright, the warning that had at last torn from her frozen lips jolting her abruptly from sleep to heart-pounding, sobbing wakefulness.

At once, comforting arms went about her. A plump bosom pillowed her head.

"Hush, hush, little one, it was only a dream—a bad dream, *ewellah,* but a dream nonetheless! There, there, Zerdali, my princess."

Alexa was trembling violently as she clung to Fatima's motherly figure, her face buried deep against the woman's breasts, fingers digging like claws into the cloth of the woman's night robes. Her heart still raced, out of control.

"Oh, Fatima, Fatima! Tell me, am I awake, or dreaming still?" she moaned.

"Awake, and safe besides! Fear not, little one, your Fatima is here. Whatever it was that frightened you has gone now. Come, let me go to light the lamp. Its glow will scare away the shadows and your fears."

She untangled herself from Alexa's tight grip and went to light the dish-lamps. In moments, the chamber was bathed in their warm, comforting radiance.

Alexa forced herself to smile, blinking back tears and trying to get her trembling body back under control. She felt foolish for being so afraid still, now that she was awake, but she was.

"That's much better. But, oh, Fatima, it all seemed so real! I saw Sharif and his men in my dream. They were climbing a rocky path—a goat path that twisted up through the mountains, I think it was, and I was floating above them, looking down. You know how it is in dreams, how things like flying can seem quite ordinary?" Seeing Fatima nod in understanding, she continued, "And then, just as I heard them talking back and forth between themselves, I saw t-two shadows ahead of them move into position. Oh, Fatima, there were robbers hidden there, bandits waiting to ambush my husband and his men, and suspecting nothing, they were walking right into their trap! I knew they'd all be killed, and so—oh, Fatima—I tried to warn him! I tried to scream, to make some sound to alarm them, but nothing would come out! My throat was numb, my tongue tied! I tried and tried, but by the time I finally managed to cry out his name, I was awake again." She shuddered, hugging herself about the arms. "It was awful!"

Fatima smiled in understanding, and patted her cheek. "It must have been. The terror in your cry roused me even in my room! But you're awake now, and quite safe. The nightmare is gone, Zerdali. Perhaps your fear for Sharif's safety was so great, the frightening dream grew from that fear, yes?"

"Fears for Sharif?"

"But of course! What woman wouldn't be afraid for her husband, if he'd been missing for so many hours under such circumstances?"

"But you said yourself—and Kairee agreed—that the *amir* believes Sharif and his men rode into the desert in pursuit of the last of the attackers."

Alarm stirred uneasily in Alexa's belly. Did Fatima and Kairee *really* believe that, or had they simply given her a plausible explanation to set her mind at rest, thinking she was concerned for Sharif's safety? Such an idea was ridiculous, of course! She didn't really care what happened to him, she told herself firmly. She didn't love him, husband or no, so why would she be worried about what happened to him?

Yet despite her convictions, her fingers twined nervously together, and her heart skipped a beat or two before thundering on.

"Isn't that what happened?" she whispered, her eyes carefully watching the expression on Fatima's face.

Fatima shrugged and sighed, her expression purposely

285

bland. "I pray it is so! But—neither Sharif nor the handful of men who went with him have returned as yet to tell their tale. And so, we can only hope that we are right, and that soon he'll return with his prisoners, or come back empty-handed but unharmed. Now, the night is yet young, and you need your sleep, my pretty. Back to bed with you! Shall I bring you some warm milk to soothe you?"

Alexa grimaced. "Warm milk? Yuggh, no, thank you! Go on back to bed yourself, Fatima. I'll be all right now. And thank you for coming to comfort me. You're a dear, always so good to me, always there when I need you, though I don't deserve it. Whatever would I do without you?" She reached out, took Fatima's plump hand in both her own, and kissed it affectionately. "Good night, dear Fatima. Sleep well!"

Fatima left, and Alexa lay down again, yet sleep refused to come, partly because she feared if she slept she would dream that horrible dream again, and partly because the gnawing anxiety in her belly refused to be stilled by Fatima's reassurances.

What she'd dreamed *had* been only a dream, hadn't it? Sharif wasn't out there somewhere in the mountains, dead under the cold moonlight, his beautiful body broken and bloodied by an assassin's blade? Tears choked her throat. It was only a dream, she repeated to herself silently. It wasn't so. It wasn't! In the morning, he'd return, arrogant and teasing, wearing his most wicked, lecherous grin, and she'd laugh at her foolish—fears.

Sharif came to, and saw the pale stars of dawn shining directly above him in the charcoal sky. His vision was blurred, the single dawn star multiplied to a dozen or more! He blinked and flicked his head to clear it, feeling stabs of fire needle into his skull. He reached up to touch his temple, and his hand came away with the stickiness of his own blood. He groaned with the pain the movement sent shooting through his ribs and lungs.

Stirring gingerly, he raised himself to a sitting position at last, remembering then the search for the fugitive al-Tabor tribesmen that had brought him here, to this godforsaken, desolate mountain pass where only the pluckiest herdsmen grazed their goats, for it was rumored that ghosts and strange monsters, half-animal, half-human, inhabited the painted caves here, and perhaps it was so. The shrill cry of some nightbird—unlike any he'd ever heard before—had alerted him as their attackers leaped from cover, but its call had come too late. The ambushers had used the element of surprise to overcome him and his men, for all that they were outnumbered two to one. The thought reminded him. By the Prophet, what of his men, his faithful companions? Where were they now?

Staggering to his feet, he saw them, flung over the boulders that littered the path. They were unmoving, with arms outstretched to the heavens or else hanging limply to the earth from where they'd come. Dead, they were all dead! he saw, and bitterness, grief, fury rose in his throat like gall. Some had been bludgeoned with rocks. Others had had their throats cut, slashed like sacrificial sheep. Another had been knocked senseless and his neck twisted awry. Six men had gone with him, and only he was left alive.

He swayed where he stood, feeling tears water his cheeks although his jaw was set hard, his teeth clenched. Unaware that he wept, he wondered from where it came, that salty river coursing down his cheeks.

"Sir?" came a quavering voice.

A gladness filled his breast. His heavy heart leaped. He swung about to greet the other survivor, a broad smile of joy lifting his lips. Not alone! Not the only one left alive, praise be to Allah!

But the smile faded as if it had never been, for he saw there only a stripling boy he vaguely knew—a slender goatherd, poised upon the twisting path like a nervous bird ready to take flight. His silly beasts were bleating and leaping from boulder to boulder and crag to crag, their demon-eyes shining in the pale light of pre-dawn.

"Ah," he muttered, clenching his fists to control the crushing disappointment that hefted through him. "Coman, son of Fadil, is it not?"

"Ewellah, sir, it is I."

"You know me?"

287

"But of course, my lord Sharif! Everyone knows you, my lord." His brown eyes nervously flickered from his master to the bodies littering the path. His wind-browned urchin's face paled, and his gaze moved quickly back to Sharif. "You were ambushed, sir. Praise Allah, you escaped with your life!"

"Praise Allah indeed, good Coman. Tell me, did—did you pass anyone as you came up the path! Did you see anyone a-at all?"

"No one, sir, but I found something. Look!"

But young Coman's revelation was destined to be postponed, for Sharif's knees suddenly buckled. The world reeled crazily, as if tilted on its axis by a giant hand, and he folded senseless to the ground.

When he awoke again, it was full daylight. Opening his eyes, he discovered he was back in his own chambers at the Palace of the Clouds.

His head throbbed as if Ahoudan was pounding his anvil within his skull! Each stroke made him wince. Bandages swathed his head, and more swathed his bare chest, binding his broken ribs so tightly, it was difficult to breathe. He winced and closed his eyes, but not before the woman and the man who sat anxiously at his bedside were aware that he had awakened.

"Thanks be to Allah, he has come to!" Kairee exclaimed. "Look, Master Hakim, is his color not better?"

Hakim, the priest and physician, stood and leaned over his patient, peering intently into his face. He peeled back a closed eyelid to inspect the eye beneath.

Sharif glowered ferociously back at the sage's rude intrusion. He rolled his bared eye horribly and muttered a string of colorful curses before he thrust out a weighty arm to ward the irritating fellow off. But rather than taking insult, Hakim smiled amidst his beard.

"Better indeed, my lady. Recovered sufficiently to take the name of Allah in vain, *wellah!* The crisis is safely passed now, I think. Our lord is young and healthy, and will recover fully from his wounds. Give him food, if he asks for it, but sleep will prove the finest medicine for him."

"Our thanks, Hakim."

Hakim made a deep bow, touching brow, then breast. "To serve the family of the *amir* is an honor, and thanks are neither needed nor expected, my lady. By your leave?"

After Hakim had left, Kairee smiled fondly down at Sharif. "Well, well, son-of-my-husband, it appears we are not rid of your rascally self as yet. Allah has mercifully spared your life, so that you may live to tease me yet again!"

For once, Sharif did not return her affectionate smile. "So it would seem, my aunt," he said soberly. "But alas, He was less merciful with the lives of my companions."

Kairee bit her lip. "I know, Sharif. And I know that you are grieving for your men. But if it was the will of Allah that they should die, what can we mortals do about it but accept His decisions for our lives? The Persians believe that there is a Sky-Tree in the heavens above, which bears upon its branches a leaf for every person in this world. On a chosen night in their calendar, they say that a number of leaves fall from the Sky-Tree's boughs, determining those who will die in the year to come, and the very day and hour of their deaths. No mortal man can control which leaves will fall, nor decide which will remain upon the bough. It was Allah's will that your fellows should die and that you should survive, Sharif. Their leaves must have been amongst those that fell from the Sky-Tree."

"The will of Allah?" he growled sourly, ebony eyes smoldering. "No! I cannot believe that, Kairee. It was not by God's will that they died, but by the will of men, the greed of men, the covetousness and deceit of men, curse their souls!" Despite his Imochagh vows, he took no pains to conceal his fury this morning. His fists were clenched by his side, but of a sudden he pounded the right one against the divan beneath him, making Kairee gasp. "I will revenge their deaths, Kairee, I swear it! I shall take two of those jackals' lives in payment for the life of each friend they robbed me of!"

"Please, Sharif, you must calm yourself and not get excited nor move about so!" Kairee insisted, pressing him back down when he would have sprung from the divan. "Hakim says you will recover, but in order to do so fully you must rest until you grow strong again, and your broken ribs and that awful gash on your head are mended. Forget about revenge for now, and lie quietly. I'll fetch the lady Zerdali to your side. That poor girl! Only one day a bride, and already she feared she'd been made a widow! She tried so hard to be brave and not seem concerned in front of me, but I could tell. She's been so anxious for your safety—"

"Zerdali? Concerned for me? I sorely doubt it, Aunt!" Sharif gritted, but little by little his steely expression softened as his thoughts turned in a different direction. Zerdali. His reluctant bride. His unwilling wife. He frowned thoughtfully and did not speak for several moments. When he did he said, "I think it better you not bring my bride here, Kairee! You may tell her that I am returned, and that I have been wounded, but you will not permit her to see me, not even should she beg to do so, is that understood?"

"What? *Ewellah,* of course I understand, but—might I ask *why* you give such an order?" Kairee's beautiful, composed face was for once thoroughly unsettled, her expression dismayed by his commands, and Sharif could not help a small grin at her loss of control.

"You may ask, my dear aunt, but I will not tell thee," he teased softly. "Only do as I ask, and we shall see what Zerdali does," Sharif promised, "and in the process learn once and for all if she cares for me or nay. You see, Aunt, in the desert after I captured her and claimed her as my woman, she called me a savage brute, incapable of love, for all that I offered her my heart. And on our wedding night, she said she had no fondness for me, could never grow to love Sharif the Defender, nor the world he laid at her feet, for all that I had made her body sing with desire. She wanted no part of a desert prince nor his kingdom, she swore it! And then, the morning after we were wed, after a night of joy and pleasure in my arms, she pleaded with me to let her go, to leave her alone, and would not admit the joy I had shown her. And so, I have decided that this might be the perfect time to grant her her wish."

"You mean to free her?"

"Free her? Never, Aunt! No, I have merely decided to leave her alone, as she asked me to do."

"And what do you hope to prove by doing that?" Kairee

inquired, tight-lipped.

"Perhaps nothing. Perhaps everything!"

"Such foolish games are not fair to your little bride! They could prove more harmful than enlightening, you mark my words! She has pride, that one, and will see your commands only as a rejection of her, not as a challenge to be overcome. Her pride will not let her disobey your orders. Believe me, I know her, Sharif."

"And is my little bride fair to Sharif?" he demanded. "What of the games she plays with me, eh, what of them, after I have waited half a lifetime to be with her? By day, my aunt, she is as cold as the snowy peaks of our mountains, yet by night—ah, by night she burns hotter than the desert sun, and forgets the harsh words she speaks when the sun is risen! She may think she can continue to play her little games with Sharif," he added, smiling wickedly, "but she will learn she cannot! *Ewellah*, we shall see, my lady aunt. Pride or no, we shall see! But for now, where is my lord father? I would speak with him at once!"

"What! He *refused* to see me? He *forbade* me to go to him?"

"Alas, yes, my little one!" Fatima confirmed, squirming in discomfort at being the bearer of such unwelcome tidings. "The lady Kairee was most insistent that I tell you exactly what he said. You are forbidden to enter his chambers, my dove."

"But why would he give such an order? Why? Surely there must be some mistake!"

"I do not know why," her companion admitted. "But it has been given, and we must obey."

"Oh, rubbish!" Alex said irritably. "I've spent the last two days pacing a hole in my carpet, worrying myself sick about what the devil's happened to that—that rogue! Then, when he shows up at long last, Kairee tells me he's been wounded in an ambush, but that he's given orders that I'm not to see him! Me, his own wife!" Her slanted green eyes, beneath which faint lavender shadows betrayed her sleepless nights, crackled with indignation. "Confound that man! He can't have it both ways,

Fatima! Either I'm his true wife, as he insists, in all ways and every way, and will be accorded the respects and rights and considerations that title entails, or else I'm not. Now, which is it to be?''

Fatima hid a smile and shrugged, thinking Sharif was craftier than she had given him credit for being, by Allah! "That is up to you and your lord husband to decide, *habibah*. Not Fatima.''

"Hmmph. Help me to dress, then, won't you? I intend to pay our high and mighty al-Azim a visit immediately, and sort this misunderstanding out once and for all!''

Minutes later, she stood dressed in her most becoming *caftan* of peacock blue—a color that deepened the green of her eyes and made the red highlights in her chestnut hair seem more predominant. The hems and sleeves were embroidered with clever trellises of chain stitch worked also in peacock-colored threads, and with bands of diamonds and eyelet stars after the Tuareg designs. Fatima threw a bluish-green shawl from Kashmir over her golden-chestnut hair.

"There! I just need some perfume, I think, Fatima, and I'll be ready,'' she decided, eyeing herself critically in a small silver-backed hand mirror and wishing she did not look so weary, that the circles about her eyes would disappear. Would Sharif be recovered enough to notice whether she was beautiful or not this morning? Would he be conscious enough to even care? She bit her lower lip, her belly doing a sudden flip-flop of anxiety. Kairee'd said he'd suffered a nasty head wound and some cracked ribs. Was he scarred, his handsome, swarthy face and magnificent body forever marred? She couldn't bear it if that were so. . . . Oh, Lord, what was wrong with her? She had to get a grip on herself, to control the trembling of her hands! "The attar of roses would be perfect,'' she suggested, more curtly than she intended.

"Perfume, mistress?'' Fatima asked slyly, bringing her the flagon nonetheless. "Your most becoming garments?'' She chuckled. "Do you but plan to speak with your husband, or to seduce the poor man upon his sickbed?''

Alexa flushed bright pink at the older woman's outrageous suggestion, but snatched the perfume phial from her and applied the crystal stopper to her wrists and throat and earlobes even as she retorted waspishly, "To speak with him, of course, and inquire after his injuries—for courtesy's sake, naturally, as his wife. What else would I want of that hateful man?"

"I thought perhaps to see with your own eyes that he is recovering, and to lay your fears to rest."

"Oh, poppycock!" Alexa insisted hotly. "Now, are you coming with me, or must I go to his apartments alone?"

"I think I will come with thee, little one. It might prove interesting," Fatima decided, muttering her reply as she flung a striped veil over her own gray-streaked black hair.

"What did you say?"

"I said that I will accompany thee, my lady Zerdali."

The two massive Negro guards who flanked the entrance to Sharif's private apartments were respectful but firm. They crossed their lances over the arched doorway and remained obdurate despite first Alexa's polite request—and then her heated insistence—that the two women be allowed to pass through it.

"By the orders of our lord, no one is to enter his chambers unless he permits it, my lady!" Alabi, the tallest and blackest of the pair, insisted.

"But surely such orders can't extend to his own wife!" Alexa sputtered. "Step aside, Alabi, and permit me to enter—I command it!"

"Alas, we dare not! It would mean our heads to let you pass, my lady!" Ahmad, the shorter guard, explained. "Forgive us, but we must respectfully refuse to obey you, my lady."

"I see," Alexa gritted, her small fists clenched at her sides. "Well, far be it for me to cause you to lose your heads! Come, Fatima! I believe I have better things to do than waste my time here. If Sharif doesn't want to see me, he can rot, for all I care!"

The horrified guards' eyes boggled at her flippant words and they exchanged glances as she turned and swept down the long, tiled corridor with all the hauteur of a queen, a surreptitiously grinning Fatima waddling after her.

But as they were about to turn the corner to their own

apartments in the Mist *serai*, a serving girl hurrying in the opposite direction toward Sharif's private quarters almost collided with them. She cradled a goatskin *anzad* in her arms, and as she reeled aside to avoid barreling into the pair, the instrument collided with the wall and emitted a deep, discordant "thwang" of protest.

"Aiee!" the girl squealed.

"Why *La Bes*, Raisha!" Alexa exclaimed, glad to see a friendly faee in her pique as she recognized the girl. "I haven't seen you for days!"

"*La Bes*, it is so, my lady," Raisha agreed, recovering and modestly lowering her eyes. "I was most unhappy when the lady Kairee told me I must leave the *hareem* and return to my father's house, for it meant leaving Zerdali, my closest friend, behind without any explanation. But, as you well know, your lord husband has summoned me back to the palace to entertain him while he recovers from his wounding, and so here I am! I cannot thank you enough for allowing me to serve your lord husband again, my lady! He told me that you'd personally mentioned how you missed me, and would be happy to have me return!" Raisha dropped to her knees and lifted the hem of Alexa's filmy veil, kissing it. "I can never repay you, never!"

"Come, come, Raisha, on your feet, there's no need for that!"

"No need?" Raisha smiled brightly, standing. "But of course there is! You are my mistress now that you are the wife of Sharif al-Azim, are you not? Oh, but forgive me my rudeness!" she hurriedly amended. "I have not yet congratulated you on that good fortune, mistress! Peace be unto you, and to your new husband also. I wish you both great happiness, and pray that Allah will bless you and make your union fruitful."

"Thank you," Alexa said sourly, fervently hoping that she hadn't already been made "fruitful" by that desert scoundrel! To be carrying his child was the very last thing she needed, for he'd never let her leave al-Azadel if she were.

"And how was your lord husband when you visited him this morning, my lady? Did he seem much improved since last night, to your eyes?" Raisha asked innocently.

Alexa smothered a scowl, reluctant to admit she had not been granted admittance to his lordship's presence, and so was unable to judge his health! "He seemed quite able to hand out orders, Raisha, and to see them enforced—a sure sign that he is fast recovering, I'm certain," she replied evasively.

"Then forgive me, but by your leave," Raisha babbled on again, "I must be on my way! Last night, he bade me bring my *anzad* with me this morning, that I might play and dance to soothe him to sleep. With his head wound making him so out of sorts and ill-tempered, he will be very angry if I delay."

"Then please, hurry along!" Alexa gritted. "Let it not be said that I detained you from bringing the—comfort—my poor husband receives from your playing!"

Raisha bowed her head respectfully, hiding a smug smile, before racing down the corridor, back the way Alexa and Fatima had just come. The two towering black guards stepped aside at once, and allowed her to pass them unchallenged.

"Well!" Alexa snapped, her cheeks hot, her eyes snapping as she saw Raisha's long black hair and trim derriere disappear into the forbidden zone.

"Well, indeed!" Fatima echoed, a grin tugging at the corners of her lips. "Did I not advise thee to learn to play the *anzad*, little one? Such a talent would have profited you today, eh?"

"*Anzad*, my foot!" Alexa hissed, stamping her foot in emphasis, bitter tears choking in her throat. "I sorely doubt it is Raisha's *anzad* with which Sharif wishes to play—oh, no, not him, that lecherous goat! And the nerve of him to tell Raisha *I* wanted her back here!"

Fatima chuckled. "Ah, but then, what do you care what the little witch does with him, eh, *habibah*, since Sharif means nothing to you?"

The woman's casual words served to curtail Alexa's temper, which had been dangerously close to bubbling over. "Yes, you're quite right! What do I care?"

"Now that Raisha is back in her lord's favor, you will be relieved of the distasteful duties of a wife that you so despised, and all will be well for everyone. Sharif will find ease and pleasure upon her eager body. Raisha will likewise satisfy her she-cat's lust for Sharif, and you—ah, you will be left quite alone, as you always wished. Yes, it is for the best that she's back, I think." Fatima made to go on toward the Mist *serai*.

"Back? What do you mean, Raisha's 'back'?" Alexa spat. She took Fatima by her plump upper arm and spun her around to face her so forcefully, the Bedouin woman all but lost her balance and toppled.

"Why, did you not know, *habibah?* Did you not wonder at Raisha, an Inandan, having the luxury of an apartment in the palace *hareem?* Why, that sly little witch was Sharif's bedmate for many months—ever since she danced half-naked for him at the lady Drisana's wedding."

"Bedmate?" Alexa ground out, a horrible sick feeling making her stomach turn over.

"*Ewellah!* In fact, she pleased him so very well, he favored her almost every night afterward—right up until the time he went into the desert and returned with you, *habibah.* He gave her many gifts as a mark of his pleasure with her too—oh, little jewels, a few cages of pretty songbirds, phials of perfume, some Cathay cloth too, I believe, and—"

"That's quite enough, Fatima!" Alexa's voice was shrill. "I don't think I care to hear anymore, thank you. In fact, I believe I have a headache coming on. Come, we will return to the *hareem* at once. Perhaps the waters of the baths and a massage might ease it. . . ."

"Perhaps they will ease your head, but it will take more than water to soothe your jealous heart, *habibah!*" Fatima muttered, hurrying after her mistress, who marched along as if at the head of an enormous army, her back held ramrod straight, her chin carried high, her skirts swishing.

"What?" she snapped suspiciously over her shoulder, catching the tail end of Fatima's mutterings.

"I said only that the waters might prove soothing for a start, Zerdali," Fatima lied smoothly, and hid yet another smile as they swept down the sumptuous mosaicked hallways to the *hareem.*

To her thinking, a second war had been declared today—and this one had nothing to do with the al-Tabor!

Chapter Twenty-One

Sharif leaned up on one elbow upon his divan and watched with a sour, bored expression as Raisha pirouetted and twirled about his apartments, hummed under her breath, and flung her filmy veils seductively about her. She was going to great lengths to arouse him, tossing her long, silky black hair, pouting provocatively, thrusting out her breasts and undulating her belly, but for all the attention Sharif paid her, he could have been a eunuch, Raisha thought miserably!

For a week now, she'd done everything in her power to arouse him, to make his ebony eyes flame with desire for her. She'd sung as sweetly as a nightingale, as melodiously as she knew how; played her *anzad* with exceptional talent and harmony; engaged in witty and, she believed, intelligent conversations with him; beaten him brilliantly at chess—oh, everything! And it all came to naught. When she sang, Sharif listened with only half an ear. When she danced, he watched her artful, graceful movements with a faraway expression, as if he saw another in her place: one with long chestnut hair, skin the creamy color of fresh *léban,* and eyes as green and slanted as a *jinn*'s. Curse Zerdali! Curse her for her beauty and for the love Sharif felt for her! Why, he even muttered her name in his sleep! She'd heard him as she slept alone on a hard pallet by the brazier in his chambers, yearning with silent tears for the warmth of his bed, for his comforting arms, and the delights of his body. Zerdali had won, curse her! For as long as she remained at al-Azadel, for as long as she lived and breathed, Sharif was lost to her, for he loved the foreign woman as he'd never loved *her.*

She stopped dancing and scowled fiercely at him, her cinnamon eyes blazing with hatred for her rival. His expression was bored, his eyes distant.

"I am finished dancing, my lord!" she gritted, fists on hips.

"Mmm? Ah, yes. Your entertainments have been most pleasing to me," Sharif observed distantly. "You must dance for me again very soon."

He hadn't even watched her, she knew, and bitterness welled in her heart. "Thank you, my lord. I would be honored to do so. But—I cannot dance for you again today. By your leave, my lord, I am unwell," she lied, her lower lip trembling—not with sickness but with trampled pride.

"Unwell?" Sharif frowned with concern, looking at her and truly seeing her for the first time in several days. She did seem somewhat flushed, he noted, and there was a slight feverishness to the brightness in her eyes and to the flush in her cheeks. "Then I insist you rest for the remainder of the day, and not tire yourself further on my account. I will have the lady Kairee see you made comfortable in the *hareem*, and medicine prepared for you by Master Hakim."

"Oh, truly, my lord, there's no need to go to such trouble. My mother, Boucha, is skilled with herbs and healing grasses, and I—I have a great hunger to visit with her, my lord." Her cinnamon eyes glistened wetly. "I was wondering, please, my lord, if I might be allowed to go home for the remainder of the day? My mother has been nervous even since the al-Tabor attacked our city, and would welcome my companionship. I swear I'll return here first thing in the morning," she pleaded, and a tear slipped down her dusky cheek.

"Of course, little Raisha," Sharif said fondly, chucking her beneath the cheek. "I'll pray for your swift recovery, and eagerly await your return to my side."

He took her hand and led her to the arched doorway. "Ahmad, the lady Raisha has been taken unwell. Find someone to escort her to her mother's house on the Street of the Silversmith's. Tell them I ordered that she is to be taken there upon a litter, and given every comfort she requires for her recovery."

"Your will is done, sir!" Ahmad vowed smartly.

"You spoil me, Sharif, my lord," Raisha said, blushing and lowering her eyes.

"Not so! You've served me well and loyally always, Raisha, and if it were not for this cursed head wound and my broken ribs, I would show you how greatly I appreciate your tender care and your graceful dancing." His black eyes smoldered. His voice was husky, his meaning plain and intimate, and tingles ran up and down her spine as he leaned down and pressed his lips to her brow in farewell. Hope swelled anew in her wounded, jealous heart as he added, "You are deserving of much more than I can offer you," and died as he continued, "A rich husband, honor as his wife, children at your breast."

"But I want only to serve thee, my lord!" pleaded Raisha brokenly. "No other man."

Sharif sighed. "And so you will," he hedged, "when you're feeling better. Go with Ahmad now, and give my greetings to your mother, girl."

Raisha left, and after she'd gone Sharif heaved a sigh of relief. He felt far less guilty for using her to make his wife jealous when she was not so close, when that look of longing in her eyes was not so readily seen! He ran his hands through his curly black hair in an irritable gesture. He needed shaving, and the soothing, cleansing qualities of a soaking in the baths, rather than the daily cat-licks with a cloth and basin by a body-servant that his cracked ribs had necessitated.

Seven days had passed since the attack of the al-Tabor and his wounding. Seven endless, inactive days he had been cooped up here, waiting for his ribs to knit. Seven days spent waiting for his Zerdali—his own wife!—to force entry into his apartments and prove her love for him by her determination to disobey his orders and reassure herself with her own eyes that he was healing. *Fool! You may wait until the desert freezes over, Sharif,* he told himself, *and the oases give Christian wine instead of water, but she won't come! Her heart is as cold as the wintry land from which she came to you!*

Cursing under his breath—a lengthy, foul curse which did full justice to the descriptive Tamahaq in which it was voiced—he went to the windows that looked out over the mountain valley.

The grassy *shott* between the ridge on which al-Azadel was built was yellowed by the summer sun, and beyond it the next range of mountains were a hazy lavender-blue in the distance. Goats and sheep dotted the *shott,* the faint clanging of the bellwethers carrying to his ears. Close by, on the cultivated, terraced slopes just below his windows, purple bougainvillea rambled in vivid sprays, and the song of birds taking noisy dust baths filled the air. He glanced disinterestedly at the scene, for he had seen it countless times before, but then he suddenly stiffened like a hunting hound scenting game, eyes narrowed. He'd spied a small figure scrambling in the sandy dirt and rocks below the terraces where no one should have been, except perhaps the gardeners who pruned the bougainvillea and weeded the terraces—and this was certainly no gardener!

He watched, and saw how a playful stray breeze whisked the veil from the figure's head, betraying the small, determined person as definitely female, with chestnut hair that shone like burnished copper and gold in the sunlight, and stirred delightfully in that same breeze. A broad grin spread from one of Sharif's ears to the other. His black eyes sparkled, and he gave a loud whoop of wicked triumph. Just when he had been about to despair of Zerdali ever betraying her feelings for him in action, she was coming, scrambling up the difficult, rocky slopes, working her way steadily but surely to the terraces fronting his apartments, there to—what? To spy upon him and Raisha? he wondered mischievously. To surprise him in adultery? To convince herself he was recovering? *Ewellah,* then she would not be disappointed, he vowed, pulling a gauzy hanging across the opening to dim the sunlight that filled his chamber. . . .

Alexa was red-faced and perspiring long before Sharif spotted her, and already regretting her decision to see exactly what her husband was up to with his cinnamon-eyed dancing girl for herself!

Fatima had argued with her, trying to talk her out of such an outrageous plan when she had told the woman of her decision, but Alexa had been adamant that her way was the only way.

"Nonsense! There are other ways to discover if Sharif

pleasures himself with the girl, little one!" Fatima had argued. "Ways that do not require my lady to scramble up a mountainside in such an undignified fashion!"

"Very well, Fatima. Name one!"

"Well, er, umm, well, you could—well—er—"

"You see, you can't think of any! I know you can't, because I've racked my brain thinking of a way to get in there for the past week, but there's nothing else that will work! No, I'll climb up to his chambers from the gardens, Fatima, slip over his balcony into his rooms, and then he'll have to speak with me." She giggled. "After all, he'll be so surprised to see me, he'll have no choice in the matter!"

"You could disguise yourself as a serving girl, and pass the guards," Fatima suggested belatedly.

"Huh! That Ahmad and Alabi are like watchful eagles where he's concerned! They'd see through any disguise of mine in a flash, Fatima, and you know it! And besides, Sharif and that— that Raisha would have the satisfaction of knowing I'd tried to see him and failed, and I just can't stand the idea of the two of them laughing at me together!" Or the idea of them together at all, for any purpose, come to that, she added silently. "Do you know of a means to hide this fair skin, this hair, that will pass muster?" she challenged.

Fatima did not, and so she'd gone along with her mistress's hare-brained plan. Secretly, she found it highly amusing that Alexa—who continued to insist she felt nothing for Sharif— should be planning to make a surprise visit on her lord husband's apartments, and was burning to discover what the outcome of her Zerdali's unscheduled visit would be. She grinned slyly. Knowing that lusty Sharif—who was all man, and one in love with his beautiful young bride, besides!—the encounter would probably end up with Zerdali being carried to his couch to while away a lazy, sunny afternoon in ardent lovemaking, after a long, tense week spent apart. She hoped so. She did so long to hold their babe in her arms, and the sooner they settled their differences and got that little one started, the better, to her mind!

Alexa shaded her eyes and straightened up, trying to gauge

the distance she had yet to climb. Oh, Lord, she grumbled silently, all those rocks, and what a steep incline to climb on such a cursedly scorching day! She longed suddenly for the mossy banks of the river that flowed dreamily past the bottom of the gardens at Harding House, and the curling green ferns and watercress that fringed its banks. Here the merciless sun beat down, its heat burning through her clothing to her aching back. Perspiration poured from her brow, gathered between her breasts, trickled down her spine, making her *caftan* stick uncomfortably to it. But then, of a sudden, a welcome little breeze lifted her veil from her head and carried it away down the valley like a floating wisp of mist. She made a grab for it, but it slipped through her hands like water and wafted away. Oh, well, let it go. She wasn't about to go climbing all that way back down for it!

She again turned resolutely forward and shaded her eyes, squinting against the dazzling light to face the white, onion-bulb turrets of Sharif's apartments. Frowning, she fancied she saw a dark silhouette standing by the windows, looking out over the valley. Sharif? Who else could it be but him? she thought, and her heart skipped a beat. Was he recovered well enough to leave his bed already, then? Apprehension made her mouth drier than dust—even drier than it had already been made by her exertions. Damn him! What if he coldly sent her packing, after this ridiculous charade? It would all have been for nothing then, every graze and scrape and tingling strawberry to her knees or elbows from those cursed little rocks that had made her lose her footing and sent her slithering back down the rocky hillside more times than she cared to count! Still, nothing ventured, nothing gained, she decided stoically, for she was not and never had been a quitter.

Gritting her teeth, she started up the last stretch of open ground. Beyond lay the cultivated terraces, like giant steps hewn from the mountain slopes, shored up against avalanches in rainy seasons by restraining walls of white rocks, prettily placed, with thorny bougainvillea making a riot of purple color there below Sharif's windows. Fatima had warned her to be careful of the thorns, and she promised herself she wouldn't forget that warning as she crouched amongst the brilliant sprays to catch her breath and recover her composure before forging on, into the very "lion's den" itself.

Long and grueling moments later, she knelt below the stone wall beneath Sharif's window at last, breathing heavily with exertion. Livid red welts scored her bare arms and there was a shorter, deep one on her face, evidence that Fatima's warning had not sufficed against the wicked bougainvillea thorns! Still, her minor wounds and discomforts were utterly forgotten as she held her breath and listened to the hypnotic cadences of Sharif's voice, rising and falling from within the room beyond as if he recited a poem to someone. Heat flamed in her cheeks. Why, that—that unspeakable, false, adulterous reptile! He wasn't reciting poetry, he was making love to someone with flattering flowery compliments—and she knew exactly who that cinnamon-eyed someone was, blast her soul!

Trembling with fury, she listened, each word piercing like yet another thorn plunged into her aching heart, each word twisting the knife of jealousy deeper and deeper into her aching soul:

"Behold, thou art fair, my love . . . thou hast doves' eyes within thy locks. . . ."

Alexa gritted her teeth, and squeezed her eyes tightly shut to keep hot tears of rage from leaking out. "Doves' eyes?" Ye gods and little fishes, how nauseating the man was!

"Thy lips are like a thread of scarlet, and thy speech is comely. . . ."

"'Thread of scarlet' indeed!" she muttered, wanting to turn and bolt, but riveted in her uncomfortable crouch beneath the windowsill. She'd strangle that sloe-eyed Inandan chit on threads of scarlet, given half a chance! But—what if they discovered her here? What if they saw her and realized she'd spied upon them? She couldn't stand the pair of them knowing: Raisha's smug, mocking smile, Sharif's amused and wicked grin. . . .

"Thy two breasts are like two young roes that are twins, which feed among the lilies. . . ." the deep, caressing voice continued from within the chamber. "Thou hast ravished my heart, my sister, my spouse. . . ."

Spouse! He dared to call that—that sly-eyed creature his

spouse? Ooooh! She'd "ravish" her blasted eyes clear out of their sockets, given half a chance!

She managed to force herself to stand and backed away, trembling all over, sickened to her stomach by the thought of Sharif and Raisha together upon his divan, making love in the afternoon shadows; of him caressing and fondling that dusky body, running his fingers through that tumbling black hair and over her plum-sized, dark-nippled breasts as he'd once made love to her. . . .

She took a couple of too-forceful backward steps, and lost her footing on the steep, dusty ground. Thrown backwards, she thumped painfully downhill on her bottom over the last few terraced steps, traveling so swiftly and so violently with the steep incline that her teeth were snapped together on her tongue.

Where the terraces ended, she pitched forward with the momentum and rolled over and over like a child's hoop down the rocky hillside, all dignity and pride lost! She landed with an unladylike grunt and a screech at the bottom of the hill, where Fatima hovered in the shade of a pomegranate tree.

In all honesty, the Bedouin woman could not say she'd been anxiously awaiting her mistress's return, for she had not expected her to return at all—or at least, not until some time after dawn of the following morning!

"My poor lady!" Eyes round with dismay, Fatima hurried to help her up. She took in her mistress's face, scratched and bloodied by the bougainvillea thorns and streaked with dirt that had become muddy smears with her furious tears. She took in the long, chestnut hair, now snarled with twigs and leaves, the veils lost Allah-knew-where. She noted the slender alabaster arms, marred by dirt and still more angry scratches, and the long, bared ivory legs revealed with the skirts of her robe hiked up about her thighs, both equally scraped and bruised, and suddenly had to fight back the wildest desire to giggle, for her lovely, refined mistress now looked no better than the lowliest beggar girl in the bazaars!

"Oh, my lamb! Up, up on your feet, little one, and tell your Fatima what happened to thee?" she crooned. To be honest, Fatima enjoyed an occasional nap in the shade of a spreading tree during the hottest hours of the day, and she'd taken advantage of her mistress's absence to indulge herself, waking only when she heard the girl cry out!

"I tripped backward and fell!" Alexa muttered, still furious. "Surely that much is obvious!"

"Alas, yes! I saw thee spinning like a dervish, my poor angel," she fibbed, drawing on her healthy imagination to supply the missing details. "But what of Sharif? Did you see anything—did you speak with him, learn if he is yet healed?"

"Huh! I do believe he's healed quite well enough, curse him, Fatima! Certainly well enough to spend the afternoon dallying with that—that Inandan witch anyway!" She smoothed down her skirts and gave a haughty little toss of her head. "It's quite obvious that your lordship has entirely forgotten he has a wife, nor does he seem in any dire need of one! The reason for his orders forbidding me entry to his quarters is obvious, so let him whisper his sweet nothings to that dancing girl from now on, if that's what he wants. I wouldn't go to his chambers now, not even if he were at death's door and begged me on bended knees!"

She stalked away from Fatima, striding up the twisting path that led back to the palace gardens proper and the courtyard that fronted the *hareem* quarters, brushing herself down as she went.

You lovesick goose! she upbraided herself. What a fool you are to have wasted a single second of your concern upon that lecherous scoundrel! He doesn't love you, and he's certainly unworthy of your love! While you worried that his wounds were graver than Kairee had revealed, or that he was horribly scarred for life, he was busy wooing his former mistress back to his bed, flattering her with syrupy words that had sounded suspiciously familiar to her ears. She drew up short. Were they—oh, surely not!—but hadn't they been the *very same words* with which he'd charmed her out in the desert, and again on the night they were joined in that secretive travesty of a marriage, that—that snake? They must have been, to have sounded so predictably familiar! A quotation of her own leaped to mind, one that was peculiarly fitting for the way she felt right now. She muttered it under her breath with enormous relish as she slipped back through the garden gate and into the courtyard, where Drisana and Hestia, Muriel and the other women were reclining and resting in the fronded shade of the date palms, cooled by their Inandan maids waving enormous ostrich-plume fans.

". . . jealousy is cruel as the grave; the coals thereof are coals of fire, which hath a most vehement flame."

Oh, she burned, all right; she flamed cruelly! And oh, Lord, yes, how those jealous coals burned! Enough was enough, she decided, her temper like an unreasonable demon unleashed now, no longer confined by the promises she'd made her mama so long ago. She'd endured all manner of insults and unpleasant surprises since being carried off in the desert and brought here. For weeks and weeks she'd tried to cooperate with these devious people, to do their bidding for her good, or for Sharif's, or whatever, and where had it brought her? What had it brought her? Nothing and nowhere, and naught but pain! From now on, she'd be like any other captive. She'd do her damnedest to escape this cursed place, and to the devil with the lot of them!

Chapter Twenty-Two

She waited until they'd returned to her apartments in the Mist *serai* before putting her decision into action, enjoying a leisurely bath and a brisk massage with fragrant oils at the hands of a skilled Inandan masseuse while she plotted and schemed.

Afterwards, she faked a huge yawn and told Fatima she was exhausted by her adventures that morning and would sleep until the evening meal, stretching her arms languorously as if scarcely able to stay awake.

"You go and rest too, Fatima, my dear," she urged airily. "I won't need a thing until after evening prayers, I'm sure, but then, if you would, you may help me dress for supper."

Fatima nodded doubtfully. Alexa's sugary-sweet smile and sudden fatigue seemed suspicious, to her mind, after her blazing anger a short while earlier, but perhaps the baths and massage had soothed her wounded pride and her temper along with her scratched and bruised body.

"Very well, if you're certain . . . ?"

"Quite certain, thank you. Enjoy your nap!"

As soon as Fatima had left her alone, Alexa gathered up a spare *caftan*, a cloak, and a couple of veils, and all the jeweled clasps and baubles she had been given since her arrival in the city, and rolled them into a tidy bundle around a sharp little knife used for paring fruit, but which she also hoped would serve to protect her, if needed. She fastened her knapsack with a cord belt, then mounded some pillows in her divan and threw a light coverlet over them. To all intents and purposes, the lady Zerdali appeared fast asleep on her bed! Smiling in satisfaction, green eyes sparkling with the heady excitement pounding in her veins, she threw a light cloak over her shoulders and attached the bundle to her belt beneath it by a loop of cord. It bumped against her legs when she walked, but was small enough to be hardly noticeable under the cloak's full folds except to the keenest eyes.

Taking a deep breath, she slipped down the tiled corridors of the *hareem*, blessing Imochagh custom that such quarters were not heavily guarded—as had been the Turkish seraglios of old—by enormous eunuch guards, armed to the eyeballs, and that the Imochagh nobles, unusual in their Eastern lands, gave their womenfolk considerable freedom and privacy to pursue their own interests. Both factors would serve her well now!

It seemed only minutes later that she was free of the palace and slipping through the narrow flagstoned streets of the city, her veil fastened across her lower face, her eyes modestly lowered to conceal their startling color from any curious passersby.

As she'd anticipated when considering the timing of her escape, she'd not gone far through the crowded narrow street when the *muezzin* began his wailing cry from the slender minaret adjacent to the mosque, calling the faithful to noon prayers. The streets suddenly emptied of people, everyone going inside their dwellings to wash, unroll their prayer rugs, find a private place, and perform their devotions toward distant Mecca, leaving their stalls and beasts—camels and oxen, asses and horses—unattended in the street.

Alexa ducked into a dark little alcove between a money-lender's stall and a bread vendor's, helping herself to two of the flat loaves while she waited breathlessly until the street was completely deserted. When it was, she darted from conceal-ment and dashed for the mount she'd chosen, a young, docile-looking white camel unburdened by anything other than its three-pronged saddle and tasseled halter, a large saddlebag of embroidered white wool, and a pair of goatskins swollen with water.

She unfastened the halter and commanded the animal to couch, giving its rump a swat with the flat of her hand to urge it to do so with all possible haste. Merciful Allah, the animal obeyed without preamble, and reins in hand, she scrambled up into the saddle, wedged the sole of her right foot firmly against its neck, secured her stolen loaves in the conveniently empty saddlebag, and commanded it to rise. It did so beautifully, and almost bubbling over with glee at her cleverness and the smooth going of her plan, she swung its head around and kicked the beast into a swift, bone-jarring trot that carried her out of the little fairy-tale city's deserted streets and into the desolate valley below.

Craggy rock formations the color of ochre or ruddy as rust rose on either side of the winding path. Stones littered the edges of the trail, and gnarled bushes sprouted from between some of them, and tufts of yellowed grass, bleached by the sun. Lizards and scorpions scuttled amongst the rocks, and once she spied a yellow pariah dog, its ribs showing horribly beneath its mangy fur, standing over the rotting remains of a dead bird with its teeth bared and strings of foamy saliva drooling from its lips. It made a low snarl deep in its throat as she neared it, warning the woman on her camel that it would not share its meal. Frightened, Alexa kicked the camel into a lope and hurriedly moved on.

The gateways to al-Azadel lay ahead of her down these twisting, well-worn mountain paths, which were—fortunately for her—easily followed, worn smooth as they were by the passage of many feet and still more hooves over centuries of usage. But the gates—oh, Lord, they were a different matter altogether! There'd be guards manning them—probably double the number she'd seen on her arrival in the mountains, since the al-Tabor attack on the Prosperous Kingdom—a further obstacle she'd have to circumvent to make good her escape. How on earth, she wondered, was she to tackle them? They'd certainly not allow an unescorted woman to pass through the gates and continue on her way into the desert unchallenged, and particularly not one whose description matched that of the foreign bride of their arrogant Tuareg lord! Since she couldn't hope to disguise either her complexion or her eye coloring, a direct confrontation with any guards was out of the question. Stealth was the only way. She sighed heavily. Her flight from the palace, stealing a mount, and leaving the city had all been ridiculously easy, but this next part, she knew without a shadow of a doubt, would not be nearly so trouble-free, and her belly churned with apprehension.

Soon after, she spied the towers of the gateway rising above the rocks ahead, and realized with a sinking heart that she was there, and still had no feasible plan in mind. She turned her camel off the well-worn path and into a grassy, sandy little spot fringed with thornbushes and enclosed on three of its sides by concealing rocky walls. It was a stone's throw from the gates, but hidden from sight of the guards manning them, and as good a place as any to stop for a while and think out her next move.

She halted the camel, dismounting and tethering its reins to a low bush and grabbing one of the flat loaves from her saddlebag. She sat with bent knees on the ground, her chin resting on her fists, munching thoughtfully on the bread. Now, how on earth could she get past the guards? she wondered, racking her mind for a way. How?

The idea, when it came to her much later, was—as the best ideas often are—triggered by nothing more spectacular than the mundane bleating of a sheep way off in the distance, of all things! Her situation, trapped here on one side of the gates while the eagle-eyed guards patrolled up and down, had brought back to mind the Greek myths her father used to read to her, wonderful translations of Homer's *Odyssey*, tales of Odysseus and his crew and their valiant attempts to return to their native Ithaca and reclaim their leader's faithful wife, Penelope. The sheep's silly bleating brought back the story of how, when Odysseus and his fellows had been imprisoned in a cave by the evil Cyclops, they had poked out the giant's single eye with a tree trunk, and escaped the monster by clinging to the underbellies of the sheep when they were released from the cave to graze each morning. She had no bloodthirsty intention of poking anyone's eyes out, thank you very much—except, perhaps, Raisha's!—but surely the herders of al-Azadel would have to bring their flocks back into the city at dusk. And surely, in the confusion of the herds' reentry into the city, she could slip out in the opposite direction, unnoticed. Oh, yes, she was certain she could! It would mean leaving her camel behind, but what other choice did she have? She'd survive without it somehow, she felt it in her bones.

The afternoon passed on feet of lead, each minute hobbling by. It seemed an eternity before the blue of the sky began to wane and take on the pinks and vermilions of sunset as the sun began its lazy decline toward the horizon; another lifetime before the rosy hues began to change to the ominous charcoal and sooty hues of approaching night. Then, sure enough, she heard on the still, sultry air the muted "clang-clang" of goat bells and the bleating of the animals and the cries and shouts of their herders, growing louder by the minute as the herds were driven toward the gates.

Her heart began a loud thumping in her breast. Her mouth felt suddenly dry, though her palms were slick with sweat. Very soon, she would have to make her move, or give up her bid for freedom once and for all and return to al-Azadel in ignominious defeat. No, not a chance! she vowed, and resolutely swung the saddlebag containing the remains of her stolen bread loaves and one of the goatskins of water over her shoulder. Keeping to the shadow cast by the rocks, she edged forward until she was directly below one arm of the towering gateways, no more than a dozen feet from the gate itself, where she crouched down and began yet another interminable wait.

The sound of clanging little bells, of bleating goats and baaing sheep, grew louder, closer, more strident, and with it came the rank smell of the beasts themselves, warm and pungent and thick on the warm dusk air. Alexa's belly rebelled as the malodorous wave swept full into her nostrils. She clapped her hand over her mouth and tried to quell the violent urge to throw up, knowing if she retched she could not help but be seen or heard or both by the watchful guards above her. With supreme effort, she forced her belly to obey her and pinched her nose tightly to keep out the stench. Then, tensed and ready, she waited, poised for the heart-stopping minute when she'd spring from cover and plunge into the thick of the animals.

One guard yelled to another as the herds reached the city gates. They climbed down and together manned the heavy wooden structures, swinging them wide to permit the flocks to enter in a sweeping rush that was like floodwaters unleashed from a dam.

The black goats came pouring through the opening first, bleating noisily as they bounded hither and thither. Close on their heels milled the dirty-yellow sheep, baaing and bleating and smiling their silly, permanent smiles. Among them, thigh deep in the animals, strutted the herders, wielding their sticks or crooks and yelling curses at the stupid beasts in an attempt to guide them through the gates in orderly fashion. Their dogs, shaggy-haired, scrawny hounds, nipped at the heels of any stragglers, and barked furiously to chivy them on.

Oh, Lord, the dogs! She hadn't expected dogs! Nevertheless, her mind was made up and Alexa tensed, waiting until a good half of the beasts were through and milling excitedly all about before she crouched over and sprinted straight into the fringes of them, keeping low as she began to duck and weave her way between the beasts that milled about on the perimeters of the crowd. She hugged as close to the walls as she could, knowing the guards still atop them could not see her from that angle.

Meanwhile, the two sentries craned over the walls and exchanged greetings with the herders.

"*La Bes*, Coman! How was it today, eh, boy? Did you see the al-Tabor hiding behind every rock then?" He nudged his fellow and winked.

"*La Bes*, Talman, of a certainty I did—but none that I could not handle with my slingshot and one hand tied behind my back, those skulking wolves!"

The guard named Talman laughed at the lad's extravagant boast. "I'm glad to hear it, my modest young friend. By the way, be sure and offer my greetings to your pretty sister when you get home tonight, eh? Tell the lovely Zel that Talman asked after her health!"

"I'll be sure to tell her, sir—but don't be surprised if she answers me, 'Talman who'?"

The other guard guffawed at his companion's crestfallen expression, and while they were occupied with their banter, Alexa seized the moment and all but dove into the thick of the herds. Halfway, she was already halfway through the gates! Another few yards and she would be clear of the beasts and on the trail that led down the mountainside to the *sahel*. The stink

312

of goats and sheep was everywhere about her, clinging to her clothes, to the hands that she'd used to thrust the woolly beasts aside to clear her path, filling her nostrils and throat, but none of that mattered now—nothing mattered, except the knowledge that she'd almost done it, that she'd as good as made her escape!

And then, when only a few tardy sheep blocked her way, around the bend in the serpentine path ahead came yet *another* herd, this one larger than all the others combined, a sweeping tide of goats and sheep jumping and butting and leaping about! She saw them, but could do little to halt or avoid them!

Just scant feet from freedom, when she could almost savor its sweet flavor on her tongue, the tide of beasts swept her backward, jostling and shoving and pushing her back and still further back, with no means to escape them or avoid the onrushing flood!

She lost ground steadily, being pushed further and still further back toward the gate, twisting and turning in an effort simply to stay afoot, helplessly yet silently screaming a furious protest. To have come so close, so damned close—she couldn't lose ground now, she just couldn't! And then, one particularly rambunctious billy goat took offense at the strangely garbed human-creature tottering and teetering in the midst of his harem of nanny goats, and perceiving her a threat, he sneaked around her and butted her soundly from the rear!

Alexa lurched forward with a shriek, sprawling on her belly in a flurry of soiled skirts amidst whisking tails and swollen udders, reeking, greasy fleeces and cloven hooves, and other unpleasant goatly residues. And, at the same fateful moment, one of the guards spotted her, his cries of alarm rising stridently above the cacophony of noisy creatures swarming around or hopping nimbly over her.

"Hey, you! What's that foolish *bint* up to down there? Talman, you see the wench?"

"*Ewellah*, I see her!"

"Get her and bring her out of there, on the double! Chances are she's a spy from the al-Tabor, by Allah, trying to sneak into the city!"

Alexa, who'd managed by now to struggle groggily to her

feet, dimly heard the excited exchange and tried to break and run for it. But in moments, a herder had stretched out his arm and deftly hooked her about the neck with his sturdy crook, bringing her painfully up short. He jerked her backward and reeled her in like a fish, hand over hand, while Alexa struggled to draw her shredded veil back over her face and by so doing conceal her identity.

"So, girl!" Talman roared when she was dragged before him by the goatherd and another of his fellows. "Try to sneak into our city, would you?" He gripped her cruelly by the chin and jerked her head back, peering into her face, though only half of it was revealed above her veil. "We'll see what our lord Sharif has to say about this, you green-eyed, spying witch! Chances are, he'll have you whipped within an inch of your life if you refuse to talk, you mark my words!"

"I wasn't trying to sneak into the city, you dolt!" Alexa hissed in her best Tamahaq, her green eyes crackling with thwarted rage. "I was trying to sneak *out!*"

"Out? Ha! A likely story!" Talman jeered, his expression frankly disbelieving. "If that's true, then I'm Sharif al-Azim, defender of the city," he mocked, giving her a lewd wink.

"That, sir, you certainly are not!" Alexa snapped, furious that these muscle-bound louts had apprehended her so easily.

"Is that so? And how would the likes of you be after knowing that, eh, girl?" he jeered.

"Because Sharif, tyrant that he is, nevertheless has a keen mind, while you, soldier, obviously have nothing more than brawn and an empty space between your ears, *ewellah!*" she tossed furiously back, and for good measure stamped hard upon his instep, forcing him to release her with a yelp and a little hopping dance of pain.

"My thanks, *habibah!*" came an amused voice behind the pair. "I do believe that's the first compliment you've ever paid me!"

"Sharif!" she exclaimed as her head jerked forcefully about and she saw him there, seated aloofly upon the most magnificent white racing camel she had ever seen, looking more lordly in his indigo-blue robes than she had ever seen him—and ten times more intimidating. Her mouth went suddenly dry.

"Who did you expect, O Most Obstinate One?" he inquired mockingly. "Your Major André Larousse and the French Foreign Legion, come to free you from the villainous Tuareg bandit? Alas, Zerdali, I'm afraid not! There is only the wicked Sharif, your cruel husband, come to bring you—home."

He gestured the guards away, ordering them with a nod to return to their posts, then tapped his camel's side with a quirt of braided leather and growled out a command for it to couch. The camel folded to its knees, and Sharif stepped from the saddle, striding slowly across to where Alexa waited, her chin defiantly raised, her green eyes blazing.

In the dusky half light, he made an imposing figure indeed, swathed in his mysterious dark robes with his fists balled on his hips, and something deep within her quailed before him, wondering if this time she'd gone too far; if this time, she would feel the full weight of al-Azim's displeasure with her, and pay for it with her head. She gulped nervously, fighting the urge to bolt as he stepped toward her and towered there, without speaking, for several moments.

He raised the braided quirt and used it to flick the veil neatly away from her lower face, baring it to his dark eyes. A smear of something revolting and greenish daubed one cheek, and there was more of whatever it was plastered across her chin. His lips twitched beneath his *tagilmust*. Her clothes were torn and dusty and stained with sheep droppings, her hair a long, disheveled nest. Never, he thought, had she looked more like a dirty beggar girl and less like an Imochagh princess than she did now—yet never had she looked more beautiful, more dear to him than she did in that moment, standing there so forlorn and yet so proud. She might be dirty and reeking of sheep, but she was unharmed, and he had feared—by Allah, how he had feared!—since Fatima had discovered her missing and sounded the alarm, that against all odds she had evaded the notice of his guards, slipped through the city gates, and fled into the desert, there to find herself at the mercy of the scorching sun and the sands, or the bloodthirsty, pitiless jackals of the al-Tabor. And like a parent who finds a missing child safe and unharmed after many endless, anxious moments, hot on the heels of his relief came anger, which this time he made no attempt to conceal or control.

"I should have thee whipped for foolishness, *marra!*" he snapped. "Whipped until the flesh of your pretty back is laid raw under my lash!"

"Fatima told me the Imochagh never beat their wives!" she retorted, too angry in her defeat to mind her tongue.

"And Fatima is right," he agreed, tight-jawed. "But you, my pretty, defiant little one, do not consider yourself the wife of Sharif, do you, eh? You consider yourself nothing more than my helpless prisoner, my unwilling captive, and my slave. Perhaps that is how I should treat you from now on, eh, girl— as my slave?" He lightly ran the quirt down her arm, outlining her body to the hip, and then he brought it back and dealt her a stinging little slap across the bottom.

"Ow! That hurt!"

"As it was intended to hurt, *slave* girl! As your master, I have a master's right to beat you soundly for your attempts to escape me, and for your disobedience and your defiance." He scowled, his swarthy, handsome face becoming decidedly evil and threatening. "I think I'll exercise that right, and tame your rebellious heart!"

Suddenly, his arm snaked out, gripping her by the wrist and spinning her sharply into his arms. Before she could react, she found herself lifted by the waist, hefted under his arm like a sack of Egyptian wheat, and hauled away to a nearby rock, where Sharif sat and shoved her face down across his steely thighs with no attempt at gentleness.

"Try to escape me again, and know that this awaits you when I find you—as I will find you, no matter how far you may run—each and every time, *marra!*"

So saying, he yanked up her skirts, flung them over her head, and brought his palm down across her bared bottom in a stinging swat that made her yelp with embarrassment more than pain, and wriggle furiously to escape him, her legs flailing.

"You—you brute! Let me go!" she shrieked, yet his other arm held her as securely as a band of steel about her waist, and she could not escape, no matter how hard she tried.

"Know that as you are my *captive* and my *slave,* it is within my power to do as I wish with you, Zerdali," he gritted, and gave her another hard paddling that left a scorching, hot-pink palm print across one ivory little cheek of her bottom.

She clenched her muscles with the stinging pain, and he heard a roar of pure outrage ground out against his thighs, felt the scalding wetness of her enraged tears dampen his leg.

"Since you believe you are my property, rather than my bride, and since you are undeniably a woman and not quite ugly to look upon, you are therefore valuable merchandise, girl. Your attempts to flee into the desert might have robbed me of your worth, and for that you must pay!"

Gritting his teeth, he spanked her a third time, ignoring the furious wails and colorful curses she shrieked at him while he admired the plump, wriggling pink globes beneath his hand. By Allah, even in his fury she aroused him, far more potently than Raisha had ever done! "Your foolhardiness in risking your life by trying to escape is inexcusable, girl, and warrants far more than this little thrashing. We will return to the palace at once and continue your punishment there."

He landed two more lusty swipes, far harder than all the others, across her buttocks, and then stood, letting her fall ignominiously from across his knees to the dirt. She sprawled in a heap of tangled clothing at his booted feet, as if she were truly a slave of little consequence except for the high price she would fetch in the secret slave markets of the cities.

Dismay filled her, choked her speechless, but her pride and her wounded dignity stung far worse than her bottom. As she scrambled to her feet, she seethed and fumed—but in abject silence, afraid if she uttered even a single word in retaliation, he'd bare her bottom before the staring guards and spank her again!

"You see, men? A woman is much like a rug," Sharif remarked casually to the openmouthed guards who were standing and gaping at the scene with eyes round with astonishment. "She should be soundly beaten at regular intervals to return her to her former softness and compliance." He turned to Alexa, who stood glowering at him as if she would have liked to tear him limb from limb, to pluck out his eyeballs and feed them to the goats at the very least. "Come, girl!" he snapped, striding for his camel as if he had no question that she would obey and follow him.

Alexa looked with longing over her shoulder at the winding mountain pathway, unraveling in serpentine curves to the *sahel* far below, its paler twists growing darker by the second, and for a fleeting moment, it seemed possible she might yet break and run. But the low growl of one of the herders' mangy dogs and the stern glare of the guard named Talman doused any last-minute hopes for escape she might have harbored, and with an angry toss of her head, she followed Sharif to his camel, trying to discreetly rub the smarting cheeks of her bottom and mentally consigning him to every horrible fate imaginable as she did so.

Alongside Sharif's camel, Alexa gave a resigned sigh and extended her arm to him, seeking his assistance in mounting behind him.

"What, O Unfragrant One? You think to ride with your master, slave girl, reeking worse than any ewe? By Allah, you will not!" Instead, with an expression of distaste, he gingerly grasped her arm and slipped a noose of cord over the wrist, yanking it tightly before she realized his intent. With eyes that had not softened by so much as a fraction above his mask, but remained a dark and disturbing jet black, lit from deep within in some peculiar fashion, he held her eyes captive while he fastened the other end of the cord to the rear of his saddle. "A slave is what you considered yourself, was it not, Zerdali? Then a slave you shall be henceforth—my *personal* slave." His eyes twinkled above the *tagilmust*. "And slaves, *habibah*, do not ride—they walk! *Imshy hal-ak!*" he commanded the camel, and the beast rose and lurched forward, tugging a fuming Alexa after it over the steep and winding paths back to al-Azadel.

Two hours later, bathed and perfumed and dressed in a gauzy green robe that revealed more of her nudity than it hid, she was delivered to his chamber to continue what Sharif had ominously termed her "punishment."

318

Fatima had not been permitted to help with her mistress's toilet, having received stern notice that for the time being, Raisha would be summoned from her sickbed in the city to attend her in her place. The lady Kairee had told Alexa and the teary-eyed Bedouin woman that Sharif was furious at her for allowing her charge to escape her care and wander about the city unescorted, and wringing her hands and weeping, Fatima had been banished from the Mist *serai* to her own little room. Alexa had felt enormously guilty that Fatima had been blamed for her escape attempt, and had sworn to Kairee that Fatima was not at fault. She'd even begged her on her knees not to hold the woman responsible, but her entreaties had had no effect. Sharif had given orders, Kairee had said sadly, and he was so angry she dare not disobey them.

Soon after, Alexa had been forced to grit her teeth and submit to the ministrations of the baths' servants, who labored under Raisha's eagle eye to see her thoroughly scrubbed free of any lingering traces of sheep or goat. Having her rival in authority over her only added to the smoldering fury and resentment in Alexa's soul, yet she gritted her teeth and submitted to the vigorous scrubbing of her body, the painfully thorough washing of her long hair, and the depilation of her legs, underarms, and sex that Raisha, cinnamon eyes aglitter with jealousy, ordered the servants to perform. Alexa had sworn a promise to herself that she'd utter no protests whatever they did to her, for she'd sooner die than give her attendants or that—that Inandan witch the satisfaction of seeing her upset or in pain! But even now, over two hours later, her perfumed, pummeled, and denuded body still tingled from the punishment she'd received at their hands! The diaphanous garment they'd given her to put on afterwards had done little to improve her temper either, for it denied her even the dignity of modesty.

"There!" Raisha had spat when she was finally readied to the girl's satisfaction. "I believe you are as ready as you'll ever be to serve our lord's needs, my lady!" she'd snapped, unable to conceal her hostility from Alexa. "Akli, you will deliver the lady Zerdali to her lord—and be certain she does not escape you, or you'll be sorry!"

She'd turned to Alexa then with a malicious smirk. "Your escape angered our lord Sharif a great deal, you know, my dear mistress," she'd informed Alexa silkily. "It was a foolish thing to try, for it displeased him more than anything else has ever angered him to date, to my knowledge. Alas, I fancy he will not be content with those playful little slaps he laid across your bottom, but will seek a far more exacting punishment from you in his chambers." She'd rolled her eyes, which glittered with malice. "Ah, how I pity you the long night to come, Zerdali, for you will be naked and helpless in his power, and he will be able to do any *manner* of terrible things to thee! May Allah protect you, my poor, dear lady!"

Not deceived by Raisha's silky tone, Alexa had nodded haughtily, looking down her nose at the jealous girl as if she were not one iota concerned, although her belly had churned with apprehension.

"Why, thank you for your concern, Raisha, my dear, but there's really no need for it, you know. I'm certain I'll survive Sharif's wrath somehow, whatever distasteful turn his anger might take, lusty or otherwise. Perhaps it will help if I think of you all alone, husbandless, and ailing in your little sickbed in order to take my mind off my own predicament?"

She'd feigned a heavy sigh, secretly astonished to realize she was quite *enjoying* the opportunity to be openly spiteful and catty to her rival, Raisha, though she'd never been maliciously inclined in her entire life until this moment, and couldn't comprehend why it was she wanted to be so spiteful now, since she certainly wasn't jealous of Sharif's fondness for the girl. Nevertheless she'd continued, "You really don't know just how fortunate you were, my dear, to be only Sharif's—er—companion rather than his bride, with all the unpleasant little duties that entails in his bed."

With that telling jibe, she'd turned brightly to Sharif's body servant, ignoring Raisha's fuming expression, and giving him a dazzling smile. "Well, Akli, we must not keep your lord waiting, must we? Lead on! Oh, and a very good night to you, Raisha. I do hope you're feeling recovered by morning! I'm sure I shall be utterly exhausted, if I know my lusty lord and his idea of 'punishment'!"

With a syrupy smile and an air of bravado she was far from feeling, she'd swept from the Mist *serai* and followed Akli to Sharif's apartments. And alas, here she was now, waiting for that black-eyed brute to do God-only-knows-what to her, and far more afraid than she'd ever let on!

"Ah, my slave girl comes, at long last," Sharif drawled, eyeing her with a lecherous grin he made no attempt to disguise. He was lounging on one elbow upon his divan, and as she stood there, his gaze traveled from her thinly veiled face on down, lingering at the pale moons of her breasts playing hide-and-go-seek through the folds of her sheer covering, which was in truth hardly more decent than a long strip of filmy, jade-colored cloth with a hole in the middle for her head, and a girdle of silver links for a belt at her hips.

The rising blush in her cheeks deepened as his ebony eyes moved down over her, with an insolent lack of haste, to her concave belly, and to the newly denuded little mound of her sex below. Never had she felt more naked than she did now, not even on her wedding night! The heated paste the servants had applied and then peeled quickly away had left her as hairless as a grape, she realized, squirming inwardly with shame as Sharif met her eyes and licked his lips wolfishly, as if in wicked anticipation of the delights yet to come. He made a sweeping gesture with his hand.

"Your garment, girl—remove it," he commanded casually.

Surely he wasn't serious. "But—I have nothing on underneath!" she protested hotly.

"*Ewellah*, I had noticed, girl! But I wish you to serve me pomegranate juice, and I have a whim that you should do so naked. I am your master, and you will not defy me! Strip, I say—or I will strip thee naked myself, and beat you for your disobedience a second time today!" His smoldering midnight eyes brooked no refusal.

She was half-tempted to rebel nonetheless, but then decided against it. After all, what good would defying him do now, except get her another of his embarrassing spankings? And besides, he'd seen her naked more than once before, so what had she to hide, really? The sooner she got it over with, the better. Lips pursed, she unclasped the silver girdle at her hips and let it fall with a tinkle at her feet, then lifted the wisp of gauze over her head and let it drift to the floor like a streamer of mist.

"Satisfied, O Master?" she gritted with heavy sarcasm, standing proudly before him like an exquisite statue of ivory marble, her golden-chestnut hair flowing over her shoulders to tease the coral points of her breasts before her, and the topmost curve of her still rosy bottom behind.

"Satisfied?" He chuckled scornfully. "Truly, *marra*, I have not begun to seek satisfaction of thee yet—and rest assured, you will know it when I have, and without need of asking!" He lounged indolently back on one elbow upon his blue divan, and snapped his fingers. "Juice, slave! Fetch your master a glass to quench his thirst!"

I'll pour the whole damned flagon over his cursed head if he continues this nonsense! Alexa plotted, seething at his arrogance. Yet without a word, she glided across to the low table and leaned gracefully down to do his bidding, well aware that she was torturing Sharif with the slight jiggle of her breasts, the graceful swing of her glorious hair, the play of her supple leg muscles shivering under creamy skin, and the pear-shaped perfection of her bottom's curves as she did so.

Steeling herself to turn and approach him without garments to hide behind, she padded barefoot to his divan and offered him the glass of pulpy, purplish-red juice she'd poured, muttering with heavy sarcasm, "As you commanded, sir."

"Very good, wench! Perhaps you might be capable of learning your place after all," he said patronizingly, and saw how her eyes flashed. "And now, hold the glass to my lips, so that I may drink."

Banking the smoldering coals of her temper at his outrageous request, she lifted the glass to his mouth. Surprisingly, she found her eyes drawn to his finely chiseled lips as she drew the glass away, and memories of his kisses danced like sugarplums in her head, distracting her. His eyes holding hers, he licked all traces of pulpy juice from his lips in a peculiarly greedy, noisy, and vulgar manner—but one which was also so very erotic and disturbing that she could not look away, and thrills of something dangerous and

322

melting licked through her belly, spreading heat through her.

"Another sip!" he ordered sharply, and jolted her attention back to the task at hand.

She tilted the rim of the glass again to his mouth, and when he waved her away, withdrew it.

"This time, I will allow you to remove the traces of juice from my mouth yourself—no, no, girl, not with a cloth, with your lips! Do it, at once!" his lazy drawl commanded.

Sucking in a breath, Alexa rebelliously considered telling him to go to hell and take his juice with him—but what worse punishment might he decide upon if she refused? She steeled herself to obey, ducking her head. Her mouth hovered a hairbreadth from his. She hesitated for an instant, but then his palm clamped around the back of her head and he jerked her head sharply down to his. "At once, I said, slave!"

Tentatively, she stuck out the very tip of her little pink tongue and traced it gingerly along the joining line of his lips, tasting no traces of pomegranate juice, but only the warmly masculine, salty flavor of his flesh. "There's n-nothing there!"

"Continue!" he growled in a thick tone, and she dipped her head obediently to continue her peculiar task.

But as she stooped over him, one of her palms resting now on his shoulder to support herself, she felt the hot curve of his hand enclose her left breast. He fondled it casually, and tweaked the nipple. She jumped in surprise, and the juice spilled, splashing over his throat and shoulders and over his bared torso, yet he gave no sign that he was aware of her clumsiness, or even angered by it.

Instead, his lips parted as she ran her tongue-tip along them, and of a sudden his own tongue darted to meet hers, warring with it playfully in a way that raised goose bumps on her arms. But just when her senses were so shattered she might have given in to her impulses and kissed him, he drew away from her and lay back on the divan, looking up at her with a wicked, sensual gleam in his eyes.

"No, don't move!" he commanded as she made to turn away and hide her embarrassment. "I am not done fondling your breasts yet, slave. When I am, I will give you leave to make amends for your clumsiness and cleanse the spilled juice from my chest.''

He continued to fondle first one of her uptilted breasts, then the other, squeezing gently, rubbing and tweaking her screaming flesh until the treacherous peaks ruched and blossomed with a will all of their own and an embarrassing, impudent prominence that could not possibly be hidden from his all-seeing eyes.

''Ah, my little slave, for the beauty of your breasts alone, I could forgive thee much! They please me with their ripe firmness and their exquisite form. But, alas, that clumsiness of yours, that willful pride, must not go unanswered!'' He tapped his chest. ''The juice, girl. See to it at once!''

''H-how?''

''In the same manner as you cleansed the traces from my lips, foolish one! Now, begin!'' He lay back expectantly, dark eyes closed, a suspicion of a grin—or was it actually the beginning of a scowl?—tugging at the corners of his lips.

Alexa wet her dry lips on her tongue, staring at the magnificent bare chest and hard belly spread out before her, at the golden-bronze flesh streaked with the purple juice of the pomegranate, as if mesmerized by him. Why, her reluctance had vanished! It had become, in the twinkling of an eye, eager anticipation instead, for he was gloriously handsome, impossibly, wonderfully male, broad-chested and hard-muscled as a Greek god, and those wicked, wanton instincts she'd tried so hard to stifle were thundering out of control again, damn them!

She knelt alongside him and slowly lowered her head, darting her tongue out and working it thoroughly down each purplish trail that stained his smooth, brown throat, tasting the sweet fruitiness of the juice mingled with the warm saltiness of his clean taste on her taste buds. More shreds of pulp clung to the flesh of his chest, and she worked her mouth down to cleanse him of it, her tongue lapping and flickering back and forth like a delicate little cat enjoying a dish of cream until she lapped hesitantly at a flat brown nipple to remove it, and saw how the tiny nubbin of flesh suddenly hardened beneath her tongue-tip, exactly as her nipples hardened under his caresses. As she did so, she felt how his lean, muscular body tensed under her steadying hand; saw the rising hardness of his rigid staff outlined beneath the cloth of his dark-blue *sirwal*, the only garment he wore.

Her eyes widened. Her heartbeat raced. The breath strangled in her throat. Her breathing came thick and shallow as she danced her tongue down the narrow line of black hair that adorned his lower chest and hard, flat stomach, dimly aware that he continued to fondle her breasts and nipples in a maddening, arousing way as she worked diligently to cleanse the juice from his belly. His clean masculine scent, of sandalwood and soap and salt and pomegranate juice, and the silky-smooth texture and taste of him flooded her senses. The feel of him, of his hard male body, lying quite still beneath her lips and tongue, was a sensation voluptuous beyond belief! She felt quite dizzy and weak with wanting, warmth rising through her, sizzling in her veins, tingling in that secret place between her thighs as if a fever raged through her. . . .

"Enough!" he growled, his voice thick and unsteady with some emotion she could not name, but he had to repeat himself twice before she could be persuaded to cease her ministrations. As she reluctantly straightened, he patted her buttocks and rose from the bed, padding across the room to rummage in a coffer of carved rosewood from Cathay that stood in one corner of the chamber, until he found what he was searching for.

"Since it seems you enjoy my 'punishments,' I must try another you will not find so welcome! Here! Give me your arm, *marra!*" he ordered crisply when he returned to her side.

Still dazed, without really thinking, she obeyed, and offered him her arm as if she were still in a trance, drugged from the taste of him. He fastened lengths of silk cloth—sashes, apparently—about both her wrists, but left the long, loose ends trailing. "Now, you will lie down, slave wench."

Too late, she realized his true intent, the meaning of those silken bonds with which he'd tied her, and sought to escape him, darting suddenly to the left, then the right, without success. He easily overpowered her and caught her up, swinging her high into the air before he dropped her heavily upon the divan, the breath bounced from her. Before she could roll free, he pinned her there with the weight of his chest while he fastened first one silken scarf to the little curved feet of the divan, and then the other. Arms stretched wide on either side and a little above her, she was now helpless to escape him! Still worse, her defenseless position thrust her breasts up high and full, offering the full, creamy mounds with their sensitive coral tips as an irresistible temptation to his hands and lips—a temptation which Sharif reluctantly opted to postpone, for the time being, with a will of steel. With a broad, evil grin, two other scarves materialized in his hands. He ran the silky cloth through his long, brown fingers, taunting her with the threat that soon, very soon, her ankles would be similarly bound, her body spread-eagled and helpless, his to do with as he wished.

"You rogue! Untie me!" she hissed, truly frightened for the first time since being brought to him here. She'd thought—hoped—he only intended to humiliate her verbally, calling her "slave" and forcing her to do his bidding by threats he had no true intention of carrying out, but now—oh, Lord, now it looked as if he really did plan to treat her like a slave and whip her—to lay her body raw beneath his lash, as he'd threatened to do just that afternoon! She licked her lips in trepidation, straining against the silken bonds, but damnably they held her as tight as if they were bonds of steel. She shivered away from him as he loomed over the divan, smiling down at her with a gloating smile that struck fresh terror in her heart. What did she really know about him, after all? He was still little more than a stranger to her, although she'd shared his bed. He could be capable of anything, of any cruelty or depravity imaginable!

"Let me go! This minute!" she demanded, her voice hoarse and shrieky with fear.

"No, my beloved little slave wench," he taunted, "I will not! I'll untie thee only when you swear never to flee me again—when you promise to accept me as your husband rather than your master—and when you agree to give us the chance to learn to love each other as man and wife that I asked for.''

"Never," she ground out, anger and outrage swelling through her and giving her a reckless courage now. "Never, never, never, you lawless savage! Not if you keep me tied up this way for a thousand years! Do what you want, you devil, but I'll never meekly accept being your wife, not when our marriage is nothing more than a mockery, a lie, a sham, you—you faithless, adulterous—bandit!"

"Ah!" he said, his raven brows raising in understanding. "Raisha. You are jealous of her I think, *habibah!*"

"I am not! You can have her, and she can have you, and welcome to you, for all I care! After all, she wants you—which I certainly don't!" she panted, writhing her body and flailing her legs in a desperate, final attempt to escape.

He grinned and moved to fasten her left ankle as he had her wrists, tying the loose end securely to one of the bottom feet of the divan. He inspected each of the knots he'd made, and nodded in satisfaction. She could move a little, and her circulation was unhampered, but she could not escape him.

"Ah, but you *will* want me before the night is gone, Zerdali, I promise you!" he threatened. "You will promise me anything, and beg your *husband* Sharif to make love to you, and put an end to your exquisitely painful torture!"

Without further ado, he'd grasped her other flailing foot and tied it by the ankle as he had the first, spreading her legs wide apart in the process, to Alexa's helpless mortification. Thank God, there was only one lamp lit and the room blessedly dim, she moaned silently, her body growing pink and warm with shame. And then, with a gasp of horror, she saw him move to the dish-lamps, lighting them one by one until the chamber was lit as brilliantly as it was by day, and all her charms revealed to his wicked, smoldering black eyes.

"*Ewellah,* before me lies passion's garden of delights, my little slave!" he murmured, wetting his lips with his tongue as if in eager anticipation. His dark eyes roved her pale body with undisguised pleasure. He idly touched the tip of his finger to a pert nipple, and laughed as he saw her recoil and buck against her bonds, although her body had surged under his caress. "Now! Let's be merciful and end your suspense, *aklan*. I shall begin your punishment in earnest!"

So saying, he picked up the flagon of pomegranate juice and strode slowly toward the divan, like a sleek and menacing dark panther stalking its next meal.

Chapter Twenty-Three

Alexa's heart was hammering wildly in her ears as Sharif loomed over her, holding the flagon of pomegranate juice aloft.

"A feast, beloved! You are truly a feast for my senses!" he murmured. "And what, I ask, is a feast without wine?"

With a wicked grin, he tilted the flagon and juice spilled out, splashing across her throat, running over her pale breasts, and trickling down her belly in ruby rivers to pool in her navel. Its cool wetness made her gasp and fight her restraints, and Sharif laughed deep in his throat at the startled expression she now wore.

"What, little slave? Was it the lash you expected—the harsh sting of a whip? Ah, but I have no patience with such barbaric tortures! Educated men such as myself prefer a more subtle means of extracting promises and punishment!"

She swallowed, wondering what in heaven's name he intended. Releasing a horde of red ants to feast upon the sweet juice, and in the process shred the flesh from her bones morsel by morsel? She began to tremble as he knelt alongside the divan, expecting the worst.

He leaned low over her, ebony eyes sparkling wickedly, and his lips trailed slowly over one of her burning cheeks, tracing its soft curve and lapping at a spatter of juice there before traveling with exquisite slowness up to her ear. There his tongue flicked delicately around its shell-like outer whorls before suddenly, hotly, stabbing within. His moist, erotic caress made her gasp and squirm as fierce darts of excitement knifed through her. She closed her eyes, scarce daring to breathe as he ran his tongue lightly down her throat, then back

329

up to encircle her lips again. As his mouth teased hers, she could taste the juicy sweetness of pomegranates and her own rose-perfumed fragrance on his lips and she wanted him to kiss her some more, but maddeningly his tongue flickered away, dancing downwards again, lapping in the little shadowed hollows that lay along the base of her throat, then moving inch by inch up over the lower curves of her breasts like a damp feather that tickled maddeningly. Was this how he'd felt when she ran her tongue over his body? she wondered. Had he experienced this same rising, sweet torment? Was this, then, to be her punishment, to lie bound and helpless while he drove her to an ecstasy of madness with his caresses?

He glanced up into her eyes then, and grinned, and she knew that she was right as he murmured wickedly, "Ah, yes! 'An eye for an eye,' little slave!" before he resumed his torturous kisses.

His lips traveled over her, expertly cleansing the spilled fruit juice and slivers of pulp from her quivering flesh, slowly, slowly encompassing the upper curves and then the valley between her breasts as they did so, before tantalizingly returning to the less sensitive curves of her shoulders in a way that made her groan with frustration.

With every passing moment, her breathing became more shallow and labored, a hoarse rasp of unbearable tension as his mouth skimmed lower and lower, grazing over her breasts, brushing the very tips of her nipples again and again so that they ripened to their master's fleeting caresses and stood erect, moving away, and then returning. She gasped, straining against her silken manacles, moaning thickly as his mouth at last fastened over one swollen nipple and suckled greedily there, drawing it deep into the flaming heat of his mouth with greedy smacking sounds of pleasure that excited her beyond all reason.

"Yes! Oh, Sharif, Sharif . . ." She thickly moaned his name again and again as sensation burst through her, sparking a chain of tiny, explosive tingles that radiated from her bosom to the sensitive flesh between her thighs, dampened now with anticipation.

His caresses and kisses made her squirm like a madwoman,

but relentlessly he continued them, his mouth diligently following the sweet lushness of the spilled juice everywhere over the creamy lushness of her body, until his lips fastened upon her other breast. He feasted greedily upon it, grazing the delicate morsel with his teeth, playfully nipping at the swollen coral bud while his busy hands caressed her straining curves with strokes of fire. He seemed deaf to the sobbing cries that broke from her lips time and time again as she begged him to cease his wicked torture! Beads of perspiration sprang out upon her brow, like tiny topaz jewels that glistened in the flooding lamplight. As she tossed her head from side to side, her glorious golden-chestnut hair raged like a molten sea, shimmering waves breaking upon a shore.

His tongue continued its wickedly sensual seduction, flickering over her concave belly, lapping at the well-rim of her little navel, which was wet with pomegranate juice. His mouth teased the screaming nerve-endings just below her skin with a dervish-dance that was pure fire! He bathed her with kisses and bathed her in swirls and whirls of fiery delight—tortured her with the denial of the one ultimate caress she now craved more than anything! And then—then his dark head dipped lower still. His searing lips branded the tender, forbidden softness of her inner thighs with velvety kisses of such sweet pleasure, such intimate warmth, they seemed to sear her flesh with brands of flame. She arched upward and cried his name aloud, her fingers tightening uncontrollably in the folds of the silken coverlet beneath her as her passion mounted.

Relentlessly, his kisses scorched her other inner thigh, nuzzling and savoring the fragrance and taste of her secret flesh as if she were some rare, sugared blossom he was tempted to devour petal by succulent petal. Indeed, the gentle nips he gave her inner thighs with his teeth seemed proof positive that he would devour her! And then, before her shattered senses could regroup or even anticipate his next move, his lips moved higher, to the pale pink crest of her denuded mound, where they tasted the slender, hidden crevasse within and thrilled to the liquid heat of her passion.

"No—you mustn't!" she cried. "Oh, it's wicked—you mustn't—no!"

Her answer was a husky chuckle from deep in his throat, and the growled response, "Ah, but I'm only a lawless savage, beloved, and as such, nothing is too wicked, nor any act forbidden the bandit al-Azim! *Ewellah,* I must 'punish' you, *habibah*—and I will!" he promised. "Most thoroughly!"

Her legs trembled uncontrollably as his hands slipped beneath her to cup her dimpled buttocks and hold her immobile as he teased and tasted the well-spring of her being. The flower beneath his lips grew moist with longing, flowing with the honey of her raging desire.

"I can't—oh, God, I can't bear it any longer!" she moaned throatily. She gritted her teeth and tossed her head from side to side upon the brocade coverlet as if taken by a fit. Her green eyes were dark with passion now, her body flushed and rosy with desire, the tone of her voice desperate and pleading. "Please—I'll do anything—swear anything—oh! Sharif, for the love of Allah, stop! End this torture, I beg you!"

"Say it!" he urged her huskily when he drew back and knelt between her thighs. "Say it now, swear it, beloved, and I'll end your torment!"

"You—you are my husband—!" she panted brokenly. "And—and I'll try—I'll really try—to—to—oh, God—to be a wife to you from now on!" She ground her teeth down upon her lower lip, gnawing at it in passionate anguish.

"Will you try to run away from me again?"

"No—I swear it! I—won't—won't try to escape again! Please—!"

"You will give yourself a chance to know me better?"

"Anything!" she swore mindlessly. "I promise I'll give—the two of us—a chance together, I swear it, if you'll only—end—this! Now, Sharif . . . please. . . !"

He left her for a moment, and then, wonderfully, her bonds were no more, and she was free again—free to caress him, hold him tight in her arms, as she now yearned to do.

With a deep groan that betrayed his own aching need of her, he knelt between her thighs and thrust his hips forward, plunging deeply into the tight sheath of her womanhood, withdrawing and thrusting again and again into its welcoming heat while summoning all the skills and self-control he possessed to reward her for her promises in a manner she would never, ever forget. He gave no thought to his own burgeoning release. Instead, he continued to move slowly upon her while his lips dusted her cheeks like pollen and danced with butterfly wings over her throat and breasts.

He whispered endearments in her ears and the hollows of her throat, and his words were no longer mere words but lovely, erotic poetry, spoken in the rhythmic cadences of his ancient Tamahaq tongue; endearments that sent her desire leaping to even greater heights. He no longer called her his slave. He called her his "songbird of the desert," his "Persian nightingale," his "jewel-in-the-crown-of-heaven," and his only love; his heart, his breath, his soul. He likened her breasts to exquisite pearls, her lips to coral, her eyes to emeralds, her thighs to ivory columns, her womanhood to an oasis of honey, a wellspring of joy.

Amidst a hazy pink cloud of delight, she marveled at the heady euphoria his tender words and actions now brought her, for a voluptuous, welcoming sweetness rose and flowed through her with the silken pulse of honey poured from a jar, and with it came a sudden dread of losing him. *I must love him!* she realized incredulously. *I do love him! It's not just desire I feel for him as a man, but love!* And the love she'd denied for him and fought against for so many days was at last secretly acknowledged in her heart—although she could not bring herself to admit her feelings to him, not yet. The realization filled her with joy, imbuing her responses with a tenderness that refined her need, and made their coupling an act of love, as well as a lusty, mutual quenching of desire.

A shudder rippled through her like warm rain. Her slender arms raised to curl about his powerful neck, to clasp his beloved ebony head in a fierce embrace and draw his mouth hungrily down to meet hers. They kissed lingeringly, and as they kissed her slender fingers moved over him, splaying across his broad back, feeling the dance of powerful cord and sinew beneath her caresses. She loved this exciting, virile, handsome man—and he loved her! With a cry, she gathered him closer, cradled him to her breasts, kneading his flesh as if by touch alone she could learn each part of him, weld him to her forever.

Their lips met again, brushed softly, and with a low moan of delight she shuddered and closed her eyes and drew her lips from his, instead seeking and finding the vulnerable webbing between his throat and shoulders as he began to thrust deeper and deeper between her thighs.

"I want you—I want you so!" she whispered throatily, and ran her tongue over his skin as he had caressed her earlier.

How salty he was to her taste! How rough and smooth, magnificently combined, his body felt to her lips. The texture of his skin altered from the velvet of his shoulders to the pleasant hairiness of his chest, and tapered to the smooth hardness of his belly, and then the roughness and power of his muscled legs. . . . She kissed too the angry, star-shaped scar that he now wore upon his temple, where the al-Tabor had marked him forever. Tears of sorrow filled her eyes at the thought that he had suffered, and tears of regret that she had not been there to soothe his hurt burned behind her eyelids. She kissed the mark again to heal it with the balm of her lips, vowing she'd never forsake him again. Drunk on sensation, she breathed and tasted hungrily of the clean tang of him as she planted a kiss upon his muscled shoulder, and then still another, lower, in the hollow at the base of his throat where his pulse thundered wildly, murmuring, "Now, Sharif, my husband. Let it be now!"

"I can hold back no longer, beloved! *Ewellah,* I come!"

He plunged harder, deeper, swifter into her then, her murmurs spurring him on to bring them both to tempestuous release.

Together, arms locked convulsively about each other, they soared skyward. He groaned. She sobbed. Her nails dug bloody crescents into his back. His grip tightened painfully upon her arms, his body mastered hers beneath it, but she felt no pain as the storm finally broke, rocking them both with the savage beauty of their fulfillment and the wild, heart-stopping ecstasy of release.

Later, she wept softly in reaction as she lay curled in his

arms, telling him little by little how she'd tried to see him when he lay wounded, how afraid she'd been for him, but that she'd been turned away by his guards; of her hurt and jealousy at overhearing him and Raisha making love together that morning, and her inability to share him with another. He chuckled and dropped a kiss upon her hair.

"Ah, foolish little one! Since that night under the stars, when Aswad and I pursued you across the desert sands, there has been no woman in my heart or in my arms but thee, *habibah,* I swear it. No one but thee!"

"But—I heard you—!"

"No. You heard the love-song of Solomon for his Bathsheba, little jealous one—not the words of Sharif for Raisha!" he corrected her. "I'd sent her away and was alone when I saw you clambering up the hill to spy upon me and—forgive me!—I could not help but tease you! It was wrong, I know, to want to make you jealous. In the process, I almost lost you," he said, grimacing, "just as Kairee wisely warned me I might do!"

He hugged her tighter, enjoying the way they seemed fashioned to fit so snugly together, just as they had so perfectly when making love. Her head nestled in the angle of his throat and shoulders. His arms were curled loosely about her. "But it will never happen again, beloved. From this night on, we start anew, just you and I. We will learn to know each other as man and woman, as wife and husband, and as friends, Allah willing, and forget the foolish dreams I had."

"Foolish?"

"*Ewellah,* foolish," he said firmly, "for they made me forget that you were not only the *houri* who had filled my thoughts, but also a woman, with your own wishes and ideas. In the joy of your coming to me at last, I tried to bend thee into the mold I had chosen—the one I'd always imagined you fitting so perfectly, *habibah*—instead of letting you choose your own mold."

"And are you disappointed?" she asked, half-holding her breath. Suddenly, it seemed vitally important to her that he not be disappointed.

"Only that I handled it all so badly," he confessed. "But I have hopes—great hopes, my beloved—that perhaps, although

335

passion came first for us, we can also grow to love one another, and put these bad beginnings behind us."

She giggled huskily in a way that warmed him through and through. "I confess," she whispered, "that although I'd never have admitted it before, I quite enjoyed our 'bad beginnings'!"

He grinned. "Then perhaps there is hope, *ewellah?*"

"Mmm. I think so. But—perhaps another sample of your 'bad beginnings' would convince me," she wheedled hopefully, with an arch seductiveness that both amused and aroused him enormously—as did the naughty way she wriggled her bottom against his flanks to provoke him.

He touched the end of her nose with his fingertip and clicked his teeth in mock reproof, his eyes twinkling in the shadows like dark stars. "Ah, my Zerdali is becoming a tigress, I fear. I have unleashed an insatiable woman that no man can satisfy!"

"You can, Sharif!" she breathed smokily and with absolute certainty. "Oh, you can!"

"Then let's begin again," he murmured softly, and rolled her astride his hips.

Chapter Twenty-Four

"Ah, what a trusting creature you still are, Zerdali!" Raisha crowed, her cinnamon eyes hooded, her small mouth curved in a malicious smile. "Did I not just explain to you that I too was once the favored of Sharif, until he smiled upon you and cast me aside the day you were wed? So will you in your turn be cast aside, when your body no longer delights him and your beauty palls." She inspected her manicured nails. "Truly, no one woman can please al-Azim for very long, whatever he tells you! He's as fickle as the honey bee that flits from blossom to blossom, tasting the nectar each one has to offer him before buzzing on to the next! It would be well for you to leave here before that day comes, Zerdali, while you still have your beauty. Stay, and you will end up as I have—one of the forgotten flowers of Sharif al-Azim's *hareem!*"

Raisha and Alexa were together in Alexa's apartments, a tray of honeyed sweetmeats on the small brass table between them. Alexa had ordered the tray brought in in response to Raisha's none-too-subtle hints that she'd missed the little luxuries she'd enjoyed while lodged in the *hareem.* Alexa had little taste for the sugar-coated almonds or the tiny pastries ranged on the tray herself. In fact, she had little appetite at all now, though she'd felt ravenous earlier. Raisha's spiteful observations and malicious barbs had effectively quelled her hunger, and also tarnished the rosy glow of newfound happiness that had surrounded her like an aura upon her return to the Mist *serai* from Sharif's private apartments that morning, following their passionate reconciliation, which had lasted the night long.

Instead, she sipped a cool glass of her favorite fruit juice—

pomegranate, naturally!—while Raisha licked honey from her sticky fingers and chattered away like a small parrot, interrupting her conversation from time to time only to pop another treat into her small mouth with a blissful sigh. That she could still manage to eat while she sowed her seeds of dissension and jealousy astounded Alexa!

"Well, he's never mentioned having a *hareem* of his own to me!" Alexa replied doubtfully to Raisha's earlier comment. She was reluctant to believe the girl's tales, for there was an undercurrent of spitefulness and jealousy to both her words and expression that made Alexa doubt her. Besides, the disquieting things Raisha was telling her jarred with the new and wonderful feelings for Sharif that had unfolded like bursting flower buds inside her, tender feelings that both surprised and delighted her at the same time. Truth was, she didn't *want* to believe what the Inandan girl was telling her— that Sharif had lied when he'd claimed to love her, and that she was just one more in a line of many gullible young women who'd fallen for his smooth tongue and devilish, dark good looks. No. She wanted so badly to be able to trust him. . . .

Raisha shrugged and licked her sticky fingers again. "Well, don't believe me, then! It's up to you, after all, as his wife. I was only trying to help you—to save you from being hurt by trusting him. After all, it was thanks to you that Lady Kairee allowed me to return to the palace, and I'm happy to be back, even if it is only as a lowly serving girl. One good turn is deserving of another, isn't it? At least I can say I tried to warn you later, when he finds someone else."

Alexa's expression softened. Poor Raisha! Her bitterness and resentment of her lowly new position was as obvious as her jealousy where Sharif was concerned, and her gentle heart went out to the girl, despite knowing what she was trying to do. It must be humiliating to have once been Sharif's pampered favorite, and then in the blink of an eye be reduced to nothing more than a servant. Was it Raisha's fault if she spoke the truth as she believed it, colored by her bitterness?

"I'm sorry if I sounded as if I doubted you, Raisha. I know you're only trying to help, but—"

"But you don't believe me?"

338

"I don't know what I believe! I only know that—that Sharif is kind and gentle to me, and that he says he loves me." Her lovely face glowed with the radiance of new love. Her complexion was rosy, her green eyes bright. "When I'm in his arms, he makes me feel as if I—"

"—as if you're the most beautiful woman in the world!" Raisha finished triumphantly. "As if no woman was loved before he loved you! Aiee! I know how it is, only too well. Sharif is a very devil in the arts of lovemaking—and as virile as any stallion!" She sighed deeply, as if overcome by memories of Sharif's virile talents.

Alexa's radiance faded. Her jaw tightened in anger—and jealousy—and her green eyes glittered now. "Yes," she gritted. "He is."

The Inandan girl hid a sly smile. At last, she had apparently managed to shake Zerdali's newfound confidence in her husband! Now that she'd created a little chink of doubt, it could be widened inch by inch, word by word, lie by lie, until it was a yawning hole of mistrust and jealousy and, finally, hatred for her husband. She'd have to take measures to keep them apart from time to time and prevent them from growing close, but one fine day, all going well, she would "help" a disillusioned Zerdali to escape al-Azadel and the "clutches" of the wicked Sharif, and who would be left but his loyal, devoted Raisha to console him over her loss when she was gone?

"Of course," Raisha added hurriedly in a silky tone, for it was dangerous to alienate one with Zerdali's potential for power too much or too soon, "it is also possible that he feels very differently for you, Zerdali. After all, you're so very beautiful—far more beautiful than I! And your coloring is so exquisite and rare. Perhaps"—she lowered her eyes in self-reproach—"yes, perhaps I'm just jealous that you've found lasting favor in our lord's eyes, and that he has honored you and made you his first wife. Perhaps he will never grow tired of you, as he did with me. *Ewellah*, I am wicked to have put such thoughts in your head! Please, forget everything I've said, everything! It was spiteful and foolish of me, and I already regret my words. Forgive me?" she implored prettily, a picture of contrition with her pouted lips and modestly downcast eyes.

"Don't be silly, Raisha, of course I forgive you," Alexa agreed readily. But as Raisha knew very well, the damage was already done, the seed of doubt firmly planted.

Alexa had already silently determined to broach the matter with Sharif somehow, and find out for herself if he had, as Raisha'd implied, a *hareem* of women secretly locked away in the palace somewhere to serve his pleasure! She would learn for herself if he truly meant what he'd said about there being a fresh start, founded on honesty, between them, or if he only paid lip service to the idea!

Her opportunity came the next morning, after yet another night spent in delightful lovemaking. It was the very first night she'd answered his summons to share his bed eagerly and with anticipation! Sharif had been gentle and concerned for her welfare and pleasure the night long, yet as tender and passionate as always. The following day, mellowed by the joys of the night they had shared and indulgent in his good humor, he asked her if she would like to try the mare that his father had given her as a wedding gift by riding with him. She agreed, but to his keen ears her agreement sounded less enthusiastic than he'd expected. Even after she'd dressed herself for their ride and returned to him, she still seemed remote.

"What is it, *habibah?* Are you unwell?" he asked, eyes narrowed. Was she with child? he wondered.

She shook her head mutely, wondering how on earth she was to voice the doubts that were nagging her.

"Then something is troubling you, yes? Out with it, little one, and tell me what it is!"

She looked away, quite unable to voice the question now that he'd given her the opportunity to do so. "I—it's nothing."

He tilted her chin and forced her to look up at him. "If it troubles you, who are the jewel-of-my-life, it is not 'nothing,'" he said sternly. "I want you to be happy, Zerdali. Did we not agree to start afresh? How can that be if we are not honest with one another?"

Honest! she'd thought indignantly. *Who was he to speak of honesty to her!* Her indignation gave her the courage to mumble, "It's just that, well, I'd heard—back in England, you know?—that all Eastern men of—of your rank have many

340

women to—to serve their m-male needs. Sometimes hundreds of them! I was wondering, do you—do you perhaps have a *hareem* of your own?"

There! It was out! Would he answer her honestly, she wondered, or lie?

"*Hareem?*" Sharif echoed, the dark wings of his brows rising in surprise at her question. With it, the image of Raisha's pretty face twisted with jealousy rose before his eyes. He had more than an inkling of where Zerdali's suspicions had come from, and it was not from distant England! Obviously, the Inandan girl must not be permitted to attend his wife any longer, despite his wishes to be kind to her, not if he wanted harmony in his household! He would see Kairee had her removed again at once, he determined grimly, and replaced by poor, faithful Fatima before nightfall.

But in answer to his bride's tentative question he only replied smoothly, "But of course I have a *hareem*, little one!" He chucked her beneath the chin with his knuckle, well aware of a certain green glitter filling her eyes that had nothing to do with their vivid color, but was the green glitter of jealousy! He smothered the grin that tugged at his lips. "Did you think such a powerful prince as your own al-Azim would not?"

She shrugged, her lips tightly pursed, and tried to sound casual and unconcerned. "Oh, I hadn't given it much thought, really. I was just—curious. Why, I certainly don't care if you have a hundred women in your *hareem!* It's none of my business or concern what you do."

She made a concentrated effort to turn nonchalantly away from him, aware of a gnawing pain that grew and spread throughout her breast and lodged there, heavily. Raisha had told her the truth after all! she thought, horrified by the hurt the knowledge gave her. He hadn't even taken the trouble to deny it! She was suspiciously close to tears in that very moment. Love! He'd sworn he loved her, no one but her, and that they'd start over and learn to be friends as well as lovers. But, how could they when he had any number of nubile, dusky beauties at his disposal, awaiting only the snap of his fingers to come running to do his bidding, in his bed or otherwise? That—that lying Bluebeard!

341

"Perhaps you are curious, mmm?" he asked, his eyelids drooping sensually to conceal the wicked sparkle in his dark eyes. "Come, then! Before we go riding, I shall take you to meet my lovelies. Let me see," he added thoughtfully, counting on his long brown fingers, "there is Zuleika, the Fair One, and little Zada, the Fortunate, and my favorite, the beautiful Barakah, whose grace and loveliness outshines them all, and—"

"No. Really, Sharif, I don't want to meet them!" she protested, horrified at the idea. "You promised we'd go riding, and I'd much rather—"

"Nonsense, *habibah!* You are my wife—my *first*, my beloved wife. I would have no secrets between us, as I promised. There will be time enough to try your mare after you've met the lovely *hareem* of Sharif al-Azim. They are like a flock of pretty birds, Zerdali, you will see, and be as delighted by them as I. . . ."

Delighted? she thought, fuming. Why, she'd sooner slit their throats and feed them to the jackals than bid them a good day! Or smear them with honey and let giant red ants devour them piece by piece. But so saying, Sharif took her rigid arm and led her through the palace.

Two of his newly selected bodyguards left their post at the entry to his private apartments and dogged their every move, discreet and silent as shadows but there nonetheless, armed with the ubiquitous *takobas* thrust into their belts.

He saw the startled glance she gave them and explained in a low voice, "I would much prefer to ride alone with you, Zerdali, but alas, the guards are necessary for our safety. These two men will accompany us as we ride, though at a discreet distance. You may trust them, for they are my friends as well as my guards, and have sworn to defend our lives with their own. The trouble with my cousin's tribe is far from over, you see. It stems from an old jealousy that began when Tabor and I were yet children, and our fathers still young but already sworn enemies, for all that they were brothers. My uncle, Murid, was envious of the prosperity of al-Azadel, you understand, and tried to draw the allegiance of her people away from my father, who as the eldest son of my grandfather was their chieftain and

342

the *amir* of our kingdom. He also coveted our fortress and its riches. When my father and I traveled the deserts with the herds during the winter months many years ago, he overran our mountain province, killed many of our people, and claimed al-Azadel for himself! As a consequence, my father and I were forced into exile in distant Egypt, and it was many years before Murid was slain and my father returned to his former power. Since Murid's death, my cousin Tabor has grown to manhood in bitterness and jealousy. He has rekindled old enmities, and would succeed where his father failed." He watched her face carefully.

"You passed your exile in Egypt? But I was born there, in Alexandria!" she told him eagerly, her anger at him forgotten. "In fact, my parents named me after the city," she admitted with a wry little grimace that wrinkled her nose. "I suppose I should be grateful I wasn't born in Cairo, don't you think?" The merry expression faded as she added sadly, "Cairo. You know, I'd almost forgotten that that was where my father was killed. He was an archaeologist, you know, and fascinated by the East. He was always puttering about musty old tombs and going on and on about this pharaoh and that pharaoh. I was quite old before I discovered the pharaohs he talked about so much were mummified Egyptian kings, and not just more of our absent relatives!"

He smiled at her little joke. "Your father died there?"

She nodded. "When I was sixteen. A passage in one of the tombs he was excavating collapsed. His body was never recovered."

"Ah, I see. I'm—very sorry," he said uncomfortably.

They walked on in silence after that, her lovely face pensive as she relived that awful time in her life.

As she'd said, she'd been only sixteen when the news arrived, and about to make her debut into London society—a formality her Grandmother Harding, a stickler for propriety, had insisted upon, and one she'd fought against without success. That ridiculous launching had, naturally, been postponed when they received the news—the only bright spot of that awful time. Keene had been summoned home from Hawkhaven, the expensive boarding school he'd attended, and

343

instead of a debutante's white gown, she'd donned the black of heavy mourning, plunged into a grief so deep she'd doubted at the time she'd ever recover. Her mama had never truly recovered from his death. Her papa, her dearest papa, gone—just like that, in the blink of an eye! They hadn't even been given the comfort of a grave over which to mourn his passing. A brief memorial service, a rambling eulogy by one of his museum associates, and that had been that. Her only small comfort had been the knowledge that her father had found entombment amongst the remnants of the ancient culture he'd studied and admired for so many years. . . .

"Down here," Sharif murmured, interrupting her melancholy thoughts, and they took some stone steps downward, coming outside the palace to a small, sunlit open courtyard lined with numerous outbuildings of natural reddish mud brick. The stables, she guessed, and a horse's muffled nicker confirmed her suspicions.

"*La Bes,* my lord Sharif!" greeted a short, stocky Inandan who exited one of the buildings. "Your horses are saddled and ready, sir!"

Sharif nodded. "My thanks. But before we go, I've decided to visit with my *hareem,*" he told the man, who frowned in puzzlement. Before he could comment, Sharif quickly carried on, "*Ewellah,* Kerem, my eyes are hungry for the sight of my lovelies—Barakah, Zenobia, Zuleika, and the others." And he winked.

"Ah, but of course, my lord, your *hareem!*" the man, understanding his lord's meaning, agreed with a grin. "Shall I bring your little beauties to you?"

"At once, Kerem, at once!" Sharif urged, rubbing his hands together in what appeared, to Alexa's jealous eyes, lecherous anticipation.

Sharif wore no turban or *tagilmust* this morning, and uncovered, his glossy, curly black hair shone with blue lights in the sunshine. Clothed in a short indigo tunic, belted at the waist with a braided leather belt in which he wore his dagger, and in baggy white breeches tucked into knee-high black kid boots, he made Alexa think of a handsome, swashbuckling pirate-king from bygone days. Her throat constricted. Oh,

Lord, why did he have to be so confoundedly attractive to her—and why, oh why did Raisha have to be right! Her feelings for him were so new and fragile, so very, very fragile and intensely possessive. She couldn't bear to share him, not with anyone—she just knew she couldn't!

"I'm sure you'd prefer to visit your 'little beauties' alone," she suggested stiffly. "I'd be happy to wait with the horses?"

"And deny you the chance to inspect your rivals face to face? I would not hear of it, *habibah!*"

She squirmed as they waited, fidgeting with the corners of her head covering, wondering what to expect. Naturally, they'd all be beautiful and, unlike her, simpering and grateful for the great honor Sharif had done them by making them his women; eager to please him, anxious to dance attendance on his every whim, willing to go to any lengths to avoid making those magnificent ebony eyes flash in controlled annoyance or that chiseled mouth tighten in displeasure—while she had only to open her mouth, and she would displease him. . . .

She set her shoulders squarely, bracing herself for the moment when Kerem returned with the women in tow. She wouldn't let him suspect she was jealous, she told herself. She'd be gracious, charming to each one of them, and wish them the good health of their desert prince. Lord knows, she'd wanted nothing to do with him before; she could convince herself to feel that way again, if she set her mind to it firmly enough. But still, her lower lip quivered as she recalled his silken kisses, his whispered endearments, the gentleness of the arms that had held her as she soared into rapture the night before. It was—it was just that she was so terribly alone here, that's why she'd started to think she was falling for him; why her heart contracted in agony at the thought of his lips caressing another, of another's head cradled upon his broad bronze chest. . . .

"Two of your ladies, my lord!" Kerem announced. "The others of your *hareem* beg your forgiveness, but they are unable to attend you."

Alexa swung sharply about, seeing Kerem standing there, his hands and arms outstretched and clothed heavily in leather gauntlets now. Upon each fist perched a large falcon, each one as white as a drift of snow, feathers like soft flakes nestled sleekly one atop the other. There was no bevy of giggling women, not a single one!

"May I present the ladies Barakah and Zenobia!" Kerem declared with a smile, and to her dismay, both he and Sharif laughed openly as she gawked in surprise.

"Hawks?" she exclaimed.

"Falcons," Sharif corrected, grinning broadly. "This pair are but two of the lovelies to be found in my *hareem* mews! Tell me, my bride, are you not jealous?" His black eyes were wicked with deviltry and shining with unconcealed enjoyment at the trick he'd played upon her.

Alexa bristled and clenched her teeth to keep from blasting him with a withering comment, her cheeks red with embarrassment and—yes, she admitted silently to herself—with enormous relief!

"They are both gyrfalcons, taken from the cold mountains of their native Greenland when they were fledgling eyasses. Of all my falcons, Barakah, the White One, is my favorite, the queen of my *hareem*. Look at her, Zerdali! Is she not lovely, worthy of the sultan's ransom I paid the trader for the capture of her and her sister?"

Alexa had to admit that the gyrfalcon, unhooded now, yet sitting quietly upon her handler's fist, was lovely indeed! From her neat, well-molded head to the clean sweep of her snowy tail, she must have measured at least two feet. Her wings, when spread, would probably be double that. At the sound of Sharif's voice, Barakah stirred and made throaty little purring noises of welcome, shifting her position restlessly now so that the silver bells of her leather jesses jingled. The sound reminded Alexa of the tinkling sound the women of the *hareem* made when they moved. A smile began and curved her lips, then spread to dance in her green eyes. Golden-eyed Barakah was a *hareem* beauty indeed, complete with tinkling bells!

"My *hareem*, *habibah*!" Sharif said gently, his dark eyes filled with love as they rested upon her face. He placed a hand on each of her shoulders. "Have no fear, for other than you, my beloved wife, they are my only *hareem*!"

She met his gaze, and the knot of bitterness in her breast

loosened and dispersed when she read the love in his eyes. A thrill ran through her as a tiny bolt of lightning seemed to leap from him to her, flooding her with joy. *He loves me!* she realized with a sense of wonder. *It's no lie, no pose. Raisha's wrong—he truly does love me!*

"Will you hunt today, sir?" Kerem asked, breaking the spell between them.

"I had not planned to. . . ." Sharif's doubtful voice trailed away as he glanced back toward Alexa.

"Please, bring Barakah, if you wish," Alexa urged, ashamed now of her former mistrust. "I'll try to contain my— jealousy!" And she smiled up at him, a smile that delighted Sharif with its genuine amusement and warmth and utter lack of resentment at the little joke he'd played upon her. His heart gave a peculiar little leap in his chest. Perhaps—perhaps there was love in her smile too?

"Very well! Come, let's be on our way!"

They rode out of the stables a few moments later, followed by their escort of two, Selim and Abdul, and by Kerem, Sharif's falconer and groom. Barakah rode aloofly upon Kerem's fist, while a brace of greyhounds, tails curled under their elegant, streamlined bodies, loped at their little cavalcade's heels.

They quickly passed through the tiny walled city, and made their way once more down the twisting, rock-littered paths of the mountain and clattered out beneath the gates. Remembering her abortive escape attempt amidst the goatherds and well aware of the amused smiles the guards shot her, she blushed furiously until they had passed through and on down the serpentine path.

If he wished to hunt, Sharif explained as they rode, the *sahel* below was a better place to do so, with game and wide-open spaces to fly Barakah properly and demonstrate her skills. Alexa nodded agreement, but secretly she didn't really care where they went—it was just so marvelous to be out in the open, away from her opulent cage, with Sharif riding tall and handsome at her side.

The mountain seemed beautiful beyond belief to her eyes, shafts of sunlight slanting down between its craggy formations and lighting the few wildflowers that bloomed amidst the rocks with a golden glow that made their colors twice as vivid to the eye, as if they were afire from within. Above them, the sky was bluer than a robin's egg, and unmarred by even a single cloud. She inhaled deeply, filling her lungs with the sweet scent of freedom. She'd wondered at times over the past weeks if she'd ever taste it again.

The dappled-gray Arabian mare, Rabi, was a joy to ride, her gait as smooth as the silk of her mane and tail, her personality sweetly affectionate. For all that she hadn't ridden in years, riding was a skill one never lost, Alexa realized, her former doubts vanishing. She moved easily in the saddle to the rhythmic motion of Rabi's stride, although it felt peculiar to be riding Arab fashion, without the stirrups of the English saddle that she was accustomed to. Though she'd probably be stiff all over tomorrow, she was pleased to discover she could handle her lovely mare well on the hairpin twists of the mountain passes as she followed Sharif down rock-littered tracks to the *sahel* below.

The *sahel* basked in the sun, sere golden grasses and acacias dreaming in its hot spell. England and the green gardens of Harding Hall, the river quietly flowing by and the scent of roses and lavender perfuming the air, seemed a million miles away here, she thought as her eyes swept the golden terrain that spread out all around them, broken only by the black outline of a ruined *kella*, an ancient watchtower, off in the distance, or random heaps of sparkling white boulders. Heat waves shimmered and danced over the land, distorting distance, appearing like curtains of moving water. Strangely, she felt no pang of longing to leave these vast arid wastes to return to England's damp green shores. At some point unknown to her, she must have accepted that she would— could!—never go back. Or perhaps, the desire to do so had paled beside new, more exciting desires . . . ? After all, there was nothing back in England for her now but the loneliness and narrowness of a spinster's life of good works and charity, while here there was—him. And the promise of a lifetime spent with a man she had grown to like, respect, and also—love. Involuntarily, her eyes sought out Sharif, and catching herself staring, she quickly looked away, rich, swelling emotion filling her. She wanted to tell him how she felt, but still couldn't bring herself to acknowledge what it was she felt for him out loud. She supposed she still wasn't ready to abandon the last remnants of her independence the admission would require. . . .

"What are you thinking, my soul?"

She glanced across at Sharif astride his shining black Aswad and shrugged. "Oh, I don't know. Just that I really must thank your father again for such a generous gift. Rabi's a dream!" she added, deftly changing the subject. She leaned forward to stroke the mare's silvery-gray neck. In response, Rabi tossed her dappled head and nickered in pleasure.

"You were always fond of horses, Zerdali," Sharif observed, smiling at the pretty picture she made as she rode beside him. Alexa was mounted with her flowing indigo garments billowing gracefully about her, Rabi dainty and elegantly colored, like the gray silk of the desert sands by moonlight. Another image filled his mind: of Alexa in a grubby ruffled pinafore, boots, and stockings, her apricot-colored hair dragged back into tight twin pigtails fastened with wilted green ribbons, scrambling astride a huge black colt that dwarfed her without any sign of fear. . . . "A little girl who would even put aside her anger at her playmate if it meant a ride upon his colt—yes, even when he was in the wrong, and deserved her anger!" he remembered aloud.

Her forehead knitted with a frown. "Mmm, I probably would have. I don't remember much of my childhood, to be honest, though my father used to say I was a stubborn little creature!"

She shot him a curious look, as if wondering if his peculiar comment had been only a keen observation of her character, or a question, or perhaps even—impossibly!—a recollection— and he held his breath, waiting, wondering if his words had struck some chord in her memory.

"Do you?" she asked suddenly.

"Do I what?"

"Remember your childhood?"

He drew a long breath. "Some of it, yes. The time we spent in exile is especially clear."

She nodded in sympathy. "Ah, yes, the hard times always

349

are, aren't they! I remember leaving Egypt—it had been home to me since I was born—quite clearly. I cried as our ship left the harbor, although Papa had told me that my baby brother was sickly and that he needed to go to England where there were doctors to care for him and it was cooler. But I didn't care about that! Everyone I'd known and loved since birth was there in Egypt, you see! Papa always claimed—though I don't remember saying it myself—that I wanted to send my baby brother to Grandmother by *post*, so we could stay! I suppose I got the idea from the gifts Grandmother used to send me by ship. There was a doll, I think. . . ."

"Lucy," Sharif prompted automatically, without thinking twice about what the revelation might mean. He could have bitten his tongue the minute he'd said it.

"Why, yes, I think that was her name, come to think of it!" She eyed him curiously again, adding thoughtfully, "My dear Lucy. Now, how on earth could you know that?"

He grinned, inwardly cursing his slip. "A fortunate guess, *habibah*. It is a common name amongst the *Englesy, ewellah?*" he said with a casual shrug.

"Not that common," she said hesitantly.

She stared at him long and hard, and in a suspicious way that made Sharif itch to be done with this secrecy, and tell her everything she had forgotten. But no, he couldn't do that. He didn't want her to love him for the sake of a childhood friendship, nor the claims that old and sadly forgotten, happy time would inevitably make upon her. Nor did he want her to convince herself she loved him simply because he had declared his love for her. He wanted her to love him for himself, as she had loved him in his dreams, utterly, completely, freely his, with the love of a passionate, giving woman for her chosen mate. . . .

He recalled how she had resisted him at every turn, how she'd fought him like a cornered tigress when he'd pursued her across the desert sands, and how she'd tried to claw her way free when he took her the first time. Barakah had been the same when she had first come to him, a "new" falcon having just gone through her first molt, brought on a long and frightening journey from the snowbound lands of her birth to the scorching deserts. Furious at her capture, terrified by its strangeness, she had screamed and fought back in rage and defiance, white wings beating furiously to escape him, struggling to strike her cruel talons deep into his hand while her eyes raged like golden fire. It had taken many long weeks of gentle handling, soft words, patience, and feeding by him alone before she had come to accept and even enjoy her master's touch, to welcome his visits and the thrill of hunting together that followed. But a woman, he reminded himself, was not a falcon. No amount of gentleness on his part could force Zerdali to love him, not when her will and her heart still stubbornly resisted the truth. He could only show her his love, and trust that the astrologer Maimun had not been wrong those many years ago.

"Kerem! I will fly Barakah!" he declared, and the falconer Kerem rode forward, passing Sharif a spare leather gauntlet, which he slipped onto his left hand and arm up to the elbow. Kerem passed the heavy falcon to him.

"Ah, my beauty!" her master murmured softly, his deep voice gentling and hypnotic. "Will you show my Zerdali your huntress's skills today?" The gyrfalcon, perched now upon Sharif's fist, puffed out her white feathers and purred deep in her throat.

They rode on for almost a mile, side by side, their escort of three bringing up the rear discreetly. At their approach, a brace of plump pigeons broke from the cover of an acacia bush and noisily fluttered up into the air. Swiftly, Sharif slipped the little tufted hood from Barakah's head and released the short leather leash from the jesses in almost the same move. He thrust his fist aloft, and at once Barakah left it like the bolt from a crossbow, soaring heavenward with breathtaking speed and grace.

Alexa shaded her eyes as the white-winged falcon soared and wheeled far above them, circling once, twice, cutting a sweeping silver arc from the dazzling blue that was exhilarating to see. She was almost holding her breath when the falcon suddenly dropped, "stooping" through air like a falling thunderbolt to grasp one of the pigeons and plummet with it held fast in her talons, back to earth. Once there, she perched atop her prey, calmly awaiting her proud master.

Sharif swung down from his horse and went to retrieve Barakah, returning her to his handler's fist with a low-voiced stream of praise for her skills. Kerem rewarded her with a scrap of meat drawn from his saddlebag, and replaced the feather-tufted hood when she was done eating, while one of the brace of greyhounds retrieved the game.

"Well?" Sharif asked, pride shining in his night-dark eyes. "Did you ever see such speed, *habibah*, or such a clean kill as Barakah's?"

She had to admit she had not, and said so, but in truth the falcon's merciless swoop, the sudden if clean death of the innocent pigeon, had unsettled her, for she was softhearted by nature and hated to see any living thing killed for sport.

"By Allah! My lord, look at this!" Kerem cried.

Sharif turned, and saw that Kerem was holding the slain pigeon in one hand and a small leather cylinder in another. His brows rose. "A message?"

Kerem nodded, drawing a small roll of paper from the tube and handing it to Sharif, who opened and scanned it.

His expression was closed and enigmatic when he looked up again at Kerem. "I cannot decipher it. It is written in *tenet*."

"*Tenet!*" the falconer exclaimed, shocked, for *tenet* was the secret language of the Inandan, known to no others. "Then with your permission, sir?"

Sharif nodded and handed him the paper, watching the Inandan's face as he read it. When he was done, Kerem wet his lips, glancing warily at the golden *sahel* stretching all about them dreaming in the sun, as if he expected to see something—or someone—spring from concealment there.

"Sir," he began, "whoever sent this intended it for an Inandan in our city! It came from the camp of the al-Tabor!"

"Then can you decipher it?" he asked, and seeing Kerem nod asked, "What does it say?"

"It says, sir, 'The chieftain Tabor sees the wisdom of your plan. He awaits word of when the desert hawk's mate can be easily taken, and will act upon it.'"

A faint smile curled Sharif's chiseled lips as the import of the message struck home. "'The desert hawk's mate,' eh, Kerem'?"

"Yes, my lord. But I swear to you, I know nothing of this!"

"And I believe you, old friend! But this message proves that we harbor an unknown traitor within the walls of al-Azadel— one who's perhaps sent and received other messages from the camp of our enemy! Perhaps even helped our enemies to eavde us? By Allah, I will seek the traitor out and slay him!" he swore, his swarthy face frightening with the look of controlled fury he wore.

Looking at the dead carrier pigeon hanging limply from Kerem's fist, he remembered the morning the goatherd had found him amidst his slain comrades, and how he'd asked the boy, Coman, if he'd seen anyone upon the paths as he brought his goats to grazing. The boy'd said he had not, but that he had *found* something. That "something" had been a number of white pigeon feathers, found scattered about in a little-used, difficult path where pigeons were never seen, for it was a lonely spot with little cover, where mountain hawks made their nests—and hawks were the pigeons' greatest natural threat. Had the traitor also been responsible for the escape of the fugitive al-Tabor, he wondered, and consequently the murder of his guards? Almost certainly it was so!

His jaw hard with brooding anger at their unknown enemy, he turned to Kerem. "You may return to al-Azadel now, Kerem. I've lost my taste for hunting today. But say nothing of what we have learned to anyone. I'll discuss it with my father later. For now, my lady and I will ride on."

"My lips are sealed, sir," Kerem vowed. He wheeled his horse's head around, heading it back toward the mountains.

The falconer had not ridden far when he reined his mount to a sudden halt. "My lord! Riders, to the east!"

He pointed, and Sharif followed the direction of his arm. At once, he too saw the dust rising from the distant desert. Judging by the size of the sand cloud kicked up, there were many camels in the approaching band! "Kadar?" he wondered aloud, apprehension chilling him.

"No, my lord! The al-Tabor!" Kerem answered. "They wear

the robes of the Blue Men, as do we! Look!"

Sharif squinted against the dazzling sunlight. The riders were robed in the indigo of the Imochagh people. His sharp-eyed falconer was right. By Allah, their enemies were close, and coming up fast! Could they reach the mountains before they were cut off by his cousin's warriors?

"We must ride swiftly, Zerdali!" he ground out, giving her a quick, assessing glance as he reached over and squeezed her hand. "Can you keep up?"

She nodded, her mouth suddenly dry with fear. "I'll try!" she promised. "But the *kella* is closer—couldn't we hide there and hope they pass us by?" She pointed to the ruined watchtower nearby.

"I think not. There's a well within its walls, and I'm certain Tabor, as an able chieftain, knows of it and means to use it as his camp. The well assures ample water for his men, you see. If we should be trapped there, it would mean death for me at my cousin's hands—and perhaps far worse than death for thee! We must outride them, beloved, or be cut off from our mountain stronghold! Go!"

They kicked their horses into a gallop, manes and tails streaming as they careened back across the pale grasslands of the *sahel* toward the rugged mountain foothills at breakneck speed. Tiny gazelles broke from cover and bounded away as they approached. Hidden birds erupted in twittering, flapping confusion. Selim and Abdul followed them, while Kerem rode ahead with Barakah—alarmed by the reek of danger on the wind—beating her white wings furiously from her perch upon his fist.

Alexa leaned low over her mare's neck, reins shortened, gripping the horse's sides with her thighs and knees and wishing she had stirrups to help her keep her seat. The golden ground and stones flew beneath their horses' hooves in a blurred, tawny stripe, yet their destination seemed little closer with each passing second, despite the fleetness of their mounts.

She risked a glance to the east and saw that Tabor's dark riders had spotted them! They were urging their camels and horses to still greater speeds with howling cries and whoops of excitement, brandishing rifles and lances above their heads. Their cries were punctuated by shots. Her heart pounded in her breast as she gauged first the ground they had yet to cover, and then the swiftly approaching sand cloud kicked up by their enemies. Surely they would be able to reach the narrow, rocky defile that twisted deep into the heart of the mountains ahead of Tabor's warriors, but—what then? Etched against the rocky backdrop of the mountain on that narrow, treacherous path, they could be picked off with ease, helpless as sitting ducks in a shooting gallery!

"This way!" Sharif yelled over his shoulder. "Follow me!"

She had no time to question why he had turned Aswad's head west instead of taking the crevasse directly ahead that led to the defile they'd taken before. She could only trust that he knew what he was doing, and follow him blindly!

They clattered down a sloping, rubbled incline that led deep into the foothills and exited into a narrow canyon. Walls of rock towered close on either side of them, as if the ochre gorge had been carved out by a huge knife like a slice of sponge cake. The mountain proper boxed in the far wall of the little canyon, making it a blind alley from which they could not hope to escape, and Alexa's spirits plummeted. If Sharif had hoped for a shortcut, he had failed. They were trapped!

But even as the thought crossed her mind, Sharif and Kerem had slithered from their horses' backs and were racing toward the far wall, working together to roll aside a huge fallen boulder that was lodged against it, one of many that littered the canyon's rear wall, the remnants of an ancient avalanche. A dark cave opened up behind it when, sweat streaming from their faces, the men finally hefted it aside, much to Alexa's astonishment, for their actions reminded her of the tales of Ali Baba and the Forty Thieves! Why, she wouldn't have been in the least surprised in that moment to hear Sharif thunder, "Open, Sesame!" nor to see the solid rock walls of the mountains part in magical obedience to his command!

As she was thinking this, Selim and Abdul sprang down from their horses. They took Rabi's reins from her and began leading their own horses and the mare toward the cave opening, while she held grimly to Rabi's mane for balance.

The air in the cave was stale yet pungent still with the musky scent of a mountain leopard or some other predator that had once made its lair within. Scenting this, the high-strung Rabi pricked back her ears and balked, digging in her dainty hooves and refusing to follow the other mounts inside. From afar, muffled by the canyon walls, came the faint cries of Tabor's men as they scoured the foothills for them, and muffled shots which grew closer with every passing second.

"Come, my beauty, be brave for your master, eh?" Sharif crooned, coming to help them. He cupped the mare's velvety charcoal muzzle in his large hands and fondled her nose, blowing his warm breath into the horse's nostrils. "Ah, my beauty, have no fear, for little Rabi and her mistress will be safe within the cave. . . ."

As it did with all females, human or otherwise, Sharif's caressing, soothing voice worked miracles, Alexa thought wryly, trembling with relief as Rabi responded and trotted obediently into the gaping, dark hole after the other horses. As soon as they were inside, Selim and Abdul labored to return the concealing boulder to its former position and squeezed behind it, one at a time, to join them in the musty darkness.

"By Allah, a narrow escape, was it not, my lord!" Kerem said fervently in the gloom.

"Narrow indeed, Kerem," Sharif agreed, finding Alexa in the shadows and slipping his arm reassuringly about her waist. He could feel the thunder of her heart against her ribs as he dropped a kiss to her head. "Don't be afraid. We'll be safe now, my love," he murmured. "The passageway leads to yet another cave, its entrance very close to the gardens of al-Azadel. The al-Tabor will not find us now."

"*Wellah*, that warring jackal will instead marvel at the magic of al-Azim, who can vanish like smoke into thin air!" Selim declared from the shadows, and the men laughed, the tension and fear dispersed by his boastful words.

Taking advantage of the gloom, Sharif drew Alexa into his arms. She trembled still with fear, he discovered as he embraced her. His lips found hers in the shadows, brushing against their warm softness until she parted her mouth beneath his in swift and complete surrender to the invasion of his tongue.

She shuddered as he kissed her deeply, his hands stroking the soft curves of her body in the shadows to calm her, his arms comfortingly strong as they held her hard against the broad warmth of his chest. She wanted to cling to him, to hold him tight and not let him go, not until her heart had ceased its pounding and her knees were done with their childish trembling! She also wanted him to make love to her, wanted him fiercely with every part of her, here and now, though the realization shamed her. What was she—a complete wanton— that she would crave his loving so badly when they had barely escaped with their lives moments before? Nonetheless, her reaction to his closeness was undeniable, her breasts hard and aching, the now all-too-familiar knot uncurling deep in her belly and spreading excitement throughout her. Her cheeks grew warm with shame in the shadows, and she was thankful he could not see them.

"By Allah, I desire thee, Zerdali—here and now!" Sharif whispered softly in her ear, voicing her own unspoken desires. Her heart skipped a beat as his hand enfolded her breast and fondled it, rubbing the sensitive nipple with the ball of his thumb. His caresses elicited delicious shivers that danced up and down her spine and made her press herself against him. "You will learn that danger acts like an aphrodisiac upon your husband, little one! Count yourself fortunate that there are others here with us, for if we were alone, my luscious apricot, you would find yourself upon your pretty back amidst the cold, hard stones of the mountain!" he threatened in a sensual voice.

"If we were alone," she whispered seductively against his cheek, scarcely able to believe she was saying such things to him even as she heard herself continue wickedly, "those cold stones you speak of would not be cold for long!"

His pleased, muffled laughter rose as warm breath to fan her hair. "Ah, truly, *habibah*, every day I discover something new about you to delight me! Come, take my hand. We must find our way through this dark tomb—and quickly!"

"Why? Do you think Tabor will attack al-Azadel again?" Alexa asked, suddenly breathless with renewed anxiety.

357

"No, my love. Tabor has learned his lesson, and at great cost. He will not dare lead his men deep into the mountains again, for fear of ambush or another defeat at our hands! No, *habibah*—I'm more afraid that *I* might attack *you*, and not care who sees us at our sport!"

With a deep, husky laugh that sent thrills through her, he started up the winding tunnel, his strong hand leading her surely through the darkness, while his men followed with the horses.

Chapter Twenty-Five

Their narrow escape that day brought home to Alexa as nothing else could have the knowledge that loving someone was a double-edged sword. One side was the sheer, delicious joy of loving and being loved: the unspoken sharing of each other's innermost thoughts simply by an exchange of meaningful looks, or of tender kisses and caresses. The other side was bitter and sharp: the razor-keen, terrible fear of losing the one dearest to you, and of being left alone without your beloved. Ah yes, there was an element of risk in loving someone, of caring too much. It opened one up to the possibility of pain. If the al-Tabor had overtaken them that day, Sharif would have been ruthlessly killed, she knew. And sometimes, gazing down at him while he slept beside her, or while drowning in the magnificent midnight pools of his eyes as he made love to her, she imagined that awful fear becoming reality, those wonderful merry eyes, that great, generous, love-filled heart, forever stilled by death, and wondered how she would ever find the will to go on living without him if her worst fears should ever become realized.

Hour by hour, day by day, he grew more vital to her very existence, as if they were two halves of the same whole, rather than individual, separate beings. When they were apart, she felt only half-alive, and yearned to be with him, fretted about him, thought of little things to tell him when they were reunited, and acted generally as if overtaken by a form of madness that, perversely, she had no wish to recover from, for the other side of love, the softer edge of the sword, was more blissful than anything she could have imagined! Now, at last, she had someone to shower her love upon, to protect her, to stand beside her through the hard times and share the joys in turn. It was easier to pretend the other, hurting side of love didn't exist and maintain a blissful ignorance. Her soaring emotions made her want to love everybody, to see everybody around her as deliriously happy as she was!

Fatima quickly grew accustomed to her mistress's singing like a lark as she pursued some new interest or other that the lady Kairee, on Sharif's behest, provided for her, or her sudden lapses into staring dreamy-eyed out of the window, her embroidery or the reading of some dusty tome completely forgotten. Fatima knew that these lapses had nothing at all to do with the view. Quite simply, her mistress had fallen giddily, hopelessly in love with her handsome young husband, and it was a state of affairs that she found enormously satisfying in every way. Well, almost every way, she amended, grumbling under her breath, for in her desire to make the entire world as happy as she, Zerdali had begged Sharif to allow Raisha to continue to serve her, and he, that young fool, also giddily in love and wanting only to please her, had agreed.

"No doubt she'll murder us all in our beds one fine night," Fatima muttered darkly, "that sly Inandan witch!"

To Fatima's mind, anyone but a blind man could see how Raisha resented Zerdali's newfound happiness—anyone but a blind man or Zerdali herself, she amended, who called the girl "dearest Raisha" and showered her with little gifts to soothe her hurt and jealousy, and gullibly believed such trinkets had achieved the desired effect of making a friend of her rival and enemy. Fatima, far older and wiser, had no such gilded illusions. She trusted the girl not an inch from her sight, and guarded against any possible opportunity that Zerdali might fall victim to Raisha's *tezma*, her Inandan curse of the "evil eye." And so not a morsel of food passed Zerdali's lips that Fatima had not sampled first. Not a drop of liquid quenched her thirst, but that Fatima had imbibed it before her. It would not be said that she, Fatima, had failed in her duties to the girl she loved once again. Her pride still smarted from the last time she had been sent to her rooms in disgrace!

Raisha, for her part, noted the old serving woman's amulets

and charms—talismans she'd also persuaded Zerdali to wear, on the pretext that they would help her to get with child—and had rocked with silent mirth. The old hag was half out of her mind with trying to keep her beloved mistress safe! Ha! Did stupid old Fatima truly believe her so foolish as to poison Zerdali's food or water? Never! There were far more subtle methods to bring her rival low. Boucha, her mother, had taught her that much! And, since she'd received no word as yet from the enemy chieftain Tabor regarding her plan, she'd decided she must take matters into her own hands. . . .

Smiling sweetly, Raisha returned from a visit to her mother's house one afternoon to find Zerdali lying upon her divan, her nose buried in a thick book.

"Ah, mistress, there you are, reading again! I can't understand what pleasure you find in it! Surely it is a difficult pastime, one better left to *marabouts* and other men of learning," she observed, well aware that Fatima was watching her from across the chamber, though pretending to be busy at her mending. "You should have come with me to the bazaar instead—they had the prettiest shawls from Kashmir there today, and silks from the Japans, and lovely ivory necklaces and bracelets from Cathay! There was a great doctor-*hakim* there today too—a huge black man as tall as any wall. He boasted that he could heal the beggars' sore eyes with just an ointment from his packs."

"Really? Oh, but there's nothing I enjoy more than an interesting book or an exciting new novel, honestly there isn't," Alexa denied, and Raisha saw at once that her cursed green eyes were especially bright this afternoon, her cheeks flushed prettily. What new joy could have made her so especially beautiful? she wondered. Could it be that she had conceived—was that the reason for her radiance? No, Raisha decided, remembering with relief that Zerdali's flow had come the week before. If she were with child, it was far too soon for her to know of it yet. There must be something else, then, but what?

"Then for your sake, I'm happy you enjoy it, since I know you wanted something to occupy yourself," Raisha declared silkily, the picture of a concerned friend as she set the little basket she'd brought from her mother's house on a low table and then proceeded to ignore it utterly. "Is it the book that makes you so radiant today, mistress, or something else?" she asked casually, removing the gossamer fringed shawl patterned with flowers that had covered her long, black hair.

"In a way, yes," Alexa agreed happily. "Oh, Raisha, this is one of the books my father wrote before his death—his findings from one of his very first archaeological 'digs' in Egypt! You see, I asked Kairee if there were any books written in English that I might have to read to pass the time, and she found me not only this one, but two others written by him as well. Isn't it incredible—that my poor father's discoveries should have made themselves known way out here in the deserts? Kairee told me Sharif was educated at the university in Damascus, and that he must have brought these books with him when he returned to al-Azadel. I can't wait to show him them tonight, and to tell him they were written by my father! There. You see?" She held out the book for Raisha to inspect. "It says 'by Jonathan Harding,' right here, on the spine! That was my father's name."

"Oh, I'm so happy for you!" Raisha declared warmly. "And no wonder you look so happy too. It must feel as if your father was not dead and gone after all, yes, with his words still alive?"

"Why, yes, that's exactly how it feels," Alexa agreed, surprised and warmed by Raisha's keen insight of her feelings. "I couldn't have expressed it better myself!" Guilty over her preoccupation, she carefully set the thick leather-bound book aside and perched cross-legged upon the divan. "Now, tell me! How was your visit? Is your mother well?"

"Very well now! In fact, she sent you some sweetcakes, my lady—her own special recipe—in thanks for your kindness to me here and for letting me visit her when she was ailing last week. There's honey and flour in them, and chopped figs and spices—well, here, why don't you try one for yourself, and see how good they taste?" She drew a cloth from the basket and revealed a dozen or so little round cakes, golden-brown, shiny, and studded with chopped figs.

"Mmm. They do look scrumptious!" Alexa agreed, her hand diving into the basket. Fatima practically leaped across the room as she did so.

"Ah, mistress, please, not so close to the evening meal! You'll spoil your appetite," Fatima warned guardedly, her alarm thoroughly aroused by the Inandan girl's sudden generosity, and by the sly droop of her eyelids that was, to her mind, both sinister and catlike.

Inwardly, Raisha laughed. Foolish old hag! Let her dwell on the sweetcakes! In so doing, she might well miss something else far more vital. . . .

"Oh, all right," Alexa agreed amiably, forgoing tasting the cakes. "I'll have one or two for dessert later instead. Now tell me, Raisha, did you see that handsome Selim today?" Young Selim, one of Sharif's bodyguards, was casting eyes in Raisha's direction, she knew. The men never failed to tease him about it!

Raisha blushed prettily and flicked her dark hair over her shoulder in a carefree, coquettish fashion. "As a matter of fact, I did!" she confessed, and sighed. "That Muriel was in the bazaar, talking with him—they are cousins, you know—but he seemed quite eager to escape her, that pathetic, boring little thing, once he spotted me. Well, of course, I nodded politely to them both and went on my way, but do you know what he did? He followed me, then he cornered me in a side street and paid me such extravagant compliments I blushed to hear them!"

Fatima snorted. "You blushed? By the Prophet's Loins, now I have heard everything! I'd more easily believe that painted old whore Jummar, who lives on the Street of the Courtesans, blushed than you had!"

"Fatima, stop it!" Alexa scolded, horrified by Fatima's unconcealed venom.

An angry crimson mottled Raisha's complexion. "Oh, don't upset yourself on my account, mistress. I'm used to her spitefulness after having endured it for so long. She's just jealous that you and I are friends, despite everything, aren't you, Fatima? Come, Old Aunt, have one of my mother's cakes and let's be friends too—or amicable enemies, at the very least! I'm sure they'd sweeten even your sour tongue, with all the honey in them!" She smiled such a syrupy smile, she knew Fatima would probably take the cakes and hurl them to the stray dogs in the streets, certain they were laden with poison now, after her suspiciously generous offer.

Fatima returned her smile with a false, syrupy one of her own. "I think perhaps I might take one. In fact, I think I'll take *all* of them—for our mistress to enjoy later." Snatching up the basket, she waddled away with it slung over her arm. "I'll just put them in my room for now, Zerdali, out of temptation's way until after the evening meal. Besides, it's cooler there, and they won't dry up so quickly."

"She'll probably gobble them all herself," Raisha said cattily when she'd gone, "and end up looking even more like a pregnant camel!"

"Oh, she's not so bad," Alexa denied. "You must try to forgive the things she says, or else learn to ignore them, if we're all to be together so much of the time. Now, quickly, tell me before Fatima comes back, was your meeting with Selim very exciting?"

"Exciting? That's not the half of it! By Allah, my heart was pounding as he spoke to me, and my knees were weak! I do believe—for I was married once, as you know, and have seen such a look in a man's eyes many times before—that he desired me!"

Alexa's green eyes sparkled. "And?" she coaxed.

"And I—I desire him too!" She lowered her eyes, the very picture of modesty, but secretly she wanted to laugh out loud as she remembered her and Selim's lusty bouts of lovemaking upon the rooftop of her father's house. If only that foolish, naive Zerdali knew just how far the "exciting little romance" she thought was progressing before her eyes had really gone!

"Then what happens now? Will Selim ask your father for your hand?"

"Oh, no, that's not necessary. I'm a widow, remember, and it's up to me whom I'll marry a second time. But—I'm so afraid Selim will not want me for his wife, since my first marriage proved I'm barren. I don't expect I'll ever know the joy of bearing Selim's child, of feeling a babe move in my womb."

Tears welled in the girl's huge cinnamon eyes, and Alexa's heart went out to her in pity. Poor, poor Raisha, married for the first time at the tender age of twelve to a man over twice her

364

age, the Inandan had told her, a horrible man whose only goal in life, once she had commenced her woman's flow, had been to ravish her and breed countless babes upon her. She could imagine the depth of Raisha's despair when time had passed and she was forced to admit she was barren. To her mind, much of what Fatima called Raisha's maliciousness stemmed from her unhappy past, and her efforts to prove her worth and desirability by attracting Sharif's notice were obviously also prompted by her past. And so she hugged the girl in an effort to comfort her a little. "Ah, yes. Oh, Raisha, I'm so sorry! It's very important here in the East for a woman to be able to bear children, isn't it?"

Raisha nodded sadly. "More important than any other quality she might possess."

At that moment, Fatima bustled back into the apartments of the Mist *serai,* her arms laden with masses of flame-colored roses. She was beaming like a plump-cheeked brown gnome amidst the blossoms.

"Well, look what we have here! Lovely roses, fresh from the terraced gardens of Kahlil, for my mistress from her husband. And a message comes with them too, so Akli said. He bade me tell thee that his lord Sharif said only the beauty of roses can compare with his bride, Zerdali, who is the most beautiful rose in all of al-Azadel!"

"Oh, they're marvelous!" Alexa cried, hurrying to take them from Fatima. "Look at the color—pink and orange, just like a desert sunset!"

"Careful, my dove. Even the prettiest roses have thorns," Fatima cautioned. "Raisha, fetch a bowl of water for your mistress's flowers, and don't just stand there gawping!"

"At once," Raisha promised, and hurried away.

"In my country, a gift of roses is a gift of love," Alexa said, inhaling the heavenly scent and thinking with tenderness of Sharif, who'd left al-Azadel early that morning with his father, to settle a dispute in a distant village of their province.

"And what else could they mean here, in a land where water is so scarce?" Fatima asked. "They're so very rare in our country, and must have been carefully nurtured. *Ewellah,* they're a gift of love, indeed!" She smiled fondly and smoothed a stray tendril of hair away from Alexa's cheek. "I'm so happy for you and Sharif, in love at last, Zerdali, my pet—and will be even happier when there are babes to dandle on my knee."

Alexa blushed. "Well, if there aren't any soon, it won't be from lack of trying!" she confided, and Fatima chuckled. "Ouch! You were right about the thorns—I've poked myself on one." She sucked at the scratch upon her palm, where a row of tiny beads of blood had welled.

"Is it deep?"

"Don't be silly, it's just a little scratch. If you'll lend me your shears, I'll trim the stalks for the bowl."

Raisha returned with the water then, and Fatima left the two young women exclaiming over the beauty of the roses while she returned to her own quarters to examine the sweetcakes. Something about Raisha's manner today warned her to leave nothing to chance. Those sweetcakes would be thoroughly examined and tasted, even if it meant reducing them to no more than crumbs. She'd not give Raisha the slightest opportunity to slip poison into her food, nor work her evil *tezma* on her beloved Zerdali—by Allah, she would not!

"So, my son, what action have you taken regarding the message you uncovered?" Malik ben-Azad inquired, eyeing his son expectantly over his water pipe that evening after their return.

"Nothing further than what I outlined to you before, Father. I had two of my most trusted men go through the city and note the houses of the Inandans who keep pigeons. I've ordered a guard posted at all times on the hillside overlooking the city, to watch the rooftops for the return of another pigeon. If the al-Tabor try to send word to the traitor in our midst, we cannot fail to know of it! And the guards at the gates and in the passes have been doubled since the attack, as you already know."

"And Tabor himself?"

"My spies report that he is up to something since his defeat at our hands, but exactly what that something is, they've yet to discover. But rest assured, Father, that my cousin is as cunning as any fox—far too cunning to try the same plan again when it has already failed! Whatever he might be up to, it will not involve having his men enter our city by climbing the mountain passes under cover of darkness. The severed heads of his leaders that I returned to him in baskets should have been ample warning that such methods are doomed to failure!"

He smiled grimly, and his dark eyes glittered with a ruthlessness that rarely surfaced, and would have shocked those who did not know that underneath his outward, easygoing, charismatic facade beat the heart of a born leader; one who was intelligent, who could be merciful and just, true, but also coldly calculating and ruthless, capable of emotionless decisions, if the need dictated, or if such a decision would benefit his beloved people. He placed the continued welfare of the al-Malik far above his own personal happiness, and would have fought to the death to preserve their welfare.

Sharif's father knew that from boyhood, his only son had been preparing himself little by little to one day rule al-Azadel when he himself was dead and gone to Paradise, and pride filled him as he looked across at the young man. He saw the matchless eyes of his beloved first wife, Bikkelu, bright and keen with wisdom far beyond his two-and-thirty years; saw his tall, strong warrior's body, and thought with tears in his eyes, "Truly, what a son he is!" Other men might boast of their many sons, but Malik felt himself blessed to have only this one and no other. He prayed to Allah he would live long enough to see the sons of Sharif born, and that they would be their father's sons in every way.

"Enough talk of intrigue and the al-Tabor!" Malik declared, for they had already spent long hours that same morning with the other *imaheren,* the noblemen of their Imochagh people, discussing what must be done about the rebellious tribe which strove to capture their city and bend their people to the rule of that embittered madman Tabor. His nephew had—alas!—grown to manhood in the image of his jealous father, Murid, Malik's younger brother, and appeared unlikely to change for the better at this late date. "We will talk of happier things, *ewellah!* Your bride—how is she?"

"She blooms, Father!" Sharif disclosed with a grin and a

tender look in his eyes now that spoke volumes. "Each day, she grows more lovely to my eyes."

"I'm glad to hear it! Rumors reach me, you know. Little scraps of information have a way of making themselves known. It seems I heard a whisper a week or so ago that your bride had tried to run away from our city and her husband, and return to Algiers? Something about—goats?" He eyed Sharif with an innocent expression that suggested he'd heard far more of the matter than the "whisper" he'd mentioned!

Sharif's grin deepened. "You have eyes and ears everywhere, my lord father! But yes, the whisper you heard was true. Zerdali was jealous of the dancing girl Raisha and her former place in my affections. In a fit of temper, she determined to leave our mountain stronghold. Luckily, Fatima learned of her intentions and warned me, and I was able to overtake her before she reached the *sahel*."

"And are things better between you now?"

"*Ewellah*, better than ever before! Just this morning, I went to Kahlil and asked him how the men of his land show their love for a woman. He told me that the *Englesy* send their chosen ones roses, and offered me the pick of his terraces for my bride. Selim should have taken them to Zerdali's apartments by now, with my message that she is the fairest rose in all al-Azadel, and that beside her the beauty of even the loveliest roses pales!" He winked. "She'll come to my bed tonight all smiles!"

Malik chuckled. "It would seem your quarrel is indeed mended, Sharif, and I am glad to hear it. But is she not yet with child?"

"Not yet, alas! But it is not for want of trying on our part, sir. Allah willing, it will happen soon enough."

"When that day comes, Kahlil and I will be happy men indeed. You have been all that a son should be and more, Sharif, and your Zerdali—why, I have always thought of her as if she were one of my daughters, and admired her keen mind and spirit. She will give you great sons, Sharif, and beautiful, clever daughters, I have no doubt."

"Thank you, Father."

"And what of Kadar—have you had word of him?"

"No. I've heard nothing since the last messenger he sent, telling us that the *Englesy*, Keene Harding, had fled into Tanezrouft to escape him, and that he did not intend to return here empty-handed."

Malik shook his head. "By Allah, that one concerns me! Perhaps it was a mistake to raise him as a brother to you, knowing he could not help but grow to manhood envying your place in my heart. He feels the difference keenly, you know, Sharif, and yet cannot bring himself to leave al-Azadel and take his place as the *shiek* of his Bedouin tribe, as is his birthright. This lust for vengeance will destroy him if he's not careful. . . ."

"Kadar is a grown man, Father. He is old enough to choose the path his life will follow without intervention from either of us. Now," he said, deftly changing the subject, standing, "if you are done with your water pipe, I would have you come with me to inspect the camel herds. Better calves I've yet to see than the ones dropped this spring, and each one white as milk!"

His thoughts safely diverted from Kadar, Malik rose to his feet, waved aside the servants that scuttled to attend him, and followed his son from the palace.

Chapter Twenty-Six

Alexa stirred restlessly, throwing aside the woven blanket that covered her body against the chill mountain air. Her throat felt parched, her tongue tasted furry, and heat burned and throbbed behind her eyes. With a groan, she struggled to sit up, but discovered she was so weak, she could hardly raise herself onto her elbows, let alone sit. With a moan of defeat, she fell back, trembling all over. The exertion expended for so simple an act had raised beads of clammy sweat on her brow and upper lip too, she realized. What on earth was wrong with her? she wondered dully, licking her parched lips thirstily. Surely she couldn't be ill.

She'd retired in good spirits and in perfect health, after spending the previous evening in the company of the women of the *hareem*. Drisana had played her *anzad* while Hestia, another of the lady Kairee's three lovely daughters, and Hestia's two adorable little girls had delighted in teaching her their native dances, and she'd whirled and twirled and laughed in total abandon, trying again and again until she'd mastered the intricate steps and was proudly able to dance in line with the best of them.

Afterwards, Raisha—in an unusually amiable mood—had offered her musical talents to entertain them all, and had taught them Inandan dances and songs, which had resulted in the women imploring Alexa in her turn to also teach them about her country's dances and music. Giving in to their pleading, she'd offered to teach them all the waltz, explaining that in her native England the dance was performed with male partners—a revelation that had sent the *hareem* into gales of laughter at such an outlandish idea.

"Do the men of the *Englesy* really dance with their women?" Drisana, wide-eyed, had asked. "Or are you but teasing us, Zerda? Surely that can't be so? Do the men not have their own dances, which they dance alone or with other men, as do our Imochagh menfolk?"

But Alexa had reassured them that, on the Beard of the Prophet, she was telling the truth, and she'd set out to demonstrate how it was done! First, she'd divided their number into two groups, one to act as "men" and the other as their ladies! Then, loudly humming the tune of Strauss's "The Blue Danube," which defied Drisana's efforts to follow it upon the *anzad,* she'd marched across the room to stand stiffly before a startled Fatima.

In a gruff voice she'd asked, "My dear lady, may I have the honor of the next dance?" and before a giggling Fatima could recover her composure to respond with a yes or a no, she'd made an exaggerated bow, grabbed the Bedouin woman by her thick waist, and whirled her—shrieking protests all the while—around the huge room, instructing, "Da-da-da, one, two, three! One, two, three! One, two, three—there! You see? It's easy!"

Giggling, the others had paired off and followed suit, twirling each other about the vast room until they'd fallen, red-faced and exhausted, to the floor, calling for cool glasses of sherbet to revive themselves and fanning hot faces with their hands.

"Truly, the men of the *Englesy* must be very different to our men," Drisana had declared, sipping the sweet liquid greedily, "to even consider such a strange way of dancing! I wonder—can their bodies be made in the same fashion as our men's beneath their *sirwal?*" She'd blushed and hidden her mouth behind her hand as she giggled.

"Drisana, shame on you! You hussy! What a question to ask poor Zerda!" Hestia'd scolded. "Er, Fatima—*are* they the same?" she'd quickly added, glancing at Fatima for confirmation and turning scarlet with embarrassment at her curiosity as the other women laughed helplessly.

"Indeed they are—just the same!" Fatima had divulged with

the air of one who knew much but would, out of good taste, say very little. "Except that they are not circumcised at birth, as our male babes are, Christian men are fashioned just the same."

"Not circumcised?" Drisana'd gasped.

"No!" Fatima had confirmed with a knowing grin. "Not a one of them! Their *wezands* are uncut, and remain as they were on the day of their birth!"

"And how would you know?" Raisha had demanded, curious despite herself to hear this outrageous tidbit of information.

"I have a tongue to ask, and eyes to see, do I not?" Fatima'd retorted. "When I served our lord Malik in distant Egypt, I saw an *Englesy* male child born, and asked his mother when he would be circumcised. It was then that I was told that this was not the custom for Christian males," she'd revealed with an air of triumph.

"I have also heard from Yasmeen, Kahlil's wife, that Christian men take only one wife, poor fellows, and stay with her until death, even should she prove barren or displeasing!" Hestia had announced with a pitying shudder.

"Aiee, surely that is not so? Out in the deserts, one wife could never do all the work that has to be done!" her sister had exclaimed.

"No, but you must realize, there are no deserts to the west, where I come from! The land is green and damp, with rich grass for grazing everywhere," Alexa had explained with a pang of nostalgia for Britain's green loveliness, wondering if they could possibly comprehend such a fertile land, having lived their entire lives amidst the mountains and the blazing desert sands. "And yes, my people really do believe in having only one wife for each husband, Hestia's right about that," she'd added, smiling. "In fact, it's against our laws for a man to have more than one wife at a time! If he does, he can end up in prison!"

"Prison? How barbaric!"

"Have they many camels where you come from, Zerda?"

"Not one that I've ever seen!"

"No camels?" Drisana had nodded in sudden understanding. "Ah, then the *Englesy* must be a poor people, yes, Allah protect them? The Blessed Prophet wrote that a man may take four wives to himself, but only if he could provide for each one of them equally. That must be why the poor Christian men have only one woman. Lacking the wealth of camels, they can afford only one."

Alexa had shrugged at the girl's simple logic, knowing then the utter futility of trying to make them understand her people. Such an existence was, to them, as alien as the very stars, and seemingly as distant. Limitless amounts of water in one's own dwelling? Water for drinking and bathing and laundering—impossible! they'd decide. Rivers and lakes of fresh water, and rolling meadows for the herds to graze at will year round without need to herd them from oasis to oasis— highly unlikely, a Christian fairy tale! Milk brought in pitchers to one's doorstep by a horsedrawn wagon, instead of milked from the goat or camel or sheep—unbelievable!

After a brief respite to catch their breath, the women had plagued her to teach them more of the strange *Englesy* customs, dances, and songs. Alexa had remembered then the clothing she'd brought with her from England, which had been recovered from the pack camels when she was abducted, but returned to her by the lady Kairee. They'd had the clothing brought from the Mist *serai* and passed another wild hour or two by dressing up in her stylish Victorian clothing, the woman of Malik ben-Azad's *hareem* screaming with amusement as they paraded about in Alexa's pantalets and corsets and sweeping gowns, teetered on her high-heeled, buttoned kid boots, or donned her leghorn straws or wide-brimmed hats with elegant osprey plumes, or bonnets with silk flowers, and admired their incongruous new looks in silver-backed hand mirrors. Afterward, they'd taken turns to have her dress their long black hair in ornate Victorian fashion with puffs and braids and swirls, and listened while she recited anything that came to mind that she thought would amuse or please them as she did so.

The moon had risen long since over the mountain ridges, and the stars were already peeping out one by one much later, when she'd bid them all a good night. Listening to the women still eagerly parroting her childhood's best-loved nursery rhymes and the poems of Tennyson in their sing-song, delightful English, she'd retired to Sharif's apartments. The strains of "London Bridge Is Falling Down" and the *hareem's* favorite, "Oranges and Lemons," had echoed over and over in her ears as she'd awaited her husband's coming to bed. But she'd quickly fallen asleep before he'd done so, and wakened, still alone, to this raging thirst and terrible weakness that made her bones and muscles feel as insubstantial as candy-floss.

She waited until she stopped trembling, then tried to get out of bed a second time. The earthenware flask of drinking water across the room drew her like a magnet with its thirst-quenching promise. She swung her legs over the side of the divan and stood, tottering a little, then took a first hesitant step, then another. How strange! The cool tiled floor felt like a soggy sponge under her feet, as if she were walking on quicksand! The feeling increased rather than lessened as she took two further steps, and reached out for the pitcher, set upon a low brass table beside a basket of fruit.

But as her fingers closed over the elegant handle, she realized she'd made a dreadful mistake. It wasn't a slender curve of pottery in her hand after all. It was the cool, slippery length of a little snake!

She froze, then snatched her hand away and stepped back, her eyes riveted on the cold, unwinking eye of the snake as it slithered over the edge of the pitcher, uncoiled across the table like an unraveling green ribbon, and looped its way down onto the floor, gliding smoothly toward her.

A movement caught the corner of her eye, and she saw that another had followed it, then another and another, until there were dozens of little snakes! She blinked and shook her head, unable to believe her eyes. Some of the snakes were—were cut and others uncut! Some were with two wives, others with four. Some wore straw hats and others were beplumed with feathers as they spilled from the pitcher to the table, wiggling and squirming and wriggling off it like maggots, before slipping down onto the tile. All of them were gaily waltzing and gliding and slithering toward her! Feeling the blood drain from about her mouth, she heard them all singing in little whispery voices as they came:

> "'Oranges and Lemons!' say the snakes of St. Clement's!
> 'I owe you five farthings,' say the snakes of St. Martins.
> 'When will you pay me?' say the snakes of Old Bailey.
> 'When I grow rich!' say the snakes of Shoreditch.
> Here comes the candle to light you to bed.
> And here comes the chopper, to chop off your head!
> Chip! Chop! Zerdaa—liii's—dead!'"

"Dead!" they lisped again softly.

She let out a moan of terror and backed away until she was pressed flat against the wall, trying to shrink into it, through it, babbling at them to stay away from her, for God's sake. . . .

But the snakes still followed, growing closer and closer, wriggling in a wormy, squiggly mess just inches from her bare feet. She choked on sobs of fear, shuddering with revulsion. Her wildly rolling eyes were almost popping from their sockets in her abject panic. She cold hear them hissing again now, like a thousand, thousand whispers which, taken together, made a deafening, sibilant shushing sound that roared in her ears:

> "All of us will drag you down,
> Pull you down,
> Tie you down!
> All of us will hold you down,
> Our fair lay-dee. . . !"

She flung her hands over her ears, yet couldn't block out the awful, breathless humming noise. And then she sensed a movement at her back, and saw that the walls and draperies behind her had dissolved. The gauzy hangings writhing in the draft had become snakes too; blue ones and silver ones and evil, slender black ones like shiny, slimy eels!

She was surrounded by serpents!

Everywhere.

Slithering.

Slimy.

The seething mass was all about, poisonous tongues flicking

375

back and forth like little forked whips, beads of venom clinging to them like tiny, nacreous pearls.

No way out!

No where to run!

None!

Oh, God oh Godohgod!

Another second and she'd be lost beneath them, buried by that seething mass, too terrified, too frozen to move. Then it would all be over. . . .

Over!

Sweat drenched her. Her bowels churned over. She heard a whimpering sound that went on and on, and dimly knew it was her own desperate crying. "Please!" she heard herself begging. "Please, I don't want to dance!"

Dance? She'd meant die, of course. She didn't want to die.

Suddenly, something clamped over her shoulder and she leaped with renewed terror, shrieking in alarm.

"Forgive me the lateness of the hour, *habibah*," came a deep voice she recognized as Sharif's.

Yet when she whirled around to face him, her heart leaping with relief, it was not Sharif who stood there. It was a giant silver-and-black cobra, speaking with her beloved's voice—a monstrosity straight from hell with its hood spread, ready to strike! The black eyes glittered like obsidian marbles as it hissed at her, "Come to bed, my dove, and I will warm you. See? Your little hand is cold."

"Sssee? Iss coold!" the voice hissed in her ear, cackling with smothered merriment. She struck blindly out at its head in a desperate attempt to escape the horror.

"Zerdali!" the cobra cried, and somehow it terrified her even more that it knew her name, and she struck out at it again—and again—and again, feeling snaky little bodies squashed under her bare toes as she battled this new enemy.

"Get awaay, *sheytàn!*" she screamed. "Don't touch mee!" Oh, God, Shariiif! Help me!"

She felt the coils of the cobra wind around her waist, squeezing tenderly as it dragged her hard against the cool, slippery darkness of its body. It lowered its head to hers, whispering, "What iss it, ssweet bride? What iss wrong?" and she knew, by the way its hood spread wider still, by the way its head lowered, then wavered slowly to and fro, that in another second it would strike her full upon the mouth, sink its fangs into her lips and spill its venom into her veins.

She swung back her fist and struck out at its glittering eyes with all the force she could summon, and to her relief the hooded monster recoiled in astonishment with a startled "Aaaggh!"

She wrenched free of its ghastly embrace and flew to the arched window, scrambling up onto the narrow sill. She'd throw herself through the window and escape! She'd jump out to freedom, she thought frantically—do anything to escape that—that hideous monstrosity with her dear Sharif's caressing voice!

But a hairbreadth before she would have jumped, the cobra coils clamped around her again, looping about her wrists, then her waist, encircling her hips and legs, and finally taking all of her up in another sinuous embrace.

"May I have thiss waltzzzz?" it asked, and she screamed one last time, shrieking, "Shaaa-Shaaaaa! Shaaa-Shaaaaa!" over and over again.

A moment later, something blunt and hard clipped her beneath the jaw, and she was plummeted into a starry well, which in seconds faded to the velvet black of nothingness. . . .

"By the Prophet, look at that awful bruise!" Kairee scolded. "Did you have to hit her so hard, my nephew?"

"If I had not, she'd have escaped me again and tried to hurl herself from the window!" Sharif growled, his expression dark and brooding in his anxiety, his eyes and raven-black brows turbulent as a coming storm.

Alexa lay on the divan, her golden-chestnut hair spread across the pillow, her face pale but for a livid purple bruise on her jaw. She tossed her head restlessly to and fro, all the while muttering and shrieking incoherently. Her wrists and ankles had been tied to keep her from harming herself, and Sharif, looking down at her, had never felt so helpless, nor so angered by the injustice of Kismet. What was it that had driven his beloved to this madness? What could it be? he wondered for the hundredth time, but he could think of no answer.

He'd retired to his apartments, ready to offer Zerdali his apologies for the lateness of the hour, eagerly anticipating whiling the night away with her in passionate loveplay. Instead, he'd discovered her cowering against the wall, tearing at her hair like a madwoman and screaming that there were snakes, snakes everywhere.

He'd touched her shoulder and asked her gently what was wrong, but she'd recoiled in horror when she looked into his face, before striking out at him like a wildcat and screaming *"Sheytàn!"*—which was the Arabic for Satan—at the top of her lungs! The black eye he now sported was ample proof—if any had been necessary, he thought ruefully—that she'd grown tremendously strong in her terror. So strong, *ewellah,* he'd doubted he could stop her from leaping from the window and taking her own life, if she were determined to do so. He'd been forced to knock her out until he could summon one of his guards to help restrain her.

He paced back and forth like a caged leopard, while in one corner of his chamber Fatima hovered, wringing her hands and weeping. The lady Kairee and Hakim, the physician, together leaned over the bed to examine the girl.

At last, after what seemed like an eternity, Hakim came to him, his eyes grave above his long white beard.

"My lord, we can find no sign of a snakebite upon the lady Zerdali's body, nor indeed any injury that might have caused her—strangeness. It is my suspicion now that her hallucinations are a result of some illness which has temporarily affected her reason, or that—" Hakim paused, as if uncertain, or perhaps reluctant to continue.

"Or what? Go on!" Sharif snapped impatiently. "Get on with it!"

"Or that the illness itself is of the mind, sir."

"I see. And if it is?"

Hakim shrugged uncomfortably. "At this time, far more is known of the sicknesses of the body than of the mind, alas, my lord. If I were you, I would pray to Allah that it is a sickness of the body, and that once her body is healed, her mind will relinquish its nightmare fantasies also."

"Pah! What nonsense! It is no sickness that ails my poor dove," Fatima heatedly cut in from across the room. "Her sickness is the work of that Inandan slut's *tezma*, her gift of the evil eye! Did you find any mark upon her, Master Hakim?"

"Only a tiny puncture or two on her palm, as if the lady had poked herself with a sewing needle. Other than that, her body is unmarked."

"There! You see? Not a mark! And I know she's not been poisoned, for she's eaten and drunk nothing that I've not first tasted, and I am quite well. Tell me, does her sickness resemble any you've seen before?"

"So far, no, I must confess it does not," Hakim admitted with obvious reluctance, frowning. "But I shall consult my writings again immediately. Perhaps it is a rare Christian disease—one I've never had cause to diagnose before in al-Azadel?"

"Or perhaps it really is magic, eh, Master Hakim?" Fatima crowed. "Perhaps I'm right and you're wrong, and it's the Inandan's evilness and jealousy at work here? Perhaps she's cast her *tezma* upon my Zerdali, and driven her out of her mind! Admit it—you don't know what's wrong with her, do you?" Fatima accused, and triumphantly saw the learned man shake his head. "So, my lord," Fatima demanded, whirling upon Sharif, "what are you going to do about that Raisha, eh?"

"Until we discover what is wrong with my wife, and ascertain what caused her to become this way, I shall do nothing," Sharif decided, doing his utmost to keep a cool head and his reason despite Fatima's burning eyes and heated urgings for action, coupled with his own escalating fear for Zerdali's life and sanity. "But, Fatima, just to be on the safe side, only you and my lady aunt will attend my wife. Neither Raisha nor any other is to be permitted entry to my apartments until, Allah willing, my wife is recovered once more! Is that understood?"

"It is understood, my lord," Fatima agreed. "I only pray that it's not too late for such an order to do my poor little dove any good!"

Ignoring Sharif's darkling expression, she waddled across to the divan, and took up her place at Alexa's side. She told herself silently that no matter what, not even should Sharif order her to do so, she would not leave her Zerdali until she was well again, that she would pray night and day for her complete recovery. And, just to be on the safe side, she slipped one of her most powerful amulets—a bead of blood-red carnelian, famed for restoring the health of women—into bed beside the girl. Prayers were quite good enough for diseases, but magic, she was firmly convinced, was best fought with even stronger magic!

Chapter Twenty-Seven

"By your leave, sir, the Bedouin girl Muriel bat-Hussein wishes to speak with you," Akli, Sharif's body servant announced with a respectful bow.

"Did I not give orders that I wished to see no one?" Sharif growled, his dark eyes snapping as he glared at the nervous man.

"*Ewellah,* master, I told her, but the girl was most insistent! She said she must see you, and would sit at your doorway until you agreed to do so."

"Did she, by the Prophet!" Sharif thundered, hurling aside the papers he'd been sifting through. "If you cannot take care of one stubborn little *marra,* then it looks as if I'll have to show you how it's done, *wellah!*"

So saying, Sharif strode across his chamber and down the long corridor, his boots rapping out an ominous tattoo on the tiled floor as he went.

Akli trailed after him, wringing his hands. The Imochagh nobles prided themselves on their ability to control and conceal their emotions, but as Akli had discovered before, to his ill fortune, an Imochagh warrior whose anger was so great it could no longer be contained at will was a terrible sight to behold! The farther one could retreat from it, the better, to his thinking. He would not have traded places with the Bedouin maid in that moment for a sultan's purse. . . .

"What is the meaning of this, girl?" Sharif demanded in thundering tones, thrusting aside the two guards who stood stiffly at attention on either side of the doorway to his apartments. "Be off with you to the *hareem,* before I have you removed by force!''

Muriel rose from her knees and turned to face him, and Akli saw that her large doe-eyes were red and swollen with tears, her lower lip aquiver. Sharif saw it too.

"Please, my lord, I won't go, not until you hear me out!" Muriel began bravely. "I have to talk with you about Zerdali— I mean, about your lady wife, Zerdali! She—she's my only friend here in al-Azadel, you see, and I—I heard that she's been taken very ill. Please, my lord, forgive me my forwardness in demanding to speak with you, but I have a suggestion that might help!"

To Akli's surprise, his master's shoulders slumped. His rigid stance softened. Akli shook his head in disgust. Trust a pretty woman and a sprinkling of tears, he thought, to soften even the brimming fury of al-Azim! No doubt the al-Tabor leaders would have welcomed such a charming woman as she to plead prettily for their lives that morning when al-Azim, despite having his head and chest tightly bandaged, had stood in the palace courtyard and coolly and unemotionally ordered the executioner to lop off their heads, and followed it up by returning them to their chieftain, Tabor, in a basket! Of course, those jackals had deserved no less a punishment, seeing as how six of Sharif's closest companions had been slain the night before, but still . . .

". . . you to see refreshments brought for the lady Muriel and have her mother awakened," Sharif was saying. "I would not wish the lady's reputation compromised in any way."

"At once, my lord!" Akli promised, catching the gist of his lord's instructions to him, and he scuttled off to do his master's bidding.

Sharif gently took Muriel's arm and led her down the corridor to his bedchamber, where Fatima still kept vigil beside her unconscious mistress. She would serve as an acceptable chaperone to the unwed girl until Noura, her mother, arrived to do so. Muriel at once pulled away from Sharif and ran to the divan, where she stood looking down at Zerdali with an anguished expression.

"Oh, poor Zerdali!" she whispered, blinking back tears as

she took in the uncannily still figure. "I'd wanted so badly for us to be friends, but it was so hard for us to talk together, since I can speak no English and Zerdali has learned only the Tamahaq tongue and little Arabic. Before I knew it, Raisha was her closest friend, and she had no time for me. I've seen so little of Zerdali since the lady Kairee gave my mother and my aunt and me separate apartments. Oh, the rooms are lovely, I don't mean to sound ungrateful, and I know she meant only to honor us, but . . ." She shrugged.

"But you've been lonely? Ah, little one, I understand. *Ewellah,* that Raisha!" Fatima commiserated with a grimace, patting the Bedouin girl's shoulder. "I saw how it was, how that one tried from the first to keep Zerdali from growing close to you, that jealous witch! But you mustn't be upset or resentful toward my mistress. The poor dove is cursed with a soft heart. I tried to warn her, but she quite wrongly felt sorry for the wretched Inandan because she was a widow, and a barren one, with few prospects for finding herself a decent husband or ever bearing a babe. I think too that my lady forgave her much of her spitefulness because she knew how Raisha craved our lord's attention and love, and it was denied her. My lady, forgive me, has more heart and pity in it than sound common sense! The silly girl felt sorry for Raisha, she did, and just look what her pity and compassion have done for her now!" Nothing could convince Fatima that she was wrong about Raisha.

"She is no better?"

"Earlier she was screaming and laughing like a madwoman and trying to escape her restraints. Now, she just lies there as if dead, without moving or speaking at all. I don't know which one is worse, I'm sure!" Tears filled Fatima's eyes.

"Can Master Hakim do nothing to help her?" Muriel glanced across at Sharif, who was listening to the two women's exchange. "He was very good to me when I came here." She reddened and lowered her eyes, adding in a whisper for Fatima's ears alone, "He saw to it that I was given medicine to prevent a babe from starting after the—the *Englesy* attacked me."

"Ah, yes, he is a learned doctor, but he's never attended a sickness such as this one before in al-Azadel."

"Then perhaps another physician could be summoned—one who's seen many different sicknesses, in many different lands?" the girl suggested eagerly.

"Perhaps. But where would I find such a doctor?" Sharif demanded bitterly. "The nearest city is four days' hard riding distant. My wife could die long before I found one in Sidi-bel-Abbes and brought him back here!"

"That's what I came to tell you, sir!" Muriel cried. "For the past two days, there has been a wonderful doctor-*hakim* in the city—one who travels from village to village and camp to camp, curing the ills of all he meets. Yesterday, he was in the bazaar with his box of *dawwa,* medicines. He had a flask of magical ointment which he swears is more powerful than any written spell or amulet for curing the sores that cause blindness—even more powerful than the words of the Blessed Koran read over the afflicted! One of the menfolk told me this same black doctor-*hakim* had cured his brother a year ago, and that he could now see again. Oh, please, my lord, surely this man can do something for your poor lady."

"Where is he now?" Sharif demanded, fresh hope filling him.

"Alas! I fear he left the city this morning, sir—that is why I told your servant I must speak with you at once! Perhaps it is still not too late. Perhaps you can yet overtake him and ask him to return here."

"If it will save my beloved's life, I will ask first—and bring him back here regardless of whether he agrees or nay!" Sharif threatened grimly. "Bound hand and foot, if needs be! Tell me, where was this man headed?"

"They say to the villages south of here. Exactly where, I don't know."

"If he can be found, then I will find him!" Sharif vowed, already moving to the door. He was eager to be gone without a moment's delay, now that he had a direction to move in, a chance—however slim—that he could find the one man who might be able to cure his bride. Anything was better than

384

inactivity; anything preferable to simply sitting there and watching Zerdali sleep a sleep so deep, so profound, it was akin to death, and suffering the torment of knowing he was helpless to bring her back from the brink!

True to his word, he was riding south less than an hour later with Aswad thundering beneath him, leading a spare mount behind.

None but a Tuareg, whose skills as trackers are legendary even amongst the desert peoples, could have followed the trail Sharif followed, and have done so by night. No man but one heartsick and determined to save the life of his beloved would even have tried such a difficult task!

The gray wolves that prowled the craggy mountain passes and the empty *sahel* howled at the moon as he thundered past them, his cloak whipped about him as he rode, for they sensed the melancholy in the man's soul, and the melancholy in their own howled in compassion.

In the bright moonlight that bathed the sugary sand hills, he read the signs left behind by those who had passed, and in doing so learned many of their secrets. Two men, he estimated, with four camels, headed south as Muriel had said. Two men who traveled in a leisurely fashion, one heavy and very tall, the other lighter on his feet—a boy, perhaps? The heavy man was a lover of *tittun*, Turkish tobacco, and smoked it in a pipe of clay. One of the camels was with young, the remainder all young, healthy beasts. Two were heavily laden. All this the signs told him, and more, but the one question he desired answered above all others must remain a mystery until he had found the doctor-*hakim* and brought him back to al-Azadel: could he save Zerdali's life? No sign could tell him that!

As he rode, he tried to imagine his life without Zerdali, but could not. In the short while since she had come to him, everything had changed! The past seemed like a vague dream, dimly remembered in the morning, lacking shape and substance. It was as if his life had only truly begun that night at the oasis of Yasmeen, when he had turned to see her cresting

385

the dune, and known that his dreams had been fulfilled. He could no sooner bear to imagine his life without her than he could imagine losing an arm or a leg, though he knew the loss of a limb would have been by far the easier to accept. When had she become so vital to his existence? he wondered. When had she become so dangerously important in his life? Dangerously? he asked himself. *Ewellah,* dangerously, for it was dangerous for a leader of men—one who was responsible for the lives and welfare of so many others as was he—to place the life of one woman above them all. If it should come to a choice and he were forced to choose between her life or the safety of his people, how could he bring himself to make the choice that his birth, as the son of Malik ben-Azad, *Amir* of al-Mamlaka al-Azadel, compelled him to make? Truly, love was a complex matter, as much a curse as a blessing, as bitter as it was sweet! Please Allah, such a decision would never have to be made, and he would never have to live with the choice he finally made. . . .

Dawn was lightening the sky with mauve and sulphur in the east when he saw a single goatskin tent, silhouetted dark atop the grayed sands of a flat plain ahead of him, and knew he had found the ones he sought. Four camels were crouched off to one side. Two men sat cross-legged before a fire, one a hulking great fellow as black as the night sky, the other a slimmer lad. The aroma of rich, dark coffee floated across the plain on the cool morning air and teased his nostrils.

"A traveler comes!" Sharif called out to announce himself as he drew closer, signifying he came with peaceful intentions. "I beg your protection, and the hospitality of your camp, my friends and brothers." Such was the custom of the desert.

"Whatever we have is yours!" the towering black man invited in a deep, gravelly voice, rising to his feet. "Come, get down from your horse and share with us, Brother!"

Sharif rode Aswad closer to the camp and dismounted, leaving the horse behind as he strode across the sand to the tent. There was no need to tether the animals. Both had been raised by his hand and no other's, and they would not wander off.

"*La Bes,* Master Hannibal!" Sharif greeted, fists balled on his hips, his booted feet planted apart. In his swirling indigo cloak and concealing *tagilmust,* he cut a formidable, mysterious figure. "The blessings of Allah be upon you, and peace always!"

"Likewise to you, my lord Sharif al-Azim!" the enormous black man rejoined, and he laughed, making a deep, rumbling sound as rich and dark as the coffee he sipped as Sharif's eyebrows raised upward in surprise.

"How is it you know my name?" he asked suspiciously.

Each word richly pronounced, the black man answered, "Who else but a chieftain or a highborn noble of the Imochagh would swagger so arrogantly into my camp, as if it were his right to do so? A man's walk tells one who watches carefully a great deal about that man. Your walk told me you were born and raised to be a leader of men, to give orders, rather than receive them. The direction from which you came suggested you were from al-Azadel. The rest was merely guesswork, my young lord—and apparently good guesswork, too!"

Abashed, Sharif grimaced. The last thing he'd intended was to irritate the man in any way! With unaccustomed humility, he gritted his teeth and asked, "Forgive me if I seemed arrogant, doctor-*hakim.* Believe me, that was not my intent!"

"I know," Hannibal acknowledged amiably. "An arrogant manner need not always imply an arrogant nature!" The black man grinned and winked, and his chocolate-brown eyes twinkled. "You see, a man's walk can also be as misleading as it is revealing! I have seen beggars strut, when the mood takes them—and sultans shuffle along like beggars! Now, sit down, young master, and over the cup of coffee my servant will pour for you, you can tell me how my physician's skills may be of service to you. Certainly no minor matter sent you galloping after me, eh? Who is ailing, al-Azim? Your worthy father? No, no, he was in fine health yesterday. Your son, then? Ah, but you are too recently wed, I understand, to have been so blessed! Then who?"

"It is my wife—my bride, the lady Zerdali! She is the one who needs your skills," Sharif managed to grind out, and with utmost difficulty he told the man everything. "You will return with me to al-Azadel at once!" he ended, and the arrogance was there, again, but in his tone this time. "Cure my bride, and you will have all the *tittun* you could smoke in a lifetime and more!"

It was Hannibal's turn to raise his grizzled eyebrows, and raise them he did!

Sharif grinned. "*Wellah*, you are not the only one who can read a man well, Master Hannibal!" he declared. "I knew long before I reached you that you were a giant, and that a lad rode with you. And of your four camels, one of whom is carrying a calf, is she not?"

The black man slapped his thigh and rumbled with laughter that burbled up from between his fleshy lips like an escaping rumble of thunder. "I have a feeling that a refusal on my part would not be accepted, would it, al-Azim?" he said with utmost accuracy. "And so, I agree—since it seems the healthier of my two choices!"

"I would prefer that you came with me willingly," Sharif said uncomfortably. "But if not—" He shrugged expressively. "Alas, you would leave me little choice but to—persuade— you otherwise. Zerdali is my life, my soul!"

"I can understand why you prefer I should go of my own accord," Hannibal acknowledged. "After all, a doctor who is hostile to his patient would hardly make for the best of situations, now would it? Calm yourself, young lord, and drink more coffee while I prepare my box of medicines. I'll come with you of my own free will, and I'll do everything I can for your lady, I promise you. The lad will remain here, to guard my camp. Since speed is of the essence, I will ride one of your mounts, rather than my camel—that is, if you think such a little horse can carry a great big fellow like me."

"Were I to ask it of him, Aswad would carry two your size, sir!" Sharif said stiffly and with obvious pride in his horseflesh.

"Then that black brute must not be a horse at all, but an elephant!" Hannibal bantered. "My namesake was very fond of elephants, you know," he added, and with a wink at Sharif, he went to prepare his box.

"Poison!" Hannibal pronounced solemnly after he'd completed his examination of the woman late that same afternoon. "Your wife's been poisoned, al-Azim!"

They had ridden without stopping, arriving back at the palace less than an hour before. Hannibal had wasted no time. After washing the dust from his body and changing his colorful robe for a fresh one, he'd insisted on examining his patient without further delay.

"Impossible!" Fatima argued, jumping to her feet. "Nothing passed my lady's lips that I did not taste, and I am well."

"True, O Voluptuous Brown-Eyed One, true," the doctor agreed, and to Sharif's surprise, Fatima blushed at his outrageous compliments. "But there are other methods for poisons to enter the body than by mouth. See here?" Hannibal turned Alexa's limp hand over, and indicated the two small, reddened swellings in her palm. "Here it was the poison gained entry. And a virulent one it must have been too, for such a little drop or two to cause such sickness."

"My poor lamb pricked herself on the rose thorns," Fatima protested, disappointed that this marvelous creature, who appeared more magician than learned doctor in his flowing robes of crimson and purple, could pose such an unlikely theory.

"Rose thorns?" Hannibal echoed thoughtfully. "Ah, yes, my plump little pigeon, it's quite possible, if the thorns had been dipped in the poison! A most clever strategy too, if the poisoner was in no great hurry to end his victim's life. He had to accept the possibility of failure and be certain he'd be afforded the opportunity to try again if this attempt failed, of course. To my reckoning, such a willingness to fail and try again would indicate a person who has ready access to the lady—as well as nerves of steel and the disposition of a cat, which enjoys toying with its prey!"

"I still say it's impossible!" Fatima protested. "The roses were a gift to my lady from our lord Sharif here, picked from the gardens of his friend Kahlil. Surely you cannot mean that it was one of them who wished to harm Zerdali?"

"For the moment, the identity of the poisoner is unimportant," Sharif cut in brusquely. "I would know if you can help my wife or no, Hannibal?"

Hannibal rested his elbow in one palm and tugged thoughtfully on his chin. "You say she had visions before this deep sleep came on her?"

"She cried that there were snakes everywhere, and tried to fling herself from the window to escape them!"

"Then the poison is a powerful vision-inducing drug— perhaps similar to that which the dervishes use to induce holy visions. Maybe a distillation of the potent poison found in toadstools. *Ewellah,* even a small dose in one unaccustomed to it, as is your lovely lady here, would have powerful consequences! But, Allah willing, yes, al-Azim, I believe she has a chance, and a good one. She is young and healthy, and the secret lies not in my skill or powders, but in allowing the body to heal itself. If my suspicions prove correct, she will suffer trembling fits, fevers, and other symptoms before taking the road to recovery. With your permission, I will treat each stage as it occurs, and to the best of my ability. The rest will be up to her."

"You have my permission, and anything else you might need."

"Good. Then you will leave me and this lovely vision of Bedouin beauty alone here. The two of us are more than sufficient to tend your lady—and I confess, I find it difficult to concentrate on my patient with you, my young lord, pacing back and forth with bared teeth, like a hungry tiger. Go, and leave this *houri* and myself to our work!" He chucked plump Fatima beneath the chin and rolled his great, chocolate-brown eyes lasciviously, so that the whites showed stark against the glistening ebony of his skin. Fatima almost swooned.

Tight-lipped, Sharif nodded. "Very well. But you will call on me if there is any change?"

"At once, young lord, at once!"

He turned on his heel and left the chamber, going directly to the Mist *serai* and entering his wife's private quarters without announcing himself. The suspicions Hannibal had voiced nagged at him and he almost expected to find the roses gone, all traces of their sinister secrets vanished! But no, the flame-colored roses he'd picked from the gardens of Kahlil were still there. The perfume clung heavily in the sun-warmed room. The opened buds made a glorious splash of color against the misty rose of the gauze hangings behind them. He went straight way to them, ignoring Raisha, who slept on an unrolled rug upon the floor.

Leaning down, he plucked one of the long-stemmed blossoms from the brass vase in which they'd been arranged, and inspected first the loveliness of the blossom, and then the wicked thorns that jutted from the stem. There was no visible trace of any poison, but then, what had he expected to find? Hannibal had said the poisoner was skilled at his craft, had he not?

He stared into the flame-colored blossoms, lost in thought as he casually twirled the rose stem between his fingers. He knew Kahlil would never have sought to harm his bride. And of course, he'd not done so himself. That left only one other possibility, and it was a possibility he did not want to consider. Selim had been entrusted to carry the roses to the palace and see them taken to Zerdali's apartments. He alone had had the opportunity to play the poisoner! It had been Selim too, he recalled belatedly, who'd sounded the alarm when the al-Tabor tried to infiltrate the city and attack. An act of courage and quick thinking—or a clever ploy to draw suspicion from himself, a traitor to the al-Malik?

The astrologer Maimun's words came back to him then, as clear as the crystal notes of a bell. *"Deceit and deception will flourish like wild roses in the garden of trust, and jealousy will poison their sharpest thorns and wither their brightest blossoms. It will be a time when a gift of beauty might harbor death in its perfumed bosom, so beware, young master, beware!"*

Had Maimun ever imagined that his prophecy would be translated so literally into action? he wondered. His "gift of love" had indeed harbored death in its rose-perfumed bosom, and all but withered the "brightest blossom" in his garden of trust, the woman he loved. Savagely, he tore the velvety petals

391

from the rose and flung them aside in a shower of flame-colored fragments, crushing the thorny stem in his clenched fist as anger rose through him anew. Selim would answer to him for his treachery, he swore, answer with his very life—

"My lord Sharif, take care!" cried a voice.

Startled from the red haze of fury into which he'd fallen, his head jerked up, and he saw Raisha standing there before him, disheveled and flushed from sleep.

"What?" he demanded.

"Be-be careful, my lord. The—the rose!"

His ebony eyes crackled and narrowed as she padded barefoot across the floor to his side and gently uncurled his clenched fingers from about the mangled stem, taking the ruined blossom from him. His hand snaked out to grip her wrist, squeezing it so tightly she yelped in pain. "What about the rose?" he demanded harshly. "What do you know of it?"

"O-only that the thorns are sharp, s-sir, and I—I would not wish you t-to prick yourself!" she panted, tears welling in her eyes. He stared at her long and hard, searching those cinnamon pools for some proof that she lied, yet she gazed unflinchingly back at him, and his grip gradually slackened and the blazing fury in his ebony eyes dimmed.

"My poor, poor master!" she whispered, biting her lower lip. "I know how worried you must be about your lady wife! Perhaps, in some small way, Raisha could make you forget your fears for an hour or two, yes?" She slipped the loose sleeping robe she wore down off her shoulders. It fell to the tile with a whisper of silk, and she stood before him naked, her tousled hair streaming down over her hard-pointed breasts, the brown nipples large and swollen. She held out her arms to him, offering her body to his need. "I am yours, Sharif, for whatever purpose you might need me," she whispered huskily, taking a step closer to him so that the spicy fragrance of her warm flesh filled his nostrils. She rubbed her bare, rounded hips up against him, and lightly ran her fingertips down his chest to the swelling hardness that her naked beauty had aroused. "Take me," she purred silkily, "and forget your heartache in Raisha's arms."

In his fatigued and anxious state, he was very vulnerable, as

392

she'd shrewdly guessed. Her offer of the moment's oblivion her body could provide him with tempted him. He took a step toward her, and then halted, seeing suddenly another's lovely green eyes dark with reproach and hurt in place of her cinnamon ones; a milk-white body he adored in place of the dusky-gold before him. He swallowed and drew back. How could he face Zerdali ever again, knowing he had betrayed her while she hovered close to death? Only the depth of his fears could have driven him so close to betraying her! He wet his dry lips and curtly shook his head in refusal of Raisha's offer. "My thanks, but no," he said coldly, and turned and left her standing there, naked and rejected.

She stared after him with a look of such murderous jealousy, it contorted her pretty face to a grotesque mask. She clenched her fists and lashed out at the vase, scattering water and flame-colored flowers everywhere across the blue-tiled floor. So, the black doctor-*hakim* that simpering Muriel had told Sharif about must have suspected the rose thorns were poisoned! Sharif's strange behavior with the roses certainly revealed he'd been told something! There was every chance, then, that with a skilled physician to attend her, Zerdali would recover, curse her! But the next time—! By Allah, the next time she'd not be so fortunate!

For two more days and nights, Alexa's life hung in the balance. As Hannibal had predicted, she next fell victim to violent tremors that wracked her poor body, which he treated with a powerful sedative in order to lessen their severity. When she later thrashed in the throes of a fever, he and Fatima worked side by side to bathe the sweat from her body with cool water, and lower it. Little by little, each obstacle was overcome, until her sleep grew lighter, more approaching a normal sleep, and Sharif's anxiety lifted. At last, she woke and recognized him, smiled sleepily and drifted back into slumber, her breathing regular and even, her body blessedly still.

Soon, Hannibal promised with a salacious wink, the chestnut-haired beauty would be recovered sufficiently well to fill Sharif's arms once more, adding wickedly, "Although your bride is fair indeed, al-Azim, I confess that for myself such a slender woman would hardly serve to fill *my* empty arms, alas, no! I find myself enraptured by much plumper women, ones whose form is far more generously rounded!" He'd described a curvaceous silhouette in the air with his hands. "Why would a wise man nibble upon a skinny little sparrow to satisfy his hunger, when a plump, full-breasted pigeon could offer him a veritable feast, eh? " And with this, he'd given poor, blushing Fatima such a hungry, burning glance, Sharif had been hard put to smother the roar of laughter that welled up from inside him, as much from amusement as his newfound relief.

"Friend Hannibal," he'd declared, clapping the huge black man companionably across the back, "I owe you far more than I can ever hope to repay for saving my Zerdali's life! The tobacco I promised you in return for your doctor's services has been readied for your departure. Other gifts to show my gratitude have been loaded onto a camel as well. Both beast and gifts are yours. But unfortunately, the 'plump pigeon' you speak of has a mind of her own, and is not mine to offer you! If there is some favor that you wish of Fatima, you must ask her yourself, my friend. The choice is hers to make."

"I haven't seen much of Fatima these past two days, have you?" Alexa observed, snuggling into Sharif's arms a few nights later. "I wonder where she's been, and what's keeping her so busy?"

"She had little sleep when you were ill, *habibah*," Sharif answered casually, hiding a grin. "Don't begrudge her her rest now."

"Then she's sleeping?" Alexa sounded disappointed, he thought.

"What else would she be doing, a woman of her age and a widow?"

Alexa giggled. "Oh, nothing, I suppose. But—I was so hoping she and Hannibal might—well, you know." She blushed. "After all, he did seem to like her quite well, and once, when I woke up, he was chasing her around and around the chamber, and tickling her each time he caught up with her!

394

And do you know, Sharif, Fatima seemed to be enjoying it, and letting him catch her!"

"Then perhaps she's not sleeping after all, and that is why Master Hannibal's camel still awaits his departure two full days and nights after it was first laden! Perhaps Fatima and her doctor-*hakim* are doing just as we are doing, *ewellah?*"

She sighed and lay back, her fingers drifting through his hair as he kissed her throat and nuzzled at her breasts, playfully teasing the nipples with his hot lips and tongue until they glistened damply in the lamplight. He ran his hand lightly down over her body in a fleeting caress that encompassed her hips, murmuring critically, "Perhaps Hannibal was right after all! Compared to you, my skinny little morsel, Fatima is a plump treat indeed! Your illness has left you thinner than I like my women. After all, a woman without curves is like a spavined horse—you may still ride it, but the ride is all bumps and bones—!"

"You brute!" she shrieked, and wriggled away from him, snatching up a pillow and thumping it down across his head.

"How dare you compare me to—to a spavined horse, or any horse, for that matter! 'Bumps and bones' indeed! There'll be no 'riding' for you tonight, my lord! Take that—and that—instead!"

"Enough!" he growled, laughing as he fought her for the pillow. "How can I play at pillow fights when I'm yet hard with lust?" He pulled harder at the pillow, trying to tear it from her and avoid her pummelings at the same time, but she refused to relinquish her weapon and pulled back. The inevitable happened. The pillow split, and feathers showered everywhere!

"It's snowing!" she cried, her eyes sparkling like emeralds as feathers drifted down about them.

"Maybe it is, but I'll keep you warm, *habibah!*" he vowed, and dove for her, tackling her by the waist and rolling her smoothly beneath him in one lithe move. She was giggling helplessly. "Open to me, sweetheart!" he rasped thickly, nudging his knee between her thighs to part them. "If al-Azim must be cursed with a skinny wife, perhaps he can fatten her up by filling her with a babe!"

"You're disgusting!" she accused, parting her thighs eagerly nonetheless to permit him entry, and gathering him in against her breasts. His lips sought out her ear as he slid deep inside her welcoming heat, raising goose bumps all over her as his tongue-tip flicked over the shell-like whorls, and his hips rocked back and forth to pleasure her. "Mmmm, yes, you're utterly, deliciously disgusting!" she whispered against his cheek with a bliss-filled sigh. "Ah, yes, oh, yes, that's it! Don't stop! Just like that . . . mmm, lovely, lovely . . . !"

"You're a witch! A wanton, delicious, seductive witch!" he rasped, matching his powerful thrusts to his words.

"I know!" she teased smugly. "Hannibal taught me a spell that I slipped into your coffee—one guaranteed to make you lust after me forever, and never tire!"

"Never tire? By Allah, I shall be old before my time, then!" he swore, and bit her lip and worried at it like a playful pup, growling as he swiveled his hips to drive her to sweet madness. "Will you still love me then, *habibah,* when I'm a toothless white-beard, doddering upon my staff?"

"Certainly not!" she replied airily. "I'll find myself another desert prince—one who can do more with his staff than lean upon it!"

"Why, you she-demon!" he roared. "You faithless *houri!* Take that, and this too, *ewellah,* and say again that you'll betray al-Azim!"

Their lovemaking, too lusty and too long denied, was made even more urgent by the bitter knowledge that Zerdali had almost lost her life, that he had almost lost her. They coupled energetically and swiftly, with little tenderness or time taken for finesse, caught up in a heady lust that cried out for fulfillment. Both speedily reached an explosive, noisy release that was mutually satisfying, and left them drained and shuddering. Their outrageous teasing had served a dual purpose: on the one hand, it had provided a means for both of them to hide the true strain they'd undergone those past few days of their lives, and on the other it had given them the opportunity to vent any lingering anxieties in laughter.

"Did I hurt you?" he asked tenderly later, winding a tendril of her hair about his finger. "I forgot that you're still not strong yet."

She shook her head. "Of course not—it was wonderful!" She lay on her left side, her head cradled upon his chest, tracing an idle finger across his chest in circles. Her eyes were heavy-lidded with languor, and she stifled a huge yawn.

"Did I tell you that I had Selim brought before me, and that he swore he was innocent?"

"Well, of course he did! We both know Selim wouldn't do anything to hurt me, although our first 'meeting' gave him ample reason to dislike me! You saw how the men laughed when he couldn't catch me, remember? But he thinks too highly of you to want to harm me."

"He said he stopped at Raisha's house on the way home from Kahlil's garden, and left the roses by her doorstep. He says anyone could have tampered with them while he and Raisha were together."

"She mentioned that afternoon that he'd cornered her on the street," Alexa remembered. "It must have been then."

Sharif said nothing, although Selim had implied he'd done far more than corner Raisha! The truth of it was, lusty young Selim had eagerly accepted an invitation to join the Inandan wench on her mat upon the rooftop, and in the process, two or more hours had drifted by before Selim had remembered his lord's gift for the lady Zerdali. Two or more hours in which anyone could have dipped the rose thorns in poison . . . To test his truthfulness, Sharif had employed the age-old method of having the lad place his hand in a bag of flour. Liars had something to fear, and accordingly their bodies betrayed them by sweating, and the flour adhered to the film of sweat. But when he'd withdrawn it, Selim's palm had been dry and uncaked with flour, proof enough for Sharif that he told the truth. And so, he'd grown no closer to unmasking the traitor within al-Azadel than before! He had, however, taken Fatima's suspicions to heart and rid the palace of Raisha once and for all, replacing her with the girl Muriel, who would henceforth act as his wife's companion, a change that appeared to be working very well. Fatima, for all her superstitious nonsense and dislike of the Inandan wench, was not one to form such a hatred without cause. If instinct warned her that Raisha's jealousy was a threat to her mistress, then Sharif felt better knowing she was not close to his Zerdali day in and day out. He couldn't help remembering the horrified expression on her face that day when she'd awakened to find him crushing the rose in his fists. A simple reluctance to see him pierced by its thorns, as she'd smoothly implied, or fear of some far greater hurt that only the poisoner could possibly have known of . . . ?

Chapter Twenty-Eight

"You must return to your apartments at once, little one!" Fatima urged, pouncing upon Alexa like a plump cat upon a mouse when she returned to the palace after visiting the bazaar. "Aiee! I searched every nook and cranny of the bazaar for you and Muriel! I was frantic when I could not find you! What is Sharif thinking of, to permit you so much freedom when your life may be in danger yet again!"

"What danger?" Alexa demanded calmly, swinging abruptly about to face her. "Fatima, I only went to the bazaar, and I didn't go alone, as I promised. I just can't stay penned up here between these four walls, day in and day out!" She grimaced. "Sometimes, I feel like I'm under a magnifying glass, I really do, what with you and Kairee and Sharif watching over me all the time! I know you have my best interests at heart, but it's stifling! Believe me, Fatima, I'm not a delicate hothouse flower that you have to pamper and see to every five minutes anymore! I'm a grown woman, and I can take care of myself." She turned to the serving girl carrying her purchases as she swept into the Mist *serai*, Fatima toddling along behind her. "Just leave everything on the divan for now, Leila, and you may go. I'll see to them later. By the way, Fatima, we saw Raisha in the bazaar, with Selim! She was trying to sweet-talk him into buying her a shawl from Kashmir, but I thought he seemed quite anxious to be rid of her. The interesting thing was that Muriel seemed a little—oh, jealous and put out, I suppose I'd have to say! I do believe Muriel likes him—and not just as a cousin—far more than she'll admit!"

"Hummph. And did that know-it-all Inandan witch not

somehow find a way to tell you the bad news?" Fatima demanded.

"What bad news?"

"That Kadar ben-Selim returned this morning to al-Azadel!"

"What?" Alexa's face had been flushed from her excursion, but now she paled. She bit her lip anxiously, her gossip forgotten. "Oh, Fatima, what of my brother? Did Kadar find him? Did he—is Keene dead? Oh, quickly, tell me what you know! Everything!" she insisted, tossing her purchases to the divan and grasping the plump woman by the upper arms. Since Hannibal's departure two weeks ago, Fatima had been quite impossible, either overly solicitous, as grumpy as a bear, or brooding and silent! The urge to shake her in an attempt to wring some speedy answers out of her now was enormous.

"No, no, he didn't find him! I talked with some of his men, and they told me—" Fatima wet her lips, nervous, and fingered the amulet at her neck. "They told me that half their number are now convinced the *Englesy* is a *sheytàn*, a devil, part-man and part-demon, for they say he does things and takes risks that no mortal man would dare to take—and succeeds! Weeks ago, as they pursued him across the desert, he turned in his tracks and coolly demanded the hospitality of Kadar's camp Of course, Kadar had no choice but to offer it! Near   he la-in their camp for 'two nights and two days, and ther like a night-phantom, he rose when all were sleeping, slew the guard withou* waking anyone. and escaped with fresh camels."

"Oh, no!" Alexa whispered.

"It is true! He took with him garments and weapons and provisions. Since then, they've been unable to find him. They do not know if he's fallen victim to the desert and is now dead, or if he's merely gone into hiding in a village somewhere, for he's vanished like the wind!"

"And—and Kadar?" Alexa asked, the question sticking in her throat.

"Kadar demanded audience with the *amir* immediately he rode into the city. He's sworn he'll not rest until he sees justice done, but if he cannot find your brother, then who else will his anger fall upon but thee, Zerdali? He has audience with the *amir* now, and your lord husband has gone himself to see what

400

can be done. Aiee, Zerdali, this is the moment we've dreaded since your arrival here! Never have I seen Sharif so grim and stern-faced!"

"By seeing justice done, I suppose you mean Kadar's howling for my blood?" Alexa said bitterly, far more frightened than her outwardly composed expression suggested.

Fatima shrugged and sighed. "That is so, yes."

"Where are the *amir* and Kadar now?"

"In the grand hall, of course, Zerdali, where the *amir* always judges the disputes of his people. But why do you want to know—? Oh, no, no, that's quite impossible! Zerdali, please, no, don't even think of it! Sharif has ordered me to see that you do not leave your apartments! Zerdali, you foolish, stubborn girl! Come back here at once, I say, at once!"

"Come with me if you must, but I won't stay here and wait while my fate is decided by others, like a little child sent to her room!" Alexa vowed over her shoulder, throwing a pale green veil over her coppery-chestnut hair and drawing the loose folds across to cover her lower face as she sped to the arched doorway of her tower quarters. "I just want to listen—and make certain Sharif isn't drawn into a fight over me, that's all. He's been overly protective since my illness, as you know. I'll keep quiet as a mouse, I promise, Fatima," she coaxed, but knew in her heart that whether the woman agreed or no, she was going to see for herself what was going on.

"Oh, very well," Fatima grumbled. She could never refuse the girl anything, and it was futile to start now, when she was so obviously determined. "I suppose you'll go, whether I forbid you or no, but I'm coming with you! By Allah, what a fool I am to love such a worthless girl, who cares nothing for her old Fatima! It will mean my head if Sharif finds out what you've been up to—aiee, my head *and* my tongue!" she grumbled.

"Since you won't need one without the other anyway, stop your grumbling and hurry up!" Alexa scolded as they hurried down the long, tiled hallway toward the palace proper.

"Explain yourself, Kadar!" Malik ben-Azad was saying with

401

a frown when Fatima and Alexa arrived. The *amir* was seated cross-legged upon pillows and rugs which had been strewn over an ornate dais at one end of the vast grand hall, and with his straight back and imposing manner, he appeared every inch a prince, Alexa observed.

She and Fatima hovered on the fringes of the large crowd of townspeople that had gathered in the grand hall to hear the *amir* pass judgment on various matters as he did every month, much as medieval English lords had once sat in judgment over their serfs, as Alexa remembered her father telling her once. Numerous disputes that had arisen in the past three weeks had already been judged by the *amir,* but the proceedings had obviously been disrupted a short while earlier by the explosive return of *Sheik* Kadar ben-Selim to al-Azadel.

Disgruntled merchants and their irate customers were forced to forget their own complaints of shoddy workmanship, failure to pay, and false weighing, and now watched the proceedings with avid interest—as did Alexa and Fatima, skulking by a fat stone pillar that helped to hide them from the main participants of the drama unfolding in the grand hall.

"Not a word!" Fatima cautioned in a whisper, her plump face nervous. "It would not be wise for either of them to know you are here."

"Not a word," Alexa promised. "Now, shush! I can't hear!"

"Explain how my son's bride is involved in this matter. What has the lady Zerdali to do with any of this?" the *amir* continued, and Fatima nudged Alexa so hard in the ribs, she gasped aloud, drawing far too many curious glances.

Before Kadar could answer, Sharif stepped from between the knots of men that made up the gathering, striding slowly to stand before his father with his powerful arms crossed over his chest. His bearing—the aloof, proud stride of the Imochagh lords—seemed to add to his already considerable height. He towered above the heads of the crowd, stern, lean-faced, and as darkly handsome as a hawk. Unflinching, he met his father's troubled dark eyes, and read the questions, the confusion, the accusation in their depths, as he offered his father a deep, respectful bow.

"By your leave, my lord father, I will answer your question.

402

Zerdali, my bride, is the woman of my dreams, the one I have awaited for half a lifetime, as I told you. But what I did not tell you is that she is also the sister of the one Kadar seeks for revenge. An *Englesy* named Keene Harding!" he declared in a loud, carrying voice so that all might hear. "He and his companion, a *Franziwa* Legionnaire, were the ones who slew the father and kinsman of Muriel bat-Hussein and violated the maiden at the oasis of Yasmeen."

"Aiee, by Allah, what is this Sharif says?"

"The lady Zerdali—that mad-dog Englesy's sister? Who would have thought it!"

"Ewellah! I just knew something was amiss all along—all that secrecy surrounding the wedding!"

"And what will our prince do? How can he decide?"

"Will his head rule with wisdom as always, I wonder, or his heart, with the weakness of a father's love for his only son and the woman he has chosen?"

The ripple of astonished comments ran through the crowd, an excited, loud buzzing that Malik silenced with an upraised hand as he rose to his feet. The mutterings were silenced as surely as if he had raised his *takoba* and threatened them to the last man with beheading.

"Is this so?" Malik demanded incredulously of Kadar, the Bedouin he had raised from infancy along with his own son. His eyes searched the man's face, hoping to find some denial in his expression that would prove Sharif wrong, for the alternative—that Sharif had deliberately concealed the truth from him, and with it the identity of the man Kadar sought—was one too unpleasant to contemplate. He knew Sharif would not have done so, unless Kadar's claims to the girl were compelling ones.

"*Ewellah,* my lord, it is so!" Kadar acknowledged, his eyes seething black pools of hostility as they met Sharif's. "At the oasis of Yasmeen, I gave the captive woman into your son Sharif's care. I entrusted him with the task of bringing her securely to al-Azadel, there to await my return from the desert and your judgment on this matter. He knew when he accepted that trust that the girl was mine by the laws of the desert, to do with as I saw fit. 'A life for a life'—is it not so written, my lord

403

prince? By taking her as his bride, knowing full well my own intentions toward her, he has foully betrayed my trust! He has spat upon the brotherhood that has been between us since the days of our birth!"

Kadar's black eyes glittered like one obsessed as he stood before the judgment of Amir Malik ben-Azad al-Azadel, his robes still stained with the dust and sweat of travel, his handsome, hawk-like face worn and lined in the aftermath of the debilitating sweating-fevers that had periodically delayed his search and his return to the mountains for so long. His fingers curled over the jeweled hilt of his dagger. "Justice!" he spat again. "I demand justice of you, my prince, according to the ancient laws of our desert peoples! The woman you call Zerdali must be handed over to me! Her life shall be forfeited in exchange for the life of the *Englesy* dog who has evaded my capture! They are of one blood, one seed. It is fitting that she should pay the price for the sins one of her blood has committed!"

"And what proof do you offer that this *Englesy* is the one responsible?" the *amir* asked quietly, trying to bring a measure of calm and reason to the proceedings, and also desperately seeking some alternative to the inevitable choice he'd soon be forced to make.

Kadar smiled wolfishly and jerked his head, beckoning to someone. Muriel, unnoticed until now and obviously deathly afraid, came forward, threw herself down on her knees, and made a deep bow to the prince.

"Well, my daughter? Do you have the proof I ask for?"

"*Ewellah,* my lord prince. It is here."

"Then show us, child," Malik urged gently, well aware of her terror.

Muriel was still trembling from her shock at discovering, on her return from the bazaar, that Kadar had returned to the city. Her summons to the great hall to appear before the prince had done little to settle her nerves! Trembling all over, she obediently raised her slender arm aloft and unfastened her tightly clenched fist. A flash of silver flowed from it, and then all saw that what she held was a silver chain, from which dangled a small, round talisman, shining in the sunlight that streamed through the lattices as it swung to and fro.

Another ripple of excitement and a shocked gasp coursed through the crowd, fortunately muffling the agonized cry Alexa gave as she saw what it was the girl had produced: Keene's St. Christopher medal—the one she'd given him on his sixteenth birthday!"

"No, oh, please, no!" Alexa murmured brokenly, her belly churning as Muriel's words and the medallion confirmed her most deeply buried fears. She would have left her concealing pillar had Fatima's fingernails not dug sharply into her wrist. The pain forced her to her senses and jolted her into silence once more. Fatima's anguished, pitying eyes beseeched her charge to stifle her grief for safety's sake, for the mood in the hall was ugly now. . . .

"Tell us how you came by this Christian amulet, Daughter," Malik said.

"My lord," Muriel murmured, her husky voice little louder than a whisper, "I tore it from the throat of the man who—who gave the command to slay my father and uncle, when he—he—violated me!"

Kadar nodded in curt dismissal, and the girl fled like a frightened doe, back to whatever nook she had appeared from. That she was terrified of the *sheik* was obvious to all gathered there.

"You asked for proof, my lord prince, and it has been shown thee! The Frenchman confessed under torture before his death that his companion wore such an amulet. It was clasped in Muriel's fist when we found her. The woman Zerdali must be brought before you, to confirm that the amulet belongs to her brother and acknowledge his guilt. I demand it!"

"No!" Sharif thundered, his ebony eyes twin dark flames with his outrage. "She is my wife now, Kadar, and I have sworn to guard her life with my own. She has no part in this, as she had no part in what happened at the oasis of Yasmeen. It is between you and me, and as her husband I forbid that she be brought here!" He strode to face Kadar, eye to eye. "Your thirst for vengeance has embittered you, my brother, and twisted your reason. Your lust for revenge has made you forget that there are other, equally honorable ways to settle this matter between us—ways that do not call for bloodshed!"

Fatima, holding Alexa fiercely to her breast to keep her silent where they were hidden behind the farthest pillar, held her breath and prayed that, for once in his hotheaded life, Kadar would listen to reason.

"You ask me to accept a blood-price for the lives of my betrothed's kinsmen? For my betrothed's lost virginity?" Kadar scoffed.

"Is that not also the custom of our people?" Sharif reminded him softly, his voice the only calm amidst the storm of emotions in the hall.

Kadar eyed him with contempt. "Pah! It is as I said once before, Sharif, my brother—in your desire to embrace the Western world and a Christian woman, you have grown as weak and womanish as the gelded eunuchs of the Turkish! Can silver and gold return life to the dead, or innocence to the defiled?"

"Can the murder and blood of an innocent woman accomplish these things?" Sharif counted, ignoring Kadar's bitter insults against his manhood, which stemmed, he knew, from his anger. "You know in your heart it cannot! Put up your dagger unblooded, Kadar, and instead accept an honorable blood-price for your losses." In a lower voice he added, "Zerdali is beloved by me, my brother—beloved by me above all women! For the sake of our friendship, for the sake of the many years of our brotherhood, don't ask me to give her into your hands, knowing to do so can only end in her death!"

"It is my right! She is of the *Englesy's* blood!"

"And I am also of their blood," cut in a low, foreign-accented voice, shocking the gathering once again. "If you would claim vengeance, Kadar, take me. I offer myself to your blade!"

The one known as Kahlil had stepped forward. As Kadar regarded him, he unwound the white length of the *tagilmust* from his face and head and set it carefully aside. An angular, deeply bronzed face was revealed, peculiarly light-skinned where the flesh had long been hidden from the sun and curious eyes by the veil. The sad, hooded gray-blue eyes were its dominant features.

A female cry of astonishment rang out on the silence as he revealed himself, but was quickly muffled by a serving woman who clamped her hand over her mistress's mouth and bustled the protesting, veiled woman out of the grand hall. The lady Kairee slipped from her cushion and followed them.

"Kahlil?" Kadar murmured in confusion meanwhile.

"Kahlil, the Friend. Yes, that is the name by which I have been known here these many years," the man confirmed. "But the name I had before I came here was Jonathan. Jonathan Harding. I am—"

"Enough, Kahlil!" Sharif cut him off abruptly. "You are my father's oldest, dearest friend, and my own. Without you, our years of exile in distant Egypt would have been cold and empty. We owe you much that we can never repay, and I will not let you offer yourself in place of my wife!"

"And you and your father have also proven my dearest friends. But Kadar thirsts for the blood of Keene Harding, Sharif," the old man said sadly. "He craves vengeance upon my seed, and so I offer him instead the very tree from which that seed sprang! The woman Zerdali and the man Keene are my son and daughter, Kadar! I give you my life for my daughter's, in payment for the sins of my son, who eludes you. What say you?"

All eyes in the hall turned to Kadar as they awaited his decision.

Chapter Twenty-Nine

"That man, Kahlil!" Alexa whispered, pale and clammy with shock. She fought off Fatima's restraining hands, trying to evade the woman and return to the hall they'd just left. "That man—he's my father!"

"Hush, now, hush, *ya habibah!*" Fatima crooned, desperate to still her distraught mistress's tongue and at the same time get her away from the great hall. "Of course he's your father—and a good friend he's been to the *amir* and Sharif these many years too! Calm yourself now, little one, or I'll have to beg a powder from the lady Kairee to quiet you."

"I don't need anything to calm me!" Alexa insisted hotly, fighting off Fatima's hands as the woman tried to chivy her back to her apartments through the long corridors. "I want to see him—I have to talk with him!" Her eyes shone with tears, but whether of joy at finding him alive after believing him dead for so long, or of grief over her father's desertion, Fatima was uncertain. "Why?" Alexa asked aloud. "Why did he let his family believe him dead all these years? Do you know why, Fatima? Tell me!" she insisted brokenly.

"Alas, that question you'll have to ask your father when the time comes, for I swear I don't know the reason. I do know Kahlil, however, and he's a good man, a man of honor. For a long, long time after he came here to al-Azadel, he was very ill—so ill that the *amir* feared for his life. I'm certain that whatever Kahlil did, he did because he had to, and was given no choice. *Ewellah*, Harding-Pasha would never have deserted his beloved wife and children except for the very best of reasons, silly girl! Now, come along with me, do! I know you've had a great shock, but Kadar is even now demanding you be handed over to him, child, and I want you gone as far from here as possible before the *amir* makes his decision! Doesn't the possibility that you could be given to him frighten you at all—not even a little?"

"Of course it does!" Alexa agreed, her expression more sober now. "It's just that—oh, Lord, seeing Papa after all those years of believing him dead and gone—! I can't think straight about anything else! Oh, Fatima, you can't imagine how it felt! It was like—like seeing a ghost!"

She bit her lower lip to keep from crying, but tears of emotion, of shock and joy, streamed down her face regardless. Her father, alive and well, after she'd believed him dead for almost nine years! And not only well, but happy too, apparently, she reminded herself, with a new wife, the lady Yasmeen, whom she'd glimpsed at her wedding feast. A sudden horrible suspicion flared up inside her. Could the sad-eyed lady Yasmeen be the reason for her father's disappearance? Had he perhaps staged his own "death" just to be rid of her own dear mama, and to circumvent the prolonged and messy proceedings that accompanied a divorce? Had he hidden himself away here in order to live in the mountains with his Eastern mistress? "Fatima, when were the lady Yasmeen and my—Kahlil wed?" she demanded suddenly.

"Oh, I believe it'll be two years this summer," Fatima replied, and realizing immediately why the girl had asked the question, she added crossly, "For shame, you foolish girl! How could you think such things of Kahlil? Is your father not an *Englesy*, and are the *Englesy* not an honorable people?"

"Not all, no!" Alexa said dryly, and Fatima snorted as she ushered Alexa ahead of her into the Mist *serai*.

"Whatever you believe, I tell you, Kahlil is a good, honorable man! He didn't marry the lady Yasmeen nor take her as his woman until several years after the lady Elizabeth-Pasha had already gone to Paradise, have no concerns about that! The lady Yasmeen was a widow herself, but very much in love with Kahlil. It is said, however, that he yet mourns his first wife, and that it is because of this the lady Yasmeen always appears so sad."

"Elizabeth-Pasha! I've never spoken of her, so how did you know my mother's name, Fatima?" Alexa demanded, whirling to face her.

"I did?" Fatima echoed lamely, her mouth an astonished O.

Alexa sighed in exasperation. "Yes, and don't try to deny it! What is it about the people here anyway! Everyone seems to know so much about me—you and Sharif, and even the lady Kairee too—while I know so very little abou . . ."

Her voice trailed away as all the pieces suddenly dropped into place, and with a fit that was too, too perfect to be mere coincidence.

"Fatima?" she began threateningly. "When was it you lived in Egypt? Was it when Sharif and his father were exiled? Was it, perhaps, twenty-four years ago—when I was born? When I was a little girl? Answer me, Fatima, or I'll shake you until you rattle!" she threatened, only half-joking as she grasped Fatima's plump arms. She appeared to intend to do exactly as she'd threatened.

"Yes! Yes!" Fatima confessed, moaning. To Alexa's horror she began to cry, covering her face with her head veil. "I told Kairee I was no good at keeping secrets," her muffled voice cried, despairingly, "and this one is so old, so very old! What harm can it do to tell it, since you will learn the whole truth soon anyway, eh? Come, come, sit beside me here, on the divan, and I'll tell you everything while we wait." She took a seat upon the plumply cushioned divan and patted the spot next to her. Alexa went and sat beside her, tense with expectation.

"As you guessed, I was in Egypt with the *amir* and his people when they were exiled," Fatima began. "Oh, I could have gone back to my people, the Bedouin, then, for I was given leave to do so, but I had grown too attached to my charges, Sharif and Kadar, by that time—and such dear little boys they were too! Perhaps you have wondered why Kadar and I are among the few Bedouin here at al-Azadel, yes, when all else are Imochagh or Inandan?"

"I had wondered, to be honest. An Arab guide I knew told me that the Tuareg tribes and the Bedouins are old enemies, isn't that so?"

"That is so—but Kadar and I were fortunate. We found

places amongst the Imochagh for ourselves, and wanted for nothing more.

"You see, when I was yet a young wife—wedded less than a year—a band of Murid ben-Azad's Tuareg brigands attacked our Bedouin camp as we traveled the deserts with our herds. My husband and little daughter were slain in the attack, as were Kadar's parents, the *sheik* of our tribe and his favorite wife. Kadar was left an infant without a mother, I a mother with full breasts that had no babe, and so in the aftermath of the attack, I took him to my breast to nurse. Soon after, the Tuaregs who had captured us—they intended to sell us into slavery in the secret markets of Morocco!—were themselves attacked by their chieftain's own brother, Malik ben-Azad, and his men—the people you know now as the al-Malik tribe of al-Azadel. Malik was yet a handsome young man with a tiny newborn son whose mother, like Kadar's, had recently died in the desert, though Bikkelu had succumbed to childbirth-fever when the babe was but hours old.

"The *amir* Malik, in accordance with his philosophy of a new way of life for his people, released the prisoners Murid had taken, except for myself. He asked me if I would wet-nurse both children until we reached his mountain kingdom of al-Azadel, promising me rich rewards if I agreed, and my freedom when he had found another to take my place as his son's nurse. I had lost one child, but Allah the Merciful had repaid my loss with not one, but two fine, strong boys, so what could I do but agree? I promised to nurse them, and have been with them ever since. I told the *amir* that Kadar was not my own child, but the orphaned son of a Bedouin *sheik*, and so Malik raised Kadar as his own until the boy was twelve years old. Then, when he and Sharif were forced into exile by his brother Murid, he returned the *sheik*'s grown son to his own people, hoping that in time he would take his proper place as their leader. That is why Kadar never came with us to Egypt. Alas, Kadar stayed with his own people for only a few short years before he returned to al-Azadel. He considers the *amir* his father, you see, and in his love for him has always been envious of Sharif."

"And when you were in exile with the *amir's* family, you lived with us in the white house in Egypt that I remember, didn't you?" Alexa said accusingly, memories of a plump young Arab woman tending her, humming and singing while she did so, flooding her mind.

Fatima nodded, and a tear escaped the corner of her eye and trickled down a plump cheek. "Ah, more than that, *ya habibah*—I was your nurse for four years, from the very day of your birth until the day we returned to al-Azadel, when you were taken by your father to England. Aiee! It was as painful to lose you then as it was to lose my own little daughter!" She encompassed Alexa in her plump-bosomed embrace, and for a moment Alexa melted into her motherly warmth. But—only for a second.

She drew away and stared at the woman a moment, before saying excitedly, "But Fatima, if you were my nurse, then that means Sharif must have been the hateful boy I vaguely remember—the one who always loved to play at battle and broke my new doll in the process!"

"*Ewellah*, it is so!" Fatima confirmed, smiling fondly. "Your baby tongue could not pronounce his name, and so you called him—"

"Sha-Sha!" Alexa finished softly with a gasp of laughter at the idea of calling the proud Imochagh lord such a name now! "I called him Sha-Sha, and he called me Apricot Hair, I remember. Oh, how I hated him!"

"Ha! Hated him so much you were his shadow! Hated him so much that never was he seen anywhere without you! Hated him so much you cried for three days and three nights when you learned you had to leave your beloved Sha-Sha to go to the *Englesy's* cold, far-off lands. Hated him so much that the little girl you were then swore to me that she would never, ever forget him, that she'd come back and marry him some day when she was all 'growed-up.' Pah! Never since then have I seen such 'hatred'!" Fatima teased gently.

"Sha-Sha," Alexa murmured aloud again, smiling a dreamy, silly smile. Had her dreams ever really been dreams at all, she wondered now, or her most secret wishes to return to the happy childhood she remembered so little of? Longings so deeply rooted in her memory that while waking, she had never suspected their existence? No wonder the "Tuareg bandit" had seemed so familiar to her from the very first! Some sixth sense within her must have recognized him, even after all those years, as her childhood companion and protector. . . .

"Quickly, girl! Pull youself together!" Fatima whispered suddenly, springing to her feet. "Someone's coming!"

Alexa heard the tramping of boots in the tiled corridor beyond her apartments and darted her serving woman an apprehensive glance. "Who?"

Fatima shrugged. "Perhaps it's nothing—and then again, perhaps it's cause for alarm! Perhaps—aiee—perhaps the *amir* has seen justice in Kadar's demands, and has ordered you to be given over to him! I pray to Allah that it is not so, but we will trust nothing to Fate. Better we be prepared for either good news or bad! Quickly, Daughter, out into the gardens with you! Stay nearby and listen well. If you hear me say that I do not know where you are, but that I believe you've gone to the baths, that is your signal that you're in danger, yes? If all is well, I will come for you myself—"

"But where am I to go if—"

"Use the passageway that tunnels down through the mountains to the *sahel*—you remember it?"

"The cave Sharif and I used the day the al-Tabor pursued us? Yes, of course, but—"

"Good! Then wait there, and I'll send Sharif to find you. Aiee, quickly, child, go!"

No sooner had Alexa slipped through the portal leading out to the terraced gardens than she heard Fatima's voice raised in outrage:

"What is the meaning of this intrusion? How dare you enter my lady's private apartments unannounced and uninvited! The *hareem* quarters are forbidden all men but the *amir* and his son, as well you know, you rogues!"

"We are here by order of the *amir* himself, woman! Where is the lady Zerdali?"

With bated breath Alexa, pressed up against the portal, heard Fatima answer slyly, "Why? What is it you want with her?"

413

"That is not your concern, my aunt!"

"Pah! The girl is my charge, even as you were once dandled upon my knee, Akbar, you great oaf! Do you forget I changed your soiled breechcloths and wiped the drool from your little chin? Tell me why you want her, and I'll tell you where she is! That's fair enough, isn't it?" Fatima grinned impishly, her dark brown eyes twinkling in her plump, merry face as she added, "After all, my nephew, what else has a lonely old woman like your 'aunt' Fatima to enjoy but gossip and everyone else's secrets, since she's grown too wrinkled and fat to stir any but a blind man's *wezand!*" She chuckled wickedly, and Akbar, the towering, muscular guard, grinned at her bawdy remark.

"You are a wicked woman, as ever, my aunt, and a liar, for all in the city know of the doctor-*hakim's* great passion for thee!" he said with a chuckle, grinning and winking at his two companions. Leaning down a little, he confided, "*Sheik* Kadar has returned. He told the *amir* that our lord Sharif's bride is sister to the *Englesy* who slew his betrothed's kinsmen and dishonored the maiden Muriel. Kadar has demanded she be handed over to him in payment for his losses, and the *amir* had no choice but to judge the matter in Kadar's favor, since he refused to accept a blood-price in the woman's place. We're to take the lady Zerdali to him at once!"

"Ah, a juicy tidbit indeed!" Fatima cackled. "And what did our lord Sharif have to say about that?"

"He would have taken Kadar by the throat and slain him with his bare fists where he stood, had the *amir* not ordered him forcibly restrained! *Wellah*, tempers are short and hot today, and it'll cost me my head if I don't carry out my duties at once, Aunt. Enough of this idle gossip! Where is the lady?"

Fatima frowned. "In truth, I'm not certain! But—" She raised her voice a little here. "The lady Zerdali mentioned the baths. I think you'll find her there, my nephew."

Akbar nodded. "Then it is to the baths we go! Live in peace and prosper, my aunt—and may your lovers be many!"

With a wicked chuckle, Fatima nodded, holding her ample sides with forced laughter until the palace guards had exited the apartments.

Once they'd gone, her smile quickly faded. She sped across to the arched portal that led out to the gardens and softly called Zerdali's name several times. To her relief, there was no answer. Thanks be to Allah, as she had advised, Zerdali had gone!

Chapter Thirty

To Alexa's surprise, she found the lady Kairee waiting for her as she slipped silently through the gardens.

"Shsh!" Kairee urged with a finger across her lips, stifling her cry of surprise. "Come, I'll show you the way to the cave. Follow me—quickly now!—before we're spotted."

Alexa followed her and the two women scrambled down the little stone-flagged paths that meandered between the terraced gardens, overhung with brilliant magenta and purple sprays of bougainvillea. They skirted the little waterfall and made their way, twisting and turning, from the gardens and out onto the rolling *shott*. There, in a hollow carved by rain and wind, Kairee drew aside bushes and vines to reveal the opening of the secret passage through the mountain by which Alexa and Sharif and his men had escaped Tabor and his tribesmen just a few weeks ago. It was so cleverly and naturally concealed, she would never have found it again alone.

"The *amir's* guards came for me!" Alexa explained to Kairee as they entered the gloomy tunnel. They were the first words she'd spoken since she left her apartments, for her thoughts and emotions were in turmoil with her father's return from the dead and Kadar's explosive demands for her life. "Fatima— Fatima thought it best I should hide here."

"Yes, my daughter. Fatima and I have been dreading Kadar's return for many weeks. We'd planned between ourselves weeks ago to hide you here if things went wrong, and so I knew where I could find you. Wait here one moment while I light the lamp." She shivered. "This old tunnel is dark and silent as any tomb, by Allah!"

Alexa halted. Moments later, the little brass lamp set high on a rocky ledge sputtered into life, its puny circle of amber revealing a large, irregular cavern. By its light, Kairee's expression was grim. "There! Is that not a little better than darkness?"

"Much!" Alexa agreed, trying to smile. She failed, and swallowed. "Oh, Kairee—you said you'd planned to bring me here if things went wrong. Have they? Gone badly wrong, I mean? Fatima made me leave before the *amir* made his decision."

Kairee nodded quickly, her handsome features drawn. "Very wrong, I fear! Fatima and I—and Sharif too, for that matter—had hoped all along that Kadar's love for Sharif would persuade him to accept a blood-price in return for your life when the time came to confront him, instead of yourself. The two of them were raised as brothers, you see, and so it was not unreasonable to hope Kadar would soften." She sighed.

"But he hasn't?"

Kairee shook her head. "Alas, no, far from it, my dear. When I saw you leave the hall with Fatima, I too left. I lingered only long enough to hear my husband's judgment in this matter." She wet her lips, and eyed Alexa intently. "You must understand, Zerdali, that he had no choice. As the prince of al-Azadel, my husband is bound to uphold the laws of our land. He must be just to all, beggars or lords, even if his judgment should seem cruel, and even if it should sometimes hurt the ones he loves most."

Alexa's heart began to pound horribly. "So he decided in Kadar's favor," she whispered in a dull voice. "He ordered me given over into his hands!"

"*Ewellah*, it is so," Kairee agreed sadly. "But as I said, he had no choice! If he'd ruled in Sharif's favor, his decision would have created chaos. The people would have seen that their *amir's* justice was colored by ties of blood and swayed by his heart, rather than founded upon reason. And in these difficult times, when our enemies wait like hovering vultures to feast upon the fat pickings of the Prosperous Kingdom, he dared not risk appearing weak in any way, though his fondness for you is without question, and the decision saddened

417

him deeply."

"Poor Uncle Malik!" Alexa whispered softly, vaguely remembering she'd once called the stern *amir* "uncle" as a little girl. She bit her lips. As Kairee had said, he'd been fond of her once. She believed he was still fond of her, even if only as the bride of his beloved Sharif. His decision couldn't have been an easy one, she thought miserably, and she did not envy him having to make it, yet by so doing, he had as good as sentenced her to death at Kadar's hands! She covered her face with her hands. "Oh, my God, Kairee, what am I to do?"

"Nothing, yet. You will wait here until Sharif comes to you. Promise me you won't leave here, nor show yourself outside?" The girl nodded and Kairee added, "Meanwhile, I must return to the palace before my absence is noticed and questions are asked. Fatima and I will try to convince my husband and Kadar that you did not return from the bazaar. We'll persuade him that somehow you got word of Kadar's return and fled in terror. The subterfuge will buy us a little time, with any luck, until Sharif can take you to safety. There's enough oil in the lamp to last until nightfall"—she dropped a kiss to Alexa's brow—"and Sharif should be here long before then. May Allah protect you and keep you safe, Daughter," she whispered as she straightened up, and there were tears in her eyes.

"Peace unto you too, dear Kairee!" Alexa replied, the answering sparkle of tears making her own eyes bright in the shifting gloom. "Thank you for—for everything you've tried to do for me! I was angry at you and Fatima for going behind my back and arranging our marriage without my consent, but I see now that what you did really was for my own good. Forgive me for doubting you?"

With a sad nod and a rustling whisper of her flowing robes, Kairee was gone, swallowed up by the darkness of the tunnel, and Alexa was left alone with her thoughts and her fears.

The draft from above stirred the lamp's small tongue of light, and made grotesque, giant shadows leap and shimmy over the craggy walls. Alexa trembled and sank down, her legs shaking too badly to support her any longer. What if the guards should find her here? Or Kadar himself? It was very possible they would think to search here. After all, the existence of the tunnel seemed to be well known, at least to those who lived in the palace, as Kadar once had. And in that event, there'd be no escape. She'd be killed as easily as a fish in a barrel!

There was no way to judge time, not there in the darkness of the tunnel. She sat and thought, going over and over in her mind the day's shocking events: her dread fulfilled by Kadar's return; the sudden joy of seeing her father alive; the knowledge that she and Sharif had known and loved each other as children. Oh, so many different things to think of! *Too* many. Would she ever have the chance to speak with Sharif again, to tell him at last how very much she'd grown to love him? And what of her father, her dear papa? Had she found him alive only to face the very real, cruel possibility that she would lose him again, once and for all? That awful Kadar might well decide to accept the brave offer of her father's life for hers, if she were not found! But knowing that, how could she run away? She clenched her fists, trying to fight down the urge to scream aloud with the questions and fears that choked her. Her head ached from thinking. Her body felt drained with reaction to the surprises she'd received, one after the other, which had made her fragile emotions swing from joy to terror, terror to joy, back and forth like a violently swinging pendulum. Tears began and flowed freely, easing the choking knot of agony in her throat and breast a little until at last, exhausted by her weeping, she fell asleep, crouched down against the rough wall of the cave with her head bowed upon her chest.

"Alexandria? Wake up, poppet!"

"Papa?" she slurred groggily, hearing the voice calling to her down the long tunnel of sleep as if calling to her down through the years. "Oh, Papa, I'm so tired."

"I know, darling, I know. But you must wake up now. Sharif sent me here to keep you company. We must talk and decide what to do. Come along, Alexandria, open your eyes!"

She opened them, and found herself looking into the haunted gray-blue eyes of her father.

"Oh, Papa!" she cried, sobs overwhelming her as she let him take her in his arms and enfold her. "All this time, I thought you were dead! Oh, Papa, I'm so glad, so glad you're alive, that you're here with me. I've felt so alone these past years—and I—and I needed you after Mama died!"

She looked up through her tears, and saw that her father was crying too.

"Oh, Dear Lord, Alexa, what did I do? What in God's name did I do?" he whispered, his voice muffled as he held her fiercely to his chest. "At the time, it seemed the only possible way! I believed I had no choice, you must believe that!"

"Choice about what?" she asked him, confused. "Was there—were you in trouble, is that why you—why you let us think you were dead?"

Miserably, he nodded. "Enormous trouble. So enormous, it seemed overwhelming at the time. But at what price I kept the secret from your mama, Alexa! What terrible price! Perhaps it would have been better to have told her everything. Perhaps, if I'd done so, my darling Beth would still be alive! But at the time, I was afraid the truth would destroy her. . . ." He shook his head. "I suppose I did what I felt was best, under the circumstances. And hindsight is always perfect, isn't it, and cruelly judgmental."

"Papa, you're not making sense!" she cried. "What trouble are you talking about? What truth would have destroyed Mama?"

"Why, the truth about Keene, of course," he answered as if she should have known all along. "All that trouble."

"What trouble? When?" Was he rambling? she wondered, afraid for her father's sanity now. "You mean, the trouble with Muriel bat-Hussein?" Her father couldn't be referring to that earlier mess Keene had gotten himself into with Polly the parlormaid; he could know nothing about that.

"No, no! It all began long ago—long before this distressing incident."

"What is it you're trying to tell me about my brother, then?"

He sighed heavily again. "Well, for a start, that he's not your brother, poppet. Or at least, not your natural brother."

"Keene's not my brother? But of course he's my brother!" Alexa cried, certain beyond doubt now that her father had lost his reason.

Her father shook his head wearily, gesturing her with a wave of his slim hand to be seated beside him on one of the soft rugs he'd brought.

Biting her lips to keep the questions that clamored to escape them confined, Alexa did so, wondering what her father was about to tell her that made him appear so exhausted, so gray and ill. Surely not the burden of guilt, she thought, butterflies of apprehension fluttering in her belly. He'd never harmed so much as a fly in his entire life, that she was aware of! Her heart went out to him. In the past few hours since Keene's guilt had been proven beyond doubt by Muriel's possession of the damning silver St. Christopher medal, from the moment she'd first seen him again, her papa seemed to have aged a lifetime. . . .

"Do you remember anything at all of the time when Keene was born, shortly before we left Alexandria to go home to England to live?"

She frowned. "Very little. What vague bits and pieces I remember are of Sha-Sha—I mean, Sharif—and me playing and quarreling together as children. I think leaving him, my only playmate, must have hurt me more than I could bear. I'd buried almost all of my memories of those times, until Fatima brought them back today. My only clear recollection is of the day we played at battle and he broke my doll—Lucy, her name was. How I hated him for it!" She ventured a smile.

"Ah, yes, 'my dear Lucy' you always called her!" her father reminisced fondly. "You were such a serious little creature, yet you had a formidable temper even then, much to your dear mama's despair. Despite your quarrels, you and young Sharif were close—closer than many brothers and sisters. He'd defend you and protect you, and you—less than half his age and size!—would stubbornly do the same for him! As I recall, that rascal Sharif had made a sizable crack in poor Lucy's porcelain cheek that day, and you were determined never to forgive him! If memory serves, you were still pouting over the incident when we left Egypt!" His smile ebbed away and he seemed weary and depressed again. "That incident with the doll—it happened the very day your brother was born. The day

421

that marked the beginning of what has sinced proved to be a nightmare lasting over two decades!" He closed his eyes, and for a moment was silent and still.

"Papa? Are you ill?" Alexa asked, leaning forward to touch his shoulder. Her green eyes were dark with anxiety. "Shall I go and find Fatima, and have her call Hakim to tend to you?"

"No, no, poppet, I'm not ill. Just old and feeling my years. Besides, it's far too dangerous for you to leave here just yet! But—I keep remembering, keep thinking how very different our lives might have been if only I hadn't done what I did!" He shook his head. "Who knows?"

"Tell me what it was you did, and let me be the judge," Alexa pressed, certain her beloved father could not have done anything too terrible. She'd always remembered him as a gentle, studious man, preoccupied with his writings and with uncovering the secrets of the dusty tombs and ancient cities of dead civilizations. Far too preoccupied to concern himself overmuch with the present, or with intrigue of any sort.

"As I said, it all began the day your little brother was born. The doctor told me he was frail, that there was a very real chance he might not survive his first few days of life. Your mama's physician advised me to take her and the child home to England if the boy pulled through. He felt the cooler climate there would be better for the babe's health, you see. We were hopeful when Keene seemed to rally a little, and clung to life for the first week. With Malik's assistance, I made the arrangements for our departure, and soon after we'd exchanged farewells with the *amir* and his household, we left our home in Egypt for England.

"Your mama was confined to her bunk in our stateroom aboard the *Neptune*, since she was still in delicate health following Keene's birth, and in that period which you women call the 'lying-in.' A day out of Alexandria harbor, she began running a high fever. The ship's doctor diagnosed childbed fever. Now, whether it was truly childbed fever, or some other virulent tropical disease, I don't know till this day, but she grew sicker and more delirious by the hour, calling for you, Alexa, and for our newborn son. It was as if, somehow, with some part of her consciousness, she knew that I was half out of my mind with dread for the two of them, for you see by then, the baby's health had also taken a turn for the worse."

Tears filled Jonathan Harding's eyes. He wiped them away adding huskily, "The poor little mite had no reserves of strength whatsoever to draw upon, Alexa. Less than forty-eight hours after the start of the fever in him, your little brother was dead."

"What?" she exclaimed. "How can that be?"

"I'm coming to that, my dear," her father promised, his voice thick with emotion. He took a moment more to compose himself before he continued, "I was distraught with grief, as you can imagine. My son was gone, your mother close to joining him in death, calling her baby's name from the depths of her fever. Alexa, oh, Alexa—I didn't know what to do, where to turn!" He wet his lips. "The captain of our ship was a German, Klaus von Krug, a fine, intelligent fellow. He stopped by our stateroom en route to his cabin that night to inquire after my wife and little son's health. When he saw what had transpired—that my child was dead and how very, very ill your poor dear mama had grown—he was filled with Christian pity. God help me, I remember that awful night as if it were but yesterday. . . ."

The bearded blond captain pressed his hand to the brow of the auburn-haired woman who tossed and turned amongst the coverings on the bunk, and brought his hand away slick with sweat. He lifted her limp, white hand, and found the thready pulse at her fragile wrist. When he turned back to Jonathan, his expression was deeply concerned, his blue eyes filled with pity.

"*Herr* Harding, your wife is gravely ill—far worse than I had been led to believe."

"She is, von Krug, she is. Your ship's doctor was here with her all day, up until an hour ago when exhaustion forced him to turn her care over to me. He—he is deeply concerned." Jonathan sighed, a man tormented. "It—it was shortly after he left us that my little son—!" He shuddered. "The babe didn't even have the strength to struggle for life, nor fight for another breath. He simply sighed, and was gone!"

With tear-filled eyes, Jonathan looked toward the corner of the stateroom where, hidden under a veil of mosquito netting, the tiny body of his infant son lay in a heavy wooden rocking cradle, as still and waxen as a doll. He fiercely gripped the backrest of the chair before him, and fought to control the weeping that threatened to unman him.

"If she senses that her child is dead, I'm afraid *Frau* Harding will lose the will to fight for her own life," von Krug observed slowly.

Their eyes met.

"God help us, von Krug, don't you think I know that!" Jonathan told him harshly. "But my son is dead! No amount of grief or wishing it were not so can change that."

Von Krug's mouth tightened a little. "Alas, *mein herr*, sadly it cannot! But for your wife's sake, you must do something, if you would give *Frau* Harding the will she needs to fight for her life. What better reason than her child cradled in her arms, needing her? With your permission, I have an idea."

"Anything, captain, I'll try *anything!*" Jonathan whispered, the desperation like an open wound upon his haggard face.

The captain nodded gravely. "Very well. I'll tell you my idea and let you be the judge of whether to try it or not, *ja?*

"There's a young woman in the steerage quarters of this vessel, *Herr* Harding. She is unmarried, and obviously of a somewhat soiled reputation since although single, she has with her her infant son—a babe less than a month old, I believe. One of my crew told me the young woman came out to Egypt two years ago as a lady's maid, and was in domestic service to the wife of a Colonel stationed with a British regiment in Cairo. With so many lonely young soldiers dancing attendance on her, our pretty young maid obviously lost her head to one of the glib fellows. The child was the consequence of her dalliances. A child, I might add, that she appears to have very little fondness for, and which, according to the sailor who struck up an acquaintance with her, she would be ony too glad to be rid of. The babe is fair-haired, though I cannot attest to the color of his eyes." He paused, letting the Englishman absorb the import of what he had said.

"Surely you're not suggesting that I replace my—my son with this young woman's child?" Jonathan cried, aghast at the idea. "That's unthinkable!"

"Perhaps, but I am suggesting it nonetheless—if the young woman can be persuaded to part with the infant, which I am certain, for a price, she will. And if you are, as you said, prepared to do anything to give your lovely wife the will to live. Are you, *Herr* Harding?" His expression was stern.

"My God, von Krug, I couldn't possibly make a decision like that without enormous consideration of all the implications of such an act!"

"Alas, my dear fellow, time for consideration is not available! Look at your wife! If something is not done soon, you and I both know it will be too late. And, I regret to remind you, we cannot postpone the disposition of your—" He coughed, obviously uncomfortable. "—of your son's body indefinitely in this climate, sir, as I'm sure you are aware."

Jonathan's shoulders sagged. He looked down at Elizabeth's waxen face, beaded with drops of sweat, and at that moment, as if on cue for her part in the tragic drama unfolding out of control all around him, her lovely sea green eyes had opened.

"Jon!" she cried, restlessly tossing upon the pillows. "Please, Jon, where is he? Let me hold him! Where is my baby, Jonathan? Alexa! Jon!"

Looking down at her, Jon's heart had given a great twist of agony in his breast. How could he bear to lose Elizabeth, when there was the slightest chance his actions could save her? She was everything to him, had been since the first moment he had set eyes upon her. Life without her was not worth contemplating. . . .

He'd wet his cracked lips and turned to von Krug, his mind made up. "Do it, then, man. For God's sake, do it, before I come to my senses!" he'd whispered. "Talk to the young woman. Offer her anything she wants—anything!"

The captain nodded soberly. He clamped his beefy hand over Jonathan's shoulder and squeezed it in a comforting gesture. "*Ja*, I will see to it at once. You're making the right choice, *Herr* Harding," he observed.

Early the following morning, the crew and a few of the passengers from steerage had gathered on deck to hear Captain Klaus von Krug solemnly read the funeral service over a tiny body sewn into a canvas shroud: the body of Albert Smith, infant son of Jewel Smith, who had passed away suddenly some time during the night previous. After the touching funeral service was over, the tiny bundle consigned with respect to a watery grave, the few curious mourners departed to their quarters, leaving the decks almost deserted. The captain took the young, fair-haired woman who was the child's mother aside and handed her an envelope containing a sheaf of crisp pound notes.

"As agreed upon, *fraulein*," the captain said sternly, watching as, her gray eyes bright, she shrewdly counted her payment. He added, "And be warned, young lady! Any attempts on your part to try to locate the child or to discover his new identity will be dealt with most—severely. I have eyes and ears everywhere in Europe, *Fraulein* Schmidt, in each and every port! Any such actions on your part will not go unnoticed." It was an empty threat on von Krug's part—one made in an attempt to ensure Jonathan Harding's secret remained a secret for all time, for he liked the archaeologist. But the girl didn't know that, and there was something about the young chit's sly smile that alerted von Krug's suspicions.

"Right you are, Cap'n," Jewel Smith said pertly, flashing him an insolent grin as she tucked the bulging envelope down her bosom. "Mum's the word! Fact is, I reckon you've done me a good turn, takin' the lil' bastard orf me hands. Nothing but trouble his randy young pa brought me, and I was bloomin' well sick an' tired o' the brat's bawlin' and wettin' night 'n' day." She fluttered her sandy lashes. "I'd be happy t' prove to a handsome sailor like you just 'ow grateful I am, luv, if ye've a mind fer a bit o' sport . . . ?" She eyed him archly, her eyes and expression inviting, but von Krug declined with an unconcealed expression of distaste.

"Thank you, no. Just remember what I said!" he ground out, clicked his heels together as he bowed smartly, and strode away across the decks, mindful as he did so of the tall, fair-haired man who stood by the taffrail, staring blindly out over the

426

vivid, sparkling blue of the Mediterranean Sea as tears streamed down his sunburned cheeks.

"Come, come, my friend," von Krug offered, a gentle giant of a man as he took Jonathan's elbow. "It has been a long night for us both, *ja?* The doctor is with your wife at the moment, I understand, and your charming little daughter is safely in the company of Colonel and Mrs. Waters and their boisterous brood. I have some fine schnapps in my cabin, *Herr* Harding, and you look to me like a man in need of a good, stiff drink, *nein?*"

"By God, yes! Damned decent of you, von Krug," Jonathan said gratefully, allowing the captain to lead him away.

"And Mama never suspected the baby wasn't her own?" Alexa asked incredulously when her father had ended his story.

He shook his head. "Never! She was still weak when we arrived in England, and it was a month or so before she was fully herself again. When she recovered, she accepted the child without question."

"And you?"

He nodded. "And I too. It was easier, less painful, to forget the truth, you see. I grew to love Jewel Smith's baby as my own, and after a time, when he grew to a little boy and people would remark how like his papa he was, it seemed as if God had also played along with my subterfuge by making the boy resemble me. And then, when Keene was nine, Jewel Smith showed up on our doorstep out of the blue. . . ."

"There's a young woman requesting to see you, sir," the butler announced that fateful day.

"A young woman?" Jonathan echoed, sifting absentmindedly through the papers that littered his desk, an accounting of his widely acclaimed latest "dig." "Did you take her calling card?"

"She had none, sir, but she insisted you see her in quite an aggressive manner, sir." The butler coughed. "She said she'd tried to visit you some while ago, but that you had already returned to Egypt on that occasion. If I might be so bold, sir, she is somewhat coarse and definitely not a young woman of breeding or education."

"Don't be such an old snob, Clarke!" Jonathan said with a grin. "I doubt she's planning on marrying into the family, so her pedigree is hardly a matter of concern! Did you manage to get her name?"

"I did. It's Smith," the butler divulged with a sniff that betrayed his conviction that the name was not genuine. "A Miss Jewel Smith."

The name seemed vaguely familiar, though Jonathan could not recall any reason why it should be. "Show her in then, Clarke, and we'll see what all this is about, shall we?"

The young woman who sidled into his study was every inch as coarse as Clarke had implied. Tall for a woman and stringy of build, she was clothed in a wine-colored bombazine gown that had seen far better days and had grown shiny and threadbare in places. It was surmounted by a patchy velvet jacket, and thrown carelessly about her angular shoulders was a moth-eaten fox fur. Her narrow and equally fox-like face was sly beneath the paint and powder she'd lavishly applied to her features, which did nothing to enhance her faded looks. Any claims she might once have had to beauty or even a sharp-featured prettiness had long since been lost, coarsened beyond redemption. She looked, Jonathan thought uncomfortably, like the young women who strutted the streets of Whitechapel and Soho by night, selling their favors.

"Miss Smith, won't you sit down?" Jonathan offered politely, but to his surprise, the young woman shook her brassy blonde head.

"I'd rather stand, if it's all the same t' you, gov'na. What I've got ter say won't take long!" She said it in a bold and somehow threatening way.

"As you wish," Jonathan said mildly. "Now, what can I do for you?"

"I won't beat about the bush," Jewel Smith began. "Fact is, I've come about my Albert."

"Albert? There's no one here by the name of Albert,

madame. I'm afraid you must have the wrong—"

"I hain't got it wrong, mister!" the woman snapped, her muddy blue eyes hard. "Maybe his name hain't Albert no more, but I'm still talkin' about the same lil' bastard—the one you bought orf o' me for two hundred quid, remember?"

Jonathan's mouth dropped open in shock. It was several moments before he could find his tongue, and when he did, his tone was uncharacteristically hard. "Believe me, Miss Smith, I am not and nor have I ever been in the habit of buying babies, bastard or otherwise! If you have nothing more to discuss, my man will see you out. Good day!"

He rang the tasseled bell-pull to summon Clarke and resolutely turned his back on the woman, pointedly dismissing her. But his hands shook as he did so.

"No, you don't! Not s' bleedin' fast, mister!" Jewel Smith exploded, her cheeks darkening with anger beneath the rouge. "You hain't gettin' rid o' me as easy as all that, let me tell you!"

Jon swung around to face her. "You think not? On the contrary, madam, if you do not leave my house immediately, I'll have you thrown out! The choice is yours." His mild gray-blue eyes were unusually steely with anger—and more than a suspicion of foreboding.

"Go ahead an' bloody well throw me aht then!" she hissed, advancing toward him so that he could smell the sickly-sweet cheap perfume she'd doused herself with. "Do it—an' I swear I'll find a way t' tell my story t' your fancy wife! I wonder what yer dear, snooty Elizabeth would say if she knowed all about a certain Captain Klaus von Krug, and about how you an' 'im buried her dead brat at sea, an' bought my bastard brat Albert t' take her sickly babe's place!" she crowed.

In the thundering hush that followed in the wake of her accusations, both heads jerked sharply about as a rap sounded at the door.

"Enter!" Jonathan barked, casting a glare at the Smith woman that dared her to say another word in the butler's presence.

"You rang, sir?"

It was Clarke, responding to his summons. The tension in the room crackled.

"A mistake, Clarke," Jon said heavily after a pregnant pause. "I'd thought Miss Smith was ready to leave. I was wrong."

Clarke glanced at his employer and then at the woman, whose expression was gloating. "Is everything all right, sir?" he inquired, convinced everything was not "all right" at all, not by a long chalk, if the atmosphere in the study was anything to go by.

"Quite all right, Clarke, thank you," Jonathan replied curtly. "Leave us, would you? I'll ring for you again when we've completed our—business."

"Very good, sir." The butler left.

"La-di-da! Must be nice, havin' servants t' fetch an' carry fer you?" Jewel Smith remarked, examining a priceless little Greek statuette that Jonathan had recovered from a youthful "dig" in Athens with heart-stopping lack of care. "An' having all these expensive knickknacks lying about t' look at—coo, I wouldn't 'alf like some o' them meself!"

She let the statuette slip from her fingers to the polished wood floors, watching Jonathan's anguished expression as the centuries-old figure shattered. "Oops! What a bleedin' clumsy thing fer me t' do!" she said coldly, her eyes like flint in her foxy face. "I bet that were worth a packet an' all, weren't it?"

"It was," Jonathan gritted. "And you've made your point, Miss Smith. How much to insure your silence?"

"Oh, I reckon two hundred quid'd do it—just fer starters," Jewel had suggested, her eyes brightening with avarice, her mouth puckering up like a miser's purse string as she considered her demand. "And then fifty pounds a month, payable on the first, each month after."

"What? You're mad if you think I can afford your blackmail!" Jonathan exclaimed in horror. "I'm an archaeologist, woman, not a millionaire!"

"If you want me t' keep me mouth shut, you'll find a way, fer yore precious Lizzie's sake, if nothink else! You can send the money to this address—it's a public house. The owner's an old friend o' mine, an' he'll see I gets it. The first of each month, remember that, all right, gov'na? If the second comes 'round an' I hain't bin paid, your bloody wife'll be hearin' from me on the third."

She came toward him, waggling a bony finger, her mouth a leering slash of crimson, hard as nails. "And by the way, *Mister* Jonathan Harding, ark-ee-ologist, don't let it inter yer clever 'ead t' try any funny business where I'm concerned. If, fer some reason, I don't show up t' collect me money on schedule, I've left a letter in me friend's care, telling him all about the rum doin's aboard the *Neptune!*" She smiled, revealing small, crooked teeth that were peculiarly feral. "So ye see, mister, you'd better be a good lil' boy an' pay yer bills on time, or the cat's out o' the bag! An' meanwhile, you'd best pray nuffin' 'appens t' Jewel, or else!"

Rearranging her moth-eaten fur about her scrawny shoulders, she flounced to the door, opened it, and turned back to face him one last time before passing through it. "The first o' the month is eggzactly a week from now. I'll expect to be hearin' from you then. An' don't bother t' ring fer old Clarke. I can see meself out. Ta ta!"

Reliving that awful afternoon, her father seemed to have shrunk unto himself, Alexa thought, becoming an empty shell. Although stunned, she was more concerned for his health in that moment than the secrets he'd spent half his lifetime to keep hidden from her mother.

"Papa, don't try to tell me any more. None of that matters, don't you see? It's past, done with. You did what you felt you had to do, because you loved Mama and wanted to protect her. To protect all of us! I understand," she told him, putting her arms about his shoulders.

"That woman, that terrible, coarse woman—how I hated her!" Jonathan shuddered. "She bled me dry over the next few years, Alexa, sucked the money and the zest for life from me like a leech! Oh, we were never well-to-do, never any more than moderately well-off. My brother Daniel, being the eldest son, had inherited the small Harding fortune and cotton-importing business, while I'd been left Harding Hall. The money on which we lived came from grants allotted me for my livelihood and my studies by the British Archaeological Society and the

British Museum, from a few private backers, and the income from a small piece of property that I'd inherited from my grandmother, which was leased. Fifty pounds each month—oh, Alexa, my dear girl, it was a small fortune to me! I lived in terror that some day I would be unable to meet Miss Smith's demands, and that my darling Elizabeth would learn the truth about—about Keene!"

"That's why you let us believe you'd been killed out in Egypt?"

Her father nodded, ashen-faced in the lamp's sickly light. "Yes! And believe me, nothing has ever pained me so deeply as did that decision, poppet. Leaving you and your mama and—and Keene too, for even as wild and troubled as he was, I'd grown to love him as my son—was the hardest thing I've ever had to do. And yet, it was the only way in which I could protect those I loved from pain and scandal! There was nothing left, you see. I'd used up my funds. I'd sold the few pieces of jewelry I'd given your mama over the years of our marriage and had them replaced with cheap paste copies. I didn't dare ask your uncle or any of our friends for a loan, though our financial situation was quite desperate by then, because it would have meant having to tell them why I needed it. Worse, your mama had started to voice her concerns for our future. By then, all that I had left of any value was Harding Hall, which I owned outright—and the insurance policy I'd taken out on my life years before. But in order for my family to benefit from those funds, I had to be dead!

"The more I thought about it, the more convinced I became that if I *were* believed dead, my blackmailer's demands would also have to cease. After all, even the shrewd Miss Smith would be hard put to wring money from a dead man, and it would profit her not at all to tell your mama Keene's true identity after my death. The more I considered the idea, the more it seemed my only way out. . . .

"Night after sleepless night I wrestled with my conscience," her father continued, "but I could think of no other alternative. I had either to turn my back on my dear wife and the family I loved more than anything, and in so doing save them, or I could watch them sink with me into poverty and heartbreak, the innocent victims of my well-intentioned duplicity and of Jewel Smith's greed. My mind finally made up, I wrote a letter to my bankers, instructing them that, in the unlikely event of my death, they should send notification of the event to a certain Miss Jewel Smith, in care of a public house near Clapham Common. Two more months passed, and then fate stepped in and gave me the chance I'd been waiting for. The tomb I was excavating in the Valley of the Pharaohs collapsed, burying several of my native assistants inside, alas. I was above at the time, dusting off some potsherds I'd discovered earlier that day. There was nothing I could have done to prevent the cave-in, or to save my men, but I saw my chance, knew I might never have another, and took it. I wore native dress to conceal my true identity in the alarm that was raised following the cave-in, and fled across the desert with the first caravan that would have me. By the time word reached Elizabeth that I had been killed and my body never recovered from the ruins, I'd reached al-Azadel and the protection of the province's *amir*, my old and dear friend, Malik ben-Azad. I told him my story, and he granted me permission to remain here for as long as I wished to do so."

Chapter Thirty-One

After her father had ended his story, there was silence between them.

Jonathan seemed utterly exhausted now that he'd unburdened himself to her after carrying his secret for so long, while for her part, Alexa was stunned by his revelations.

It wasn't what Jonathan Harding had done that left her so stunned. No, she could understand what his desperation had driven him to do, to save her mother's life. Would she do less, in order to save Sharif's? Never! It was the thought of all the lonely, difficult years she'd spent since her mother had died, trying single-handedly to be a good guardian to Keene when all the time her papa had been alive that numbed her.

She remembered her frustrating attempts to balance their household accounts each month, her struggle to make ends meet on little more than a pittance. Well, she'd succeeded in that much, she thought with a stirring of pride; they hadn't been forced to leave their home and go to the poorhouse. But— she'd paid a price nonetheless. Would-be suitors, attracted by her looks, had quickly turned their attentions elsewhere when they'd learned that not only would marriage to Alexa bring them no dowry, but there would be the additional burden of her young, incorrigible brother to support. In the end, she'd abandoned all hopes of a life for herself with a family of her own, and resigned herself to a spinster's life, spent caring for Keene and trying to keep him on the straight and narrow. Oh, she'd tried so desperately to keep the Harding name untarnished, for the sake of her father's memory, and it had been a hard burden for a girl of sixteen to carry alone! Each scrape Keene had gotten himself into had seemed only further proof to her that she'd failed miserably in her duties and promises to her parents to care for her younger brother. Was that why she'd denied Keene's guilt so long and hard—because to do so would have meant admitting that despite everything, she'd failed?

Her father's confessions had lightened her burden of guilt somewhat, and yet she could not deny the twinges of resentment they'd also stirred in her. Surely, if her father had wanted to, he could have contacted her—at least let her know he was alive and where she could find him. Just knowing she was not alone when things were rough over the years would have made all the difference! All the difference in the world, she thought, a little bitterly, wishing her father had been a stronger man, one who would not have meekly bowed to a blackmailer's dirty demands. Sharif, she knew with absolute certainty, would never have done so. He'd refused to bargain with the al-Tabor when they'd taken hostages to buy their way out of al-Azadel, hadn't he? He would have dealt with someone like that Jewel Smith woman in short order too, and no mistake!

Thinking about Sharif softened the sharp edges of her fears. The tender warmth of her feelings eroded the chill that anxiety instilled in her. When she saw Sharif again, she'd finally say it; she'd somehow find the words to tell him she loved him and was proud to be his wife, she promised herself, if it was the very last thing she ever did.

Surely it must be close to nightfall by now. Soon, he'd be here with her, she thought confidently, and with his strong arms about her, everything would be all right! Yes, he'd come soon, and he'd know what to do about Kadar, about everything. If only he were here with her, it would all work out. They'd work it out together. Meanwhile, there was her father to consider.

"Papa, we're all human," she began, and with the words she knew that she could forgive him, that love could overcome and outweigh almost any difference, any difficulty. "And as such,

435

all we can ever do is our best! The time has come now to put the past behind you once and for all, and to forget. . . ."

Raisha sat cross-legged upon the flat rooftop of her father's house, her chin resting sulkily upon one fist while she popped figs into her small red mouth with the other.

The date palms, tossing fronded heads far above, shaded her from the afternoon sunlight as she chewed, deep in thought, trying to make some semblance of order out of all that had happened that day.

Early that morning, the *amir* had gone to the great hall to sit in judgment on the cases set before him by the citizens of al-Azadel, as he did each and every month. Then, at mid-morning, *Sheik* Kadar ben-Selim and his men—all appearing travel-worn, ragged, and exhausted—had at last ridden into the city, without, she'd learned, the hated fugitive Englishman they'd hunted for so long.

Not even stopping to bathe the sweat and travel grit from himself nor change his robes, Kadar had straightway stormed into the great hall and demanded audience with the prince—no doubt to settle the question of his claim upon the foreign woman once and for all, Raisha guessed. But—what had transpired afterward? What decision had the *amir* come to? Had Kadar and Sharif fought over the woman—had they drawn daggers, even let blood? Aiee, she'd give every silver bangle she possessed to know the answer to that!

She looked up sharply as a whirring sound stirred the sultry air far above her, and saw one of her messenger pigeons fluttering in the sky above her neighbor's house on the Street of the Silversmiths, headed home to the rooftop cote she kept her pigeons in. At last, word had come again from Tabor, she realized, springing to her feet!

But her heart skipped a beat as she also saw, high above the fluttering pigeon and silhouetted black against the sky, yet another massive wingspan. It was Barakah, Sharif's white hunting falcon, she realized with a gasp of dismay! But who had flown the bird here, in the crowded city, and why? Hunting was impossible here! She licked her suddenly dry lips. Had someone been lying in wait for one of the pigeons she'd given the al-Tabor to return? she wondered, her heart thumping crazily now. Did that explain what had happened to the first message Tabor had sent, the one that must have gone astray? Had Sharif intercepted it somehow? Her palms were slick with sweat as she ducked back into the shadows cast on the roof by the palms, and shaded her eyes against the bright sunlight.

Sure enough, by scanning the other rooftops and the mountain slopes that ringed the city, she spied Kerem, Sharif's Inandan falconer, standing on a rocky ledge that commanded a view across al-Azadel. Even from here, Raisha could see that his fists were gloved. *So! As she'd feared, somehow Sharif knew!* she realized with a thrill of forboding. Obviously, he'd been waiting for just such a moment as this: for another pigeon to bring word to the traitor within al-Azadel, and he had craftily stationed Kerem in that lofty perch to keep watch. By marking where the pigeon flew home to roost, he'd planned to unmask the traitor and take him—or her!

Her heart pounded madly as the pigeon, unnerved by Barakah's screaming death-threat, finally managed to land on the rooftop of Ahoudan the Silversmith, seeking the safety of the familiar cote and its companions with feathers ruffled and a nervous, twittering sound. A curse on the confounded bird! Raisha thought. It had betrayed her! Sharp-eyed Kerem could not have failed to see where it flew to roost! Yet there was still a chance. Kerem could not know she was responsible; he'd probably suspect her father, not her.

She saw Kerem turn and begin scrambling quickly down the mountainside, and while he was so occupied, she sped across to the dovecote and removed the message from the pigeon's foot. She unrolled the slip of paper she found in the leather cylinder fastened to its legs and read the message. *"Act tonight,"* it read. *"Two have been sent to aid you. They await in the* sahel.*"*

Tonight! she thought as she quickly wrung the pigeon's neck and tossed the limp body down into the street, where one of the starving mongrels that roamed the city limits would find it in short order and dispose of the damning evidence. *Tabor wanted her to bring Zerdali to him tonight!* That jackal's timing could not have been worse, she thought, her mind racing furiously as she scrambled down the outer steps that led from the rooftop to the street below.

First, she'd have to seek out that gullible fool, Selim, and find out what had transpired in the great hall and the whereabouts of the lady Zerdali. Wheedling that necessary tidbit from him would take precious time. Though at any other moment she would have welcomed such news, she prayed Selim would not tell her that the *amir* had ordered the woman confined to the dungeons beneath the palace, pending his judgment of the matter! It would be next to impossible to carry out her plan, if that were so. . . .

"Why, Kerem! Greetings to you, my brother!" she exclaimed, pulling up short as she saw the falconer in the street before her. He was breathing heavily with exertion from his climb while her eyes, gaping up at him, were enormous, startled cinnamon pools ringed with kohl. She made a sketchy salaam. "You honor our humble household with your visit, my brother!"

"Yes, yes," Kerem snapped, glancing over her shoulder. "Where is your father, girl? I would speak with him on matters of great importance." His dark face was almost black with controlled anger, his brown eyes stern indeed. She shivered inwardly, though Kerem did not notice. In his anger that a fellow Inandan, his friend, Ahoudan, had betrayed their Tuareg lords, he could think or see nothing else.

"My—my father? Why, I'm not certain, Kerem. I believe— *ewellah,* I'm almost *certain* he was up on the roof a short while ago, fussing with his beloved pigeons, but he isn't there anymore. Perhaps he's gone to the forge," Raisha suggested slyly. "If I see him, I'll be sure to tell him you're looking for him—"

"There's no need for that, girl. I'll find him myself, that treacherous dog!" Kerem gritted grimly. He turned on his heel and left her alone.

With a sigh of relief, Raisha drew her shawl over her head and sped up the narrow, winding streets of the city toward the palace. Perhaps Tabor's timing was not so bad after all, she thought as she scurried along, breathless in her fear and haste. Her days were surely numbered if she remained in al-Azadel

438

now. Once her father had convinced them of his innocence, their suspicions would fall on her! She must be far from the mountains before then. Aiee! Her neck prickled beneath her hair as if the executioner's blade already caressed it. . . .

Both Jonathan and Alexa glanced up nervously as footfalls sounded in the tunnel much later that afternoon. Their hearts thudded in apprehension until Raisha appeared in the dimming circle of light shed by the lamp.

"Oh, thank God, it's only you!" Alexa exclaimed with relief, sinking back down onto the rug beneath her. "I was afraid you were Kadar and his men—or the *amir's* guard, at the very least!"

Raisha smiled. "My poor Zerdali, I'm so sorry! I didn't mean to frighten you! The guards are searching the city, but don't worry, they won't come here. The lady Kairee and that Bedouin serving woman of yours have convinced everyone that you never returned from the bazaar this morning, and that little fig-brain Muriel backed them up. It'll be morning at the very least before anyone thinks of coming here to look for you. See, I've brought you some food. Eat up, and then I'll take you to Sharif."

"Did he send you to escort my daughter?" Jonathan Harding asked from the gloom beyond the lamplight, and Raisha jumped like a startled cat.

"Why, Master Kahlil, I did not know you were here!" she exclaimed. "Why, yes, he did. He knew no one would think twice to ask where a serving maid was going, and so he sent me to lead the lady Zerdali through the tunnel to the foothills. He'll be waiting there at moonrise with mounts and provisions to see your—your daughter taken to safety." She voiced the lie smoothly but with just the right amount of breathlessness the tense situation warranted, and was relieved to see the blue-eyed Kahlil's shoulders loosen.

His initial suspicions eased, Jonathan nodded in complete acceptance of her lies. "There, my poppet! You see? You'll soon be safely away from here!"

"Oh, yes! Isn't that welcome news, Zerdali?" Raisha purred.

"Soon you'll be well out of Kadar's way, and the danger over and done with! But meanwhile, Sharif ordered me to see that you eat and drink something, and to remind you that it may be many, many hours of hard riding across the deserts before the two of you are able to stop to eat, and for you to take your fill now."

"I understand, but I'm so nervous I really don't think I could eat a bite. . . ."

"Nonsense! You want to be strong for Sharif, don't you? You wouldn't want to let him down and fall from the saddle, weakened by hunger! Come, see what I've brought," she tempted. "There's bread and spiced chicken, some dates and apricots and a flagon of pomegranate juice—your favorite, yes? Kahlil, won't you join her?" she wheedled. "I'm sure if you were to eat with her, the lady Zerdali might be tempted to take a few bites? She really needs to strengthen herself for the journey, you know."

"Raisha makes sense, poppet. You'll need your strength if Sharif is to get you away from here tonight," Jonathan coaxed fondly. "Come on, love. I'll eat a bite or two with you to keep you company."

Alexa gave in under their concerted pressure, and managed to swallow a few mouthfuls of chicken and even an apricot or two, then some bread, yet in her nervousness the dry, unleavened crusts lodged dryly in her throat. Choking, she gratefully accepted the flagon of pomegranate juice shining-eyed Raisha handed her, and swallowed several gulps of the cool, sweet juice.

"Ah, that was good! I didn't realize I was so thirsty."

"Nor I," her father admitted after accepting the flagon from her in his turn and wiping his lips on his fist when he'd drained it. "Did your master mention where he intends to take my daughter, Raisha?"

"Alas, no, sir. Perhaps he felt it was better not to say. The fewer people who know, the easier it will be to keep the secret, yes?"

"Mmm. You're right there." Jonathan yawned hugely and stretched. "Lord, I'm tired! All this blasted excitement, and the worry! I suppose I'm not as young as I used to be," he added with a rueful smile for his daughter.

"Too much excitement does tire one out, Master Kahlil," Raisha agreed silkily. "Why not relax? There's an hour or two left before moonrise—plenty of time to say goodbye to your daughter before she leaves."

"No, no, I wouldn't dream of sleeping, not now! Why, we've been apart for too long to waste these few precious moments together, haven't we, Alexa?"

"Far too long," Alexa agreed readily. "And all too soon, I'll have to say goodbye to you again." She bit her trembling lower lip. "Oh, Papa, do you really think Sharif will be able to settle things between himself and Kadar so that we can return here one day? I'd only just—just realized that I love him, Papa, and now, oh, now it all seems so hopeless for us! Papa?"

But her father, she saw, had not heard her. He'd slumped down where he sat. His chin was lolling on his chest. A loud snore buzzed from him. "Why, he's fallen asleep!" she exclaimed, a little hurt that he should do so under the circumstances, and so soon after insisting he wanted to waste none of the time they had left together in sleep.

"Oh, don't be angry with him! Kahlil is no longer a young man," Raisha observed, "and old men often fall asleep when they least expect it or want to, do they not? You must try to forgive him, Zerdali, for he cannot help himself. Here, if you're done eating, I have a fresh cloth for you to bathe your face and hands and refresh yourself. And then, if you're ready, we will go through the passageway to meet Sharif."

"So soon? But, I thought you said we had an hour or two to wait until moonrise?"

"Oh, we do! But I was thinking, I've never used this tunnel myself before, and so perhaps it would be better if we set off now, in case the oil in the lamp burns down to nothing and it's too dark to find our way. You see—the light's already beginning to grow dim."

"Lord, so it is! Then—then I'll wake my father and tell him goodbye now," Alexa said, returning the wet cloth to Raisha. Her heart was heavy. It was so hard to tell her Papa goodbye again so soon after finding him alive. . . .

"Must you? Poor Kahlil, he looks so peaceful, so happy!

441

Why not let him sleep, and spare him the pain of another farewell? Were he my father, I wouldn't wake him merely to say goodbye. I'd let him keep the memory of us talking and eating happily together, until we were united again, instead of burdening him with the tears of my farewell—though, of course, that is up to you, my lady."

Alexa smiled doubtfully, feeling selfish and guilty now for wanting to wake her father to say goodbye when it would only heap more heartache upon them both. "I suppose you're right. Well, goodbye again, Papa," she whispered, leaning over her sleeping father and kissing his brow. "Allah willing, we'll be together again very soon." She straightened up. "There. I'm as ready as I'll ever be, I suppose. Shall we get going?"

Raisha's eyes were narrowed slits in the dwindling lamplight as she answered, "Let's! We don't want to keep Sharif waiting, do we?"

As Raisha had anticipated, the oil in the lamp failed when they were only three quarters of the way through the tunnel. They fumbled the last stretch in total darkness, feeling their way on hands and knees through its twists and turns, until at last they came out into the wide cave mouth where Alexa and Sharif and his men had once concealed themselves from the al-Tabor.

Flaring torches, their flames writhing in the draft, had been fixed into sconces mounted on the cavern walls. Alexa looked about her expectantly, but the torchlight revealed only two fierce-looking men she'd never seen before, both of them grinning broadly.

"*La Bes*, Raisha. I see you handled your part of it without trouble, after all!" one of the men observed.

Raisha gave a smug smile. "Did I not tell you earlier that I would, Ali, and yet you doubted me."

"I did, and that's no lie! By Allah, our chieftain will be pleased with us when he—"

"Where's my husband?" Alexa demanded, cutting the man off. "Raisha?"

She looked to the girl for an answer—any answer that would

allay her growing doubts. But the girl only smiled, her cinnamon eyes glowing almost golden in the torchlight with her glee.

"I asked you—where is my husband?" Alexa repeated, looking frantically about her, but there was no sign of Sharif, nor, for that matter, of anyone else she recognized. Her green eyes flared like emeralds, widening and catching the hissing torchlight in mounting apprehension as she realized that she was quite alone in the cavern save for Raisha and the two men; uncouth, disreputable-looking fellows she did not recognize as al-Malik tribesmen. Their indigo robes marked them as Blue Men, true, but they were ragged, unkempt fellows, quite unlike the men of her husband's guard. Then, who were they? Her heart started thumping so loudly in her ears it sounded like a frantically played goatskin drum. She licked her dry lips and looked nervously at the taller of the pair.

"Where—is—my—husband?" she repeated in a voice that was husky with fright and quavered a little.

The taller one, Ali, grinned again, a grin that appeared doubly evil and threatening in the shifting light spilled from the torch he now drew from a sconce and held aloft in his fist. A gold tooth winked slyly from beneath his bushy black moustache as the flame writhed snakelike in the draft.

"Husband, little one?" Ali chuckled. "Ah, my lady Zerdali, you have no husband here! There is only my humble self and my good friend, Yasah—is that not so, Yasah?"

"*Ewellah*, Ali, Just you and me—and the lady Zerdali, of course."

As their words and their sly tone confirmed her worst fears, Alexa fought back a scream, staring at them mutely.

"It is a pity our chieftain gave us orders to leave her untouched, is it not?" Ali murmured, his glittering brown eyes insolently appraising her. "I have never had a woman with such white skin as our lady's here—and her eyes, by Allah, bewitch one—like the eyes of a *jinn!* Shall we see what other treasures lie hidden, Yasah?" He reached for her veil, intending to remove it, but Alexa tossed her head sideways and evaded his stubby fingers.

"Didn't you say you had orders?" she ground out through

443

gritted teeth. "Lay a finger on me, and you'll be sorry!"

Ali gaped at her imperious tone, then snorted with coarse laughter. "Ah, she speaks our Tamahaq tongue, and like a queen too! In truth, Yasah, we've captured ourselves a prize here! What a pity we must hand her over to our lord Tabor! That one has enough girls and young boys to satisfy ten men, while we, poor fellows, do all the dirty work, but alas, have not a woman to share between us!"

He moved closer to Alexa and inhaled, the nostrils of his hooked nose flaring. "Ah, the fragrance of a woman, Yasah! Is any other perfume so sweet as a woman's musk? The lady Zerdali smells of flowers—*ewellah*, like the flowers in the walled gardens of the city. How I would love to pluck your blossoms, Green-Eyed One. To caress your hard little breasts—"

"You stupid, rutting donkey!" hissed Raisha's voice at his elbow. "You waste precious time filling her ears with your praises and threats—time better spent in getting her ready to ride far away from here, *ewellah*, and with all possible haste. Can it be you want al-Azim breathing down our necks?" Raisha harshly drew breath. "Well I, for one, am not anxious to be caught by him, not when we've stolen his woman! But perhaps you two—fools that you are—are eager to die?"

Ali scowled. "Oh, all right, bitch! Yasah, tie the lady!" he snapped, giving Raisha a black look. "Hand and foot, mind. I'll bring up the camels."

Ali moved away, disappearing into the blackness that pressed close all about the cave mouth. Soon after, Alexa heard his guttural "*Ikh-kh-kh! Ikh-kh-kh!*" commands to the beasts to crouch, and the grunts of several camels.

Yasah drew lengths of camel-hair rope from within his robes and came toward her, while Raisha, tapping her foot impatiently, glanced over her shoulder to see what was taking Ali so long. In that moment, Alexa erupted into action, knowing she might have no other chance to do so if she waited a second longer. As Yasah came toward her, she sprang forward and thrust at him with all her might, throwing him off balance with the surprise of her attack. She quickly whirled about, and struck the second torch from its sconce, sending it toward Raisha in a shower of sparks and a flare of fire as it toppled to the ground, before flinging herself about and plunging back into the darkness of the tunnel, running blindly through the pitchy blackness.

Raisha recovered quickly. With a squeal of outrage, the Inandan girl sped after her, catching up with her in a matter of seconds, for in the darkness, Alexa could not find her way. Her arms, outstretched before her, encountered a blank wall of knobby stone. She lurched against it, fumbling for the opening, panic making her breathing wheeze from her lungs as if through a pair of old bellows.

With a sob of relief, she at last encountered open space just ahead of her and threw herself forward. But in that moment, Raisha's fingers knotted in her flying hair and yanked hard, jerking her sharply backward. She twisted in the painful grasp of Raisha's fingers, the agony in her scalp nothing compared to her desperation to be free. She flailed at the girl, and wild elation filled her as her fist landed solidly against Raisha's cheek. Raisha yelped and clawed for her eyes, the two of them rolling over and over, spitting and clawing at each other like she-cats in the blackness of the tunnel.

But at last, Raisha managed to gain the upper hand, straddling Alexa's hips and using her weight to keep Alexa trapped beneath her. "Ali! Yasah!" she panted, "I have her! Quickly!" Her wiry fingers encircled Alexa's throat and squeezed.

Fighting for every breath, Alexa struggled to free one arm and clawed upward, lodging the heel of her hand beneath Raisha's chin. Raisha's fingers lost their tight hold about her throat as, groaning with effort, Alexa shoved upward and back, forcing the other girl's head back as far as she could, then heaving upward to buck her off and roll free of her weight. Scrabbling in the rubble that littered the cave mouth, she crawled away, sobbing aloud now as her clawing fingers yet again failed to find the way. Oh, God, if only she could see—! If only she didn't feel so weak, so dizzy, and could think through the cotton filling her mind. . . .

But then, even as the flare of the rekindled torch spilled across the cave walls and showed her the way, she saw Yasah's booted feet planted solidly in the path before her; sensed rather than saw Ali's bulk at her back. Lungs screaming for air in her terror, she hauled herself to her feet, ready to feint and dodge past Yasah and put every ounce of strength she had left into the lunge the moment his attention wavered. But instead she only swayed where she stood, gaping at squat Yasah, who suddenly began to grow taller and taller. His silhouette blurred in her vision and ran crazily together with streaks of brilliant torchlight and the blackness of the tunnel beyond him. Dear Lord, what was wrong with her? She suddenly felt so faint . . . and that . . . that hammering in her ears . . . what . . . ?

While she stood there, swaying groggily, Ali raised his fist and struck her hard across the temple. She gave a little whimper, swayed once more with the force of the blow, and then her knees buckled. Ali caught her as she fell, swinging her limp body up into his arms.

Raisha muttered a curse. "At last! About time you used your brawn if not your brains, you bungling fools!" she hissed. "Or is one weak and helpless woman too much for the al-Tabor?"

Ali shot her a murderous glance. "If you'd given her the sleeping draft as planned, we could have been well away from here by now!"

"I gave it to her!" Raisha protested. "But she drank only a little of the juice I put it in, curse her!" She shook her head. "Two of you, and yet *I* had to do everything, didn't I, you imbecile sons of afflicted mothers!"

"In truth, bitch, I weary of your insults!" Ali snarled, hefting Alexa over his shoulder and striding to the cave mouth. He paused as he drew alongside the Inanadan girl. "Another word from you—by Allah, even half a word!—and I will slice that ready, treacherous tongue from your mouth and feed it to the jackals! Better yet," he threatened with enormous relish, "I'll feed the jackals all of you, *marra*—fingers and toes, ears and nose—piece by pretty piece!"

She read the murderous look in his eyes and silenced the scathing retort that had sprung to her lips. Raisha was no fool. She knew Ali was quite capable of carrying out his threats. Gulping, she nodded and meekly went to help Yasah with the camels.

Moments later, they were mounted and loping across the starlit *sahel*, carrying their captive to the camp of the al-Tabor.

446

Chapter Thirty-Two

Alexa came to moments before they rode into the camp of the al-Tabor. Groggily, she found she was seated before Ali on his camel. One of his meaty arms was hooked tight about her waist to keep her from falling. He reeked so strongly of sweat and spices, of camels and rancid butter, that she wanted to gag, but forced herself not to. Instead, she remained limp and lifeless in his grip as if still dead to the world, while her eyes searched the grayed desert sands all about her for some clue to their whereabouts.

The moon shone down on a small, flat plain, from which the black outlines of a ruined *kella*, or watchtower, rose like a black thorn. She recognized it at once as the *kella* that lay in the *sahel* to the south of the foothills of al-Azadel and almost wept in relief. So, they had not ridden many miles while she was unconscious, as she'd feared.

The light of many campfires ringed the ruin. Their ruddy glow illuminated the faces of several score Tuareg tribesmen robed in the familiar indigo, several goatskin tents, and dozens of camels. She smothered a groan of despair. Oh, Lord, there were so many of them—over a hundred, she was certain— perhaps closer to two hundred! And so many enemy tribesmen congregated so close to the mountains could only mean one thing: Tabor ben-Murid was planning an all-out attack on al-Azadel very soon! Or was he? Having failed to overrun the city once, thwarted by the unfamiliar, mountainous terrain, and having endured the shame of having his surviving warriors sent running back to their desert villages with their tails tucked between their legs like whipped hounds, why had Tabor been

447

emboldened to try again? she wondered. What advantage was Tabor so certain he possessed now, that he'd not had before?

The answer, ridiculous as it seemed, could only be herself! But surely they didn't believe they could use her as a hostage to bring the al-Malik to their knees or forcing them to surrender their city kingdom. The idea was preposterous! They couldn't think for a minute that the *amir*, ever a wise and resourceful ruler, would place so high a value upon one woman's life that he would jeopardize his people and his kingdom to regain her? And yet, what other answer was there?

Several men, all armed to tne teetn with belts of cartridges slung around their shoulders and rifles or daggers cradled in their arms, came out to meet them as the camels reached the perimeters of the camp outside the *kella* walls. Each one of them stared at her with hot, black eyes as Ali commanded his camel to couch, dismounted, and dragged her after him.

"He's been waiting for you, friend!" growled one man, jerking his turbaned head toward the *kella*. "You took your sweet time getting back here!"

"If he thinks it's so cursed easy to kidnap al-Azim's bride, he should try it for himself!" Ali grumbled, crouching down to sever the ropes that bound Alexa's ankles. "Get going, my lady! That way!" He nodded toward the *kella*, slapping the flat of his *takoba* across her flank to get her moving in the right direction.

"How can I when my feet are numb, you lout!" Alexa snapped, bending to massage her ankles. "And lay that dagger acros. me again, and I'll tell your blasted chieftain you did far more than that! We'll see what a warm welcome back you'll get from him if he believes I'm damaged goods!" It was a brave boast, albeit an empty one, and Ali's eyes narrowed.

"Pah! Give me the soft-spoken, biddable wenches of the al-Tabor any day! I wish the al-Malik pleasure of their womenfolk, for to the last one they're all nagging bitches!" he snarled. "Very well, *my lady*," he sneered, salaaming scornfully, "we will wait until it pleases you to continue on."

But moments later, she could delay no longer and signaled that she was recovered. Scowling, Ali chivied her beneath the crumbling stone gateway of the tower and into the little courtyard within its ruined walls. Raisha followed uncertainly, but was smiling in triumph as she walked slowly behind them.

A huge fire burned in the center of the courtyard, its flames leaping up toward the square of star-spangled indigo sky above and lighting the area as brightly as if it were day. Several men were congregated about the huge fire, sipping thimble-sized measures of coffee and conversing. A few women—campfollowers, obviously—giggled and chattered off to one side, but their chatter was abruptly silenced by the approach of Ali and Yasah with their long-awaited prize, and they craned their necks to stare at her.

Ali, obviously out to impress his chieftain, grasped Alexa's bound wrists and shoved her roughly forward into the circle of light, swaggering a little as he did so.

"My lord Tabor, the woman Zerdali, as I promised! On your knees before our lord Tabor, wench!" he barked, and with the impetus of his shove propelling her, she had no option but to comply. She landed heavily on her knees, unable to break her fall with her hands bound behind her, her lips almost tasting dirt as she lurched forward. Her glorious mane of hair spilled over her face, but she flung it proudly back over her shoulders and raised her chin defiantly as she lifted her eyes to the chieftain, Tabor.

A gasp broke involuntarily from her lips at first sight of him, for the eyes that inspected her so coldly were not brown, but blue in the firelight. The curling hair that capped the man's uncovered head was brown streaked with blond. Fatima had told her long ago that the Tuaregs were an ancient Caucasian Berber tribe, and that some of their number had blond hair and blue eyes, but could this man be Sharif's cousin? It seemed he was.

Tabor smiled then, and she saw how femininely full yet cruel his lips were as they twisted, and how the gesture never warmed the pallor of his eyes by so much as a drop. He was a fine-looking man, his features masculine and elegant save for that incongruously feminine mouth. The combination was a chilling, sinister one.

"So, you are my cousin's bride!" he murmured as he rose to his feet, his eyes crawling over her as if she were some slave girl in a market of human flesh. "Stand, *marra,* and let me look at you. You, *aklan,*" he snapped, turning to Raisha, "remove your mistress's outer robe, that I may admire her beauty."

Raisha, stunned by his curt reception since she had anticipated praises, thanks, and rich rewards instead of being addressed as a slave, hurried to obey, drawing Alexa's swirling outer robe from her shoulders and casting it aside. It seemed she too had read something in the chieftain's face that warned her that instant obedience was the best course of action here, for she did so meekly, revealing her rival still clothed in the rose-colored *caftan* she had worn to visit the bazaar that morning with Muriel, belted at the waist with a girdle of braided wine-colored cords so that her breasts thrust high and proud against the finely woven cloth. Her hair was her only veil, glossy as a curtain of silk as it spilled almost to her waist, its color rich in the glow of the fire. Her oval face was pale, its only color the glitter of emerald that was her eyes and the rich coral bow of her lips.

Tabor rose and moved cat-like to stand before Alexa, grasping her chin and tilting her face this way and that as his pale eyes devoured her. He buried his hand in the tangled weight of her hair and rubbed its softness between his fingers, lifting it to his nose to savor its flowery fragrance.

"My cousin Sharif is a constant source of surprise to me," he observed, smiling his painted-on, mirthless smile yet again. "It is rumored in the villages of the al-Tabor that al-Azim is a lover of little boys. Could it be those rumors were false?"

"You have here his former mistress—one who would betray her own people to regain his bed," Alexa told him with no effort to conceal her contempt. "And his bride, who is al-Azim's contented wife in *every* way, my lord Tabor," she continued more softly and with obvious pride. "I will not dignify your insults by responding to them further!"

"Is that so? Then be warned, my lady, that neither your answers nor your pride are of any great consequence in my camp!" Tabor countered menacingly, angered by her composure. He had expected her to cringe in terror before him and beg for her freedom, not to coolly counter his insults with a quiet conviction that made him appear a jealous fool! Ah, yes, he would have preferred her bowed with fear and begging for her life, but it appeared she would have to learn the hard way that what Tabor wanted, he took. . . . "Pride can be crushed as easily as a scorpion beneath a bootheel! If you wish to keep that flawless white complexion unmarred by the stripes of a whip, then you would do well to comply rather than defy me. After all, you're nothing more than a hostage in my camp, woman, not a pampered princess. Your life is of little consequence to me, once you've outlived your purpose and brought al-Azim and his father to their knees."

So! Her guesses had proved correct! And if that were the case, her life would not be in jeopardy until after Tabor had sent their demands to the *amir* and Sharif, and received his answer—which would, of course, be a refusal to comply. Sharif, as his father's heir and a prince of al-Azadel, would have no choice. Still, she had a little time before then, she realized, and the knowledge encouraged her. Her jaw tightened. "If you plan to use me to force Sharif to relinquish al-Azadel, you'll wait until the deserts freeze over! My husband won't be forced into anything against his wishes, not when his people's lives are at stake."

"You think not? But perhaps you underestimate your charms, my fair cousin-in-law. According to this Inandan wench, my cousin's love for you is great indeed!"

"Oh, yes. But not so great he would betray the al-Malik, or give them over into your hands!"

"You think not? Then if I were you, my beauty, I would pray to whatever god you follow that you are wrong! As I said before, your life is of little consequence to me, except for the power it brings. Once al-Azadel is mine—as it should have been mine and my father's before me long ago—your usefulness will be at an end. Perhaps when that time comes, I'll use your lovely body and learn for myself what mystery it was that stirred my cousin's heart to love you, yes? And afterwards, when I tire of your charms, there are always the slave markets, are there not, which flourish despite intervention from your Western lands. With your rare coloring, I fancy you would bring me a good price upon the block."

He leered at her, his blue eyes bright with cruel pleasure

451

now. "How proud will you be then, woman, stripped naked before the whoremasters of Algiers or Morocco, forced to stand there in silence while they fondle your breasts and buttocks or probe deep between your thighs to test the tightness of your womanhood?" He licked his lips and chuckled with triumph as he saw heat at last fill her cheeks with fiery color, and knew his taunts had struck home. "Ah, that frightens you, I can tell! But it will not end there, for the slave market is only the beginning! If you are fortunate, you will be bought by a rich master, one who will use you often and in every way a woman can be used by a man, and perhaps—if it is to your master's tastes—as young boys are used by men. Then, when your beauty fades, as it must in time, your master will sell you again, to a less discriminating master. In time, you will fall into the hands of the cringing brother-keeper whose filthy bordellos filled with diseased whores of every race line the wharves of the cities. And from there—what else but the gutters and a miserable death await you?" He shrugged.

"You've made yourself quite clear, Tabor!" she snapped, unable to bear his filthy, silkily voiced threats any longer.

"I'm delighted to hear it," Tabor rejoined, almost amicably. "And now, with that dubious future to consider, I'll have Ali take you to your quarters! I trust they will be adequate for your needs, if not what you've grown accustomed to," he mocked, his fists planted on his hips.

"I'm sure I'll survive," Alexa gritted, some perverse obstinacy inside her refusing to knuckle under to his over-bearing, menacing treatment of her.

"Oh, but we'll go to great lengths to insure that you do, princess," Tabor agreed with a sneer, adding, "until I'm done with you, at least. Ali, take her and the serving wench up above, and post a guard over them. It might prove amusing to pen them together, betrayer and betrayed, in the same small space! Perhaps they will fight like she-cats!"

"But, my lord! I helped your men to abduct the lady Zerdali! Surely you can't mean to hold me hostage too!" Raisha protested, falling to her knees before the chieftain.

"Hostage? Oh, but of course not, little Raisha! What can I have been thinking of, eh, my pretty golden cat?" He smiled

452

down at her and stroked her dusky cheek with his knuckle. Raisha blinked through her tears and managed to smile back up at him, though her lower lip still quivered. "Your reward will be a night in my bed—and a generous reward it is too, if my contented wives and smiling woman are to be believed. Who knows? Perhaps, if you are clever and eager to do anything to please me, I might postpone the reward I'd planned for your—treachery."

"Reward, m-my lord?" Raisha whispered hopefully, then paled as he drew his *takoba* from his belt and ran his finger across the sharp blade that shone like a silver thread in the starlight.

"Why, yes. Surely such a clever little cat can see that it's far too dangerous to allow a traitress like you to join our numbers, girl," he said with feigned regret. "Having betrayed your al-Malik masters, it would be easy for you to switch your allegiance once again and this time betray the al-Tabor, would it not? Alas, I have no choice. You simply have to die."

Raisha began to tremble all over, weeping through her splayed fingers.

"Now, come, take heart, little traitress!" Tabor consoled her scornfully. "For the love of Allah, don't weep! You have a whole night of pleasure in my arms ahead of you, before you lose that pretty head—more than reason enough to smile, eh?"

He nodded to Ali and calmly returned to the fire and his companions, their coffeepot, and conversation, ignoring the two captive women and Ali and Yasah as if they no longer existed.

So, Alexa thought as Ali roughly yanked her arm to lead her to her prison cell, this foul beast was Tabor! She shivered as she stumbled along ahead of her captor, though the night was yet young and the air still sultry with the heat of day.

Ali jostled her up a flight of shallow stairs to a circular room of crumbling stone. Half of the roof had long since fallen in, and the starry night sky yawned above her. Untying her but cautioning her to make no attempts to escape or she'd be sorry, Ali left her alone, grumbling about ungrateful masters as he took up his post, squatting at the foot of the stairway. Alexa could see the top of his turban from where she sat, and much of the courtyard beyond, including the bright fire about which Tabor and his fellows congregated.

She sank down, exhausted, after making a cursory inspection of her cell and finding nothing more interesting than a few shards of broken pottery and a great deal of grit and sand that had been blown there by some *simoom* or other over the centuries. She found nothing else that would serve as a weapon when the time came and she was forced to defend herself, worse luck! She leaned back against the cold stone wall and watched the comings and goings about the campfire below, trying for a long while to make sense of the snatches of loud conversation that carried on the stillness to her in the hope that somehow, the information would prove useful. But after a while, sheer emotional and physical exhaustion from the day's harrowing events overcame her. Her eyelids drooped. Her head sagged forward on her chest. She tried to revive herself and fought to stay alert and awake, but in the end fatigue won, and she slept.

Sharif paced up and down, his expression more pitiless, more terrifying than Selim, trembling on his knees before him with two grim-faced guards flanking him to left and right, had ever seen before.

"I ask you, my young friend—how did Raisha know where my wife was hidden?" he demanded sternly.

Selim licked his lips. "I swear, I did not tell her outright, my lord Sharif!" He lowered his eyes. "But—*ewellah*, I am guilty nonetheless. Guilty for having assumed—from what Raisha implied—that she already *knew* where the lady Zerdali was hidden, and in so doing, I revealed her hiding place. Sir, believe me, I would never have endangered the lady Zerdali's life knowingly. You must believe me!"

Believe him? Ha! The irony was that Sharif could believe the young man only too well! And it was because he believed him and knew that Selim was loyal to him at heart, that he also knew he would spare the young man's life. Had he not been deceived by the Inandan girl himself, believing her capable of nothing more threatening than a jealous nature? By Allah, how badly he'd underestimated the depths of her hatred for Zerdali!

When he'd gone to the cave at sunset, he'd found only Kahlil there, heavily asleep, with no sign of his wife. He'd roused her father, and from Kahlil had learned that Raisha had come to them, that she'd lied and sworn she'd been sent by Sharif to escort Zerdali through the tunnel. He'd ordered a search made for the two women, but they had found nothing. At that time, he'd still not understood the depth of Raisha's betrayal. He'd suspected only that Raisha intended to harm his wife, and had ordered her parents brought to the palace, so that they might be questioned, and perhaps her whereabouts discovered.

To his surprise, Raisha's mother Boucha had at once tearfully confessed that Raisha had harbored two of their enemies in her household following the last attack of the al-Tabor, and that she'd later shown them safe passage down the mountainside to freedom by means of a little-used goat path— the same goat path where Sharif's faithful companions had met their deaths. He'd also discovered that it had been Raisha who'd stolen a deadly poison from her mother's store of simples and cleverly dipped the rose thorns in it. She'd hoped, Boucha said, that Zerdali would prick herself upon them and die, and that in his grief Sharif would turn once again to her for comfort. And, as a final, damning proof—if any further proof were needed!—Kerem the falconer had learned from a horrified Ahoudan that the pigeons kept upon their household's rooftop in the Street of the Silversmiths were not his, but belonged to his daughter.

And so, Sharif reflected, little by little, piece by piece, it had become obvious that Raisha had been the traitress within al-Azadel! It was she who had received messages from the al-Tabor by the ancient Arabic means of homing pigeons, she who'd plotted and carried out Zerdali's capture. And it must also be Raisha whom the astrologer Maimun had cautioned against all those years ago, for had he not foretold that there would come "*a time when a gift of beauty might harbor death in its perfumed bosom*"? His "gift of beauty," the "perfumed bosom" of the roses he had given her himself, had almost taken his beloved Zerdali's life. . . .

It seemed he had forgotten his father as he stood there, scowling; forgotten too Selim, Kahlil, Ahoudan, and the others as he paced, deep in thought. He discarded numerous plans to regain his bride one after the other, for each one posed a possibility that she would be harmed or killed in the process. But—was any plan he might hit upon foolproof? Was any plan any guarantee that she'd survive, now that Tabor had her in his power? No, he acknowledged, and his dread mounted. At the first whiff of something awry, Tabor would have her throat slit! *Ah, my Zerdali!* he thought silently and with a heart that ached with pain. *"You have become both my blessing and my curse! How can I bow to the demands that Tabor will make and betray my people? And how can I refuse them while knowing that by doing so, you—my beloved—will die?*

It was a choice he could not bear to make, yet one he'd always known he might someday be forced to make. As his father had been forced to choose between the dictates of his heart and Kadar's demands for justice, so must he choose. Such were the burdens of a chieftain, and he could not set them aside when they weighed him down. His mind made up, he finally spoke.

"If we wait for Tabor to make his demands known, we lose valuable time," he said slowly, and his father nodded agreement. "As it is, Tabor believes our hands are tied, that we won't dare risk an attack that might cost us Zerdali's life! And so, I intend to take advantage of his complacency, use it to our good, and do the last thing he expects!" His ebony eyes glittered with the thrill of danger and excitement that flowed like wine through his veins.

"Attack at once!" Malik said softly, for he already knew what Sharif's answer would—must!—be. As the future prince of al-Azadel, his way was clear. Not even his love for Zerdali could be allowed to alter that way.

"Ewellah, we attack tonight—without delay, without waiting for daylight or for that crawling worm Tabor to send us his demands! While they sit smug and slack about their campfires in the moonlight, we will set our faces to the enemy camp and ride! When they see the proud warriors of the al-

Malik Blue Men encircling their camp, they will know that to spit in the eye of al-Azim is to spit in the eye of *sheytàn*, the Devil!"

Ebony eyes fiercely aglitter, he tore his *takoba* from his belt and brandished it aloft. "Death to the rebel al-Tabor!" he roared in a voice of thunder.

The Imochagh warriors drew their daggers and echoed his challenge.

"Death to the rebels!"

Chapter Thirty-Three

Screams awakened Alexa over two hours later, a woman's screams that were high and carrying on the night air. Cold sweat broke out all over her body as she was jolted awake, for she recognized the terror-filled cries as Raisha's. Dear God, what terrible, awful thing could Tabor have done to her, to make her scream in that inhuman way?

Clinging to the crumbling stone wall for support, Alexa rose to her feet and shuffled her way cautiously to the head of the stairs, shaking the pins and needles from her cramped limbs. That awful Ali lay asleep at the foot of the stairs, his sentry's duties obviously forgotten in his fatigue. Looking down into the courtyard, she saw that the rest of the camp also appeared to have been asleep, but had now been roused by the woman's screams. One by one, she saw the al-Tabor tribesmen who'd slept rolled in their robes about the campfire throw aside their coverings and spring to their feet with their *takobas* drawn. It was then that she saw Raisha stagger through the gateway and into the courtyard, moving as if sleepwalking—or else deep in shock.

Her long, black hair was wild as a witch's mane, swirling about her blood-spattered nude body. Her dusky flesh was ruddy in the shifting flames of the campfire, her eyes demented, glittering golden pools of terror. In one fist, Alexa caught the flash of a sharp blade, and simultaneously heard a man cry out in pain and rage, "After the Inandan, you lazy dogs! By Allah, I'll have your cursed heads if you let her escape! The bitch has stabbed me!"

She saw Tabor then, and realized at once that he was

wounded. He was bare-chested and staggering as he entered the courtyard. His face was livid with fury and pain. He was clutching at his belly as he approached Raisha, and blood trickled from between his fingers and ran down his arms in dark rivers.

"Your moments of freedom are numbered, slut!" he rasped. "Stab me, would you? Refuse my commands, would you? Ha! Y-you'll plead with me to do anything I command soon enough, bitch! I'll have you lashed hand and foot, spread-eagled and helpless, and given to my tribesmen to use as they see fit!"

"No!" Raisha denied, deathly pale as she shook her head from side to side. "I will not go through that again! By Allah, I will die first, you—you animal, you foul, inhuman beast! Never again—!"

So saying, she turned and fled, weaving her way drunkenly between the goatskin tents and then running, running for her life across the open *sahel*. Alexa lost sight of her then, but the rasping sobs of her breathing carried loudly on the air for a moment longer, before Alexa could see or hear her no more. In answer to their chieftain's commands, first one tribesman mounted up and kicked his camel in pursuit of her, then another, and still another.

"The slut goes to the men who catch her first! Let them take their pleasure of her, before she dies!" Tabor gasped, and sank weakly to his knees.

His men whooped and howled their approval as they jostled their mounts out of the courtyard, each one of them eager to be the first to reach the girl.

Alexa heard his foul promise and her throat constricted. Raisha was doomed, she knew. And, despite everything the girl had done in her crazed desire to have Sharif for herself, she could not help the stirring of pity that filled her heart. No one, not even Raisha, deserved the awful death Tabor would exact in revenge for her attempt to kill him! A lone woman on foot could not hope to escape all those howling, lust-crazed men on horses or camels, and even if—by some miracle—she did, what else lay ahead of her but a long and drawn-out, agonizing death in the scorching deserts? She chewed her lower lip. Perhaps she would suffer a similar fate herself when Tabor received Sharif's answer to his demands and learned his attempts at blackmail had failed. Ah, yes, probably.

She stood there, trembling uncontrollably, still clinging to the angle of the wall for support while she tried to get a grip on herself. She stared out across the courtyard. Her view beyond it and through the crumbling archway of the gates revealed the hushed desert sands and the looming silhouette of the mountains of al-Azadel, sprawling across the deep violet horizon like a great, sleeping black leopard.

Somewhere out there, Sharif was searching for her. She knew it as surely as if she could hear his voice calling to her! And, as desperately as she feared for his life at Tabor's hands, she yearned so for Sharif, for his strength and protection, for the comforting circle of his arms about her. She blinked back her tears, willing herself not to break down, to be brave. After all, she was the wife of al-Azim, a princess of al-Azadel. She wouldn't shame him by crying! But—if only he were here, she wouldn't be nearly so afraid, she just knew it. She wished with all her heart that he would come for her and spirit her away to safety—and perversely prayed with all her strength and will that he'd do no such foolish thing. . . .

Her eyes grew accustomed to the darkness little by little, and once she fancied she saw a lighter shadow against the deep gray of the *sahel* beyond the *kella,* a small, paler oval shape that moved furtively and was swiftly swallowed up by darkness yet again. Her pounding heart skipped a beat. Her eyes narrowed as she tried in vain to discern further movement out there in the blackness, yet she spotted nothing else out of the ordinary.

Another time, she thought her straining ears caught the muffled nicker of a horse nearby, quickly silenced, but surely her eyes and ears had deceived her, for the men who'd pursued Raisha had taken the horses. She decided she must be mistaken, for the few men remaining in the al-Tabor camp gave no sign of having heard anything unusual. But then, she realized, they weren't watching and listening, as was she. They were too intent on carrying their injured chieftain back to his tent and seeing the stab wounds Raisha had inflicted quickly tended to, and so their attention was diverted. Could she have heard something they had not?

Heart pounding, she waited, her eyes riveted to the darkness that pressed close all about the *kella*, plumbing the pitch-darkness for the slightest sign—however faint—that would prove her suspicions fact, rather than wishful thinking. And, after what seemed an eternity had passed, her patience finally paid off. Excitement thrummed through her like a taut wire set to vibrating. Someone—possibly a great many someones!—was out there, moving furtively closer and closer to the *kella*, she was almost convinced of it now. . . .

"Hey, you! Back inside, mi' lady!"

Blast him, Ali had wakened! He growled at her to move away from the head of the short flight of crumbling stone stairs and return to her circular cell. Yet in the same moment, she looked beyond him and saw a circle of shadowy riders—many, many riders!—silhouetted beyond the fire and the gates, and knew that her dearest wish had been granted. Sharif had come for her!

Wetting her lips, she saw that Ali, still groggy from sleep, was looking suspiciously about him, no doubt wondering belatedly where many of his companions had gone while he lay fast asleep. If he looked too carefully, he'd be able to see the riders from here as she had, and perhaps sound an alarm before they attacked!

"You're such a fool, Ali!" she declared suddenly. "Why, you slept through all the excitement!" Her tone was taunting as she tried to draw his attention. Without further ado, she backed away as he'd ordered, removing herself from his line of vision so that in order to hear or see her, he'd have to mount the stairs. Crouching down, she fumbled in the darkness until she had two hefty fistfuls of sand.

"What excitement?" he demanded. What are you talking about?" His turbaned head appeared over the top of the staircase, then the rest of him.

"Your friend Raisha didn't care much for your chieftain's 'lovemaking,' apparently," she told him with an edge of glee to her tone. "And so she stabbed him and fled! Half the camp has gone off in pursuit of her, while you slept through the whole thing! You'd best pray to Allah that Tabor dies, Ali. He'll have

461

your guts for *agals* if he survives her attack!"

Ali was standing before her now, wearing a sullen expression that was growing uglier by the second. "What is this? Pah! I think you lie, woman!" he growled. "If what you said were true, the commotion would surely have wakened me!"

"Well, it seems it didn't! Raisha was screaming like a madwoman, Ali—and Tabor was roaring like a stuck pig—and the men all went howling after the girl like a pack of wolves—it was all quite amusing, I thought!" And she grinned broadly. "Further proof that the al-Tabor are nothing but a bunch of incompetent, lazy, worthless jackals, fit to be nothing more than—than Gatherers-of-Camel-Dung!"

"Why you—!" Ali took a step forward, and in that same moment she saw movement beyond him—sudden and swift—close by the crumbling arched gateway; saw a dark mass separate itself from the blackness of night; heard the ululating battle cry of the al-Malik ring out on the silence as they poured through the gate; and knew the moment had come to act! Before he could turn to the sound, she flung her fistfuls of sand into Ali's eyes, temporarily blinding him. He staggered backward, and while his attention was diverted, she rushed forward and gave him a hard shove that sent him tumbling down the stairs, rolling over and over like a hoop. She quickly followed him down, leaping over Ali's still form at the bottom of the stairs before hoisting up her skirts and racing out into the courtyard.

In the distorting light of the leaping flames from the fire, the courtyard was a scene of chaos. The al-Malik, mounted on the finest Arabian horses, had their *takobas* drawn and were fiercely battling the remnants of Tabor's forces. Horses screamed. Camels grunted. Men roared and yelled in triumph, or shrieked in mortal agony as they went down in the sand clutching bloody wounds. The camp-followers wailed and shrieked and fled for a hiding place. Daggers clashed and crashed, flashed and clanged, steel ringing and echoing against steel or stone. Bullets cracked and whined and ricocheted. Blood ran. Wounded men threw up their arms and crashed to the gritty earth, while the victors flung about with whoops of triumph to take on other foes.

And then, Alexa at last spied Sharif in the very thick of the battle, and her heart leaped with joy. How magnificent her husband looked, his wickedly curved *takoba* swooping like an arc of golden fire in the light as he fought his way through the gateway and into the courtyard. Never had he looked as tall and proud, as fierce and graceful as he looked now, with his indigo robes swirling about him and his powerful sword-arm weaving patterns of light in the air. Her heart swelled and sang with pride. Sha-Sha, her childhood friend and her first love, was now Sharif al-Azim, her hero, her desert hawk, and her last and only love. He was the lover she'd once only dreamed of belonging to! Brave and strong, tender and gentle, wise and funny, and oh, so handsome too, he was everything she'd ever wanted in a mate, and more!

The scene before her all seemed faintly unreal, Alexa thought, mesmerized: the firelight and giant shadows shimmying across the courtyard, the curvetting horses, the flashing blades, the cries of victory or wails of despair and defeat—like a scene straight from a picture book of the Crusades or a wonderful tapestry! But her hero was no Christian knight in shining armor, mounted upon a snow-white charger. Rather, he was the mighty Saladin upon a stallion as black as the devil, come to free his bride, Zerdali, from the wicked clutches of their greatest enemies! She saw how his ebony eyes caught the firelight and glowed above his *tagilmust* with determination and the ardent will to triumph, while between his powerful thighs, the stallion Aswad seemed carved of gleaming jet, trimmed in scarlet leather trappings, prancing and snorting as he bore his master bravely into the heat of the battle. . . .

As Alexa watched Sharif, her heart in her mouth with concern for his safety, Ali recovered from her trick. Eyes bloodshot and watering, he nonetheless lumbered to his feet and moved stealthily toward her, his dagger ready in his fist. So enthralled was she by the activity everywhere about her, she neither heard nor saw him as he slipped up behind her until it was too late. He sprang at her, and knotted a fist in her hair. His other hand brought the blade of his *takoba* in a cold caress across her throat. But he'd underestimated the woman. She'd gone beyond fear now that Sharif was nearby, and felt capable

463

of anything, filled with a reckless courage that sang through her veins. Ali wouldn't stop her from reaching his side, she swore—no one could! He'd risked his own life to save her, and she'd be damned if he'd leave here empty-handed and alone!

She struggled to escape Ali, twisting and squirming in his grip with strength born of desperation. Oh, Lord, she had to get free, had to warn Sharif not to turn his back on the desert— had to warn him that there were countless numbers of the al-Tabor still out there, where they'd gone in pursuit of Raisha! At any moment, those others could return, and Sharif and his warriors would be trapped in the courtyard between the two factions of the al-Tabor like helpless fish in a barrel!

She wormed her way around until she faced Ali, her nails clawing and scoring at his face, yet his grip in her hair remained inviolate. Finally, she brought up her foot and slammed it into his groin, using all the strength she could muster. She was rewarded far beyond her expectations! With a shriek like a wounded animal, Ali paled and doubled over, cradling his hurt, while Alexa quickly spun about, emerald eyes widening with joy at what she saw. Sharif had broken free, and was riding toward her! The stallion Aswad's racing hooves were gobbling up the shadowed courtyard between them! Closer and closer Sharif came, and then, wonderfully, he was alongside her, his strong arm outstretched to haul her up behind him onto the stallion's broad rump, his ebony eyes aflame with love and relief to see her unharmed.

"There's more of them!" she screamed above the clamor of battle all around them. "Fifty, maybe even a hundred more men! They rode into the desert, but they'll hear the shots and turn back!"

Sharif nodded grimly, and through her joy that he'd come to free her, she wondered at his silent acceptance of her warning momentarily, before she realized the reason for it; her warning had come just moments too late! Her fears had already become reality.

The remainder of the al-Tabor had heard the shots and returned posthaste to the *kella* to aid their fellow tribesmen, surprising the battling al-Malik by attacking their rear flank and sandwiching Sharif's men between them and their tribesmen still in the courtyard. With their greater numbers, they'd managed to gain the courtyard, retake it, and were even now steadily forcing the al-Malik further and further back, beneath the gateway and out into the desert from whence they'd come. Another few minutes, and she and Sharif would be cut off from his warriors, trapped amidst the al-Tabor within the imprisoning walls of the *kella*, which—thanks to the well at its heart and a ready water supply—the al-Tabor could then defend indefinitely!

"We must break through," Sharif cried over his shoulder, voicing her own thoughts, "or we'll be trapped! Hold fast to me, beloved!"

She needed no second urging, but clung to Sharif's waist like a limpet clinging to a breakwater of stone, pressing her cheek hard against the comforting breadth of his back and trying to grip with her thighs and knees as she felt Aswad's powerful muscles bunch beneath her legs. The stallion bolted forward, heading like a bullet straight for the gateway, gathering speed and momentum and kicking up dust-devils as they careened across the courtyard.

"*Stop them!*" someone screamed. "*For the love of Allah, cut them off!*"

"*Don't let them get past you!*"

"*Al-Azim and his woman are escaping! Halt him, you fools! Stop him!*"

To her horror, Alexa saw the al-Tabor wheel their horses about to face them, a flank of six or seven men ranged on either side of the roaring fire. Her heart was in her mouth with dread. It was no use! Whichever side Sharif steered Aswad toward, they were waiting for them, more than six men to one! They'd be hacked down like stalks of wheat, without a chance of putting up a fight!

Yet she had reckoned without Sharif's enormous courage and daring, had badly underestimated the ebony stallion's love for his master and the slim woman upon his back. . . .

Sharif made no attempt to steer the animal around the fire, as she'd expected. Nor did Aswad once falter or shy with fear as the fire loomed up, a huge and crackling wall before them. Sharif demanded the stallion's all, and Aswad answered with all the courage of his great, throbbing heart. Together they rode him straight for the golden heart of the fire!

"Up, my proud one, *up!*" she heard Sharif roar, and felt the valiant stallion throw itself forward in a tremendous, exhilarating jump that bore the two of them soaring to safety over the flames! For a fleeting second, she felt the scorching heat wafted against her cheek, heard a sizzle as it singed the hems of her flowing robes, and then without missing a single stride Aswad had landed safely on the opposite side of the fire! He regained his footing and galloped on, through the gateway and out into the starry desert beyond.

They left the al-Tabor staring openmouthed after them.

From that night, the stallion's fearless leap through fire and the escape of al-Azim and his beautiful *Englesy* bride would become legend in their camps, to be marveled at over endless cups of coffee through decades to come.

Chapter Thirty-Four

Alexa was still deeply asleep when the sun began its fiery arc toward the horizon, staining the pale sands garnet and rust. Sharif halted the horses at a small oasis. He swung his leg over Aswad's back and dismounted, laying Alexa gently down in the sand without waking her. Then he went to the pack camel, withdrawing and unfolding a black goatskin tent from the packs, which he quickly erected, spreading small rugs and cushions within its skirts to soften the stony ground. When all was in readiness and a small fire crackling merrily before it, with water from the goatskins given the horses and more heating in a brass kettle for coffee, he carried Alexa inside, settling her gently upon the coverings. She tossed her head and mumbled in her sleep, her speech slurred with the powder he'd given her, but she didn't awaken.

He crouched down beside her, brushed strands of damp hair from her face, and planted a kiss upon her lips, relieved that she had not roused when he moved her. The closer they came to Fort Valeureux before she awoke and realized his intentions, the better, to his mind. But, as he looked down at her, a fist of pain squeezed his heart. A flare of heat burned behind his eyelids. He swallowed, and his throat ached with the unshed pain of his imminent loss. So close! He'd come so cursed close to fulfilling his dreams of the two of them together, always. And now . . . now his dreams were vanishing, bright yet insubstantial mirages shimmering tantalizingly just out of his reach.

His heart was empty, heavy as stone. Sorrow overwhelmed him. He couldn't bear to stand there, looking down at her beloved face, knowing that by the next setting of the sun she would be gone from his life, probably forever. Never again after this night would he see her shy smile deepen and feel the warmth of it touch his soul like a ray of sunshine. Never again would he hear her laughter, nor see her eyes sparkling at some foolish, intimate little joke they'd shared. Never again would he hold her in his arms and share with her the wondrous delights of lovemaking they had known, or watch her blossom into the passionate, confident woman she was destined to become. Now would he ever plant a child in her womb, nor watch her swell and blossom with the fruit of their love.

He tightened his jaw and straightened, forcing himself to be outwardly strong, emotionless, in the manner of the Blue Men. *Ewellah,* he would be strong, no matter what, he swore, for her sake if not his own! As Maimun had long ago foretold, the greatest proof of a man's love was not in the magnificence of the gilded cage he built to keep his beloved safe and always at his side. Proof of a man's love lay in making the greatest sacrifice of all, and setting the songbird free, even if doing so meant never hearing its sweet song again. He hardened his jaw. He was Imochagh. He was of the *imaharen,* the nobles, and a man of honor. He would do what must be done to enable her to begin a new life, a life without him, as he'd planned when he rode from al-Azadel two nights ago to free her from Tabor's camp.

He'd realized before he set out that night that he must put her from him, set her free. Sadly, he'd admitted to himself that his great love for her weakened him as a leader of the al-Malik. That as long as her life and safety were at stake and uppermost in his heart, his enemies had power over him and his people through her. He'd tried to tell himself that he was still capable of making decisions based only on cool logic and reason, but it was a lie. His feelings for Zerdali colored his every thought and action; his judgment of any situation was biased by the effect such an action would have on her. Such a situation was untenable for the son of Malik ben-Azad! He had no choice. He must cut her from his life, and allow no cowardly weakening on his part.

"I divorce thee," he uttered solemnly, his voice sounding

loud on the hush of twilight, with scarcely a show of emotion other than the sudden twitch of a muscle at his jaw. He clenched his fists tight, tighter at his sides, so that the knuckles gleamed white as bare bone. "*Ewellah*, beloved, I divorce thee. I divorce thee, my soul!"

Three times, he made the vow, gritting his teeth as each word was wrung from him. And with its making, by the laws of his land she was no longer his wife, no longer bound to him in any way. She was free once more. It was done.

When the last word had trembled away into silence, he turned on his heel and ducked under the skirts of the tent, striding for the fire without a backward glance. Moments later, sitting cross-legged before it and sipping a thimble-sized cupful of scalding Turkish coffee that tasted like gall, he knew he'd never felt more alone—nor more lonely—than he did at that moment, watching the full moon rise and bathe the sands in ethereal light; watching the stars come out one by one like a million shining satin eyes in the indigo darkness above; hearing the chill night breezes whisper her name like a thousand soft sighs: Zerdali . . . Zerdali . . . Zerdali . . .

Gazing into the golden flames, he remembered that first night when he had gazed into her green eyes in the camp of Cemal and had not recognized her as the bewitching *houri* of his dreams. And then, that other time when he had chased her across the sands upon his black stallion, believing she had come to him at last. . . .

How long he sat there, seeped in memories, he did not know. But quite suddenly, he grew aware that he was being watched. His ebony eyes, gleaming in the moonlight and the flames of the fire, scanned the dunes all about their little camp, and he was certain. His senses had not played him false. Someone—or something—was out there!

The hackles rose upon his neck in response. A sense of danger, near at hand, flared his nostrils, skittered down his spine like a nervous cat upon scampering paws. Moving slowly, he shifted position and curled his fingers over the hilt of his *takoba* within the folds of his robes. Then he waited, for patience was also a warrior's virtue. Every nerve and muscle in his body was tensed. His legs were coiled, ready to spring into action. His heart thundered. Yet, to all outward appearances, he was calm, relaxed, unaware.

Was the watcher Kadar? he wondered. Had he learned of his intention to return Zerdali to her people, and come in pursuit of them? No. He thought not. The Imochagh were renowned for their skills in tracking, their ability to disappear in seemingly barren terrain, their possession of an uncanny sixth sense that forewarned and forearmed them in dangerous circumstances. His keenest instincts told him now that someone was indeed out there, but that the mysterious watcher was not Kadar. Stealth was not Kadar's way. Rather, he would have ridden boldly into their camp and demanded the girl be handed over to him, or taken her by force. But if not Kadar, then who? The al-Tabor? Instinct again said no. And so he remained, waiting and ready, for a long, long time before whoever—or whatever—had been out there in the shadows, watching him, moved away. The sensation of eyes upon him vanished as subtly as it had come.

Sharif exhaled the drawn breath he'd taken with a relieved sigh.

"Sha-Sha? Sha-Sha!"

He jumped sharply on hearing the sleepy voice, husky with alarm on the silence, calling that long-remembered name, and hurried to the tent, dropping to his knees beside Zerdali's bed of rugs and pillows. He took her hand in his own warm one and squeezed it to comfort her.

"It's all right! I'm here, beside you, *habibah*. Don't be afraid, my love."

"Sha-Sha? Oh, thank God you're here! I was asleep, and I had such strange, muddled dreams, they frightened me. When I woke up, I was so confused! Where are we? Is something wrong with me? I feel so—so tired. Have I been ill, is that it? And what are we doing here, in this tent?"

"I gave you something after we reached my father's tent, remember? Just a sleeping draft to calm you, beloved, nothing more. You were frightened and upset, and Kairee and Fatima thought it for the best that you sleep," he murmured, wrapping the falsehood in truth. "That was two nights ago. You've slept through many, many hours of travel."

"But where are we? And why didn't we go back to al-Azadel

470

after you rescued me from Tabor?"

"Alas, I dared not take you back there," he explained softly. "It has become far too dangerous for you—and for my people."

"Dangerous!"

"*Ewellah.* After Kadar left my father's hall empty-handed and in anger at your disappearance, he decided to join forces with Tabor! It is said he has become Tabor's right-hand man, and will remain so until Tabor recovers from his injuries. In return for this alliance, Tabor has promised Kadar he and his tribesmen will help him to recapture you. In other words, my love, Tabor would have given you into Kadar's hands had I not stolen you away."

In his turmoil, his accent was pronounced, his words stilted. He sounded as if each syllable was plucked from him one by one, like bloody thorns drawn from his flesh. Alexa paled.

"But Kadar was like a brother to you—you were raised together as brothers and friends! How could he think of joining Tabor!"

"When a friend becomes a foe, my Zerdali, he takes with him all the secrets, alliances, and trusts of that former friendship. In his great bitterness at being wronged, he uses those secrets to restore his lost pride and soften his hurt by bringing low his former friend. More than anyone, Kadar knows where to strike so that the hurt will go deepest—where it will do the greatest damage to his former allies. I am my father's only son, and the heir to our kingdom. And you—you are the woman I love above all others! Tabor knows he cannot attack al-Azadel with any hope of victory, for the mountains are unfamiliar to him, and the possibility that we lie in wait for his men within her passes too great. But Kadar is a different matter. Kadar knows the mountains' secrets as well as any who live within the walls of al-Azadel. With his help, Tabor can succeed. Through us, he can bring my father to his knees."

A dull pain began to throb in her temples as she saw the bleakness in his midnight eyes. What he had left unspoken was more eloquent than any words. "And through me you? Then I was right—that's why Tabor had me abducted?"

He nodded. "*Ewellah*, partly. He needed you to buy Kadar's

allegiance if his plan to ransom you to me failed. In return, Kadar would have given him his knowledge of the mountains of al-Azadel."

She drew an unsteady breath. "So you decided you must take me away, to somewhere where I would be safe and they could not use me against you. And knowing I'd refuse to leave you, you drugged me." It was a statement rather than a question. She knew him too well to even ask.

"Yes," he confirmed softly, unable to meet her eyes.

"Wh-where?" she asked, her voice breaking.

"Fort Valeureux. You will be safe from Kadar and Tabor amongst your own kind. The *Franziwa* major you once threatened me with will see you safely escorted to Algiers, I am certain." A ghost of a smile hovered about his lips.

"Algiers!" So far from him, she thought, so very far! And then—what then? She bit her lower lip, trying to stay calm as she asked, "And how long must I stay there?" but her voice came out as a strangled whisper.

"I cannot say. But it must be for as long as the danger to you still exists," he lied, knowing in his heart of hearts that the danger would exist for as long as Kadar still lived. Kadar was not a man to allow time to soften him, nor lessen his thirst for vengeance. . . ." Perhaps it will not be for long, and we shall be together again very soon, yes?" he added in an attempt to comfort her.

But she'd grown pale in the gloom of the tent and in the moonlight that streamed beneath the raised skirts, knowing in her heart that he lied, and knowing why he did so. He was sending her away, and instinct told her that he doubted they would ever be reunited again. Hurt blossomed like an ugly, unwanted flower in her breast. "And what of you? What about your safety?"

His eyes met hers, ebony to emerald, and his slid uncomfortably away first. Suddenly, she knew what he planned to do when she was safe and far from the desert.

"No!" she cried brokenly, moving to kneel at his feet. She drew his hands into hers, kissing them feverishly, pressing her cheek to their warmth and then resting her head upon his thighs. "No, no, I won't go meekly away and let you do it!" she

472

cried softly, her words muffled with tears. "You'll be killed if you challenge Kadar! I won't let you do it and risk your life! All of this was my doing, after all—mine and Keene's. If he and I had stayed in England—if I'd trusted him just that once—none of this would ever have happened."

"Hush, little one," he commanded, stroking her hair to soothe her. "You are not at fault. All that has happened is the will of Kismet. And there is more to this than you or I, or even your brother. The safety of my people is at stake too. I must go back, and do what I can to put an end to the old enmity between the al-Malik and the al-Tabor once and for all, so that we can move forward into the future in the ways my father and I had always planned, with peace and harmony between our tribes. Tabor's ways—the old Tuareg ways of robbing the caravans that cross the deserts for our livelihood—must be done away with. We must find new ways to prosper—ways that will insure a future for the children of my people, and for their children's children. Come beloved, you know that I'm no fool! Would I seek to draw Kadar out into the open—and Tabor and his tribesmen with him—unless I believed we could win?"

"But—surely there's another way, one with less danger for you."

"It is the only way, and it is the one Kismet has set down for me."

"No!" she whispered hoarsely. "No! Fate doesn't control our lives—we do! You said so yourself! You still have a choice—you don't have to send me away," she pleaded. "I could come back with you to al-Azadel. Whatever happens, I'm your wife. My place is there, beside you, whatever the future may hold for us. Why can't I be there, where I belong, with Kairee and the other women, and my father too? There's nothing for me in Algiers, nor in England, not anymore. Please don't—don't make me leave you," she begged him, her lips quivering. "My life is here, with the man I love, with you, my husband. I love you, Sha-Sha, I do! I've never been able to tell you before, but I love you so much. My heart will break if you send me away, never knowing if—if—I'll ever—!" She bit her lip, unable to voice her greatest fear.

His heart churned as she said the words. *I love you,* she'd said, *I love you so much!* He sat, looking down at her glossy head cradled in his lap, wondering how he could bear the agony of losing her. Her pale face was still blurred, soft and dreamy from her deep, drug-induced sleep in the shadows. Her eyes shimmered, emerald pools bright with tears soon to be shed as he tilted her lovely face to his. The moonlight glinted, touching her hair with a dark coppery luster through the raised skirts of their tent and lending a nacreous sheen to her bare arms. How long have I waited for you to say you loved me, my jewel? he wondered. How long have I yearned to hear you say those words and mean them with all your heart! And now, when I must give you up, my heart's desire has been granted—but, too late, ah, too late! By Allah, was Kismet not cruel and merciless? Had she no pity nor compassion? He wanted to bellow and rant with rage at the unfairness of life; to lash out and give hurt and pain in a desperate attempt to ease the building grief and pain within himself. . . .

Instead his arms found her, drew her up off her knees to nestle upon his thighs. He held her so tightly in his powerful arms, it was as if she sought escape rather than melting into them and against him with a broken cry of longing.

Sha-Sha, please, don't make me leave you, she implored silently, burying her face in the angle of his throat and shoulders, her hot tears scalding his bared neck.

I have no choice. There is nowhere I could hide thee where Kadar's assassins could not find and kill thee, little one.

I'm not afraid. We could face what comes together.

But I'm afraid—afraid for you! I know him too well. We were as brothers. He will do as he says! He will not relent, nor will he ever cease his quest for vengeance.

Come with me, then. Come with me to Algiers—or to my land, to England!

Run away? Ah, little one, I cannot! I am a hawk of the desert, you know this. And the hawk flies free, fearing no one. In a house of stone, with walls and doors to confine me, I would die, or suffer a living death. I was born of the blazing deserts, habibah, *beneath endless desert skies. And it is in the desert I must stay.*

Not a word was spoken as he drew her to him, yet their tumultuous thoughts communicated as effortlessly as if they

474

had been voiced aloud. She lifted her slender arms, twined them about his throat, framed his dear, dark head between her palms, **and** felt his glossy hair give like silk beneath her fingertips as she drew his head down to hers.

Kiss me! her eyes implored him. *Kiss me, and forget your vows! Hold me, and relent. Make love to me, Sha-Sha, my husband—and I will make love to you, so sweetly, so tenderly, so passionately, you'll never bring yourself to let me go!*

He buried his face in the soft, tangled mass of her hair, inhaling the sweet fragrance of roses mingled with the unique fragrance of her flesh. Her scent. The essence that was her. He breathed in deeply, filling his nostrils and lungs with that cherished scent. He would never forget it, never! He pressed his lips to her temples, her smooth brow, and then to each of her cheeks, tasting the salt and the warm dampness of her tears upon them as she gave way to weeping again. Desire for her rose through him like a hot flood. His grip tightened and he ground his mouth down upon hers; lashed his tongue across her lips and parted them, surging deep into her mouth, no longer gentle but stirring her tongue to a fevered, ardent response that sent yearning through him. She arched her body to his, molding its soft curves to his lean, strong angles and pressing her hips to his flanks, wanting him so. Wordlessly, he pressed her down until she lay half-crushed beneath his chest upon the heaped rugs.

With a groan, he kissed her throat, her shoulders. He needed her as never before, wanted her with the desperation of lovers everywhere who are destined to be parted from the one they love, and have only moments left to share. With hands that trembled, he bared her lovely breasts, half-tugging, half-tearing the hampering garment away as her hands helped him, showed him how, as eager and unsteady as his own. Her breath came sweet and sorrowful against his cheek, ragged with heartache and desire, when she was naked in his arms. She took his hands in hers and pressed them both over her ivory breasts, leaning upward to fill his palms with her soft mounds, imploring him with her actions to take her, to still her fears, to ease the aching emptiness in her flesh with the fullness of himself, to fill her, heart and body, with himself, and blot out fear and grief in passion—even passion as bittersweet and fleeting as theirs might prove.

He fondled her, adoring her creamy, coral-tipped breasts and belly with touch and tongue as always, but with a feverish hunger that leaped from him to her like a contagion and swept them both away. As she uttered little gasping sounds deep in her throat, her hands sought and found him, encasing the swollen ridge of his shaft in the sheath of her hand, stroking, stroking, until he was as hard and ready for her as she for him. With a drawn-out sigh, she lay back, parted her thighs, and guided him gloriously home, slipping her arms about his shoulders to gather him to her breasts like a mother embraces a child. Her slender legs cradled his hips, holding him tight within her as he buried himself deep in her moist flesh, filling her utterly. For a moment, he remained still, kissing her lips with fleeting, tender butterfly kisses, then deeper, harder ones. Their tongues writhed in a mating dance that was slick and wet and warm—and *right,* so very right—as he began to move, to plunge, each rhythmic thrust building upon the last as he rode deep within her.

The desperation of their plight filled both of them with an urgency, a sweet-savage, violent possessiveness neither had dared to express until this moment. He branded her with his searing kisses, knotting his fingers roughly in her hair and winding it about them both like bonds to bind them fast together, always. She gasped and clung and arched against him, digging her nails into his smooth back, her sobs of agony and sobs of rapture commingling, becoming one and the same, floating upon the cool night air like the cries of some exotic nightbird, calling plaintively for its lost mate, as the passion within her rose, trembled, then tore free and flung her, whirling, heavenward.

She grew still as pulsing sensation moved through her, and then in the same moment felt his fingers grip her upper arms, and knew that the rapture of release had claimed him too. A shudder wracked him, and then a low, exultant groan of completion broke from his parted lips as he thrust one last time and spent deep within her, his face buried in the angle of her throat and shoulder.

476

For glorious moments, they were one: one being, one body, one soul, without beginning or end. For glorious moments, they could pretend they would never be parted, and believe the lie.

Keene Harding slithered backward on his belly away from the crest of the dune behind which he had concealed himself to watch the little camp below. The stolen native robes he wore blended with the darkened color of the sands, and he was all but invisible in the night.

Hidden by the crest of the dune from Sharif al-Azim's piercing eyes that—as if he had powers beyond those of mortal men—Keene was certain could see through the darkness like the eyes of a cat, he rolled onto his back and lay gazing up at the multitude of stars, thinking over all that he had seen.

He replayed the images of his sister and that—that *Arab* coupling together through his mind. He'd watched them through the raised skirts of the tent. They'd believed themselves alone, but he'd watched them, all right, and he'd seen everything. He'd caught glimpses of pale flesh, bared in the moon's bright beams. Seen slender white arms reaching eagerly—eagerly, damn her harlot's soul!—for broad, tanned shoulders. Seen their two bodies moving, limbs entwined in a rising and falling dance of passion. Heard her cries of ecstasy floating on the wind . . .

Damn Alex! Damn damn damn her! He'd set her up, hadn't he? He'd run out on her and left her to the Tuaregs' tender mercies, wanting to punish her for doubting him, hadn't he? Hadn't he? He'd used her so that he could make good his escape from Kadar and the others, certain they would make her the scapegoat for his doings and that this time Father's pet—his dear little Alexa, his precious poppet!—would learn how it felt to be *him*—to be the one blamed for every wrong, the one punished for every niggling, imagined misdeed. But, yet again, she'd had the last laugh. She had triumphed, not he! She'd turned the tables and bewitched the Tuareg scum who'd abducted her. . . .

You see, sonny, she's done it again! Clever, clever witch, clever bitch, there's the hitch! She's done it again! She's made the Tuareg love her! They're laughing at you, Keene old son, lying there naked together and touching each other while they laugh at you! You've been hounded from oasis to oasis. You've hidden in filthy native villages with cringing Arab peasant-dogs who were too fearful of you to oust you out until you were good and ready to go. You've had to eat the foul, stinking swill that was all they had to offer you for food, and drink spoiled, fetid water from their dank wells or sour milk that reeked of badly cured goatskins. You were forced to find another hideout, then another, and another, and still another, as Kadar came closer and closer. It's not fair, is it, Keene old son? It's just not fair how everyone turns against you . . .

Keene listened to the voices, and an unholy grin split his lips, baring his teeth wolfishly in the moonlight. Ha! The two in the tent didn't know it, but Kadar was done hunting him now—done hunting anything ever again, for that matter! He chuckled gleefully, clutching his belly with laughter, remembering how he had enticed the Bedouin to his death just the day before.

Kadar, for some reason, had been intent on tracking his sister and the other Arab, al-Azim, when Keene spotted them. More out of perversity than for any other reason, he had followed Kadar and his handful of men for two days and nights over many miles of what was now only too-familiar desert terrain. And then, he'd remembered the deadly *fesh-fesh* that lay ahead, and had decided that he'd had enough of running, and more than enough of that hook-nosed monkey Kadar. Appearing suddenly over the crest of a dune, he'd called Kadar out, dared him to take him single-handed, taunted the Bedouin with jeers and boasts and elusive appearances and disappearances just ahead of him, all calculated to lure the Bedouin on and on, until there could be no turning back and the *fesh-fesh* lay ahead. . . .

"Oh, but she was good, your ripe little virgin *bint!* The best I've ever popped, in fact!" Keene had crowed, leering. "And you know what? That little slut loved it, Kadar! She pretended she didn't, but she loved every bloody minute of what I did to her! T' tell the truth, the more I gave it to her, the harder I gave it to her, the more that hot little bitch wanted! Don't let her

478

simpering lies fool you, old chap!" he'd goaded. "Whatever she may have told you, she was panting for it!"

Keene had noted with silent glee how the Bedouin's swarthy face had turned almost black with rage, how his eyes had sizzled with hatred beneath his flowing white burnoose. It was working, exactly as he'd planned. . . .

Seated upon his moth-eaten camel on the farthest edge of the *fesh-fesh*, Keene had continued to taunt the Bedouin mercilessly. He'd kept it up until the man could stand it no longer, until he'd grown reckless in his rage.

"Her tits were like pomegranates, you know. Nice firm little titties with nipples the size of grapes. Tasty? Ah, I couldn't keep my hands off 'em, and that's the truth! And that tight little virgin slit! Christ, she was a prime piece of arse all right, Kadar! Pity you never got into her first, wasn't it, but then I dare say she'd rather have been diddled by a white man than a blasted monkey!"

Mad with fury, Kadar had drawn his curved dagger, the blade blindingly bright in the afternoon sunlight as he swung it aloft. With a howl to his God, he'd cruelly lashed his camel into a lope that was doomed from the third stride the beast took.

Keene had laughed and laughed when he saw Kadar's eyes change in the very moment he'd realized his folly, widening first in disbelief and denial, and then, finally, in understanding and despair as the camel lost its footing. The animal had found no purchase for its hooves on the sandy terrain ahead of it. It had struggled, yet its desperate struggles, combined with the dragging weight of its rider, had only made it sink deeper and deeper as it floundered about. Little by little, both camel and rider had vanished into the *fesh-fesh*—the wide, bottomless pit of sand, sand, and still more sand that reached, it seemed, to the very bowels of the earth, and which had swallowed them up as surely as any sucking quicksand or weedy, strangling bog! The last glimpse Keene had had of his hated enemy had been his upraised dagger, still glinting in the sunshine as it slipped below the surface. The sand had been left smooth and unmarred again in its wake.

Just like Tennyson's *Morte D'Arthur,* his epic poem of King Arthur and the sword Excalibur and the Lady of the Lake,

Keene reflected with a rare, lucid flight of whimsy, and he giggled to himself. The Lady had brandished the magical sword above the Lake, and so had that dog Kadar. Ah, Hawkhaven had been a better school that he'd ever guessed, he decided now, much as he'd hated it back then. They'd given him a firm grounding in the classics—and an even firmer one in the skills of survival, equipping him with the know-how to exist amidst even the most rugged of terrains. The latter had proved invaluable these past weeks since he'd become a fugitive in the desert. He'd really have to tell old Whitey that, if he ever saw his former schoolmaster again. . . .

But meanwhile, what about dear, lovely Alexa? What was to be done about her and her Tuareg lover? he pondered.

Think of something perfect! the voices in his skull wheedled. *Something fitting for that green-eyed witch. You can do it, old son. You can!*

Keene smiled. Something perfect, eh, was that what they wanted? His blue eyes blazed with sudden cunning.

Those who'd formed his six-man squad had long since perished in the desert, had they not, victims of heat and thirst and the blazing sun? Their bones were bleaching out there on the sands. He'd seen them himself, jumbled, gleaming white heaps that the vultures had made merry havoc with. There'd been no survivors, he was certain—no one left to carry the tale of what he'd done back to the fort. Ah, yes, under the circumstances, he could do it, all right. And he would.

Would! Could? Good. Very, very good!

Chapter Thirty-Five

The guards stationed in the embrasures above the gates of Fort Valeureux tensed as they spotted the lone rider, mounted on a weary camel, cresting one of the dunes that encircled the plain on which the fort had been built.

"Look sharp, *mon ami!* I believe we are about to have visitors!" one hissed grimly to the other, and nodded his head toward the approaching rider.

The other guard reached for the bugle strung on a cord about his neck, puckering his lips in readiness to sound the call to arms, an alarm that would turn out the entire barracks, armed and prepared to fight, on the double.

"One moment, Henri! Whoever the blighter is, he's showing a white flag!"

Both men saw that the rider had drawn his turban cloth from his head and fixed a torn square of it to his bayonet, waving his rifle to and fro to make certain no one could mistake his peaceful intentions. Both men could now see his bared head, and discern that the hair exposed was white-blond, rather than the black usual for an Arab.

"God in Heaven—it bloody well can't be, but it is, just the same! It's that damned 'Le Fou'!" one man exclaimed breathlessly, unable to believe his eyes.

"Why, so it is, *mon ami!* Our beloved sergeant himself, home at last! Who'd have believed he was still alive after all this time!"

"Believe it or not, it's him, all right! You get the gates and let him in, while I go and tell the Adjutant."

The Frenchman smiled mirthlessly. "I think not, Ted. On

the contrary, I would prefer that *you* let our friend in, while I inform the Adjutant of his return."

Ted's eyes suddenly lit up with understanding. "Oh, I see! Planning a little surprise for the rotter, are you, Henri, you old rogue?"

Henri shrugged. "You could say that, my friend. You could indeed."

"Sergeant Keene Harding, returning to duty, sir!" Keene barked, snapping a smart salute.

It was an incongruous gesture, considering the man was bareheaded and wore the white robes and baggy trousers of a native. Had Captain Boch, the Adjutant, been a different type of man—one more like his absent commandant, André Larousse, who'd gone to Sidi-bel-Abbes to enjoy a long-overdue leave—he might have permitted himself a smile. As it was, he was far too insecure, too anxious to perform his duties to the letter, to permit himself that extravagance. His chance had finally come! Major Larousse's departure had offered him the perfect opportunity to prove his worth and demonstrate his abilities as a leader. Now that the chance had finally dropped into his large lap, he did not intend to allow levity to distract him from his duties.

"At ease, Sergeant," Boch said, eyeing the man standing stiffly at attention before his desk with well-concealed distaste. With his hair, brows, and beard bleached white by the Sahara sun, and his skin dark bronze and leathery with exposure, the sergeant was hardly recognizable as the same man who had left Fort Valeureux three months ago, he realized. Only the wild, unstable glitter of his piercing blue eyes remained unchanged, though they were perhaps a trifle more unstable, a touch more wild, than before.

"Please, have a seat, Sergeant! And when you've made yourself comfortable, perhaps you'll be good enough to tell me where you have been since you left here last, *ja?*" Boch's tone was amiable enough, but his iron-gray eyes were cold and hard.

"Where I've been, sir?" Keene Harding laughed, and it was a harsh, bitter sound, without mirth. "Why, I've been to hell and back—that's where I've been!"

"I do not doubt it! But, if you will, I must have the facts, all of them. Why don't you begin at the beginning, soldier, with the day you left here along with your *escouade* of six men to escort the young lady—your sister, I believe?—to Sidi-bel-Abbes. Take your story from there."

"Very good, sir," Keene agreed, and in level, unemotional tones he recounted the story of those first few days, leading up to the night their camp had been attacked. "There were dozens of those Tuareg devils, sir, all of them armed to the teeth and hiding behind their disgusting masks. My men—God rest their souls!—put up a damned good fight, but we were hopelessly outnumbered. The Arabs bound us hand and foot, and took Corporal Flechette away with them. They tortured the poor bastard to death—"

"A tragedy indeed. And why, may I ask, was the corporal singled out for torture?"

Keene shrugged and frowned. "Well, sir, as far as I've been able to figure it out since then, they seemed to have believed him guilty of killing two of their people."

"And was he, Sergeant?"

Keene licked his cracked lips and seemed a trifle uneasy. "Damned if I know, sir! I doubt anyone will ever know for certain. I believe the matter of his guilt's between Flechette and his Maker now."

"Quite," Boch agreed with a curt nod. "Carry on."

"Well, I'd been bound and dumped very near to the tent in which the Tuareg chieftain had taken my sister. She'd fainted—the shock of it all, I suppose, the poor darling!—and she'd not been tied. When she came to, she managed to free me. Naturally, I suggested we have a go at freeing the others. God knows, I couldn't have left the poor devils to Flechette's fate, could I? No man with a conscience or any sense of honor in him at all could have! Alexa argued a bit at first, but she's a game old girl, and finally she agreed. She took the less risky job, naturally, and saw to untying the other prisoners, while I laid low the two men guarding the camels and made off with a few of the beasts."

"Very admirable of you, Sergeant," Boch observed, leaning

forward over the table and forming a steeple with his fingers. He pursed his lips and regarded Keene speculatively. "And then?"

"Then, sir, everything went wrong!" He shook his head, and gave a shudder of recollection, tugging on his beard. "O'Day, Toussant, and the others tried to make a break for it. They managed to overpower their guard barehanded, but then the whole blasted lot of those savages jumped them! God, sir, it was—it was bloody awful—as I'm sure you can imagine. After that, it was all over in minutes—they'd all been hacked to pieces! I tried—oh, Lord!" He sobbed, covering his face with his hands. "I tried to—to get Alexa—my sister—away, but I was unarmed, and some of those filthy scum had her. They spotted me and came after me. What else could I do? I rode off, hell bent for leather, intending to ride back here to the fort for help—or perhaps to hide out somewhere until they'd called off the chase and I could figure out a way to free Alex—oh, I don't know! To do *something!* But their chieftain—al-Azim, they call him—was merciless. He's been hounding me across the deserts all these weeks, after my blood in revenge for his kinsmen's deaths, I suppose. You don't know what I've been through, sir! It was hell, pure hell out there! And all the time, in each and every waking minute, all I could think of was my poor sister suffering unspeakable acts of cruelty and depravity at those filthy animals' hands, and of my brave men, dead to the last one, and their deaths unavenged! I sweated it out in native villages, rode across endless miles of sand, sometimes without water, food, shelter, or rest, for days at a time. And always, they were just one step behind me. They never gave up, never! Damn that Sharif al-Azim and his men to hell!" He broke down and wept uncontrollably behind his hands.

"Come, come, Sergeant! You have been through hell, agreed, but that is all over with now," Boch said mildly, though a rising excitement glittered in the iron-gray of his eyes. He leaned back, resting his stubby body comfortably in Major Larousse's chair while he rolled and lit a cigarette. Exhaling a thin spiral of smoke he considered how well the chair fitted him—as if it had been made for one Commandant Boch, rather than André Larousse. . . . "Yes, soldier, your nightmare is all over now," he repeated.

"Is it?" Keene demanded harshly, looking up. "If only it were, sir! But that Tuareg savage still has my sister. And as long as he does, I'll never be able to rest! I came here to the fort to get help. I beg you, sir, only give me the men and the weapons, and I'll do the rest! Al-Azim's encamped not two days' ride from here, and Alexandra's with him! We could take him easily, I know we could!"

There was a long pause while Boch smoked and considered his request. At length, he tossed his cigarette butt into the spittoon in one corner of the office. "Very well, Sergeant. I'll see what I can do, *ja?*"

While Keene Harding sat with his shoulders slumped and his head bowed upon his chest, Boch stepped outside his office and exchanged a few words with Corporal Bouton, who was stationed there. When he returned seconds later, Harding had not moved. Boch took up his seat behind the desk once again and regarded the sergeant thoughtfully and silently for several moments before speaking again.

"I have decided to help you get your sister back, Harding. The men I've chosen for the duty will be here shortly. I trust they will meet with your approval."

"Thank you, sir. I'm sure they will. And I—I can't tell you how grateful I am, sir—nor how grateful Alexa will be when she's safe once again."

A knock sounded at the door, and Boch rose, barking, "Enter!" as he did so.

Three men, dressed in the smart uniform of the French Foreign Legion, filed quietly into the office and stood at attention in a row behind Keene.

"Sergeant—your *escouade*," Boch announced quietly.

Keene turned about in his chair and his jaw fell slack. He gaped in horror at the three men behind him, looking as if he'd seen a trio of ghosts. His face paled beneath its dark tan.

"O'Day? Toussant? Gianetti?" He frowned. "But how in the hell—?" he demanded angrily, springing to his feet and looking as if he intended to bolt.

"'How' no longer matters, Sergeant!" Boch snapped, enjoying the little drama. "Suffice it to say that not *all* of your men perished in the desert when you rode off and left them that day. More than enough survived to carry back the tale of your despicable cowardice, and of your desertion!"

He came around the desk and stood with his stubby body rigidly at attention. "Sergeant Harding, I wish to inform you that you are under arrest!"

André Larousse would promote him for this, at the very least, Boch thought gleefully as they marched the indignant, struggling Sergeant Harding from the office to await court-martial in a cell in the guardhouse! Now, he mused, if he could only recapture the girl Alexandra that Larousse had been so sweet on, and see her captors swiftly brought to justice, his future with the Legion would be secure!

Dare he believe that Harding had told the truth about his sister's whereabouts, and that the girl was nearby?

"*Ya habibah,* wake up!" Sharif hissed, shaking Alexa by the shoulder. "I must leave you now, and quickly!"

She came awake at once with the urgency of his tone, her heart pounding crazily. "Why? What's wrong?" she cried, looking about her.

"A *Franziwa* patrol is coming! They will be here in only a few minutes. Quickly, my love! I would say goodbye to you before I go!"

He drew her into his arms, looked at her long and hard, then knotted his fingers in her hair and kissed her fiercely, raining kisses over her lips, her cheeks, her throat. "Farewell, my brightest jewel-amongst-women!" he bade her huskily. "If it is Kismet's wish that we should meet again, I will find you, never fear. Until then may Allah guard your path, and fill my dreams with memories of thee!"

He caressed her flushed cheek one last time, his ebony eyes dark with sorrow and brimming over with love for her, and then drew the *tagilmust* across to cover his face and strode quickly out of the tent without a backward glance.

"No!" Alexa cried, scrambling after him. "You can't leave me like this! You can't! Take me with you, Sharif!"

She blinked against the harsh light as she stumbled out of

the tent, and saw that he'd already mounted his black stallion, was even now wheeling its head about and digging his heels into its flanks. In a second, he'd gallop away and out of her life—forever, she was certain.

She ran like a madwoman toward the horse, heedless of the Legion patrol bearing down upon them, and grabbed Aswad's scarlet bridle, preventing Sharif from riding away. Her eyes swam with tears as she looked up at Sharif and implored him to let her up behind him, to take her with him.

Aswad sank back on his haunches as she clung to the bridle, and his forelegs pawed the air momentarily as Sharif reined him in hard to keep the stallion from trampling the girl, who now darted forward to cling to his master's hand.

"Please!" she sobbed earnestly.

"Believe me, I would do anything rather than give thee up, beloved!" Sharif rasped. "But only amongst your own kind will you be truly safe from Kadar! Look! The Legionnaires are coming up fast! If there is fighting, you might be harmed. If you would not have them capture me, release the bridle, my flower! Let me ride!"

It was useless! He would never be dissuaded! And if she didn't let him go at once, the Legion soldiers would catch him. With an anguished sob, she stepped back, and with a tormented final glance at her ashen face, Sharif raised his hand in farewell and turned his mount toward the distant mountains of al-Azadel. He kicked the stallion into a gallop, and Aswad hurtled forward and flew across the golden sands, his midnight mane and tail streaming, his rider's indigo robes flowing behind him with the swiftness of his ride. At once, the patrol changed course, peeling away to the northwest in pursuit of him.

Sharif's leave-taking hit Alexa with the force of a deathblow. Her knees buckled and she sank, keening, to the sands, unaware that one of the Legionnaires had continued on toward her, instead of riding after Sharif. The officer—a tall, beefy fellow wearing a captain's insignia—dismounted and strode to her side.

"Thanks to the brave men of the Legion, you are quite safe now, *fraulein!*" he declared pompously. "My men will overtake that native swine, have no fear of that, and bring him to justice. He will answer for what he has done to you—and for what he did to my men—with his life, rest assured. I, Captain Fritz Boch, will see that he does!"

Alexa shook her head slowly from side to side in denial, fury rising through her at the man's smugness, his unshakable conviction that her beloved Sharif had done her—or anyone else—harm.

"You're wrong, Captain!" she cried. "Sharif al-Azim is my husband! He has harmed no one—not your men nor myself! He was bringing me back to the fort to safety, not trying to hurt me! Please, you must listen to me—you must believe me! Sharif has done nothing! I demand that you take me to Major Larousse at once, Captain! He'll sort this out, I know he will!"

"Alas, Major Larousse has gone to Sidi-bel-Abbes on leave, *Fraulein* Harding. We do not expect him back at the fort for at least another two days. Meanwhile, it is my opinion that your capture at the hands of the Tuaregs has quite understandably left you overwrought, *fraulein*," Boch said tightly, livid that the woman had implied he was incapable of dealing with the situation and had wanted to go over his head and speak with Larousse. "If this Sharif al-Azim is taken alive, he will have ample opportunity to speak in his own defense at the hearing I will convene, have no fear of that." He glanced up, saw the patrol returning with the Tuareg chieftain as their prisoner, and a smug glow of satisfaction filled him. "And then," he continued mildly, "he will of course be shot—as an example to his kind that the French Foreign Legion holds the lives of her brave Legionnaires in the highest esteem, and that those who harm them will pay the ultimate price. Now, *fraulein*, won't you take my arm?"

In an effort at gallantry, he offered her his thick elbow, but her eyes blazed with emerald fire as she ignored it and dragged herself to her feet unaided, facing him with defiance and hatred and disgust stamped on her pale, lovely features.

"Go to hell, Boch!" she hissed. "Go to hell!"

Chapter Thirty-Six

"This way, ma'am," Sergeant O'Day said, leading Alexa into the guardhouse two days later. He carried a huge ring of keys in his hand that jingled noisily. "But I—I can't give ye more than a few minutes with t' prisoner, I'm afraid," he apologized.

"I understand. You've been very kind, Sergeant."

He smiled sheepishly. "Kind? Why, 'tis no more than ye're after deservin', ma'am, Toussant and Gianetti and meself are thinkin'! Why, we'll never be forgetting how it was ye cut us free that time, and risked yer own life doing it. Never! 'Tis our opinion ye're one hell of a woman, ma'am—beggin' yer pardon for me language. It ain't right at all what that fool of an Adjutant's done here! There'll be t' very devil hisself t' pay when t' Major comes back, an' no mistake! 'Hearing,' that bloody fool called it, b' Jaysus! Why, 'twere more of a kangaroo court than a fair hearin' that the Tuareg got, I'm after thinkin'! Me and the others, we told the truth, ma'am, you know that. We did our best t' clear your—your husband, though for the good it did him, we might as well ha' kept silent!" He shook his head.

She nodded sadly. "I know you did your very best, Sergeant, and I thank you."

"Boch intended from the first t' hold him responsible for Flechette's death, and the deaths of the others who died with us in the desert, we could tell that! And an obstinate man the likes o' him—one who's got a notion stuck in his head and blinkers on when it comes t' changing it, and a good eye out for promotion—why, there's no talking sense t' him! If the Tuareg—if your husband had put in a word in his own defense,

489

perhaps it would ha' gone better on him."

"Perhaps. But I think Sharif knew the outcome was decided before he even went before them. The hearing was just a formality," she said bitterly.

"Jaysus! T' think of any decent man dying for the likes o' that scum, Flechette! Why, ma'am, it's terrible unjust, it is! I won't pretend I'm overly fond o' the natives in these parts. Well, they don't think like us, do they, ma'am—they don't put the same value on human life. Their religion has a lot t' do with that, I suppose, you know, their belief that everythin' in life or death be t' will of Allah an' can't be changed! But even so, yer man's innocent t' my mind, ma'am. He had no part in Flechette's death. No, it were the other one, Kadar, what ran the show."

"Is there a chance André—Major Larousse—could be back before dawn tomorrow?" she asked, hope in her eyes.

"Aye, there's a chance—but it's a slim one, ma'am, I'll not lie t' ye. He ain't expected back 'til the end o' the week."

He opened a door with his keys and passed through it, motioning Alexa to follow him. They were in a large, spartan room, the only furniture a battered desk and chair. Part of the room was sectioned off by heavy metal bars, and beyond them two wooden bunks had been bolted to the wall. Keene sat upon one, his eyes flaring as he saw her, though she never looked at him. Her eyes were only for Sharif. He stood straight and tall, his back to her, gazing out of the narrow slit of a window in the wall opposite. The window gave him a view through the opened gates of Valeureux: a slim vista of the flat plain and rolling dunes beyond, and a sky so blue its brilliance pained the eyes.

"I'll leave ye now, ma'am."

She nodded.

O'Day tactfully left her alone, taking up a discreet position outside the outer door. For a few moments, she was struck dumb. What could she say? What could she possibly say to him that would change anything?

Sharif turned and saw her, and a smile of welcome curved his lips. He stepped forward to the wall of bars that separated them and reached out his hand to take hers. Her hand felt cold, so very cold, in his.

"Zerdali, my beloved!" he said softly, his rich, hypnotic

490

voice laden with love. "Your beauty makes a little Paradise of my ugly prison cell!"

Her lower lip trembled. She tried to smile, blinking back tears, but could not. Any composure she had managed to salvage after that disastrous hearing yesterday had now been irrevocably lost when she saw him again.

He drew her closer until she was pressed up against the bars before him, so close and yet so far away. Her hair's fragrance rose, warm and sweet, to his nostrils, and he yearned to bury his face in its soft mass one last time, but could not. Instead, he tilted her pale face up to his. "No more tears, beloved," he told her sternly. "Rather, I would take with me the memory of your smile."

"I'll try," she promised tremulously as he kissed her hand, his lips lingering in the little well of her palm, his tongue tracing damp circles there that tickled. "Oh, God, Sharif, I'll try."

"You are the wife of al-Azim," he reminded her, "the bride of an Imochagh lord. You will succeed, for our women are as strong as they are lovely!" It didn't matter now that he had spoken the words to divorce her from him. She had never heard him, and he had never, even at the time, divorced her from his heart. She was his, and would be through eternity.

"I love you, husband!" she whispered.

"And I you, beloved."

Through the bars, their lips touched in a fleeting kiss.

"I'll keep trying," she promised. "If there's any way to stop this madness, I'll find it, I swear it!"

"And if there is none, you will not blame yourself for my death?" There was only silence. "Zerdali—promise me you will not," he insisted.

"All right. I promise."

"Then there is nothing more to be said. Go now, my little Apricot Hair."

Her mouth worked soundlessly for several seconds before she managed to whisper, "Goodbye, Sha-Sha!" in reply and turn blindly for the door.

"No farewell for me, sister? No comforting kisses nor kind words?" came Keene's voice, and he gave a derisive snort. "No, I suppose not. That would be just a little too much to expect, after what I've done to your Arab chum here, eh? Well? How come so silent? Aren't you going to scream at me, tell me how loathsome I am, and how much you hate me? Aren't you going to blame me for every miserable, rotten thing that's ever happened in your life? Go on, get mad! Let it all out, Alex, my sweet! Let your bloody hair down for once in your life, lose your temper and have a field day!"

She paused with her hand upon the door latch, and swung about to face him, retracing her steps until she was only inches from him.

"Perhaps I would have blamed you in the past," she agreed. "But—not now. Now I understand that you can't help the way you are, Keene. You're twisted and sick, very sick. I blame myself for not realizing that long ago. So you see, I don't hold you responsible, and I don't blame you, not for anything. You're my brother, and despite everything, I still love you, Keene. And," she said, looking him straight in the eye, "I forgive you. I forgive you for everything."

With one long, last look at Sharif, she turned and slipped from the room, leaving Keene gaping openmouthed after her, with a shattered look in his eyes. He stared at the door she had exited long after she was gone.

Alexa dragged herself up the stone steps as if she were mortally wounded. Movement hurt. Thought hurt. Feeling—feeling was agony. Tears blinded her. They streamed down her cheeks, falling unnoticed to dampen her robe. The playful wind whipped her hair and the cloak about her like angry ropes lashed hither and thither as she clambered up onto the embrasure and stood there, looking out over the grayed silk of the desert sands that stretched for thousands of miles in every direction with haunted green eyes swollen from crying. Her fingers were claws clenched fiercely over the crumbling, crenellated walls, the pain of her grip the only thing that kept her from screaming her agony aloud.

Her heart ached so. It threatened to burst from her breast with grief and terror as she saw what she had dreaded all night long: that sudden streak of golden light ignited like a torch's sulphur flare far to the east, the lightening of the indigo sky around that telltale flaring to a paler shade of amethyst.

Dawn, she realized. *Time was running out! O, Dear God, Sharif, Sharif, my love, my only love, this isn't happening . . . it can't be . . . No . . . !*

Another shudder of dread swept over her, making her tremble uncontrollably despite the warmth of the heavy cloak thrown hastily over her shoulders by a concerned Sergeant O'Day. Despite its thickness, her hands, her feet were cold as ice.

If only—ah, God, if only she could hold back the dawn! If only she could halt time in its irrevocable, measured march through the seconds, the minutes, remaining! Yet she was only human, and no fragile, mortal man or woman could halt time, nor delay its passing by so much as a hairbreadth. . . .

She tried to blink back her tears, failed utterly, and instead looked above her, letting her weeping continue unchecked. In the charcoal sky above, where only *zohra,* the lonely morning star, still shone out her pale light, she saw the gliding shadow of a nighthawk as it wheeled over the desert floor. In her mind's eye, she was transported back to the rocky *sahel* below the mountains of al-Azadel, and it was Sharif's snow-white gyrfalcon, Barakah, the White One, wheeling high above her. An omen? she wondered. Were there such things as omens— and if so, what did this one foretell? *What?*

She wrung her hands, fighting down the terrible, choking lump that lodged in her throat, savagely gnawing her lower lip until it bled in an effort to stanch the wails of grief that threatened to tear from her lips as she realized that there were sounds in the fort below now: the tramping of many booted feet. Barked commands, indecipherable from here. The jangle of keys and clanging cell doors. The noisy, ominous rattle of rifles being loaded and readied for firing . . .

Oh, God, not yet, not yet, please God, not so soon—! she prayed silently, her lips moving without a sound. *The sun's barely rising—! Give him—give us both—just a little more time, God, I beg you!*

Yet even as she prayed for time, the treacherous sun leaped up onto the horizon, flaunting its glorious rays in all directions to flood the sky and the world below with light and color. Saffron and mauve, the true colors of a desert dawn. She'd once loved to watch morning painting the sky with those glorious hues when she awoke cradled safe in her beloved's arms. She'd never see those colors, never welcome another dawn again, without remembering this terrible dawn. Her life would end today as surely as his, though hers would be a living death.

Her head jerked up sharply as the sound of tramping feet—growing closer and closer—broke in upon her tormented thoughts. Each footfall was a knell of doom. Each footfall reminded her that she had tried to free him, but failed. She flinched as if struck by a bludgeon as a dozen uniformed men marched smartly into the open parade ground below, a grim-faced, newly promoted O'Day at their head.

"Squaa-ad, halt!" he barked.

She slumped forward over the embrasure, sinking to her knees. Her fingers clawed over the edge as she shook her head in silent denial of the nightmare unfolding below.

As one man, the *escouade* in the parade ground below smartly halted.

"Abouuut, face!"

Another crisply barked command, and O'Day had turned his men to face the blank gray eastern wall below, the one farthest from her. The twelve men of the firing squad stood so stiff and still at attention they seemed not real men at all, to Alexa's confused mind, but painted lead toy soldiers placed in a tidy row by some industrious little boy.

None of this is real, a part of her mind clamored, denying the truth, clawing for a lie to hang on to and make the agony go away. *Soon you'll wake up and find it's all been just another terrible dream, you'll see!*

But another part of her mind reasoned that this was no dream, no nightmare from which she'd awaken to laugh at her fears. The hushed fort, the firing squad ready and waiting below with rifles shouldered—all of it was horribly real.

Real.

Oh, God, why him?

Why?

He was innocent!

Corporal Bouton appeared, the prisoner striding in his wake. The condemned man wore no chains, no handcuffs, or shackles to restrain him, nor did he need the corporal's arm to steady him on the path to his final destiny. Clad in the proud robes of his people, the Free Ones, the flowing indigo cloak and concealing *tagilmust* of a desert lord swathing his tall, lean body and swirling around him in the dawn breeze, he strode erect and unafraid behind the Legion corporal to the wall. There he turned and took his place before it.

When he faced the twelve men, he did so without so much as a flicker of fear in his stance or in his proud bearing. Rather, there was a calm acceptance and quiet courage in his eyes as he gazed one by one at the faces of the twelve apprehensive young men ranged before him and told them softly, "Come now, not a flinch, lads! Do what you must, Gianetti—and you too, Toussant—and do it well. . . ."

Alexa was frozen in place on the embrasure above. Paralyzed by terror and dread, she watched the scene unfolding before her without any outward show of emotion, as if she watched a tragic stage play. Yet her fingers were still clenched so tightly over the ragged stone edges of the embrasure they were bled white, and her face so ashen it was the ghastly gray-yellow of a tallow candle. The sensation of unreality still lingered, dulling emotion, numbing pain and sensation, as if her compassionate mind had taken pity on her and turned off in a last-minute attempt to deaden the sharp agony of grief that would soon be hers. . . .

"Sharif al-Azim al-Azadel," Sergeant O'Day's voice rang out. "Ye've been tried by representatives o' the Government of the Republic of France for the crime of murder, and have duly been found guilty as charged in the deaths of four of her loyal citizens. In accordance with that judgment, ye've been brought here, to this place of execution, on this the appointed day, and sentence will duly be carried out at dawn. Prisoner, do ye have any last requests or final words ye might wish to say?"

"No last requests," came the condemned man's voice, strong and carrying.

The prisoner glanced up to the parapet where the slender, pale-faced woman watched. The hood of her dark cloak had fallen back, leaving strands of her chestnut hair free to twist and turn in the wind. Her shoulders were bowed with sorrow, her green eyes agonized. He could see the tracks of her tears glistening in the dawn sunlight as they slid unchecked down her cheeks, and he swallowed, for her tears were not for him.

"Just tell Alexa that I'm sorry, would you, O'Day? Tell her that it's better this way, for everyone. . . ."

"I'll tell her," O'Day said stiffly, his brogue marked. "And may God have mercy on your black soul!"

"There being no further requests from the prisoner," the Irish sergeant said in a louder voice that carried to all corners of the parade ground, "sentence will be carried out immediately. Corporal Bouton, the blindfold, if ye please!"

"I need none," the condemned man insisted softly.

With a curt nod, Corporal O'Day waved back the stout corporal who'd begun to hurry forward with the folded white cloth at his sergeant's command.

"Squad, at the ready!" O'Day barked, and the twelve men dropped forward onto their right knees with the precision of a crack drill team.

"Shoulder aarms!" the second order rang out. As one man they smartly raised their rifles to their shoulders.

"Aaaim!"

The squad sighted down the long, black snouts of their weapons. A pause that was endless followed, as if time hung suspended on leaden wings.

"Fire!" barked the sergeant, and twelve fingers jerked on twelve curved triggers.

"*Noooooo!*"

The shots rang out as a single, deafening crack upon the hush of dawn. Smoke rose in the cool air from each barrel in its wake as the dull echoes of the report reverberated over and over in the squad's ears like a rolling peal of thunder.

So, too, did the heartrending wails of the woman who'd watched the execution echo again and again throughout the fort and across the desert sands, ululating over and over in their ears as the condemned man jerked once, dropped like a stone to his knees, and fell forward face down in the sand, indigo robes billowing about him.

The firing squad had done their job well. The prisoner was dead long before he hit the ground.

496

Chapter Thirty-Seven

Major André Larousse paused in the doorway to his spartan quarters, looking with profound regret down at the woman who sat with bowed head and slumped shoulders upon the very edge of the bed.

"*Ma pauvre petite* Alexa! If only I could have returned to the fort sooner and spared you all this heartache! That fool of an Adjutant will be court-martialed for his flagrant disregard of regulations, I promise you!"

"It wasn't your fault, André," she whispered, her voice wooden.

"I should have been here!"

"No. Don't blame yourself. You weren't to know."

"*Non,*" he agreed with a sigh. "I didn't know."

His cornflower-blue eyes were filled with pity for her hurt and the shock she'd suffered, for all the anguish she'd borne unnecessarily. His eyes were also filled with the love he felt for this woman. Not since she'd left Valeureux weeks—months!—ago had he once stopped thinking of her! For a moment, he was strongly tempted to leave things as they were, to comfort her and offer her his strong shoulder on which to cry out her grief—and *oui*, perhaps in the process win her for his own? But it was a temptation that was swiftly squelched. He was a man of honor, after all. And besides, he could tell by the depth of her grief that there could be no other man but the proud Tuareg chieftain for Alexandria Harding. Alive or dead, her heart belonged to him, not to André Larousse, and she would accept no other in his place.

"Your—escort—will be here for you shortly, Alexa. I sup-

497

pose all that's left for me to do is to say *au revoir* to you yet again, lovely *madame*, and to tell you that I will carry always in my heart a tenderness for you, and a dream of what might have been for us, had circumstances been different."

"No, André," she chided him gently, her green eyes lifting sadly now to his. He caught his breath, for even in her grief, she was hauntingly beautiful to him. Pale lavender shadows encircled her eyes now, and the long, tawny lashes that fringed them were spiked with tears. "Forget me! Dream a new dream, a beautiful new dream all of your own. They can come true, you know. They truly can." She gave him a brave, wan little smile that touched his heart. "Sometimes, the dream is fleeting, as mine was. But some people are more fortunate than I, André. Their dreams last a lifetime. Yours can too. I just know they can."

He smiled. "When you say such things, Alexa, even a hardened soldier such as myself dares to believe that you are right!" He lifted her chill hand, and touched his lips to her fingertips. "And, perhaps, little one, you may yet discover that your dream was not so fleeting, after all, *non?* Farewell, *madame*, and good luck and happiness to you always."

With a smart salute, André left her. Alexa stared through a mist of tears at the door he had used.

But then, as she watched—feeling emptier and more alone than ever before—a beloved swarthy face, a tall, lean frame she'd believed lost to her forever, filled the doorway in André's place. Albeit that figure was clothed in the unfamiliar uniform of a Legionnaire rather than the flowing indigo robes of a Blue Man of the Sahara, she would have known him anywhere!

A thrill ran down her spine, raising the hair at the nape of her neck and goosebumps down her arms. She gaped as if seeing a ghost, unable to believe her eyes, shaking all over with emotion as joy swelled to bursting in her heart and finally exploded through her. It was no ghost, no mirage! He was there, and alive!

"Sha-Sha!" she cried, *"Oh, thank God, thank God—!"*

She flung herself from the cot and across the room, hurling

herself into Sharif's outstretched arms, dragging him through the door and kissing him again and again, crying and laughing and kissing and embracing him all at the same time.

"*Ewellah*, it is truly your Sha-Sha!" Sharif confirmed unnecessarily, giddy laughter in his deep voice as he swung her up into his arms and kissed her long and hard. He held her so fiercely, so tightly in his arms, she could hardly breathe—not that she cared if he crushed her in that moment, for she'd never thought to feel his dear, strong arms about her again, not in this world! Tears of joy were streaming down her cheeks as she clung to him, determined never to let him go again.

"But how—? Who—? I saw—I saw what happened yesterday—the firing squad—everything!—and I—oh, God, Sharif, I was so certain you were dead!"

"And so I would have been, *habibah*, had another not taken my place," Sharif said gravely. His ebony eyes were somber now as he set her gently on her feet before him, yet his arms were still tight around her, as if he feared to let her go.

"But who'd have done such a thing? Who'd have made such a sacrifice for you—for both of us?"

It was the question he'd dreaded, but known he'd have to answer sooner or later. There was a long, pregnant pause before he did so, and when he finally spoke, it was as if each word was wrung from him.

"It was Keene, Zerdali. He was executed in my place."

Alexa's hands flew to her mouth, muffling her shocked cry. She took a step back, away from him, and the horror and betrayal that widened her green eyes struck him like a physical blow, robbing him of breath.

"Oh, my God, no, no!" she whispered, shaking her head to and fro. "Tell me it isn't true—that you're lying! *Tell* me!"

To have received the gift of her beloved's life, only to learn it had been paid for at the cost of her brother's—oh, Dear Lord, it was too much to bear! Yet there was no denial in the sorrowful dark eyes that met hers as she searched his face, and her hopes died. She began to tremble uncontrollably, and turning from him with an anguished cry, she staggered across the spartan room on legs that would no longer hold her. They buckled, and she sank to her knees on the cold flagstoned floor, and buried her face in her hands.

"Dear God, how can I live with this, Sharif—?" she sobbed, her shoulders heaving. "How can I reconcile my love for you, knowing wh—what you did to my brother!"

"*No!*" he rasped hoarsely, his voice like the crack of a whip above the sound of her weeping. He strode to her side and took her shoulder in a fierce grip that bespoke his turbulent emotions more eloquently than words. In his need to convince her, his fingers were unintentionally cruel. They bit into her tender flesh, bruising it, yet in her agony of grief she felt no pain as he almost dragged her to her feet and jerked her roughly about to face him. "If there is trust for me in your heart," he rasped, "believe me now, for I swear to you, on my honor as a man, that it was a choice Keene made for himself!" He firmly framed her tear-streaked face in his large palms so that she could not turn away from him, yet there was still doubt in her eyes and it tortured him to see it there. "Zerdali, beloved, you know the man I am—*ewellah*, perhaps better than I know myself! Am I a coward? One who'd ask another to endure the death that was mine?" he demanded.

"No, no, you could not, I know that! But why? Tell me *why*, in God's name, would he do such a thing? Keene is—he was never fond of me. He'd always resented me and my father's closeness to me. Why would he sacrifice his life for yours feeling as he did?" Her lower lip trembled. "It doesn't make sense!"

"Perhaps it did, to him! Perhaps he felt it was the last thing—the *only* thing!—he could do to make amends to you! You see, he was dying, Zerdali," he told her gently. "He'd known it for many, many months. The doctors in Algiers suspected a growth in his brain and offered him no hope for recovery. It was simply a matter of time. . . .

"After you left us yesterday, your brother seemed disturbed, quieter than before your visit. 'She forgave me!' he said, over and over. 'Did you hear that, Arab? After what I did—after everything I've done—Alexa forgave me.' It was as if he couldn't believe it—couldn't understand that you could love him despite what he'd done. And, I think, he realized then that you'd always loved him. Later that night, he began to talk.

He told me that he'd welcome death as a release from the agony he'd endured for so many years, and he made me an offer. He suggested that since he would be court-martialed and shot as a deserter at some point anyway, that by taking my place he could buy us the time we needed until Major Larousse returned to the fort." Sharif paused.

"And you accepted his offer?" she asked in a bitter, strangled tone.

"Accepted?" he demanded bitterly, aggrieved that she could still think him capable of such cowardice. "By Allah, had he begged me on his knees, I would have refused! He was your brother, Zerdali, and I knew you loved him, despite everything. And so, I told him no.

"Shortly before dawn, Keene shook me awake. He said he wanted to talk to me before they took me away, and he told me many, many things, *habibah*. He told me again of the terrible headaches he'd suffered since he was a young boy. Of how, when the pains were too much to bear and opiates failed to ease them, of voices inside his mind that spoke to him and soothed the hurt away. But he'd grown tired, he told me, of the constant agony in his skull. Of listening to the whispering voices which no longer soothed him, but told him to do evil things. He was sick of hurting innocent people, of being feared and hunted and hated by them. He wanted peace, and he said quite simply, my love, that he wanted to die. That he would welcome death when it came and granted him release from the agony of living! His last words were that he was sorry for all the heartache he'd caused you. That despite his jealousy, he'd always loved you, however shamefully his—illness—had caused him to treat you. He hoped you would someday understand, as well as forgive him.

"Then he told me he was thirsty and asked me to pass him the water dipper. I turned my back to get it for him, not suspecting he meant to jump me from behind. We struggled briefly, but surprise had given him the upper hand, and he was incredibly strong. When I came to, it was over. He'd traded his uniform for my robes—as you can see—and had taken my place before the firing squad."

Sharif, his expression grimmer than she had ever seen it

501

before, drew her hand to his lips and gently kissed her fingertips. "That is how it was, I swear before Allah! There was nothing I could do to change it. Can you ever forgive me, *habibah?*"

She swallowed and managed to nod, ashamed then as she realized the agony of guilt her doubt had put him through. Whispering through her tears she asked, "Forgive you for being alive! Oh, Sha-Sha, don't! Never ask my forgiveness for that! I love you, with all my heart and soul! However painful it is to accept, Keene's sacrifice gave you back to me! Because of it, you're alive and here with me now!"

"O'Day, Toussant, Bouton, and the others knew that Keene had switched places with me, and yet they kept silent," Sharif continued. "Except for your brother, Timothy O'Day and the other survivors are the only ones living who know the truth of what happened that day at the oasis of Yasmeen. O'Day told me he'd always felt guilty for not lifting a finger to put a halt to what happened to Muriel and her kinsmen that day. He wanted to make amends, and to repay you for trying to free them that day. They knew it was Kadar who'd ordered the attack on them, and that it was he, not I, who'd commanded them left to the mercy of the desert. And so, when he saw that Keene had traded places with me, he turned a blind eye to it and said nothing to Captain Boch. Afterwards, he would have told you the truth at once, if the fort physician hadn't given you a sleeping powder! And so, when Major Larousse rode into the fort during the night, he went to him immediately and told him everything, *habibah*." He paused and eyed her jealously. "And of course, the gallant *Franziwa* major was only too happy to have me released, and by so doing be of service to the lovely *Englesy mademoiselle!*"

"Ah, yes. He's a good man, Sharif, an honorable man," Alexa murmured as she looked up at her husband, trying to summon a smile through her tears. But she could not.

Poor, troubled Keene! He'd given his life for Sharif's in the end. She would tell her papa that he had died with great courage, and they would mourn together for the wasted life that had been his; would grieve for the lost goodness in all men, even the worst of them, which Keene's terrible sickness had driven out and denied him. She sighed deeply. Her heart ached, but grief would have to wait. For now, it was the living that should be celebrated; the joy of life, not the pain of death, that should be uppermost in her heart. Keene was at peace now, beyond all pain, and the man she loved more than anything was alive when she'd thought him dead and lost to her forever. Even if she couldn't share his life, she could wait and hope and pray that someday things would be different and they could be together again. *Thank you, God!* she prayed silently. *Thank you for giving him back to me!*

"Your Rabi and my Aswad await us," he was saying. "Are you ready to go home to al-Azadel, beloved?" he asked gently.

"Home? You aren't going to send me away?"

"I tried, did I not, O Stubborn Little One? But of what use was it, since you were determined not to leave me? I offered my songbird the freedom of an open door, and yet she chose to remain at my side. Maimun would have approved, I think!" More seriously he added, "You were right, Zerdali. We belong together, you and I, through good and bad, joy and sorrow, through whatever Kismet has in store for us. We will meet Kadar face to face when the time comes, and deal with what the future holds together."

"Then I'm ready to go anywhere, Sharif—just as long as it's with you."

With a smoldering look that promised a reunion between them that would set the desert sands aflame, he swung her up into his strong arms and carried her outside, to where their horses, both saddled and ready, waited by the opened gates of Fort Valeureux.

As André had so enigmatically implied, her escort had come to take her home. Home to al-Azadel!

Sharif tossed Alexa up onto the back of her silvery-gray mare, and vaulted astride his ebony stallion. Leaning low from his saddle to kiss her once more, he gathered the reins in his fists and kicked Aswad into a gallop. Horse and rider exploded from the gates of the fort like a dark arrow fired from a bow. Only seconds later, Alexa followed, her chestnut hair flowing behind her. She and her swift gray mare were soon lost in the drifts of sand churned up by Aswad's flying black hooves.

"*Dream a new dream, André!*" Alexa had urged the major a short while earlier. "*A beautiful new dream all of your own. They can come true, you know. They truly can.*"

From atop the fort's gray walls, André Larousse shaded his eyes and watched as the dappled gray horse drew abreast of the first, which had slowed to match the mare's shorter stride. Then, the two lovers hand in hand upon their backs, the horses disappeared over the rolling golden dunes, vanishing like phantoms into the saffron-and-mauve glory of another desert dawn, where dreams could still come true.

And often did.

Epilogue

The wail of a newborn babe carried on the dawn air. It was a lusty, indignant cry, a vigorous protest at being thrust from the warmth, safety, and quiet comfort of the womb in which it had curled for ten cycles of the moon, out into the brilliance and noisiness of the world.

Sharif's head jerked up at the sound. Thrills ran through him. He sprang to his feet, only half-hearing the sudden burst of congratulations from his men gathered about the campfire over the morning coffee; only dimly feeling the hearty slaps and back-thumpings and embraces with which they welcomed his new state of fatherhood. Indeed, he hardly gave a thought to the child which had just moments before been born! His thoughts were all for the mother of that child, his beloved Zerdali. How had she fared, he wondered, his dear, stubborn, hard-headed wife, giving birth on sandy ground apart from their camp after the nomadic custom, with only a handful of women and the Tuareg midwives to attend her? He had implored her to stay in the mountain city when her condition had become apparent, but she had obstinately refused, he remembered.

"I swore that morning I saw you alive at Fort Valeureux—after believing you'd been shot and killed—that we'd never be parted again, Sharif. The place of an Imochagh wife is beside her husband, and that's exactly where I intend to be from now on—beside you, always." Her little chin had come up in defiance, and her green eyes had flashed in a manner he had grown to recognize.

"You are my wife, *ewellah*, but you are with child, and your condition cannot be taken lightly," he'd reminded her, gently rubbing her swollen belly with fragrant oils that soothed the stretched skin. "It is my son and heir you carry here in your womb, *habibah,* and for all that you have decided to embrace the ways of the Imochagh, you were not born a nomad woman. You will find following the herds across the desert all winter too difficult in your condition, I fear. And I would prefer that Master Hakim be close at hand when your time comes. Fatima says your hips are narrow for the bearing of children, and that is was only with great difficulty that your mother brought her children into the world."

"And if I stay here in al-Azadel, quietly sewing and stuffing myself upon dishes of fruit and honeyed sweetmeats, you'll return to find a balloon instead of your wife awaiting you, Sharif," she'd threatened, "a very bored, very enormous balloon! Our son will be a desert prince, and it is in the desert that he'll be born. I won't have it any other way."

She'd remained obdurate on that point, and in the end Sharif had been worn down and given in. By Allah, how could he refuse her anything—she was his breath, his soul, his life, and all the joy in it! The past nine months had only served to deepen his love for her and, he knew, her love for him. Each passing day had brought them new discoveries about each other to be treasured and stored away in memory; each rapturous night had deepened the passionate bond between them. The child that they had conceived upon the desert sands the same golden-and-mauve dawn that they had ridden away from Fort Valeureux to begin their lives together was now born, living proof of their great love!

Sharif grinned and waved aside his men's congratulations, stepping between them and going outside to stand staring toward the place where the women had taken his beloved wife early the evening before, when it was certain her labor had begun, a little hollow in the *sahel* that he had chosen himself especially for this time. The dunes secluded it from the cold night breezes and prying eyes. The bright fires he had ordered lit would keep jackals and predatory wolves at bay. He had also made certain that the tent the women had erected there for Zerdali to give birth in had lacked for nothing by way of comforts. His preparations had not made the waiting any less nerve-wracking, however! The night had seemed endless. . . . And there was still no sign of the women yet, he realized, and sighed heavily as he gazed about him.

His grazing herds made moving blots of black and yellowish white all about the camp, their colors muted in the light of dawn. The goats bleating to be milked, the snorting of the camels, and the baaing of the sheep mingled with the clanging of the camel bells and the yells of the herd boys and all the other sounds of the Imochagh as they rose to greet a new day. Sharif heard none of them.

Muriel and her Selim would have been wed for several months by now, Sharif mused, lost in thought as he awaited the return of the women from the birthing place, and perhaps have a babe of their own started. To his mind, the shy, sweet-natured Muriel would find more happiness with her handsome, easygoing cousin than she would ever have found with her intended, the quick-tempered, somewhat dour Kadar. And since the Bedouin found matches between distant cousins much to their liking, Muriel's mother had also been pleased by Selim's request for her daughter's hand, and by the generous dowry Sharif had settled upon the girl to replace the one she had lost: double the amount of the normal blood-price the Bedouins set to recompense a family for the death of a *sheik*. Ah, yes, by then Sharif had known that Kadar was no more. That his "brother's" leaf had fallen from the Sky-Tree . . .

He had learned of Kadar's death from the *sheik's* men when he and Zerdali had returned to al-Azadel, and although he'd realized at once that Kadar's death had freed his bride from the threat the *sheik* had posed to her life, he'd been deeply saddened to hear of it nonetheless. Kadar had been as close to him as any brother, and he'd grieved for his senseless death even while knowing Kadar had brought it upon himself.

Kadar's thirst for revenge had been a madness as sick, as real and sad, as that which had tormented his murderer. That madness had lured him into carelessness as surely as Keene Harding had lured him into the bottomless *fesh-fesh* to his death. So too had Kadar's stubborn determination to follow the old, bloodthirsty ways of the desert contributed to his downfall, for if he had not determined to exact an "eye for an eye" in the ancient manner, he would yet be alive.

The old desert ways must be done away with, Sharif felt keenly, for the ways that had served the nomads so well in former years no longer did so. If the Imochagh were to survive, they had to accept the past as dead and gone, embrace the present, and look to the future for their children. Those of the desert peoples who survived would be those who could adapt, and adaptation required a people who were educated and equipped to move into the twentieth century, with knowledge as their new and shining weapon instead of the curved blade of the dagger. Sharif and his father intended the al-Malik to be counted amongst those survivors. The day of the desert pirates who'd swept down from their mountain stronghold upon their white camels to plunder the spice caravans was long past, fitted only to become the stuff of which legends are made. . . .

It was then he spotted them, coming toward him just as the sun leaped up as a golden ball on the dark rim of the mountains: three women, only silhouettes as they approached, the plumpest one—Fatima, he knew—supporting the slender woman in the middle, the other carefully carrying a little bundle wrapped in a blanket of lamb's wool. *His child!* He fought down the urge to run like a boy to meet them, for Zerdali had insisted upon doing this in the accustomed way, and he had promised to respect her wishes. But it cost him—by Allah, how it cost him to wait while they moved closer with agonizing lack of haste!

Alexa saw the dark silhouette of her husband, tense with anxiety, waiting before his tent, and smiled in exhausted satisfaction as he slowly returned to his men and the coffeepot to await her women's official announcement of the birth.

"Go, Fatima, and put him out of his misery!" she told the woman. "My poor husband has had little sleep tonight, I'd bet a hundred camels on it!"

Fatima giggled. "I would not accept your bet, my dove, for I know you are right! Give me the precious little one, Noura, and see our lady made comfortable. I will make the necessary announcements."

Smiling, the Bedouin woman took Alexa's arm, and escorted her to her own tent, while Fatima proudly carried the infant to the gathered men.

"Fatima—?" Sharif spoke as she neared them, and she saw the anxiety in his ebony eyes, the lines of fatigue about them and bracketing his chiseled lips as he half-rose to meet her. "My wife—?"

"Have no fear, the lady Zerdali is well and strong, my lord!" Fatima crowed smugly. "She awaits your coming in her tent."

Sharif nodded, his relief patently obvious. "Praise Allah, I am glad to hear it! And the babe—?"

"Your babe is as strong and lusty as any I've seen—*ewellah*, and twice as beautiful!"

"You hear that, men?" Sharif demanded of the gathering, paternal pride swelling his chest. "A strong, lusty son for your chieftain, and handsome like his father!" He grinned broadly. "I will send word at once to Ahoudan, and have him begin forging the finest little ceremonial sword for the babe's naming feast next week!"

"Allah forgive me, but did I say it was a son you have?" Fatima teased in an apologetic tone. "Of a certainty, my lord, the child has no *wezand*! On the contrary, it is a *daughter* the lady Zerdali has given thee, not a son!"

The grin upon Sharif's face did not lessen by even a fraction, much to Fatima's relief, though the men seated cross-legged all about him groaned in disappointment.

"A little daughter—and with her mother's beauty, you say? I am not displeased, Fatima, don't eye me so doubtfully! *Ewellah*, we will but have to try again for the son and heir I need!"

"And the tryin's no hardship, eh, my chief?" Talman quipped, nudging his lord with a hefty elbow and rolling his eyes lecherously.

"Indeed not," Sharif agreed with a wicked grin. "No, indeed not, Talman! Here, give me my daughter, Fatima, and find your bed. It's been a long night for us all. I will take my little daughter to her mother."

He held out his arms, and Fatima gently placed the babe in their strong cradle, tears welling as she saw how tenderly he held the infant and the dawning love and wonder that filled his eyes as he gazed down at her tiny, rosebud face, crowned with jet-black curls that were yet damp from birth. Her skin was pink and white, her little mouth a tiny, perfect bow of coral.

"Your mother is a jealous woman, you will find, my smallest jewel," he whispered, kissing the baby's flushed cheek. "I wonder how she will take the news that Sharif has given his heart to yet another little beauty, eh?"

"A heart is big enough to be shared many, many times," Fatima observed fondly, watching the pair, father and tiny daughter, as Sharif carried the babe away, toward her mother's tent. Her eyes misted with happy tears. "*Ewellah*, more than big enough!"

Alexa was resting upon her bed of tamarisk boughs spread with soft sheepskins when Sharif ducked into the tent, carrying their daughter. She had been washed, and was dressed now in her finest indigo robes, her wrists and ankles tinkling with bracelets of silver, the silver *ankh* he had given her on their wedding day resting between her breasts. Her hair had been brushed to shining glory, her skin oiled with her favorite rose perfume. She appeared every inch a desert princess, although her face was a little pale and drawn-looking still, with her eyes as radiant as twin stars, glowing as she looked up at him.

"Are you disappointed?" she asked breathlessly.

"Do I look disappointed, *ya habibah?*" he countered with a broad smile of pride for the daughter in his arms that banished any fears she'd had.

"I was afraid you might be. All men want a boy the first time, after all."

"Ah, but Sharif al-Azim is not all men," he teased. "Sharif is a law unto himself, and is very proud of the lovely girl-child you have given him!" He leaned down and gently placed the infant in her mother's arms. "My heartfelt thanks, *habibah*," he murmured, and took them both in his arms and kissed Alexa's brow, her cheeks, her nose, taking care not to crush the babe as he did so. Nevertheless, their daughter gave a squeaky

510

whimper of protest and flung out her little fists. At once, her face reddened furiously, and they both laughed.

"Ah, already this one is like her mother, is she not—protesting loudly on every side, and no doubt calling her father a 'clumsy savage'! If she keeps up that braying, perhaps we should call her 'Little Donkey'!" Sharif teased.

"Oh, you!" Alexa grimaced. "She's beautiful, and you know it! 'Little Donkey,' indeed! She deserves a beautiful name, and I have just the one picked out—and a very appropriate one too, I think you'll agree." She eyed him archly, and in a way that no woman recently delivered of a babe had any right to eye her husband.

"I will? And what is this so-fitting name you have chosen?" Sharif asked, amused by her seductive expression. His black eyes twinkled.

"Zohra."

"The dawn star?"

"Yes! Isn't it just perfect? After all, she was conceived by the desert dawn, and born under the desert dawn. No other name would be nearly as fitting as Zohra."

"I agree," he said slowly. "But it is the *marabout* who will choose her name, after our customs, remember?"

"Oh." Her face dropped in disappointment. "I'd forgotten that."

"But, there is a way—!"

"There is? How?"

"As I told you, the naming ceremony is an ancient one. A week from today, a sheep will be sacrificed for the feast. Afterwards, we, as parents of the babe, will give the *marabout* two thorns, each one marked with a symbol that represents one of the two names we have chosen. The *marabout* prays to Allah for guidance, and then he selects one of the thorns."

"And whichever one he selects, that's the name given to the child?"

"*Ewellah*, it is so!"

"But there's still a chance he'll pick the wrong one!" she wailed.

Sharif grinned. "True. But—not if each thorn bears the *same* name, O Woman of Little Faith!"

511

Alexa grinned, then giggled. "Ah, Sharif, my lord, you are truly a clever fellow, as cunning as the desert fox, as shrewd as the desert hawk—as sly as the jackal—!"

"Jackal! But you love me anyway, eh, *habibah?*"

A slow smile curved her lips. She reached out and caressed his cheek, and he took her hand and dropped a kiss in the palm, eyeing her expectantly.

"I love you," she agreed huskily, and her lips twitched. "Lawless savage or no, Zohra and I both love you!"

He pretended to scowl. "When you are recovered from your daughter's birth, I will see you soundly spanked for that insult, Apricot Hair!"

"And I, my lord husband, will look forward to it!" she retorted cheekily, and rubbed her face against the back of his hand like a kitten that wanted to be petted.

Sharif grinned. By the time they next followed the herds to winter grazing, he had a feeling her belly would be big again with child—this time a son. *Ewellah*, the way she was looking at him, it was *more* than just a feeling; it was as inevitable as Fate!